HERE is a rich, surging novel about a young Irish immigrant who clawed his way to the top to become one of the most powerful men in the world.

BUT the price he paid was devastating. It almost seemed as though he were pursued by a sinister curse. There was his marriage—a loveless union born of a promise to the only woman he loved but never could have. There were his children—and the tragedy of one son's war-time death and of his daughter's insanity.

THERE remained only Rory, whom he had sworn to make President of the United States—even at the risk of awakening the curse that seemed destined to haunt the family.

———

"AN ABSORBING STORY . . . THOUGHT-PROVOKING. THOSE WHO WERE ENTHRALLED BY THE POWER DESCRIBED IN THE GODFATHER WILL BE EVEN MORE SO WHEN THEY READ THIS BOOK."
—Cleveland Press

"THERE IS INTRIGUE, VIOLENCE, ABRUPT SHIFT OF FORTUNE, ENIGMATIC CHARACTERS, FULL DETAILS OF SCENE AND HISTORY, AND THE UNFLAGGING PACE OF VARIED ACTION."
—Buffalo Evening News

CAPTAINS
AND
THE KINGS

Taylor Caldwell

FAWCETT CREST • NEW YORK

CAPTAINS AND THE KINGS

**THIS BOOK CONTAINS THE COMPLETE TEXT OF
THE ORIGINAL HARDCOVER EDITION.**

Published by Fawcett Crest Books, a unit of CBS Publicatio
the Consumer Publishing Division of CBS Inc., by arrang
ment with Doubleday and Company, Inc.

ISBN: 0-449-24089-4

Alternate Selection of the Literary Guild, May 1972
Selection of the Doubleday Book Club, November 1972

Printed in the United States of America

36   35   34   33   32   31   30   29   28

The tumult and the shouting dies,
The Captains and the Kings depart.
Still stands Thine ancient sacrifice—
An humble and a contrite heart.

Lord God of Hosts, be with us yet,
Lest we forget, lest we forget!

—RUDYARD KIPLING

Foreword

This book is dedicated to the young people of America, who are rebelling because they know something is very wrong in their country, but do not know just what it is. I hope this book will help to enlighten them.

There is not, to my knowledge, any family like the "Armagh Family" in America, nor has there ever been, and all characters, except those obviously historical, are my own invention. However, the historical background and the political background of this novel are authentic. The "Committee for Foreign Studies" does indeed exist, today as of yesterday, and so does the "Scardo Society," but not by these names.

There is indeed a "plot against the people," and probably always will be, for government has always been hostile towards the governed. It is not a new story, and the conspirators and conspiracies have varied from era to era, depending on the political or economic situation in their various countries.

But it was not until the era of the League of Just Men and Karl Marx that conspirators and conspiracies became one, with one aim, one objective, and one determination. This has nothing to do with any "ideology" or form of government, or ideals or "materialism" or any other catchphrases generously fed to the unthinking masses. It has absolutely nothing to do with races or religions, for the conspirators are beyond what they call "such trivialities." They are also beyond good and evil. The Caesars they put into power are their creatures, whether they know it or not, and the peoples of all nations are helpless, whether they live in America, Europe, Russia, China, Africa, or South America. They will always be helpless until they are aware of their real enemy.

President John F. Kennedy knew what he was talking

about when he spoke of "the Gnomes of Zurich." Perhaps he knew too much! Coups d'état are an old story, but they are now growing too numerous. This is probably the last hour for mankind as a rational species, before it becomes the slave of a "planned society." A bibliography ends this book, and I hope many of my readers will avail themselves of the facts. That is all the hope I have.

                                        TAYLOR CALDWELL

Part One

JOSEPH FRANCIS XAVIER ARMAGH

Much memory or memory of many things, is
called experience.
            —*Thomas Hobbes,* OF MAN

Chapter 1

"Joey, Joey? O God! Joey?" his mother cried out of her extremity and pain.

"I'm here, Mum," said Joseph, holding her thin small hand tighter. "I won't leave you, Mum." She stared at him in the dimness, her eyes bright and distended and sparkling with terror. Joseph bent over her, the stool on which he sat rocking with the heavy laboring of the anchored ship. Her fingers squeezed his hand until they were like tight iron on his flesh. He felt the cold sharp tips. "Oh, Mum," he murmured. "You'll be well, Mum." His crisp russet hair fell over his forehead and his ears and he shook it back. He was thirteen years old.

"I'm dying, Jocy," she said, and her weary young voice was hardly audible. "There's Sean, Joey, and the little colleen. You'll take care of them, Joey, for himself? You'll mind them?"

"You're not dying, Mum," said Joseph. The eyes of his mother did not leave his face. Her gray lips had fallen open and they showed her delicate white teeth. Her little nose was thin and pinched and the nostrils blew in and out with her hurrying breath, and she panted. Her eyes asked him a desperate question, and they started from under her glossy black brows.

"Sure, and I'll mind them, Mum," he said. "Dad will meet us. You'll be well then."

The most pathetic smile appeared on her mouth. "Good Joey," she whispered. "You were always a good boyeen. You're a man, Joey."

"Yes, Mum," he said. The fingers that clutched his hand had become icy, and not only the tips. His mother's thick black hair, as glossy as her brows, was strewn over the dirty pillows, and faintly shone in the light of the stinking and swaying lantern which hung from the wooden ceiling.

11

That ceiling and the wet wooden walls sweated with an evil and oily moisture and the big masted ship creaked all about them. The coarse jute curtain at the end of the passage moved backwards and forwards with the slow lurching of the vessel. It was still light outside the four small portholes but little light entered here in the rancid steerage where fifty women and infants and little children slept on noxious bunks under thin and dingy blankets. The broken floor was soiled with the urine of children and scattered with sawdust thrown there for sanitary purposes. It was very cold. The portholes were blurred with spray and the little heat and breath of the bodies of the wretched creatures within. The ship was a four-master which had left Queenstown, Ireland, over six weeks ago. By standing on tiptoe the tallest could see the shoreline and wharfs of New York, the wandering yellow lights, the faint gloomy illumination of lamps, and flittering shadows. Some of the steerage passengers had been rejected twenty-four hours ago in Boston. They were Irish.

The majority of women and children on the hard bunks was sick with cholera, Famine Fever and other illnesses caused by rotten food and moldy bread, and tuberculosis and pneumonia. There was a constant frail wailing in the air, as if disembodied. Older girl children slept in the upper bunks; the very sick slept in the lower, clutched against the sides of their starved mothers. The light darkened swiftly, for it was winter, and the cold increased. Joseph Francis Xavier Armagh felt and saw nothing but his dying mother, who was hardly thirty years old. He heard bitter crying near him and he knew it was his little brother, Sean, who was scarcely six. Sean was crying because he was perpetually hungry and cold and frightened. He had had his supper ten minutes before, a bowl of thin oatmeal and a slice of coarse dry bread which smelled of mice.

Joseph did not turn to Sean. He did not hear the wailing of children and the weeping of the sick women in the steerage, nor did he look at the bunks which lined both sides of the narrow tilting deck. His mind and his passionate determination were fixed only on his mother. He willed her to live with a quiet cold will which no hunger, no destitution, no pain nor chill nor hatred could break. Joseph had eaten no supper at all, and had pushed aside the bowl which Sister Mary Bridget had entreated him to take. If he thought of anything extraneous but his mother now she would die. If he took his hand from hers and his eyes from her face, she would die. "They" would have killed her at last, Moira Armagh, who laughed when there was no occasion to laugh and valiantly prayed when there was no God to hear her.

But Joseph dared not remember that there was no God, and he was afraid of mortal sin, and only a God could help Moira now—and the will of her son. The new baby had been born at midnight, and the Sisters had taken her, and the old priest in the steerage—among the men beyond the swinging burlap curtain—had baptised the child and had named her, on Moira's whispered word, Mary Regina, which had been her dead mother's name. The child lay soundless in a cocoon of dirty blankets on the bunk of young Sister Bernarde who had given her a "sugar tit" to suck—a tied square of cotton in which some sugar had been placed—for there was no milk for such as those who traveled in the steerage. The child was too weak to cry; the young nun sat on the bunk near her and said her beads, then stood up as Father William O'Leary pushed aside the curtain and entered the quarters of the women and young children. The long passage became silent; even the sick children stopped crying. Mothers reached from the narrow bunks to touch his frayed black cassock. He had been summoned by a Sister aboard, Sister Teresa, and he carried, very carefully, a worn and ancient leather bag in his hand.

Old Sister Mary Bridget patted Joseph's emaciated shoulder timidly. "Father is here, Joey," she said. But Joseph's head moved in strong negation. "No," he replied, for he knew why the priest had come. He bent over his mother again. "Mum, you'll be well," he said. But she was looking over his shoulder at the priest and the fevered brightness of her eyes increased with fear. Sister Mary Bridget stroked the young woman's arm. Joseph brushed her aside with ferocity, his own deep-set blue eyes shining with rage in the light of the malodorous lanterns. "No!" he exclaimed. "Go away! No!" He caught his breath with a choked sound. He wanted to hit the holy old woman, in her patched black garments. Her white coif, which had miraculously remained clean and stiff during these weeks, glimmered in the semidarkness, and beneath it her wrinkled face worked in pity and there were tears on her cheeks. Joey gestured at the waiting priest, but did not look at him. "You will kill her!" he cried. "Go away." A spot of blackish oil fell from the ceiling above him and struck his cheek and left a smear as of old blood on its gauntness. It was the face of a grimly resolute man that looked at the old nun and not a boy of thirteen.

One of the six nuns in the steerage had produced a small splintered table and this she set near Moira Armagh's head. "Come," said Sister Mary Bridget, and though she was old she was sinewy and strong, having been a farm girl in her youth. The hands that had held the reins of a horse, and the handles of a plow, and had dug and turned soil, were not to be denied, and Joseph was pushed, in spite of his resistance and his firm seat on the stool, a foot or so along the side of the bunk. But he clutched his mother's cold hand as tightly as ever, and now he averted his head so that he would not even see her face and especially not the face of the priest, whom he now hated with cold and determined anger.

"Joey," said Sister Mary Bridget in his ear, for he had seemed deaf these past hours, "you won't deny your own mother Extreme Unction, will you, and deprive her of the comforting?"

Joseph's voice, as hard and ruthless as his nature, rose on a great cry. He lifted his head now and stared at the ancient nun with passion.

"And what has she to confess, my Mum?" he almost screamed. "What has she done in her life to make God hate her? How has she ever sinned? It is God who should confess!"

A nun who had been spreading the table with an anonymous square of white cloth drew in her breath at this blasphemy, and blessed herself. The other nuns did also, but Sister Mary Bridget looked at Joseph with compassion and she folded her arms in her veil. The priest waited. He saw Joseph's face, so appallingly thin and white, the broad full forehead, the deep flashing eyes, the strong curved nose, the broad cheekbones on which ginger freckles were sprinkled lavishly, the long Irish lip and the wide narrow mouth. He saw the thick crest of the ruddy hair, its roughness, and the boy's thin tall neck, frail shoulders and slender, clever hands. He saw his frantic dishevelment, the poor white shirt and rude pantaloons and broken shoes. The priest's mouth shook; he waited. Grief, revolt, and hopeless fury were not new to him; he had seen them on too many calamitous occasions among his people. It was rare, however, to see them in one so young.

Vermin ran up and down the curved wooden walls of the deck. There was a splashing sound outside in the quickening dusk. The children began to wail again. Fetid air blew through the curtain at the end of the deck and now some man on a bunk beyond the curtain began to play on a mouth organ, a dolorous Irish ballad, and a few hoarse voices hummed the chorus. The kneeling nuns began to murmur: "Holy Mary, Mother of God, pray for us sinners now and at the hour of our death—"

"No, no, no!" shouted Joseph, and he beat the side of his mother's bunk with one clenched fist. But he did not release his other hand from hers. His eyes were blue fire. They could hear his disordered breathing above the mouth organ and the singing voices of the men. His face was pulled into a terrible distortion in his agony. He half-crouched over his mother as if to protect her from mortal enemies, and he glared at the priest and the nuns with the utmost and most intense defiance and rage. But Moira Armagh lay in mute exhaustion.

The priest silently opened his case and his ancient hands trembled with age and sorrow and reverence. Joseph's eyes now fastened on him and his pale lips lifted from his big teeth in a soundless snarl.

"Joey," said Moira in the faintest of dying voices.

"Go away," Joseph said to the priest. "If she receives she will die."

"Joey," said Moira and her hand stirred in his. Joseph's eyes closed on a spasm, and then he slipped to his knees, not in piety but only in weak surrender. He put his head down near his mother's shoulder, near the young breast which had once nourished him, and her hand touched his hair with the gentle brushing of a wing, then fell. He held her other hand as if to withhold her from the darkness and the endless silence which he believed lay beyond life. He had seen many die, as young and innocent and as starving and brutalized as his mother, and helpless infants crying for food and old women gnawing their hands for hunger. He could not forgive God. He could no longer believe. He had only hate and despair to sustain him now, to give him courage.

A heavy mist was rising from the cold sea and melancholy horns began to moan in the harbor. The ship rocked. "I'll take ye to your home again," sang the men beyond the curtain, "to where the grass is fresh and green!" They sang of the land they had loved and left, because there was no bread there any longer to satisfy the body, and only rotting and blackened potatoes in the wet and ravished fields, and they sang with deep melancholy and sadness, and one man sobbed, and another groaned. Women's heads lifted from rank pillows to watch the priest solemnly, the hands raised to bless meager breasts, and there was a muffled blurt of weeping.

A murmurous sound rose, the Litany for the Dying, and the kneeling nuns and the priest formed a small half-circle about Moira Armagh's narrow bed. Beyond the half-circle little children raced and squalled and stopped briefly to stare at the black bent bodies, and then continued to pound up and down the wooden and reeking floor, scattering clouds of rank sawdust. From the deck below some cattle lowed. A night wind was rising and the vessel rocked uneasily and the foghorns moaned like a hell of the possessed. The priest had placed a candle upon the little table and had lighted it, and near it stood a worn wooden crucifix with a yellow ivory Corpus. There was the bottle of holy water, a saucer of oil, and a small dish in which the priest washed his tremulous hands, and a nun reached up to give him a clean and ragged towel. The old man leaned over Moira and looked into her eyes, on which a film was rapidly gathering. She gazed at him in a mute plea, and her mouth stood open with her panting. He said in the gentlest voice, "Peace be to this house— You shall sprinkle me with hyssop, O Lord, and I shall be clean. You shall wash me, and I shall be whiter than snow—"

"No, no," whispered Joseph, and his head nestled deeper against his mother's breast and he frenziedly clutched her hand even tighter. The Litany for the Dying rose clearer and stronger as Moira sank into darkness, and now she could not see but only hear. Some woman, not as sick as the others, had drawn little Sean to her bunk on the opposite side of the deck, and she held him there as she knelt, and he clutched her arm and whimpered in bewilderment, "Mum, Mum?"

Joseph held his mother, praying and blaspheming in his boy's heart, and believed that he could bar the way into death by the strength of his young body and his silent inner cries. All became a murky and anguished confusion. A fainting sickness came to him. He, from the corner of his half-shut eyes, saw the flickering of the candle, and it greatly enlarged so that it became a monstrous and moving yellow blur at once nauseating and dizzying. The lanterns swayed and threw down their shifting pallid light and the stench of offal flowed through the deck from the two wooden latrines that stood between the men's and women's quarters. Timber groaned. Joseph drifted into a hazy dream of pain and despair.

The priest administered the Sacrament of Extreme Unction and Viaticum to the dying woman, whose white lips barely moved in her extremity. Then the priest said, "Go forth from this world, O Christian soul—"

Joseph did not hear this. He was saying to his father, Daniel, who was to meet his little family in New York, "I brought her to you, Dad, and Sean and the little colleen, and now you and I will take care of them, in the house you provided, and we'll be free and never hungry or homeless again. No one will hate us and drive us from our land and tell us to starve— Dad, we've come home to you."

It was real to him, for he had dreamt that scene a thousand times on this sorrowful voyage. His father, his young fair father with the singing voice and the strong thin arms and the gay laughter, would meet his family on the dock and enfold them all, and then he would take them to the "flat" in the Bowery where he lived with his brother, Jack, and it would be warm and there would be soft beds and a hot stove and joy and the fragrance of boiling potatoes and turnips and beef or lamb and Moira's light songs and, above all, safety and comfort and peace and hope. Had they not received letters from him, and money, and had he not told them of this? He had a good job as janitor in a small hotel. He ate to repletion for the first time in years. He worked hard, and received money for his labor. He would provide for his family, and no more would they be hunted like vermin and despised and execrated for their Faith, and thrown from their land to die on the highways of exposure and hunger. "Ah, and it is a land for free men," Daniel had written in his careful hand. "The lads will go to school, and the little one will be born in America, and we will be Americans together, and never part again."

The dying woman suddenly moved so convulsively that Joseph's dream abruptly ended, and he lifted his head. His mother's eyes, no longer filmed and dull, were gazing over his shoulder with an expression of profound joy and surprise, and her gray face flashed with life and rapture. "Danny, Danny!" she cried. "Oh, Danny, you've come for us!" She lifted her arms, wrenching her hand from Joseph, and they were the arms of a bride, rejoicing. She murmured something deep in her throat, confiding, half-laughing, as though she were being embraced by a dearly beloved. Then the light faded from her eyes and her face, and she died between one breath and another, though the smile remained, triumphant and fulfilled. Her eyes still stared over Joseph's shoulder. Her glossy black hair was like a shawl about her face and shoulders.

Joseph knelt beside her, no longer conscious of any pain or grief or rebellion or despair. All was ended, and he was emptied and there was nothing else. He watched old Sister Mary Bridget close those staring eyes and fold those rough and little hands across the quiet breast. The nun reached under the blankets and composed the long legs. She was one of the company of the Sisters of Charity in this steerage, but even she winced as the back of her hands and her fingers encountered the blood-soaked and vermin-infested straw mattress. So much blood from so young and fragile a body—but at last the girl was at peace, safe in the arms of Our Lord who had come for His lamb. The nun gently drew the blanket over the smiling face and it seemed to her that it still glowed with joy. Sister Mary Bridget, who had seen so much death and so much torment and so much hopelessness, wept a little in spite of her stoicism.

The priest and the nuns were muttering half-heard prayers, but Joseph stood up. He tottered for a moment like an old man, then straightened stiffly. His face was as gray as the face of his dead mother. At the end—and as usual—God had betrayed the innocent and had left them comfortless. Joseph knew only one desire now—vengeance on God and on life. He crossed the aisle between the teeming bunks and without a word he took the dirty hand of his young brother and led him from the steerage section of the women and young children. He pushed aside the ragged cloth that hid one of the latrines—a mere wooden affair like a country privy, and stinking beyond endurance—and he signed to Sean to use the hole. He helped the child let down his pantaloons—which were belted with rope—and assisted him onto the narrow shelf, and he was not aware of the stench but only stared at the wooden walls and saw nothing. "Mum, Mum?" Sean whispered. Joseph put his hand on the child's shoulder, not in comfort but in restraint, and Sean looked up at him blankly. He followed Joseph into the men's quarters, and the men were silent and no longer sang, but gazed at the two boys in speechless pity. Joseph did not see their pallid and emaciated faces, both young and old. He had gone beyond them. They hoped, but he had no hope. He was as removed from them as a stone image is removed from life. It seemed to him that he was filled with echoes, and he had only endurance left and one absolute resolution: To deliver the family to his father.

He removed Sean's pantaloons and shirt and shoes, leaving him dressed only in ragged underdrawers and darned long black stockings. He pushed the child down on the dark and smelly blanket and the stained striped pillow. Sean's large blue eyes questioned him in silence. Joseph had always been a formidable older brother who knew all things and must be obeyed, but was ever ready with a kind brief word and encouragement. Joseph had taken care of the family since his father had left for America nearly eight months before. Even more than the father had Joseph been the head of the house, his mother's guardian, the protector of a brother. Sean trusted Joseph as he trusted no one else, and leaned on that indomitable strength. The child did not know this new Joseph, so fixed and implacable of feature, so frighteningly silent. The lantern light swam over that austere face and then retreated as it swung, and Sean was afraid and whimpered again.

"Hush," said Joseph.

Unlike Joseph, Sean was a delicately made child, with thin bones and long, and translucent flesh, easily flushed, easily warmed, easily expressing radiance of mind and body. He resembled his young father, Daniel Padraic Armagh, who awaited his family in New York. Daniel's fairness had incited the suspicion in Ireland that he had some Sassenagh blood in him, and he had had to fight with fury to disprove this evil and insulting canard. He, with English blood! May God forgive the sinners who said this, though he would not! Sean had inherited his aristocracy of flesh, his fine golden hair, his patrician features, his hesitant, charming smile with lips that were softly colored, his dimpled left cheek, his air of gaiety and trust and joyful abandon, his impertinently tilted nose, his thick fair brows and milky skin, his quickness and eagerness, and his pale large blue eyes. Father and son possessed a graceful elegance which the tall but sturdier Joseph did not. Even patched pantaloons and ragged shirts acquired a smooth charm when they assumed them, while Joseph's clothes were merely utilitarian over an impatient body hurrying to accomplish something or to set things to rights. Daniel and little Sean spoke softly and beguilingly, in the way of enchanters, but Joseph spoke abruptly for he was, instinctively, always pressed for time. Daniel, and Sean, believed that life was to be enjoyed. Joseph believed it was to be used. He loved and honored his father, but had never been unaware of the happy faults Daniel possessed, the procrastination, the belief that men were better than they obviously were, the optimism in the face of the most appalling and cruel disaster. It was Joseph who had said to his father, eight months ago when he had still been only twelve years old. "Go to Uncle Jack, in that New York, Dada, for we will die here, I am thinking, and there is no future on this land."

Even the Famine had not stirred Daniel overmuch. Tomorrow would be infinitely better. God would perform a miracle and the black and soaking fields would flourish again with white fat potatoes and the corn would rise and the hearths would be red with peat fires, and there would be lamb stew in the pot and a bit of bacon for breakfast, with rich eggs and oat cakes, and there would be new thick blankets and the languishing fruit trees would be heavy with apples and pears and cherries—in short, there would be a blessed tomorrow.

"We can't wait," Joseph had said. "We are starving."

"Ye have no faith," said Daniel. "Ye are a hard boyo."

"There is no bread and no potatoes and no meat," said Joseph.

"God will provide," said Daniel kindly, and with a large paternal gesture.

"He has not provided, and Ireland is dying of hunger," said young Joseph. "Uncle Jack has sent you the money, may the saints bless him, and you must go to America."

Daniel had shaken his head with loving admonition at his older son. "Joey, you are a hard man, and I say this though you are still a lad." He looked at Joseph who had stared back at him with his relentless and darker blue eyes. Within two weeks Daniel was weepingly on the way to Queenstown to the ship for America. He embraced his beautiful Moira and his son, Sean, but had avoided looking directly at Joseph. At the last Joseph stiffly extended his hand to his father and the tender-hearted Daniel had taken it, and with a little sudden fear. "May the wind be always at your back, Dad," said Joseph, and Daniel, suddenly feeling far younger than his son, replied, "Thank ye, Joey." He had then stood tall and fair and beautiful, like a knight, his eyes fixed on a glorious future.

"It is said that in America the streets are paved with gold!" he exclaimed, and had smiled his radiant happy smile. "And some of it will be mine, I am praying!"

He had been imbued, then, with magnificent hope and animation, and Joseph had gazed at him with the reluctant pity such as an adult bestows on a buoyant child who knows nothing of life and nothing at all of terror. Daniel saw mansions and black horses and phaetons and curved green lawns and clinking gold pieces, and Joseph saw a rich Irish stew of potatoes and lamb and turnips and parsnips and a warm shelter free from alarms in the night and street-murder and starving hordes of men and women and children on the muddy highways of a desolate Ireland. Daniel saw ease and fawn-colored pantaloons and a shining tall hat and a cravat with a pin of pearl and diamonds, and a walking stick of gold and a swagger, and Joseph saw nights without the brutal fist at the door and desecrated churches and the hiding in the bogs with a priest who had a terrified face. Daniel saw big warm rooms glinting with candlelight and Joseph saw chapels where the Host was not stamped upon and a man could walk free to the worship he desired. In short, Daniel saw joy, and Joseph saw liberty, and only Joseph suspected that they were one and the same.

At the final moment before parting Daniel had smiled warmly but with unease, at his older son, "I pray you are not a Covenanter, Joey."

Joseph's pale lips had contracted at this insult. "Dada," he had replied, "I do not believe in dreams. I believe in what a man can do—"

"With the Grace of God," said Daniel, dutifully blessing himself. Joseph smiled grimly. The blessing was automatic and graceful, and therefore meant nothing. It was the gesture of a pagan. "With the grace of will," said young Joseph.

Moira had watched this encounter with anxious eyes, then she had embraced Daniel and her tears came. "Joey will be the man whilst you are working for us, Danny," she said.

"It's afraid, I am, that he was always the man," said Daniel and his gaiety left his face and he looked earnestly at his older son, and with a curious sad respect mixed with self-reproach. He knew that Joseph had considered him at least partly at fault for being unable to retain Moira's inheritance of some thirty acres of land, five head of cattle, two horses, a flock of chickens and rich soil which could bear good potatoes and other vegetables and grain, and a small, tight thatched cottage in the midst of it all, with sound outbuildings. The Famine had not struck here too harshly in the first years and the village nearby had not been too stricken then.

Daniel had been an optimistic farmer. When the potatoes and other vegetables rotted in the black and sodden fields and the rain never ceased, the sun would be warm in a few days and new crops could be sowed. When the cows ceased to give milk, sure and they would soon be freshened. When the trees bore little fruit, the next year their boughs would be bending with the harvest. When the Sassenagh taxgatherers became brutally insistent Daniel talked with them in shining friendship in the pub, and paid for their poteen and smiled into their scowling faces. Next spring he would have more than enough for two years' of taxes! A little time, gentlemen, he would say with that large eloquent wave of his arm and a conciliatory twinkle on his handsome face. Daniel was also a millwright. When the Sassenaghs suggested that he go to Limerick and seek employment he smiled at them with incredulous indulgence.

"I am a farmer, sirs!" he exclaimed, and waited for them to smile in return, but their scowls deepened.

"A bad farmer, Armagh," one answered. "You paid but a portion of your taxes two years ago, and a year ago you paid none, and you have no money this year either. Like all the Irish you are improvident, careless, roistering, and sanguine. We know of the Famine. Who does not? The Irish wail about it without ceasing. But—what do you do?"

Daniel's face darkened and became somber and very

changed, and his family would not have recognized it, nor would he, for suddenly he faced reality.

"Now, you must tell me, sirs," he said and his melodious voice was rough. "The whole land has been cursed by an evil, and what can we do? We can only wait for it to pass, like all evils. We cannot hurry time, gentlemen. What would you have us do? You have said I must go to Limerick and work at my trade. Matters, I have heard, are very bad in Limerick, and there is starvation there."

"There is work at your trade, in England," said another of the taxgatheres.

A white shadow struck Daniel's mouth and his pale blue eyes narrowed. He said with the utmost quiet, "Had ye asked me to go to hell to work, gentlemen, you could have said nothing more insulting." He had thrown down his last shillings on the table and had risen with dignity and had left. As he had walked home in the dark and teeming twilight his optimism returned, and he chuckled. He had had the Sassenaghs there! He would forget them at once, for they were not worth remembering. He had begun to whistle, his hands in his pockets, his head tilted, his woolen cap at an angle. Moira would laugh when he told her. And tomorrow, surely, this miserable day would be in the past and the future would open again, beaming, and the fields would dry and the Famine be over.

Joseph remembered the telling that evening, and he remembered his mother's wide and alarmed eyes and the way she bit her lip. But Daniel was endearing, and she went into his arms and kissed him and agreed with him that he had been a fine boyo and that he had crushed the Sassenagh with his haughty words, and see, was not that the moon between that rack of black clouds, an omen for the morning's sun?

Joseph, in the chimney corner with Sean, whom he was teaching his letters, had watched his parents and his young lip had lifted with mingled scorn and dread. He knew that his mother knew all about her husband. He would not add to her dejection with the sharp and blunt questions he wished to throw at his father, who was jauntily munching on a piece of dark bread and basking in the admiration of his beautiful young wife, and shaking his wet frayed coat in the small warmth of the peat fire on the hearth. The white plastered walls were stained with damp; there were cracks in the ceiling and on the walls. Daniel never saw these things; it never occurred to him to repair them. He constantly spoke of the larger stone house he would build—"soon"—and the slate roof. The money? It would come. The next harvest would be more than bountiful. There was a good piece of lamb boiling in the pot tonight, though unaccompanied by potatoes, and the turnip cooking with it was plentiful, still, and before the last four turnips were consumed God, in His goodness and providence, would provide.

The brick floor was cold and damp, as always, and the rush chairs needed repairing, though covered with the gay little cushions Moira had made from a last bolt of cloth, and the table was carefully spread with the colorful plates and cups she had inherited, and there was tea simmering in the brown earthenware pot on the hob. The feather-beds were still intact, and there were blankets, and Daniel saw no farther than these, for he believed that fate was kind and one had only to endure in patience.

Had Daniel been a fool Joseph could have forgiven him. Had he been illiterate, as were so many of his neighbors, there would have been an excuse for his hopeful folly. Fools and illiterates looked no farther than the moment's comfort. But Daniel was not a fool. There was poetry in his heart and on his tongue, and he had had the advantage of attending a Sisters' school in his original home in Limerick for eight or more years. He had a little store of cherished books which some priest had given him, books of history and literature. He had read them over and over, especially the books on the history and glory of Old Ireland. He could quote passages at will, and with passion and fervor and pride. So, there was no excuse for his refusal to face reality and his confidence in some happy tomorrow.

Daniel also had faith in God. It was not the faith Moira had, devout, a little fearful of sin, and possessed of an enduring steadfastness. Rather, it was a gay faith, as lavish and as expansive as himself. He could readily conceive of mercy, but not of justice and retribution. God was a benevolent Father, and in particular He loved the Irish, so what harm could come to their dear land and this dear people so trusting of Him? One, Daniel had said earnestly to Joseph—in whom even he suspected cynicism—had only to lie in the arms of Our Lord, like lambs, and He would care for His little ones.

Joseph had said, "And the 'little ones' who are dying, we

are hearing, of the Famine on the roads, and the priests who are hunted like mad dogs, and the hangings we are knowing, and the desecration of the churches, and the beating of women and the little colleens in the cities when they cry of hunger and beg in the streets?"

Daniel had shaken his head gravely. "We hear, but have we seen? Sure, we know it is very bad, but men will make big tales of little matters. The Faith is attacked by the Sassenagh, who, poor soul, believes that if it is killed we shall be more humble and willing to serve in the Sassenagh's army and work in his mines and his fields and manufactories, and receive little for our labor. But God is stronger than the Sassenagh and his Queen in London Town, and He will not desert us."

Then some of the starving, what was left of them, had come to the village of Carney, and a number had lain in Daniel's rotting fields and had sought shelter in his barns and had begged him for bread—which he no longer had. They had lifted their limp infants to him, and the babes had sucked their hands greedily, and they were all eyes in small sunken faces, and the old men and women were too weak to walk any longer. Among them were two or three priests, as starveling as themselves, and they spoke of terror in the other counties and in the towns and cities, and the scaffolds and bloody murder in the streets, and the proscription of the Faith. Those who had taken refuge on Daniel's farm were ragged, and though it was winter they had no coats or shawls or gloves, and their boots were broken and their flesh frost-bitten, and their bodies and faces were those of skeletons. And he had nothing to give them but the cold shelter of his barns, and they stayed there and they died, one by one.

Before they died, these destitute and homeless, Moira and Daniel and Joseph had gone to neighbors imploring any help at all, but the neighbors had their own famine-stricken in their empty barns and could only weep with the Armaghs. The village was starving also. The shopkeepers had little to sell, even if there had been pounds and shillings and pence. The land was not producing; it was black and wet and dead, and the Sassenagh would not send his wheat and meat to save the survivors in the land he hated. His sovereign, Queen Victoria, regretting that the Irish Rising had not materialized after all, had written to King Leopold of Belgium to the effect that if the Rising had occurred, the trouble-making Irish would then have been destroyed once and for all, "to teach them a lesson." (Her own Prime Minister had hoped for such a fatal insurrection so that the Celt would finally perish, and a new Plantation, settled by the English, would flourish in Ireland. He had not looked kindly on the foreign ships, even from India, which had brought some food to the dying land, and he had spoken to ambassadors with contemptuous hauteur.) The desperate Irish leaders had been publicly hanged in Dublin and Limerick, after a farce of a trial. Priests fled and hid in hedgerows and in ditches for their very lives. Nuns were driven in derision through the towns, yoked together like oxen. Many were violated by soldiers and thrown from their convents and their schools, to die and starve with their people on the highways. It was a fearsome thing and Daniel Armagh faced reality for one of the few times in his life and he knew a brief despair. However, the mood did not last too long in spite of all the evidences of disaster. But Joseph heard and his young soul had hardened and quickened.

Daniel's brother, Jack Armagh, had gone to America five years ago and worked on the steamcars in the State of New York and he, in solicitude, though poor himself, had sent Daniel some dollars in gold and Daniel had exclaimed with joy and had cried, "Sure, and I never lost hope and here is the Mercy in our hands, and all will be well!" He had then gone to Limerick on the coach and had returned with a basket of bread and some eggs and a little lamb and bacon and a few gnarled vegetables, and he was as ebullient as ever though the dead lay buried at the bottom of his garden, unshriven and as dry as juiceless twigs, mother with babe in her withered arms, old husbands and wives pressed together. Daniel remembered them at Mass each morning, but it was as if they had never truly lived and had died in his barren barns.

Chapter 2

Joseph, now sitting on the edge of the bunk where his little brother slept with tears on his wan cheeks, remembered all the dolorous suffering of Ireland and his father who waited for his family. He remembered, also, that the English Queen had contemptuously offered multitudes of the Irish free passage to America to escape starvation and oppression; it was evident that she considered America still a penal colony as her grandfather had so considered it, and still a British possession though a worthless one. The multitudes who had no alternative but death and brutality and starvation had fled their stricken land, with weeping. But Daniel's brother had sent passage money for the steerage. Daniel, hopeful always, had hesitated. Sure and matters were not so evil now in Ireland. Some farms were producing again. It was "best to wait." The Sassenagh was tiring of his vindictiveness.

Then the little family was evicted for taxes and a cousin of Moira's in Carney took them into his crowded small cottage. For once Daniel was more discreet. He did not squander the passage money. He shared a portion of it with Moira's cousin for necessary bread and a handful of vegetables—half-rotten—once a week, and a slab of bacon. When that was gone, and the passage money in danger, Joseph had confronted his father. Moira had not told her husband that only yesterday an English soldier had accosted her in the main street of Carney, that little village, and that when he had dragged insistently on her shawl she had struck him in the face with her last strength. He had punched her, then, in the breast until she screamed in agony, and then had kicked her to the stones, and had left her, shouting with mirth and execrations and foul epithets. Moira's cousin's wife had seen this, and had assisted the weeping crouched woman home, and Moira had begged

27

her not to tell Daniel, and Joseph had heard. The shawl was moved aside, and the buttons of the ragged bodice opened, and Joseph saw the black and purple bruises on his mother's young white flesh, so shrunken with starvation now, and he had clenched his fists and he had known his first lust to kill.

So Daniel, packing his few clothes in a black cardboard portmanteau, had left his country with tears in his eyes, and had glanced for the last time at his son, Joseph, who seemed to him to be an old and unrelenting man and not a child, and the innocent reproach in Daniel's eyes had not touched Joseph at all. For fear that his father might turn back at the very last Joseph had accompanied Daniel to the pub in the stark cold wet dawn, and there had waited with him for the coach to Queenstown, and the ship. The rain struck their faces and Daniel had tried to whistle, but it was a sad sound. When the coach rumbled up, and Daniel had thrown his luggage on the roof, the father had turned to his son and said, "Ye will be the father to your mother and Sean, Joey, and bring them to me in America."

"Yes, Dad," said the boy. He looked at the four great horses, steaming and stamping in the half-light, their hides agleam with water and sweat, and at the white faces staring through the running windows at the new passenger. The coachman cracked his whip and it was a cutting sound in the village silence, and Daniel had hesitated for a final word, and then had smiled his radiant smile, climbed into the coach, and was gone. It was as if, to Joseph, a charming but incompetent older brother had departed, and he shook his rain-wet head and smiled a little in love and reluctant indulgence.

He knew that the charming and the lovable had their place in life, but it was a trivial place and the first to be shattered when disaster struck. It was a village of gingerbread, where they lived and had their uncertain being, and the roofs were only sugar-icing. They were like flowers, the adornment of gardens, and so were not to be despised, except when life demanded that food be planted in their place for sustenance. If they were then uprooted, it was sorrowful but inevitable. Joseph did not fault them. They had been born so.

Now, as he sat with his little brother, Sean, who was fitfully sleeping, he feared that Sean was too like the father and he vowed in his desolate and emptied heart that he would teach Sean to face truth without fear, and despair with resolution, and to despise false words of hope. The world was an evil place, and did not he, Joseph, know it surely? It was a dangerous place. Only courage and will could conquer it or at least cow it so that it withdrew from a man's throat with a snarl and crawled away for a time on its belly. But it always waited and lurked for a moment of weakness on the part of its victims, a moment of expansive optimism and buoyancy and belief in a rainbowed future. Then it struck the fools to the death. Joseph had read his father's books, not with Daniel's interpretation that man became better and nations more civilized as time passed, but with cynical understanding. Tyranny was man's natural mode of government and his secret desire, and liberty was always threatened by men, themselves, through their governments and through their easy acquiescence and lack of fortitude. On realizing this, Joseph became a man and was no longer a child or even a youth.

Joseph sat in the deepening cold of the men's portion of the deck, and thought. The sick moaned in their pain-racked sleep. The men no longer sang, but sat mutely side by side on the lower bunks, their heads and hands hanging, or they, too, slept. The ship groaned and creaked. The cattle below lowed uneasily. Joseph sat near his sleeping little brother, his eyes fixed, almost without blinking, on the gritty deck beneath his feet. Where would they go, now? Where would they be permitted to land, if ever? Joseph knew of the many little ships that had put out from Ireland during the Famine, only to be broken on reefs or to founder in the ocean, or to bring a dying cargo back to the stricken shore. He knew that a half or more of those who had sailed for America on great ships had died before their arrival of disease and Famine Fever and slow starvation, and had been buried at sea. (Many of those on this ship had suffered that and had been lowcred quickly into the water at night, accompanied only by the prayers of the old priest and the Sisters.) The survivors, he had learned, had been forced to take shelter in cold sheds on the wharf, there to suffer or die without food or water or warm clothing, until "authorities" could determine whether or not they were a danger to the cities with their cholera and "consumption" and fever. The healthy, and the lucky, then had been permitted to join relatives and friends who waited for them and who could take them to warmth and fires and

food. The dead were shoveled into mass graves, anonymous
and forgotten. Many of the ships, too, had been turned
back at various ports in America. They were not wanted.
They were the destitute and the starveling, and they were
"Romans" and Irish and trouble-makers and strange. The
Religious were especially despised and secretly feared.

. Was Daniel Armagh still waiting for his family on the
wharf in New York? Did he know they had been rejected,
and could not land? It was winter: Was he standing at the
door of one of the sheds and staring hopelessly at the big
anchored ship with its slack sails and its wet fortress-like
hull? Was he doing, thought Joseph with an acrid taste of
bitterness in his mouth, anything at all for his imprisoned
family except praying? Did he know that his young wife
was dead? Dead. Joseph squeezed his dry eyes shut and his
chest became tight and smothering with his huge hatred
and sorrow. Oh, Mum, he said in himself. They could not
consign her to the ocean in the harbor. They would wait
until they were at sea, again. They would bind her in a
ragged blanket and fasten her body to a thin frame of
wood, and she would go into the cold and blackness of the
water just as her soul was in the cold blackness of nothingness now.

But he dared not think of this yet. There was the immediate calamity to be faced. Would they be returned to Ireland, and would they then all perish inevitably on the way
back, or on landing? Joseph did not ask himself: "Is there
no pity and mercy among men, no help for the helpless, no
justice for the innocent?" That question was for men like
his father and those who had unrealistic hope, and the
weak and sentimental and stupid. The real question confronted him: How was he to assure the survival of his
brother and his infant sister, and himself? If he were alone
or had only Sean to consider he might contrive, in the
morning just before dawn, to steal from the ship when it
moved to the wharfs to unload the cattle and the passengers who comfortably traveled on the upper decks, from
which steerage passengers were excluded. Authorities were
not too difficult to circumvent, if one assumed a confident
and assured appearance and was clean and quiet. However,
there was the baby, and even the dullest of authorities
would be curious about a youth with an infant in his arms,

and accompanied by a young child also, with no apparent guardians. Though he, Joseph, could doubtless manage to provide some food and shelter for two boys, the little girl needed womanly comfort and care, and where were these to be found for the derelict?

A sick man nearby began to cough violently, and at once the suffering and restless sleepers about him stirred and began to cough also, in tearing and rasping and spitting chorus. One by one the convulsion of misery spread through the men's quarters, then was taken up by the women and children beyond the jute curtain, until the dolorous echoes went back and forth incessantly. Only one lantern had been left lighted in the men's quarters and it enhanced the cold and shifting dimness rather than relieved it. Joseph remained unaware, except that he tucked the blanket closer about his sleeping brother. He, himself, had not put on his thin coat; he sat in his shirt and traced, over and over, a stain on the knee of his pantaloons with his index finger. His mind was one intensity and focus on his predicament. Weeks ago, at the beginning of the journey, he had felt compassion for his fellow travelers, especially the children, and fear that his family might acquire one of their diseases. But now his compassion was ruthlessly quelled in his own struggle to survive. He had no time even for grief or despair.

The four portholes began to emerge grayly from the gloom as dawn approached. The stench from unwashed and dying bodies and from the latrines filled the cold dank air. The wooden ceiling dripped. The sawdust on the floor was smeared ominously with the blood from diseased lungs. Joseph traced the stain on his knee with rising quickness. His strong and russet hair hung in ragged points over his forehead and ears and neck.

He felt a touch on his shoulder and looked up with blank and sunken eyes. Old Father O'Leary was standing before him, in his long nightshirt. "You haven't been to bed," said the priest. "Sure, and you will be sick, too, if ye do not rest, Joey."

"How will we let my father know we cannot leave the ship?" asked Joseph.

"In the morning, I will go ashore—it is permitted for me for an hour—and I will find Danny and tell him, and we should know, then, where we are going. It is to Philadelphia, I think, and let us pray that they will permit us to land. Joey, you must rest for a bit."

"Philadelphia?" said Joseph. "Is it far from New York? It has a pretty sound."

The old priest smiled painfully, his ancient and haggard face falling into deep gray lines. His shock of white hair was disheveled and as ragged as Joseph's, and his nightshirt dragged on his skeleton body. "Philadelphia," he said. "It means the City of Brotherly Love. Pray they will have some 'love' for us, Joey. We must trust in God——"

A flick of wild impatience touched Joseph's eyes. "If it is far, how then will my father reach us and take us home to New York?"

"Trust in God," said the priest. "Nothing is impossible with Him. Joey, there is some hot tea the women are brewing, and I will bring you a cup, and then you must rest awhile."

"We will travel to New York," said Joseph. "I have fifteen dollars, which my mother gave to me for keeping." It was as if he were speaking aloud to himself, and the priest's face trembled with sorrow and pity. "It is a lot of money, Joey," he said. "Be comforted. I have spoken to a seaman and he will bring some milk for the baby before the cattle are taken ashore, if he can manage to steal below. I gave him four shillings."

"I will repay you, Father," said the boy. He looked down at his sleeping brother. Was the child's face flushed with fever? Joseph touched his cheek.

"When will they throw my mother into the sea?" asked the boy, raising his head and staring at the priest.

"Joey," said Father O'Leary, and he felt a pang of fear for the boy, for this dead composure was unnatural. He had not shown a tear or displayed any anguish. "It is only your mother's body, but her soul is with God and His Blessed Mother. Let that comfort you, that her earthly pain and striving are over, and she is at peace. I have known her since she was a babe, and I baptised her, and never was a sweeter colleen and a woman. Her memory will bless you, and from the radiance of heaven she sends her love to you."

"It will be when we sail, will it not?" said Joseph. "You must let me know." Nothing stirred on his face nor in his dark blue eyes, so gritty now with black fatigue.

"I will, that, Joey," said the priest, and again he touched Joseph's shoulder timidly. But it was like touching rigid stone. "Will ye join me in prayer for your mother?"

"No," said Joseph. His young voice was the voice of a man, and indifferent.

"It is that you believe she has no need of prayer, my child?"

"There are steamcars from Philadelphia to New York, are there not?" said Joseph.

"To be sure, Joey. All will be well, if we trust in Our Lord. Joey, it is cold. Put on your coat. And the seamen will be bringing our breakfast before we sail."

He helplessly patted the boy's shoulder, then sighing he turned away, for a sick man had weakly called him in his extremity. He wore old carpet slippers and he shuffled on the sooty floor. Out of exhaustion, the coughers were now quiet and some were lifting themselves on their elbows, or rising and shambling to the latrines. Joseph felt for the packet which hung on a string around his neck, and against his chest. The gold certificates were safe. Fifteen dollars. Three pounds. It was a lot of money which his father had sent to the family before they had left Ireland. And his wages were but two pounds a week. It had taken Daniel Armagh several months to accumulate such a sum.

One porthole was suddenly rosy with dawn, and Joseph stood up on his tiptoes and looked outside. Almost imperceptibly the ship was moving to a pier among a forest of bare masts and crowded hulls. Sailors were already working on the anchored ships, and their rude hoarse voices came faintly to Joseph whose face was pressed against the salt-crusted thick glass of the porthole. The slow oily water of the harbor was black and sluggish, but its small crests were lighted with cold pink. Now Joseph saw the long piers and wharfs and warehouses in the growing light, and beyond them crowded brick houses and other low buildings. Their roofs were wet with moisture and here and there a street could be seen from the ship, narrow and cobbled and winding, with patches of gray leprous snow piled along the curbs. Drays and wagons were beginning to move along those streets, horses straining. A nearby packet, soaked sails billowing, bowed and withdrew from a pier and Joseph could hear the shrill hiss of its passing, so near did it venture. Curious seamen's faces peered at the desolate Irish ship which was to take its place at the pier. Some of the vessels were of the new steam variety and they suddenly poured black smoke and soot into the silent morning air, and their horns bellowed for no reason at all.

Foot by foot the *Irish Queen* moved to the docks and the long sheds upon them, and Joseph strained fiercely to see the faces of the lonely crowds gathered on the wooden wharf. Was his father among them? There were many there, including some women, and they were weeping, for they already knew that the steerage passengers would not be permitted to land. Some forlorn hands waved in greeting. A man was raising a flag on a staff nearby and for the first time in his life Joseph saw the stars and stripes whipping wetly in the cold wind of winter and unfurling heavily to the new and hopeless day.

"So, and that is the brave flag," said a man at another porthole, and other men joined him to gaze at the forbidden land. One laughed derisively, then burst into a fit of coughing. Others joined him, as if a signal had been given. "They don't want the likes of us," said another voice. "Sure, and they do, and we go to Philadelphia," said still another. "I have heard it, meself, with these ears, from Father."

The door at the end of the deck opened and three seamen appeared with a cart on which steamed bowls of oatmeal and fresh tea, and there were tin plates of hard biscuits and bread. The men and boys rushed eagerly to seize the food but Joseph did not move. Was that his father there, that tall man whose fair hair showed under his workman's cap? Joseph struggled for a moment with the fastening of the porthole, but the iron had corroded and it could not be moved. Ah, yes, it was surely Daniel Armagh there waiting, for the quickening light showed his fine features and Joseph's eyes were keen. Joseph's thin fist beat impotently on the porthole, and he shouted. His cries awakened Sean, who began to whimper, and Joseph pulled him upright in the bunk and forced his face against the porthole.

"There!" he cried. "There is Dada, Sean, waiting for us!"

Sean wailed. "It's not Dada," he protested. "I want my brekky."

Joseph had forgotten. He looked about him anxiously. The cart with its steaming but depleted load was about to pass behind the curtain to the women. Joseph raced after it. "My little brother," he said. "He has not eaten."

The seamen, in their dirty and crumpled uniforms, glared at him suspiciously. "You'll not be wanting extra for yourself, then?" one demanded. "There's not enough."

"I don't want it for myself," said Joseph. He pointed at Sean who was sitting and crying on the edge of the bunk in his drawers. "My brother. Give him mine, too."

A hot bowl was thrust into his hands and a hunk of moldy bread, and he was pushed away. He carried the breakfast to Sean who looked at it and whimpered again. "I don't want it," he wailed, and retched.

Joseph's heart clenched in fresh dread. "Sean!" he exclaimed. "You must eat your breakfast or you will be ill, and there is no time."

"I want Mum," said Sean and turned away his pretty face.

"But first, you must eat," said Joseph with sternness. Was that indeed fever on Sean's thin cheeks? Oh, God, Joseph muttered with hatred between his clenched teeth. He felt Sean's brow. It was cool but sweaty. "Eat," Joseph commanded, and the new note in his voice affrighted his little brother who began to cry again and sniffle. But he accepted the tin bowl and the big spoon and, sobbing, forced the porridge into his mouth.

"Good boyeen," said Joseph. He looked at the bread in his hand and hesitated. There was a gaunt hollow in him. But if he sickened, himself, then there would be no help for the other children. He began to chew on the hard bread, and now and then he rose on tiptoe to watch the slow moving of the ship to the wharfs. The man with the fair hair had disappeared. Then there was the rattling of chains, a loud thump, and the broad wooden gangplank was lowered to the wharf. A chorus of voices rose, and disturbed gulls began to wheel in clouds above the ship and against a sky from which the red light had faded and had now become dun and threatening. Joseph could hear the cheeping of the gulls, and from below the movement of cattle. A wet sail fell to the deck. Water muttered and hissed about the hull. The harbor waters were filled with refuse and floating wooden beams, and now the ocean was the color of pewter. In a moment it was pitted by a harsh and driving rain mingled with snow. Joseph shivered, and chewed somberly. This was not the golden land of which his father had written. The streets looked alien and sullen and deserted for all the wagons and the carts and the occasional gleaming umbrella that scuttled along the cobblestones or on the bricked walks. The land was little and low and the skies were immense, and there was only desolation and icy chill and loneliness and abandonment.

This was no green Ireland with enormous skyscapes of fairyland and the fresh fragrance of grass and trees and the still metallic glitter of blue lakes and snug thatched roofs and gardens knee-deep in bright bloom and racing streams filled with fish and herons, and songs of larks and hedgerows shining with buttercups and the pungent smell of burning peat and warm little fires and laughter in the pubs and the gay lilt of fiddlers. Here were no mysterious lanes overhung with oaks and hollyhocks, no welcome cries, no songs, no smiling lips. Joseph, still peering out at New York, saw the coming to life of factories and their heavy black tides of smoke darkening a sky already torn with storm. A mist was beginning to rise from the water and soon there would be fog as well as rain and snow. Joseph could hear the winter wind, and the ship rocked against the wharf. The boy's mouth opened in soundless pain and misery, but he immediately quelled the shameful emotion. He had terrible news for his father, and now he thought of Daniel as a child who must be protected.

There were hurrying loud footsteps on the decks above, and calls, and Joseph knew that the fortunate passengers were disembarking and their trunks and boxes with them. By straining he could see the first passengers leaving, the women in furs, the men in thick greatcoats and tall beaver hats. Carriages were appearing on the wharfs, with coachmen. The wind whipped coats and the men, laughing, held their hats to their heads and helped their ladies against the blast and to the carriages. The horses' sleek bodies smoked. The water smoked. The sky appeared to smoke. And the morning steadily darkened.

Luggage was taken ashore, and waiting crowds embraced the passengers, and even from the closed steerage Joseph could hear laughter and excited twitterings, and could see the happy movements of snugly clad bodies. The crowd waiting for steerage passengers had retreated like a frightened band of cattle, and huddled together to let the fortunate pass to the carriages, followed by carts of leather luggage and trunks banded in iron and brass. These were not those whom the Queen called "the Irish peasantry," but were landed gentry or Americans returning from sojourns abroad. Joseph watched them enter their closed carriages, laughing at the wind, the ladies' bonnets whirling with ribbons, their skirts ballooning. The carriages rumbled away at last, and now there was only the wretched crowd who would not be permitted to enter the ship nor even to see their relatives in the steerage, for fear of contagion. Nor were steerage passengers, not even during the long voyage, ever permitted to climb to the upper decks for air and sunshine.

For the first time in his life Joseph felt the awful sickness of humiliation. True, in Ireland, the Irish were despised and reviled and persecuted by the Sassenagh, but then one in turn stoutly despised and reviled the Sassenagh, himself. No Irishman ever felt inferior even to his "betters," or to the English. He walked and lived proudly, even when starving. He never raised a piteous cry for succor and sympathy. He was a man.

But Joseph now guessed that in America the Irishman was not a man. Here he would be permitted no pride in his race and in his Faith. He would meet only with indifference or contempt or rejection, less than the cattle which were now clambering down the oily wet gangplank, accompanied by amorphous figures huddled against cold and storm. How Joseph guessed the truth he never fully understood, except that he suddenly remembered that though his father had written joyously of warmth and "good wages" he had not written of the people among whom he had found himself but only of brother Irishmen who had fled the Famine. There had never been any mention of Americans nor gossip of neighbors nor bits of news concerning fellow workers. There had been one remark about the "little church" near the rooming house where Daniel worked as a janitor, and where he attended Mass. "But it is closed in the day, and there are no visits to the Blessed Sacrament but on holy days," Daniel had written, "and there is but one Mass on Sunday." Daniel had spoken often of the freedom in America before he had left Ireland. He had not written of it but once during these last months. Joseph looked at the flag twirling and tugging in the wind on the wharf.

Now nothing was on the wharf but piles of freight and seamen pushing barrows and carts, and the silent and rain-soaked crowd of wretched folk still hoping and praying numbly for the sight of a beloved lost face on the ship. The heavy dimness of the stormy morning was too deep now for the identification of any features. The watchers seemed but of one body and one mass, hopeless and unmoving. Fog mingled with smoke. The water quickened and began to boom restlessly.

"There is naught here for us, I am thinking," said a man near Joseph, and his voice was sick with despair. But Joseph's young face grew smaller and tighter with resolution, and his exhausted eyes were charged with angry bitterness. Sean moved against him, whimpering insistently. "I want my Mum," said the child. "Where is Mum?"

I do not know, thought Joseph. Sure, and it must be nowhere. He said to Sean, "Soon. She is sleeping." The child had left a spoonful or two of the cold porridge in the bowl and Joseph ate it. Sean watched him, then he began to cry. "Mum," he sobbed. "Mum?"

"Soon," said Joseph again. He thought of his infant sister. He hesitated. Then he said to Sean, "I will look for Mum. Stay here a bit, Sean." He gave the child a hard and commanding look and it was frightening to Sean who saw it in the swinging light of the lantern on the ceiling. The child shrank and watched his brother go down the deck.

The women's quarters were silent and muffled in the total surrender to hopelessness. Some sat on their bunks, nursing or soothing little children in their arms. Some only sat, staring at wall or ceiling emptily. Some wept without sound, the tears dripping down their faces, to be wiped away with quiet hands. Even the children were still, as if recognizing calamity. Joseph found Sister Mary Bridget, who was administering to a sick woman and her child. She turned her old head and looked in silent compassion at the boy.

"The babe?" said Joseph.

The old nun tried to smile. "She is with Sister Bernarde, and there was warm milk, and she is a lovely babe, Joey. Come, and see for yourself." She led the way to the bunk of the young sister who sat like a childish Madonna with a bundled infant in her arms. She lifted her beautiful pale face to Joseph and her blue eyes sparkled bravely. Slowly she unwrapped the ragged wool bundle and showed Joseph his sister. "Mary Regina," said Sister Bernarde with maternal pride. "And is she not a darling?"

"And she is an American too, for sure she was born in American waters," said Sister Mary Bridget.

Joseph was silent. The child had been born under disastrous circumstances, but there was no mark on her waxen little face. She slept. Long golden lashes lay on her cheeks but her wisps of hair were glossily black. "She has eyes like an Irish sky," said the young nun and gently stroked the small white cheek with her finger. Joseph felt nothing at all except a fierce resolution that this daughter of his mother must survive.

The curtain was pushed aside, and Father O'Leary's face peered around it. "Joey," he began, and then faltered and bowed his head and he let the curtain fall. But not until Joseph had seen his devastated face clearly.

Joseph returned to the men's quarters, his thin shoulders squared, and he went to learn all that he needed to know, and he knew it would be evil.

Chapter 3

Father O'Leary was sitting in a broken attitude on the edge of Sean's bunk, and he held the little boy on his knee and stroked his bright hair with a tender and shaking hand. He saw Joseph approaching. He saw the strength in the thin rigid body, the set of the shoulders, the fixed hardness of the young face, and the freckles that seemed to protrude on the white cheeks, and the mouth that was as firm as stone, and as implacable.

Joseph reached him and stood before him. "Well, and you must tell me," he said, and his voice was the voice of a man who can endure. "And is it my Dad?"

"Yes," said the priest. He patted Sean's cheek and piteously smiled. "It's a good boyeen, this," he said. "He will not cry while Joey and I speak together." He fumbled in the pocket of his frayed habit and brought forth an apple and held it high, and Sean looked at it with wonderment, his mouth opening.

The priest put it with a flourish in Sean's hands, and the little fingers stroked it with awe, and puzzlement, for he had never seen an apple before. "It is good, Sean," said Father O'Leary. "Eat it slowly. It is sweeter than honey." Sean stared at him and then at Joseph, and clutched the fruit as if in fear that his brother would take it from him. The priest said, "I bought it on the wharf, for Sean." His old voice strived for lightness, and pride. "Fifty cents, and that would be two shillings, I am thinking, for it is not the season and it was in gilt paper." He showed Joseph the paper but the boy said nothing.

The priest stood up, and then he staggered with weakness and he bowed his head as he caught at the edge of the upper bunk to steady himself. Only yesterday Joseph would have helped him, but now he held himself away, and stiffly, as if he feared he would shatter and this was no time to shatter. "Come," said the priest, and led the way down the deck to the end near the door where they could have a small privacy. Once there Joseph said in a rough voice, "You did not see my Dad."

"No," said the priest. He lifted his head and his dim eyes were filled with tears. Joseph considered him without pity or emotion.

"You saw my Uncle Jack," said Joseph. "It was him I saw, on the wharf."

"Yes," said Father O'Leary. He wet his lips with the tip of his tongue. He studied the floor. Then he reached into his pocket again and brought out a crumpled green bill. "Two dollars, almost half a pound," said the priest. "It is all your uncle could spare." He pushed the money into Joseph's hand.

Joseph leaned against the door and folded his arms across his bony chest. He surveyed the priest with what the old man knew for cold hate and revulsion.

"And my Dad?" he said at last, when the priest did not speak.

The priest's mouth shook, and he squeezed his eyes together. "You will be remembering, Joey," he said in a very low voice, "that your mother, before she was taken, and after she had received, looked beyond us and cried out to your Dad, as if he were there, and she smiled and died with a smile of joy, recognizing him." He paused. The coughers had begun again, drearily.

Joseph did not move. "You are telling me, I think, that my father is dead, too?"

The priest spread out his hands humbly, but could not meet the boy's stare. "I believe she saw his soul, and he was waiting for her," he whispered. "It was a joyful reunion, and you must not grieve. They are safe with God." Now he looked at Joseph and what he saw made him wince. "It was two months ago, Joey. He died of the lung fever."

I must not think, yet, thought Joseph. I must hear and know it all.

"I believe he came for her, with the Mercy of God," said the priest.

Joseph's white mouth twitched, but it did not lose its fixed sternness. "And my uncle, Father?"

The priest hesitated. "He has married, Joey."

"And he has no room for us."

"Joey. You must understand. He is a poor man. The two

dollars he sent you is a sacrifice. This is not a land of gold at all, at all. It is a land of bitter labor, and the worker is driven like cattle. It is all your uncle can do for you."

Joseph chewed his underlip and the priest wondered at his impassiveness. The lad was young, and an orphan, and he was unmoved. Joseph said, "Then I need not spend the fifteen dollars to come back to New York from Philadelphia. There is naught to return to. There is no one."

The priest spoke with compassionate eagerness. "You must keep the money, Joey. There is an orphanage in Philadelphia, managed by the Sisters of Charity, where these with us are bound. I, too, am to live there. They will welcome the children of Danny Armagh and love them as their own."

He paused. "And it is possible that some good man, with money, will be joyful to adopt the little colleen, and Sean, and give them rich homes with warm fires and fine food and clothing."

For the first time Joseph stirred and showed emotion. He stared at the priest in total amazement and outraged fury. "And is it mad you are, Father?" he exclaimed. "My brother, and my sister, my flesh and blood, given to strangers so that I will not know how they fare or where they are? Is that permitted in this America, that my kin be taken from me? If so, we will return to Ireland."

"Joey," said the priest sadly, "I have the paper from your uncle, consenting."

Joseph said, "And let me see that famous paper."

Father O'Leary hesitated again, then felt inside his habit and brought forth a paper and silently gave it to Joseph. The boy read: "I hereby grant to religious authorities the privilege of conveying adoption in the matter of my deceased brother's children, Daniel Padraic Armagh, for they have neither father nor mother. Signed, John Sean Armagh." The paper was written poorly but clearly, and dated this morning, March 1st, and signed.

Joseph, slowly and deliberately, and watching the priest balefully all the while, tore the paper into shreds, over and over, and then stuffed the remnants in his pocket.

The priest shook his head. "Joey, Joey. That will do no good. I have but to send to your uncle for another paper. Ah, Joey, you are not dull. I taught you myself for nine years. You are but thirteen. How can you care for Sean and the babe?"

The blows of the last hours now began to ache agonizingly in Joseph, but he held himself still. His heart had started to run like a racer's, and his voice was stifled and gasping when he spoke. "Father, I will work. I am strong. I will find work in this America. The children will be with the Sisters until I can provide a home for them. I will pay the Sisters. They will not be on charity. I will pay. And if I pay they cannot be taken from me."

The priest could have wept. "And what can you do, Joey?"

"I can write a find hand, and that you taught me, Father. I can work in the fields and in the manufactories. Perhaps there will be work in the orphanage a strong man can do, fire to keep, walls and roofs to repair. I have worked, Father, and I know what work is, and I do not fear it. But you must not take my brother and my sister from me! If you do, Father, I will kill myself, and that I swear to you!"

"Joey, Joey!" cried the priest in horror. "It is a mortal sin even to speak of that!"

"Mortal sin or not, that I shall do," said Joseph, and the priest, with dread, knew that he was not speaking as a child but as a man. "And you will be responsible for my lost soul." He made a small secret grimace and something in him smiled with rage and contempt as he saw the priest's old anguished face.

"You do not fear God," said the priest, and blessed himself.

"I never feared anything," said the boy. "I shall not begin now. But mark me, Father, what I must do I will do." He looked at the priest with renewed hatred. "And that was what you were doing so long, Father, with my uncle this morning, while I waited. You were plotting against the children of Daniel Armagh, and telling my uncle how to write the letter. You were uncommonly sly, Father, but it has come to nothing."

The priest studied him with both pity and dread. "We thought it best," he murmured. "We thought it best. It was no wickedness we plotted against you, Joey. But if it is your will, then so be it."

He left Joseph then and returned to Sean who was licking his fingers after eating the apple. The priest's eyes filled with tears again, and he held Sean to his breast.

"Mum?" said Sean, and his face twisted as he began to cry. "I want my Mum."

Joseph stood beside the priest. He thrust the two-dollar bill into his hand. "This I owe you," he said. "I take no charity. Say a Mass for my mother for what is left." He looked at the priest with daunting strength and aversion. Then he took his brother from the priest's knee and held his two hands in his own and looked down into the large tearful eyes.

"Sean," he said, "I am your father, and your mother, now, and we are alone together. I will never leave you, Sean. I will never leave you." He lifted his hand less than in a vow than an imprecation, thought the priest with a dim terror.

The ship was weighing anchor. It began to move from the harbor and the snow and rain hissed at the portholes and the wind howled in the lifted sails, and their last hope gone the men and women in the steerage put their faces in their hands.

Chapter 4

"No," said Joseph Francis Xavier Armagh, "I am not Irish. I am a Scotsman."

"Well, you don't look Irish, that's for sure. But that's a funny name, Armagh. What is it?"

"Scots," said Joseph. "An old Scots name. I am of the Established Church of Scotland."

"Well, that's better than Irish," said the fat man, with a smirk. "Still and all, you're a foreigner. We don't like foreigners, in this country. What do you mean, the Established Church?"

"Presbyterian," said Joseph.

"I'm nothing, myself, though I'm no atheist," said the fat man. "Anyway, you're not a Roman. Hate Romans. Trying to take this country over for the Pope. And, you know what? What they do in them convents of theirs?" He snickered and leaned towards Joseph across his huge belly, and whispered obscenities to him. Joseph's face remained shut and smoothly bland. He kept his hands loose, for he wanted to kill.

The fat man tilted his cigar and chuckled. "Well, anyways. How old are you?"

"Eighteen," said Joseph, who was sixteen.

The fat man nodded. "Big strong fella, too. And you got the mean look I like. Hold your own. That's what I need, driving these big wagons. Know anything about horses?"

"Yes."

"Don't talk much, do you? Just yes or no. Like that, too. More men been hung by their tongues than by the rope, heh. Well, now. You know how these blue-noses in Pennsylvania are. The blue-noses are agin drink of any kind, with them Pennsylvania Dutch and their funny hats and hacks. Amish." The fat man spat into a spittoon lavishly. "So, the po-leese don't like wagons hauling beer and such on Sundays. Godless." The fat man laughed again, and then fell into a fit of asthmatic coughing, his puffy face and bald head turning scarlet. "But there's folks who need their drinks on Sundays, and who should be agin them? And saloons run short. So, we haul the beer and likker on Sundays when we get calls. Saloons ain't supposed to stay open on Sundays, but they do a good back-door business. That's where we come in. You haul the beer and likker in a nice respectable-looking wagon with 'grain-feed' on it, and you deliver and collect, and that's all there is to it."

"Except the police," said Joseph.

"Yeh," said the fat man, suddenly and sharply scrutinizing the boy again. " 'Cept the po-leese. Ain't likely to bother you, though. Just drive sober and straight. Farm boy going home or something, or out for a Sunday lark, driving his boss' wagon. Just don't lose your head. You don't look like the kind, though, that would. Feed bags on top of the stuff. Let 'em look if they want to. Invite 'em to. That makes them sure it's all right. Then you drive on."

"And if they do more than just take a look?"

The fat man shrugged. "That's what I'm paying you a whole four dollars for one day's work, a week's wages, son. You get stupid. Someone gave you a little money to drive down a few streets. You don't know where, and you're supposed to meet a fella somewheres on a corner, and he's supposed to take over. That's all you know, see? The po-leese confiscates the stuff, and you get thrown in the pokey for a couple days, and that's all. When you get out you get ten dollars, from me. And the next Sunday you're on the job again. Simple. On a different route."

Joseph considered. Four dollars a week! He made but four for six days a week, twelve hours a day, in a sawmill on the river. It would come to eight dollars a week, a fortune. He looked at the fat man and loathed him. It was not just the fact that Joseph suspected that here was no mere grain-and-feed and harness merchant but a probable bootlegger transporting illegal whiskey from Virginia and adjoining states. (Joseph, remembering Ireland, had no reverence for duly constituted authority, mainly British.) But that man exuded a dirty slyness and crafty evil that revolted him.

"If you're thinking that I wouldn't pay you the ten dollars," said the man.

"I've no fear of that," said Joseph. "After all, if you

didn't, I'd go to the police, myself, and let my tongue wag."

The fat man howled with laughter and slapped Joseph's knee. "That's what I like! A man with spirit. Loyal, that's what it is. I treat you fair, you treat me fair. No quarrels, no argufying. Fair and square. And you'll deliver right, too. I'm a man that keeps my word. And I got friends that help me, if a man does me wrong. Understand?"

"You mean thugs," said Joseph.

"Hell, you're a man after me own heart, Joe! I love you. Call 'em thugs if you want to. Who cares? I put all my cards on the table, see? Nothing up my sleeve. Come next Sunday. Six in the morning. 'Til six at night. Then you get your money, see?"

Joseph stood up. "Thank you. I will be here at six next Sunday, Mr. Squibbs."

He walked out of the gloomy anonymous little building that stood on the edge of the small town of Winfield, Pennsylvania. It was a wooden building and held but two offices and two desks and a few tables and chairs. On the side in huge white-washed letters was the legend: SQUIBBS BROS. DEALERS IN WHOLESALE GRAIN AND FEED. HARNESS. Behind the office building was a vast and well-kept stable of big dappled horses and vans. Behind this building was a warehouse of bagged corn and other grains, and harness. It was seemingly very legitimate. The warehouse and stables were full of men, not openly working—for that was forbidden on the Sabbath in Pennsylvania—but merely caring for the horses and watering and grooming and feeding them. Some saw Joseph emerge from the offices and studied him acutely, smoking their pipes, their caps pulled down over their brows. New fellow. Tall and hard-looking, and steady. Trust old Squibbs to pick them right. Never made but one mistake, and that was a smooth Federal spy, and nobody ever saw that one again anywhere. Nobody.

And trust old Squibbs, too. If a wagon was ever traced back to him—and that was easy, his name on the wagons— he didn't know nothing, either. Some trusted employee had taken advantage of him, that's all, doing some illegal work for some bootlegger or somebody on Sundays. Old Squibbs had the chief of police in his pocket, and was a big contributor to the Party. Even knew the mayor, Tom Hennessey. Of course, the police, and everybody, knew it was old Squibbs all the time, but he never got hauled in, no sir. And none of his men ever served more than a day in the pokey, either. All the police and the Big Fellows asked was that nobody talked and made no fuss, though they had to take a little action when some blue-nose suspected and complained. Just a little action, every now and then, to keep the citizens quiet, and besides old Squibbs did do a feed and grain business open to anyone's inspection, and very profitable, too. It was the "Sunday lads" who sometimes got into trouble, not the regular boys on the weekdays. Old Squibbs took care of his own, and you could say that for him, and the good wages.

Winfield was one hundred fifty miles from Pittsburgh, a dun little town which had no major industry but the sawmills on the river. Yet, it was a rich town, for many of its men dealt in illegalities, including slaverunning, and other vices such as the transportation of farm girls and women to the large cities. The inhabitants preferred that the town seem to be poverty-stricken and humble, unworthy of notice and scrutiny, supported by its mills and the prosperous farmers beyond its confines. Even the very rich men lived in plain clapboard gray houses or small houses built of yellow sandstone on small lots, and their women dressed plainly and they had only traps or inexpensive buggies and one or two horses, usually kept in the local livery stable. No one was ostentatious. No one displayed lavish jewelry, or silk gowns or elegant shoes or the latest fashion or stocks fastened with pearl and diamond pins, or brocaded cravats or vests. And everyone spoke in subdued and decent voices and no one was louder in denunciation of "fast horses and fast women" than the men who dealt in them, and their friends. "Dens of vice" were almost unknown and never spoken of, though they flourished also, discreetly, and expensively and prosperously, and opulent enough for Pittsburgh, Philadelphia, and New York. Everyone supported the churches, and everyone attended services on Sundays, and everyone cultivated the reputation of being "God-fearing." All the ladies belonged to temperance societies, especially those ladies whose husbands dealt in the enormous bootleg trade and owned the condemned saloons. All decried slavery and were prominent in abolitionist organizations, especially those who, taking advantage of the Dred Scott decision of the U. S. Supreme Court, hunted and then returned slaves across the borders, and collected large sums for their efforts. Some of them, who knew an excellent thing when it presented itself under their respectable noses, even had agents in the South who induced slaves to run away and paid for their passage across the border, there to be held for a few days and then returned to their owners. All spoke of "tolerance" and "brotherly love" and honored William Penn, and no community was more ruthless and exploitative and bigoted than Winfield.

It was a gritty, dusty, barren little town, ugly even under summer skies and beside the rushing green river. The churches appeared drab and listless; the public buildings showed a penurious hand, the cobbled streets were usually dirty and ill-kept. There was no grandeur or pleasant vista anywhere, no parks, no open flowery spots or many trees. It was avoided by travelers, which was exactly what the inhabitants desired, and so there were few inns and no "wicked" theaters or halls of music. Its square, on a Saturday, teemed only with farmers who "came to town" to gawk or drink or lean against buildings and talk, while their women shopped in the plain poor stores for necessities.

The streets were narrow and dull, faced with smeared windows and doors opening directly on planked and broken walks. There were few gardens in the rear, for grit was everywhere from neglect and from the small factories and sawmills. The only bright and interesting spectacle in the town was on the riverfront where the squatters dwelt in shacks and the steamboats paddled noisily up and down the stream to other and more interesting cities.

The rich authorities of the town really lived in Pittsburgh or Philadelphia, or they had homes in the radiant green hills some three miles away where beauty and gaiety and lavishness were not limited. For the great majority of the poor inhabitants there was no joy and little pleasure but the saloons and walks through the streets and endless "prayer meetings," and endless sermons and devotions in the many churches, and family gatherings for Sunday dinner in dark little rooms, or solemn discussions of the "Roman Menace," and missions to the heathen and the iniquity of slavery and the corruption of "that dinky little government in Washington," which was far, far away. Mr. Lincoln had just been elected President but even those who had voted for him denounced him now though he had not yet taken office. Many of the inhabitants had come from the stark hills of Kentucky or the Tidewater area of Virginia to "work on the railroad" or in the factories and the sawmills, and for them the natives of Winfield had adopted the Southern appellation of "white trash." These people carried with them their folkways of speaking and life and so the men and women of Winfield were titillated by a sense of superiority to the "hillbillies."

To Joseph Armagh, Winfield was repulsive, alien, and lightless. Its ugliness and lack of color disgusted him. The voices he heard were strange and discordant. Its lack of human diversity and lively movement depressed him. It was a gray prison and often he felt that he was smothering. His loneliness frequently overwhelmed him with despair of so active a nature that it was like an ague. The sweltering summers made him gasp beyond endurance and the winters were a long suffering. He had lived here for three years and knew no one but the Sisters in the St. Agnes's Orphanage, and he had little conversation with his fellow workers in the sawmill. They shunned him, for he was a "foreigner" and therefore suspect. He was never seen to laugh or to engage in gossip nor heard to utter an oath. This was more than enough, with his lilting brogue, to incite enmity and ridicule.

To the few who knew of Winfield it was known as a "real quiet small town," but to the people of Virginia who had to deal with it it was "that there mud hole up North."

The Sabbath evening was closing in this late November day while Joseph walked towards the orphanage which he visited once a week. He hurried, for it would soon be too late for visitors. A dim and dirty drizzle began to fall and there was a dank wind from the river and the houses and streets became increasingly blank and glum and anonymous. A slimy moisture began to glisten on the stones where a dull lamppost blew down its feeble light. The few trees flung their stiff webby shadows on brown walls and gloomy little houses, and they uttered a dry and crackling roar. The last daylight showed a racing mass of black clouds against a pallid grayness. Joseph plunged his chilled hands into the pockets of his too-short greatcoat which he had bought, secondhand, nearly two years ago. Even then it had been thin and cheap and of the shabbiest material, blackish and coarse, with a grubby velvet collar. Now it barely covered his knees and hardly stretched across his broad shoulders. He wore the woolen cap with a visor that all workingmen wore, as brown as earth. He possessed no gloves, no waistcoats, no cravats. His sleazy shirts were clean if cheap. To Joseph a man did not reach total degradation until he neglected soap and water and to that degradation he would not fall. A cake of pungent soap cost three cents, the price of a cup of coffee and a slice of bread and cheese. When he had to choose between them he bought the soap. But hunger was an old familiar to him and had his young appetite ever been satisfied he would, now, not have recognized the sensation or it would have made him uncomfortable. It had been years since he had eaten his fill and the memory was becoming vague. Still, he was always haunted by a sick craving and sometimes a shaking weakness, and sometimes he would be covered by a prickling sweat, the result of weariness and semistarvation.

He walked proudly and swiftly, not bowing his head before the drizzle. He could smell the wet dust of the streets, and the dead leaves in the gutter. The river wind exhaled an odor of fishy cold water, and a rancid stench of oil blew from somewhere. His pale young face was set but otherwise it expressed no emotion. He had learned that he must endure, and the Irish genius for endurance was strong in him. He passed a small livery stable in which a yellow light burned, and he saw the accustomed sign on the closed doors: No IRISH HIRED. With this, too, he was familiar. He felt himself fortunate that he had his job on the river sawmills and never could regret that he had called himself a Scotsman in order to obtain work. A man must do as he must do, old Father O'Leary had once told him, but hardly in the context in which Joseph now found himself. However, it became the interior warrior cry of Joseph Armagh. He had not created the world in which he was forced to live, nor did he feel, or ever feel, that he was truly a part of it. He must survive. Self-pity was as repulsive to him as sentimentality, and a compassionate glance—which he received only from the nuns and the priest of St. Agnes's Church—filled him with a bitter rage as at a monstrous insult.

He passed the filthy little saloons with the shut doors and the dark windows, and knew that in the rear revelry "on the Sabbath" was in full voice. He hesitated. He was thirsty, and a mug of beer would be satisfying. But he had but fifty cents in one pocket, and payday was not until Tuesday, and in the meantime he had to give his aching stomach some sustenance. In another pocket, pinned securely, was the two-dollar bill which he would give to the

Sister Superior tonight for the weekly board of his brother
and sister. So long as he supported Sean and Regina they
could never be taken from him on the plea that they were
indigent orphans.

He was recovering from a cold. He coughed harshly and
noisily once or twice, and then spat. The rain was now pelt-
ing. He began a half-run. Against a sky becoming steadily
darker he could see the steeple of St. Agnes's Church, a
miserable little building which had once been a barn, all
gray walls and peeling paint and narrow plain glass windows and shingled roof which leaked during bad storms. It
was open only for Sunday Mass, a single Mass, and for the
morning Mass during the weekdays. Otherwise it was
locked, for fear of vandals. An old watchman slept behind
the sacristy armed with a club, a venerable and penniless
old man whom a heavy winter gale could make stagger or
fall. But he believed both in God and his club, and slept
sweetly. Next to the church stood an equally miserable
building, a little smaller, which had also been a big barn
long ago, but which now housed five nuns and some forty
children without homes or guardians. Somehow the nuns
had gathered together enough money to enlarge the barn
and make it a two-story and ramshackle affair of wood and
odds and ends of curious lumber, and somehow they had
furnished it cleanly if meagerly. It stood, with the church,
on a small plot of land which the men of the parish kept
green and neat in the summer. The women of the parish,
almost as destitute as the Sisters, planted flower seeds
against the sifting walls of both church and orphanage, and
during the summer the desperate poverty of both buildings
was partly alleviated by the living light of blossoms and
green leaves.

The people of the parish, to the rest of the inhabitants of
Winfield, were pariah dogs, fit only for the dirtiest and
most revolting work which not even the "river scum"
would accept. They were also the poorest paid. Their
women worked in the houses of their superiors for small
rations of food and two or three dollars a month. They
brought the food home nightly to their families. The only
joy any of them possessed was an occasional mug of beer,
and their Church, and their Faith. Joseph Armagh never
entered that church. He never mingled with the people. He

regarded them as dispassionately as he did the other people of Winfield, and with the same far indifference. They had nothing to do with him, and his life, and the thoughts he thought, and the stony determination that lived in him like a dark fire. Once Father Barton, accosting him deliberately as he left the orphanage, had tried to soften that taciturn and obdurate young man and had attempted to engage him in conversation beyond the few words Joseph would give him. He asked Joseph why he never attended Mass, and Joseph said nothing.

"Ah, I know it is the Irish bitterness in you," said the young priest with sadness. "You remember Ireland, and the English. But here, in America, we are free."

"Free—for what, Father?"

The priest had looked at him earnestly, and then had winced at the sight of Joseph's face. "To live," he had murmured.

Joseph had burst out into ugly laughter, then, and had left him.

The priest then spoke of Joseph to the Superior of the combined convent and orphanage, Sister Elizabeth, a small portly middle-aged woman with a kind and sensible face and gentle eyes, but also with a grim mouth and a will that, Father Barton suspected, not even God could bend. She was not the conventional docile and obedient nun whom Father Barton believed had comforted his bleak childhood. She feared no one—and possibly not even God, the priest also suspected with some interior misgivings, and she had a worldly brief smile and an impatient air of tolerance when he delivered some small homily or pious aphorism to her. When he became particularly ethereal she would say quickly and with an abrupt motion of her small fat hand, "Yes, yes, Father, but that will not buy any potatoes, I am thinking." It was her famous reply to any maudlin remark or sentimental dithering on the part of anyone.

Father Barton had said to her, "Joseph Armagh, Sister. I confess that he troubles me, for though he is very young he seems to have had experiences far beyond his age, and has become hard and vindictive over them, and unforgiving, and perhaps even vengeful."

Sister Elizabeth considered, fixing her eyes upon the priest for several moments. Then she said, "He has his reasons, Father, with which you and I may not agree, but they are his reasons, born out of sorrow, and he must find his way alone."

"He needs the help of his Church, and his God," said the priest.

"Father, has it ever occurred to you that Joseph has no church, and no God?"

"At so young an age?" The priest's voice trembled.

"Father, he is not young, and it is possible that he never was." With that reply she had closed the conversation and had bustled away, her wooden beads clicking, and the priest had gazed after her and had wondered, wretchedly, how it was that in these days the Religious seemed more concerned over matters of the world than in their hope of heaven. Smarting a little, he remembered: "But that will not buy any potatoes." Once he had thought to say, "God will provide," but he guessed at once that Sister Elizabeth was waiting for him to make just that remark so she could pounce, and so he had refrained, flinching.

Joseph was not thinking, tonight, of either Father Barton or Sister Elizabeth, for they were no more to him than anyone else. They merely existed, as others in his world existed, and he never permitted them to approach him, not because he resented or respected them—for he did neither—but because he knew they were not part of his life at all and represented nothing to him of any value except that the nun sheltered and fed his brother and sister until the day when he could take them from her. He had no more animosity towards them than he had for the rest of the world of men and women, for he knew now that personal animosity brought people more sharply towards you, made you aware of their being, and there was no time for this or any other wasteful emotion like it. There would be no intrusion into his existence by any stranger, for that weakened a man. He had no curiosity about others, no sense of fellowship with those about him, no pity, no hostility, no longing for companionship for all the loneliness that tortured him frequently.

On another occasion Father Barton had said to him, knowing his history, "Joseph, there are multitudes of people in this country, and not only from Ireland, who have suffered and have lost as you suffered and lost. Yet, they do not turn away from others."

Joseph had stared at him without expression. "I neither

turn away nor turn to, Father. I am as I was made. The same anvil and hammer create horseshoes and knives and harness and nails and a thousand other things, and not only one. The same experiences turn one man this way, and another the other way, and it is in their nature."

The priest had marveled at this, for Joseph had been but fifteen then, and then he was frightened for he vaguely felt that he was confronting a phenomenon new to him, and terrifying, for it was like a natural force which no man dared refute or defy, but only accept. The thought filled the priest with sadness and fear. Then he remembered that one young nun had shyly told him, "Joseph loves his brother and his sister, Father, and he would die for them. I have seen it on his face, the poor lamb."

But lately the priest had begun to believe that the nun was mistaken.

Joseph reached the orphanage with its faint yellow lamps shining through the clean bare windows, and its whitened stone steps and its bare façade. Then he paused. Standing at the curb was a wonderful equipage which he had never seen before in America but only coming or going to the great houses of the landed gentry in Ireland. It was a sleek and blackly polished closed carriage, with a coachman on its high seat, and with glittering windows and varnished wheels. Two horses drew it, as black as the carriage itself, and as sleek, and their harness gleamed like silver in the faint lamplight nearby.

Joseph stared, and the coachman, in his thick greatcoat and tall beaver hat, stared back at him. His gloved hands held a whip. Now, thought Joseph, what is such a carriage as this doing here, before this orphanage, and on this street? It is fit for the Queen, herself, or the President of the United States of America.

"And what'll ye have?" said the coachman, in an unmistakably Irish brogue. "Get on with ye, boyo, and stop gowpin' like a fish. Or I'll fetch ye a clout."

The first curiosity Joseph had felt for years stirred him, but he shrugged and went up the shallow steps of the orphanage and pulled the bell. A young nun, Sister Frances, opened the door and smiled at him, though he never smiled in answer. "And it's very late, Joseph," she said. "The children have supped and are at their prayers before bed."

Joseph entered the damp hall without reply, though he wiped his feet on the bristled rug at the door very carefully.

The nun closed the door after him. "Only five minutes,
Joseph," she said. "You'll wait in the parlor, as usual, and
then I'll see."

The bare and splintered wood floor was painfully clean
and polished, and so were the wooden walls. To the left
was Sister Elizabeth's special "parlor" where she had mysterious and weighty discussions, and to the right was a
small "reception room," as the young nuns called it, for
such as Joseph. At the end of the hall was a long narrow
room, hardly more than a corridor for indeed it once sta-
bled a number of horses in their stalls. Now the nuns called
it "our refectory," and here they ate their sparse meals and
here, with them, ate the orphans. At the end of the "refectory" was the kitchen which, in winter, was the only really
warm spot in the orphanage, and a favorite gathering place
for the Sisters who sewed here and spent their recreation
time and chatted, and even laughed and sang, and discussed their sad little charges and even, though this was
sinful, Sister Elizabeth. Some kind and partially affluent
soul had donated the three rocking chairs near the huge
black iron stove which was set in the red brick wall, and
the nuns' hands had cleaned and polished the brick floor.
There was always an enormous iron pot of soup steaming
away over the embers in the stove, and to nuns and children it had the most delightful scent in the world. On the
second floor slept the children in their crowded cots, and
beyond a door slept the nuns in similar community. Only
Sister Elizabeth had privacy, her space hidden behind a
heavy brown curtain. The schoolroom for the children was
the church, itself, "while we wait," said the nuns, "for a
real school to be built." Their hopes never faltered though
Sister Elizabeth was less sanguine. "We will make do," she
would say.

The outside privies were sheltered from public gaze by
being enclosed at the end of a rough wooden tunnel built
by the nuns, themselves, and it led from the kitchen door.
Bare and cold though the orphanage-convent was, the
nuns, several of them from Ireland within the past few
years, thought of it as the dearest and most contented
home, and their faces, in the warm kitchen, were bright in
the lamplight as they worked and innocently gossiped.
Sometimes a sick and very young child would be brought
here, wrapped in shawls, to be rocked by a nun, and

soothed and petted even at night, until he slept against the immaculate but maternal breast and was carried upstairs to the murmur of a prayer. No hunger of the stomach was ever fully appeased in this building but the nuns counted themselves as blessed in this community of genuine hope, faith, and charity.

Joseph went into the little reception room which was as chill as death and dank, and smelled of beeswax and generous amounts of soap. The walls were white-plastered, and nothing the nuns could do could remove the stains of damp permanently. The floor was polished to a dark brightness, and the room contained a table covered with a coarse linen cloth bordered with coarser lace, and held the convent's cherished Bible bound in moldering red leather, and nothing else except a lighted kerosene lamp. A tiny window near the ceiling let in the only daylight but never any sun, and there were four straight kitchen chairs ranged stiffly against the walls.

But on a wall pedestal stood a small and badly executed statue of Our Lady Help of Christians, all cheap gilt and poisonous blue and glaring white, with a gilded halo. In the very center of the same wall hung a very large wooden crucifix of dark wood, and the Corpus upon it was miraculously executed in old ivory. This had belonged for generations to Sister Elizabeth's family in Ireland, and she had carried it to America when she was a very young nun and it was her treasure, and the treasure of the convent-orphanage. It had been suggested to her that the high altar in the church was the most fitting place for it, but Sister Elizabeth sought out the dingiest room in the convent in which to place it. No one knew her reason and she never replied to questions, but almost all who entered the reception room were moved by it, some to sorrow, some to rebellion, some to peace, and some to absolute indifference, such as Joseph Armagh.

He sat on one of the stiff chairs and shivered, and he wondered, with alarm, if he had got another chill in the rain. The only fear that he ever allowed himself was the fear of desperate illness and unemployment and beggary, for he believed that in that event he would never see his brother and sister again, and they would be given for adoption to strangers whose names he would never know. None in Winfield had ever mentioned or hinted it, but he was convinced of it, remembering old Father O'Leary who had brought the family to this place and then had died but a month later.

Joseph waited for his family, and he shivered again and remembered that he had had but one small meal today—all he could afford—and that a poor one of bread and cold bacon and black coffee in his boardinghouse. He was also cramped by pangs of hunger, and he rubbed his cold hands together and tried not to think of food. He raised his eyes and they encountered the crucifix, and for the first time he was aware of it clearly and there was a sudden and darkly violent convulsion in him.

"Sure, and You never helped anyone," he said aloud. "It is all lies, and that I am knowing and none can tell me anything else."

His mother's face, young and dying and afflicted, shone sharply before him and he squeezed his dry eyes shut for a moment. He said in himself, "Mum, I've minded them and I always will, as I promised you." He had bitten down on the pain of grief for three years now and thought he had lost the capacity to feel it, but it returned like a blow against his heart, a savage blow which rocked him in his chair and made him grip the sides as if in fear of falling from it. Then when he could he bit down on the terrible pain again and again until it was numbed.

Three years, he thought, I have been in this country three years, and I've not been able to put my family in a home of my choosing, but only in an orphanage. How am I to get this famous gold that will protect us? I am trained for nothing but hard work, though I have a neat hand and could be a clerk. But none will give me such work, at better wages, because I am what I am, and what I was born. Is it always to be so? I have looked and I have thought, and there is no light and no hope.

He remembered how it had been three years ago when those who were not sick or dying were permitted to enter America through Philadelphia—a very few. Father O'Leary and the Sisters had surrounded the boy and his brother and one of the nuns had carried the baby, and Father O'Leary had declared that the three orphans were in his care, and they had been admitted. But the orphanage in Philadelphia had been overflowing, and so the old priest, in the first stages of dying from deprivation and sadness, had brought the three children to this town on the stagecoach, a long and wretched journey in the midst of winter. Two of the nuns had accompanied him in order to help. Joseph had insisted on paying his own passage out of the fifteen dollars his father had sent his mother, and when they had arrived in Winfield he had but two dollars left, for food had had to be bought at taverns and inns, and milk for the baby.

He, himself, had remained at the orphanage while he looked for work. "Stay with us for a year or so, Joseph," Sister Elizabeth had said, "and work for us, and we will teach you. We cannot pay you, for we are very poor and are dependent on charity."

But Joseph found his first job in a stable for three dollars a week, one of which he gave to Sister Elizabeth in spite of her protests. He remembered how he had lived, in the stable with the horses, sleeping in a hayloft. When he was fourteen he knew he had to have more money and went to work in the sawmill. He was promised a dollar more a week in May.

He looked at the crucifix and at the marvelously detailed and suffering Face.

"No," he said again, "You have never helped anyone. How is it possible? You are only a lie."

The door opened and he looked at it eagerly, for what he would see was his only comfort and the source of his desperate cold determination. But it was Sister Elizabeth who was entering and he slowly rose to his feet and his face was as neutral and closed as always.

Chapter 5

"Joseph, lad," said the nun and held out her hand to him. It was a hand callused and scored by endless hard work, but warm and strong. His own was cold and flaccid in it, and the nun was aware of the fact. But she smiled her deceptively sweet smile and blinked behind her polished glasses, and her rosy face dimpled and her face was affectionate under her coif and black veil. Though she ate less than anyone in the convent her short body was plump, which was an unending miracle to the young nuns under her care.

"Where is Sean, and Regina?" Joseph asked with no replying smile. He stood before the nun in threatening challenge and the old fear returned to him.

"Joey, sit down, do, and let me talk with you," said Sister Elizabeth. "Have no fear. The little ones are expecting you and they will be here presently. But I have something important to tell you."

"They are sick!" said Joseph in a loud accusatory voice, and his brogue roughened it.

"Not at all," said Sister Elizabeth, and no longer smiled. Her face became stern and commanding. "Stand, if you will, and not sit. You are a very stubborn lad, Joey, and I am displeased with you. I thought I would speak with you as I would speak to a sensible man but I am afraid there is little hope of that! Ah, well.

"Did you notice that handsome carriage and all, outside, waiting?"

"What has it to do with me?" demanded Joseph. "Or has someone a fine job to offer with good wages, Sister?" and he smiled with derision at such a golden idea.

"Ah, Joey," sighed Sister Elizabeth. She loved the boy. He reminded her of her relentless brave brothers in Ireland, all of them dead now of disease and starvation. "Life is not that easy and fanciful."

"You have no need to tell me that, Sister."

"Yes, Joey, and that I know." She regarded him with hidden compassion. "Well, I must tell you. There is a beautiful lady here, young but truly genteel, the wife of a gentleman of excellent prospects. She is, herself, rich and it is her house in which they live, and her servants, and she is almost the sole support of our church in Winfield, and it is she who pays for our food and shelter and clothing and boots, and she gives to the Missions and a seminary. But there is a bottom to every purse, I have heard, and she does all she can.

"She has a little daughter, the age of Mary Regina, but alas, she can have no more children. Her great heart longs for another little one, but it is not to be. It is God's will. So she wishes to adopt—"

"Regina?" said Joseph in a tone like a curse. He made a wild gesture almost as if he would strike the nun before whom he still stood. "Is that what you would tell me?"

"Joey—"

"How dared you show Regina to her!" His voice rose to a broken shout of rage and affront. "Do I not pay for my sister? You would steal her from me, in spite of your mealy promises. You lied to me!"

She reached out, her face as hard as his, and she caught his thin arm and shook him. "Speak to me not like that, Joey, or I shall leave you and say no more. In truth, I would leave you now were it not for Mary Regina and her future. I did not show your sister to this lady, whom I must call Mrs. Smith, for you are not to know her name. She saw the child on one of her missions of mercy to this orphanage, bringing us rolls of wool and flannel, and some money, and she loved the child at once and thought of her as a sister for her own little one.

"Hark, Joey. Let the madness go from your mind a moment. What future has Mary Regina here, and in this city? You are only sixteen, poor lad. You are half-starved and live miserably, and though you have not told me I know. You have a brother, also. Life is not good for the Irish now in America, as you have discovered for yourself, and it may never be. Do we not have to keep the doors of the church locked except at Mass, and the doors of this orphanage, also? It was but two months ago when evil men forced their way into the church and threw down the altar and desecrated the Host, and beat Father Barton who tried, in vain, to restrain them. They stole our candlesticks and broke our crucifix and befouled the sacristy. You know of this, Joey, and I have heard it is as bad in other cities in America, against the Catholics and the Church. But a month ago the Sister Superior in her convent in Boston was beaten almost to death, and her nuns attacked, and the Hosts in the adjoining church were fed to horses, or stamped in the gutter."

She lifted her eyes to the crucifix on the wall, and her face was pale and there were tears on her lashes. But she continued to talk quietly and resolutely.

"What life opens before Mary Regina, who needs a home and a mother's love and care and a future of peace and comfort, and education? At the best you may make some higher wages, but short of a miracle you will be hard pressed to support yourself and Sean for many years. In the meantime, you will live as you live, and there will be no hope for Mary Regina, and little for yourself and Sean.

"Do not the children of your dead parents deserve more than this? You are a man, Joey, and Sean will soon be a man, and life is not so hard for men as it is for women, and that we know. You will manage for yourselves. But what of Mary Regina? Do you dare deny to her what the little love may have—warmth and good clothing and care and affection, and teachers and gentility, and later a fine marriage? You would deprive her of this, Joey, and condemn her to lifelong misery instead. Have you thought what the years will inevitably bring her if she remains here? We can teach her her letters and domestic duties, but when she is fourteen we can no longer keep her here, for her place must be given to a younger girl. We have no choice. So Mary Regina, as do all our girls, must go into service and be a despised servant the rest of her life, and her way will be humble and she must bow before those who will abuse and scorn her and treat her with less kindness than they treat their horses and dogs.

"You have told me, Joey, that when Mary Regina is fourteen you will be able to give her a good home of your own making. That is in less than eleven years. Do you believe this truly, Joey?"

"Yes," said Joseph, and in the dim lamplight and half-darkness which now filled the reception room his face was the face of a man much older, and set.

The nun sighed again and looked down at her clasped hands. "You do not know the world, Joey, in spite of what you have already endured. You are very young, and so to you nothing is impossible. But, Joey, almost all of the dreams of the young come to nothing, and I have seen that for myself. I have seen hundreds of high young hearts broken, and die in the breaking. And I have heard the silence of despair, more times than I dare think of." Her round voice, usually so full and assured, now sank into melancholy.

"Joey," she continued after a moment, "I do not deny that you may make your way, and well. But not with a sister to care for and protect. You must also think of Sean. Do not deprive Mary Regina of the mother and the love and the home this beautiful lady has offered her out of the goodness and tenderness of her heart. You dare not, Joey."

A wizened tautness drew the boy's features together and his pale cheeks seemed to sink in like the face of an old man. His deep-set blue eyes fixed themselves with unmoving intensity upon the nun, and his wide thin mouth was like a blade. He had removed his workman's cap when he had entered the room, and his ragged thatch of russet hair hung in points over his wrinkled brow, over his ears and the back of his neck. His was a face of both black desolation and concentrated anger.

"Think, Joey, before you speak," said Sister Elizabeth, and her voice was gentle and moved.

Joseph began to walk up and down the little room, firmly and slowly, his hands in his pockets, his stare fixed blindly ahead of him. Sister Elizabeth saw his sick pallor and his ginger freckles and his fearful thinness and shabbiness, and her heart sickened with grief and pity. So brave a lad, with so strong a soul—yet he was but a lad after all, an orphan little older than many now in this orphanage. She closed her eyes and prayed: "Dear Lord, let him make the right decision, for his sake above all others."

He suddenly halted before the nun and again made that fierce and intimidating gesture. His large, almost hooked, nose was a gaunt and glistening bone in his stark face.

"Let me see this precious lady," he said.

Almost crying out in her joy Sister Elizabeth bounced to her feet and waddled swiftly from the room. Alone again

Joseph turned and surveyed the crucifix. It seemed to flicker with life as the waning and brightening of the lamplight washed across it in waves. Joseph smiled, and he shook his head as if with somber amusement at something which had no meaning for him but which had suddenly called itself to his attention.

The door opened and Sister Elizabeth entered, and a young lady with her. Joseph opened his eyes—they were sunken now as if from a profound illness.

"Mrs.—Smith," said the nun. "This is Joseph Armagh, Mary Regina's brother, of whom I have told you. Joey?" She looked with dismay at the boy. Joseph was leaning against the wall and did not move and gave no response. But he was gazing with complete fixity at the young woman who stood, smiling hopefully, near Sister Elizabeth.

She was young, possibly nineteen or twenty, and tall and slender, with a fine and sensitive face of rose and pearl, with large and shimmering dark eyes and a scarlet mouth like a leaf in autumn. Under a bonnet of rich pink velvet, tied with pink satin ribbons, her hair curled in tawny waves and little ringlets. She wore a short jacket of some smooth dark fur, shining and expensive, and her elegant hooped skirt was of black velvet trimmed with gilt braid. She carried a muff in her gloved hands, and the muff was of the fur of the jacket. There were diamond and ruby earrings in her ears, and a little scarlet light was reflected on her beautiful cheeks. Her slippers were of velvet, with low heels, and beneath her skirt there was a hint of pantalettes of lace and silk.

She studied Joseph with almost his own concentration, and her timid smile disappeared and her delicate face became beseeching and diffident.

Joseph had never seen any woman so lovely, no, not even his mother, nor one so richly clad. A faint odor of violets floated from her, and his nostrils distended, and not with pleasure. She was as far removed from him as any point in space that he could think of, and as alien as another species. He hated her and the hatred was like acid in his throat. So, it was her money that could buy flesh and blood, was it, like some well-fed and brocaded Sassenagh who bargained for the hands and back of a starving Irishman for his mines and his armies and his manufactories, and left nothing but dead bones behind.

The two young people regarded each other in silence,

and Sister Elizabeth looked earnestly from one to the other and prayed inwardly. Then Joseph said:

"And so you would buy my sister?"

Sister Elizabeth caught her breath, and Mrs. Smith turned to her impulsively and with a kind of timorous fear that implored help and made her look like a young and frightened girl. Sister Elizabeth, responding, took her hand and held it encouragingly.

"Joey," she said with quiet sternness, "that is most uncivil and wicked. There has been no talk of 'buying,' and that you know." She tried to meet Joseph's eyes to command and reprove him, but he did not look away from Mrs. Smith. It was as if he had not heard. He lifted himself from against the wall and folded his lean arms across his chest and they could see his red wrists and the scars upon them and upon his long thin hands.

"Would you have my sister as a toy, a servant, for your own child?" Joseph asked. "A Topsy, as it was written in that book I have been reading about the slaves? *Uncle Tom's Cabin,* is it?"

Sister Elizabeth was aghast. Her round full face deepened in color and her eyes were wide behind her glasses. But Mrs. Smith, to her amazement, pleadingly touched her arm and said, "Sister, I will answer Mr. Armagh," and the nun was more amazed than ever that this shy creature had suddenly become so bold.

Mrs. Smith faced Joseph again and drew a long breath and her eyes met his widely. "Not as a toy, that dear child, but as my own loved little daughter, sister to my own little Bernadette, cherished, guarded, protected with tenderness and devotion. She will inherit as my daughter will inherit. I have seen her but once and I loved her immediately, and it seemed to me that she was my very own, Mr. Armagh, and my arms ached for her, and all my heart. Beyond that, I can say no more."

Joseph's pale mouth opened to speak, and then he said nothing for several moments while the women waited. The falling and rising lamplight rippled over his tight features. A spasm distorted his face, as if he were in extreme pain. But his voice was quiet.

"Then, you will give me a paper," he said, "written as I say, or there will be no more talk. My sister will keep her name, though you take her, for it is a great name in Ireland and proud I am of it, and my sister will be proud. She must always know that she has two brothers, and that one day we will claim her, and until that day I must see her as I see her now, and Sean must see her also. I will lend her, then, for the advantages you can give her now, as a companion to your own child, but only lend her."

"But that is impossible!" exclaimed Sister Elizabeth. "An adopted child takes the name of the adoptive parents and her new sister, and she is of the family and has no other, and must know no other! It is a protection for the child, herself, so that her heart is not divided nor her thoughts troubled. You must understand that, Joey."

Joseph turned to the nun with huge repudiation. "It is my flesh and blood we are speaking of, is it not, Sister? The flesh and blood of my own parents, the body of my sister Regina! It is you who cannot understand, I am thinking. A man does not give away what is of his flesh and blood and turn and never see it again, as if it was the family pig or goat going off to market! I swore to my sainted mother, on her deathbed, that I would mind the little ones and never leave them, and I will not break my word. Regina is mine, as Sean is mine, and we belong to each other and never shall we be parted from each other. That is my final say, Sister, and if Mrs. Smith refuses, then that is the end of it."

Mrs. Smith spoke again in her timid and imploring voice. "You must not think me insensible, Mr. Armagh, or a female fool. I know how it will tear your soul to part with your sister. But consider what she will possess, which you cannot give her; consider what your own mother would desire. I was not always rich. My mother and father went to the Territories, for the lumber, and they lived in squalor, as my father told me, and when I was but a babe in arms my mother died of cold and homesickness and destitution. It was not until I was ten years old that my father made his money, and I was left with strangers when he was in the forests for a very long time, and I did not know him when he returned for me. So I know the sensibilities of a homeless child. Do you think, Mr. Armagh, that you are being just to Regina to condemn her to live in an orphanage with no hope for her future? Do you think your mother would wish that?"

"My mother would wish her children to know each other and remain together," said Joseph, and he made a rude gesture of dismissal of the two women.

"Wait. Please," said Mrs. Smith, and she put out her small gloved hand to him. "My husband and I—we are leaving Winfield, and it may be that we shall never return. We are going to—to a distant city—for my husband is a man of consequence and has many ambitions. Regina would have to go with us—"

"No," said Joseph and his voice was rigorous and loud. "We have talked too much. I have nothing more to say. I am here to see my brother and my sister, and I will see them alone—if you please."

Mrs. Smith bent her head, fumbled in her muff and brought forth a scented handkerchief which she put to her eyes. She burst into soft weeping.

"Joey," said Sister Elizabeth, and she was very touched. "It's a proud lad you are, and of proud blood as you have said yourself. But be careful that it does not lead you astray. And now, you cannot dispose of Mary Regina's fate as lightly as this."

The boy said with ridicule, "There is more than money, Sister, and is it I who should tell you that? There is a man's family, and he does not sell that family. I have nothing more to say."

Sister Elizabeth put her arm about the sobbing young woman and led her away, murmuring consoling words. But Mrs. Smith would not be consoled, and Joseph heard her darkly to himself. He sat down again on the stiff chair and gripped his raw hands on his knees, and waited. His exhaustion became deeper. His body shivered and trembled, and it was not fear again that he felt for himself but for Sean and Regina.

The door opened and the two children came in, running, and calling his name, and he could not get up as yet to greet them, but held out his arms to them without a word and they ran to him. He lifted, with an enormous effort, the little girl to his knee and put an arm about Sean, Sean tall and very thin and fair and nine years old, and Regina but three.

"They made us wait a long time to see you, Joey," said Sean, and leaned against his brother's shoulder. He had the beguiling and enchanting voice of his father, and his father's endearing smile and Daniel's dimpled cheek and large shining eyes, pale and blue, and his fair hair curled over his head and ears and nape. He wore the poor coarse garments of the orphaned children, clean and patched, and he wore them like a knight in silk and velvet. His tilted nose gave his face a gay expression even when he was wretched, which was not often, for he possessed his father's optimistic and hopeful character and was rarely in tears or sulks. Joseph, as usual, could not prevent himself from smiling, and remembering, and he hugged Sean closer to him, then pushed him off with gruff affection.

"I had affairs to discuss with Sister," he said, and turned all his attention to Regina, and his deep-set dark-blue eyes softened. For Regina, as the Sisters all said, was "a little love," a delightful grave child who seldom smiled, and who was unusually beautiful, with her long mop of curling and glossy black hair, white skin and rosy cheeks and lips, and eyes as dark a blue as Joseph's, but larger and rounder. She seemed to understand almost everything that was said, and appeared to reflect on it, and so the nuns said "she is listening to the angels, that darling one, who is an angel, herself." They found it of portent that the child's lashes were a vivid gold, unlike her hair, and the unusual color gave her a shining regard. Her expression was not childlike, but was often somber, and she was usually very quiet, though not retiring, and liked to play by herself. Her face was the face, not of a very young child, but of a girl approaching puberty, and very thoughtful, and at times sad and remote.

She was, to Joseph, dear above all other things in the world, dearer even than Sean, and far dearer than his own life. Her small body was thin, as all the orphans' bodies were thin, and she wore a brown woolen frock much too large for her, a donation of some charitable mother to the orphanage. The material had chafed the silken whiteness of her little neck, and her stockings had been knitted of black wool by the nuns and her shoes were too big and she had to wiggle her toes constantly to keep them on her feet.

As if she knew that Joseph had undergone some recent travail she looked up silently into his face, and then she touched his cheek lightly. Sean was moving restlessly up and down the room, and endlessly chattering and questioning, but Joseph held his sister to him and felt that he had rescued her from something direful, and the very thought made him shiver again. He took her little hand and felt its chapped roughness and he saw the small broken nails, but when he looked at her face again she smiled at him suddenly and it was like light to him and a blessed consolation. He pressed her almost violently to his own body, and though she must have felt considerable discomfort she did not protest, but nestled against him. My darling, my darling, said the boy to himself. And they would take you from me, would they? But never, until I die. So help me God, never until I die.

Sean stopped before his brother, jealously. "And where is that fine home you have been promising us, Joey?" he demanded. His tone was light and wheedling.

"Soon," said Joseph, and he thought of the three years he had been in this country. Three years, and there was no home as he had promised his mother and then these children, but only an orphanage for Sean and Regina, and only a miserable tiny room for himself under the eaves of a widow's decaying house more than a mile from the orphanage. He was one of her three roomers, and he paid her a dollar a week for the bed in that room, clean but sagging with its old straw mattress on a web of rope, a chair and a commode which held all he possessed. It had no heat even in the winter, and no curtains at the one small window, and no rug on the cold floor, but it was all he could afford, and more. It took all his fortitude, now, thinking of that room, thinking of his brother and sister in this destitute orphanage, to keep from breaking down in despair.

The old priest and the nuns always said, steadfastly, that honesty would be rewarded by God, and faith would never be disappointed, and a man of industry and integrity would rise to riches and to honor before his fellowmen. Sometimes, when he remembered those innocent aphorisms, Joseph would suddenly laugh aloud, his brief fierce laughter in which there was no merriment but only a bitterness. To Joseph Armagh the naïve were not pathetic. They were contemptible. They made a parody of reality. At these times Joseph would remember his father, but not with love.

He remembered that next Sunday he would receive four dollars for twelve hours of somewhat dangerous work, and he felt a sudden relief. He said to Sean again, "Soon. It will not be long, now. I will bring you a cake next Sunday, and a cake for Regina."

He put his arm about Sean again and held him to his side, and he held Regina to him also, and the children were silent now, watching him with quiet curiosity for they felt the hard concentration in him and Sean, more volatile than his sister, became afraid as often he was afraid of Joseph.

None heard the door open and none saw Sister Elizabeth for a moment or two, on the threshold, and she stood there and watched that pathetic tableau and her eyes burned with tears. Then she said briskly, "And it's still up, are you, Sean and Mary Regina, when you should be in bed? Off with you, and kiss your brother good night for he is tired, too."

She bustled into the room keeping her mouth pressed tightly together for fear of its trembling, and she ruffled Sean's light hair with her plump hand, affectionately, and smoothed Regina's curls. She was not a woman to show sentimentality but suddenly she bent and kissed the two children, then as if annoyed with herself she hurried them out and closed the door smartly after them, grumbling. She had placed two parcels on one chair as she had entered. Joseph stood before her with cold and silent hostility, and she sighed.

"Well, Joey, all's been said that could be said, and I pray that you will not be regretting it. And now, we are not going to be silly tonight, are we, and refuse the little dinner Sister Mary Margaret packed for you, saying you are not hungry when I know you are, and raising the pride up in you again. For it's very thin and sickly you are, with your cold, and if you fall ill who then will care for the little ones?"

It was an artful plea and Joseph glanced at the parcel on the chair and tried to prevent himself from shivering.

"And I have the usual books for you, too, Joey, left for you by a good man."

Joseph went to the parcel and tried to ignore the thick bread and cheese and slice of fried pork fat, though his mouth watered for them instantly. He looked at the books in their separate parcel, wrapped in newspaper. There were four of them. There was always at least one every Sunday, and some he sold for a penny or two after he had read them and some he kept for rereading. Tonight the parcel contained a book of pious reading with a frontispiece of a group of asexual angels standing on a pillar of white fire, a volume of Shakespeare's sonnets, thin and worn, Charles Darwin's *Voyage of the Beagle*, almost new which he examined with sharp intentness, and the fourth was a volume of the philosophies of Descartes, Voltaire, Rousseau, and Hobbes. As always, he felt a deep thrill of anticipation and excitement at the sight of books and the feel of them in his hand and the rustle of paper. They were like food and drink to him. He put down the book of pious readings with a small gesture of scorn, and wrapped up the other three books in the newspaper. Then he hesitated. Finally, with real reluctance, he lifted the parcel of food also. He said, "Thank you, Sister." But his white cheekbones flushed with mortification. "I can afford my dinners, Sister, but I am hungry tonight, and so I thank you."

He tucked the parcels under his arm and removed his cap from the table.

"Joey," said Sister Elizabeth, "God go with you, my child."

He was surprised at the emotion he saw on her face, for she was always so full of common sense and never uttered pious aphorisms and blessings. He was not sure that what he felt in response was contempt or embarrassment, but he ducked his head and passed her with a final "thank you." She watched him go, not moving for a few moments. As he went by her secluded "parlor" he heard Mrs. Smith's soft mourning and now the voice of a man comforting her. He left the convent-orphanage, and the fine coach was still waiting. Joseph hesitated. All at once he felt the power of wealth as he had never felt it before, and he was suddenly choked with alarm. A man who had money could take what he wanted and the devil take the rest. It was possible that that rich man and woman in Sister Elizabeth's parlor could seize, law or no law, the sister of Joseph Armagh and spirit her away, and there would be naught he could do.

A thin cold sweat broke out on his forehead and between his shoulders. He walked slowly towards the carriage, smiling as pleasantly as he could, and the coachman watched him come with sharp alertness and clutched the whip. Joseph stopped near him and stood back on his heels, and laughed. "A noble carriage for Winfield," he jeered. "Does the gentleman keep it for his lady-love, perhaps, but not to be seen on the streets in the day?"

"It's a foul tongue you have in your head, boyeen!" shouted the coachman, and glared down at the haggard face below him and raised his whip. "This is the carriage of himself, the Mayor of Winfield, and his lady, Mrs. Tom Hennessey, and it's not in Winfield they live," and he spat, "but in Green Hills where the likes of you would skulk at the back door begging for bread! And be kicked off, down the road!"

Now Joseph's alarm reached icy terror, but he merely

stood there and grinned up at the coachman. Then he finally shrugged, gave the carriage a last sneering glance and walked off. The Mayor of Winfield, and his lady, and they coveted Regina and would steal her if they could, like a pickaninny in the hands of a blackbirder! Joseph hurried through the streets, panting, clutching his parcels, senseless fright snapping at his heels. It was not until he was near his rooming house, in the darkest and most poverty-stricken part of Winfield, that he was able to control himself.

So long as he could afford to pay for his brother and sister at the orphanage they could not "give them away," like puppies or kittens. It was true that Sister Elizabeth had never once hinted such a thing, but Joseph distrusted all people without exception, and the fear he had felt on the ship was with him always. No one knew now where his uncle, Jack Armagh, was, so he, Joseph, was Sean's and Regina's true guardian, but he was only sixteen. One never knew what horrors and perfidies and crimes could be invoked against the helpless, even from such as Father Barton and Sister Elizabeth.

He needed more money. Money was the answer to all things. Had he not read that somewhere, probably in the Bible his father had cherished at home, and which had gone with all the other Armagh treasures? Sure, and there it was that he had read it: "A rich man's wealth is his strong city." He had been determined from the beginning to be rich some day, but now his determination was complete, confirmed. He thought of his mother, given to the sea after the ship had left New York, and his father in a pauper's grave, without stone or remembrance, and Joseph's mouth became a slit of pain in his stark face. He must have money. It was the only protection, the only God, the only fortress, a man had in this world. Before this, Joseph had believed that very soon he would find a way to earn a comfortable wage and give his brother and sister a home and shelter and warm fires and good food and clothing. After all, there still lingered in him the belief that this was a land of opportunity, and he knew there were rich men in Winfield even if they did conceal their riches.

Now he no longer cared how he would obtain, not a comfortable wage, but money in profusion. It was a matter from this night on of discovering the secret, and he would find it. He would surely find it.

He thought of Mr. Tom Hennessey, the Irishman who

had made his fortune, it was said with truth and knowledge, in blackbirding, and so had his father before him, and he had many interests in the great Commonwealth of Pennsylvania, and all of them, it was hinted, equally nefarious. It was his money which had made him mayor of this town, and which had given him a luxurious home in Green Hills, he the son of an Irish immigrant like Joseph Armagh, himself. The townsmen spoke in awe of him, while they sneered at his origins—but with a sort of indulgent fawning. Even an Irishman with money was to be respected and honored, and caps lifted at his passing. What was it his lady had said? They would be going to another city, far away. Joseph could not afford the penny for a newspaper but he had heard the men at the sawmill discussing that "Papist" who had just been appointed by the State Legislature as one of the two senators to go to Washington. They pretended to despise him, but they were proud that a senator—something like a member of the House of Lords, Joseph had thought—would be from their town and so add polish and pride to it. Besides, he had been born here, and he had been a less venal mayor than most, and had often expressed his "fraternal interest" in the poor workingman "and the conditions of his work." The fact that he had done nothing to help either was not held against him, and in spite of the general loathing and fear of "Popery" Tom Hennessey was not suspected of secret unspeakable crimes except the ones less appalling, which were at least understandable and even to be admired as "cuteness," and obsequiously envied.

To deal in flesh and blood, even if it were "black," had always seemed to Joseph to be the vilest and most unpardonable of crimes. Oppressed, himself, from birth, his rare cold sympathies had been with the fleeing slaves, who could now be captured and returned to their owners in the South. There had been times when he had sickened over the thought, and had hoped that at some near time he would be able to help a desperate slave to reach Canada, and safety from the viciousness which was universal man. But tonight he envied Tom Hennessey whose fortune, and his father's, had begun in blackbirding. The mayor was far cleverer than Joseph Armagh, and his father certainly more intelligent than Daniel Armagh, who would have been stunned to learn that in the world there lived men so detestable and degraded.

"An honorable man, lifted above sin and meanness, who had never raised his hand against the helpless but had given them all he could, was greater in the sight of God and man than a lord of Norman blood, and the Royal Family, itself," Daniel had said once, long ago. Joseph had not really believed that nonsense. But it was Daniel Armagh, thought Joseph on this ashen and raining night, who had innocently betrayed his family with his silliness of thought and word and deed and had never told them the truth. In these tormented minutes Joseph felt his first hatred for his father—and was not ashamed and was not aghast.

He crossed the mean town square with its slippery cobbles and its black storefronts. A statue of William Penn, badly executed in bronze, stood in the center, the latrine of birds. No one was abroad on such a gloomy night of drizzle and chill, and Joseph's pounding footsteps echoed throughout the square. A street, among others, led off it, named Philadelphia Terrace, and here was the gritty and forlorn rooming house in which Joseph Armagh lived, and where he had had his determined and hopeful dreams for nearly three years.

It was a little woeful house, more decayed than its neighbors, and sagging and dilapidated, its clapboards pulling from the walls, its door splintered. One streetlamp, belching the odor of gas, lighted it feebly, which was an advantage for there was not a light in the house. It was past eight o'clock and all decent folk were in bed for the work tomorrow. Joseph pushed open the unlocked door and by the light of the streetlamp he made his way to the table on which his own lamp stood, filled and cleaned and ready to be carried up the creaking stairs which reeked of mold and dust and rodents and cabbage. He fumbled for the lucifers which were deposited in an open—nailed—tin box on the table, and lighted his lamp, and the yellow light smoked for a moment or two. He closed the door and lifted the lamp and made his way upstairs, every step snapping under his feet. The still cold inside the house was more penetrating even than that outside, and Joseph's shivering returned.

His room was hardly more than a closet and smelled of sifting dust and damp. He put the lamp on the commode. He looked about the hopeless dreariness of his "home," and at the pile of books neatly stacked in one corner. Sudden heavy sleet began to hiss and rattle against the little window. Joseph took off his coat and covered the one blanket on his sagging bed with it, for extra warmth. Autumnal thunder, one loud and explosive clap, followed on a brilliant flare of lightning, and the wind rose and the glass in the window shook and one loose shutter banged somewhere.

Joseph was conscious of a nauseating ravenousness, and he sat on the edge of his bed and unwrapped the parcel of food. He stuffed the stale bread and sour cheese and cold pork into his mouth rapidly, hardly chewing, so great was his hunger. It had been a generous parcel, and it had been sacrifice from the kind nuns, but it was not quite enough to satisfy him. However, it was more filling than the dinners he ate in this house seven nights a week, for seventy-five cents a week, and he had not spent his fifty cents. He licked the crumbs of bread and cheese and fat from his fingers, voraciously, and was immediately strengthened.

The oily newspaper lay on his bed. An item caught his quick attention. He read it over and over. Then he lay back with his arms under his head, and he thought and thought and continued to think for at least an hour more. He thought only of money, and he had found the first step towards it. It was a matter, now, only of a little more patience, a little more knowledge, and much planning. Even when he blew out his lamp he continued to think, for once unaware of the sick smell of his flat pillow and the hammock-sag of his bed and the thinness of the blanket and coat which covered him. Out of terror and despair and hatred—he had found the way. If it was not the one extolled in theology, it held, for Joseph Francis Xavier Armagh, far more truth and practicality.

Chapter 6

The next night on returning to his boardinghouse Joseph was met at the door by his little landlady, an elderly widow with an innocent, pure and chronically apprehensive face, for life had been no gentler to her than to Joseph, himself. However, it had had the reverse effect on Mrs. Alice Marhall: It had made her so compassionate of others that she wept when accepting the money her boarders paid her weekly, knowing their endless hard labor and their desperate plight—these young and old men without kin or comfort. As she had neither herself—though she never knew a paroxysm of self-pity—she mourned over them. No bitterness had settled in her timid soul, no hatred of God and man, no vengefulness. Part of this was due to the fact that she had very little intelligence and part to her faith which never questioned. To Mrs. Marhall "God knew best, our Consolation and our Help," and she prayed fervently not only for "the heathen" and the black slaves but everyone whom her small mothlike mind brushed for an instant.

She would have incurred Joseph's immediate contempt —for her conversations were always full of pieties and biblical aphorisms—had she not reminded him of his mother's mother who had died in the Famine of starvation. There was the same unshakable simplicity, the same patience and sincerity, the same far distant look of one who had known and had seen unspeakable pain and suffering and had accepted it with heartbreaking endurance. But the apprehensive expression of the brutalized innocent remained on her small pallid face, in the anxious look of her dwindled gray eyes, in the nervous placating smile, in the aimless little movements of her hands. Her black crinoline was greenish in its ancient folds and threadbare, but her mobcap was always white and tied with old-fashioned ribbons, and her apron glistened with starch and was never stained. She

76

seemed like a starved old bird to Joseph, and her hands were scorched with homemade soap and labor, for no one helped her in her dying house and she did all things connected with it—including emptying the slops—without aid.

She sometimes irritated Joseph with her homilies and her concern for him and the other boarders—when she could waylay him—but he never dismissed her with a sharp word or overtly showed her impatience. He had lost his own innocence long ago but the innocence of such as Mrs. Marhall always touched him. Moreover, he had been brought up to respect age, even if senile, and to honor the old if only because of the evil life had inflicted on them through long and monstrous years. For, had they not mastered the secret of endurance, and were they not brave?

She accosted Joseph tonight as he entered the house—wet and chilled—with her outstretched gnarled hand which, however, did not touch him. She had early learned that he flinched at contact with others, so the hand, meant to reach in sympathy and maternal consolation, did not even approach his streaming sleeve. She held a corked bottle in her other hand, and she smiled tentatively.

"Mr. Armagh," she said, in her voice which was barely more than a whisper, "I heard you coughing all night, as you have coughed for weeks, but it was terrible, last night, truly it was. And I—I mixed an old elixir for you, my father's remedy for all ills, but mostly for the lungs and the throat, and I hope you will take it kindly and not think I am interfering—" (In spite of her lack of keen intelligence she had the elemental perceptiveness of a young child, and she knew Joseph for a proud young man and one as remote and as indifferent to others as a tower on a hill.)

Joseph's lips tightened, and then he saw her pleading eyes, always so watery and shrinking, and he thought again of his grandmother who had given her last loaf of bread to a pregnant girl. So he took the bottle. She said, "It's very good, truly. Thyme and horehound and honey with a little sorrel. So harmless, but so very effective."

"Thank you," he said. She liked his "foreign" voice, deep and resonant and polite, with its undertone of lilting music. "I should like to pay you for it, Mrs. Marhall."

She was about to refuse, hurt, when she remembered his pride. She averted her eyes. "It was nothing, truly. I grow the herbs in my garden, and I had a little honey left over from the summer, a kind friend who keeps bees—" She looked at Joseph then, and blurted, "Three cents will be more than enough, Mr. Armagh!"

She added, "On your payday."

He put the bottle in his pocket, gravely inclining his head as he prepared to mount the steps to his room to wash and then to join the other boarders in what Mrs. Marhall somewhat grandly called her "dining room." But Mrs. Marhall, deprecatingly clearing her throat, said, "You had a caller, Mr. Armagh, but it seems to me a very peculiar caller—"

Joseph thought immediately of Mayor Hennessey. "A policeman?" he asked, and he left the first step of the stairway and returned to Mrs. Marhall and she saw his face and was frightened, and retreated.

"Peculiar?" he demanded in a loud voice. "What do you mean by that? What was his name, his appearance?"

She put up her hands to him, palms outward, as if she would fend off a blow, and again when Joseph saw this he felt a poignant twinge. He tried to smile. "I am a stranger," he said, "and I know no one, so how could I have a caller? I was just surprised."

But Mrs. Marhall was from childhood acquainted with fear, and she saw the acute fear in Joseph's eyes and trembled, herself. She said in a quick and stammering tone, "Oh, I am sure it wasn't anyone alarming, Mr. Armagh, not a policeman for what would a policeman want with you? It was just a—gentleman—a rather rough gentleman, not really a gentleman— Oh, dear, I'm afraid I am muddled! Just a big—man—nicely spoken but a little crude in manner, and he held his hat in his hands and bowed to me, and said he was a friend of yours. He asked if you lived here."

Joseph controlled his quickened breathing. Mayor Hennessey need not have sent a man for that information. Sister Elizabeth could have given it to him, and now the absurdity of the mayor sending a messenger to him struck him and his rigid body relaxed.

"What was his name?"

"A Mr. Adams. That's what he said. An old friend. He seemed to know you, Mr. Armagh. He described you to me, and it was just so, eighteen or thereabouts, and tall and thin with thick auburn hair—that is the color, isn't it?—and you worked in a sawmill. Dear me, I hope I did no wrong admitting you lived here, Mr. Armagh! And I told him you lived here for nearly three years and was very respectable, and minded your manners and paid promptly and I had no complaints and he said he was glad to hear it, and it was truly you. I asked him if he wished to leave a message, and he said no, but that he would see you on Sunday."

She was so heartened at Joseph's sudden bleak smile that she tittered and applied her apron to one eye. "Oh, you know who he was, Mr. Armagh, and I am so relieved!"

So, thought Joseph, old Squibbs is making sure of me, is he, and satisfying himself that I lived in this house for some time, and am honest, and no thief who will skip with his swag of a fine Sunday.

"He called you 'Scottie,' " said Mrs. Marhall, "which I think was disrespectful. Nicknames are always uncivil—unless they are used by friends."

"Oh, he is an old friend," said Joseph, and smiled again without much humor. "Did he ask if I had a family, or something of that nature?"

"Indeed, and I was a little surprised at that, if he was an old friend, he would know, would he not? And I told him no, you had no family, you were an orphan from a place in Scotland—?"

"Edinburgh," said Joseph.

Mrs. Marhall nodded. "Edinburgh. Yes, that I told him. You had no kin, I said, leastways you'd never mentioned anyone, and it is very sad. He agreed with me."

Joseph, taciturn by nature, had not spoken of his brother or sister to anyone in the town but the Sisters at the orphanage. The less anyone knows of you the better for you, was his complete conviction, and the fewer attempts they will make to be friendly and intrusive and later, perhaps, dangerous. He had learned, as a child, to be silent in the presence of the Sassenagh, or, if viciously questioned, to tell as little as possible. This lesson fortified by his natural discretion concerning himself and his natural mistrust, was one never to be forgotten. Daniel Armagh had not been able to understand the reserve of his older son and his carefulness even in the presence of his family, for Daniel by temperament had accepted and trusted all men—and had, Joseph often thought, dearly paid for his folly. "You cannot suspect, Joey, like some unshriven miser or thieving vagabond, and have no confidence in any creature. What would the world be like, Joey, if everyone mistrusted everyone else, and had no love and no faith?"

Safer, the child Joseph had thought. But he had only said, "It's sorry I am, Dada, and I meant no disrespect."

There was none to connect Joseph Armagh of Philadelphia Terrace, the young Scotsman of Edinburgh who worked in a sawmill on the river and had no kin of his own, with St. Agnes's Orphanage, an obscure and stricken and hidden little building in the worst part of the town, and one not known except to Catholics. None knew of his brother and sister and that he was an Irishman and a "Papist," if only a nominal one.

"So, he will see me Sunday," said Joseph to Mrs. Marhall. "I expected him then. Not today. And a good evening to you, Mistress Marhall."

The word "mistress" instead of the American "missus" always made Mrs. Marhall preen as at a grand compliment. It had a gay and a vaguely forbidden but an exciting intimation. She folded her wounded hands under her apron and watched Joseph ascend the stairs with the foolish fondness of a mother. A very likely boy, and a proud clean one, and he would go far, for he was a gentleman in spite of his work and his poverty, and she prayed a little innocent but fervent prayer for him and was comforted.

Joseph washed at his commode and neatly emptied the bowl into the slop pail and rolled down his blue sleeves. He looked at the bottle of "elixir." It would do no harm. The old ladies, including his grandmother, in Ireland, were fine ones for gathering herbs which they mixed in evil-tasting brews, but he remembered that they were often efficacious. At least, he had never heard that they had killed anyone. His cough was becoming more annoying and exhausting since his cold, and he thought of the "consumption" so rife among his people. So he uncorked the bottle and drank some of the contents, and to his surprise it was not vile and it soothed his raw throat. He would remember to take it to work tomorrow together with the lunch—newspaper wrapped—which Mrs. Marhall prepared for him.

The name of John Tyler, the names of the seven seceding Southern states of the Union, the initial affair at Fort Sumter, the agony of President Lincoln, were all unimportant to Joseph Armagh while the winter deepened. The world of men except as it pertained to himself and his family was unimportant. He wasted no penny on a newspaper; he never stopped in the streets of the town to hear the shouts and angry words of new crowds; he did not listen to his fellow workers who talked excitedly of Buchanan and Cobb and Floyd and Major Anderson. They were aliens in an alien world, to him, which concerned him not at all. The language they spoke did not resound in him, their lives did not touch his nor did he permit them to touch his. When Mrs. Marhall said to him once, fearfully, "Oh, is it not terrible, Mr. Armagh, this threat of War between the States?" he had replied with impatience, "I am not interested, Mistress Marhall. I have too much to do." She had stared at him then, disbelieving, and then, incredulously, believing, and though she had always considered him enigmatic and beyond her simple comprehension, now she felt as if he were not of flesh or blood and did not possess any of the sentiments of men or any of their concerns, and she was almost as deeply frightened then as ever she had been in her suffering life. She silently retreated, and pondered and could come to no conclusion.

Mr. Lincoln's train passed through Winfield on the route to Pittsburgh, and a holiday was given so that men could go to the depot for a brief glimpse of the melancholy man who was on his way to Washington for his inaugural as President. The majority wished him well, especially now that the threat of war was increasing, but the hint of assassination excited them and they would not have been too grieved had it come to pass. Their lives were so dingy, so obscure and so lacking in gaiety or any joy or notable event, that a national calamity would have titillated them. But Joseph Armagh, as indifferent to Mr. Lincoln as he was to the existence of the farthest star, did not go to the depot. He had no interest in events except as they threatened him and Sean and Regina, for too deeply and at too young an age had he experienced anguish and frenzy and grief, and if he thought of his relationship to the world at all it was as its enemy.

There was not even any active love in him for Ireland any longer, only memory like a dream. If he had been forcibly questioned he would have said, "I have no country, no allegiances, no loyalties, no kinsmen among others. The world rejected me when I was defenseless, and so I reject it now with all my heart and with any passion I still retain, and I ask of it only to remain apart from me as I do what I must do. Do not try to stir up in me any commitment to any man or any nation or any faith or any cause; do not try to draw me among you, or speak to me as one of you. Let me alone, and I will let you alone, because if I should become any part of you or engage myself among you I could not bear to live any longer. So, let us live in a truce."

He read the books which Sister Elizabeth had managed to procure for him, but he would not read of current affairs and the growing fear and distress in the country. He read philosophy and essays and poetry and literature—all of the past—for now only they had eternal verity to him and could interest him. As for the future, it belonged to him alone and nothing must move him from his course, not war or blood nor the convulsions of men.

"I thought him a lad of intelligence and mind," Father Barton said to Sister Elizabeth. She cocked her head at him and said, "Yes, Father? And is he not?"

"I tried to speak to him of the threatening war and what it portends, Sister."

"Father," said the nun, as if speaking to a child, "Joseph left the affairs of the world long ago. He is like a sextant pointed to one star only. Let him be." When the priest still could not understand, she said to him gently, "He dares let nothing approach him, for his soul is like worn thin crystal which could shatter at a touch."

"He is not the only one who has suffered in this world!" the priest replied with unusual asperity.

"We each respond to events," said Sister Elizabeth, "according to our nature—some of us with fortitude and faith, and some disastrously. Can any man understand another? No, only God, and what is between Joseph and God is theirs alone."

"I fear for his soul," said Father Barton.

"I also fear for his soul," said Sister Elizabeth, but the priest suspected she feared for a different reason than his which he could never comprehend. He could only complain, "I doubt he has a soul like crystal. Stone, Sister, is more like it. You are fanciful."

This conversation would not have interested Joseph in the least had he even heard of it. He paid the convent an extra dollar a week for his family now, as the long torture of the winter drew towards spring. For fear of falling ill he spent fifty cents extra a week on food for himself, and bought a stout pair of boots to protect his feet from the snow. He grew two inches that winter and appeared years older than his actual age of seventeen.

Each Sunday, armed with a truncheon that never left the seat beside him, he drove a van or a wagon of ostensible feed and grain to the various saloons in the town. Each Sunday he collected the forty or fifty or sixty or even the one hundred dollars in payment for the true illicit load he carried under the burlap bags. The money was given him in brown paper, which he kept in his pockets—tight rolls tied with thick string. He delivered the money to Mr. Squibbs, who was highly satisfied with his latest employee, and to such an extent that after the first few months he did not even count the money in Joseph's presence. He allowed his "Sunday lads" fifty cents extra for a lunch, but Joseph did not spend it. He saved it, along with two of the four dollars he made on Sunday, and he had contrived a money belt of sorts to tie about his waist, for he would not leave the bills in his boardinghouse. Nor did he consider the bank, and for a reason pertinent to him.

The police never stopped or questioned him, and he was too indifferent to wonder why, though the ten dollars promised by Mr. Squibbs would have been welcome even at the cost of a night in jail. But for some reason he was not halted.

"He looks stupid, like a dummy," said Mr. Squibbs's brother. "That's why the po-leese don't even see him. If they did they'd think we'd have more sense than to hire him to carry likker."

Mr. Squibbs chuckled. "All the better. But he don't look stupid. Looks kind of like he don't even live here. Got a mean look in his eye, though, if you just try to be pleasant or make a joke, and he looks at you like you're pizen or somebody from the moon."

The thoughts of Joseph Armagh were long thoughts, which would have appalled Sister Elizabeth. The money increased in his money belt. He counted it every day or two, greasy bills of a great size which were more precious to him than his own life. They were the passports which guaranteed entry into living for his brother and sister. Without them, they would be barred forever from the world in which they must live—which would never be his world. And as the months passed that which was within him became more taut and rigid, and more dangerous.

The Confederacy was making active plans for war. Not

long after Mr. Lincoln's inauguration three members of a Southern commission went to Washington to discuss with the President a more or less amiable agreement concerning public debts and public property, agreements which would go into effect after total separation of the Confederacy from the Union. They informed Mr. Lincoln that "we are the representatives of an independent nation, de facto and de jure, and we possess our own government perfect in all its parts and endowed with all the means of self-support, and we desire only a speedy adjustment of all questions in dispute on terms of amity, good-will and mutual interest." To which Mr. Lincoln sorrowfully replied that his new Secretary of State, William H. Seward of New York, would answer in due time.

The President understood the pride and the deep anger and affront which the South cherished, and he knew that according to the Constitution it had every right to secede from the Union. To object, to use force against the South, was un-Constitutional, and none knew this better than the President. But as he loved his country, both North and South, he was as terrified as any man of his character could be. Beyond the Atlantic lay the old lustful nations, the imperialistic nations, who craved this new and burgeoning country, and desired nothing more than to have her sundered and weakened or fighting a bloody fraternal war, so that they could fall upon her and divide up her members among themselves. It was at this point that Imperial Russia casually mentioned to the British Empire—through the tactful offices of ambassadors—that should Britain overtly and covertly take an active part in the approaching conflict, and seize before others also had an opportunity to seize—Russia's sentiments would not be lukewarm. Britain, never impulsive, sat back to consider, though she openly declared her sympathy with the South, a declaration which made the Czar smile in his magnificent beard.

This episode, vaguely mentioned in American newspapers, ought to have interested Joseph Armagh. It did not. He was as removed from and as dispassionate about this world as a shadow. He lived his internal and secret life, and had his deadly concentration of will which had been trained on the world like a great weapon ready for attack.

On the warm April day when Captain George James fired on Fort Sumter, Joseph Armagh, after his day's work, set out on the three-mile walk to Green Hills, where the

Mayor of Winfield lived. The roaring excitement in the town was, to him, like the far barking of dogs, and just as significant.

Chapter 7

Though Joseph had rejected the world of men as no part of his own being, except to accede to his secret ambitions, he could not be insensible to the beauty of the land. His innately poetic Irish nature could not detach itself, however he consciously tried, telling himself that nothing mattered or really had any existence beyond what he must accomplish. All else was trivial and a waste of time and strength.

He was going today for a look at the mansion of Mayor Tom Hennessey, for he had heard it was the most lavish in Green Hills and he needed another emphatic sword of desire in his growing arsenal. He wished to see how rich men lived and in what surroundings, and to study the environment in which he was determined that his family must live. As for himself, he had no yearning for luxury or beauty or ease. He wanted them only for Sean and Regina, whose lives depended on their brother.

He had never been in this particular territory before, beyond the confines of the flat monotony and grit of Winfield and its ugly little houses and unkempt square. He was soon in the countryside, brilliantly green in the spring, lush, leaping with life and urgent wild flowers and patches of wild violets and random pools of daffodils and trees golden with unfurling leaves, and little rills and brooks wandering through copses and even spilling over onto the uneven road of mingled stone and drying mud. It was still shiningly bright and the sun was just beginning to lower in a glitter of radiant orange behind the western trees, and the air was lively and murmurous and piercingly sweet with excited bird calls. In the distance stood the misty softness of green hills, and the ground and road rose towards them. Joseph passed a large pond as purely blue as an Irish lake, and the young yellow leaves of willows bent over it and were reflected in its stillness, and from its proximity now began to rise the chorus and hosannah to life of the peepers. From nearby fields came the nostalgic music of cowbells as cattle prepared to go to their paddocks, and wind stirred the tall new grass at the borders of the road and above it all was a sky faintly green and luminous.

Joseph had long forgotten the feeling and meaning of peace. But now he suddenly knew it, and it was accompanied by a pang of such sorrow that it was like a fresh agony. He stood and looked about him, and listened for several minutes, alone in a fresh new world. Then the peace and even the sorrow left him as he thought: This is only for the rich and not for the poor. They live in silent green contentment, but we live in dust and murk and ugliness—for they are the fortified and we are the helpless. For a brief moment or two he had made contact with the world, and it had wounded him once more, so he set his face and stared only at the road as he went on. But he could not shut his ears to the jubilation of young life, nor his Irish soul to the scent of innocent carnal earth and the fecundity of that which lived. Yet he felt that this all mocked him, the destitute and the homeless. The poetry of sound which he heard, the fragrance of the earth, the very poignancy of tree trunks and blue shadows on the grass and the quiet dim hollows of silence in the woods, seemed to cry out to him, "These are not for you, for you have no money. You have no money!"

But I will have it! he thought with familiar savagery. I will have it, no matter how! And he lifted his face and his hand to the sky in hatred and determination.

Now he was approaching the rich residential area of Green Hills, where the safe lived and had their tranquil existence far from Winfield. The road began to wind, and other roads left off from it, and at near or far distances Joseph saw the white brick or sandstone mansions of the fortunate and the cynical, and the gravel walks that led across lawns like green water and past gardens filled with the purple and gold of iris and daffodils and red tulips in spring beds. Almost every estate was guarded by wrought-iron and ornamental fences and tall gates which did not shut out envious glances but announced to passers-by that they must not trespass. The fire of the approaching sunset ignited tall mirror-like windows with its own color, and slate roofs glimmered and occasionally a red brick chimney emitted a feather or two of soft gray smoke. It was very silent and full of peace which Joseph could no longer feel.

He knew that Mayor Hennessey lived on Willoughby Terrace, and he watched for discreet board signs as roads were increasingly named. Then he came on it to his right and he turned off the rough main road onto a narrower but smoother road, very winding and overhung with oaks and elms and maples. A low graystone fence followed the road instead of iron fences and gates and over this he could see the mansions, some sunken below the rising ground of the distance, some bold and standing like monarchs on their land. Dogs barked warningly, and some collies raced across lawns to the stone walls and challenged Joseph's passing. He did not pause nor even look at them. He was watching for an iron shield embedded in the wall with the number eighteen upon it in Gothic scroll. He finally found it, and stopped to look past the lawns which rolled and spread serenely over several acres.

The mayor's white house was the largest and most imposing of any which Joseph had seen so far, and the most opulent and pretentious. Its center was of the classic outdoor portico type of ancient Roman fashion with thick and smooth white pillars and Corinthian capitals and frescoes and ponderous carved bases. The floor within was of white stone, gleaming and polished as marble, leading to mighty double bronze doors of Italian origin. On each side of the tall porticoed entrance structure stretched a two-storied wing, broad as well as high, with ornamental friezes near the eaves and a wide balcony at the end, extending from the upper floor. Every window was partly shaded by shirred gray silk, glimmering as silver; flowering spring shrubs, yellow and snowy, pressed against the shining walls. Great pruned trees were scattered in groups of twos and threes on the lawn, and every blade of grass had its own iridescence in the lowering light of early evening. A marvelous tranquillity lay over everything like a blessing, heightened by the deep sweet sadness of descending robin song.

So, thought Joseph, himself lives here and his money came from human misery and death and despair, as always it does. Yet, there is none to reproach him, neither God nor man, and all fawn upon him and he will be a senator and crowds will laud him and he will have the ear of the President and all will honor his riches and consider him worthier than other men because of it. I, too, honor him, for he is a thief and a murderer and a mountebank and a whoremonger—and does the world not prefer such to an honest and devoted man? It can only be that the good and noble man is a fool, despised by God, Himself, for does not the Bible say, "The wicked flourish like a green bay tree" and their children dance with joy in the streets? It is true.

He leaned his elbows on the wall and contemplated the grounds and the mansion and listened to the evensong of the birds. Here would his sister, Regina, have lived had he permitted it, slowly forgetting that she was of another family, lost to him and Sean forever. She would have slept in one of those chambers of the upper story, and would have run on these lawns. But, she would no longer be Mary Regina Armagh of a prouder name than Hennessey and it would be as if she had died, and she would finally have believed that those within were her family and she had no other, and her love would be for unworthy strangers.

Not for an instant did Joseph regret his decision concerning his sister. He could only smile grimly at the house and nod his head over and over as in secret agreement with himself.

He heard the shrill ringing sound of a young child's voice, and a very little girl came suddenly running across the grass towards the wall where he stood, and she was followed by an elderly woman in the blue cotton dress, white apron and cap of a nursemaid. Joseph stood in brushy shadow and he looked at the child, who was about Regina's age and screaming with malicious mirth. She was somewhat smaller than Regina, but plump, and she wore a frock of white silk and a little jacket of blue velvet trimmed with silver embroidery and as her tiny petticoats swayed they revealed the ruffles of lace pantalettes and little black slippers and white silk stockings.

She had a round golden little face saucy and rather flat, and merry hazel eyes, and her smooth brown hair had been trained into glistening curls that reached almost to her shoulders. Her lips were full and red and showed bright teeth, and her nose was tilted. It was not a pretty face, but she had a look of constant mirth that was very attractive and even fascinating. Regina was grave and thoughtful. This child—Bernadette, is it?—had probably never wept for fear in her life and probably had no thoughts but of her own babyish satisfaction. Like Regina, she was four years old.

She had almost reached the wall but did not see the watching Joseph in the shadows. She looked about her with gleeful mischief, and as the nursemaid, uttering loud reproaches, was almost upon her, she darted away like a squirrel, squealing with impish laughter, showing her pantalettes up to her fat thighs. She ran very fast and soon she was lost among the trees and the panting old nursemaid stopped to catch her breath and shake her head.

The slow spring twilight began to flow over the lawns and Joseph turned away and began his long walk back to Winfield. A mist was rising over the ground now and the joyous cries of the peepers were louder and more insistent. The sky was a pure soft green and the orange of the west had turned to scarlet. A wind came up, heavily scented by warming pines and living plants.

Joseph had just reached the intersection of the private road with the main road when he heard the rattling of wheels and the rapid pound of hoofs. He looked down the broad road and saw an open victoria approaching pulled by two beautiful white horses. A coachman, young and in fine livery, was driving the horses and he looked at Joseph out of a broad and bellicose face, snapping his whip, as the carriage turned in on Willoughby Terrace. But Joseph did not look at him. He was staring at the occupant of the victoria, and he had no doubt at all that this was Mayor Tom Hennessey, for he had once seen his woodcut in a newspaper page which had enclosed his lunch.

As Mrs. Hennessey was young Joseph had thought to see a young husband, for the photograph had been flattering. But Tom Hennessey appeared to be a man approaching forty, at least, a big, wide handsome man with a wenching and florid face and slate-gray narrow eyes, and an exigent, even brutal, mouth. He had the Irish long lip, as Joseph had also, but a thick ridge of a nose protruded above it, giving his face an arrogant and scoundrelly expression. His chin was smooth-shaven, as was his lip, and heavy and dimpled, and it indicated common blood.

He was clad in fawn broadcloth with a greatcoat of brown velvety cloth, and his waistcoat was richly embroidered. He wore a tall and shining hat, and from under it flowed his brown and waving hair and his brown sideburns. He looked potent and virile and cruel, though his mouth was automatically arranged in a look of amity and humor. His gloved hands rested on an ebony walking stick with a gold head, and his jewelry was flashing and considerably vulgar.

Foot travelers were few on Willoughby Terrace and Tom Hennessey's attention was caught by the sight of this tall thin youth with the beggarly clothing and workman's boots and woolen cap. A servant? A gardening hand? Tom Hennessey had the born politician's powers of keen observation and he missed nothing, no matter how unimportant. The sunken blue eyes of Joseph were met squarely in sudden confrontation with the merciless gray eyes of the older man. It was absurd to the mayor, but something which had quickened shot between them and the mayor was fully conscious of it as was Joseph. The mayor touched the rump of his coachman with the tip of his cane and the man brought the wonderful horses to a halt very close to the stranger.

The mayor had a round and sonorous voice, the voice of a blackguard politician, and it was mellifluous and fruity in addition, trained as it was by ruthless guile. He said to Joseph, "Do you live on these estates, my lad?"

Joseph wanted to go on with a mumble but his own interest in the mayor held him near to the horses' heads. "No," he said. "I do not."

Tom Hennessey had been born in Pennsylvania, but his father had been born in Ireland and he well-remembered the rich brogue and it echoed now in Joseph's voice. Tom's eyes sharpened. He studied Joseph calmly but completely from his seat in the victoria.

"What is it, then, that you do?" he asked and smiled his engaging smile. But the smile did not have the innocent charm of Daniel Armagh, but the charm of the born rascal.

Joseph looked at him in silence and not with trepidation. His thin wide cheekbones, sprinkled with freckles, seemed to become more noticeable.

"It's out for a walk, I am," he replied. Now he became wary. If this man spoke to his wife of Joseph's appearance, and his Irish intonations, then she would immediately suspect Joseph's identity. There would be no danger in that, but to Joseph the whole world was dangerous and should not be informed. He added, "I am a gardener's helper."

"Hum," said the mayor. Had not the news been so portentous today, and were he not returning hurriedly home from Winfield to pack for a fast journey to Washing-

ton—as a senator just confirmed by the State Legislature—
he would have taken the time to satisfy his curiosity about
Joseph. Abruptly, he ordered the coachman to drive and
the horses skipped on. But Joseph stood and watched the
vehicle until it was out of sight beyond a bend in the road.
He smiled a little. His conviction that he had been only too
right concerning Regina's adoption was confirmed. A father like that—he would inevitably have poisoned that
young soul with his own sensuality and coarseness. Shanty
Irish, commented Joseph to himself, in scorn, as he walked
rapidly towards town. Did America, then, have no pride
that she should honor such as Tom Hennessey and raise
them to high estate? Joseph, for the first time in years,
began to whistle as he walked back to Winfield, and his
young heart was lighter than it had been since he had been
a child. If the Tom Hennesseys could become rich and famous and honored in this America, then an Armagh could
also, and easier.

He thought of what he had seen, and he looked back
over his shoulder at the silvery mist which was blowing
over the softening green hills, and it seemed to him that
this was the fairest sight he had ever beheld and that he
must live here one day, and on not too far a day. It would
be the home of Sean and Regina with himself as guardian,
behind high walls, and perhaps the peace he had momentarily experienced an hour or so ago would return to him
until the end of his life. Not joy, not wealth for wealth itself, not laughter and songs and travel and beauty and ob-
sequiousness and servants, not love—no, he wanted only
peace and forgetfulness until the blessed time when he
could turn his face away from it all and be done with it.

It was dark when he reached his boardinghouse and
again he read what he had first read last November on a
black and sleeting night in the midst of his suffering, and he
thought and said to himself, It will be next Sunday.

Chapter 8

On Saturday night, after work, Joseph counted up the money he had saved. It amounted to seventy-two dollars, after nearly six months of Sunday work, and sacrifice and the payment of three dollars a week to the orphanage. It seemed an enormous sum to Joseph, but he knew it was not enough.

He carefully wrote a letter, bought a stamp at the post office, near the depot, and mailed it. It was the first posted letter he had ever written in America. Absently, he noted the large poster in brilliant red, white, and blue on the post-office walls, urgently calling for volunteers for the Army and the Cavalry and the Navy, but it meant nothing to him though he was surrounded by men who excitedly discussed it. He went out, unseen and himself indifferent. He stopped on the street, standing on the brick sidewalk, and the barrenness of the town struck him again, the absence of vital color, the few isolated and drooping trees leafing listlessly in the late May twilight. Men passed him, reading newspapers with large black print, and there was a sense of hurry in the air and elation. For an instant Joseph felt it, for it was almost palpable, and he reflected with his usual dark irony that death and war and disaster had their own impelling excitement which stirred and lifted the dull mind.

He suddenly thought of his great-grandfather's wake, before the full Famine—Moira's grandfather. He, himself, had been but five and his parents had taken him with them, for Moira was a realist and believed children should early know about death for, was it not as natural as life and birth, and was it not the soul's introduction into life everlasting? Daniel had demurred, for he was softer of nature than Moira, and Joseph had felt his first wild impatience with his father, his first repudiation of sentimentality. The wake had begun somberly among a large crowd in the snug small house, and even the walls were lined with mourners, for the old man had been cherished. Then the poteen was passed about, and a table of cold funereal meats was discovered, and shortly thereafter the drama of death had become melodrama, not only a solemn occasion but a theatrical one in which the corpse was the leading character. Poteen flowed, tears flowed, cries and exclamations rose, loud keenings were like flutes and trumpets. The mourners mourned with exaltation. Daniel Armagh had been present at many wakes but they never failed to shock him and convince him of their impropriety, but Joseph, cynical from birth, and understanding, knew that men can find piquant stimulation even in calamity. Later he was to know that were it not for these men would go mad, for life would be totally unbearable. Unlike the bewildered Daniel, Joseph could understand why Moira and her mother could push Daniel away with a quick wrath when he tried to comfort them and hush their wailings. In their doleful way they were enjoying themselves and resented interference, and their tears washed away their pain and made them important. Even the two priests present looked at Daniel with annoyance, as if at an uncomprehending stranger, and eventually one had led him away and had gently put a large mug in his hand.

In his long reading Joseph had read somewhere, "Life is a comedy for the man who thinks, a tragedy for the man who feels." To Joseph life was a black comedy, if a tragic one in its overtones, and he accepted it. He kept himself apart from it for it would sap his strength. He remembered another aphorism: "That man is strongest who is alone." He had long ago refused to feel the immanence of tragedy as it concerned others, and he turned from the fatal involvements of mankind and felt only contempt.

He went to the orphanage, though this was but Saturday night, and Sister Elizabeth was surprised to see him. "The children are in bed," she said. "But, I will ask Sister to bring them to you if you cannot see them tomorrow, Joey."

"No," he said. If he saw his brother and sister now it would be a weakness he could not afford, and might hold him back.

He said, "Sister, I am going away for a little while, a few months, perhaps a year. I have another job, in Pittsburgh, which will pay me better."

"Capital, Joey!" she said, and looked at him searchingly. "Oh, Joey, you are going to join the Army?"

"No." The idea amused him, and he gave the nun his dark unmirthful smile. "But it is connected in some fashion, Sister. It will pay me very well—in Pittsburgh."

"You must write as soon as you are settled," said Sister Elizabeth. A peculiar uneasiness came to her, which she dismissed at once, being a sensible woman.

"I will." He looked down into her shrewd eyes, and hesitated a moment. "I hope, in the near future, to send for Sean and Regina."

"I see," said the nun. "You will send your address?"

Joseph paused. "I will not be staying, Sister, at one place, but I will send money now and then." He put a roll of bills into her hand. "There is fifty dollars here, Sister, for Sean and Regina, for their board. When that is gone there will be more from me."

Her peculiar uneasiness sharpened. "I wish I could know that all will be well for you, Joey."

"Sister, your meaning of 'well' may not be mine, I am thinking."

She looked at the height of him, the breadth of his thin shoulders, his hungry slenderness, and then she saw, as always, the power in his set face, the cold blue glimmer of his sunken eyes. But for the first time she felt that Joseph Armagh was dangerous. Instantly she chided herself for her absurdity: A young man, only seventeen! A hard-working and sober young man—dangerous! But she had known danger many times in her life and however she laughed at herself she remained apprehensive.

He went out into the early night, unaware that Sister Elizabeth was watching him from the doorway, and he looked back at the façade of the convent-orphanage for the last time. He knew he would never see it again, and he was thankful. He thought of his brother and sister asleep behind those frail wooden walls, and he pressed his lips together against a wince of pain that he was leaving them without a goodbye.

He returned to his boardinghouse and looked at his few belongings. He would have to leave his beloved books. He laid out his one change of clothing beyond what he already wore. He packed these tightly in a cardboard box, pitifully small, even though it included another pair of mended boots. He was glad that it was cool enough, at night, to wear his patched greatcoat. He lay down on his bed and went to sleep at once, for long ago he had taught himself to sleep immediately and on demand. The violet twilight deepened outside and the swallows blew against a purpling sky, and the town murmured with the excitement of threatened war. But Joseph Armagh slept with resolution for it had nothing to do with him.

"Go with God, Joey," Sister Elizabeth had murmured as his tall emaciated body had swung down the street, but Joseph had not heard her and he would not even have smiled had he heard. She no longer existed for him.

It was only faintly light, faintly gray, when Joseph awoke in the morning. The silence was total, for it was too early even for church bells. The air, he was pleased to feel, was a little chilly and so his greatcoat would excite no attention. He wrote a note on a piece of brown paper to Mrs. Marhall: *I am sorry to leave you, Mistress Marhall, but I have been offered an excellent post in Pittsburgh and will leave for it today. I could not give you notice, but kindly accept, with my compliments, this ten-dollar gold certificate. I will not be returning. I am grateful for your kindness to me in the past. Your obedient Servant, Joseph Armagh.*

His handwriting, so meticulously taught to him by an old priest he no longer remembered, was copperplate and careful, as well as bold and strong and clear.

He looked thoughtfully at the gold certificate he had placed on his note. He could not understand this rank mawkishness of his, for he owed the woman nothing. He took it in his hand and debated. It was precious; he had earned it. He despised himself as he put it back on the paper, and then he shrugged. It was the utmost folly to see that poor frightened face so sharply now, and the wavering and placating hands. But, she was an innocent and to the end of his life Joseph was moved by innocence and only by innocence. She too had owed him nothing, but she had prepared an "elixir" for him, and had placed a ragged afghan on his bed during the coldest nights this winter, and he suspected that it had come from her own bed. More than anything else, however, she had never threatened him with sentimentality or intrusion, except on those two occasions, and had granted him the dignity of letting him alone. Maudlin she might be, but insistent never.

He looked at his books. He lifted the thin volume of Shakespeare's sonnets and pushed it under his blue cotton shirt. He picked up his cardboard box and stole silently from the house, never looking back. Like Sister Elizabeth, it no longer existed for him. The street lost its familiarity. He was done with it. Again, he was an absolute alien in an alien land.

He had always carried his lunch in the cardboard box which now held his few possessions, so no one at Squibbs Bros. Grain and Feed, Harness, noted it as he arrived at the stables and office. His wagon and the horses were waiting for him in the new light. The first pale sun was touching high chimneys and the tops of trees, but the earth was still in morning twilight. There was a hint of the coming hot summer in the air, for the smell of dust and dryness was pervasive.

"Good load, today, Scottie," said the foreman. "People are thirsty, thinking of the war," and he chuckled. He gave Joseph the customary few cents for his lunch and Joseph nodded, tucked the coins in his pocket and lifted the reins. "Big load," said the foreman. "Could be you'll be getting back late."

"It doesn't matter," said Joseph. "But do not forget the extra fifty cents if I am."

The town was still silent though here and there flutters of gray smoke were rising from chimneys. Not even the horse-cars were running as yet. Joseph tied up the horses six streets from the depot, then ran swiftly. The depot was just opening, for the 7:10 was expected in an hour from Philadelphia. He hurried to the counter and asked for a ticket to Pittsburgh on the late afternoon train, and paid for it: two dollars from his store. He put the ticket in his pocket. The old stationmaster would remember, if asked, that a young man he had never seen before had that morning bought a ticket to Pittsburgh for two dollars. But it was very improbable that he would be asked. Moreover, Joseph had carefully tucked the last thread of his russet hair under his workman's cap and he appeared insignificant enough, and the stationmaster had seen no wagon and no horses. Ah, thought Joseph, poverty is marvelously anonymous.

He raced back to his tethered horses and found them peacefully cropping some blades of grass that had forced themselves through the bricks of the road. He looked about cautiously. The gray-faced little houses were quiet, a door banged somewhere but no one was about. He climbed onto his seat and set about his deliveries. By ten o'clock he had collected sixty dollars. At this time the people were going to church in the quiet and sunlit town, most on foot, a number in buggies or carryalls or shabby surreys, and all dressed respectably and all with pious downcast eyes. They did not notice the heavy wagon lumbering slowly along the curb or if they did they ignored it. They did not speak of the approaching conflict or even of the beset President for such was "unseemly" on the Sabbath. Church bells began to ring, competing stridently from steeple to steeple, and Joseph could hear the solemn murmurings of organs through doors open to the warming air. Children walked decorously with parents. Feet shuffled on brick. Carriages rattled by importantly. Sunshine lay on the trunks of trees or like bowers of light in the branches. There was a warm smell of manure in the streets and the ever-present dust and heated brick. Birds darted from bough to bough and an occasional squirrel was pursued by a stray dog or cat. To Joseph Armagh it was a street scene that might have been but a mural for all it had life to him and he did not hear the loud fervency of the singing which burst from door and opened window in the churches.

By three o'clock he had collected over one hundred and fifty dollars and had watered his horses at a street trough and had fed them their oats in the bags. He had also eaten his dry lunch. At four he admitted to a furtive saloonkeeper that he was thirsty and hungry and accepted, for thirty cents, two large mugs of foaming yellow beer and a package of hardboiled eggs, four ham sandwiches, a German sausage in a long bun, and two pickles and one salt herring and two slices of seed cake, including a package of potato salad, a German delicacy he had never eaten before. He complained about the price, and so the saloonkeeper returned five cents and magnanimously included another mug of beer. He gave Joseph forty dollars. At the next saloon, at five, Joseph collected another fifty dollars. It had been a very successful day, and the load had been twice as much as usual as Mr. Squibbs had learned to trust his newest "Sunday lad."

Two hundred and forty dollars. With the twelve dollars in his money belt it reached the enormous sum of two hundred and fifty-two dollars. At half-past five he turned his wagon about, reached a street of warehouses completely barren on this Sunday of any passers-by or vehicles, abandoned the horses after patting them, and ran for the depot. He reached it just as a train in the station, with its gigantic funnel and blinking headlight, was shrilly sounding its bell and letting off painful shrieks of steam. Its wheels were already grinding as Joseph leaped aboard the last coach. The conductor, about to shut the door, growled at him, "Almost got kilt, you did, and where's your ticket?" He suspiciously examined it front and back and glared at Joseph who muttered something in what he hoped would pass as a foreign language. The conductor sniffed, said, "Foreigners! Cain't even speak a word of English!" Joseph humbly touched his cap, gabbled again pleadingly. The conductor roughly pushed him inside the coach and forgot him.

Joseph, whose breath was short from his long run, found the coach partly empty and so he chose a seat in the rear and huddled down, pulling his cap as far over his eyes as he could. He did not sit up until he was certain that he was beyond the confines of the town, and then he looked through the filthy window at the countryside. He listened to the howl of the whistle as the train gained speed and rocked on its roadbed. The coach was hot and airless. He tried to open the window but a gush of black soot and steam blew by it. He did not take off his cap but he loosened his greatcoat. He discovered that he had not only taken his cardboard belongings, but had accidentally included the truncheon as well. This amused him. Cautiously, watching his fellow passengers all the while, he pushed the weapon into the long side pocket of his coat. It seemed, to his Irish soul, that this was some sort of an omen, though he usually despised superstition.

He hoped that the horses, intelligent beasts, would eventually grow tired of waiting for him—for he had not tethered them—and would find their way back to their stables. By now it was past time when he should be arriving at the stables, himself, with that great sum of money. He knew that the other men would be looking up the street for him. By eight o'clock they would be searching and would be making the rounds of the saloons. By ten they would be convinced that he had departed with the collections. By eight tomorrow Mr. Squibbs would receive his letter:

I have not stolen your money, sir, but have only borrowed it, on my honor. I have been offered a fine post in Pittsburgh and needed some money to tide me over until I

*have become settled. You may find this very reprehensible,
sir, but I beg of you to trust me for a few months, when I
will return your money with six percent interest. I am no
thief, sir, but only a poor Scotsman in desperate circumstances. Resp'y your Servant, Joseph Armagh.*

Mr. Squibbs would not dare to go to the police for a variety of reasons, and his thugs would not find a Joseph Armagh in the big city of Pittsburgh, for the simple reason
that Joseph's destination was not Pittsburgh at all. He felt
in his pocket for the worn newspaper clipping he had kept
these long months and reread it:

"More and more fine oil wells are being drilled at Titusville monthly and are richly yielding, some of them thousands of barrels a week at least. The little town is booming
as the Klondike in '45, and workers are receiving unbelievable wages. Men are flocking from all over Pennsylvania
and other States to work in the fields, and regrettable Vice
is accompanying them as it always does Riches. Incredible
wages of up to twelve and even fifteen dollars a week are
being paid for mean labor such as hauling the oil barrels to
the flatboats and loading them. Those engaged in drilling, it
is rumored, receive far more. So close to the surface is the
Rich Oil Deposit that it gushes out of the ground on mere
drilling. But a few of the wells are much deeper, and these
have the best of oil, more refined. So some are being
'blown' by nitroglycerin, though not many, and it is quite a
novelty. Intrepid young men, with apparently no regard for
their Lives, are willing to haul nitroglycerin, a very dangerous Element, for the wells, and it is said that they can receive up to twenty dollars a week, unheard-of Recompense.
No wonder Corruption is an inevitable Companion, and
there are now more saloons in Titusville than there are
churches, impossible though this may be in the opinion of
Our Readers. It is fortunate that Titusville still has only
one train a week, on Sunday night, but it is expected that in
a few months it will have daily runs and our Fears mount
accordingly. It is hoped that young Men of Decorum in
other sections of the State will not rush to Titusville to
make their fortunes but to imperil their Souls.

"It is rumored that Pithole, a few miles from Titusville,
has even more astounding Oil deposits, but it is in rough
country and is arduous to reach over some formidable hills
and rude territory. Men from Titusville and other parts of
the State, it is said, are buying up land near Pithole and

hope to do what, in their parlance, is called 'wild-catting.' It is said that 'oil lies on the very ground and in holes and pits, ready for the taking, without drilling, in Pithole.' Alas, if it is so, for a quiet and God-fearing community of a few souls. If enough oil is discovered there a shuttle may be run to Pithole, but that, we hope, will never transpire. There are enough ruthless Entrepreneurs and Gamblers already in Titusville, with eyes on Pithole, and are selling stock certificates hand over fist for Enormous Sums. Yet the Standard Oil Company, we have heard, is evincing interest. So far the owners of the oil fields in Titusville have resisted the blandishments of the Standard Oil Company, so the battle continues for control of the new wealth which will soon entirely eliminate, it is believed, the market for whale and other oils. We are not that sanguine, for we have heard that the odor of crude natural oil is beyond bearing and creates Hazards of smoke and fire.

"While we all rejoice at the abounding wealth of our Great Commonwealth, we must also mourn that its Cohorts abound also, women of unspeakable morals and cardsharps and the vendors of liquors and beer, and dance-halls and opera houses and other dens of Vice. We pray with the deepest piety and apprehension, for the Souls of—" But Joseph had torn off the rest and had kept the clipping.

He tucked the paper in his pocket again. Months ago he had decided to become a "ruthless Entrepreneur" as soon as possible. Men do not get rich by honest labor, he had often thought. They study and then gamble cautiously, but not too cautiously. He knew the danger of failure, but he did not intend to fail. He thought of Pithole as well as Titusville, and the oil which lay there for the taking. He had no grandiloquent dreams of sudden fortune, but he had the intuition of the Irish for the place of eventual fortunes, if a man used his intelligence and overlooked no opportunity. For a beginning, he was willing to do any work and had discovered that willing and able and industrious workers were not as plentiful as employers always desired, and if a man had intelligence, too, then employers were inclined to regard him favorably. Joseph had seen languid, impertinent workers at the sawmills who would work only when under constant supervision, and not even poverty could drive them to greater efforts, nor could the threat of discharge. They were of feeble character, even the most burly, and grumbled and short-shrifted their work, so Joseph had slowly come to the conclusion that they were not worth more than they were paid and were not exploited. By their very shiftless being they were hindrances to such workers as Joseph Armagh, and his kind had to redouble their efforts to attract the benign—more or less—eye of ambitious employers.

It was dark beyond the train window. Joseph opened his parcel of food and devoured three hard-boiled eggs, all the ham sandwiches and pickles and herring and the sausage and its bun, and then finished the meal with the cake. He discarded the potato salad. This done he looked furtively about him at the stinking coach with its poor and nodding passengers, its rattan and broken seats, its floor covered with straw and the ends of cheroots and tobacco-stained spittle. The conductor had lighted the three lanterns that hung from the round wooden ceiling, and the smell was intense in the sooty heat. The whistle howled as the train pounded through the hidden countryside and past little villages where it did not stop, and tiny lighted depots, and the rocking of the coach almost threw Joseph from his seat. The steam and soot spewing past the window were lighted with red sparks, and some of the filth found its way even into the shut coach and the murk and smoke set all to coughing. Joseph saw that his hands were already blackened and he suspected that his face was, also. He had no watch. He did not know the time and dared not ask the trainman for fear of revealing that he understood English. But he knew that the train stopped at a small town in about two hours, and had a shuttle to Titusville, and that it met this train before it turned east towards Pittsburgh.

He thought of Corland, twenty miles from Titusville, and he said to himself, I have found a way to be rich, and nothing will stop me! It needed only what Americans called "a stake," and that he would have in a very short time. It needed concentration on the only thing which mattered in this world.

Joseph, watching the backs and heads of the other passengers, felt for the twenty-dollar goldpiece in a pinned pocket. It was secure. He felt for his money belt, heavy now, and that was secure too. He was on his way, and he smiled and waited.

Chapter 9

The train for Titusville had not yet arrived when Joseph's train reached the little town of Wheatfield. So, with others, he left his train, pulled his cap down lower on his forehead and tried to appear as inconspicuous as possible as he entered the hot little depot, which was well lighted and crowded to its walls. Joseph had never seen such a bewildering gathering of men as he saw now, to his astonishment. There were men in silk and tall beaver hats, rich greatcoats and florid waistcoats and splendidly pinned cravats and fawn pantaloons, men fat and red and sweating of face and with flowing hair and sideburns and exquisitely trimmed beards and mustaches, and carrying Malacca canes with gold or carved silver heads and with fat fingers loaded with sparkling rings and with watch chains embellished with jeweled charms, and conversing with each other with jovial laughter and hoarse joking voices, their avid eyes glittering over strangers. They all smoked thick cigars or cheroots and they smelled of bay rum or racier perfumes, and their boots shone daintily. A considerable number of their faces were pock-marked, but they exuded excitement and confidence and money. Among them milled workmen in cloth caps and patched coats and blue shirts stained with sweat and oil and dirt, and ebullient men in shirtsleeves and with loud hectoring voices demanding and commanding, their fat legs moving constantly. There were also the quiet and deadly men in subdued but rich clothing along the walls, watching all newcomers closely, their rings shining, their shirts ruffled and fluted, their cravats and pantaloons and waistcoats elegant. These were the hunters and gamblers.

Posters imploring enlistments covered the dirty stained walls of the little depot and in one corner stood a young lieutenant in blue with his forage cap smartly over his forehead, a little table before him and two soldiers soliciting the younger men to join "the patriotic service of your choice." Several youths jested with them lewdly; the young lieutenant sweated in the hot rank air but he remained composed and serious though his aides grinned and spat. His eyes glowed with the fervor of the dedicated soldier, and it was obvious that he was a graduate of West Point and not a mere enlisted man. His shoulder patch read, THE ARMY OF THE UNITED STATES. He was proud of it.

All the narrow benches were occupied, though men, as if overcome with impatience, would rise and join the milling crowd, their seats immediately confiscated. The uproar was appalling with the constant crescendos of masculine voices arguing, wheedling, boasting, promising, and raucous. Spittoons were ignored. The floor was almost covered with blackish-brown slime. The stench and the heat overpowered Joseph and he kept near the door in spite of the jostling he received. Men raced out onto the wooden platform with papers in their hands, or carpetbags, cursing the tardy train to Titusville, then raced back inside, their eyes goggling as they sought out friends they had just abandoned. Another smell rose above the smell of bay rum and chewing tobacco and smoke and sweat, the smell of money-lust and greed, and it was insistent. The lamps overhead stank and flamed brightly; a wind blew in cinders and hot dust and chaff. Somewhere a telegraph chattered like an insane woman. Men shouldered others aside, were cursed or clapped on the back. There was an odor of raw whiskey as men tilted bottles to their mouths. The depot was like an enormous monkey house, seething with heat and movement and restiveness and vehement roars and impassioned shouts and great belly-laughter and good-humored imprecations. The old stationmaster crouched like an animal trainer behind his counter, his mouth working silently, his spectacles glimmering, as he tried to placate constant besiegers who demanded an explanation for the delay. He shrugged, he shook his head, he threw up his hands, and looked about him helplessly. Men fell over luggage on the dirty floor, cursed, laughed or kicked aside the portmanteaus and bags. The young Army lieutenant, momentarily discouraged, surveyed the dazing movement in genteel bafflement, for it was apparent that he was a gentleman among men who were certainly not gentlemen. He had been taught goodwill by his mother and his mentors, and he struggled to maintain it, keeping a reserved but friendly half-smile fixed on his boyish mustached face. But his expression was becoming haunted. The flag at his right hung limply in the suffocating and noxious air. The two windows of the depot were open but no cool breeze entered.

After a little Joseph could endure it no longer and he went out on the platform and looked down the tracks which were silvered by the moonlight. Here, at least, there was the cleaner smell of steel and cinders and dust and warmed wood and rock. The lights of Wheatfield glimmered dimly in the distance. The moon rode in a black sky seemingly without stars. Occasionally the platform vibrated as clots of men exploded from the depot to look down the tracks also, to speak to each other in loud excited voices, to joke, to brag, and then to rush back inside as if something of stupendous import was going on in there.

At last Joseph became aware that someone had been standing silently beside him for several minutes and would not move away. He ignored the presence, continuing to stare glumly down the tracks. He was very tired after his long day, and he knew he would have a miserable ride to Titusville, and he was becoming afraid that if he were not vigilant there would be no room on the train for him. He was thirsty. He had seen a pail of water on a bench and a chained tin cup attached to it but he shuddered at the thought of drinking from it. Light spilled through the window nearby onto the platform. Joseph kept just to the rim.

"Got a lucifer, mister?" the presence asked at last in a very young voice.

Joseph did not turn. "No," he said in his usual short fashion when approached by strangers. A small fear came to him. Had he been followed after all? It was this fear and not mere curiosity which made him cautiously move his head a little and glance sideways through the corner of his eyes. But what he saw reassured him. The presence was smaller than he, and infinitely more shabby, even ragged, and it was only a boy about fifteen years old, a boy without a cap or hat or coat, and very thin. He had a starveling appearance but not one of degradation nor had he spoken with the sniveling importunity such as the very poor affected.

His whole appearance and manner were astonishingly lively, even gay and lighthearted, as if he were perpetually happy and interested and cheerful. Joseph, accustomed to the bland anonymity of the Anglo-Saxon appearance in Winfield, was surprised at the elfish face which hardly rose to his shoulder, a dark face, almost brown, the great black eyes gleaming through thickets of girlishly long lashes silken and glimmering, and the electric mop of vital black curls and the prominent "hooked" nose. The undisciplined and obviously uncombed hair spilled over the low brown forehead, over the ears and rioted over the scrawny nape and straggled in vibrant tendrils against the thin flat cheeks. A pointed chin with a dimple, and a smiling red mouth, added reckless gaiety to the impudent face, and white teeth shone eagerly between moist lips.

"I don't even have a cheroot or a stub," said the boy, with actual glee. "I just wanted to talk." His voice was light, almost as light as a girl's, and faintly and exotically accented. He laughed at himself. But when he saw Joseph's truculent expression and his cold, half-averted ironic eyes, he stopped laughing though he continued to smile hopefully. "I just wanted to talk," he repeated.

"I just don't want to talk," said Joseph, and turned aside and studied the rails again.

There was a little silence. Then the boy said, "My name's Haroun. You goin' to Titusville, too?"

Joseph's mouth tightened. He debated a lie. But this strange boy might be on the same train and he would appear foolish or a suspicious runaway or a criminal in flight. So he nodded his head.

"Me, too," said Haroun. Joseph permitted himself to glance swiftly at that remarkable young face again. The boy was encouraged. He gave Joseph a very large smile. "You can make lots of money in Titusville," he said. "If you've got a mind to, and I don't have nothin' else to put my mind to so I am goin' to make money!" He laughed joyously and Joseph, to his own amazement, felt his face move into a smile.

"I can say that, too," he said, and was again amazed at himself.

"All I got in this world is six bits," said Haroun. "All I make is two dollars a week in the blacksmith shop, and a bed in the hayloft and some bread and bacon in the mornin'. It wasn't bad, though. Learnt how to shoe horses and that's a good trade, yes sir, and you can always make a livin' at it. I'da saved money from the two dollars but I had my old granny to take care of, and she was sick and there was medicine, and then she died. God rest her soul," added Haroun with no melancholy in his voice but only affection. "Took care of me after my people died, here in Wheatfield, when I was a little shaver, washin' clothes for the quality folk when she could get work. Anyway, she died, and she's buried in potter's field, but I think like this: Where does it matter where you're buried? You're dead, ain't you? And your soul's gone off someplace but I don't believe up in any heaven as my granny told it to me. Anyway, after I bought my ticket today I've got six bits until I can find work in Titusville, or maybe Corland."

The recital was so artless yet so explicit and so full of confidence and inner surety that Joseph was reluctantly intrigued. Here was one who totally loved life and believed in it and found it blithe, and even Joseph in his youth could recognize the soul which was not only indomitable but lighthearted.

Haroun permitted himself, without resentment or uneasiness, to be inspected thoroughly by Joseph's small eyes which were like bright blue stone between the auburn lashes. He even seemed amused.

Joseph said, "How far do you think you can go on six bits?"

Haroun listened acutely to his voice. "Hey, you're a foreigner, too, like me, ain't you?" He stuck out his small brown hand frankly and Joseph found himself taking it. It was like hard warm wood in his fingers. "Where you from?"

Joseph hesitated. His associates at work in Winfield had known him as a Scotsman. Now he said, "Ireland. A long time ago. And you?"

The boy answered, shrugging eloquently. "Don't know where it is, but I heard it was Lebanon. A funny place, near Egypt or maybe it was China. One of them places. What does it matter where you're born?"

Joseph, the proud, looked at him coldly then decided that one so ignorant deserved no rebuke but only indifference. He was about to turn finally away and into the depot to escape the boy when Haroun said, "Hey, I'll share my six bits with you if you want to."

Joseph was freshly amazed. He looked over his shoulder and halted and said, "Why should you do that? You don't even know me."

Haroun grinned whitely and the great black eyes

laughed. "It'd be Christian, wouldn't it?" and his voice rippled with mischief.

"I'm not a Christian," said Joseph. "Are you?"

"Greek Orthodox. That's what my folks were, from Lebanon. That's where I was baptised. Haroun Zieff. I was only a year old when they come here, to Wheatfield. My Pa was a weaver, but he and my Ma got sick here and died, and so there was just me and granny."

Joseph considered him again, half-turning. "Why are you telling me all this?" he asked. "Do you tell every stranger your whole history? It's dangerous, that it is."

Haroun stopped smiling, and though a deep dimple appeared in each cheek his antic face became grave. He, now, studied Joseph. His full red lips pursed a little and his long eyelashes flickered. Then he said, "Why? Why's it dangerous? Who'd hurt me?"

"Best to keep your own counsel," said Joseph. "The less people know about you the less harm they can do you."

"You talk like an old man," said Haroun, kindly and with no rancor. "You can't sit around all the time and wait for someone to knife you, can you?"

"No. Just be prepared, that's all." Joseph could not help smiling a little.

Haroun shook his head violently and all his curls fluttered over his head. "I'd hate to live like that," he said. Then he laughed. "Maybe nobody ever hurt me bad because I didn't have anything they wanted."

One of the young soldiers sauntered out on the platform, taking off his forage cap to wipe his wet forehead. He saw Joseph and Haroun and brightened. He said, "You men want to join up? Looks like we're going to have a war."

"No, sir," said Haroun with much politeness, but Joseph showed only contempt.

"Pay's good," said the soldier mendaciously.

"No, sir," repeated Haroun. The soldier peered at him with suspicion, at the dark face and the mass of black curls. "If you're a foreigner, you can get to be a 'Merican citizen quick," he suggested after he had decided that Haroun, though obviously dark, was not a Negro.

"I'm already American," said Haroun. "My granny made me one, couple of years ago, and I went to American schools, too, in this here town, Wheatfield."

The soldier was doubtful. Haroun's appearance made him namelessly uneasy. He turned to Joseph who had lis-

tened to this exchange with harsh amusement. Joseph's face
and manner appeased the soldier. "How about you, sir?"

"I'm not interested in wars," said Joseph.

The young soldier flushed deeply. "This country's not
good enough for you to fight for, is that so?"

Joseph had not fought since he had been a young lad in
Ireland, but the memory of combat made his fists clench in
his pockets and the hair at the back of his head bristle.

"See here," he said, keeping his voice quiet, "I'm not
looking for a quarrel. Please let us alone."

"Another foreigner!" said the soldier with disgust.
"Whole country's getting overrun with 'em! The hell with
you," and he went back into the depot. Haroun looked
after him, shaking his head merrily. "Only doin' his duty,"
he said. "No call to make him mad. D'you think there'll be
a war?"

"Who knows?" said Joseph. "Why should it matter to
us?"

Haroun stopped smiling again, and his young face was
suddenly enigmatic.

"Don't anything matter to you?" he asked.

Joseph was startled at the perceptiveness of one so young
and he retreated in himself. "Why do you ask that?" he
said. "That's impertinent, I'm thinking."

"Now, I didn't mean anything," said Haroun, spreading
out his hands in a gesture Joseph had never seen before.
"You just don't seem to care, that's all."

"You are quite right. I don't care," said Joseph. A group
of bellowing men erupted onto the platform and they
glared up the tracks and cursed futilely. They were very
drunk. "Won't get in 'til noon, now!" one bawled. "And got
a derrick to deliver 'fore that! Ought to sue the railroad!"

They returned in a sweaty rout to the depot. Joseph followed them with his eyes. He said, as if to himself, "Who
are all these people?"

"Why, they're prospectors—oil," said Haroun. "They're
going to Titusville to stake out a claim or buy land around
there and start to drill. That's what you're going there to
work for, ain't you?"

"Yes." Joseph looked at Haroun fully for the first time.
"Do you know anything about it?"

"Well, I heard a lot. There's not much work in Wheatfield, with the Panic, and people don't even keep their
horses shod right, and I'd like to make more than two dol-

lars a week," said Haroun, cheerful again. "I aim to be a millionaire, like everybody else who goes to Titusville. I'm going to drive one of them wagons with nitroglycerin, and when I get a stake I'm going to buy a drill myself or go into partnership with somebody, and take options on the land. You can do that, if you can't buy the land, and be sure nobody around Titusville or even Corland is selling out his land right now! You take options, and if you strike oil then you give the owner of the land royalties. I heard all about it in Wheatfield. Lots of men going there now, to work in the oil fields. Some of the men in the depot already struck it rich, real rich, and they're here to buy more machinery cheap, and hire help. I'm already hired," he added, with pride. "Seven dollars a week and board to work in the fields, but I'm going to drive the hot wagons. That's what they call 'em."

"They let a young lad like you drive those wagons?"

Haroun stood up as tall as he could, which was not very tall. The top of his head reached only to Joseph's nostrils. "I am almost fifteen," he said, very impressively. He is not even as tall as Sean, thought Joseph. "I been workin' since I was nine, but I've had five years of schoolin' and can do my letters and figures right well. I'm no greenhorn." Now, to Joseph's surprise, the black eyes were wise and shrewd as well as straight in their regard, but they were not hard or malicious. There was a deep maturity in them, and an awareness without wariness, a pride without mistrust. All at once, to his own confusion, Joseph felt a thick warmth in his throat and the sort of tenderness he experienced when he saw Sean. Then he was frightened at this humiliating assault on his emotions by a mere unimportant stranger, and alarm made him want to retreat.

Suddenly there was a howling and clanging and ringing and grinding on the rails, a clamoring like an outbreak of furious metallic madness. A huge and blinding white eye roared out of the darkness around the bend and the rails trembled and so did the platform. Joseph could hear the rattling of coaches, the hiss of escaping steam as brakes were applied, and there was the train to Titusville screaming towards the depot, the squat black engine dwarfed by the gigantic smokestack which was retching smoke and fire into the night. The engineer, in his striped cap, vigorously pulled the whistle, and the unbearable sound pierced Joseph's ears and he put up his hands to protect them.

Now the platform was boiling with masses of men, all shouting and blaspheming and struggling and carrying bags. Haroun pulled Joseph by the arm. "Get over here," he shrieked over the noise. "Second coach stops right there, and you'd better move smart." He left Joseph for a moment for the side of the door where he had deposited a small cloth bundle and rejoined the older boy immediately with the air of a protector and a guide and a man of the world. He had darted like a cricket, and for a moment or two Joseph thought that he had resembled one, and Joseph saw the small thinness of bare wrists, and bare frail ankles above broken boots. Again he felt that weak degrading twinge which he could not understand.

The strong adult men exploded in masses towards the coaches and the two thin youths were no matches for their strength. The men thrust them aside and boiled into the coaches, kicking and pushing Joseph and Haroun in the process and banging them with their heavy luggage, and cursing them as they struggled to board the train. Joseph found Haroun clinging desperately to his arm and he restrained the angry impulse to shake him off. Once Haroun fell to his knees, punched in the back by a swearing brute of a man, and Joseph felt instinctively for his truncheon. Then he knew that neither he nor Haroun would be able to board except by extreme and punitive measures, so he pulled out his truncheon and literally beat his way through the masses, his young arm flailing. Some of the men fell back, howling, and Joseph pulled his companion through the narrow passage between heavy bodies and helped Haroun to climb the narrow steep steps. The train was already snorting for departure. The coaches were loaded now with seated and bawling and laughing men, and the aisles were crowded and smotheringly hot. There was no place in the coaches for Joseph and Haroun, though men continued to push by them to try to enter the coaches and then clot about the open doors, which could not be shut.

Joseph was panting. He muttered, "God damn them." The sleeves of his greatcoat were torn. He had lost his cap and his russet hair spilled all over his head and nape and cheeks, and he was wet with sweat. Haroun was sallow with pain. But he tried to smile. His breath was heavy and painful and he was holding his thin back in the region of his kidneys, where he had been punched. "Lucky we got this far," he said, "thanks to you. What's your name?"

"Joe," said Joseph. The train started with a lurch. The two boys fell against the rear wall of the coach ahead. They were marooned on the sliding platform between the coach ahead and the one behind. An attempt had been made to overcome the danger to those standing on the platform, a new invention over the coupling and its pin: two moving plates of metal which met occasionally then slid back with the movement of the train. The plates were slippery, and Joseph had to cling to the handhold of the coach ahead. Haroun leaned against the rear of the coach behind, his face running with cold sweat, his breath loud and wheezing and irregular, his feet holding to the moving plate under them. But he still smiled with admiration at Joseph. "You got us aboard," he said. "Never thought we'd make it."

"We may be sorry we did," Joseph grunted. "We'll have to stand out here all the way to Titusville, I am thinking."

Then Haroun uttered a desolate cry. "My bag! I dropped my bag. Now I got no clothes!"

Joseph said nothing. He clung to the iron handhold of the open coach ahead. He must shake off this importunate boy who had apparently decided to adopt him. He would only hamper and make demands and intrude his friendship and so weaken him, Joseph. He looked into the coach, but there was no longer even standing room. Heat and stench poured from it, and the effluvia from the one latrine at the end. The men were all smoking. The lantern light was misty and swaying, and the noise was intolerable. Joseph saw clouded heads wreathed in smoke; smoke billowed along the greasy ceiling. He saw broad shoulders bending and moving and swaying in unison and always he heard the roar and tumult of voices. The coach following was no better. But despite the discomfort the men were hilarious and rowdy and Joseph knew now that there was no greater excitement and joy and cheer than that surrounding the hope of money and the possession of money.

"My bag," wailed Haroun. Wild with impatience Joseph looked down at the dangerously sliding plates, and the narrow opening between them as they slid. "You shouldn't have dropped it," he said. The passage was open to the night and wind and soot and cinders and smoke poured onto it and Joseph coughed spasmodically as he clung precariously to his handhold. "You should never let go of what belongs to you," he added, in a strangled voice.

If he could just find a corner into which he could flee from Haroun! But not even a garter snake could have entered either of the stuffed coaches. Then Haroun screamed, a scream of mortal pain and terror and Joseph turned back to him.

One of Haroun's thin feet, in its broken boot, had been seized at the ankle between the jostling and sliding steel plates on the platform, and he had fallen on his knees. Light spilled from the coaches and Joseph saw the boy's anguished and terrified face and then the blood oozing from his captured foot. The plates still slid backwards and forwards but now they did not entirely close because of the frail flesh and bone caught between them.

"My God! You fool! Why didn't you hang on?" Joseph shouted with mingled rage and fear. He dropped his box and fell to his knees beside the screaming boy. When a plate receded slightly he tugged at the caught foot, but it was wedged. The opening was not wide enough, and each lurch of the pounding train and each sway around a curve and each of Joseph's tugs only enhanced Haroun's agony, and he screamed without let. Now the blood splashed Joseph's pulling hands and he suddenly thought of his mother's blood which he had seen, and he became sick. He tugged harder. He clenched his teeth and despite Haroun's pleas of agony to desist he turned the small foot, telling himself that what had entered could be released. "Shut up," he commanded Haroun, but the boy was beyond hearing anything but his own pain and his own terror.

Joseph soon saw that he'd need help. He shouted over his shoulder at the coach ahead. Three heads emerged and saw what was to be seen, but no man offered to help, though one jeered hoarsely, "Cut off his foot, damn you!" The others laughed, drunkenly, and watched with interest.

Then Joseph thought of his truncheon. He pulled it from his pocket; he waited until the plates slid apart at their widest aperture and thrust the truncheon between them. Then he wedged the steel-shod heel of his sturdy boot into the opening also, and pulled it from his foot. He looked down into the gray darkness between the plates, closing his ears to Haroun's shrieks. He bit his lip. He would have to reach down into the forced opening and push off Haroun's shoe, which was hopelessly caught in the metal. In doing so he risked having his own hand caught and perhaps losing it between the jaws of the plates. He hesitated and a lightning thought rushed through his mind, Why should I risk this for a stranger who is nothing to me?

He looked at Haroun's face, lying now near his thigh, and he saw the tortured innocence of it, the brutalized innocence, and he looked over his shoulder at the laughing and jeering men who were enjoying the spectacle of childish suffering. The edges of the stout leather and steel truncheon were already being chewed by the plates, and so was the heel of Joseph's boot. He would have to act at once. He closed his eyes and pushed his hand between the plates, caught the back of Haroun's shoe and waited for an instant until the orifice widened slightly again. Then in one rapid motion he pushed off the shoe and tore Haroun's foot from the aperture and released his own boot. The truncheon broke and fell down upon the track. A moment later and it would have been too late.

Haroun lay on his face on the sliding plates, shocked into mere whimpering, his tears running over the metal. His ankle was turned and heavily bleeding, his bare little foot piteous in the lantern light which swayed onto the platform. Gasping, Joseph put on his boot and sat beside Haroun. He stretched out his hand and held the other boy's shoulder. "It's all right now," he said, and his voice was low and gentle. He frowned at the flowing blood and at the dirt mingling with it. My God, how had he become entangled in this dangerous situation? He should never have spoken to the boy in the beginning. This is what came of becoming involved with others, and it weakened and destroyed a man. One thing led to another. He would have to do something, now, for the wounded and suffering boy, and he despised himself. He dimly heard the raucous comments and jeering of the men who had watched the struggle.

Haroun was no longer whimpering. Shock had overcome him. He lay flaccid and prone, his meager body moving rhythmically on the sliding plates. The train shrieked into the night. Clouds of smoke gushed onto the platform. The feeble light of a small depot fled by the train. Wheels pounded. Joseph's breathing began to slow.

Then a rough coarse voice sounded over Joseph's shoulder. "What's all this, eh? What's wrong here?"

A stout short man had appeared in the doorway of the coach ahead, a man of about forty, a man richly dressed but with a bald head like a huge pear rising from broad thick shoulders. His wide face was florid and jowled above a folded silken cravat held with a diamond pin. He had tiny eyes like wet raisins, and restless, and enormous pink ears and a fat pursed mouth. A watch chain loaded with gemmed trinkets spread across a bulging waistcoat dazzling in its brocaded colors. His plump hands, which clung to each side of the doorway, glittered with jeweled rings.

He was a man of authority and importance, for the men he had pushed aside stood behind him, still grinning, but respectful. Joseph looked up at the glistening and well-fed face. "He caught his foot. He hurt his ankle. He's bleeding. I got him out just in time," said Joseph with hard and contemptuous curtness. "His foot's hurt. He needs attention."

The man's face quickened at the sound of Joseph's voice. A big cigar was held between stained teeth. He removed the cigar with his sparkling fingers. He grunted then. He looked down at the prostrate Haroun. He said, "Got him out, did you?"

Joseph made no reply. He suddenly felt spent. He hated this bloated man who could do nothing but smoke and stare while Haroun bled and lay in a half-faint on the plates, and was choking and coughing between muffled sobs.

The stranger suddenly shouted in a voice louder than the uproar in the coaches and the howling of the train. "Come on, here!" he bellowed, looking over his shoulder. "Clear another seat, damn you all! Lift this boy and take him inside, or I'll have your lights and livers, damn you!"

No one contested or argued. Men rose in the billows of cigar smoke and a seat was miraculously vacated. The stranger gestured. Two of the men who had watched, jeering and laughing, picked up Haroun and bore him inside the coach and sat him on the seat. The boy's eyes, flooding with tears, remained closed. Blood dripped from his torn ankle. "And in with you, too, boyeen," said the stranger. Disbelieving, Joseph struggled to his feet and entered the coach, and there was a little silence among the crowd and a wider staring, surly and curious. Joseph fell into the space beside Haroun. The back of the seat ahead was reversed and the stranger sat down ponderously upon it and surveyed the two boys. Crowded faces peered. The stench of sweat and smoke and pomade and whiskey choked Joseph's breath. Voices called inquisitively from the front of the coach, and were answered. The lanterns' light was the light of lamps in a twirling fog.

"Well, now," said the stranger, planting his fat hands on his fatter and gleaming knees. "We gotta do something for this spalpeen, don't we? Don't want him bleeding to death. Where you lads from?"

"Wheatfield. Going to Titusville," said Joseph. "To work."

The man bellowed again, without looking away from Joseph and Haroun. "Whiskey, damn your hides, lots of it, and clean kerchiefs! Fast!" There was a flurry behind and about him. He smiled at Joseph. "And what's your moniker, eh? And his?"

His teeth were small and stained and crooked, but there was a certain rude geniality in his smile.

Joseph said, "Joe Francis." He nodded at Haroun. "He says his name is Haroun Zieff."

But the stranger was staring at Joseph intently. "Joseph Francis Xavier—what?"

Joseph's internal muscles contracted. He looked more closely at the broad and glistening face opposite him and at the little dark eyes, so shrewd and cynical. "Just Joe Francis," he said.

The stranger grinned knowingly. "Now, then," he said, "I'm an Irisher, meself, though born in this country. Dada came from County Cork. Name's Ed Healey. Never been on the ould sod, but heard enough from Dada. So I know an Irisher when I meet one. Afraid to say you are, is that it? Don't blame you, in this country. But an Irisher is match enough for anybody, ain't he? But don't never be ashamed of your name, boyeen."

"I'm not," said Joseph.

"But you're running from something, is that it?"

"Perhaps," said Joseph, and thought of Ireland and not of Mr. Squibbs. He also thought of his father.

"Not a long tongue in you, is there?" said Mr. Healey, in a tone of approval. "That's what I like: A man of few words. So, Joseph Francis Xavier something-or-other, you're going to Titusville with this lad with the heathen name?"

"He is no heathen. He's a Christian," said Joseph. He was still wary. And his profound exhaustion was growing.

He looked up at the crowding and avid faces clustered around their seats and they were like faces in a nightmare, and as alien as the countenances of hell. Mr. Healey's crimson and enormous face swelled and retreated before his eyes.

From a sudden vast dark silence Mr. Healey's voice roared in on him. "Eh, you drink this, boyo! Can't have you dying on me!" Joseph became aware that some hiatus had come to him, a dim unconsciousness, a mindless blank. He felt the edge of a tin cup against his lips, and he turned his face aside. But a gigantic pink hand was pressing the edge again to his mouth and he had to drink to escape it. A scalding and smarting and burning liquid ran into his mouth and then into his throat, and he gasped. Then there was a widening warmth in his empty stomach, and he could see clearly again.

"Need your help," said Mr. Healey. "Irishers don't faint like the ladies. Now, look here. I'm going to give this lad of yours a jolt, too, but a bigger one, so he won't feel nothing. You've got to hold him for me. Can't trust these drunken sods of mine."

Even Joseph, resentful of and resisting always the force of authority, instinctively obeyed. He said to Haroun, "We are helping you, with your foot." He put his arms about the whimpering and weeping boy, tightly. Haroun opened his wet eyes and Joseph saw the trustfulness in them, and he frowned. "Yes, Joe," said Haroun.

Large and clean and scented kerchiefs had been produced in profusion. Mr. Healey kept them folded on his knee. He gave Joseph the tin cup again, with swirling pale liquid in it, a considerable amount. "Bourbon, best white mule," said Mr. Healey. "Make him drink every drop." He held a large jug in his hand and nodded and smiled encouragingly.

"It'll kill him," said Joseph, whose senses had become exceedingly acute after his own drink, and were painful.

"Life's no bargain," said Mr. Healey in a voice of reason. "But never heard of a man dying of good ole Kentucky brew. Not even anybody with a heathen name."

Joseph said to Haroun, "You must drink this. Quick, now."

"Yes, Joe," said Haroun in such a meek and trusting voice that Mr. Healey blinked. Haroun held his breath and drank quickly. After the cup was empty his face bulged and his great black eyes started from his head, and he strangled and held his throat. Mr. Healey chuckled. "In a minute he won't have no pain," he commented.

Mr. Healey, smiling widely, soaked two or three kerchiefs in whiskey from the jug he held. Joseph was still holding Haroun who was slowly subsiding though still coughing.

"Why do you do this for us?" asked Joseph. "We're nothing to you."

Mr. Healey studied Haroun keenly, but he said to Joseph, "It's like that, eh? If you don't know, boyo, don't you ask."

Joseph was silent. Mr. Healey still studied Haroun, lying in the circle of Joseph's arms. He said, "This heathen ain't anything to you, either, is he? But you got his foot out and saved it. Why? Don't you tell me, now. You think on it."

Haroun's eyes closed. He lay limp in Joseph's arms. Then Mr. Healey became brisk. He leaned forward, muttering, and wiped the dirty and bloody ankle quickly and expertly. Haroun moaned once, but did not move. "Best thing for anything," said Mr. Healey. "Beats the divil for curing." The kerchief was soon soaked with blood and filth. Mr. Healey wet another. "Don't think there's anything broken," he said. "Just tore up. Bad, though. Could have been cut off. Now, it's clean."

He deftly swathed the lacerated ankle in fresh white kerchiefs and generously poured raw whiskey on them. Haroun was now in a stupor. His little toes emerged from the kerchiefs in a pathetic fashion. He seemed to have shrunk. He was hardly more than a starved child in Joseph's embrace. Mr. Healey contemplated him, ignoring the jostling faces all about them.

"Well," he said, "seems I heard that the meek'll inherit the earth, and maybe the helpless, but not until the rest of us have eaten the lion's share and don't want no more. But no use quarreling with things as they are. Only a fool does that." He looked at Joseph. "You ain't no fool, and that's for sure, boyo."

"I am going to survive," said Joseph, and suddenly, his head fell back against the rattan seat and he slept. The train screamed on into the night like a triumphant banshee. Flickering red fire glared briefly at the windows.

Chapter 10

Joseph was awakened by brilliant sunshine lying on his eyes and face. Stiff and aching and weary, he moved on the rattan seat where he and Haroun had spent the night in heavy slumber. The younger boy's head lay on Joseph's right shoulder, as a child's head lies, his dusky face empty of everything but innocence and pain. His thick curling hair, black as coal and as shining, spilled on Joseph's arm and neck. One of his hands had fallen on Joseph's knee.

The iron wheels of the train rumbled and clattered; the engine howled and pounded. The bright air outside was frequently dulled by smoke and steam. Most of the men in the crowded hot coach still slept, snoring and grunting. Empty bottles rolled and collided over the filthy straw-strewn floor. A rancid wet ceiling, occasionally splashed by sunlight, was still lighted by the kerosene lanterns, and appeared to drip. The wooden walls of the coach were thick with filth and the accumulations of soot, dirt and smoke, and tobacco stains. The door of the latrine banged persistently and each breath of wind carried the effluvium into the coach. Joseph looked about him with dull and sunken eyes.

Mr. Healey slumbered peacefully and noisily on the reversed seat opposite the boys, huge fat legs spread wantonly, bulging waistcoat moving rhythmically, the jeweled trinkets and seals on it winking in the sun, soot-filled white silk cravat loosened, fat arms slack against his big though short body, polished boots dusty but still shining, fawn pantaloons stretched, coat creased. His great rosy face was like an infant's, and his fat sensual mouth drooled a little and his big gross nostrils expanded and contracted. One large pink ear was crumpled against his bald head. Pale short lashes flickered, and there was a pale stubble on his cheeks and double chin. Porcine, thought Joseph, without malice

119

or disgust but just as a matter of fact. He looked at the
short thick fingers with their glittering rings and the jeweled
buttons that fastened the fine linen of the fluted shirt at the
bulky wrists.

Joseph's eyes narrowed thoughtfully as he studied Mr.
Healey. His instincts told him that his benefactor was a rascal, but unlike Tom Hennessey's rascality Mr. Healey's
was open and frank and in a way admirable and a sign of
strength. He was a man who would use but probably could
not be used. There was a strong shrewdness in him, an alert
intelligence, a benign implacability—in short, a man to be
feared, a capricious man perhaps, a man who had authority
of his own and therefore did not fear authority and could
outwit it, and who had little regard for stringent opinions
concerning wrong and right. Mr. Healey, it was possible,
ran his affairs dangerously close to the cutting edge of the
law, and no doubt he had defeated it many a time. Men in
this coach had deferred to him, had obeyed him without
question, even the deadly quiet men who saw and knew everything, and all of them were scoundrels in their own
right. Scoundrels did not respect, obey, and admire probity: Therefore, Mr. Healey did not possess probity.

But conscience, Joseph reflected, and in the words of Sister Elizabeth, "bought no potatoes." He suddenly felt for
his money belt and his concealed twenty-dollar goldpiece.
The train was full of sleek robbers. The money was intact.
Who would think that a hungry and ragged boy would possess money, anyway? Still, Joseph was relieved. He looked
again at Haroun, and frowned. He was still resentful and
now even more so that Haroun had attached himself to
him, had involved him in dangerous difficulties, had artlessly confided in him and so had made him in a way responsible for his troubles. Haroun now possessed only the shirt
and the pantaloons on his body, and only one boot, and the
"six bits" in his pocket. It is none of my business, thought
Joseph. He must, as the Americans say, take his lumps like
anyone else, and his lumps are not mine. As soon as the
train reached Titusville he, Joseph, would immediately
abandon Haroun. Mr. Healey was another matter. He exuded wealth, competence, authority, and strength. Joseph
continued his study.

Musing, he looked at the passing countryside through the
evilly stained window. The land was rolling and green here
in early summer, and appeared colder and more northern.

Cattle walked amiably in the valleys; an occasional gray farmhouse huddled under sparse trees and feathers of early smoke fluttered from their chimneys. A boy here and there, barefoot, leaned on a rail fence to stare at the noisy train, idly chewing on a slice of bread. There was a dirt road nearby, and a loaded wagon or two ambled along it. Farmers waved; the harness of the horses shone and sparkled in the early sunlight. There was a herd of sheep in the distance. A dog ran barking for a few feet beside the train, then fell back. The sky was polished, cold and blue like steel.

"And what will you be thinking, with that look on your face?" Mr. Healey inquired. Joseph flushed. Apparently Mr. Healey had awakened recently and had studied Joseph in his turn. "Joseph Francis Xavier What?"

"Joe Francis. That is all," said Joseph. He was vexed. It was all very well for him to reflect and weigh others, but his pride rose at the thought of being so inspected himself. It was an affront, and unpardonable.

Mr. Healey yawned vastly. He appeared amused. He leaned forward to inspect the sleeping Haroun's foot. It was swathed in kerchiefs no longer immaculately white, and it was badly swollen and appeared red and hot. "Got to do something about your friend," Mr. Healey remarked.

"He is not my friend," said Joseph. "I met him on the platform last night, and that is all. And why should you help him?"

"Well," said Mr. Healey, still examining Haroun's foot, "what do you think? Out of the goodness of my heart? Brotherly love or something? Touched by a lad so young and his plight? Wanting to help the unfortunate? Kindness of my big soul? Or maybe I can use him? You pays your money and you takes your choice, as the horse-race fellers say. You figure it out, Joe."

Joseph was increasingly annoyed. It was apparent that Mr. Healey was laughing at him and that was unendurable. He said, "Are you a wildcatter, Mr. Healey?"

Mr. Healey leaned back in his seat, yawned again, produced an enormous cigar and carefully bit off the end and then lit it from a silver box containing lucifers. He contemplated Joseph.

"Well, boyo, you can call me a Grand Panjandrum. Know what that means?"

"Yes," said Joseph. "It was a burlesque title of an official in a comedy by an English playwright, long ago. It means," said Joseph with a cold smile, "a pretentious official."

"Hum," said Mr. Healey, looking at him in shrewd disfavor. "Educated feller, ain't you? And where did you acquire this famous education? Yale, maybe, or Harvard, or Oxford, in the old country?"

"I read a lot," said Joseph, and now he stared at Mr. Healey with derisive amusement of his own.

"So I see," said Mr. Healey. He moved one bloated hip and produced Joseph's thin leather-bound book of Shakespeare's sonnets. He rubbed one fat finger on the binding, never moving his little black eyes from Joseph's face. "And you had money to buy a book like this, Joe?"

"Books were given to me by—I don't know," said Joseph, and tried to take the book from Mr. Healey. But Mr. Healey deftly put the book behind him.

"You don't know, eh? Some kind soul, who had pity on a boyo like you, and wanted to help him? But you feel grateful, anyways?"

Joseph said nothing. His small blue eyes glinted in the sun.

"You don't think anybody does anything out of goodness of heart, eh?"

Joseph thought of his father. "Yes, I do," he said in a loud uninflected voice. "My father did. And that's why he lies in a pauper's grave, and my mother lies in the sea."

"Ah," said Mr. Healey. "That explains a lot. That happened to my father in Boston, too, where he landed. And my mother, when I was seven. Pauper's graves for both. Was on my own when I was seven, working in Boston at anything I could turn my hand to. Never regretted it. Nobody owes anybody anything, in this world. Anything good comes, it is a blessing out of the blue. Fit for pious thanksgivings. Except you don't believe in thanksgivings?"

"No," said Joseph.

"And nobody did nothing for you, all your life?"

Joseph unwillingly thought of the Sisters of Charity on the ship and the old priest, and Sister Elizabeth, and the unknown man who had supplied him with books, and the nuns who had occasionally forced a dinner on him. He also thought of Mrs. Marhall.

"Think it over," said Mr. Healey, who was watching him closely. "It may be important to you one of these days.

Now, I'm not one of them who thinks you should slink around with prayers and talk sweetness and light all the time. It's a bad world, Joe, and I didn't make it, and I learned soon not to quarrel with it. For every good and charitable man there's a thousand or more who'd steal your heart's blood if they could sell it for a profit. And ten thousand would sell your coat to the pawnbroker for two bits, even if they didn't need the money. I know all about this world, boyo, more than you do. Eat or be eaten. Your money or your life. Thieves and murderers and traitors and liars and grafters. All men are Judas, more or less."

Joseph had listened intently. Mr. Healey waved the cigar and continued in his resounding and suetty voice.

"Just the same," he said, "you sometimes find a good man, and like the Bible or something says, he's worth more than rubies, if he ain't a fool who is feckless and thriftless and believes in a wonderful tomorrow that never comes. A good man with a head on his shoulders is worth something, and that I know. Could be all the good people you met were fools?"

"Yes," said Joseph.

"Too bad," said Mr. Healey. "Maybe they wasn't though. Maybe you just thought they was. That's something for you to ponder on, when you have the time. You never had much time to ponder on anything though, I'm thinking."

"True," said Joseph.

"Too busy," said Mr. Healey, nodding his head. "I like men who are busy. Too easy to lie down in the gutter and beg. Find lots of them in the cities. Well, anyways, it was bad for the Irish in Boston, so I worked my way down to old Kentuck and that's where I grew up, Louisville and Lexington, and such. And the river boats." He winked amicably at Joseph.

"A gambler?" said Joseph.

"Well, say a gentleman of fortune. A Grand Panjandrum. I always thought it meant a man of affairs, but then I'm not educated like you though I know my letters. Some."

He looked at his gold watch, then clicked it shut. "Soon be in Titusville. Say I give Grand Panjandrum a new meaning: A man with lots of affairs. Finger in every pie. Politics. Oil. River boats. Retailer. Name it. I'm it. Never turn down an honest penny and maybe never turn down a dis-

honest one, either. And another thing: Find out the skeleton in every man's closet or his favorite vice or weakness,
and you've got him in your hand," and Mr. Healey's fat
fingers closed quickly in the hand he suddenly held aloft.
"Do him favors, but make him pay for them one way or
another. Best way to get rich, though, is politics." The gesture of the ringed hand was both cruel and rapacious.

"So you are a politician, too?"

"No, sir. Too dirty for me. But I control politicians, and
that's better."

Joseph was becoming extremely interested in spite of his
aloofness. "Do you know Senator Hennessey?"

"Ole Tom?" Mr. Healey laughed richly. "I made Ole
Tom! Knew half a dozen of the Pennsylvania Legislature.
Been living in Pittsburgh and Philadelphia last twenty years
or so. Worked like hell to stop that yokel, Abe Lincoln, but
it didn't turn out. Anyways, all for the best. We're in a war
now, and there's always a lot of money to be made out of
wars. Know them all. Did a lot of business in wars in Mexico and other places. People say they hate wars, but governments never made a war and nobody came. That's human
nature. And when we win this war, there's going to be lots
of good fat pickings in the South, too. That, boyo, is what
the war's about, though you hear a lot of drivel about slavery
and the Rights of Man. Et cetera. Lot of dung. It's money,
that's all. South too prosperous. North in an industrial panic.
Simple as that."

"I'm not interested in wars," said Joseph.

"Now that," said Mr. Healey, "is one Goddamned stupid
remark. If you want to make your mark, boyo, you've got
to be interested in every last Goddamn thing the world
does, and see where it will turn a profit for you if you're
smart. You got to learn a lot, Joseph Francis Xavier."

"And you intend to teach me?" said Joseph, with contempt.

Mr. Healey studied him and his eyes narrowed so much
that they almost disappeared. "If I do, son, it'll be the luck-
iest day of your life, sure and it will. You think you're
tough and ornery. You ain't. Not yet you ain't. Tough and
ornery folks don't appear to be. It's the soft ones who put
on the front of toughness and hardness, to sort of protect
themselves from the real murderers, who are all sweet talk
and kind smiles and helpfulness. It don't do them no good,

though. The tough fellers can see right through all that shell to the tasty oyster inside."

"And you think I'm a tasty oyster?"

Mr. Healey burst out laughing. He pointed his cigar at Joseph, and he laughed so heartily that tears filled his little eyes and spilled out onto his fat full cheeks. He shook his head over and over in uncontrolled mirth. Joseph watched him with mortified and furious anger.

"Son," gasped Mr. Healey, "you ain't even a morsel of shrimp!" He pulled out another scented and folded kerchief from his hip pocket and wiped his eyes and moaned with delight. "Oh, my God, oh, my God!" he groaned with rich feeling and pleasure. "You're killing me, son."

He looked at Joseph and tried to control himself. His whole body quaked with joyous laughter, and he belched and gulped. Then he pointed the cigar at Joseph again.

"Son," he said in a strangled voice, "I'm interested in you because you got the makings of a scoundrel. Besides, you're an Irisher, and I always had a soft spot for an Irisher, feckless or not. You can do something with the Irish. And you can depend on their loyalty, too, if they like you. If they don't, you're a dead man. Now, look here, you helped this boy, though he's no kin or friend of yours. Maybe saved his life. I'm not asking for an explanation, because you can't explain it. But I liked that in you, though I don't say I admired it. What is he, anyways, a Turk?"

Joseph, in his silent rage, could not speak for a moment. "No," he said at last, in a voice full of hate for Mr. Healey, "he's a Lebanese. I told you he was a Christian, if that means anything. Do you know," said Joseph with unusual malice, "what a Lebanese is?"

But Mr. Healey was not humiliated or annoyed. "No, boyo, I don't. Don't even want to know. Never heard of anyone like that, though, come to think of it. He looks like life dealt him a dirty hand, too. Know anything about that?"

"A little," said Joseph.

"Bad as your own, eh?"

"Perhaps."

"But he don't look sour like you, boyo, and maybe there's something in that for me, too. Would you say he was soft?"

"Perhaps. He supported an old grandmother on two dollars a week, working in a stable."

"And you never supported anybody, and you a grown man seventeen, eighteen?"

Joseph said nothing.

"Heard that men seventeen and eighteen, married, and with kids, opening up the West," said Mr. Healey. "Covered wagons and all. Wilderness. They got guts. Think you got guts, Joseph Francis Xavier?"

Joseph said, "I'll do anything."

Mr. Healey nodded. "That's the password, boyo. That's the password of the men who survive. If you'd said anything else I'd not have bothered with you any longer. Think you'd like to join up with me?"

"Depends on the pay, Mr. Healey."

Mr. Healey nodded again with great approval. "That's what I like to hear. If you'd said that it depends on anything else I wouldn't waste my time on you. Money: that's the ticket. Looks like your Turk is waking up. What you say his name is, his moniker? Haroun Zieff? Heathen name. From now on he's—let me see. Harry Zeff. That's what we'll call him. Sounds more American. German. Lots of Germans in Pennsylvania. Good stuff in them. Know how to work, they do, and how to turn a profit, and never heard them whining, either. If there's anything I hate it's a whiner. What's your Turk trying to say to you?"

The men in the coach were awakening, too, groaning, cursing, grunting, complaining. A long line of them formed for the latrine at the end of the coach, as they fingered their buttons impatiently. They exuded the old stink of sweat, tobacco smoke and stale perfume and wool. Some of them, pressed more than others, frankly exposed themselves in readiness and roared for loiterers to hurry. The prudishness which lived darkly in the nature of Joseph was affronted at this brutish display, and he turned reluctantly to Haroun who had begun to whimper with pain though his eyes still remained shut. The men jostled in the aisle, swaying with the sway of the slowing train, and some of them obsequiously nodded and grinned at Mr. Healey and some looked with indifference at the two youths opposite him as if they were no more than a pair of trussed chickens. Their immediate interest was their needs, and their importunities became increasingly obscene. The raw sunlight showed their swollen and gross and rapacious faces, and when they spoke or laughed the light glinted from large white teeth which resembled, to Joseph, the teeth of predatory beasts.

"Hang it out the window!" bawled Mr. Healey in his genial fashion.

This evoked fawning laughter and admiring comments on his wit. Mr. Healey spoke in a just perceptible brogue, and his mixture of Southern and Irish usage apparently charmed those who hoped to make a profit from or with him in Titusville. "You got a dirty mouth on you, Ed," said one man leaning over to slap Mr. Healey on his thick shoulder. "See you tomorrow?"

"With cash," said Mr. Healey. "Don't do business 'cept it's cash."

He looked at Joseph with a contented and important expression but Joseph was distastefully examining Haroun. Haroun's dark face was deeply flushed and very hot. His forehead gleamed with sweat and tendrils of his black hair clung to it as if stuck by syrup. His tremulous mouth moved and he spoke but Joseph could not understand his imploring words, and now his whole body moved restlessly with pain and distress, and sometimes he groaned. His toes had purpled and extruded through the kerchiefs which swathed them. Mr. Healey looked at him with interest, leaning forward.

"Now Joseph Francis Xavier What," he said, "what do you propose we do with this boyeen—who's no concern of ours, eh? No friend of yours. Never saw him before, myself. Leave him on the train for the conductor to dispose of like rubbage?"

Joseph felt a rush of the deep cold fury he always felt when anyone intruded upon him. He looked at Haroun and hated the boy for his present predicament. Then he said with anger, "I have a ten-dollar goldpiece. I'll give it to the trainman to help him. That's all I can do." He had a sick sensation of helplessness and wild impatience.

"You got ten-dollar goldpieces? My, that's surprising," said Mr. Healey. "Thought you was a beggar, myself. So, you'll give a piece to the trainman, and you'll get off this here ole train and forget your little Turk ever lived. Know what I heard once from a Chinaman working on the railroad? If you save a man's life you got to take care of him the rest of *your* life. That's for tinkering with the fates, or something. Well, the trainman takes that nice yeller piece of yours, and what's he supposed to do then? Take the little Turk home with him in Titusville and dump him into his wife's bed? Know what I think? The trainman will take your money and just let the spalpeen die here, right in this coach, peaceful or not. It don't run back to Wheatfield for six whole days. Nobody's going to look in this coach until Saturday."

Despairing, Joseph shook Haroun, but it was evident that the boy was unconscious. He kept up a steady moaning and muttering in delirium. He lay flaccid against Joseph's greatcoat except when he struggled in his suffering. Joseph cried, "I don't know what to do!"

"But you are real mad that you have to do anything, is that it? Don't blame you. I feel the same about people don't belong to me. We're coming into Titusville. Get that box of yours from under the seat. We'll just leave the Turk here. No use even to use that goldpiece. Lad looks like he's done for, anyways."

But Joseph did not move. He looked up at Mr. Healey and his young face was gaunt and drawn and very white, and the dark freckles stood out on his nose and cheeks. His eyes were blue and enraged fire.

"I don't know anyone in Titusville," he said. "Maybe you know somebody who'd take him in and care for him until he's better. I can give them the money."

"Son," said Mr. Healey, standing up, "you don't know Titusville. It's like a jungle, it is that. I seen many a man, young as this and you, dying on the streets from cholera or ague or something, and nobody cared. Black gold fever: That's what got this town. And when men are after gold, the devil take the hindmost, specially the sick and the weak. Everybody's too busy filling his pockets and robbing his neighbor. There ain't an inn or hotel in Titusville that ain't crowded to the doors, and no new-fangled hospital, if that's what you're thinking about. You take people who are living peaceful in town or country, and they'll help a stranger—sometimes—out of Christian charity, but you take a madhouse like Titusville, a stranger is just a dog unless he's got two good hands and a good back to work with, or a stake. Now, if your Turk was a girl I'd know just the place who'd take him in. Own four or five, myself," and Mr. Healey chuckled. He pulled up his pantaloons and chuckled again. The train was moving very slowly now and the men in the coach were gathering up their bags and talking and laughing with the exuberance only the thought of money can induce. The coach was hurtfully glaring with sunlight but the wind that invaded the coach was very cool.

Joseph closed his eyes and bit his lip so hard that it turned white. Haroun's restless hands were moving over him, as hot as coals.

"Well, Joe, here we are, depot riding right in. Coming?"

Joseph said, "I can't leave him. I'll find a way."

He hated and detested himself. It would take very little, he thought, just to lift his box and walk from this coach and never look back. What was Haroun Zieff to him? But though he actually reached for his box his hand fell from it, and despair swept him like the intensity of physical illness. He thought of Sean and Regina. What if they were abandoned like this, in the event that he, Joseph, was no longer able to protect them? Would any Mr. Healey or even a Joseph Armagh come to their aid and save them?

"I'll find a way," said Joseph to the standing man near him. He saw only the big belly in its silk brocaded waistcoat and the jeweled trinkets of the gold watch chain which sparkled in the sunlight, and he smelled the odor of the man, fat and rich and sleek.

"Now," said Mr. Healey. "That's what I like to hear a man say: 'I'll find a way.' None of that, 'For the love of dear Jaysus, sir, help me, 'cause I'm too damned lazy and stupid and no-account to do it meself. I appeal to your Christian charity, sir.' Any man says that to me," said Mr. Healey with real pent emotion, "I say to him, 'Get off your ass and help yourself as I did and millions afore you, damn you.' Wouldn't trust a psalm-singer or a beggar with a two-cent piece, no sir. They'd eat you alive, come they had the chance."

The train had halted at a dismal makeshift depot and the men were running from it with shouts to acquaintances and friends they had seen from the windows.

Mr. Healey waited. But Joseph had not been listening closely. He saw that Haroun had begun to shiver and that his child's face had suddenly turned gray. He tugged off his old greatcoat and clumsily wrapped Haroun in it. A trainman was coming down the aisle with a basket, in which he was depositing the empty bottles on the floor. Joseph called to him. "Hey, there, I need a hand with my sick friend! I've got to find a place for him to stay. Know of any?"

The trainman stood up straight and scowled. Mr. Healey uttered an astonished grunt. "What the hell's the matter with you, Joe?" he demanded. "Ain't I here? Too proud to ask, eh, and me your old friend, Ed Healey!"

The trainman recognized Mr. Healey, and came forward, bowing his head and tugging at his cap. He looked at the two boys. "Friends of yours, sir?" he asked in a groveling whine. He looked more closely, and was astonished at the sight of the two ragged youths, one of whom was obviously almost moribund.

"Bet your life they are, Jim," said Mr. Healey. "My carryall out there with my shiftless Bill?"

"Sure is, Mr. Healey, I'll run get him and he can help you with—with your friends," he added in a weak voice. "Give you a hand too. Glad to do it, sir. Anythin' for Mr. Healey, anythin'!" He looked again at Joseph and Haroun and blinked incredulously.

"Capital," said Mr. Healey, and shook hands with the trainman and the dazed Joseph saw the gleam of silver before it disappeared. The trainman ran like a boy off the train, shouting to someone and calling.

"Nothing like good silver, as every Judas knows," said Mr. Healey, chuckling. He picked up his tall silk hat and set it like a shimmering chimney over his enormous rosy face.

"Whatever you do," said Joseph, finding his voice and using it with hard and sullen pride, "I'll pay you for it."

"That you will, boyo, that you will," said Mr. Healey. "Eh, here's my Bill." He said to Joseph, "I ain't a man for sweet talk, but I'll tell you this, Irish: A man who don't desert his friend is the man for me. Can trust him. Would trust him with my life." Joseph looked at him with the calm and enigmatic expression he had had to cultivate for many years and behind which he lived as if in ambush. Mr. Healey, seeing this, narrowed his little dark eyes and hummed under his breath, thoughtfully. He thought that there were a few men still in the world who were hard to fool, and Joseph was one of them. Mr. Healey was not vexed. He was amused. Never trust a simpleton, was one of his mottoes. He can ruin you, the simpleton, more devastatingly with his virtue than any thief with his thieving.

The air was chill and bright outside the train, and the new rough depot platform milled with excited men carrying their wicker luggage and portmanteaus. Carryalls, surreys, carts, wagons, buggies, and a handsome carriage or two, horses and mules, awaited them, and a number of buxom women dressed gaudily and wrapped in beautiful shawls, their bonnets gay with flowers and ribbons and silk and velvet, their skirts elaborately hooped and embroidered. Everything dinned with ebullience and loud fast voices. If there was any thought of the fratricidal war gathering force in the country there was no sign of it here, no sober voice, no fearful word. A golden dust shimmered everywhere in the sunlight, adding a carnival aura to the scene. It was as if the insensate length of the train, itself, was quivering with excitement also, for it snorted, steam shrilly screamed, bells rang wildly. Everyone was in constant motion; there were no leisurely groups or easy attitudes. The scent of dust, smoke, warmed wood, hot iron, and coal was pervaded by an acrid odor Joseph had never encountered before, but which he was to learn was the odor of raw black oil. Just perceptible to the ear was a dull and steady pounding of machinery at a distance.

Titusville, set among circling hills and valleys the color and gleaming texture of emerald velvet, was hardly a frontier town, though the normal and settled population was just in excess of one thousand, more or less. It was about forty miles from Lake Erie, and had been prosperous even before oil, being noted for its lumber production and its sawmills and its busy flatboats carrying wood down Oil Creek for distant parts. The farmers were prosperous also, for the land was rich and fertile, and life, to the people of the pretty village, had always been good and never arduous. They were of industrious Scots-Irish stock, with a few Germans equally sound and sober.

But the newcomers from nearby states, and the oil frenzy, gave it the air of an exploding frontier town of the West, in spite of noble old mansions scattered at intervals throughout the town behind great oaks and elms and smooth lawns, and proud old families who pretended not to notice the raw newcomers and their frantic ways and their bawling voices. They also pretended to be immune to the new commerce on Oil Creek. They affected to be unaware of a recently unemployed trainman known jocularly as "Colonel" Edwin L. Drake, who had drilled the first artesian well in Titusville two years before. (They had heard, however, that he was keeping the Standard Oil Company at bay, and John D. Rockefeller, reputedly a nobody and a vulgarian and gross entrepreneur who thought of nothing but profit and exploitation, and recklessly destroyed beautiful countrysides in his delirious and insatiable search for wealth.) No one spoke of the new ten saloons and eight brothels in the town, two "op'ry houses," four inns, and one fairly new hotel. If these seemed unduly busy no one seemed to notice. These were for "outsiders," and did not exist for ladies and gentlemen who had vowed to keep Titusville Pure and Untrammeled, safe for Christian Families.

There were six churches, filled at the two services every Sunday, and for Wednesday "meetings," and the many socials. The village, even with its new banks founded by "outsiders," was only the periphery of the churches, which dominated social life and its affairs. The cleavage between the "old residents" and the "outsiders" was apparently impassable, and both apparently ignored the other, to the "outsiders" knowing winks and bawdy hilarity.

"Ain't nothing funnier than a big-mouth Christian," Mr. Healey would often remark. "And more murderous and greedy, neither. Just quote the Bible at them and you can get away with anything you got a mind to." Mr. Healey, during business sessions with the natives of Titusville, always quoted the Bible, though nobody could ever discover the text he had quoted so sonorously and with such evident reverence. He rarely, however, quoted the Bible to business associates, who were busy with the same deceit as himself.

It sometimes annoyed Mr. Healey that after he had wasted time quoting the Bible at some apparently docile and gentlemanly native of Titusville and had invented sections which had won his own admiration for their eloquence and wisdom, the natives had gone out to gather up options in the countryside for themselves, "and their mouths looking just like they'd just drunk milk and eaten fresh bread," he would recall bitterly. "It just makes you remember," he would add, "that not every man who chews a straw is a greenhorn, and there's many a woman you think is a lady who can outsmart you and leave your pockets empty."

Mr. Healey's "Bill" was a William Strickland from the stark hills of Appalachia, a Kentuckian. Joseph had never seen a man so tall and so excessively thin and lank. He was like a skeleton tree, narrow and fleshless and without juice. He had a face like the head of an ax, and hardly wider, and a shock of black hair stiff and lifeless like the quills of a porcupine, and as erect. His eyes, though not intelligent, were brilliantly intent and hazel, the eyes of an avid and predatory beast. His shoulders, including his neck, were no more than sixteen inches broad, and his hips appeared even more meager. But he had gigantic hands, the hands of a strangler, and feet resembling long slabs of wood crudely fashioned. His skin was withered and deeply lined, and he possessed few teeth and those like fangs and stained with tobacco juice. He could have been aged from thirty to fifty. His impression on Joseph was of a creature of witless ferocity.

But Bill was strong. A word from Mr. Healey and he lifted the delirious Haroun in his arms without strain and carried him from the depot. He smelled of dirt and rancid sow belly. His voice was soft and subservient to Mr. Healey, and never questioning. He wore a filthy dark blue shirt, the sleeves rolled up over brown tendons and elongated muscles, and blackish overalls, and nothing else. His feet were bare. A thin stream of tobacco saliva dribbled from a corner of his mouth. He had glanced once at Joseph and that glance was as opaque as wood, and as interested. He showed no wonder at the sight of Haroun. Apparently what Mr. Healey ordained was sufficient for him, however strange or foreign, and Joseph thought, He would kill on command. When he found out later that Bill had indeed killed he was not surprised.

Everyone appeared to know Mr. Healey's fine carryall with its fringed top, for there was an empty circle about it. Not looking to right or left Bill carried Haroun to the vehicle, which was drawn by two fine gray mares with silken tails and manes. He laid the boy along one side and tucked Joseph's coat about him, then climbed down and awaited his employer, looking for him with half-wild and doglike eyes. Mr. Healey was a procession in himself, accepting greetings affably, bowing and doffing his hat to the ladies, smiling and joking and smoking one of his endless rich cigars. Joseph walked at his side and attracted no more attention than if he had been invisible. In the presence of the gorgeous Mr. Healey all other human beings, and particularly a shabby and ragged youth, disappeared.

Bill tenderly helped Mr. Healey into the carryall, then seemed startled when Joseph followed as if the youth had not been encountered before. Then he climbed to his seat, struck the mare with his whip and the ironshod wheels rolled off smartly.

Seeing that Haroun rocked on the long opposite seat and was in danger of rolling off, Joseph braced the boy's middle with his boots. Haroun never ceased his feverish moaning, and Joseph watched him with an inscrutable expression.

"He'll live, strong and healthy, and if he don't there's no loss," remarked Mr. Healey. "Look about you, Irish, you're in Titusville now and ain't that where you want to be? We brought some life to this hick town, and you'd think they'd be grateful, wouldn't you?"

Joseph thought that Winfield had been barren and repulsive enough, but he saw that what the "outsiders" had made of a once lovely and charming village was nothing short of desecration—in the name of progress and money. An apparently new and raw community had grown up swiftly in the vicinity of the depot, and the cold northern sun glared without the softening effects of trees and grass on wooden walks. The carriage rolled over broken slabs of stone and long dusty planks laid roughly and in a haphazard fashion on bare packed earth. Cheap houses, still unpainted, fashioned of crude siding or logs, huddled sheepishly between noxious saloons and tawdry shops. Small copses of trees had been chopped down to make plots of grassless clay, waiting for new and ugly buildings, a number of them in various stages of construction, and being built without regard for gracious space, inviting vistas or even regularity. Some had already been finished and Mr. Healey pointed to them and said, "Our new op'ry houses. Lively every night 'til early morning. Liveliest places in town, 'cept for the whorehouses, which does a good business all the time. Saloons never empty, neither. Even Sundays," and he chuckled fatly. "We put this town on the railroad, that we did."

The "outsiders," who had come to ravish and exploit and not to create homes and churches and flowered lawns, had only alleys and bare ground and broken barrels where there should have been gardens. Swarms of dirty children played on the walks and on the streets. "Work here for everybody, even the town folk," said Mr. Healey, with pride. "You should have seen it when I first come. Like a graveyard; no life. Nothing."

Joseph looked up at the green hills, steep or sloping, which surrounded the village, and he thought of the beautiful hills of Ireland, which were no greener nor more inviting. Would they soon be destroyed also, and left desolate and denuded of all that soft serenity? Joseph considered what greedy men can do to the holy earth and the splendor of the world, and to the innocent creatures who inhabited it harmlessly and had their simple being apart from men. Man, he reflected, destroys everything and leaves a wasteland behind him, and congratulates himself that he has improved the earth instead of raping and scarring it. In his hand lay the ax of death and desolation. The desert which was the mind of man made a desert beyond that mind, fruitless and evil, filled with burning stone and vultures. Joseph was not accustomed to mourning the wickedness of his fellows, for he was inured to it, but he felt a surly rage against what he saw now and what he suspected had already been done in other communities. Forests, hills, mountains, rivers, and green streams had no protection in the face of rapacity. Was it possible that most men were blind and did not realize what they were doing to the only home they could ever know, and the only peace available to them?

He said to Mr. Healey, "Do you live here, sir?"

"Me? Hell, no. Got a house here where I stay in town, bought it cheap from some high-and-mighty snot-nose never worked a day in his life and went bankrupt. Hard to believe in this here territory where there's so much lumber, and salt mines and good land, but he managed, that he did. Feckless. That was before the oil come in. I live in Philadelphia and sometimes Pittsburgh, where I got a lot of interests, too."

Joseph reflected that Mr. Healey told as little about his affairs as did he, Joseph, and he smiled sourly to himself.

"Now here's the square, as they call it, and the City Hall, and the best stores and the law fellers' offices, and the doctors," said Mr. Healey as the carryall entered the square. It was apparent that once this small section of land had been as entrancing and gently lovely as any other spot in the vicinity, for trees still stood on it in cool dark clusters, their leaves glittering in the sunlight, and there were gravel paths winding through dead earth which formerly had been green and soft. There was a broken fountain in the center, and a stone plinth with carved words on it, and nothing else except clay and weeds. The square was surrounded by buildings which still hinted of grace before the "outsiders" had come, ravening here, of fieldstone, and the windows were still bravely polished, but there was a sad look about them as if they were shrinking.

The square was full of traffic, high bicycles, buggies, carryalls, hacks, surreys, and even a few handsome carriages

of shining black lacquer with gorgeously painted scenes on
their sides and drawn by lively horses in silver harness.
People moved rapidly on the bald walks. The wind was
strong, and it lifted the women's shawls and tossed their
wide skirts and showed yards of ruffled petticoats, and bonnet ribbons streamed from bent heads. Men held their hats.
Here the atmosphere was harsh with voices, the rattle of
iron-shod wheels, the rumble of loaded wagons, and it
smelled highly of manure. Doors swung open and banged
vehemently. Everything was much louder than in drab and
staid Winfield, where vice and avarice lived quietly. Joseph
suspected that here they lived noisily and with gusto and he
wondered if that were not an improvement. At least there
was something rawly innocent about open vileness. The air
of festival and anticipation was almost palpable here, and
all faces reflected polished greed and lively busyness, even
the faces of young girls. Everyone seemed to skip, as if
about to break into an eager and laughing run, full of excitement and hurry. Voices, greeting others, were quick
and breathless, and men raced off replacing lifted hats.

The carryall moved briskly towards the opposite end of
the square and suddenly Joseph, half-disbelieving, caught
the scent of grass and fresh trees and roses and honeysuckle. The carryall swung down the far street and at once everything changed abruptly. Pretty small houses and lawns
and gardens and tall elms and oaks appeared as if one
walked from a prison yard into comparative and blooming
heaven. The cobbled street began to broaden, as if smiling
as it revealed treasures, and the houses became bigger and
taller, the lawns wider, the trees higher and more profuse
and the gardens luxurious. This area was not Green Hills in
the least, but to Joseph it was a refreshment to the eye and
a green touch on the spirit.

"Pretty, ain't it?" said Mr. Healey, who noticed everything. "Old families. Own lots of farmland, good rich
lumber farms, and fields where we're drilling. Been here
before the Revolution, and sometimes I think none of them
ever died but just live on like mummies or something, or
what is that thing that turns to stone?"

"Petrified wood," said Joseph.

"You're right smart, ain't you?" said Mr. Healey, with a
little friendly rancor. "Never held it against a man, though.
What else do you know besides everything, Joe?"

"I've read a lot most of my life," said Joseph. "And I write a fine hand."

"Is that so? Need an honest man to keep my books. Maybe you'll do."

"No," said Joseph. "I'm not going to be a clerk in some dark office. I am going to drive one of the wagons to the oil fields. I hear the wages are very good."

"You want to blow all those brains of yours to kingdom come, eh?"

Joseph shrugged. "Better that than live the way I have been living, Mr. Healey. I need a great deal of money. I want to make my fortune. The little life is not for me. That is why I came to Titusville. As I told you before, I'll do anything—for money."

Mr. Healey squinted at him. "It's that way, eh?"

"Yes," said Joseph.

"Reckon I can use you," said Mr. Healey. "I'll think on it. But don't despise ledgers. You can learn a lot that way."

He thought a moment or two, as he clung, swaying, to the straps of the vehicle. Then he said with a positive air, "The law for you, boyo. That's the ticket."

"Law?" said Joseph, his small blue eyes widening in incredulity.

"Why not? Legal plunder, that's what it is. Don't dirty your hands, and gold sticks to 'em. Other people's gold." His body shook with his fruity laughter. "It ain't necessary to be a lawyer to go into politics, but it helps. Don't look at me as if I'm demented, boyo. I know what I'm talking about. We'll put you to study law with some fine thief of a lawyer, and your fortune's made." He slapped his fat thighs happily. "I need a private lawyer, that I do.

"Of course," said Mr. Healey, "that ain't tomorrow. In the meantime, we can make a good thing together, you working for me."

"At what?"

"My interests," said Mr. Healey. "Collecting, managing, and such. Had a feller up to a month ago and he stole me blind. Almost. Got sent up for twenty years and he was almost hanged." He looked at Joseph intently. "In places like this, they ain't soft on thieves—except legal ones. Ever stole anything, Joe?"

Joseph immediately thought of Mr. Squibbs. He said, "I borrowed some money—once. At six percent interest."

"All cleared up now?" He winked knowingly. But Joseph remained without expression.

"No. And that is why I've got to make a lot of money, soon."

"Why'd you borrow the money?"

Joseph considered him. "Mr. Healey," he said at last, "that is my own affair. I've not questioned you about your affairs."

"Sassy tongue on you, don't you?" said Mr. Healey. "Well, I like a man with spirit. Knew you had guts minute I saw you. Hate snivelers. Would you say you was an honest man, Joe?"

Joseph smiled his cold and ironic smile. "If it is to my interest, yes."

Mr. Healey laughed. "Knew you was a born lawyer! Well, here we are."

It was a ponderous three-story house, baronial, in Joseph's first appraisal, of rose brick and white stone, tall if narrow, with pedimented windows and white shutters, and a wide porte cochere of brick and snowy pillars. It did not have the smooth grandeur of Tom Hennessey's house in warm Green Hills, but it had a hard and compact strength, and lace curtains and velvet hung against polished glass and the doors were double and white and high. It stood like a wall, a sentinel, somewhat forbidding, beyond a rolling lawn, and a winding gravel driveway moved towards it past a clump of stiff green poplars, sentinels themselves. No flower beds softened the hard light on the grass. Joseph could glimpse a glass conservatory in the rear, and a number of outbuildings including a stable. The house spoke of age and solidity and money.

"Nice, ain't it?" said Mr. Healey as the carryall rolled towards the porte cochere. "It does me well when I'm here. Got it for a song."

The carryall passed under the roof of the porte cochere and the door flew open and on the threshold stood a young lady of uncommon beauty and obvious vivacity. Joseph's mouth opened in surprise. Mr. Healey's daughter? She was no more than twenty, if even of those years, and had a lovely figure which her rich gown of wine-red merino draped over enormous hoops could not entirely hide. There were deep cascades of weblike lace about her throat and wrists, and the throat and wrists were remarkable for their whiteness and delicacy, and were jeweled. Her pointed face glowed and dimpled, and her cheeks were the color of apricots and so were her beautiful lips which had parted in a smile of great delight, showing her square white teeth. Her nose was impertinent, her eyes extraordinarily large and shiningly brown, with shadowy long lashes. Glossy ringlets of brown hair tumbled to her shoulders. She had a look of intense life and gusto, and she stood on the middle step of a white flight of four, laughingly holding out her arms and regarding Mr. Healey with radiant glee. He climbed from the carryall and bowed and lifted his hat, and shouted, "Miss Emmy! God bless you, my child!"

Joseph had not been prepared for such a house nor for such a girl, and he stood dumbly beside Mr. Healey, conscious as never before of his shabby state and dirty boots and soiled shirt and scarf, and hatless head, his cardboard box under his arm. The girl looked at him with open surprise, at his shaggy mass of russet hair tumbled and uncombed, at his pale and freckled face, at his general air of indigence. Then she ran down the rest of the stairs and flung herself, laughing and trilling, into Mr. Healey's arms. He kissed and embraced her with enthusiasm, then smacked her on the backside with pleasure.

"Miss Emmy," he said, "this here is Joe. My new friend, Joe, who's thrown in his lot with me. Look at him, now: Gawking like a chicken with the roup. Never saw such a pretty sight as you, Miss Emmy, as he sees now, and his mouth's awatering."

"Pish!" exclaimed Miss Emmy, in the prettiest voice, like that of a happy child. "I swear, sir, that you make me blush!" She dropped a light little curtsey, full of demureness, in Joseph's general direction, and he bowed his head stiffly, full of silent bewilderment.

"Joe," said Mr. Healey, "this here is Miss Emmy. Miss Emmy, love, I don't rightly know his name, but he calls himself Joe Francis, and he's got a close mouth and so we make the best of it."

Sunlight flashed on the glossiness of Miss Emmy's ringlets and on the side of her bright cheek and now she looked at Joseph with more interest, seeing, as Mr. Healey had already seen, the latent young virility of him and the capacity for violence about his eyes and wide thin mouth. "Mr. Francis," she murmured.

Bill appeared with the unconscious Haroun in his arms, Joseph's greatcoat swathing the slight body. Miss Emmy was astounded. She looked to Mr. Healey for enlightenment. "Just a young spalpeen, penniless beggar from the train," he explained. "Joe here's friend. Think we got a bed for him, and a bed for Joe?"

"Why, Mr. Healey, sir, it is your house and there is room for all—for all your friends," said the girl. But her fair brow puckered in bafflement. "I will tell Miz Murray." She swung about, hoops and ringlets and lace swaying, and ran up the stairs and into the house, as blithely as a kitten. Mr. Healey watched her go, fondly, his face suffused and contented, and he went up the steps motioning for Joseph and Bill to follow.

"Bought Miss Emmy from a whorehouse when she was fifteen, three years ago," said Mr. Healey over his shoulder, and without the slightest embarrassment. "Come from Covington, Kentuck, raw as an egg. Cost me three hundred dollars, but cheap enough for a piece like that, wouldn't you say, Joe?"

Joseph was not entirely unfamiliar with the traffic in white flesh, though he had only heard of it in Winfield from the snickering men at the sawmill and knew of the discreet houses which harbored unfortunate girls. He stopped on the steps. "You bought her, Mr. Healey? I thought only blacks could be bought."

Mr. Healey had reached the door. He looked down at Joseph with impatience. "That's what the madam said she was worth, but more, and I own the whorehouse and Miss Emmy drew a lot of money and she was young, and the madam had cleaned her up and dressed her and taught her manners like a lady, and so she was worth the money. Not that I own her like you mean, boyo, like a nigger, but I own her, by God I do! And God help the man who looks at her now and licks his lips!"

Joseph had not read many pious books recommended by the Church, and only when he had been bereft of other books, and it had been his conviction that "women of shame" were drabs, and tortured with remorse and despair and showed the marks of evil and degradation on depraved countenances. But Miss Emmy was as fresh as the blue wild flowers along the roads in Pennsylvania, and as fair and gay as spring, and if she felt "remorse" or bewailed her condition it certainly had not been evident in that brief encounter of a few moments ago. Happiness and exuberance had sparkled visibly from her, and she had left a trail of haunting and expensive scent in her passage. He felt like an uncouth and ignorant bumpkin when he entered the long and narrow hall behind the white doors. He looked about him with increasing uneasiness and confusion.

The hall was dim after the glare of sunlight outside, but after a moment Joseph could see that the tall walls were covered with red silk damask—he had read of such in romantic novels—and were profusely covered with landscapes, seascapes and classical subjects, very decorous, in heavy gilt frames. The walls were also lined with handsome sofas and chairs in blue and green and red velvet, and the floor under Joseph's feet was soft and he saw the Persian rug in many different hues and of a tortuous pattern. At the end of the hall an overpowering staircase of mahogany rose and turned upwards in the direction of the second and third stories. Joseph could smell beeswax and old potpourri and cinnamon and cloves, and something else which he could not as yet define but which he later learned was gas from the oil wells of Titusville. Behind him waited, in that sinister and patient silence of his, Bill Strickland with Haroun still in his arms.

A door banged open in one of the walls, and Joseph heard Miss Emmy's teasing and laughing voice, and another voice, rough and strident and protesting, and he was taken aback when he saw the owner of the voice for he had thought it had come from a man. But a middle-aged woman was entering the hall with a rocking tread, like iron, and the old polished floorboards creaked. Joseph's first impression of her was that she was a troll, short and wide and muscular, the torso like two big balls superimposed one above the other, the billowing black taffeta skirts made huge by many petticoats, the two balls parted by a white frilled apron. There was, too, the third ball which was her oversized head set squarely on corpulent shoulders straining against black silk. A white ruffle puffed out under the roll of flesh which was her chin, and jet buttons winked over her truly awesome bosom.

But it was her face that immediately caught Joseph's attention. He decided he had never seen an uglier, more belligerent or more repellent countenance, for the coarse flesh was the color and texture of a dead flounder, the nose bulbous, the tiny eyes pale and vicious, the mouth gross and malignant. Her hair was iron-gray and like unravelled rope, only partly seen from under a mobcap of fine white linen and lace. Her peasant's hands were as broad as they were long, and swollen.

"Miz Murray, ma'am, it's home I am," said Mr. Healey in a most genial voice, and he doffed his hat in a gesture both mocking and elaborate.

She stopped in front of him and made fists of her hands and planted them on her splayed hips. "So I see, sir, so I see, and welcome, I suppose!" she said in that repulsive voice Joseph had just heard. "And what's this about unexpected visitors, sir?" It was as if Joseph and Bill and Haroun were invisible, but Joseph had caught the malevolent glitter of her eyes for an instant when she had appeared in the hall.

"Now, Miz Murray, these are my friends, Joe Francis here, who's joined up with me, and little Harry Zeff you see in Bill's arms. It's ill, he is, and needs care, and so Bill will go for the doctor when the lad's in bed." Mr. Healey spoke genially as always, but now his own face had become rosy rock and the woman's stare faltered. "You'll do your best, as my housekeeper, Miz Murray, and ask no questions."

She dared not show further umbrage towards her employer, but she affected to be disbelieving at the sight of Joseph and Bill and Haroun, and let her mouth fall open in absolute disgust. Miss Emmy's face, vibrant with happy mischief, now appeared over the woman's shoulder, and glee danced in her girl's eyes.

"These, sir, are your friends?" said Mrs. Murray, pointing stiffly.

"They are that, ma'am, and it's best you hurry before little Harry dies on us," said Mr. Healey, and laid his hat and cane on a sofa. "Call one of the girls."

"And their wicker baggage, sir, and their portmanteaus? Or perhaps their traveling trunks are on the way from the depot?"

"That they are," said Mr. Healey and most of the geniality had left his voice. "Miz Murray, Joe Francis here, and Bill with little Harry, will follow you upstairs and Miss Emmy can call one of the girls. We're all aweary from the long train and need a wash and refreshments."

The woman turned like a gray and black monolith, swishing in all her skirts and petticoats, and marched towards the staircase, followed by her master and the sad little procession led by Joseph. She walked heavily on her heels and her manner suggested that she was marching towards the scaffold with determined courage and valor. Mr. Healey chuckled, and they all walked up stairs padded with Persian carpets. Smooth mahogany slid under Joseph's hand in the duskiness of the stairwell. Now he was beginning to feel his familiar harsh amusement again, and a loathing for Mrs. Murray.

The upper hall was dim also, lighted only by a skylight of colored glass set high in the ceiling of the third story. The passageway was narrower than the one downstairs, and colored light from the skylight splashed on thick Oriental runners and on walls covered with blue silk damask. A row of polished mahogany doors lined the walls, their brass knobs faintly gleaming in the diffused light. And now, a very thin and frightened little housemaid, in black and with a white apron and cap, literally bounced into the hall by way of the rear staircase, all eyes and moist mouth, and cringing. She was hardly more than thirteen, and there was not a single curve on her flat body.

"Liza!" roared Mrs. Murray, seeing an object for her rage. "Where were you? You need a strapping agin, within an inch of your worthless life! We got company, hear? Open those two back rooms, the blue one and the green one, and quick about it, my girl!"

"Yes'm," whispered the child and raced to one door, throwing it open and then to another, and Joseph thought, And this is what Regina will come to if I do not make money for her, and very soon. Liza stood aside, cowering and with bent head, but her humble attitude did not save her from a resounding slap on her cheek, bestowed by Mrs. Murray. The girl whimpered, but did not lift her eyes. Joseph now saw pockmarks on her thin pale cheeks, and her young face was plain and fearful. In about eight years, thought Joseph, who had seen scores of abused children in America, Regina will be her age, and only I stand between my sister and this.

"Now, here you are, Joe, my lad," said Mr. Healey, and waved majestically at one open door. "You'll do with a good wash, and then we'll have our breakfast like decent Christians, and Bill here will put little Harry down and go for the doctor."

Joseph fumbled at his pinned pocket and took out his treasured twenty-dollar goldpiece. He held it out to Mr. Healey and even Mrs. Murray's malign attention was caught.

"What's this, what's this?" asked Mr. Healey in surprise.

"For our expenses, Mr. Healey," said Joseph. "I told you I take no charity."

Mr. Healey lifted his hand in protest. Then he saw Joseph's face. Mrs. Murray had sucked in her vindictive mouth, and was staring blankly at the youth, while behind him Bill waited with that sinister patience of his and appeared to see nothing.

"All right," said Mr. Healey, and he took the shimmering golden coin and tossed it in his hand. "I like a man with pride, and have no quarrel with it." Now he looked more closely at Joseph, and with curiosity. "Some of the money you—borrowed?"

"No," said Joseph. "I earned it."

"Hum," said Mr. Healey, and put the coin in his pocket, and Mrs. Murray regarded Joseph with squinted and wicked eyes and nodded her head in affirmation of some invidious remark she had made silently to herself. Liza gaped abjectly at Joseph as at an apparition, for now she saw his ragged appearance and his shock of hair like a dull blaze under the skylight.

Mr. Healey turned. "In half an hour, Joe, in half an hour."

Mrs. Murray followed Mr. Healey to the door of his own room and then stood on the threshold.

"That one's a thief, sir," she said. "Plain as day."

Mr. Healey began to loosen his cravat. He looked at himself in a long mirror on the silken wall. He said, "Possibly, ma'am, very possible. And now please close the door behind you. Unless you'd like to see me nekkid, like Miss Emmy does." He looked at her blandly, and she rumbled away.

Chapter 11

It had not been impulse or the bravado of pride which had made Joseph force his hoarded twenty-dollar goldpiece on Mr. Healey. It had been the instinct of perceptive genius. Shrewdly, Joseph understood Mr. Healey; under all that jocular good-will and Irish sentimentality lay a cunning man who could be ruthless and probably frequently was, a man who could be a jaunty bully but a bully for all that, a man who respected no other man but one who stood toe to toe with him and would not give an inch, a man who would exchange something for something and honored only men who were similar. For a fool or a weakling, or a witless man who did not know his own worth or permitted himself to be cheated, or who stood solely on principle and even then not with strength, Mr. Healey had the most honest contempt. Mr. Healey might praise "gents with scruples" but Joseph suspected that Mr. Healey despised them open-heartedly.

In giving Mr. Healey that money Joseph had given him silent notice that not only was he prepared to pay his way but that he would not be another Bill, a sycophant or unreservedly devoted follower. He would serve Mr. Healey if it would also serve himself, equal for equal. His loyalty was not for sale, and could not be bought with fair words, promises, affectionate laughter, moneyless generosities and rich hints, and avowals of friendship and facile agreements, or any other lying beguilements of no value which men like Mr. Healey would use to exploit and deceive the unwary and trusting. Joseph's loyalty was for "cash on the counter," as Mr. Healey would say.

Joseph also understood that it was not Joseph's angry and forced concern for Haroun that had touched Mr. Healey's sensibilities. Had Joseph been maudlin or entreating and had begged for help, Mr. Healey would not have concerned himself for a moment with him. He would have been only another ragged pauper, a sniveler, to be kicked aside. Yet Joseph also knew that Mr. Healey, when the spirit moved him, as he would call it himself, could be kind provided it did not inconvenience him for an instant, cost him anything of moment, or distract him. His own kindness flattered him, raised a self-esteem already high, and was a personal indulgence such as a stout women feels in the presence of bon-bons, and then against all sense takes one. It sweetened Mr. Healey's nature for days, and he was pleased with himself.

It was not a paradox, Joseph reflected, that he found himself respecting Mr. Healey also for what he was: A strong and exigent man, inexorable in the pursuit of his own interests. Mr. Healey, in behalf of his own affairs, might attempt to inspire trust, but he would never trust the man who took him simply at his word, for that man would be an idiot fit only for the plucking. "Always get it in black and white, with witnesses to the paper," Mr. Healey would say. "That's the only way to do business."

On the other hand, if Joseph should tell him—Joseph suspected—that he, Joseph, had borrowed money from Mr. Squibbs and intended as soon as possible to return it, with scrupulous interest, Mr. Healey would approve immediately. One must not become indebted, through open theft or otherwise, to men such as Mr. Squibbs, who was only a small and unimportant scoundrel.

He looked about him in the "blue room" to which he had been assigned. He had read about houses like this, and the Tom Hennessey's houses, in the many books he had read, but he had never been in one before. Yet, from his reading and some stir of aristocratic blood, he recognized and accepted it at once, with one of the few grudging pleasures he had ever known. It was a tall square room, and had obviously not been furnished by Mr. Healey who liked only opulent and obvious luxury. Here was all the muted color, restrained and haughty, from the pale blue silk walls to the same blue of the draperies at the window, and to the darker and softer blue of the antique rug. The furnishings were plain and spare and not crowded with expensive furniture as the hall below had been crowded, but the wood gleamed like dark honey and the brass trimmings were delicate but solid. The bed had a blue velvet coverlet, worn but still handsome, and the posts of it were uncarved. There was a rosewood desk here, the desk of a lady, and some fine steel etchings on the walls, and a fireplace of black marble adorned only by two brass candelabra and a black marble clock ticking defiantly against the profanation of usurpers.

Joseph drew a deep breath then let it out slowly. The room seemed to know him, as he knew it. Then he saw that there was a bookcase in the far corner and he went to it at once. A lady may once have occupied this room, a banished or dead lady, but her taste in literature had been sophisticated, and all the books in the case were classics bound in blue and gold leather. For a moment, Joseph, handling them, even forgot the room and even where he was.

Among many others he saw Goethe, Burke, Adam Smith, and the *Aeneid,* various Greek dramas, the earlier Emerson, Manzoni, Aristotle's *Ethics,* Washington Irving, *Two Years Before the Mast,* the *Odyssey,* and Spinoza. He hungered for them with a deeper hunger than the voracity of the body. He touched them as a lover touches a woman.

There was a timid knock on the door and he answered it and saw the little maid there, Liza, with a copper can steaming with hot water, and fresh towels. He had forgotten her existence, and the existence of everyone else in the house, and so stared blankly at her for a few moments. "Hot water, sir, and towels," she whispered. "The gong will sound in a few minutes."

He had not eaten since early last evening, and suddenly he was conscious of hunger. He stood aside and the girl came in and poured hot water into the china bowl on the commode and put the towels neatly beside it. She pointed to the commode, and blushed. Then she ran from the room. He wondered why she had blushed, and so opened the bottom compartment of the commode and saw the chamber pot there. He laughed aloud, for there had been no chamber pots in his room at the house of Mrs. Marhall, such luxuries being reserved for more affluent boarders than himself.

He took off his grimy shirt and bathed, and used the highly scented soap and the soft warm towels. He had but one clean shirt in reserve so he opened his cardboard box and put the shirt on and fastened it with a button. He had no cravat. He brushed down his worn coat and wrinkled pantaloons, then took out his steel comb and ran it briskly through his thick russet hair. He was still shaving but twice a week, and as he had shaved last Friday and this was Monday there was a soft faint stubble of reddish hair on his pale young cheeks and chin. Though he had scrubbed his long slender hands with their finely shaped fingers there was still grime under his nails which could not be removed.

A brass gong hit vigorously below startled him. But he had read of such in novels and was not confused. He went downstairs.

Mr. Healey, jauntier and more pleased with himself than ever—due to the occasions Joseph had given him to be kind—was waiting in the long hall dressed in fresh pantaloons of a Tartan any Scotsman might have admired, a deep red silk waistcoat and a long pale-gray coat. His white cravat was pinned with a diamond horseshoe. Beside him stood the demure Miss Emmy with her mischief-brimming eyes and her sparkling smile.

He said, "Though you've not asked nor seemingly cared, boyo, I've had the doctor for your Harry Zeff. The lad's in a bad way, that he is. Blood poisoning and such. But, he'll live, with good care. Miss Emmy will see to that, and Miz Murray and the maids, and my Bill, when I can spare him." He chuckled. "I paid the doctor out of that money piece you gave me. That's what you wanted, didn't you?"

"Yes. Thank you," said Joseph, without much interest. Haroun was out of his hands. He hoped the matter would remain that way.

"You like your room, eh?"

"Very much." Joseph looked at him blandly. "The other people furnished it, didn't they?"

"Well, yes," said Mr. Healey, with superiority. "Not so fine as the rooms I done over, myself, but adequate, boyo, adequate, for a lad your age. Comfortable. Now we'll go into the dining room."

Mr. Healey had furnished the dining room with stupendously large pieces of furniture of ornate and expensive taste. The mahogany sideboard covered one wall almost entirely, and was loaded with glistening silver of an elaborate pattern. The china closet was filled with gilt cups and saucers and other objects not so easily identified, and the round and pedestaled table was enormous and wore a stiffly ironed white linen cloth with napkins folded in a lily design. There were crystal goblets and gold-bordered plates and heavy silverware and an epergne and a bowl of roses also, and the chairs were of black leather with studs of bright brass. The old rug was scarlet, overlaid with a pattern of flowers, and the walls were of yellow silk. Mr. Healey looked at it with pride, believing that it all had evoked Joseph's humble awe, but Joseph was not awed. He had never been in a dining room of the gentry, but instinctively he knew this was grossly vulgar. He also knew that Mr. Healey was "shanty" Irish, and not the "lace curtain" Irish of his mother's family. Puffed with importance, Mr. Healey gallantly seated Miss Emmy on his left and indicated Joseph's chair on his right, he taking the huge armchair at the head of the table. Mr. Healey was not without sensitivity, himself. Without consciously knowing or understanding it, he had felt that Joseph was of superior lineage. Had anyone suggested this he would have hooted loudly, but the impression was there, a little galling, however.

There were three tall windows on one wall and a luminous green light from the trees and the gardens filtered into the room very softly even through lace of a tortuous pattern. It was, as Mr. Healey frequently mentioned, real Venetian lace. He pointed it out without modesty to Joseph, who looked at it with indifference. Joseph said, "Are your houses in Pittsburgh and Philadelphia as fine as this, Mr. Healey?" If his tone was ironic Mr. Healey did not discern it. He beamed happily.

"Well, now, sir, not quite," he said. "I live in hotels in them cities. More handy. I don't throw my money away. I like to move around, quick like, and houses hamper a man. I come here to rest, and do business in Titusville. Besides, I don't think Miss Emmy would like Pittsburgh or Philadelphia, would you, love?"

"Fie!" said Miss Emmy, coquettishly slapping the back of Mr. Healey's fat hand. "You never showed me, sir."

Mr. Healey colored with self-satisfaction. "Never intend to, either, love. I know cities too well. Too distracting for the young."

Two little maids, one of them Liza, came in with silver and porcelain dishes of food, and immediately Joseph was ravenous. He had never smelled such delicious odors in all his life as those steaming from the vessels. Mr. Healey filled a small glass with whiskey for himself, then filled one for Joseph. "Real good bourbon," he said. Joseph was never to develop a taste for "spirits" or even for wine, but he lifted the delicate crystal glass and sipped at it. It made his stomach revolt. But he had disciplined himself for too many years to permit a mere stomach to dictate his actions. He drank the whiskey and carefully refrained from even a grimace or a cough, and drank a little water. Mr. Healey watched him cunningly. A cool customer, this one. A hard-headed young cockerel. He'd never give anything away, and a man like this was a man Mr. Healey needed urgently.

A vast silver tureen was set before Mr. Healey, and with dramatic and operatic gestures he ladled soup out into frag-ile soup plates. With a flourish, he served Miss Emmy first, to be rewarded by a simper and a bridling. He next served Joseph, and then himself, while the two childish maids hov-ered anxiously. Mr. Healey covertly watched his guest but Joseph had had thirteen years of his mother's training and so did not furiously fall on the food as Mr. Healey had hoped he would. Joseph ate the thin soup, which was excel-lently flavored, and he recognized thyme though he had not tasted it for years. Miss Emmy ate with that excessive dain-tiness which only reformed whores can display, her little finger thrust out stiffly from her hand, and she preened with that gentility found exclusively among prostitutes. She, too, watched Joseph but with a different sort of inter-est, one of which Mr. Healey would not have approved.

"Miz Murray is one fine cook," said Mr. Healey, with an expansive air. "Pay her six dollars a week, a fortune, but she's worth it."

There was roast lamb with dressing (and Joseph was acutely reminded, and with pain, of his mother's kitchen) and roast potatoes, turnips, parsnips, and cabbage. The whiskey had made him lightheaded. He could smell peat fires, damp plaster, rich grass and lilacs in the rain, and earth voluptuously carnal beyond any ground in America. The coffee cups, with their faint festoons of little rosebuds and green leaves, were of the same pattern and vintage of his mother's china, and all at once his chest was filled with the swelling of misery and sorrow.

"Don't like your dinner, maybe?" asked Mr. Healey, freshly pleased.

But Joseph raised his eyes and Mr. Healey, taken aback, saw the deep blue fire hidden behind those auburn lashes, and he became confusedly silent for a few moments. Up-start, above himself, Mr. Healey grumbled inwardly. Pre-tends, like all this is nothing to him. Know these high-nosed

Irish; lords of the manor—they think. Well, we'll take him down a peg, soon. I've taken down better men than this spalpeen who forgets I've took him right out of the gutter.

He's right pretty, thought Miss Emmy, and right smart, too. She smiled brilliantly at Mr. Healey and again touched the back of his hand with her coquettish gesture. He eats like a hawg, thought Miss Emmy of her master. Mr. Francis is a real gentleman, and he's got a fine figure, though skinny like a squirrel out in the rain. Don't talk much, though. I wonder what he'd be like—

After the heavy dinner had been concluded by a hot apple pie and coffee Mr. Healey gallantly dismissed Miss Emmy and invited Joseph into his "lib'ry to talk business." It was indeed a handsome library and Joseph immediately noticed the walls were filled with books, and that the leather furniture gleamed softly and the tables glowed. Here was a room, like his upstairs, which soothed his abraded sensitivity, and he resented Mr. Healey who sat behind a low long table and proceeded to preside, his cigar smoke blue in the rays of sunlight which came between long blue velvet curtains.

"Do all my business here," said Mr. Healey, leaning back in his chair. His rings glittered and so did the trinkets on his watch chain. "Now, then. I don't do business with mysteries. I got to have answers to my questions. You see that, don't you, Joe? I like open things, before I hire a man. So, I'll ask the questions, and I'll take it kindly if you answer them in the spirit they're asked." He was no longer so easily affable. His little dark eyes pointed. His mouth had assumed a tight look, though he smiled.

"Yes," said Joseph, and hid his hard amusement.

"I got to trust a man," said Mr. Healey, admiringly inspecting the long ash on his cigar. "Can't trust anybody right off the street. I got interests, confidential, and I got to trust. That's understood."

"Yes," said Joseph.

"Shut-mouthed, and that's what I like," said Mr. Healey. "Never did like a wagging tongue. All right. How old are you, Joe?"

"I'll soon be eighteen."

Mr. Healey nodded. "Not too old, not too young. Can be trained. All right, Joe, what's your full moniker?"

"For the present," said Joseph, "I am Joe Francis."

Mr. Healey pursed his lips. "Police looking for you, Joe?"

Joseph thought of Mr. Squibbs. "No."

"Nobody else?"

"No."

"What've you been working at?"

"Sawmills. Taking care of horses. Driving wagons."

"What did your Dada do, on the ould sod?"

"He was a farmer, and a millwright."

"You mean he grubbed for potatoes, what there was?"

Joseph's face stiffened. "I said he was a farmer, and a skilled worker."

Mr. Healey waved his hand. "No offense. Where you from, Joe?"

"Wheatfield."

"How'd you get there?"

Joseph could not help himself. "On the train," he said, and smiled his short and taciturn smile.

"Getting things out of you, Joe, is like digging with a bowie knife in a coal mine," said Mr. Healey. "Got any reason for not opening up, like?"

"Just my nature," said Joseph, and smiled again.

"No kin?"

Joseph's face became shut. "No," he said. "I am an orphan."

"Not married, and running away?"

"No."

"That's sensible. I'm not married, myself," said Mr. Healey, and chuckled. "Never did believe in it. Here, Joe. Write something on this paper. Anything."

Joseph picked up the quill pen with the new steel tip which Mr. Healey had rolled towards him across the burnished table. He considered Mr. Healey, and with growing and amused contempt. Yet, for some reason even he could not understand, he felt a stab of unfamiliar pity. He considered, his ruddy brows drawn together.

He wrote: *No man is contented until at least one person knows how dangerous he is.* He was careful with flourishes and neatness and artistic shadings. Then he pushed what he had written on fine vellum to Mr. Healey, who read it slowly, his fat mouth moving over every syllable.

"Right smart sentiment," said Mr. Healey at last, with

heartiness. But he glowered a little at Joseph. "Your own sentiments, eh?"

"No. Henry Haskins."

"That feller," said Mr. Healey, who had never heard of Henry Haskins. "Now, I never wanted any feller to think I was dangerous. It's bad for business. Ain't no place in business for dangerous fellers. Word gets around. Can't be trusted."

"I thought you said it was a smart sentiment," said Joseph.

"For city slickers. I ain't one." He scrutinized the writing closely. "You write a fine hand, Joe."

"I am not a clerk," said Joseph. "I do not intend to be one."

"Joe, how much money did you make at your last job?"

"I worked a full week, and I received eight dollars a week. That isn't enough."

Mr. Healey's mouth made a soundless whistle. "Nearly eighteen, and eight dollars a week ain't enough! A man with a family's mighty lucky, Joe, to make that. Hard labor, too."

"Not enough," said Joseph.

"What do you aim to make?"

"A million dollars." His square white teeth suddenly flashed in his face.

"You're mad," said Mr. Healey, with simplicity.

"Mr. Healey, don't you want to make a million dollars?"

"I'm older'n you. Got more experience."

"I am younger than you, sir, and so I have much more time. And experience comes with living, and doing."

"Hum." They regarded each other in a short silence. Joseph thought, If he had not had to fight the world as I am fighting it he would have been a good man, for he'd prefer to be kind. We make scoundrels of each other.

"You're a hard customer," said Mr. Healey.

"If I weren't, I'd be no use to you."

"You never said a truer word, I am thinking," said Mr. Healey. "I see we understand each other. Here's my idees: I show you around. You help manage my business. You study law with a smart lawyer feller. I pay you seven dollars a week until you're worth more."

"No," said Joseph.

Mr. Healey leaned back in his chair and smiled sweetly. "That includes room and board."

Joseph had had no intention of remaining in this house longer than he could find a boardinghouse in Titusville. He wanted to be, as always, his own man, and not "beholden" to anyone else. But he thought of the books in this house, to which he would have access, and he hesitated. Then he said again, "No. I want eighteen dollars a week, and to pay five for my board. In one month I want a four dollar raise —a week. Then we'll discuss just how valuable I am to you."

Mr. Healey ruminated, his beefy face as closed as Joseph's own. He said, "You got a right high opinion of yourself, don't you, Irish? Well, I like that, too. How about the boyeen upstairs?" and he tilted his head at the ceiling.

"I've paid you for his room and board, until he can work."

"And who's he going to work for?"

Joseph shrugged. "He said he has a job in this town."

"How about him working for me, too?'"

"Mr. Healey, that is entirely your affair, and Haroun's, not mine."

"You don't want no burdens?"

"That is right."

Mr. Healey smoked thoughtfully. He said, "Eighteen years old, and talks like a sharpie with pockets full of gold. Well, how do you expect to make a million dollars?"

"When I have enough money I intend to buy a string of tools, myself, and drill."

"In competition with me and the other lads?"

"Mr. Healey, I'll never cheat you. On that you can rely."

Mr. Healey nodded and said again, "We understand each other." He considered. "All right, eighteen dollars a week, and you pay five for board. For yourself. Then I'll find out if you're worth a corncob to wipe my ass. If you ain't, we part. If you are, we'll talk again. Now"—and he leaned back in his chair and assumed a very open expression, candid and even a little pious—"I believe in laying my cards out on the table so a feller can see them. They call me 'sincere' around here."

Joseph immediately became wary.

"So you can trust me, Joe."

Joseph said nothing. Mr. Healey laughed gently. "A real sharpie. You don't trust nobody. You must've had a hard life, Joe."

"I did."

"Want to tell me about it?"

"No. It isn't important."

"You got to trust some people, Joe, or you won't get nowhere."

"Mr. Healey, the less we confide in each other about our private affairs the better friends we'll be. We'll just discuss our work together, frankly."

"You ain't even prepared to trust me, and I've laid everything on the line to you, Joe. I'm sorry you think everybody's a rascal."

Joseph could not help smiling. "Let's say," he said, "that we may learn to trust each other."

"Good enough," said Mr. Healey, with heartiness, and slapped his fat hand on the table. "Let's get down to business. I'm the president of eight oil companies. Ever since 1855. Started in Pithole, with the oil coming right out of the ground. No need to drill. Pithole ain't developed yet. But I got my options out there; first one to do it. Just scoop it up off'n the water and out of the holes. For twenty-five dollars I sell twenty-five thousand shares in my companies. Can't get out the certificates fast enough, that's how good business is in Titusville. And I've got three distilleries, too, right on Oil Creek. Up to date, we've been shipping out the barrels on flatboats all over the state and country. Kerosene. And just the crude oil to distilleries elsewhere. Kerosene's going to replace all other fuel for lamps, and the crude oil's being used for lubricants instead of more expensive oils being used. I got part of a patent for burning kerosene—since 1857. Saw the possibilities at once. I call that the Healey Kerosene Company. And helped develop better lamps than the old ones burning whale oil and such.

"When they run the railroad regular from Titusville in a few months, instead of one train on Sunday, my business will be ten times as much. Quicker and more than the flatboats. I got an interest in the railroad, too. You might say I got many interests. Did a lot of business in Mexico not long ago." He stared expressionlessly at Joseph.

"Legal, sir?"

"Well, it wasn't oil. I told you: I never miss a chance at turning a penny."

Joseph thought. He remembered reading, in a newspaper, of men like Mr. Healey who had made fortunes gun-running in Mexico. But he held his tongue. It was none of his affair just yet.

"I own salt mines here too," said Mr. Healey. "And I do a good business in lumber. Lumber's what made this town, before oil. Wide interests, Joe. All in all, I got about two hundred men working for me, townsmen and outsiders. I'm a director in the new bank, too. Own a couple of lawyers, but they ain't smart. But one of them can teach you what you need to practice law, yourself. If I was you, Joe"—and Mr. Healey leaned forward in a most paternal and confidential manner, as one speaking to a beloved young relative, perhaps a son—"I'd concentrate on patent laws, criminal laws."

"Especially criminal law," said Joseph.

Mr. Healey laughed expansively, and leaned back. "Well, I don't do nothing downright criminal, you understand. But every businessman runs close to the edge, or why else is he a businessman? Couldn't make a living if he didn't. Now law's law; you got to have laws, or the country wouldn't hold together. But sometimes law can be—well, can be—"

"Ambiguous," said Joseph, with a little malice.

Mr. Healey frowned. He did not understand the word. "Well, anyways. I mean you take two lawyers, and they can't agree what's legal and what ain't, and that goes for judges and juries, too. Laws're written funny, sometimes. And it's the funny part that's profitable, if you're smart."

Joseph nodded. "And if you have a good lawyer."

Mr. Healey nodded and smiled also. "And there's this here war I hear we're going into, right now. Lots of profit there for a smart man. I hear there's a patent in England for a six- or eight-chamber rifle—but that ain't for tomorrow, Joe."

Joseph suddenly became intensely interested. "And Washington will buy the rifle from England?"

"Well, sir," said Mr. Healey, "the Sassenagh ain't particularly fond of the Union, boyeen. His sympathies are with the South. Already said so, he did. Still, being a Sassenagh —there ain't anyone keener for a dollar or a sovereign than the Sassenagh in spite of his piety and all them churches of his, and the Queen—he might sell to both sides. I hope not."

"Which is the most prosperous side, the Union or the South?"

"The South, son, the South. South wasn't hit by the Panic that's here, like the North. King Cotton. Slave labor.

Farming. The South's where the money is. And that's what makes the Northern factory owners and businessmen madder'n a hornet. They ain't worried about slave labor because it ain't moral, or something. They just wish they could have slave labor, themselves, though that's just about what they have right now, with the foreign labor they're importing from Europe, foreigners can't speak English, and starving. Still, they got to pay some wages, and that's killing them. No, sir, ain't morals and the rights of man them there suffering Northerners care about. It's the cost of labor. Profits. Joe, if you want to use just one word"—and Mr. Healey wagged a huge finger at Joseph—"to describe wars and the making of wars, it's profits. Nothing else. Profits."

"And this war, too?"

"Joe! What else? Sure, and Mr. Lincoln talks about saving the Union, and a house divided against itself must fall, and the immorality of slavery, and from what I've seen of him I reckon he speaks without lying and hypocrisy. He's kind of simple, in a way. Businessmen always like simple politicians; they're easier to manage and persuade. So, they give Mr. Lincoln highfalutin' slogans and talk moral-like to him. But all it is is profits. King Profits. Kill off slavery in the South and the South ain't got the big factories and businessmen, and where does that leave the South? The South's where gentlemen live, and gentlemen ain't up to managing business. And so the Northerners can go down there and get rich. Profits, again. Do you follow me?"

"Yes," said Joseph. "Who do you think will win?"

Mr. Healey winked. "Well, the North, of course. They got the factories for munitions. It ain't fair, it ain't. Somebody ought to even up the balance."

Joseph nodded solemnly. "Only fair," said Mr. Healey. "Provided there ain't no interference in honest trade. But we won't know about that for a little while."

"And Mr. Lincoln wants to abolish slavery?"

"Well, not rightly. That ain't exactly what he's saying. It's preserving the Union. Did hear he said that if slavery would preserve the Union he wouldn't interfere with it. But the South's sick and tired of all them howling preachers up North screaming for abolition, and the hungry businessmen and factory owners, and interference, and being called names, such as murderers and Simon Legrees. As I told you, the Southerners are gentlemen. The South wasn't used much for the dumping of English whores and thiefs like the North was. Easier to ship them here, the Sassenagh thought, than hanging all of them. So the South sort of despises the North besides being mad at the interference. The South knows what it's all about, and they want an aristocratic nation of their own. Of course, that ain't democracy, and me, Ed Healey, I'm for democracy, too. Didn't vote for Lincoln, myself, that Republican." He nodded virtuously. Then he stood up, and pulled down his florid waistcoat and took out his thick gold watch and sounded the repeater. "Well, Joe. It's three o'clock, and time's apassing. What say we go out and look around a little, so you get the feel of the town and some of my business?"

They went downstairs, Mr. Healey shouting for his surrey and Bill Strickland. Joseph saw the almost mute Bill sitting like an image in the hall, waiting. He stood up, galvanized, when he saw his master, and Joseph observed the absolute devotion and blind dedication on the man's ugly face. The back of his neck prickled for no reason he could feel consciously. Then Bill turned his head slowly in Joseph's direction and stared at him emptily.

Joseph saw the killer's fervid eyes and an icy finger touched him between the shoulder blades. Mr. Healey laid his hand with affection on Bill's incredibly narrow shoulder, and he smiled at Joseph.

"Bill," he said, "would do anything for me. Anything." His smile widened as he and Joseph regarded each other in a little silence.

The surrey was standing on the wooden bridge overlooking Oil Creek. The green stream was stained with oily rainbows, and the banks were poisoned with oil so that the shrubs and plants and trees drooped in deathly attitudes, and many of them were already dead. Barges and flatboats filled the narrow and curving stream, and were being rapidly and noisily loaded with barrels of oil, and lumber. Joseph looked up at the unravished hills with their bowers of light and at the distant folds of tender valleys, and at the polished blue sky which would always resist the horribleness which was man. "It is beautiful," he said, and Mr. Healey nodded with satisfaction and pride.

"We made this town," he said, and shifted his cigar. "Nothing but greenhorns sleeping their lives away, and standing on the black gold all the time! I tell you, Irish, people are real dumb."

"Yes," said Joseph. He clenched down on all the spiritual anguish in himself and thought of Sean and Regina and what he must do for them in this place. But the hills haunted him. If he permitted them to haunt him there would be no rescue for his brother and his sister. He looked at the narrow little river and forced himself to observe the noisy busyness of the flatboats. "We got enough oil here," said Mr. Healey, "to light every town in the U.S.A. Ain't that a wonderful thought?"

"Yes," said Joseph.

A tall thin man with a beard was standing on the bridge taking wet photographs of the creek and the flatboats. His enormous equipment stood about him. "That's Mr. Mather," said Mr. Healey. "Takes pictures in five minutes! Ain't that incredible? Five minutes!"

"Does he think it's pretty, down there?" asked Joseph.

"Prettiest thing you ever saw, boyo! Money!" said Mr. Healey.

I must remember that, thought Joseph. I forgot for a few minutes. Your money or your life. He watched the lean black-clad figure of the young man feverishly darting under a black cloth that covered the lens of his camera, which stood on a tall tripod. The surrey rolled on.

"Now I'll show you one of my oil wells," said Mr. Healey.

They drove out into the countryside, which was, to Joseph, no countryside at all but a raped Eden. Derricks and well houses filled a landscape once placid and silent. Here and there at a distance he could see rich fields filled with black and white cattle, and the shine of a blue pond and meadows with rising corn and clumps of trees. But the air was permeated with the sick and pungent stench of crude oil; smoke, black and oily, poured from the steeples of the well houses which, incongruously, resembled miniature brown churches. The new God, thought Joseph, and oil is His prophet. The white farmhouses had a false tranquillity, as if immune to all this, but Joseph now knew enough to understand that the farmers were equally involved in this havoc, and had connived with it for money.

And here, as always, lay the embrace of jasper and aquamarine hills beaming as innocently as though man had never been born and was not a lethal menace to them, and lifting their iridescent flurries of leaf to the sky, as if glorifying a God who cared not in the least for them, but conspired with His human race to cancel it all.

"Well, here we are," said Mr. Healey. They had arrived at a large cluster of housed oil wells and Joseph could hear the rhythm, like mechanical heartbeats, of machinery. The primeval stench was thicker here as the decayed and oleaginous vitals of ancient animals and plants poured to the surface after millions of years of quietude, to give wealth to a race who had never known the riches of their being. Who am I to quarrel with God? thought Joseph with bitter cynicism.

He followed Mr. Healey into one of the housed oil wells. He saw the great wheels being turned by leather belts and the sweating attendants and heard the monotonous and imbecile pound of the pumps as they sucked up the black blood of the earth. He saw the donkey engine being fed sedulously by young men, naked to the waist. He smelled the smoke and the acrid odor of oil, and the wood which was being burned to move the wheels and the pump. He looked up at the tall wooden chimney which spewed out billows of black clouds. The workers had the intense and dedicated appearance of priests, their faces and their bare arms stained with streaming wet moisture as black as coal, their brows sooted. They looked at Mr. Healey and their white teeth glittered in their young faces. They were just as avid as he, but they were also subservient. "Hundred barrels so far today!" one of them shouted at Mr. Healey. "And more to come, sir!"

Mr. Healey nodded. He said to Joseph, "It's all surface oil; just pump it out. Maybe lakes of it. Perhaps the whole damned world is filled with oil. Never can tell." He smiled widely at Joseph and his small dark eyes squinted. "Want to work here, for eight dollars a week or keep your hands clean and make more?"

Some of the young men working about the well were not more than fifteen years of age and Joseph felt old as he watched them. "I heard tell," said Mr. Healey, "that John Rockefeller said a man's worth a dollar a day from the neck down but there ain't no limit to what he's worth from the neck up. Muscles don't get you anywheres, Irish. Brains do."

"I knew that when I was in nappies," said Joseph. "I thought this was all settled today."

Mr. Healey inclined his head. "Just thought I'd show you, if you had any funny idees." He chewed on his cigar, ruminatively. Then he grasped Joseph's arm. "Ain't never been married. Don't have no sons. I aim to make you one I never had. But you be square with me, hear?"

"I told you, I'd never betray you," said Joseph, and Mr. Healey smiled. "And remember what I told you, too, Joe. All men are Judas. Every man has his price. Mine's higher."

They returned to the town and Mr. Healey took Joseph into a three-story building near the square. The wooden steps were gritty and dusty; the halls were narrow and lightless. Splintered doors lined them, and Mr. Healey flung one open. "Here's where I really conduct my business," he said "My house is just for important folks."

The door opened on what Joseph immediately saw was a series of small adjoining rooms. The dirty windows were shut tightly and the air was heavy with heat and smoke, and if these rooms had ever been cleaned in a decade it was not evident. The floors were filthy with tobacco spittle, though cuspidors were placed here and there, and the walls were a dull brown and the ceilings were of dark-brown tin. Every room held a roll-top desk stuffed with papers and a high bookkeeping desk with a stool, and a dilapidated chair or two. Mr. Healey's own office was little better but it did have a long table as well as a desk and a comfortable leather chair. The light that seeped in through the gray-smeared windows was like light struggling through fog. Joseph also noticed that the windows were barred, as if the offices held prisoners, and that the one door leading into the series of rooms was steel-sheathed on the inside and had a number of complicated locks. Garish calendars hung on some walls, and Mr. Healey's room held a bookcase full of law books.

But what caught Joseph's interest at once was not so much the decrepit and ugly and polluted atmosphere of the rooms as the inhabitants of them. He saw at least fourteen men there, and not one was over forty, the youngest being in his early twenties. However, they had various things in common, so that they seemed of one family, one breed, one blood and mind: They were all tall, slender, elegant and deadly and dispassionate, and their faces were as unreadable as his own. They were richly dressed, though they had discarded their long coats because of the heat. All wore fawn or gray or discreetly plaid pantaloons, and their immaculate white shirts were ruffled, their cravats smoothfolded perfection, their waistcoats beautifully embroidered, with watch chains across their lean middles; their fluted cuffs showed no stain or gritty deposit. Their jewelry was most decorous, unlike that of the flamboyant Mr. Healey, yet obviously expensive, and their black boots were brilliantly buffed and narrow. Their figures were the figures of gentlemen, or actors, and they moved with the sure grace, restrained and economical, of the professional assassin. Their eyes might have been of different colors, their features might not have been identical nor their heights exact, yet Joseph caught the impression of oneness and affinity, which had no need for many words or explanations. Handsome though they were, and smooth and polished, they exuded cold menace. Joseph recognized them as the sort of quiet men who had waited in the depot at Wheatfield, the men who had been pointed out to him as gamblers and other unscrupulous men who lived by their wits.

They did not move as Mr. Healey entered with Joseph, though those who had been sitting rose and stood. They said nothing. They did not smile. It was as if the king wolf had come among them and they waited for his orders, which would be obeyed instantly and without question. Some of them were smoking the long thick cigars Mr. Healey favored, and they removed them from their mouths and held them, in their long and extraordinarily aristocratic hands. Their black boots twinkled in the muted light from the dirty windows, but did not stir. Their attitudes were supple and quiet and attractive. Their thick hair, of many different shades, was fashionably long, covering their napes, and marvelously burnished and sleekly waving. With the exception of neat sideburns they were all clean-shaven, and all complexions were uniformly pale and unblemished and displayed minute care. From them all exuded faint perfumes and the scent of expensive hair tonics.

They were incongruous in these close and filthy and crowded rooms, like patricians, or parodies of patricians, caught in noisome alleys or lurking fitfully in dark doorways in dangerous sections of a city. But Joseph felt the incongruity only briefly, and then he intuitively understood that this indeed, was their proper milieu.

Mr. Healey boomed affectionately, "Lads, I want you to meet this here spalpeen, Joe Francis he calls himself, and he's going to help keep the books while I'm off making money for all of us!" He laughed happily. "Then I won't have to strain my eyes over all those details. You just tell him. He'll boil it down. Smart, and sure he is. Fine hand, too. He'll give me in an hour what takes me, now, a whole day to get into my head," and he tapped his rosy and glistening temple. His attitude was affable and easy. "My manager, you can call him. Kind of young, but he ain't young in his mind, are you, Joe?"

None said a word but Joseph was suddenly the target of narrowed and intent eyes and merciless speculation. If any man present felt the matter was incredible no expression at all appeared on his face. Here was a youth, much younger than the youngest, meanly dressed, shabby and patched, with no ruffled shirt, no watch chain, no silken cravat, no jewelry, his thick boots dusty and broken, his pantaloons of a coarse brown cloth and stained, and with a pallid, ginger-freckled face that betrayed his immaturity, and surely, thought Joseph, they must feel some surprise. If they did, they did not reveal it. No one moved, and except for their roving and sharply observant eyes they might have been elegant statues.

Joseph was to learn later that none of these men ever questioned or doubted Mr. Healey's decisions or wisdom, or ever protested or ever ridiculed them privately. He ruled them absolutely not because he was rich and potent and their employer, but because wolves, themselves, they recognized and honored a more puissant wolf who had never, as yet, made a mistake. Had they once discovered a weakness in him, a hesitancy, a stupid blunder or an uncertainty, they would have pulled him down and destroyed him utterly. Not from malice or greed or thievery would they have done this at once, and instinctively, but because in his self-betrayal he had betrayed the pack and endangered them. He would have no longer been master, and for abdication they knew but one remedy: execution.

Joseph waited for a protest, for a subtle smile or one half-hidden, for a wink of disbelief, or a murmur. But there was none. It was a long time before he understood that a few had recognized him almost immediately—not a criminal like themselves—but as powerful and more dangerous even than the most dangerous among them. Moreover, Mr. Healey had chosen him and they never were dubious about his methods or decisions. He had proved himself too often to them, and they were certain he would continue to prove.

Joseph saw no signal, but the men came together in a thin-hipped queue and held out their soft gamblers' hands to him and bowed a little. He took their hands. He still felt the incredulity of the whole affair. There were a few men here old enough to be his father, yet they lowered their tall heads in respect. They felt his lack of fear for them, but if they guessed it was because he did not know exactly what he should fear, they did not show it. However, a number of the more experienced silently decided to test this newcomer very soon to see if Mr. Healey had, at last, made a stupid mistake.

Joseph heard names mentioned by Mr. Healey's jovial voice, but he did not really listen. Later, he supposed, he would know them by name, all of them. If he did not, it did not matter. What was important was what they could teach him and tell him. However, he did observe that Mr. Healey, still smiling like the sun but with cold blank eyes, drew two of the older men aside and spoke to them almost inaudibly, and that once or twice he made a ruthless chopping motion with his jeweled hand. He suspected that he was the object of these quiet conversations and it annoyed him, then he shrugged mentally. Of what importance was it? If he failed, then he had failed. If he succeeded, then he would be on his way. He determined not to fail. A man who refused to fail was a man who did not fail. Once he had read an ancient Roman saying. "He is able who thinks he is able." I am able, said Joseph to himself. I dare not be anything else but able.

A young man gracefully offered him a cigar, but Joseph shook his head. He looked at the man and said, "I do not smoke. I never intend to smoke. I don't want to waste my time and my money." Mr. Healey overheard this and sauntered back, beaming and chuckling. "And that, boyo, is just my sentiments, too. But everybody to his own pizen, I say."

He said to the company, "Joe, here, this miserable young spalpeen, is eddicated. He reads books. Now, lads, don't hold that agin him!" and he held up his pink palm in a parody of defensiveness. The gentlemen dutifully laughed. "I don't hold with book-learning as such," Mr. Healey continued. "Softens a man's brains and makes him a fool. But it done the opposite with Joe, this Irisher. It toughened him. Made him ambitious, like. Taught him what things was all about, it did. And he's got an Irish head on his shoulders and I'll tell ye this, lads, you don't beat an Irisher at any game. Not ever, not once. Don't I know it, being Irish, myself? We burn like peat but like peat we never just flare up; we keep on burning until there ain't nothing left. And Joe here don't like whiskey. If there's one mortal thing bad for an Irisher it's whiskey, though I ain't found that out for myself!"

He beamed and patted his enormous paunch. "But I don't drink the booze when I'm working, and you know my sentiments about that, too. No whiskey in these offices. Pistols yes, but no whiskey. And no hangovers tolerated. This is just for Joe's information, lads. And now, I want Joe to have my office, beginning tomorrow, and my desk, but not my table. That's mine. He'll be on hand at seven in the morning."

He looked at Joseph, then indicated the man nearest him. "This here is Mr. Montrose. We never call each other by Christian names, Joe. Just Mister, and God knows if their monikers is the ones they were born with. Don't matter, anyway. Mr. Montrose will take you to the shops tomorrow morning and buy you clothing fitten my men."

"Not unless I can pay for it myself," said Joseph.

Mr. Healey waved his cigar. "That's understood. Get off your high horse, Joe," but he was pleased and looked at the others with a self-congratulatory smirk.

He took Joseph by the arm, nodded to his employees, and led the young man out into the gritty corridor. "Finest lads in the world," he said. "Smart as turpentine, too. Don't fear God or man, or the police. Just fear me. I reckon there's not one but police are looking for them somewheres. Maybe like you, Joe, eh?"

Joseph said, "No police are looking for me, Mr. Healey. I've told you that before. Nor am I running away from anyone, nor have I ever been in jail. Nor will I ever be."

"No shame in once being in jail," said Mr. Healey and Joseph at once knew that his employer spoke from experience. "Finest men in the world, been in jail. No disgrace on them, I always say. There's better men been in jail than ones never been there, I'm thinking."

The air was blessedly cooler and cleaner than the air in the offices and Joseph breathed of it deeply. There were hollows of bright gold in the tall trees and the western sky was deepening into a bluish purple in which small flecks of rose floated. Bill Strickland was waiting in the surrey. His attitude was as still and as removed as an Indian's, and Joseph wondered if there were not Indian blood in him as well as Anglo-Saxon of a degenerate sort. Certainly he had the capacity for infinite patience and immovability.

They drove home, Mr. Healey placidly smoking and relaxed. But Joseph could feel him thinking, and thinking intensely and with absolute precision. A soft and benevolent smile touched Mr. Healey's fat gross mouth, behind which he thought and thought and made plans. Joseph did not speak. He knew that Mr. Healey had temporarily forgotten him and that he had compartments in his mind which he closed when he thought out some problem or made some plan. He, Joseph, had just this genius and he respected it in others. A man whose mind idly wandered was feckless and of no importance.

They arrived at Mr. Healey's house. The tall thin upper windows blazed like fire in the increasing sunset. The lawns appeared greener and thicker than ever, and the trees glittered with fresh and blowing gold. But for some reason he could not explain to himself Joseph felt a sudden desolation at the sight of the fortress-like house, as if no one lived there at all, and it was hostile in its isolation. There were neighboring old houses on the same street on their own vast lawns, yet Joseph had the eerie conviction that they were not aware of Mr. Healey's house, and never saw it. He looked up at the hills, which were turning violet in the evening light and they seemed far and cold to him, unaware also. It was these mysterious insights which had plagued Joseph all of his almost eighteen years, and which were to plague him, despite angry rationalizations, all his life. He thought, neither nature nor God seem to know or care anything about us, though they care about other things, such as the earth. His Irish soul was struck by an inexplicable sadness, a sense of total alienation, a sense of exile, a sense of heartsick yearning which had no words.

"Now, we'll wash and then we'll have our supper," said Mr. Healey, who apparently never experienced any of these emotions. " 'Early to bed, early to rise, makes a man healthy, wealthy and wise.' George Washington."

"Benjamin Franklin," said Joseph.

Mr. Healey's bright smile became fixed. "Smart, ain't you? Who cares who said it? True, ain't it?"

They went into the hall with its immense sofas and chairs and rugs. Mrs. Murray was there in her black crinoline and her ruffled white apron and cap. She made a little grudging curtsey to Mr. Healey, but gave Joseph a malignant glance. "Supper in ten minutes, sir," she said. "It's late."

He laid his hand genially on her shoulder, which was as broad as his, and her formidable face softened for an instant. "Miz Murray, ma'am," he said, "you'll pardon me, I know, and begging your pardon, too, but when I come down you hit the gong. Not before."

She curtseyed again, but gave Joseph a murderous look as if it were all his fault.

"It's a hard day we had," said Mr. Healey to his housekeeper, as he began to mount the stairs with Joseph. "Got to forgive us businessmen."

She snorted then disappeared down the hall. Mr. Healey laughed. "I'm always kind, that I am, to folks who work for me, Joe. But there's a limit. You get familiar like with them and first thing you know they're running you and you not running them. It hurts me, Joe. I'd like to love everybody, but it don't do. Got to have authority. Got to show them the nine-tails once in a while."

Mr. Healey went to his own quarters in the front of the second story and Joseph walked down the hall to his own room. He was about to open his door when he heard a weak and fretful voice behind the door of the green room, and a soft young female voice answering. He said to himself, It's none of my business any longer, what happens to Haroun. I have my own self to consider, and no involvements. But still he hesitated. He remembered what he had felt outside this house a few minutes ago, and then with an imprecation against himself he went to Haroun's room and opened the door, throwing it open angrily as if driven not by his own will but by the power of a stupid stranger.

Vivid red sunlight poured into the room and Joseph noticed at once that this room was as beautifully serene and as austere as his own, but in green shades. Haroun was lying in a magnificently carved poster bed made of some black wood, and he was resting on plump white pillows. Beside him sat little Liza, holding his hand and soothing him and talking to him in the gentlest and sweetest of voices. They were both children, and Joseph, in spite of himself, thought of Sean and Regina.

Liza jumped to her feet in obvious terror when she saw Joseph, her thin flat body quaking in its black cotton uniform, her starved face tremulous. She shrank; she tried to make herself invisible, and cowered. She dropped her head as if awaiting a blow.

But Haroun's fevered face, the huge black eyes shining, brightened with delight. He was ominously sick; he appeared to have dwindled in size and shape. He held out his dusky hand and quavered, "Joe!"

Joseph looked at Liza. He said, "Thank you for taking care of—for taking care of—" She lifted her head a little and glanced with fearful timidity at him. "I just been talkin' to Mr. Zeff, sir. I didn't do no harm. I'll bring him his supper," and she fled from the room like a meager small shadow in apprehension of violence. Joseph watched her go, and his face darkened and tightened. You fool, he said to himself, what does it matter? These are of no consequence. They ought never to have been born. He turned to Haroun and felt umbrage because Haroun, though now conscious, was evidently suffering and it was no affair of Joseph Francis Xavier Armagh's, who had been intruded upon.

Haroun still held out his hand and Joseph was forced to take it. "I don't know how I got here, Joe," said Haroun. "But I reckon you did it."

"It was Mr. Healey. This is his house, not mine."

"But you did it," said Haroun with the most absolute conviction. "He'd never look at me 'cept for you."

"Well, get well, Haroun, and you can repay Mr. Healey. I did nothing."

"You saved my life, Joe. I remember the train."

It was then that Haroun looked up at Joseph with a glowing look, a deep and intense devotion, a total trust, a passionate fervor. It was the look which Bill Strickland gave Mr. Healey, unquestioning, dedicated. It was not to be shaken, that faith. It was beyond reason.

"I am your man," said Haroun, in a whisper. "For all my life."

Joseph pulled his hand from Haroun's "Be your own man, for life," he said in a harsh tone. But Haroun still glowed upon him, and Joseph almost ran from the room.

Chapter 12

Joseph discovered that Mr. Healey had been somewhat modest about his holdings and activities and financial worth and prospects. He had hinted that his main interests were in Titusville, but Joseph found that Titusville was merely his base of operations and that he preferred not to conduct his business in Pittsburgh and Philadelphia because of a certain stringency on the part of the police and political enemies. However, his operations in Titusville were only a small part of his affairs. In Titusville he could protect himself from impertinent investigations with the aid of the men he employed. He also "owned" the sheriff and the latter's deputies, something he could not do in Pittsburgh and Philadelphia where the thieves were bigger than himself and had greater financial resources even than his. Yet his fortunes came from Philadelphia and Pittsburgh, and even from New York and Boston.

"Everything is organization, wit and an eye for opportunity, Irish," he would say to Joseph, and Joseph soon understood that this was a profound truth.

In most ways he was typically Irish, but not an Irish which Joseph knew, which was reserved, cold, restrained, melancholy, powerfully but secretly emotional, aristocratic, disdainful, proud, unforgiving, unrelenting, austere, "high-nosed," poetic and reluctantly mystical. Mr. Healey understood, if humorously resenting, Joseph's Irishness, but Joseph could never accept Mr. Healey's kind of Irishness which he considered vulgar, ostentatious, demeaning, and noisy.

Mr. Healey's steel files were kept in a room next to his "suite of offices," as he called the dirty and dingy rooms he rented, or owned. There were bars on the windows here, too. There was a cot with blankets. In this room each man in his employ slept for two nights a month, or at least

169

dozed, with pistols and a shotgun. Mr. Healey dealt with banks in Pittsburgh and Philadelphia, and with a new one in Titusville, but he always kept a large sum in gold in the enormous iron and steel safe in that central arsenal in his offices. His men had orders to shoot to kill any intruder, and this was known well in the township. Each of his men was an expert marksman, and practiced in the country at frequent intervals. Joseph was not exempt. His immediate mentor, Mr. Montrose, was his teacher, and Mr. Montrose reported to Mr. Healey that "that boy has an eye like a hawk, and never missed from the beginning."

"Never mind the law if you should shoot somebody trying to get into this room," Mr. Montrose said to Joseph who had proffered the suggestion. "Mr. Healey is the law hereabouts. Besides, it's legal to kill a thief on your own property. Or maybe you don't like the idea of killing?"

Joseph thought of the desperate and murderous and bloody battles between his people and the English military, and he said, "I have no objection to killing. I just wanted to be sure that I wouldn't be hanged if I did it."

"Careful, aren't you?" asked Mr. Montrose, but not with ridicule or rancor. "Only a fool is careless and doesn't know the odds before he acts."

Joseph soon learned that Mr. Healey despised rashness and impulsive actions, and as he disapproved of them himself he cultivated his native cautiousness.

None of the men knew the history of his companions, and none confided in anyone. It was obvious, however, from their accents that they had come from various sections of the country. Mr. Montrose had a soft deep-South accent, was courtly of speech and had gentle natural manners. He was also the most deadly of Mr. Healey's men, in spite of his Cavalier appearance, his fascinating voice, his air of polite consideration, and his unfailing civility and the unmistakable signs of superior breeding. He was always urbane and elegant and quietly patrician, so Joseph guessed that he had come of a family of gentlemen and had chosen to be a rascal either out of sudden poverty or innate inclination. He guessed the latter. Mr. Montrose's allusions were the allusions of a well-educated man, and not the absurd pretensions of a vulgarian.

He was a man about thirty-eight and very tall and slender with graceful postures and movements. He dressed expensively, but with taste. Joseph thought of the ginger cat which his grandmother had owned in Ireland, or, rather, who had owned her in the way of cats. Mr. Montrose had light ginger-colored hair and wide yellow eyes and dainty if effective mannerisms. His face was long and creamily pale and unreadable in its expressions, and his nose was almost delicately fine and his mouth handsome with its good teeth. He was rarely known to frown or to raise his voice or to speak insultingly or to show anger. His attitude was disciplined yet strangely tolerant. A man might make a mistake once, but only once. If more than that Mr. Montrose was his enemy. Joseph found something military about him though Mr. Montrose smilingly denied that he had ever been in the Army. However, Joseph did not quite believe this. Authority and discipline over self and others came from command, and Mr. Montrose, in spite of his elegance, was commanding.

His companions respected him and feared him, and he was their superior. They knew that he was even more ruthless and lethal than themselves. They remembered two of their number who had inexplicably disappeared from one day to another in the recent past and Mr. Montrose had expressed no surprise. The two were soon replaced.

For Mr. Healey all the men had devotion. Joseph had at first thought they only feared him, but Mr. Montrose enlightened him.

"The man they fear and detest and who is the subject of their nightmares is not Mr. Healey, who is a considerate gentleman," Mr. Montrose told Joseph. "They know he is human as they are human themselves, and is frequently sentimental. They trust him. Certainly, they will avoid any opportunity to annoy him—for various reasons. Their real hate and fear is Bill Strickland, the white trash with the soul of a tiger." (It was the first time that Joseph had heard the term "white trash," but he understood it at once.) "Bill Strickland," Mr. Montrose continued, with the first glare Joseph had ever seen in his eyes, "is atavistic. He is mindless, as you have possibly observed yourself, Mr. Francis. He is a living and murderous weapon and Mr. Healey holds the trigger. There is something in mankind, Mr. Francis, which is horrified at primeval wildness and unthinking savagery, no matter how contemptible a man is, himself, or how despicable and conscienceless. If men have enemies, they know that those enemies are impelled by something they, themselves, can understand, for are we not all men? But creatures like Bill Strickland are outside humanity, and are incapable of even the most distorted reason. They kill impersonally without malice or enmity or rage—and that is something other men cannot comprehend. They kill like swords or cannon or guns—at the pull of the trigger of the man who owns them. They ask no questions. They do not even demand money for their slaughter. They simply—are. Do you understand me?"

"Yes," said Joseph. "Is he an idiot, or feeble-minded?"

Mr. Montrose smiled, showing his excellent teeth. "I have told you: He is an atavism. Once, I have read, all men were like that, before they became fully men, homo sapiens. The alarming thing is that their number is not small. You will find them among the mercenaries, and you will even find them in the best of families. You will find them everywhere, though frequently they are disguised as men."

Mr. Montrose smoked reflectively. "I have never feared any man in my life. But I confess to fearing Bill Strickland —if he is behind my back. He makes my flesh crawl."

"And Mr. Healey employs him."

Mr. Montrose laughed, and touched Joseph lightly on his shoulder. "Mr. Francis, he employs him as men employ guards or guns. He is a weapon. If Mr. Healey carried a pistol you would not fault him, would you? You would say he is a man careful of his safety. Mr. Healey does not carry a pistol. He has Bill Strickland."

"Why is such a creature devoted to Mr. Healey?"

Mr. Montrose shrugged. "Ask that of a dog, Mr. Francis, who has a good master."

It came as a mortifying shock to Joseph, who had reached his conclusions about Bill Strickland through his own reason and observation and the conversation with Mr. Montrose, that young Haroun Zieff knew all about Bill by pure and artless instinct. Yet Haroun was the only one of Mr. Healey's entourage who felt no mystic horror of the man or instinctive revulsion and loathing. "I'd never cross him, and I'd stay away from his muzzle," he told Joseph. His great black eyes shone with a light that Joseph could not interpret. "But I wouldn't run away from him. You don't do that—with a jackal." For the first time Joseph encountered the quiet courage and peculiar ferocity of the desert-born, though he did not recognize it as such at that time. "Don't you ever be afraid of him, Joe. I'm here, your friend."

Joseph had laughed, his brief cynical laugh which was only the slightest sound. For the first time he was unpleasantly aware that he was beginning to trust Haroun, who now answered to the name of "Harry." To trust was to betray one's self. He tried repeatedly to mistrust Haroun, to find occasions when the boy was ambiguous and devious, or to catch a look in his eye that would reveal the general malice of men. He never found them. He did not know whether to be relieved and touched, or vexed.

Haroun now occupied a small but comfortable room over Mr. Healey's stables. His wounds had healed, though sometimes he limped. He never complained. He accepted life with high-heartedness and a simple wisdom which was beyond Joseph's capabilities. He was never resentful nor grudging. He gave largely of himself and his big glowing smiles, and his native merriment. He appeared to trust everyone, and to take them to himself, which was deceptive. He had his secret thoughts, but never betrayed the more somber of them except to Joseph, who, startled, would stare, and this would make Haroun burst out laughing—another thing which baffled Joseph. "You are never serious," he said once to Haroun, to which the boy answered, "I am always serious." It was not for many years that Joseph began to realize that Haroun was subtile and not to be understood completely by the Western mind. Haroun was proud, but it was not the pride of Joseph Armagh. It had something of the Spaniard about it: a point of honor.

Mr. Healey, on Joseph's insistence, paid Haroun ten dollars a week to haul nitroglycerin from the depot in Titusville to the deeper-drilled wells. Mr. Healey had looked with smiling meditation at Joseph. "Now, then, your lordship is very concerned with the vassals—is that the word? —all at once. Are you not the one who told me that Harry was nothing to you, and that you wished to be rid of him? Yet now you say 'a laborer is worthy of his hire.' Irish, you are a conundrum."

"If you hire Haroun, he must not be robbed, as he has been robbed all his life."

"It's the soft Irish heart in you that makes you say that?"

"Mr. Healey, Harry could get that much money from other drillers. Do you want to keep him? If not, I'll tell him to go. Why should he not make as much money for dangerous work as other men do?"

"So, it's fairness, is it?"

"Fairness has nothing to do with it. Money has."

Mr. Healey smoked for a few moments. Then he said, "Irish, you are not as tough as you believe you are, I am thinking. You've got wounds, you have, and they don't heal, so you stand guard over them with your pistol cocked for fear of them bleeding again. Boyo, every man has his wounds, even me. And that explains a lot about human nature which the Religious don't know about. When you talk about 'fairness' to Harry, you are thinking about yourself, and damn me if I don't think that explains the saints, too!"

He was elated with his sudden intuition and insisted on Joseph joining him, in the study, for a glass of brandy. "Yes, sir," he said, "a man don't want something for somebody else unless he thinks of himself in the same hole. Drink up, Irish. Life's not as sour as you think it is. At your age! Damn me, but I was a fine cockerel when I was eighteen, and not a monk like you!"

That had been ten months ago. Haroun was now earning eighteen dollars a week and Joseph—who did not consider it surprising though his associates did—was receiving thirty-eight dollars a week. In a town where a doctor or a lawyer felt affluent if his earnings were thirty-five dollars a week this was remarkable. Joseph paid Mr. Healey five dollars a week for his board, something which Mr. Healey found hilarious though Joseph could see no occasion for amusement. He put his savings in the bank. He would not have spent money on clothing had not Mr. Healey been insistent. "I'll have no ragged beggars working for me!" So he dressed somberly and plainly and cleanly. Not for him the ruffled shirts of the men in the offices or the rich jewelry. He wore modest clothing of a dark cut, unbedecked white shirts and a cheap watch across his lean middle. His boots were inexpensive but polished. His russet hair might be shorter than was fashionable but it was well-barbered. His changes of pantaloons and waistcoats were fewer, but the clothing was meticulous and spare. He was never to have the easy grace of his father, but he did have something of Mr. Montrose's obvious discipline of movement and economy of words. He was invariably grave and unsmiling, and sleeplessly industrious and aware. Mr. Healey, regarding him covertly, often nodded to himself.

But he could not understand Joseph's joylessness. The saints know, Mr. Healey would think, I've had as rough a road as this young spalpeen, but it never took away my appetite and my enjoyment in living. There's fury in this boyo, I'm thinking, but the fury will never get in the way of what he wants. It'll only kindle it higher.

In an effort to awaken Joseph's joy in living—which Mr. Healey fully believed lay latent in every man—he gave Joseph a silver token which would admit him to any brothel he desired in Titusville, and to the prettiest girl, and at no cost. "I've got the handsomest wenches in the whole Commonwealth," he said. "Never one over sixteen, youngest about twelve. Farm-fed, rich with butter and cream, plump as doves. Makes a man smack his lips. They know all the tricks. I've got madams who teach 'em. No gutter drabs in my houses! All clean and scented and healthy, and not cheap. You go and have a good time, boyo."

"No," said Joseph.

Mr. Healey frowned. "You ain't got a hankering for—? No, reckon not, though you never can tell. Well, you're only nineteen still. Hell, they say that's the hottest time. Think so, myself. Couldn't stay away from the wenches, when I was eighteen, nineteen. Just about used myself up." He chuckled. "You keep that token. One of these days, you damned monk, you, you'll look at it, spit on it, and polish it, and off you'll go just like everybody else."

On three nights a week after supper at five o'clock, Joseph went to the office of Mr. James Spaulding, a lawyer whom Mr. Healey "owned." He also spent two hours on Saturday afternoon there, and half a day on Sunday. Here he studied law with Mr. Spaulding as his teacher.

Mr. Spaulding was a man to whom the word "creamy" could be most aptly applied. He was as tall as Joseph, but pleasantly massive though not fat. Not one of his expressions was sincere, except avarice. He was fifty years old and kept his long, waving gray hair dyed a rich chestnut, and it flowed to his nape. He was clean-shaven; his features were big and somewhat rubbery, which gave them their mobility. There was nothing edgy, awkward, abrupt or combative about Mr. Spaulding, and no one, not even his wife and his wenches, ever guessed his true nature. Blanc Mange, thought Joseph on first seeing him, remembering his mother's pale bland pudding which quivered slightly when moved and had no character or no emphatic taste. He almost immediately revised his opinion, and for Joseph to revise his opinion was an event that was deeply disturbing to himself, for it lowered him in his own rigid estimation.

Mr. Spaulding had a large face in proportion with his bodily measurements, the face of a blackguard or a successful politician, and his eyes were the same color as his hair. His expression was one of composed amiability and sweetness, enhanced by a tender smile and a deep dimple in his chin and one in his left cheek. His voice was velvety and rich, like warm chocolate, and resounding and even musical, never grating, never quickened, never hostile even to the most recalcitrant. He invariably wore black and gray-striped pantaloons, nicely cut, a long black coat, a shirt with a wide soft white collar, and black silk cravats fastened with one pearl pin of impressive size. Always suave, always considerate and polite, always deferential, speaking in periods, always sympathetic and conciliatory and attentive, he was a most dangerous and clever man. Truth to him was an uncivilized attribute and a gentleman never used it if a colorful lie could be used instead, and he had no honor and no principles and was always for hire. He knew law thoroughly and had a memory which none could surpass. He admired but two categories of men: the very rich who could pay well and so had power, and the intelligent. This did not mean that he liked them. Mr. Spaulding never liked anyone but himself and love was a word he used only in the courtroom to move "the jackasses" to tears and a favorable verdict. His opinion of judges was little less unflattering. If they could be bought he respected them. If they could not be bought he despised them. He had two sons who lived in Philadelphia, and were as unscrupulous as himself. They sought his advice on the most difficult cases —and paid well for the advice. Mr. Spaulding was not one for family feeling, nor were his sons. They were very successful but they did not make, together, half the money Mr. Spaulding made in Titusville, and Mr. Spaulding's interests were not confined to Law. (He spoke in capitals.) He and Mr. Healey were as much friends as two such men could possibly be. There was a symbiosis between them.

When Mr. Healey brought Joseph to him Mr. Spaulding thought, What's the old bastard up to behind my back? He smiled happily and gave Joseph a warm and meaty hand to shake and made his eyes shine paternally. "Jim," said Mr. Healey, "this here boyo is Joseph Francis, he calls himself. Good enough moniker if he likes it. Ain't in no trouble with the police; no one's looking for him. Teaching him my business. Mr. Montrose thinks he's right smart and no fool. So I thought, seeing he's learning to handle my business, he ought to learn law, too, and who's better to teach law than old Jim, I said to meself."

Mr. Spaulding had long wanted to "handle" Mr. Healey's business, and so had one of his sons. Mr. Spaulding's smile grew wider and more glistening, and fonder as he studied this raw youth in plain clothing. Was old Ed getting senile? Then Mr. Spaulding remembered that Mr. Healey was a considerable number of years his junior. He wafted the two visitors to two of the six black leather chairs in his office, sat down behind his mahogany desk, folded his hands as if preparing to pray, and suffused his face with love and attention. His office was large and warm in the October chill, and a fire rustled briskly in the grate of the black marble fireplace. There were several worthy Currier-Ives prints on his paneled walls, and a noble view of the distant gaudy hills—resplendent in autumn fire—through his wide window. It was a brilliant day with a sky like blue polished enamel.

"Sharp as horse-radish, this boyo," said Mr. Healey. "That's what Mr. Montrose says."

"No one," said Mr. Spaulding in a middle-octave organ note, "has a higher respect for Mr. Montrose's opinion than I have. No indeedy." He wore a signet ring and a watch chain and everything about him was decorous, solid, and reliable. Sunlight lay on his imposing wall of law books and on his deep crimson thick rug. His fingernails, broad but shallow, were faintly tinted pink and shone with buffing. What the hell? he thought and looked more closely at Joseph, who was scrutinizing him in turn. This took Mr. Spaulding aback somewhat. He was not accustomed to strangers, and especially callow strangers, studying him coldly and showing no signs of being impressed with his office or his person. Joseph suddenly seemed hostile, to him, and this was sheer impudence. Who did the young rat think he was, to stare at James Spaulding in such a cynical fashion? Weighing him, by God! Looking him up and down as if he were a houseman humbly searching for a job! Mr. Spaulding did not like small sunken blue eyes, and particularly not these with the darker spark glittering in their depths. He did not like reddish hair on a man, nor freckles, nor stark pallor which hinted at an uncomfortable asceticism. A sharpie, thought Mr. Spaulding, city scum picked up from God knows where by this fool of a Healey. Perhaps a wood's colt, Mr. Spaulding's thoughts continued, and he smiled benignly at Joseph who did not smile in response.

Joseph thought, An actor, a smooth criminal, a liar and a thief, and never to be trusted for one instant.

Mr. Healey leaned back expansively in his chair. "He can come couple of nights, and time on Saturdays and Sundays. Teach him fast, Jim, and you'll not regret it. Criminal law, and such. And a lot about politics. Aim to make him governor some day," and Mr. Healey grinned. "Could use a governor in my business."

A sum was named, hands were shaken, cigars passed, and little glasses of brandy. Joseph accepted his glass and sipped at it slowly, watching Mr. Spaulding openly or covertly as his rapid thoughts continued. Mr. Spaulding in his turn watched Joseph, and all at once he said to himself, aghast, This one's meaner than a rattlesnake!

Mr. Spaulding was shaken as he had not been shaken for many years. He reconsidered Joseph and now it seemed to him that Joseph was not a callow youth but an aged and powerful man, crusted with experience and knowledge as a rock is crusted with shells. It was incredible!

This impression did not diminish when Joseph became his student. Joseph seemed not to enjoy the study of law, but he pursued that study with intense concentration as a means to an end, and this Mr. Spaulding guessed almost at once. Then Mr. Spaulding acquired a hating respect for the youth, for Joseph's mind raced but not with immoderation or facility. He seized a problem in law, as it were, with his teeth and shook it until it gave up its solution, and often that solution had not occurred to Mr. Spaulding, himself. His memory was apparently as prodigious as Mr. Spaulding's own.

Once he said to Joseph, "It is not what the Law *says* that is important. It is how it is interpreted, how it is used—"

"Yes," said Joseph. "Law is a harlot."

Mr. Spaulding cleared his throat and assumed a shocked expression. "Hardly that, dear boy, hardly that. No indeedy. But the Law, it has been said, is a blunt Instrument. One must learn to soften its Blows or turn them aside, if possible."

"And it is for sale," said Joseph, pointing out a case which they had just been studying.

Mr. Spaulding pursed his large flabby lips. Then he could not help smiling and winking. "To the highest bidder," he said. "See, it is like the Constitution of the United States of America. The Constitution guarantees to the individual States that they have the sacred right to secede from the Union whenever they Desire, and no Hindrance shall be put upon them. But Mr. Lincoln has decided otherwise, for his own reasons, which we hope are Just. We can only Hope. If a President, or the United States Supreme Court, can decide at random what is Constitutional or un-Constitutional, to suit their whims or their convictions or their expediency—in spite of express wordage simply and explicitly given in the Constitution—then Law, too, can be decided on the basis of personal convictions and expediency, or whims. One must suit the Law, or the Constitution, to suit the case."

"Prologue to chaos," said Joseph.

Mr. Spaulding said, "What did you say?"

"Nothing," said Joseph. "I was just talking to myself."

Mr. Spaulding said, " 'The quality of mercy is not strained. It droppeth as the gentle rain from heaven—blesseth him that gives and him that takes'. The Bible."

"Shakespeare," said Joseph. "Portia. *Merchant of Venice.*"

"Smart as paint, aren't you?" said Mr. Spaulding. "I was testing you, dear boy." He gave Joseph a smile of loving malevolence. "Joseph, you and I did not make the Law. Now, any fool can pick up a law book and read what the Law *says* and what its apparent intention is, but will that stand up in court? No, sir, not always, rarely ever. It is a lawyer's function to convince judge and jury that the Law did not mean exactly that, or perhaps meant even the complete opposite. Only idiots go by a strict interpretation. A wise lawyer can make ducks and drakes out of any law."

"The Devil's race," said Joseph.

"What's that? I do wish, Joseph, that you would lose that annoying habit of mumbling to yourself. Judges don't like it. To continue: The Law is only what people agree it is, mainly juries, after they have been persuaded by a smart lawyer, though tomorrow they will agree it is something else again when they are in the hands of another lawyer.

That is the beauty of Law, Joseph. Its flexibility. The same Law can accuse a man of being a criminal and the very same Law can declare him innocent. It can hang or release in the exact same words. So you must always decide at once what you wish the Law to do for you, and your Client, and convince yourself that that is the only solution. All my Clients," said Mr. Spaulding, "are innocent."

Joseph soon discovered in full why Mr. Spaulding was so necessary to Mr. Healey. The evidence was in the files in the locked room. He often found himself sickened at the evidence of collusion between Mr. Healey and Mr. Spaulding and the two local judges. For certain favors the judges owed their elections to Mr. Healey, and Mr. Healey owed considerable to the judges, and all this was presided over by the massive realism of Mr. Spaulding. He once said to Joseph, in a rare moment of vulgarity, "It's a case, dear boy, of you scratching my back, and me scratching yours, and what is wrong with a little proper scratching at the right time and in the right place? You can't always reach the itch, yourself, and you need help, and in a way it is Christian reciprocity. Joseph, if we all adhered to the letter of the Law, which I think Christ Himself condemned, there would be precious few of us left free in this world, and very little joy. Or profit."

The months went by and Joseph learned in the offices of Mr. Healey and in the richer office of Mr. Spaulding, and what he learned, in spite of himself, made his nature harsher than it was even by birth, and bitterer than he could ever have imagined. More and more he was convinced that as an inhabitant of this world, for which he was not guilty, he must live by its laws and its exigencies if he were to survive and save his family. His last chance for personal happiness winked out and the ponderous darkness settled upon his spirit.

Chapter 13

Joseph, out of desperate necessity, had finally been forced to trust the first person, with the exception of his mother, he had ever trusted in his life. It was a trust that was really only partial mistrust, but it had to be risked.

He needed to send money to Sister Elizabeth for his brother and sister. He knew that there was only a slight chance that Mr. Squibbs would ever discover that "Scottie" was really an Irishman and that he had a family in St. Agnes's Orphanage, and that through them he could trace the man who had absconded with his money. Still, there was that chance, and life was grotesque enough to permit it, and Joseph dared not risk such Hogarthian jokes. He was saving everything he could, and soon he would have enough for Mr. Squibbs plus interest. In the meantime there was Sean, and Regina, and his unshaken belief that in the event money was not received by Sister Elizabeth they would be separated and adopted, or worse.

He considered. Every two months or so Mr. Healey sent Haroun and two older men to Wheatfield to buy equipment for his wells, or other of his enterprises, or to deliver messages. (Mr. Healey did not trust the United States Post Office, nor even the Wells Fargo Express.) Joseph had once suggested that he would not mind such a journey occasionally, himself, but Mr. Healey assured him that his time was too valuable in Titusville. So Joseph had recourse to Haroun, whose dedication to him was frequently embarrassing. ("You've got yourself your own Bill Strickland, ain't you?" Mr. Healey asked once, with immense amusement.)

Joseph wrote a letter to Sister Elizabeth in which he said he sometimes "passed through" Wheatfield on business from Pittsburgh, and he enclosed a full year's payment for his family in gold bills, and extra money for small luxuries for them for the coming Christmas and their birthdays. He added that he was sealing the letter in red wax in three places, and that he'd be obliged if Sister Elizabeth would inform him if the letter had been tampered with and if anything had been taken from the envelope. Then he went to the stables over which Haroun slept and lived in a small hayscented and manure-pungent room and Haroun was happy to see him for never before had Joseph visited him here. Joseph sat with the letter in his hand and studied Haroun with the intensity he always gave those he was judging and weighing.

He saw the boy's glowing devotion and the wise candor of the huge black eyes. Mr. Healey trusted Haroun to the small extent of the boy's duties, and so did the men with whom he worked in the well houses and in the field. It was as if, to Joseph, he had never seen the boy fully before. He did not often encounter him, and Joseph did not linger for idle conversation on the few occasions he saw him. His indifference to Haroun had not diminished, nor did he think of him for weeks at a time. Had Haroun vanished mysteriously he would have shrugged and forgotten at once. But now he must consider Haroun for Haroun was necessary to him. The boy had lost his starved appearance, due to plain but sufficient food and reasonably comfortable shelter, and a little money. His always hopeful and expectant expression had brightened as his optimism grew. Joseph marveled at the implicit vitality of the boy, the innate exuberance for life, the appetite for living, and the laughter that lay so close to his lips and rarely left his eyes. The crop of thick black curls had become glossy with health, the dusky skin was browner and sleeker, the mouth as red as a girl's and almost always smiling. He looked like a lively cherub though the eyes were hardly angelic. What he did with his small free time was a mystery, to Joseph, who had never thought of it before. Haroun was now sixteen, and still small for his age, but he seemed to vibrate with animation and vigor like a young colt eagerly pawing the green pasture. Haroun suddenly impinged on Joseph's consciousness like a highly colored and unexpected portrait, and he did not like it. But his liking or disliking must not interfere with necessity.

Joseph sat on the edge of Haroun's narrow cot and Haroun sat on the wooden crate which was his only chair and which held his few belongings, and in the light of the kerosene lamp Haroun's delight at this visit was embarrassing to the older man. He held the letter to Sister Elizabeth in his hand, and he looked into Haroun's eyes and said, "I want you to mail this letter in Wheatfield tomorrow, when you go there early in the morning."

"Yes!" said Haroun, and held out his small brown hand for the letter. But Joseph still held it. Would Haroun ask why it should be posted in Wheatfield? If he did then he could not be intrusted with the posting. But Haroun did not ask. He only waited, his hand still extended. If Joseph wished something it was enough for him, and he almost palpitated with the pleasure of the thought that he would be helping his friend.

"You must not let anyone else see this letter," said Joseph.

"No!" exclaimed Haroun, shaking his curls until they flew.

"You will take it to the post office," said Joseph. "And there you will arrange for a postal box for me, Joseph Francis. I will give you the two dollars rent for the year."

For the first time Haroun was puzzled. "I do not understand this, about a box," he said. "You must tell me so I can be sure."

So Joseph explained and Haroun listened with the older boy's own intensity and concentration, and then Joseph made him repeat the instructions at least twice. Then he gave the letter to Haroun who tied it in a kerchief and stuffed it into the pocket of his only coat. Joseph watched him closely, but the boy showed no curiosity, no slyness, no speculation. He was only happy that Joseph was with him.

"How do you like your work for Mr. Healey, Harry?" Joseph asked, not with interest for he could feel none, but he felt that some amenities should be included.

"I like it," said Haroun. "I am making money, and isn't that enough?" He laughed and his white teeth shone in the lamplight. "I will soon be a rich man, like Mr. Healey."

Joseph could not resist smiling. "And how do you think you'll manage that?"

Haroun looked wise. "I save almost all, and when I have enough I will buy a string of tools for myself. One of these days."

"Good," said Joseph. He did not see that Haroun had stopped smiling and that he was regarding Joseph with earnest attention as if listening to something that had not been spoken. Joseph looked at the floor and thought, rubbing his foot against some straws on the wood. Then he glanced up at Haroun and was a little confused at the boy's expression, for it was both sad and very mature, the expression of a man who knew all about the world and was not enraged at it but only aware.

"Harry, here are two dollars for you, yourself, for doing me this favor." Joseph held out two cartwheels, for one must always pay for what is received or one becomes the lesser, and nothing but money bought loyalty.

There was a sudden sharp silence in the little musty room as if someone had slammed a brutal hand on a table in threat or anger. Haroun looked at the money in Joseph's hand but did not take it. His face became absent, averted.

Then he said in a very low voice, one Joseph had not heard before, "What have I done to you, Joe, that you insult me, your friend?"

Joseph started to reply, then could say nothing. Something moved in the cold stiffness of him, something painful and unfamiliar, something infinitely melancholy and ashamed. He stood up, slowly. He felt a vague anger against Haroun that the boy should touch him so acutely, and presume to call him "friend," a silly incredible word.

"I'm sorry," he said in a cold voice. "I didn't mean to offend you, Harry. But you are doing me a great favor, and then—"

"And then?" repeated Haroun when Joseph stopped.

Joseph moved his head restlessly. "You don't make much money, Haroun. I—I haven't seen you for a long time. I thought perhaps the money—I thought you could buy something for yourself with it. Call it a present, if you want to, and not payment."

Haroun stood up also. His head hardly reached Joseph's chin but he was suddenly endowed with dignity. "Joe," he said, "when you really want to give me a present I'll like it and take it. But you don't want to give me a present now. You want to pay me for doing something for my friend, and friends don't take pay."

Joseph felt another unfamiliar emotion—curiosity. "What is the difference between payment and a present, Harry?"

Haroun shook his head. "Maybe, sometime, you'll know, Joe. If you don't ever, then don't try to give me money."

Joseph could find nothing more to say and so he turned and went down the ladder to the warm dark stables and heard the stamping and the snufflings of the horses, and he went out into the cold night and stood for several minutes on the packed clay of the ground and did not see anything at all.

"Nothing like a good war for prosperity!" said Mr. Healey to Mr. Montrose, showing him an advance cheque on a British bank for delivery of four thousand eight-chamber repeating rifles which had been manufactured by Barbour & Bouchard, quite illegally, considering that the British owned the patent entirely at present. (Barbour & Bouchard, munitions makers in Pennsylvania, were quite realistic about the "temporary appropriation" of the patent, as they also had a large interest in Robsons and Strong, British munitions makers, who did own the patent. It was only a matter of time until amicable arrangements would be made, which could not now be made in view of the War between the States and the blockade against all ships, mainly British, which Washington had promulgated.) No name was issued on the British bank draft, but Mr. Healey quite understood. The rifles were to be delivered to a small unbusy port in lower Virginia, where Mr. Healey had done business in some trifles before, none of which would have received the hearty approval either of the police or the Federal military. "And this is just the beginning," added Mr. Healey with satisfaction. "What's four thousand rifles? Hardly a flea bite. Of course, Barbour & Bouchard are doing their own gun-running and arrangements with the Confederacy, and making millions. Maybe they want to be generous and let me and other small fry make an honest dollar." He chuckled.

"And perhaps," said the elegant Mr. Montrose, "Barbour & Bouchard are testing us to see if we can be entirely trusted with the gun-running, and perhaps they have heard that so far we have been discreet and bold enough to do other running to the Confederacy of contraband, without being caught once."

"Knock wood," said Mr. Healey. "And that means that B&B, if we do this right, will have more work for us. Sure, and that it is." He puffed on his cigar, thoughtfully. "When I was younger I did a bit of blackbirding in my time. After all, the black savages were better treated and fed here than in their jungles, where they were the slaves of their cannibal chiefs. Still and all, it came to me at last that they were human, too, and I was brought up a strict Catholic and it went against the grain. I regretted the money, but there's things a man can't always force himself to do."

Barbour & Bouchard sold the eight-chamber repeating rifles in enormous quantities to the Federal Government in Washington. Whether or not the four thousand rifles now waiting in New York in a discreet warehouse—the boxes labeled MACHINE PARTS—were rifles stolen by interested parties from the Federal allotment, or whether Barbour & Bouchard had delivered those weapons themselves to that warehouse, was something Mr. Healey would not have dreamed of speculating about. That would have been uncivil, ungrateful, unrealistic, and unworthy of a businessman. Besides, the bank draft was solely for successful delivery and demanded no investment of Mr. Healey beyond the lives or liberty of his agents. Nevertheless, one had to be careful in choosing those agents.

"It is time to break young Francis in," said Mr. Montrose. "I have kept my counsel for two years about him, giving him only temperate commendations to you, but now I am certain not only were you completely correct about him in the beginning but that he has improved so he is, himself, a formidable weapon, or henchman, or whatever you may wish to call him. My trust is rarely given in full, but I think we can trust young Mr. Francis to the utmost— so long as we continue to pay him well and he can pick our brains."

"Um," said Mr. Healey. He considered the ash on his cigar as he and Mr. Montrose sat in his study over brandy. "Perhaps it is right you are. I sent him to Corland to buy up some leases, but before he went he said to me, 'Mr. Healey, I want to buy some leases on my own, and next to the leases you want. I do not yet have the money. Would you lend me two thousand dollars?'

"Well, sir, I thought that was mighty cool on the part of the spalpeen, whom I pay forty dollars a week now—under duress, you might say." Mr. Healey smiled, but not with annoyance. "Mighty cool. Twenty dollars a week to be returned from his pay, with six percent interest. Well, sir, I did."

"I know," said Mr. Montrose.

Mr. Healey was not surprised. What Mr. Montrose did not know was of the very least significance.

"I had a small talk with him," Mr. Montrose said. He

preferred narrow and scented cheroots to the thick and robust cigars Mr. Healey favored. "No, he did not tell me of the loan. I said to him, 'All leases, to be legal, must be in your full and correct name in the courthouse, or later—er, scoundrels—might dispute the matter.' I like the young man, and wished to help him and prevent him from doing himself a grave mischief. He appeared somewhat disturbed at this. To make certain he visited the courthouse himself. He trusts no one, and that is in itself commendable. Apparently he discovered that I had given him correct information."

Mr. Healey sat up. "Yes? And what is his correct name—" Mr. Healey knew Mr. Montrose too well to question how he had come by the information.

"Joseph Francis Xavier Armagh. That is a strange name."

"A high-nosed Irish name!" said Mr. Healey, delighted. "County Armagh. Not your County Mayo or Cork or such. High-nosed. Damn me if I don't have a lordship working for me! I always knew it."

Mr. Montrose, as an aristocratic Southerner of Scots-Irish stock—he was related to the Carrolls—was a little impressed, though not too much, as he was an Episcopalian born.

"Lots of Protestants, though, in County Armagh, and among the Armaghs," said Mr. Healey with unusually prejudiced feeling. "Got a feeling, though, that Joe's not a Protestant."

"No, he isn't," said Mr. Montrose, smiling slightly. "As you know, the court records demand to know a man's baptismal name as well as the name he is—ah—assuming for various reasons, and where he was baptised. Young Joseph was baptised in St. Bridget's Church in Carney, Ireland. His writing was almost illegible when he gave this reluctant information, and possibly he gave it truthfully after my warning. But I have never been balked by illegible writing. It is one of my hobbies."

"And not even a Rosary in his room, or a holy medal or picture," said Mr. Healey.

"Nor in yours," said Mr. Montrose, smiling again.

"Well, I am—different," said Mr. Healy. Mr. Montrose saw that Mr. Healey seemed somewhat depressed, or hurt, and this amused Mr. Montrose. He loved paradoxes, especially those concerning human nature. "Young heathen," said Mr. Healey, and Mr. Montrose assumed a grave expression. "Excommunicated, perhaps."

Mr. Montrose said, "Certainly, we will not betray to young Mr. Francis that we know his true and full name. That would be most vulgar of us. It is none of our business, as you know, sir."

"True, that it is," said Mr. Healey, but he fumed slightly. "Well, I never took a false name, or shortened mine, but once, and that was when I had a little difficulty with the police in Philadelphia, when I was very young. I had a little pride, I had."

"We shall not question young Mr. Francis's reasons," said Mr. Montrose. Mr. Healey looked at him curiously. What was Mr. Montrose's true name? But no one ever asked. Mr. Montrose owned no leases; he had no businesses with the courthouses. He dealt only with banks. Mr. Healey, though it was difficult, always suppressed his normal Irish inquisitiveness, for inquisitiveness could be dangerous.

They settled down to business. Gun-running to the embattled South was somewhat different from running in food supplies, wool lengths, tools and such, in which Mr. Healey had been heavily and profitably engaged since the outbreak of the war. For contraband such as weapons Washington had threatened the death penalty. Still, at this time, the Federal Government was in dire difficulties with the wild and chaotic draft riots all over the North, and the constant threats against the life of Mr. Lincoln—in the North—and the various victories of the Confederacy. (Mobs in the North were carrying placards around courthouses and Federal buildings depicting Mr. Lincoln as "The Dictator," for he had suspended the law of habeas corpus among other Constitutional guarantees, and the American people were still suspicious of government, remembering that governments are usually men's deadliest enemies.)

"I don't want anybody killed, or caught," said Mr. Healey. "Or anybody who would talk. You are right, you are. I'll have a talk with Joe Francis Xavier. Sound him out."

"I want you to do something for me," said Mr. Healey to Joseph, after he had called him into the study. "A little— dangerous. And no questions."

"What?" asked Joseph, frowning.

Mr. Healey raised a pacific hand. "Now, now, don't you get on your high horse. I'm not asking you this time to look about you in Pittsburgh and bring some nice pretty little girls to some of my boardinghouses, where they'll be well-fed and protected and make a bit of solid cash. I don't understand you," complained Mr. Healey. "The girls I have always—protected, call it—come from wretched homes or have no homes, or are in slavery service, starving and what not. What's the harm in their earning some good money and having a gay time with many a spark? But not you, you monk, you Joe St. Francis Xavier, not you. It ain't moral, or something, you think. But I have my ears out, and you didn't find it amiss just lately to use that there little token I gave you, did you?"

Joseph was silent. Mr. Healey laughed, leaned across his table and slapped Joseph on one of the cold slender hands which rested tensely on the wood. "Don't give it a second thought, Joe. You're young, and it's only envious I am. What it is to be young! Never mind. The job I have in mind for you, Joe, is something you never dreamed of before, and I never engaged in it, myself. Not out of your morality, you righteous humbug, but out of lack of opportunity. Now, no questions. It's gun-running down to a little port in Ole Virginny, as they call it."

Joe studied him. His expression did not change. He said, "And how will I manage that?"

Mr. Healey, before replying opened his desk drawer and removed a packet of gold bills from it and a new pistol and a box of ammunition. "Now here," he said, "is what you will use to grease your way, if things get a little sticky, which we hope they won't. Never saw a man whose eyes don't shine when he sees these. And this here gun is for you. It's yours, for always. Fine gun, isn't it? Best made; Barbour & Bouchard, right here in this here Commonwealth. They made those four thousand eight-chamber rifles you'll be delivering down South. Mr. Montrose will go with you. Time you faced a little danger, took on some of the responsibilities my other lads have been doing right along, as you know only too well. But you've been snug in my offices, like a flea in a dog's ear, and the only danger you ever had was when you spent those two nights a month in the file room. My lads're not getting younger, and you're young, and it's hard to recruit the proper men for the proper jobs. Haven't found anyone but you in three-four long years, and that's a compliment, sir, that's a compliment."

Joseph thought of his brother and his sister, and then he took the pistol in his hand and tested it. It had a fine balance, an excellent "feel," a certain competent smoothness, a certain deadly reassurance. "You've said no questions," said Joseph. "But I need to ask a few."

"Go ahead," said Mr. Healey, with a large wave of his hand. "But that don't mean I have to answer them."

"Is there any chance I may be killed, or caught?"

Mr. Healey watched him closely, then nodded. "I'll be honest with you. Yes, Not a big chance, but some. Depends on what you do, what you say, how you conduct yourself, and your luck. But you got the luck of the Irish, don't you?"

Joe's hands caressed the pistol but he looked silently at Mr. Healey for several moments. He said, "And how much will you pay me for this?"

Mr. Healey affected incredulous astonishment. "You get your pay, don't you? Pay my other lads didn't get until they'd worked for me at least ten whole years, and you've been around only little over two. It's the soft heart I have, and I'm getting sentimental in my old age. I'll forget you ever asked that question."

Joseph smiled faintly. "I owe you one thousand eight hundred dollars still. You've treated me fair and square, as you call it, Mr. Healey, and you've collected your interest, too, which is only right. So, to be brief, when I return after this job you will cancel the balance of my debt to you." He lifted his own hand. "I take care of your books, Mr. Healey. You do pay the men a handsome salary, but for certain tricky jobs you give them a fine gift. I know. I write out the cheques myself, for your signature. I may be your eyes and your ears, as you have kindly mentioned yourself several times, but I do have eyes and ears of my own, too, though I keep my tongue to myself."

"You're mad, that you are," said Mr. Healey.

Joseph said nothing, but waited.

"Your first important job, and God knows if you'll do it right, and you want one thousand eight hundred dollars for it!"

"Mr. Healey, there is a good chance, and that I know, that I may never come back. I will leave a letter with—

someone—who will deliver my options to another person in another city, if I am killed or caught. You need have no anxieties. I will not tell that—someone—where I am going or what I am going to do. I will only tell him that if I don't return he is to go to you and you will give him the canceled agreement, and he will send it off to another person. You see, Mr. Healey"—and Joseph smiled his grimace of a smile again—"I am giving you my absolute trust that you will act honorably."

Mr. Healey was alarmed. He sat up straight, his face swelling and turning crimson. "And who, may I ask, is that person in another city?"

Joseph almost laughed. "Only a nun, sir, only a nun."

"A nun!"

"Yes. A harmless old nun—she once did me a great favor."

"I think," said Mr. Healey with awe, "that you're daft. A nun! You! And who's your messenger right here, who'll take the papers to that nun, not that I believe a word of it."

"Harry Zeff."

"And he knows that nun?" Mr. Healey slapped his forehead in despair.

"No. He does not. He won't even need to know her or see her. He will only send her the papers when he reads her address in the letter I will leave him."

"Good God, why all these secrets?"

"No secrets, Mr. Healey. A nun is not a secret, and we Irish do have a penchant for the Religious, don't we?"

"What's that—that pen—?"

"A weakness for, let us say."

"So, you want to be charitable, to an old nun who probably never saw twenty dollars in her life!"

"No. Not charitable. Just a—remembrance, I'll call it."

Mr. Healey repeated, "I think you're daft." He chewed furiously on his cigar, then spat. He glared at Joseph. "You're deeper than a well," he said. "Maybe deeper than hell, even. Any connection of yours, that nun?"

"No."

"I don't believe any of this," said Mr. Healey.

"Nobody, sir, is going to force you to believe anything. I just want your word of honor that you will deliver that canceled agreement to Harry Zeff to be sent to that nun, if I don't return."

"You think of everything, don't you?"

"Yes."

"What makes you think you can trust Harry?"

"What makes you think you can trust Bill Strickland?"

"Hah!" Mr. Healey leaned back in his chair. "I saved Bill from the gallows."

"And I saved Harry's life, or at least his leg."

"But Harry's sharp, and Bill's a dog."

Joseph did not answer. Mr. Healey studied him. "So you finally got yourself to trust somebody, eh?"

"I tested him, and he asked no questions."

"You could take a lesson from him," said Mr. Healey with sourness.

When Joseph made no comment Mr. Healey said irascibly, "Why can't you leave that letter with me, and not with Harry? Don't you trust me? And I don't like that smile of yours, I'm thinking."

"Mr. Healey, you once said the fewer people you need to trust the better. I've already trusted Harry. Besides, you are a busy and important man and I don't wish to burden you with trifles like this."

"Hum," said Mr. Healey. "Trying to diddle me, are you? You got a right sarcastic mouth on you, Irish, for all your smooth way of speaking."

"I am not planning on being killed or caught, Mr. Healey. The letter is only for an unforeseen emergency, which I hope will not occur. I can trust Harry to return that letter to me unread in case I return. I've trusted him before. I didn't like to do it but I was forced to."

"All I know," said Mr. Healey, "is that in some way you outsmarted me and got me to say you can have that money I lent you. I didn't intend to. All right, get on with you. Get out of this room."

Joseph stood up and said, "Thank you, Mr. Healey. You are a gentleman."

Mr. Healey watched the young man leave the room and silently close the door after him. He ruminated. He began to smile, and it was both a rueful and affectionate smile, and then he shook his head as if laughing at himself. "The damned Irish!" he said aloud. "You can't beat us."

Chapter 14

Joseph wrote the letter to Sister Elizabeth, and enclosed the deeds to the options he had bought near Corland. He wrote that the options were to be held for his brother and his sister, and then offered for sale in a year for a certain price to Mr. Healey. He mentioned that a cheque would be reaching her shortly in the amount of several hundred dollars, for the board of his family. "This will protect their future, which I leave in your hands," he wrote, "for if you receive this letter I will probably be dead." He sealed the letter carefully and wrapped paper about it, which he sealed also.

Then he wrote a short note to Haroun Zieff and sealed it also, the hot red wax dripping on his fingers. The candle he had lighted for this purpose flickered and smoked. On the envelope he wrote, *Not to be opened unless I am dead.* He blew out the candle and the wan and sharper light of his table lamp filled his bedroom. A fire burned quietly in the grate. It was April 1, 1863, a cold bleak April after a desperately bitter winter. Joseph put the two packets together, placed them in a drawer of the rosewood desk and turned the key and pocketed it. The packets would be given to Haroun on the day he left for New York.

He threw more coals on the fire and opened a book and began to read. He had marked a place with Sister Elizabeth's last letter. He would reread it again, then burn it. He never left any incriminating item behind him. He had put the thought of his coming mission to New York, and then Virginia, out of his mind for there was no need to think of it at present. Unnecessary thought was an impediment and made one too hesitant about the future.

He had given a very brief consideration as to what he would do on his return, for now he owed no one anything and could borrow again, probably from Mr. Healey, for a string of tools and the hire of a few men to work them on the property on which he held options. However, there was a good possibility that he would not return, and there was no intelligence in planning unless there was a sound assurance behind the planning. Until he returned he would waste no time even on probabilities. A week from today he would be in New York. He did not even try to remember New York. If a vague and uneasy pain touched him occasionally from the suppressed remembrance he was hardly aware of it, though he moved restlessly once or twice in his green velvet rocking chair. He had learned how to deal with sorrow; of that he was certain. One had only to make up one's mind that nothing in the world would ever hurt him again, not even memory, and that was sufficient.

If natural apprehension nibbled a little at the edge of his intense concentration on the book he ignored it and dismissed it. Fear did not make him stare sightlessly at the page. What had to be done must be done, and as his life had always been joyless and he knew nothing of laughter and gaiety he found nothing particularly vulnerable in it for himself. He had money in the bank in Titusville; he had his options. All would be used for his family's future, combined with the sale of the options to Mr. Healey if he, Joseph, did not return. The options, a year from now, ought to be worth twice what he had paid for them and far more, for drilling had already begun in Corland and wells had come in in a very satisfactory way. All in all, the family was protected. It did not occur to Joseph, who trusted no one very much, not even Haroun, that he was trusting Sister Elizabeth to use the money wisely and well in behalf of Sean and Regina. Deep in his hidden consciousness lay that trust, though he did not know it consciously.

He was reading Macaulay's Essay on Machiavelli, and it came to him with grim humor that he, himself, was not of the cut of a Machiavelli. The airy and delicate art of supreme irony—in contrast with the acid irony of the Irish—interested him and pleased him, as one would be interested and pleased by a ballet full of grace, gauzy gestures, pirouettes, and collected harmony. Having read much of Machiavelli himself, Joseph found Macaulay's treatise somewhat heavy and pedantic, though Macaulay had indeed suspected that Machiavelli's gravest advice to princes was given with tongue in cheek. But Machiavelli's dancing-eyed mockery was not Joseph's, for Joseph understood, himself, that his own mockery of men and life came from hatred and pain while Machiavelli's came from sophisticated amusement. Joseph was well aware that he could never laugh at the world. To be the total ironist one had to possess that gift no matter what wounds lay under the laughter. To be a Machiavelli, then, with plots and counterplots, one had to be objective, not an objectivity that came from uninterest, as in his own case, but the objectivity of a man at once apart from the world and subjectively involved in it.

Only a few months ago the Union troops under Rosecrans had forced the Southern "rebels" to retreat after the Battle of Murfreesboro. Mr. Lincoln, in January of this year, had issued the Emancipation Proclamation, and a few weeks later the Union had passed a draft law which had resulted in many bloody riots throughout the North. Burnside's Union Army had been almost annihilated at Fredericksburg. The Union, though grief-stricken at the death of its sons, was engaged in merry money-making and a war prosperity which elated almost everyone. There were constant bands, exhortations, the movement of troops and excitement in the Union, and particularly in Pennsylvania so near to the field of battle. Yet to Joseph Armagh they were events that had been taking place, and were taking place, on Arcturus and engaged his interest not at all. He was not even a citizen of the United States of America nor did he consider the possibility of becoming so. If he thought of the situation in the most passing way it was with the thought that he was an alien in this world and its affairs were not his affairs, and that he had no country and no allegiances.

He got up from his rocking chair for a moment to throw a new handful of coals on the fire. He sat down and opened his book and saw the last letter from Sister Elizabeth, dated ten days ago. He opened it and reread it. She thanked him for the money for Sean and Regina, who were now boasting that they had a rich man for a brother, and their teachers had warned them of the sin of pride, Sister Elizabeth added with a touch of humor. Sean still remained of a "delicate constitution, not, perhaps, physically, but of a too intense sensibility found very rarely in a lad and not approved by the other Sisters." Regina, as always, was somewhat too quiet but still "an angel, devoted to prayer, modesty, gentleness, and a sweet demeanor, a true daughter of the Blessed Mother."

Joseph frowned. He stared at the carefully written pages for a moment before continuing. Sister Elizabeth went on to relate, with sadness, of public buildings being turned into hasty hospitals to accommodate the desperately wounded and dying soldiers, and of the Sisters' service in those hospitals, nursing, tending, feeding, comforting, praying, sustaining, the washing of wounds and the writing of letters to mothers and wives. "We are hard-pressed," wrote the nun, "but we thank Our Lord for this opportunity to serve Him and to console the dying and to sustain the living. Trains arrive daily with their burdens of the wounded and the suffering, and the ladies of Winfield give of their money, their hearts and their helping hands. Rich or poor, all divisions are forgotten in these dire times, and we are but servants of the suffering, and we are not concerned whether they are of the Union or the Confederate armies. Captured Confederate physicians work nobly side by side with their Union brothers, to save as many of the young boys as possible, and they toil in their uniforms and there are no reproaches, no cruel glances, no quarrels. Truly it has been said that in the presence of pain and despair all men are brothers, though sadly they are not brothers in health and prosperity and happiness. That is a most mysterious and fatal flaw in human nature. Ah, if this wicked war would but end, and peace be restored! So we all pray, Union or Confederate, and our little church at Mass is filled every day with the Gray and the Blue kneeling side by side and receiving Holy Communion together! Yet tomorrow, restored to health and their respective armies, they will seek to kill each other. Never was there a holy war, Joseph, never a just war, despite all the slogans and the banners. But men love war and though they deny it vehemently, as I hear daily, it is rooted in their Nature, alas." She added, "If you can, say five Hail Marys a day for the souls of the sick and dying, for I cannot believe, in my heart, that you have totally forgotten—"

Joseph had sent her ten dollars extra in his last letter and in accordance with his request Sister Elizabeth had sent him a daguerreotype of Sean and one of Mary Regina, somewhat highly colored, by hand, by the photographer. But not even the too-florid and vivid touches could conceal the smiling and poetic face of Sean Armagh, overly sensitive and refined, and the shining gaze and immaculate countenance of Regina, fragile yet exquisitely strong and softly ardent. It was the face of Moira Armagh, yet not her face, for there had been a sweet and tender earthiness in Moira. There was no earthiness in Regina's luminous eyes, blue and fearless, nor in the carving of her nose and the firm innocence of her beautiful child's mouth. In contrast, Sean was another Daniel Armagh, full of grace and light and hopeful merriment. Sean was now almost thirteen, his sister, seven.

It was the portrait of Regina that held Joseph's attention, though the dark and suppressed pain always struck at him in spite of self-discipline even at the thought of her. He studied the black glossiness of her long curls, the smoothness of her white forehead, the blue large stillness of her eyes between her golden lashes and for some reason Joseph was suddenly frightened as if by some foreboding undefined by his consciousness, and formless. He forced himself to look at the likeness of Sean and tried to feel the old bitter resentment he had felt for his father. All at once—and he was incredulous at the thought—he believed that he would always have to protect Sean but that Regina was beyond his protection and had no need of it. What nonsense, he thought with some anger. I will make a man of my brother if I have to kill him doing it, but Regina will always need me, my darling, my sister.

He went to his coat which hung with his other few items of clothing in the rosewood wardrobe and brought out his leather pocketbook and he put the portraits of his brother and his sister in one side and tried, with sternness, to control the sudden turbulence of his foolish thoughts. He returned to his chair and gloomily studied the fire, then reread the final page of Sister Elizabeth's letter.

"Among our dearest and most devoted helpers is Mrs. Tom Hennessey, the wife of our senator. So kind and gracious a lady, so dedicated and tireless! Sometimes she brings her little girl, Bernadette, to our orphanage, for you cannot instill too soon a spirit of charity and love and kindness in a Child, and Bernadette, a most charming Child, is as thoughtful as her mother and brings gifts to the Little Ones who have no one to remember them. She and Mary Regina have become friends, for all Mary Regina's natural reserve and reticence, and it is well for Mary Regina to have so blithe a spirit sometimes near her, for she is often too grave. I have often heard Mary Regina laugh, her quiet little laugh, and it is music to my heart. We love her dearly."

His first vexed thought when he had originally read this letter was to command Sister Elizabeth to keep his sister from the daughter of Senator Hennessey, that corrupt man. But his realism soon convinced him that his real impulse was jealousy, and he was mortified. Still, he could not suppress that jealousy, for Regina was his own and she belonged only to him, and the very thought that others saw her when he could not was misery to him. He had not seen her for several years, but he wrote her a small note to be enclosed in his letters to Sister Elizabeth, and he never once thought of writing to Sean though Sean wrote to him.

Looking at the fire now he said to himself that time was growing short and that when he returned from his mission he would go on business for Mr. Healey to Pittsburgh and have another conversation with the man he had met there. Having decided this, he picked up his book of essays, closed his mind to all other thoughts, and read. The carved clock below in the hall struck one, two and then three, and the fire died down and the room became cold and Joseph still read.

Mr. Healey did not come to his offices the next day as was his usual custom. Nor had he been present at breakfast with Joseph. Little Liza timidly informed Joseph, on his indifferent question that no, Mr. Healey was not sick. He had but gone to the depot to meet an Important Personage who would be a guest in this house for a few days, a very Important Personage. No, she did not know his name. (Joseph had not asked.) But Miz Murray said that before she, Liza, had come here the Personage had been a frequent visitor, though now Mr. Healey visited him instead. As Liza sounded somewhat breathless at the honor about to be bestowed on this household, Joseph glanced up at the girl and saw that she was quite flushed with importance and that her color made her plainness attractive and even appealing. She was barely sixteen now but her slightness, her immature figure, her air of old starvation and remembered cruelty and her chronic fear, still gave her the look of an abused child. She had thin but bright light brown hair under the oversized mobcap, and there was something clean and touching about her, and her shy smile had the poignancy of unforgettable suffering. Her eyes were big and brown though they had a tendency to flutter between their lashes.

Miss Emmy came yawning into the dining room, her pretty hair rolling down her back, her naughty eyes heavy as if with recalled and recent pleasure. She wore a morning gown of deep blue velvet laced with cherry ribbons and her face bloomed though her glance at Joseph was old and wise and teasing. She touched him lightly on the shoulder as she passed him on the way to her chair, and he drank his coffee hastily in preparation for departure. Miss Emmy saw this, and was amused. One of these days, she promised herself, he would forget to be indifferent and uninterested. Had she not already driven him to a brothel? At least that had been her conjecture when Mr. Healey had boisterously confided in her. She was becoming somewhat impatient. She had but to glance at the other men to cause them to lick their lips and shift their pantaloons, but this one looked at her as if she did not really exist. She told herself that she was not fooled. He rarely, now, replied to her most pointed remarks, and that was an excellent sign. Sagacious in the ways of men, she hummed softly under her breath as Liza served her, and when Joseph almost fell over his chair in his haste to leave the room she nearly burst out laughing. The next moment she pettishly but painfully slapped Liza's hand when the girl poured her coffee a little too fast.

The April morning had suddenly turned warm and balmy, and Joseph put his greatcoat over his arm, and then settled his tall sober hat over his brows. Mrs. Murray came into the hall and said in her detesting and sullen fashion that he was not to go to Mr. Spaulding's office tonight but to return to this house at half-past four. There was a Visitor and lateness on Joseph's part would be uncivil if not unpardonable. Joseph said nothing, and did not acknowledge this message from Mr. Healey. He ran down the steps outside and began to walk rapidly. Mrs. Murray stood in the doorway and watched him, and her face took on its usual gray malevolent look when she encountered the young man. Joseph knew that she hated him, but did not ask himself why, and he knew that Bill Strickland, in his mindless way, was also aware of him and hated him also. But Joseph had encountered too much hatred in his life to be concerned at this, in Mr. Healey's house. He accepted unmotivated malice as part of human existence.

After Mrs. Murray shut the door, muttering in a malign

undertone, she went upstairs to her daily task before Liza or the other little maid began theirs. She entered Joseph's room and carefully and quickly searched every drawer in his commode, deftly opened the locked desk with a similar key and started at encountering within the drawer a thick sheaf of gold notes and a new pistol and a box of ammunition. "Ahah!" she cried aloud. Then to her immense disappointment she saw Mr. Healey's handwriting on the band which held the notes and the words, *Joe Francis*. She relocked the drawer and her thick whitish lips moved in and out surlily and with resentment. Mr. Healey should have told her last night. She moved to the wardrobe and searched every pocket lingeringly, and felt every seam, hoping for some evidence which would convince Mr. Healey that his protégé was a thief or perhaps a murderer, or some other kind of criminal. Diligently, she ran her hand over the tops of books, almost praying for a forgotten and incriminating letter. She shook Joseph's book of essays which he had left on his bedside table. She turned up the mattress and felt between it and the bed boards, then looked hopefully under the bed itself. She felt the pillows, examined the seams for an entrance. She lifted the corners of the rug, felt behind the one large picture on the wall which depicted a pale woodland scene. She examined the backing. She searched behind the draperies at the window, and at the window ledge on top. All this was familiar to her and she searched deftly. More and more disappointed— though she was positive that on one of these days she would uncover some baleful proof of her intuition regarding Joseph—she glanced down into the cold fireplace. Aha, he had burned another letter, as he had burned others, the sly cunning fox! She crouched fatly and with difficulty on the hearth and turned the black flakes over with the poker. Her breath stopped when she found a torn piece which had been only charred at the edges, a small but clear piece with chaste writing upon it. Snatching up the scrap she read it: "Sister Elizabeth."

So, he had a sister, had he, hidden away probably in jail, or perhaps in a brothel. Yet he had told poor, trusting Mr. Healey that he had no kin! Men did not conceal the existence of blameless sisters or deny that they possessed any. The drab had been kept out of sight, though she probably advised and guided her brother into plots and schemes and infamy. Why, they could be conspiring together at this very minute to rob and murder Mr. Healey in his bed! Why else would a man hide such a relative? Trembling with triumph and joy she carefully wrapped the scrap of paper in her kerchief and rumbled rapidly out of the room. She met Miss Emmy in the hall and abruptly came to a halt.

Miss Emmy smiled at her bewitchingly. "Anything found today?" she asked.

Mrs. Murray said in a surly voice, "I don't know what you're talking about, Miss Emmy. I was just making certain that the girls do not fault their cleaning." Then she could not contain herself. "I always knew he was a sly deep one, probably a thief or a murderer! I did find part of a letter he had burned, but he overlooked this! See it!" She gave the scrap to Miss Emmy who examined it curiously. Then the girl laughed and returned it. She said, "Why, Mr. Francis is Irish and a Catholic, Mr. Healey told me, and 'Sister Elizabeth' is probably a nun! He'd know them, just as Mr. Healey knows some in Pittsburgh. He even sends them money at Christmas for orphanages and such."

Seeing Mrs. Murray's bloated face becoming grayer and grayer with frustration, and her eyes blinking rapidly, the girl asked with sharper curiosity, "Why do you hate Mr. Francis so much? I've seen you looking at him, and you'd like to stick a knife in him."

Mrs. Murray lifted a massive hand and shook a finger at the girl. "I've lived a life, Miss Emmy, and I can tell a criminal when I see one, and you mark it, it will all come out one of these days, and maybe then you'll be sorry you laughed at me." She trundled off with her behemoth tread and the floorboards shook and her whole thick body expressed her malignance and hate. At the head of the stairs she stopped, swung about with amazing rapidity and said to the girl who was still standing watching her:

"And don't think, ma'am, that I haven't noticed you watching him, too! But you're one, Miss Emmy, who don't want to stick a knife in him."

Why, the horrid old bitch, thought Miss Emmy, and the two women's eyes held together and Mrs. Murray smirked knowingly and went down the stairs. Miss Emmy was frightened for a little while when she returned to her bedroom, which was all gold and blue and white. She sat on the edge of her rich flounced bed with its plump pillows. She would have to be careful, very careful indeed. She ought to have remembered that Mrs. Murray had once

been a Madam in one of Mr. Healey's brothels, and Mrs.
Murray knew all about the glances and gestures of men—
and women, and what they meant. Fool, fool, thought Miss
Emmy and she lay back on the bed and smiled as she considered Joseph sharing it with her on some hot midnight
when Mr. Healey was in Pittsburgh or New York or' Boston. Her erotic thoughts became wilder and more acute,
and soon she was panting and sweating, and Mr. Healey
had never seen her face as it was now and the languishing
humid eyes and the swollen red mouth.

Joseph thought of Sister Elizabeth's last letter, and his
family. He had written her upon opening the postal box in
Wheatfield that he "traveled" and had no permanent address, and that she was to write letters to his box number.
Sister Elizabeth had then inferred that he was a "drum-
mer," "that is," she wrote, "a man we call a 'traveler' in
Ireland, one who sells. I understand it is a very precarious
means of making a living, Joseph, but I pray for your success. I also pray that you do not encounter rude and uncivil
and rough people who could wound you when they reject
your offerings. It is possible that Our Lord, when He was a
carpenter, did not always find customers for His wares."
This had made Joseph smile.

He had always mistrusted Sister Elizabeth, in the belief
that if he did not send funds regularly for his brother and
sister they would be separated or adopted by strangers. Yet,
paradoxically, he also believed that when Sister Elizabeth
received money for Sean and Regina she would do the very
best for them and that she could be trusted. It was always
money, he would think, when the paradox emerged to his
conscious mind and demanded reconciliation. Aware of the
paradox, if only briefly, in his own mind, he became more
and more aware of the paradoxes among those with whom
he was forced to associate, not with sympathy but with impatience for himself and others.

When he arrived at Mr. Healey's offices Mr. Montrose
accosted him and invited him for a consultation in an
empty room. Mr. Montrose said, "We leave, as you know,
very soon. We are to travel in the private coach, at Mr.
Healey's order, for, are we humble and unknown travelers?" Mr. Montrose smiled, and his cat's eyes gleamed at
Joseph. "We are gentlemen, and important as Mr. Healey's

employees. When we arrive in New York we will stay at the best hotel. Our wardrobes will be irreproachable."

"My wardrobe is sufficient," said Joseph, thinking of his saved money.

"No," said Mr. Montrose. "What is it Shakespeare said? I believe it was something regarding the glass of fashion, rich but not gaudy. Mr. Healey has commissioned me to be certain that you are attired so. It is not 'charity,' Mr. Francis, for I, too, must dress for the occasion, at Mr. Healey's expense."

"I thought," said Joseph, "that dangerous work demands anonymity."

Mr. Montrose looked at him as one looks at a child. "Mr. Francis, when we travel for Mr. Healey we are not on dangerous work. We are agents traveling on his very respectable business, and so we stay at respectable hotels, and conduct ourselves respectably and noticeably in New York, or wherever. We consult with others concerned in Mr. Healey's affairs; we dine with them; we converse with them; we walk with them. Mr. Healey is not unknown in New York, Mr. Francis. When we do our other—shall I say manipulations—we do it quickly and unseen, and who is to suspect us, we who are on important business in New York, admired and esteemed, above reproach or suspicion?"

Joseph considered this, frowning. Then he said, "I am not being foolish in believing that those with whom we will associate also have a dangerous side to their 'business?' "

Mr. Montrose laughed softly. "On those aspects we are silent, for it would be crude of us to suggest, would it not? Mr. Francis, there is not a rich and powerful man alive who arrived at that sumptuous estate who could bear scrutiny. But, when one comes down to that, who could? You? I?"

Joseph said nothing and Mr. Montrose studied his shut face with inner amusement. He said, "You will acquaint yourself with the—ah—equipment Mr. Healey gave you. You understand, certainly, that I am to familiarize you with certain aspects of this new work, but later you will do it yourself, alone."

"I understand," said Joseph. "I have heard you permit only one mistake."

"True," said Mr. Montrose with an amiable smile.

Joseph's teeth clenched together as he thought of Mr. Healey, the benevolent, the generous and even sentimental, the paternal and jocular. He thought of Bill Strickland.

"You are young," said Mr. Montrose. "But not too young to learn. Only the stupid believe that the young should be indulged and their errors condoned. Mr. Francis, your errors will never be condoned."

Joseph spent the rest of the day studying and searching the reports of Mr. Healey's men who worked for his various enterprises. Eight thousand dollars income the last ten days from the brothels of Titusville and vicinity, over and above expenses. Illicit gambling was another huge source of income, and there were discreet notations to the effect that "drinking supplies" were vastly increasing, also the incomes of saloons. These did not include revenues from Pittsburgh and Philadelphia and New York and Boston, which were separate items and kept under lock and key, nor the income from oil wells. Joseph summarized the ones on his desk; it was a monthly task. The April day was becoming warm and stuffy and though the sun shone brightly there was a dull mutter of thunder in the air.

The wages of sin, thought Joseph, are not hell. They are a comfortable old age and universal respect and admiration and accolades and, at the last, an impressive funeral. He thought of Sister Elizabeth and all the Religious he had known, and smiled in himself. Their wages were humble or unknown graves after lives of adversity and service, remembered by none, not even by their God. I did not make this world, thought Joseph. But, I have come to terms with it.

He left early, remembering Mr. Healey's message. The sun was brighter, yellower, more vivid, than in the morning, because the eastern sky had turned purple and ominous. All things, buildings, streets, people, walks, the dusty roads, were suffused with an especially hurting light. Even Joseph noticed this, though usually he ignored his fellows and their habitations. He saw the patriotic banners flowing from windows, standing at doors, the Stars and Stripes he had first seen on that bitter morning in the harbor of New York. He heard martial music at a distance. He passed a little starveling newsboy, not more than six years old, who was selling newspapers with the urgency of hunger. He had seen the boy scores of times but now he was aware of him, and angry at his awareness. The boy proffered him a newspaper. He shook his head, then reached into his pocket, found a fifty-cent piece and dropped it on the pile of newspapers, which all proclaimed the latest war news in huge black headlines. The little boy stared, stupefied, at the money, then at Joseph. Joseph went on, but he saw that the boy had pounced on the coin like a hungry magpie, and that he was holding it in cupped palms as surely as no one had ever held the Host. Joseph looked up at the tall hills, and saw that they were appareled in the gold of early spring though yesterday they had been black and bleak and empty. Above them towered the dark purple clouds of the coming storm, and their gentle color was more intense for the contrast. Joseph could not understand why he felt a sudden and grieving yearning, a sudden and abysmal sadness, and why he thought of the little newsboy with sharper cognizance.

Mrs. Murray met him in the hall with hateful rebuke. "You are late," she said. "You have kept the gentlemen waiting." The clock chimed. Joseph was five minutes early.

Chapter 15

"Three hundred and one men you wish to keep from the draft," said the Important Personage. "That will be very costly, Ed. You will have to buy substitutes for them. The price is high. One hundred dollars apiece, at the very least. That is what they are asking now in New York. Some ask for as much as five hundred dollars and find five offers." He laughed. "I have heard that some millionaires are offering as much as five thousand dollars for a substitute for their sons! Yet you offer only twenty dollars. Come, Ed, you must be jesting."

He sipped the excellent whiskey and looked at Mr. Healey with humor. "What are you saving it for? Neither wife nor children nor kin."

"I was poor once," said Mr. Healey. "You were never that, and you don't know what it means. I do. I can understand why men offer their souls to the devil. You don't."

They sat in Mr. Healey's library and the walls were bright gold in the stormy light. Windows were open and everything had come profoundly alive, filling the room with the scent of new grass, warming earth and steamy wind. There was a vase of hyacinths on Mr. Healey's long table, seeming to gleam with heliotrope radiance and pervading the air with perfume.

"I think," said the Personage, admiring one of Mr. Healey's cigars which he held in his fingers, "that every man, if he could, and knew how, would sell his soul to the devil. That is why the devil is discreet. He'd have too many customers if he proclaimed that he was in the market for souls. Well, Ed, are you ready to put up the money?"

"To you? Or to the substitutes?"

"Now, now, Ed, no need to be uncivil."

"You owe me a lot," said Mr. Healey. "I don't want to mention how much. That would be 'uncivil,' as you call it, and impolite. I helped you. You wasn't too smart in many ways. I didn't ask you to meet me here to discuss money for substitutes. I asked for your influence in Washington."

The Personage inclined his head. "The price of my influence comes high, Ed. We have Mr. Lincoln to deal with and he abhors the reality of substitutes, though he has to accept it. The Army needs men. We've suffered great losses. Recruiting does not fill the ranks any longer. People are realizing now that war is no lark. Its price is blood and death. When you buy a substitute you buy the possibility of a man's life, and a life is all a man has. Call it a worthless life—it is still the man's life, and all he knows. Now, don't be huffy. It is true I have influence, as do others. But this is a dangerous and delicate business, Ed, and needs the aplomb of a thousand Philadelphia lawyers, not to mention their fee. If I should undertake this for you I would put myself into jeopardy. There are already disagreeable rumors about others in my position, and Mr. Lincoln is getting wrathy, to put it very mildly. If the ax falls—I don't want it to be my head, and I am sure you will understand."

Mr. Healey looked at him with blunt rudeness. "How much do you want?"

"Two hundred thousand dollars, in gold, not bills, not in notes, nor cheques."

"You are daft," said Mr. Healey. His visitor shrugged fine brown broadcloth shoulders. "One hundred thousand."

"For my whole career, if it is found out?"

"For your whole career—which I could stop on a word."

The visitor laughed gently. "You are not the only one who has a Bill Strickland, Ed."

"But you have more to lose than I do. As you said, I have neither wife nor child."

There was a sudden black chill in the library though the golden light increased in intensity against the walls.

Then the visitor said in a soft voice, "Are you threatening me, Ed?"

"I think we are threatening each other. Let's be sensible. I will make it one hundred thousand but not a penny more. Take it or leave it."

The visitor frowned as if with pensive pain, as if musing

on the infidelity of old and beloved friends who are hinting at betrayal. His face became sad. Mr. Healey smiled and refilled their glasses.

The visitor sighed and said, "I will do what I can, Ed. I can't promise success—"

"For one hundred thousand dollars any man would cut his wife's throat, turn traitor, become an assassin, blow up the White House. Anything. I don't pay for promises of doing one's 'best.' I've been robbed too many times by the 'best' a man can do. I pay on delivery. I will pay when all my men receive notice that a substitute has offered himself to the Army in his place, and that the substitute has been accepted. Is that clear?"

"Ed, you have always made yourself eminently clear. You've never been obscure."

"It is a bargain, then?"

The visitor reflected, then with an air of indulgent surrender and deep brotherhood and affection, he reached across the table and shook hands with Mr. Healey. "A bargain, though God knows what it will cost me."

"You mean what it will cost me, I am thinking," said Mr. Healey. "What the hell. I wonder if my lads are worth it."

"You've bought them, Ed," said the visitor. "They're yours."

"Um," said Mr. Healey, looking at his friend with sharp dark eyes. "I've learned one thing, that I have. When you buy a politician he doesn't stay bought. You have to keep on buying him."

The visitor laughed. "But it's worth it, isn't it? Three hundred and one men; you'd have a hard time replacing them in these degenerate days. There's hardly a man you can trust."

"It's not you that should be telling me," said Mr. Healey with a significant glance which made his visitor laugh, a rich unctuous laugh like flowing treacle. Then Mr. Healey nodded at the thin sheaf of delicate paper near his elbow. There were fine inked drawings on the papers, intricate, numbered, explained in careful printing. Mr. Healey examined them, and the patent numbers, turning them over slowly. "Yet, there is one. Yes, I do believe there is one. Thank you for the copy. Must've been a sight of work, getting them from the Patent Office."

The visitor laughed again, cynically. "Well, we'll see. You aren't getting maudlin, are you, Ed?"

"There's a great trouble with you, sir. You think everyone is like yourself." Mr. Healey smiled without illusion at his visitor. Then he turned his large rosy head. "I think the boyo is here now. Not that you can change my opinion, but I'd like yours, honest if it isn't too much to ask."

There was a knock on the door and Mr. Healey bellowed genially, "Come in, come in!" He shifted his great bulk on his chair. The door opened and Joseph stood on the threshold and he saw the visitor, after his first glance of greeting at Mr. Healey and the first inclination of his head.

Mr. Healey saw no overt change in Joseph, no sudden tensing, no change of color. He had not expected these in any event, but intuitive as he was, perceptive as he was, he felt a change, sudden and even drastic, in Joseph, as if he had received an enormous shock. Mr. Healey's little eyes widened in surprise and he was intrigued and interested. As for his visitor he merely looked with aloof and very faint speculation at the young man. Mr. Healey saw this, and an instant later his guest was slowly sitting up in his chair and was regarding Joseph acutely, and slightly frowning.

Mr. Healey said, "This here's my right hand, Tom, Joe Francis Xavier I call him. Joe, be on your mark: This gentleman is our esteemed senator, Tom Hennessey, come to visit his old friend."

Joseph did not stir or even appear to breathe for a moment or two. He did not look away from the senator. Then, stiffly, as if he had become wood, he bowed a little and murmured a respectful greeting, to which the senator replied with a gracious inclination of his head and a winning smile. But now the expression on his large and sensual face was puzzled. He said in his fruitiest tones, "Happy to meet you, Mr. Francis. I have heard very flattering remarks about you from our dear friend, Mr. Healey."

"What're you standing there for, like a ninny, a gowp?" said Mr. Healey, becoming more and more intrigued. He looked from one man to the other. "Here's a chair, Joe. We're just having a little talk. Here's the glass waiting for you." He poured whiskey into the glass.

Joseph moved to the chair and sat down. He appeared brittle, and the senator thought with surprise, Well, he has distinction at any rate, and doesn't look like a fool. But I have seen him somewhere before. I am certain of that. Joseph lifted the glass and sipped at the whiskey and Mr. Healey watched him with affection and the senator with growing sureness. This Joe was trying to avert his face, not openly, not obviously, but the senator, wise in the ways of men like a whore, saw the slight averting. Now, a man who tried to hide himself was an interesting person to the senator. Young, yes, but the senator had known clever and dangerous men who had been young in years but old in evil and trickery. He had certainly met this Joe before; he needed only to hear his voice and the senator smiled viciously in himself because Joseph had not yet openly spoken. Had old Ed been made a victim at last, and by one so much younger?

The senator leaned his still handsome body back in his chair, with easy negligence, and he smiled at Joseph with all his captivating charm.

"Mr. Francis," he said, and his voice was as soft and lulling as down, "haven't we met before? I never forget a face."

Joseph lifted his head and faced the senator for there was nothing else to do. "No, sir," he replied. "We have never met." His eyes met the senator's straightly.

The senator's ears were keener even than his eyes and he said to himself, I've heard that voice, not recently, but I have heard it. It is an Irish voice, and there is the Irish accent like my father's, and it is a strong voice and I have an impression of trees. But where, when?

Now, then, this is very interesting, thought Mr. Healey and watched with acute attention.

"Were you ever in Winfield, Mr. Francis?" asked the senator, leaning forward now so as not to miss the slightest change of expression on Joseph's face, the slightest hesitation in his voice.

"Winfield?" said Joseph. He wondered if the savage bounding of his heart was audible in this room. His whole body felt numb and cold and prickling.

He's afraid, thought the senator. But a hard-nosed Irisher who wouldn't flinch if a Sassenagh thrust a red-hot poker up his ass—that he is. He's like my father, who would take on ten men in a saloon in a fight and never even notice if he had a broken leg or a bashed nose. So would this one, though he's lean as a starved dog—like my Dada.

"Ain't Winfield near Pittsburgh?" Mr. Healey asked Joseph, who turned to him as if he were afraid that he would break if he moved rapidly.

"I think so, Mr. Healey."

You damned well know so, thought the senator, and his loving politician's smile did not harden. Joseph looked at the senator, at the florid face, the long Irish lip, the heavy nose, the narrow light eyes, and the waving and flowing brown hair and sideburns. Everything about him was too large, except for the eyes, too studied, too embellished, and the mouth had known too many women and the heaviness of his jowl testified to too much dining, too much wine and whiskey and brandy, and he was still as Joseph remembered him—potent and cruel and totally without any benevolence. He made the dangerousness of Mr. Healey appear as minor as the mischief of a young boy, as insignificant as a thumbed nose and a childish threat. For behind him was the power of manifest government and Joseph knew that such power was the greatest thing a man had to fear, for all it was concealed by an air of candid kindness and gentlemanly interest, and friendly ease. Now Joseph's fear was overwhelmed with disgust as he remembered that this man had desired to beome the adoptive father of little Regina, and the senator saw the sudden tightening of the young man's features and saw that the fear had left his eyes. He saw challenge there, not the challenge of youth, but the challenge of a peculiar integrity. He had seen that challenge before in one or two men's eyes, and he had set out with smiling mercilessness to destroy those men. They were a menace to such as Tom Hennessey even if they had made no gesture of attack.

Yet the senator recognized something in the young man which was growing more and more obvious: His resemblance to Old Tom, his father, the one man whom the senator had loved and respected and honored. Old Tom had not had this ambiguous integrity, this elusive probity, but he had had this pride, this staunchness, this refusal to cower, to retreat, to turn and run, to placate, even in the face of danger. That Joseph had recognized him not only as dangerous to others but dangerous to himself, the senator had understood almost at once.

Now, how could I be dangerous to a fellow like this? thought the senator. Recognition of him? Exposure of him? He can't be much over twenty, and I think that it must be several years since I first saw him.

"You were born in Ireland, I believe, Mr. Francis?" said the senator.

"Yes, sir." The voice was stronger than before, and the challenge was there also. "In Carney."

The senator quickened. "Carney? My father spoke of it once or twice. County Armagh."

It was Mr. Healey's turn to quicken, and he stared at Joseph openly.

The dread was on Joseph again, and he felt hatred for himself that he had been so indiscreet. But he said with quietness, "Armagh. Yes."

The senator gazed at him, musing. Armagh. Where had he heard that as a personal name before? He would remember soon; he always remembered. He would remember where he had seen Joseph before, too. Their eyes did not move from each other and Mr. Healey watched. Then he was surprised. The senator was a mountebank and could assume any expression at will, all of them lying, and hypocritical, as needed for the occasion. But the expression now on the senator's face was unguarded and, for the first time, honest, and Mr. Healey recognized this astutely. It was as if he were remembering someone for whom he had had some genuine affection, some close emotion, some unforgotten fondness. Then, as if conscious of his own self-revealment, the senator's face almost immediately changed and became false again.

Joseph rose and turned to Mr. Healey. "If you will excuse me, Mr. Healey, before supper? I must wash and change."

Then he half-turned to the senator and bowed in his direction and said, "I am happy to make your acquaintance, sir."

I bet you are, thought the senator, but without contempt and even with humor. I don't think you are a thief or a scoundrel, now, nor hiding from the law. But you are hiding, my lad, and I will know why, and from what and from whom. He inclined his own head graciously. "And I am happy to make your acquaintance too, Mr. Francis."

They watched Joseph leave the room and shut the door behind him. "Now," said Mr. Healey, "what was all that?"

"I could swear I've seen him before, and heard his voice, Ed. But I can't remember."

"We don't get younger, Tom."

The senator gave him an unfriendly look. "I'm not senile yet, Ed. Yes, I've seen him before. I'll probably remember."

"You don't think he can be trusted? I want your opinion, Tom."

"You mean you want my corroboration. Very well. He won't knife you in the back. I've—known—one or two, one at least, like that. He won't sell you out, Ed. But he's his own man. He'll never be anyone else's. When the time comes for him to move, he'll move, but he'll give you warning."

Mr. Healey's own face became as florid as the senator's with pleasure and satisfaction. "That I always knew, always believed." He looked at the thin fine papers on his table and nodded his head. "But we'll see, soon. Can't always trust your own judgment."

He said to the senator, "I don't want you to think I've been hard on you, Tom, making you take only one hundred thousand dollars, which is a sight of money anyway you look at it. I'll throw in Miss Emmy. You haven't seen her in two-three years, but she's a prettier trollop than ever, and you've wanted her for your very own. She's yours, to take back to Washington. Right in your own pocket."

"Now," said the senator, affecting Mr. Healey's own Southern phraseology, "I take that right kindly, suh. But there's folks down there in that thar Washington who're out after my hide. They know I hate that damned Lincoln, for good and sufficient reason. And he hates me in return. Tried to be decent to him, but he looked me in the eye and said, 'Humph,' and that was all there was to it. He don't even recognize me when we meet."

Mr. Healey laughed. "He ain't no joy to me neither, Tom. But what's that got to do with Miss Emmy? Plenty of you fellas down there, wenching."

"True. But Mr. Lincoln doesn't like it. Baptist, probably, or maybe Free Methodist. He'll overlook it a little in others. But not in Tom Hennessey. He's trying to find some way of getting rid of me. I think he heard something about me—and some others—cornering the wheat and meat market so we can make a little money out of his damned war, too. Now, Ed, you know I'd never connive to do such a thing, don't you?"

Mr. Healey laughed again. "Especially not raising prices so that the widders and orphans would suffer, and the Boys in Blue. Not you, Tom. So, you can't take Miss Emmy."

"I've a nice little colleen of my own in a discreet house, Ed. But I'm getting tired of her. How about sending Miss Emmy down to me in about four weeks? Are you tired of her, yourself?"

"Miss Emmy? Love the ground she walks on. If I didn't I'd have packed her back to the house where I found her."

The dinner gong sounded, and they stood up. "More than one wench at a time would right rile Mr. Lincoln, if he found out, and he has ears everywhere," said the senator. "But Miss Emmy was trained to be retiring, and he won't find out. Wish to God somebody would murder him."

"Amen," said Mr. Healey without real rancor.

As they went to the dining room they heard the faint thump and trumpeting of a martial tune, coming from a distance accompanied by a dim far cheering:

> "When Johnny comes marching home again,
> Hurrah! Hurrah!"

The senator did not notice nor apparently hear. But Mr. Healey did. His jovial face, for an instant or two, became curiously melancholy.

Joseph did not speak a dozen words at the table that night and avoided direct glances at the senator. But Miss Emmy preened coquettishly and smiled at the senator, for she knew he admired her. She hoped Joseph was watching. Joseph was watching only the senator from the corner of his eye. So, the bastard hadn't remembered yet. It was possible he never would. In a few years it would not matter if he remembered. He, Joseph, would be safe, no longer vulnerable to idle malice, no longer vulnerable to Mr. Healey's anger at being deceived, if only by a name.

At the end of the dinner Mr. Healey laid his hand in a fatherly fashion on Joseph's shoulder and said, "I'd like a minute of your time, Joe, in the lib'ry."

For an instant Joseph stiffened, but there was nothing in Mr. Healey's face which was false or unkind, and he followed him into the study, or the library.

Mr. Healey sat down at his table and faced Joseph, and smoked contemplatively on his cigar.

"Joe," he said, as if asking the most innocent question, "who is Sister Elizabeth?"

Again Joseph's heart jolted in his chest. He looked at Mr. Healey, and now all his caution returned to him. "Sister Elizabeth?" he repeated. What Mr. Healey said next would reveal what he really knew.

"Come on, Joe, you know very well who Sister Elizabeth is."

"If you know that name, Mr. Healey, why do you ask me about it? Where did you hear it, and from whom?" Now Joseph understood that in some way Mr. Healey had learned of the name, but knew nothing else. Joseph's thought ran to Haroun, then dismissed it. He suddenly remembered burning the letter last night. It had never been out of his hands or his pockets since Haroun had delivered it to him, fully sealed. Joseph could see the fireplace. Had a scrap remained, a shred of paper? He kept his face still. He waited.

"Now, Joe, don't you trust me?"

So, he doesn't know anything but the name, and how did that come about?

Then he recalled that Miss Emmy had told him weeks ago that Mrs. Murray searched his room every morning for some unknown reason. She could have found only a scrap of paper in the fireplace, and he cursed his carelessness in not making certain as he usually did.

He said to Mr. Healey, "You remember our conversation last night, Mr. Healey. I told you of a nun I know, to whom my money will be delivered if I do not return from my—mission. She is Sister Elizabeth."

"Where does she live? Where's her convent?"

Joseph simulated profound surprise. "What does that matter to you, Mr. Healey? That is my own affair. But I will tell you a little. She was kind to me when I was a boy fresh from Ireland."

Mr. Healey's face was no longer so pleasant. "All right, Joe, I'll believe that part. Never caught you in a lie yet. But you don't get no letters around here. I see all letters first."

Joseph made his voice very quiet. "Let us say that I have a post office address in another city. It is my affair, Mr. Healey. It has nothing to do with you in the least. I know, from the papers I manage in the offices that you, also, have post office boxes in other cities. It is no affair of mine. I ask no questions. I have no curiosity."

Mr. Healey's gaze was still narrowed on him. Joseph added, "If you feel you cannot trust me, Mr. Healey, I will resign—if you wish."

Mr. Healey considered. That damned old whore, Miz Murray, and her whispered message to him tonight, and her triumphant showing to him of that little scrap of paper! Now he might lose Joe, that damned proud Irisher, and all at once, to his baffled amazement, Mr. Healey felt a bereavement so sharp that he was frightened.

"Nothing to do with me, eh, Joe?"

"None at all, Mr. Healey."

"You never told me your real name."

"Joseph Francis is my name. That is no lie."

Mr. Healey smiled. He almost laughed. "Joe, you're always up on your high horse. Climb down. Never mind how I knew about Sister Elizabeth. It'll be our own secret, eh? And one of these days maybe you'll tell me all about it—confiding like."

So, Joseph thought for the first time, the senator had not remembered. Had he remembered and told Mr. Healey the latter would not now be so paternal and kind, even wistful. It was the wistfulness that astonished Joseph. He had seen it before—on his father's face, in Ireland, and he had not understood it then, either.

Chapter 16

Mr. Healey had bought a private coach for himself, and for the use of the more important of his employees, and his friends, a year ago. Now that the Pennsylvania Railroad ran regularly between Titusville, Wheatfield, Pittsburgh, and Philadelphia, and then to New York, with adjacent stops depending on demand, Mr. Healey had decided to indulge himself, "at my age, and when will it be earlier?" It was a handsome coach, painted black with touches of crimson and gold on the outside, and contained two fine bedrooms, a room with a lavatory and flush toilet and a bath, an astonishingly large dining room, kitchen and parlor, not to mention a "conference room" containing businesslike chairs and table. All these were on one side of the coach with a corridor running along them, and doors were installed for privacy and discretion. It was heated by steam from the engine, and all rooms were decorated and furnished lavishly so that the coach was, indeed, as Mr. Healey said with happy satisfaction, a hotel in itself. Walls were paneled with oak and mahogany, floors were covered with Oriental rugs, and fine pictures were installed on the walls and the kerosene lamps everywhere were of crystal and gilt and silver in intricate patterns. Windows were wide and curtained in expensive brocades. The furniture had been made in New York, to Mr. Healey's ostentatious order. It was, to use his own adjective, "grand." Mr. Vanderbilt and Mr. Astor may have had solid gold handles on doors and in the bathroom, but Mr. Healey had well-plated gold over silver.

Joseph had heard of the coach but had not seen it. He was amazed at the luxury of it all, for he had not believed the colorful reports. Now it would be his habitation for fifteen hours or perhaps longer. He did not care for the ornate furnishings of the bedroom assigned to him and thought them absurd, but the bed was wide and comfortable. There was even a bookcase in the room but a glance at the contents did not arouse his interest. Mr. Montrose knocked on his door and entered and sat down on a brocade chair near the window, where Joseph also sat. The door had been carefully shut. The coach was still on a siding and would not be attached to the train, near the caboose, for an hour or more.

"How do you like it?" asked Mr. Montrose, smiling.

"I remember the night I first came to Titusville," said Joseph. "I have traveled since for Mr. Healey, but not in this coach, in the new Pullman cars. But I did not believe coaches like this existed."

"I think they are ridiculous," said Mr. Montrose. "I am not one to deprecate luxury and ease and civilized amenities, but they should be discreet, especially in war time. Less—fortunate—people are inclined to become envious, not asking themselves, of course, why others had more than themselves and what industry, intelligence, and sleepless ambition produced such luxury and how it was earned by sweat and self-denial and superior intelligence, or what superb villainy. But every man who has to count his pennies feels that in some fashion those who surpass him in mind and will and ingenuity have 'exploited' him, and by their wealth have taken money from his own pocket. You feel this sentiment especially insistent in the North, though not in the South. It has been encouraged by Mr. Lincoln, and the 'new men' in the universities who are, themselves, envious of greater ability than their own, and more energy. There is nothing more dangerous than an inferior man who has been convinced that he has been deprived of what he feels is due to his humanness."

Mr. Montrose laughed, and then said immediately, "It is no matter for laughter. Forty years ago a famous Frenchman said America is doomed because she draws no distinction between those who are naturally preeminent and those born to be obscure. That, sadly, is called 'democracy,' which is the common denominator of the barnyard."

"I have lived in the country, for my father was a farmer," said Joseph, who was drawn into less reluctant speech by Mr. Montrose. "It was a matter of observation that animals established their own hierarchies of the superior and the inferior in character and dominance. There was always a bell cow, the queen, who controlled the herd, and horses are very determined who shall lead, and chickens have their pecking order. Dogs soon decide who rules a given territory, and birds, in the spring, stake out their areas of food and fight off intruders. This is a world not only of men but other animals who are governed also by instinct, set down by nature, and I have come to terms with such a world."

"You are no idealist," said Mr. Montrose, looking more closely at the young man.

"Idealism is for those who cannot come to terms with reality," said Joseph, "nor the world as it is."

Mr. Montrose nodded. "Such men are mad. But madness is spreading, ever since Karl Marx promulgated his Communist Manifesto fifteen years ago. I am no prophet, but I can say this: Since the French Commune in 1795 the world has begun to lose its reason.

"Would you say," asked Mr. Montrose, lighting one of his perfumed cheroots, "that Christ was an idealist?"

He saw that Joseph's face, never open, had closed tightly. Then Joseph said, "I do remember that He said to a young man, 'Why do you call Me good? None save God is good.' This is hardly the remark of an idealist."

"It is the remark of a sensible Man," said Mr. Montrose. "If there are angels I believe they denounce fools more than any other sort of criminal." He puffed thoughtfully at his cheroot. "I think, in the future and beginning now, that America will be ruled—and ultimately destroyed—by fools. Do not denigrate Mr. Lincoln too much, though I confess to despising him. He said that America will never be conquered from without but by the Vandals within. I fear he is only too right."

Mr. Montrose had brought a thick portmanteau into Joseph's room. He opened it now and showed Joseph the contents: gold bills of denominations not less than one hundred dollars each, and some of a thousand dollars. Joseph saw this wealth and said nothing. In the words of his father, it was a king's ransom, and this did not include the money he also carried.

Mr. Montrose said, "If I should not—survive—guard this with your life and return it to Mr. Healey." He leaned back in his chair. "You will be taught much on this journey. You have only to refrain from asking questions. You have only to listen. And to act."

Joseph nodded. Mr. Montrose locked the portmanteau

and stood up. The train was moving out of the yards. Joseph saw the hills and the town as they slid by his window. It was late afternoon and everything shimmered in a golden dust. It was unusually warm for April. He saw a long line of recruits marching raggedly down a narrow street and fainty heard martial music. He saw the flags. He shrugged. They had nóthing to do with him.

Joseph and Mr. Montrose met for supper in the dining room. The train was gathering speed and roared through the countryside, howling and pounding. Two tall young Negroes served the supper, dignified men with watchful eyes, and silent and swift. There was whiskey, and wine, both of which Joseph refused, to Mr. Montrose's silent amusement. Mr. Montrose saw that Joseph was not aware of the rich meat, the hot breads, the vegetables swimming in butter, the delicate pastries. He ate as a necessity, not as a pleasure. A man who is not discerning about food, thought Mr. Montrose, is not necessarily a dolt. He may have grimmer objectives. He was slightly curious concerning Joseph, but he did not deprecate him. Such commanded respect, though never admiration, for they were beyond pleasure, beyond gratification, beyond the usual joys of the world. This man is young, thought Mr. Montrose, but there are empty chasms in his soul, and so he is, perhaps, more dangerous than all the rest of us. He has not yet been tested. We shall see.

They went together into the small but luxurious parlor of the train, and Mr. Montrose busied himself with certain records and Joseph watched the early evening landscape beyond the polished windows. The sky had the poignant shine of deep aquamarine, flushed with rose in the west, and the trees of the spring were bright gold against it, and the earth had turned brilliantly green. Cattle roamed the pastures and stopped beside the reflected blue of streams and ponds, and farmhouses stood at a distance, white and placid, their huge red barns towering over them. Hedges were touched with yellow or soft green; here and there lay pools of tiny purple wild flowers or freshly minted dandelions. Beyond all this lifted hills of lavender and heliotrope, and woods as dense as dark-green jungles. Wide peace lay over all, as tranquil as still water, and shining. In this coach no sound from outside could enter and so there was the illusion of radiant silence about the countryside.

Watching, Joseph was taken by the old dark melancholy he knew, and hated, so well. Were Daniel Armàgh here he would break into poetry, his musical voice both moving and hushed. He would speak of the perfection of nature, which reflected the perfection of God. But Joseph knew that beneath all that bright tranquillity, that green and gold and purple beatitude, writhed a savage struggle for life, for prey, for food. There was not a root, however frail or red or brown or timidly green, on which some death battle was not taking place, minute perhaps but as surely lethal as any battle engaged in by man. There was not a leaf which was not being attacked, not a drop of water but in which a Waterloo was taking place. In that aquamarine vault so benignly beaming above hawks were swooping on defenseless birds, and buzzards were wheeling, gazing for carrion. Some of the cattle munching there were themselves battlefields and were themselves dying. The bark of the new trees was being riddled by insects who were drinking of the sappy lifeblood, and many of the trees would die before autumn. The flowering hedges were the flowers of a graveyard. Daniel Armagh had spoken of nature's celebration of life. Joseph thought of it as the celebration of eternal death, forever triumphant. We have this moment's breath, he said to himself. It may be stopped the next instant. We, too, are celebrants at an endless funeral.

Mr. Montrose put aside his books and said quietly, "And now we must have a talk before we go to bed, for this is a long journey and so far the coaches ahead are not yet filled with listening ears or curious ones." He began to speak and Joseph listened with that focused intensity of his. He said nothing. His face did not change; it was not possible to read his thoughts nor conjecture on them. He sat as still as stone beside the window in his dark and newly rich clothing—which Mr. Healey had bought—and never did one of his black and polished boots twitch nor did his hands stir nervously. The last light died in his russet hair and his face was hidden.

"You see, now, that there is much for us to do, besides this personal mission. Mr. Healey wished you to know. He places great trust in you."

He smiled faintly at Joseph. "You are permitted two questions."

"No," said Joseph.

"You understand?"

"I understand that I am to learn and watch and show no curiosity."

"Good," said Mr. Montrose. The landscape had turned gray and black and dim beyond the windows. At a knock on the door one of the young Negroes entered and lit the crystal lamp which hung from the polished ceiling. Mr. Montrose gathered up his books. "I think I shall retire," he said and looked at Joseph with his yellowish eyes. "I suggest you do so also, for we shall be very busy when we arrive in New York."

Joseph sat for some time alone in the parlor and saw his own somber reflection in the black mirror of the window. Even alone as he was his face showed no emotion. But a peculiar weariness, not of the body but of the mind, began to burden him. He stood up and felt old and tired. He went to his bedroom, undressed and went to bed. The rails sang under him; the joints clicked like castanets. The bedroom swayed like a ship. It was very warm in the room. Joseph lay on the top of the soft blankets and stared emptily at nothing.

A long time passed and he still did not sleep. His nightshirt felt cold against his body for all the warmth in the room. He was not what the Irish called a "sleeper" under the best of circumstances, and tonight he could not even feel drowsy. He heard the soft step of the young Negroes in the corridor outside as they patrolled the rich coach and inspected the dimmed lamps that flickered in the ceiling. Once or twice Joseph heard their muted voices, melodious and light, and once they laughed lightheartedly, and he briefly wondered at them and why they should laugh at all. The train moaned through the night and there was no answer.

Now the train was slowing and Joseph half-sat up to look through the window over which he had not drawn the curtains. He saw the glisten of many rails in the moonlight and beyond them the feeble light of some little unknown depot. Then between his train and the depot clattered another train, lighted from every window, and nearly every window was open to the warm and suddenly oppressive night. Joseph could see clearly into the many slowly moving coaches. They were filled with young soldiers, all bandaged, all wounded, lying asprawl on makeshift beds, and on wicker seats. He saw staring and sightless boys' faces under reddened cloth, faces as pale as linen and as bereft of life; he saw trussed arms and legs. He could not hear groans or cries of anguish, but he could sense them. Through the bloody clutter of the suffering and the dying moved young women in caps and white aprons and among them were the black habits of young nuns and their white wimples. They carried basins and jugs of water and towels and sponges. They bent over the boys, stroking cheeks, holding wet hands, talking soundlessly, smiling, sometimes weeping, opening or closing windows, holding water to fevered mouths, cheering, grimacing with amusement to hide their pain, consoling, sponging away blood.

Both trains had halted uneasily, side by side, for a moment or two. Joseph knew this was a troop train going into the nearby and anonymous town, a hospital train. A young woman in cap and apron straightened up from a youth she was attending, and there were tears on her cheeks. She, for some reason, looked directly through the window at Joseph's darkened coach, and he moved a little from the window though he knew she could not see him. I have seen her before, thought Joseph, but he could not remember.

The coach opposite was aglare with the yellow light of numerous lanterns and seemed to steam with heat. Joseph forgot the misery and suffering he had seen and stared at the tall young woman, who seemed to be exhausted beyond endurance. She stood in a drooping attitude, a bloody bandage in her hand, her head lifted, her eyes holding the expression, far and distant, of one who has looked on too much pain. She gazed at Joseph's sleek coach with the indifference of despair, her eyes hollowed, her nose pinched, her pretty mouth as dry and white as cotton. But her tiredness, her drooping posture, her manifest depletion of young vitality, and her coarse apron and cap, could not hide the slender loveliness of her body, the beauty of her face. Her loosened hair rolled in tawny ringlets and damp curls to her shoulders, and her eyes shimmered like dark opals above her finely boned cheeks, now sparkling with fire, now dimming, now taking on the amber of her hair, now expressing intense sweetness and hidden glowings. Her neck was long and graceful, and as soft as silk, and her hands, as she held the bandages, were narrow and finely tapered.

She seemed to look directly at Joseph with those remarkable eyes of hers, those unmurky and innocent and tender eyes, so alive, so brilliant. They expressed strength as well as delicacy, courage as well as sadness, and a frailly indomitable spirit. There was one gemmed ring on her left hand, a dazzle of diamonds and emeralds.

Joseph sat up straighter, and looked deeply into the girl's face. She was not much older than himself, perhaps two or three or four years, yet to him she appeared as young as his sister, Regina. She would not submit to exhaustion. She would go on after a moment. The coaches, though not moving, rocked a little. A soldier spoke to her, a man out of sight and Joseph saw her bend her slight body and he saw the outline of a perfect young breast under a dark blue cotton dress. The lantern light lay in a little pool, shivering, in the hollow of her throat. Her face was full of pity; it trembled with mercy and quickened concern.

Then the troop train moved on to the depot. Joseph still half-sat, stiffly. The girl was lost in the glare of following coaches. He lay down, very slowly. He knew that he knew her; he could almost hear her voice, soft and low, beseeching. Then all at once he was taken by something he had never experienced before, and did not know. It was a wild and passionate surge in him, at once desirous and lost and aching, fiercely devouring, making him alive as he had never been alive before and conscious of his own body and his shouting mind. He pushed open his window. He saw the diminishing lights of the other train as it neared the depot, and suddenly he wanted to jump from his own train and race after the other. So hot, so demanding, so turbulent were his feelings, so hungry and emphatic, that he lost his reason, his cold aplomb and disciplined self-control. Even in his turmoil he could dazedly ask himself what had struck him like this, and with wonder, and to marvel at his emotions.

It had not been the girl's beauty alone which had bludgeoned him, for he had seen prettier and younger and certainly more blooming in Mr. Healey's brothels. He had seen gayer—this girl was not gay in the least. He had known her, but where he could not remember. Her name would not come to him. In the streets of Boston, New York, Philadelphia, in a carriage? She was obviously a lady of breeding and gentility. Had she passed him somewhere? For an instant he could smell violets, and see a cheek rosier than the pearly one he had just glimpsed. Yes, he had seen prettier and more girlish. But they were nothing to this young woman who had such gentle pride, such selfless compassion, such determined desire to serve and console.

Then Joseph was outraged at the thought that she was attending sweating, bleeding, and stinking men straight from the battlefields, was touching them with her soft hands, was wiping away their grime and was carrying odorous vessels away from them. Where was her father, her guardians, that they permitted this disgusting labor in the abattoirs? He hated them. Again he longed to leap from his train and go after the girl and take her—

I have lost my mind, he thought, and forced himself to lie still. What is she to me, a woman I'll never see again? Then, at that thought he felt bereft, torn with grief, savaged by longing, and, to his immediate horror, by desire. He told himself it was shameful, then the next moment he buried his face in his pillow. He said, aloud, "I have seen her. I have heard her name. Sometime I will remember. Then I will find her again, I will find her—"

And what will you do then? asked the cold voice in his brain which was always ready to admonish and to mock him and to control and advise him.

The train moved on into the night, clattering with gained speed. It had been sidetracked briefly to permit the troop train to pass. Joseph's eyes strained after the other train, now just a twinkling shadow in the distance. He did not even know the name of the town he had passed. He saw the bell on the wall near his bed, and he pulled it. In a moment or two one of the young Negroes entered, saying, "Sir?"

"That town we just passed—what is its name?"

The Negro looked beyond him through the window. "I don't know, sir. We never stop there. Perhaps just a junction." His voice did not possess the slow music of Mr. Montrose's voice, so Joseph knew he had never lived in the South. "I heard," the steward continued, "that there is an Army encampment there, for the wounded troops."

"Would Mr. Montrose know?"

The Negro's eyes looked baffled. "I don't think so, sir. We never stopped there. We were just put on another track so that troop train could use ours. Is there anything else?"

"No." Joseph was angrily embarrassed, and he was enraged at this evidence of his new vulnerability. He tried to relax on his bed. He was an imbecile. The girl was nothing to him; he would never know her; he did not want to know her. His bare life was enough for him, austere and orderly. It needed no permanent woman, but only a transient one of no account and no meaning.

But he could not suppress that mysterious throbbing and incandescent heat in him, the curious hot excitement, the yearning, the wild anxiety to hold and press, the desperate insistent hunger. He had no absolute words for all this, no explanation. He had come under an enchantment, not a happy one, but terrible and driving.

He awoke in the grayish twilight preceding dawn. The train was not moving, and Joseph had the feeling that it had not moved for some time. They were standing on a track near a depot, and he suddenly saw the sign: *WINFIELD*.

In that uncertain light the depot was almost deserted, though it was hung with bunting and with flags just stirring in the dawn's faint wind. However, there were many wooden boxes and crates on the platform and a few yawning men were unloading more from the freight cars. Their voices came, muffled, to Joseph. The engine was spitting languidly, and steam rolled up from the wheels. Beyond the depot Joseph could see the dreary town and a few of its gritty streets.

Joseph thought, I have not seen my brother and my sister for years. Is it possible that I could see them now? He rang the bell and the steward came in. "How long are we staying in this town?" Joseph asked him.

"I reckon we're leaving soon, sir. We've been here nearly two hours. Delay on the tracks. Troop trains, I think."

If I had woken only an hour ago I could have seen them, thought Joseph. Regina thinks of me, but she can't remember me, surely, as a brother and a person. I have grown dim to Sean, too. His self-control had been broken last night, disastrously, and now it was broken again, and he smiled with disgust at himself. But the empty longing and urgent hunger was mauling him and once more he felt horror and dread at being assaulted by something he thought had long been buried and subdued.

He sat up and covered his window again with the draperies, and then lay, rigid, fighting himself, shouting inwardly at himself, ridiculing himself, cursing himself. The train began to move; bells rang; steam shrilled; whistles blew. It was too late to see Sean and Regina. Thank God, thought Joseph. He fell asleep again when the train gained speed.

When he awoke the spring sun was glinting through the draperies. He was wet with sweat, and trembling with weakness. But he clenched his teeth and went to the bathroom to wash and dress. He could not look at himself even with indifference. He averted his eyes.

Mr. Montrose was waiting for him in the dining room. The older man was surprised at the appearance of the younger, for Joseph's usually gaunt and pallid face was streaked, as if bruised or chapped, with a harsh crimson, narrow and sharply defined, on the hard cheekbones. He looks, thought Mr. Montrose, as if he had slept with a woman in the night, and Mr. Montrose was amused. He was even more amused when he saw that Joseph's fingers were faintly tremulous and his look uncertain, as if he were embarrassed or had been humiliated or had indulged himself in an unspeakable manner.

"Long travel is wearisome," said Mr. Montrose. "Did you sleep well?"

"Very well."

"These war-time delays are very tedious," said Mr. Montrose. "There was another troop train a few hours ago. My steward brought me a newspaper. There are very bad riots in New York, against the draft. It is rumored that over eight men were killed on the streets last night by the police and the military. Do you think, then, that the rioters are in sympathy with the South, and so desire not to serve?"

"I never thought about it," said Joseph.

"Be sure they were not in sympathy," said Mr. Montrose, "or they would have rioted over two years ago, in protest. They are only afraid to fight, afraid of death. When others fought, and died, it was nothing to these protesters, but when the demand was made to them they went berserk. Now, they shout, it is an 'unjust' war. It is 'Lincoln's War.' They scream that he is a dictator, a man on horseback. They demand his impeachment. It is an unConstitutional war, they proclaim with placards. What they truly mean is that they do not want to serve their country, that they have no love for their country, and wish only to be let alone to enjoy the fruits of others' deaths and sacrifices, and to bask in the security of a war prosperity and to make money and pursue their own interests."

Joseph forgot his own turmoil and looked with the first

focused curiosity at Mr. Montrose. He hesitated. Questions were not encouraged by Mr. Healey's men. But Joseph heard himself saying, "Pardon me, Mr. Montrose, but I was always under the impression that you were a Southerner, from your accent and your manners. If I am correct, do you have no sympathy for the Confederacy?"

Mr. Montrose lifted his yellow brows. He carefully cut off the end of one of his cheroots, then lit it. He studied the end thoughtfully for a few moments. Then he smiled, his feline smile, as if Joseph were a trifle absurd but he had decided to indulge him.

"Mr. Francis," he said, "I have no allegiances, and never had, either to God or man or country. It was not that I was an object of their famous ferocity, nor had I suffered because of them. I never wanted, was never robbed, never betrayed, never made to suffer. Therefore, I am not vengeful. Therefore, I am not defenseless. I chose my way of life calmly. I never permitted myself to owe any other man, nor have I permitted others to be in debt to me. I live only my own life, and I enjoy it immensely and would have no other. Does that answer your question?"

Joseph did not reply. He was considering and weighing every one of Mr. Montrose's words, and he was a little confused. He suddenly realized that he had believed that Mr. Healey's men were like himself, at war with the world for grim and disastrous reasons, reasons in some way similar to his own. Is it possible, he thought, that if I had had this man's hinted life I would be what I am, or someone entirely different? Are circumstances always our driver, our jailer, our motives, and are we molded from without or from within? Do we choose to become what we are—or are we forced into that becoming? Are we victims, or masters? He was again mortified in that he had not thought of this before, but had assumed that men were only victims of calamity and that their response to it was not their fault or of their choosing, and that if anyone was to be blamed it was "God" or arrogant and stronger men.

Mr. Montrose, in his elegant way, was at war with a world which had never harmed him, had never tortured him or bereaved him, had never ridiculed him. He was superbly compact. He would never be ripped by upheavals, torn by circumstance. No one would ever be able to touch him. He did not know fear, and had never known it. If he struck back at the world it would not be out of rage and injustice, but out of self-interest and self-protection. And it would be done without vengefulness and without hatred or emotion.

As if he had heard what Joseph was thinking Mr. Montrose said, "We all choose what we wish to be. No one impels or compels us. We may delude ourselves that it is so, but it is not. The same wind which blows a ship on the rocks could blow it into safe harbor. In short, it is not the wind, it is the set of the sail. A man who denies that is a weakling who wishes to blame others for his life."

He smiled a little. "When I was a boy an old illiterate Negro said to me, 'Young Master, remember this surely: The Recording Angel will not accept your excuse that others made you what you are, and that you are blameless.' I never forgot that, Mr. Francis."

Joseph, with rough impulsiveness, said, "But there are those who were born in slavery, those who were born into misfortune—"

Mr. Montrose shook his handsome head. "And there are those who refuse to be slaves in their hearts or their minds or their souls, whichever you wish to call it, and there are those who use misfortune to educate and elevate themselves. It is still your choice, Mr. Francis. If I believed in any Deity I would thank and bless Him for this liberty of choice, for otherwise we would be slaves indeed."

"I did not choose—" said Joseph.

Mr. Montrose arched his eyebrows again, coquettishly, at Joseph. "Did you not, sir? The sooner you ask yourself that question the sooner you will be safe from the world. A thousand choices are daily open to every man, and we make our choices. No one, for instance, is compelling you to go on this mission, Mr. Francis. No force has been used on you; you are not helpless. If you desire, you can leave this train at the next stop and none there will be who will dispute you."

"If others are dependent on you, Mr. Montrose—?"

"There," said Mr. Montrose, "you descend into sentimentality. A truly strong man is never sentimental. He never considers others. He never fights for others. He considers and fights only for himself. All the rest is weakness."

Chapter 17

Something sick and nagging lingered in Joseph's mind, and would linger for the rest of his life. Remembering what Mr. Montrose had said to the end of his days, Joseph became more merciless without understanding the reason: That other men also make their choices, and should not accuse him, Joseph Francis Xavier Armagh. "No man corrupts another. He corrupts only himself, and therefore he should not plead for compassion." In one day Joseph became much older and much more relentless.

They stopped briefly, near midnight, at Philadelphia, not leaving the coach, which was shifted to another train, and looked only at the vast grayness of the gaslighted station filled with moving troops and smoke and flags and banners and martial music and the uproar of voices and the howl of other leaving or entering trains. They waited, in semidarkness, the lamps of their coach wavering and flickering. They waited, in quiet luxury, not part of the turmoil outside, the crowds of weeping girls and women, the crowds of young men in blue uniforms. Mr. Montrose watched it all tranquilly, smoking and reading, apart and only vaguely interested. Joseph watched it without tranquillity and with another turmoil in himself. He thought, for the first time vividly, of the contraband munitions in the port of New York.

He said to himself—though not without a dim inner protest: We are our own destiny. If we are victims at all, or conquerors, we have done it in our minds and our will, or with our faulty judgments or our illusions. If we permit others to exploit us, in private life or in government, we chose it. Or we made the fatal error of acquiescence, and for that we should be condemned. The world forgives everything but weakness and submission. It forgives everyone but a victim. For there is always battle, even if you die in it. In any event death came to all men. How you died was your own choice, fighting or submitting.

Joseph thought of the woman he had seen in the coach opposite him, and he clenched down on the memory and refused to think of her, and thought he had·banished her for all time, for she was irrelevant to him and there was no place for her in his life. It was not his fault or of his choosing that he dreamt of her that night, beseeching, gentle, full of pity and sorrow, not only for those she tended but for him.

They arrived in New York in the early morning. Joseph had watched the red morning light on the peaceful Hudson River and on the green Palisades with their white and gray mansions and great gardens overhung by enormous glistening trees. The river was full of steamboats and small sailing vessels and flatboats, their reflections gliding with them on the water, so still was it. It is a beautiful world, thought Joseph, with that mystic deep melancholy of his which had no name. He sat by his window and waited until he heard Mr. Montrose go into the dining room, and then he followed him. They had an early breakfast, for they would soon be arriving.

"I do not like New York," said Mr. Montrose. "It has become a polyglot city, far worse than Pittsburgh or Philadelphia. As it is on an island one feels crowded, and so do the inhabitants, and crowds are always hysterical and womanish. They are happy, the New Yorkers, when there is an opportunity for uproar, and if that opportunity does not come often enough they will create it. You have never been there?"

Joseph said, "No," and thought of the harbor those years ago and the wet black wharfs and the multitude of rocking ships and rain and snow and despair.

"As so many of them have come—brought in by cattle-boat and steerage—from the oppressed and semi-enslaved countries of Europe, they carry with them both a hatred and a fawning towards all government, even American. They will occasionally riot, as they did in their old countries, but it is an instinctive rioting and not based on an awareness of where they really are now. The next day they will cringe before the most contemptible politician for his favors, remembering the headman of their village and his whip, or the ruler of their province, or their vicious mayor.

They came to what they knew was a free country, but their impulses still govern them and they respond to their new freedom with the old cunning subservience, fear, suspicion, and truckling."

"The Irish have been persecuted and beaten and killed, too," said Joseph, and the red stain was on his cheekbones again. "But though they do, still, band together in America, I have heard, they are not fawners nor trucklers nor are they suspicious and cowering."

"Ah, yes, you were born in Ireland, were you not?" said Mr. Montrose. "My grandfather came from there, from County Galway, I believe. He settled—" He stopped and frowned through the window. "Ah, I see we are arriving." He looked at Joseph. "Some men are born free even in ghettos, even under persecution, even in slavery. I should think it is a matter of spirit."

The station in New York at 26th Street and Fourth Avenue was even more tumultuous than the stations in Pittsburgh and Philadelphia, and far larger. The noise of bells, whistles, voices, and trundling carts and leaving and departing trains was overpowering. Joseph saw a vast welter of confusion, of running men, of lanterns, of gaslight, and the sides of coaches sliding past his window, rumbling and squealing. And, as usual these days, troops were climbing into standing trains, and hordes of young girls and women and older men, smiling, cheering, reaching up hands to windows, clasping young hands they might never touch again, trying to laugh, to joke, to send sons and husbands and lovers and brothers away with the same lighthearted feeling that they were on an adventure but would soon be home. The women smiled widely under April bonnets of velvet and silk and lace, trimmed with curling plumes and bright flowers. They wore brilliant shawls over their shoulders or small velvet capelets or jackets, and their many-colored swinging hoops collided with each other and revealed pantalettes and little black slippers. Their gloved hands held up wrapped gifts to the young men teeming at the opened windows, and though the women smiled or flirted or cooed, their eyes were filled with tears. Beside them stood fathers and husbands in tall silk hats, and in respectable city clothing of black broadcloth or fine brown wool, with watch chains decorously spread over decorous brocaded waistcoats of black or brown or gray. Their bearded faces were fixed in determined smiles, like the

smiles on the faces of corpses, and they blew their noses as
they tilted their heads to the youthful ones above them and
spoke in slow, full and reassuring voices as if they were
only bidding goodbye to sons on the way to visit beloved
relatives or to enter a university. They swung ebony or Malacca canes with gold or silver handles, and sometimes
slapped their calves with them, or held them out quickly to
guard a lady against a new surge of people hurrying along
the platforms.

The station platforms were heaped with wooden boxes
and cartons and luggage, and men in crude workmen's
clothing sweated them onto flat wagons and struggled with
larger pieces. Steam gushed from the wheels of trains,
screaming thinly. Smoke from stacks billowed in black
gushes through the station. Somewhere a bugle sounded,
then a rattle of drums, and somewhere a whole group of
people laughed, or there was a sharp uncontrollable cry, or
a called message. Everywhere hung the red, blue, and white
bunting, and the limp lengths of flags, sluggishly stirring in
the wind created by movement of trains and people. Now,
through far distant doors the morning brightened and with
it entered unseasonable heat on an almost visible wave of
soot-speckled air. And always the hurrying groups, entering
or leaving, the thrusting heads, the portmanteaus, the wicker suitcases, the scurrying carts filled with anonymous objects, the shouting of porters, and the sudden splitting howl
of a train on the move.

As detached as inhabitants of another earth Joseph and
Mr. Montrose left the train to be met at once by a uniformed coachman who touched his hat and took their luggage. His face was heavily pocked and swollen by old
smallpox. Mr. Montrose seemed to have expected him. He
led them outside on Fourth Avenue to a hot and pounding
and blazing welter of sun, blasts of heat from brick walks
and cobbled streets, multitudes of glittering carriages, vans,
wagons, hacks, cabs, victorias, drays, buggies, and surreys,
and endless surging crowds of people who appeared to trot
and half-run rather than walk. The side streets, filled with
tall chocolate-colored attached houses, three stories tall,
were hardly less quiet, and every flight of brown steps was
vivacious with ladies in fashionable clothing and children
and bustling men, and the curbs were littered with vehicles.
The roar of wagons and the voices of people and the rattle
of wheels on cobblestones made a heated confusion in the

air. Though every street was lined with newly blooming trees and though little lawns were greening before the brownstone houses and on Fourth Avenue, the swirling air was choked with yellow dust and a pervading stench of sewers and manure and simmering stone. Horses clopped or trotted, hoofs striking fire on brick and cobbles, and drivers yelled from vans and wagons and drays and whips cracked. Joseph had seen other cities but not such an intense and blinding and noisy and driven city as this. Everywhere hung flags and banners and again there was a burst of martial music from a little distance.

A fine closed carriage awaited the two men from Titusville. The coachman disposed of their luggage and they climbed into the carriage. The windows were dusty even this early in the day and the fastidious Mr. Montrose rolled them up. "Better to suffocate in quiet and clean air than to be smothered to death," he said. Joseph was already sweating but Mr. Montrose was as serene and cool and scented as a white gardenia in some hidden and shadowed garden. Heat, apparently, was familiar to him.

The coachman fought his way to Fifth Avenue with lashings of a whip and the strong menace of his two huge black horses. Mr. Montrose lit a cheroot and leaned back on crimson leather cushions. The harness of the horses was so polished and so brilliant in the sun that it shot back lances of light into the carriage and Joseph's eyes smarted. Then they turned into Fifth Avenue, "as famous, in its way, as the Strand in London," said Mr. Montrose. Though the windows were closed Joseph could hear the unresting bellow of the city and its traffic. Then he could see up the length of Fifth Avenue, cobblestoned and with endless marches of trees and small lawns enclosed in bronze railings, and the ranks of elegant white and graystone mansions with scintillating polished windows and grilled doors and whitened steps and the pouring traffic between curbs and the flagged walks filled with seething crowds. Above them all leapt the many steeples of many churches, the tallest structures in the city, their crosses and their pointed towers catching the almost tropic sun and intruding into the white-hot sky. So tall were they that the buildings about them were diminished.

"The street of the new millionaires, the glorious entrepreneurs, the gilded and revered thieves, the true rulers of America, the commanders of governors and Presidents and government," said Mr. Montrose. "The Vanderbilts, the Astors, the Goulds—the new aristocracy of wealth, the new patricians from old gutters. In Europe, because of their enterprises, they would be hanged, but in America they are adored. Look at the opulence of their mansions, fit for princes, filled with servants of far better ancestry—honest, at least. Yet, when they visit the capitals of their forebears in Europe they are received by kings and emperors. Has this war sobered their greed, quieted their avidity, darkened their vast and gold rooms and polished floors? Not in the least. It is only an occasion for importance and profit and excitement. Their sons buy substitutes for the battlefield, though I admit their ladies are engaged in lively bazaars and dances and theatricals to make money for those they call 'our boys.' "

Mr. Montrose spoke without bitterness and even mirthfully. "I heard," said Joseph, "that the cities are filled with gloom and shortages of food and clothing."

"Not in New York, Mr. Francis. At least, not on these streets. There are possibly regions of the slums here and the dwellings of the poor and the perpetually indigent, who find it almost impossible to buy bread or meat or vegetables even with the little they earn. The clergy insist it is no crime to be poor but no one believes that. Wars do not devastate the fortunate. Devastation is for those who have no money, either in the cities or in battle."

He puffed contentedly, and his excellent profile, so delicately drawn and attenuated, showed no rancor. "It was always so," he said, and thought: Luane. Luane.

The respectful and watching police were everywhere with their long blue coats, belts, helmets, and mustaches, carrying their clubs openly, for none knew when, even here, the draft riots might break out and ragged rascals attack these great houses. Joseph could see their wet and heat-reddened faces and recognized them as Irish, a well-fed if not respected Irish. In Ireland they fought arrogance and power. In America, they guarded it. Am I to quarrel with them? thought Joseph. Do I not wish that I lived behind those bronze carved doors and those silk-hung windows?

As Joseph had made no remark Mr. Montrose glanced sideways and he thought, I have a sapling his age. Did my father sell him—and Luane? Or did my mother—incredible!—for once open her foolish mouth and defy my father? Where are they now, my son, and my Luane, my dar-

ling? He smiled as if his thoughts were peaceful and not
grinding.

When they arrived at the ostentatious pile of the Fifth
Avenue Hotel at 23rd Street, Mr. Montrose left the carriage with the agility of a youth and Joseph followed, bending his angular body from his lean waist. Grandeur had a
fascination for him, even the grandeur made by men. He
looked up at the whitish grayness of the building, and at
the steps swarming with yellow-coated servants busy with
the unloading of many carriages drawing up and with the
assisting of gentlemen and ladies to alight. The ladies
laughed and fanned themselves with dainty little fans or
perfumed kerchiefs, and the gentlemen also laughed and
pushed their silk hats back on their wet ridged foreheads.
The high twitterings and dainty laughter were totally alien
to Joseph and though he hated himself he felt like a
ploughboy among these *élégants*, these insouciant young
men with canes and jewelry, these assured creatures who
had never known want or despair. The women's bright
faces were even brighter than their silks and their satins
and their fluttering colorful mantles. Among them were
graceful military officers in exquisitely tailored uniforms,
and full of courtliness and gallantry, chattering like actors,
their gilt buttons sparkling. They wore swords, and their
legs were perfect in their tapered pantaloons and their
pointed boots dazzled the eye, and their epaulets were
brave on wide shoulders.

They looked suddenly irritated when Mr. Montrose, with
murmured apologies, glided through their ranks, but a
glance at his face impelled them instinctively to allow him
a passage. Joseph followed him deftly and he thought, That
is authority. Yet, it was something else, also. It was intangible breeding; it was an absent hauteur as if those men and
officers were inferiors. Many looked after him in curiosity,
wonder, or resentment, and the ladies gazed on him with
interest and whispered among themselves, "So distinguished! Who is he?" Some straightened bonnets or adjust-
ed ribbons under soft round chins. "At least a diplomat, a
person of consequence," one said. Joseph and Mr. Montrose heard and Mr. Montrose glanced at him with a silent
laugh, as if at a ludicrous joke, and then he turned and
bowed elaborately to the young lady, who blushed with
pleasure and tittered, while her gallant scowled.

For the first time, to his dismayed surprise, Joseph found

himself liking Mr. Montrose, the man from nowhere, the chivalrous blackguard and gambler, the man without family or home or kindred, the man whom many would consider a criminal.

They entered the lobby and Joseph felt himself immediately inundated by an enormous redness and at once the air, to his senses at least, was far hotter and more overwhelming than on the avenue. The walls were of dark mahogany and red satin damask under a domed ceiling of gilded wood. The carpet was scarlet, the great chairs of mahogany were cushioned in the same color. Those monster tables were surely created for giants and not men, and they overflowed with spring flowers and masses of ferns and vases; they were intricately carved with bowed legs and gilded clawed feet. All the huge portraits on the walls showed men or women dressed in various shades of red, with glowing backgrounds which suggested fire. Between them were sconces of polished and gilded bronze holding tall white candles. Here and there stood sofas fit for Goliath, covered in crimson silk. The eight mighty chandeliers, dripping crystals and faceted balls of glimmering light, dropped from the ceiling and each could have lighted a ballroom alone. Here they appeared of only ordinary size. At the end of the lobby moved three caged elevators of gilded bronze, and five men in ruffled shirts and the finest of black broadcloth and the most discreet jewelry waited behind a desk with a dignified subservience to receive guests. Their mustaches were waxed to a glitter; their eyes saw everything and missed nothing.

The lobby was one movement of men and women coming and going, laughing and talking, greeting and saying farewell. There was such an air of festival here that Joseph wondered if there was a holiday in progress peculiar to New York alone. Then he remembered that this was the joyful air of war prosperity, despite the shortages of goods and food, and the new income tax which Washington had desperately imposed to pay for the conflict. From behind some gilded screens came the soft singing of violins and a piano, unobtrusive but adding their own sweet comment to the happiness and gaiety here, the air of well-being and riches and importance and excitement. All the ladies were beautifully and expensively dressed, their silk hoops draped with contrasting colors, and beaded and embroidered, their mantles bordered with gold or silver ornamentations, their ears and necks jeweled, their parasols of many bright colors, and all were scented so that the lobby seemed to be one hot flower garden blowing in full sun. Young or not so young, every face was beautiful and every woman, apparently, tried to resemble a soubrette. Their gestures were pretty and animated, their voices like birds. Their fans fluttered; embroidered reticules swayed on their gloved wrists. There was not a sad or anxious countenance among them. Their gentlemen were equally splendid and as marvelously arrayed and dashing, and when they were not speaking they were laughing or bowing to some lady or displaying a handsome leg in tight pantaloons.

Joseph had never seen such vivacity and joyousness, and though he had read of these in connection with lavish balls he decided that the reality was far more vivid than any written word or painting. The florid hue of everything and the colors on the ladies made him feel dizzy and overheated, and the babble was too close and intrusive.

As if the lobby were empty Mr. Montrose moved smoothly to the desk where at least two of the gentlemen recognized him at once, and bowed. He said, "Mr. Francis, my associate, is with me, gentlemen, and I will have the customary suite." One man produced a thick book and wrote in it swiftly, nodding his head with respect at Joseph. Behind them stood two men in the yellow uniforms which Joseph had seen outside, holding their luggage.

They entered one of the gilded caged and grilled elevators, and the operator pulled on his rope easily and they ascended. "How do you like it, Mr. Francis?" asked Mr. Montrose. Joseph considered. He looked down through the grill at the red falling lobby and its many-colored and milling inhabitants. "I don't think I do," he said.

"Mr. Healey holds it in high regard," said Mr. Montrose, and smiled a little.

"War time is no longer grim," said Joseph.

"It never was and never is, except for those who fight the wars, pay for them, die in them, and lose all in them," Mr. Montrose remarked. "But they, certainly, are of no importance."

General Grant's Army was entering Mississippi for the siege of Vicksburg, and every step was being bloodily contested. Thousands were being slaughtered in the scarlet lightning of cannon and in the deathly fog, and rifles were obliterating young life and towns were burning and fields, greening and burgeoning just hours before, were black and trampled, and rich forests were smoking under the smiling sky. But those below in the disappearing lobby, all red and crystal and carved wood and gilt, cared nothing for this. In spite of himself Joseph felt cold bitterness and even hatred for those who joyfully profited from wars, and then he was derisive with himself. These, at least, were sensible and pragmatic.

The two men and their two escorts with the luggage left the elevator at the fourth floor, and they walked down a corridor paved with red carpeting and bounded by walls of polished mahogany. One carved door was unlocked and flung open. Mr. Montrose was about to enter when an Army officer, apparently in haste, suddenly left the room opposite and collided with the small caravan in his way. He was a short youngish man with a full clean-shaven and pugnacious face and eyes of a darting and restless intelligence, and of a peculiar sharp and piercing blue.

He halted and bowed to Mr. Montrose. "My abject apologies, sir," he said.

"Accepted, sir," said Mr. Montrose with a responding bow.

The officer looked swiftly at Joseph, inclined his head, then raced down the corridor in the direction of the elevators. "These soldiers," said Mr. Montrose. "They move as though there is a battlefield around the corner." His voice was indulgent. But Joseph remembered the searching and penetrating glance the man had given him, as if judging him.

The expansive suite was mercifully decorated in dove gray and soft green silk and velvet, with not a single touch of red, for which Joseph was grateful. Three big windows, draped in Cluny lace, were partly opened to the steaming outside air, and the green velvet draperies were looped back in carved golden metal holders. The gilt chairs were gracefully formed, and so were the gilt tables and sofas, and the ornaments were costly and in good taste. A big round bowl of tulips and narcissi stood on the central table. Off this living room opened two bedrooms of a size that was astonishing to Joseph, and each bed had curtains and coverlets of Brussels lace and green satin. There was a marble bathroom between the two bedrooms, with faucets and appointments of gold plate, and it was the first bathroom Joseph had ever seen in a hotel or a house. The tub was encased in a frame of mahogany, the commode was marble with a chairlike seat made of gilded wicker, and the lavatory was marble. There was a stained-glass window for privacy and the hot increasing sun struck it and made small rainbows dance over all that white stone, that expensive luxury of towels and flowered rug.

The uniformed attendants quickly and expertly unpacked the gentlemen's luggage, and put the contents in wardrobes and chests with gilt handles. Joseph went to the window and stared down at the welter of Fifth Avenue and its small front lawns and iridescent trees and its endlessly moving crowds on the walks and its fiercely congested traffic. As so many ladies had opened colored parasols against the sun it was like looking down on a clanging garden on a rampage. Suddenly Joseph felt that he was being suffocated. He closed the windows, and the noise was muted. He felt Mr. Montrose near him, and he turned and said in a stiff voice, "Mr. Healey does himself well."

Mr. Montrose raised his yellow eyebrows. He had poured a glass of cool water from a decanter on one of the tables, and he sipped at it thoughtfully. Then he said, "And why should he not, Mr. Francis? Has he not earned it honestly—or even dishonestly—himself? To whom is he accountable? Is there some virtue in abstemiousness, some nice compliment in austerity? He is less—venal—than those who live in the mansions you see from that window, but venality is not the question, is it? It is a matter of taste. Mr. Healey likes opulence and why should he not indulge himself? If you and I have different tastes, does that make them superior?"

Joseph was mortified. Mr. Montrose had spoken in the gentlest voice, like an older brother or a father, but his feline eyes were glinting with amusement and something else which Joseph could not interpret. "I am sorry," he said stiffly. Mr. Montrose shook his head.

"Never apologize for your own opinions," he said. "That is akin to feeling remorse. Was it not Spinoza who said that a man who feels remorse is twice weak? As for opinions, yours may be more, or less, valid than the opinions of others, but they are still your own and you should respect them." Now he looked at Joseph directly, but with kindness. "There are times when I suspect you do not hold yourself in the highest esteem, and that is dangerous—for yourself—and sometimes for others. It is a fault you must correct."

Joseph had now detected a note of warning in Mr. Montrose's voice.

But he said, and the sharp stain so narrow and burning appeared on his cheekbones again, "I am not so egotistic that I think I am never capable of making a mistake."

"That is not what I mean, Mr. Francis. If you do not have superb self-esteem others will have no esteem for you, and therefore they will doubt you and your word and your actions, and will hesitate when you give them orders or be mutinous. You must first convince yourself that you are above all others—even if you know it is not so—or you must act as if you are so convinced. Tolerant men are not to be trusted for they sometimes doubt themselves. I know that is a refutation of copybook headings, but it is quite true." He sat down negligently on the arm of a sofa and studied Joseph with a smile. "You may also think it is a paradox, or very subtle, but I suggest you consider it. It has intimations beyond just the mere words."

Joseph considered. Then he said, "You imply that tolerant men are milksops?"

Mr. Montrose lifted a thin forefinger with an expression of delight. "Exactly! Tolerance is the refuge of the fearful. You are tolerant of only those who can injure you, and so you placate them. It is on a par with altruism, and we know that altruism is self-serving and vainglorious, and also a gesture of fear."

Now he opened his hand and consulted the merest scrap of white paper in it. "We shall have a visitor in exactly five minutes. Perhaps you would care for a glass of this water, and then a quick washing?"

Joseph thought, But we were very late on the train and no one knew when we would arrive, and so there could have been no definite appointment, and no messages were asked for or delivered at the desk downstairs. Nor did I see a paper or an envelope in these rooms. Yet a visitor will be here in exactly five minutes!

He went into the bathroom and washed himself. He went over the last hour or so in his mind. No one had given Mr. Montrose an envelope; he had spoken to no one except on the business of obtaining the suite. No one had discreetly passed him a paper, not even in passing—

Joseph wiped his hands slowly. Except that one had collided with him and spoken to him in the corridor outside: the Army Officer. One had apologized, one had accepted the apology, and then they had disentangled themselves. Joseph smiled. He went into the parlor again and looked at Mr. Montrose who was as fresh as if he had just arisen. Joseph hesitated. He wondered if Mr. Montrose was waiting for him to comment, and to approve the comment, or if he would be vexed if Joseph spoke, and would think the less of him. But Joseph was smarting from the older man's remarks, so he said, "Ah, yes, a visitor. The Army officer, I assume?"

Mr. Montrose looked up alertly. He said, "Were we that clumsy or obvious?" But he seemed capriciously pleased.

"No, not at all," said Joseph. "It is just my deduction from the events of this morning."

"I always knew you were clever, Mr. Francis, and astute and shrewd and intelligent. I am glad that you confirm my opinion. And I must admit that you are far more intelligent than even I knew. Best of all, you are magnificently observant, and that is a rare gift and cannot be overvalued." He looked at Joseph with a curious pride, and this baffled the young man. "Colonel Braithwaite has been waiting for us since last night, and we were very late and our arrival uncertain. He had to let me know when we could have our meeting. Otherwise, I should not have known and wasted time waiting."

When Joseph did not comment Mr. Montrose was pleased again. Someone knocked on the door and Mr. Montrose stood up and went to it.

Chapter 18

Colonel Elbert Braithwaite literally burst into the room when Mr. Montrose opened the door, and he threw a last blazing blue glance over his shoulder as he bounced over the threshold. The air in the suite was far cooler than on the avenue below, but the colonel was sweating profusely and his pugnacious face gleamed. He shook hands heartily with Mr. Montrose and bowed and grinned, showing a vast amount of large and glistening white teeth. His manner was boyish and happy and excited. "I waited all day yesterday and all night!" he exclaimed, and looked at Mr. Montrose with laughing reproach. "I assume, sir, that the train was very late due to the troop trains and such."

He had the New Englander's sharp clear speech and brisk manner. Boston, thought Joseph. For a reason he did not know himself he took an instant aversion to the effervescent colonel, for he had never liked exuberant men or men with round short faces. He knew this was unreasonable and that it was only a matter of temperament; men, however, had murdered each other for far less. Too, the colonel seemed to be a merry man, not with the merriment of a Mr. Healey which was natural, but with a calculating merriment which Joseph suspected could change instantly into cold brutality and meanness. Though he was too short and broad to set off a uniform handsomely his own was so excellently tailored that it gave him a certain impression of height. He wore the usual sword with dash and his gray gloves were delicate. He pulled them off now, as daintily as a woman removing her gloves, and smoothed them and laid them carefully on a table. All this time he regarded Mr. Montrose with hearty affection, and this too Joseph felt was contrived and used for effect, and his whole manner was agreeable and expansive, and extremely soldierly. A patch on his arm proclaimed that he was a member of the

Army of the United States, and not merely a member of the U. S. Army, and so he had been graduated from West Point and was a professional military man.

His short broad nose had a way of expanding and contracting at the nostrils over his widely smiling mouth and his penetrating blue eyes sparkled with well-being and friendliness and extraordinary health—he was probably in his late thirties—and Joseph disliked him more and more. He had removed his wide blue felt hat and his hair was curling and bright. He had a way of chattering boyishly, and he complimented Mr. Montrose on his apparent good health and how happy he was to see him again, and Mr. Montrose listened with smiling courtesy and little comment. He towered over the colonel who continued to chatter, his hand on Mr. Montrose's arm. In all that chatter he was like a woman and said nothing of consequence at all, which Joseph again felt was design. A disastrous man, thought Joseph, and his men probably detest him.

The colonel had ignored Joseph's presence, and Joseph waited. Finally Mr. Montrose detached himself from his friend and gestured towards Joseph. "Colonel Braithwaite," he said, "this is my new associate, Mr. Francis. He is also in my utmost confidence and so you can trust him. Mr. Healey, who never makes a mistake, as you know, chose him."

The colonel swung at once to Joseph, bowed deeply, and held out his strong short hand in utmost fellowship and greeting. "My compliments, sir!" he exclaimed. "I am happy to make your acquaintance!" His teeth, like white porcelain, glowed.

Joseph bowed also, touched the hand quickly and withdrew. He repeated, "I am happy to make your acquaintance."

The colonel listened acutely. It was his theory that you could discover considerable by listening to a man's voice and not his words. His thick pink ears seemed to peak as he heard Joseph's lilting accent. Then a quick look of incredulity ran over his face. He had heard that accent tens of thousands of times in his native Boston. He heard it every day among his men. His nostrils twitched with distaste and the broad good humor of his countenance hardened.

"You are from Boston, sir?" he asked.

Joseph said, "No, from Titusville, Pennsylvania." He knew that expression only too well. He had seen it on the faces of British officers, who resembled this one, and he knew the reason. Mr. Montrose's ever-ready deviltry came to the surface and he said, "Mr. Francis also comes from Ireland, I believe."

"I thought so," said the colonel, with mingled self-satisfaction and a contempt which was so obvious that Mr. Montrose's usually serene and aloof face became somewhat stern. "I can always pick them out."

He then turned his back on Joseph and began his fast chattering again with Mr. Montrose, giving him news of the city and the war. Then he said more slowly and with loud emphasis, "You will be glad to know, sir, that we have finally put down the Irish Rebellion in this city. It was not done, however, until we were given orders to shoot rioters on the spot. Excellent! They soon enough retired to their hovels and gutters and caves in Central Park with their rats' tails between their legs!"

The insult was so palpable, and so intended, that Joseph's fists clenched and he started blindly towards the colonel, and the lust to kill he had felt in the past rose up in him and reddened his eyesight. The colonel had the soldier's instinct, and he turned immediately and said with the most open and happiest smile, "Present company excepted, of course, Mr. Francis!"

Joseph stopped, shaking with his cold anger. He looked down into those mocking but contemptuous eyes and said, "Present company is not excepted, sir, when I say soldiers are brutes and not men, and that they are incapable of reason and have no capacity for thought and obey orders as mindlessly as a gun. They are never masters; they are slaves."

"Come, come, gentlemen," said Mr. Montrose. "I am certain that no one intended to insult anyone else in this room. Are we not gentlemen here? Do we not have business to transact, and is not business transcendent over mere pique and misunderstandings?" He looked at the colonel straightly and there was an expression on his face which Joseph had never seen before, but the colonel's figure seemed to diminish. "I have told you, sir," said Mr. Montrose, "that Mr. Healey has chosen Mr. Francis, and he would be extremely—disturbed—if he heard that his choice has been deprecated. I am sure, Colonel, that that was not your intention?"

"Not at all!" cried the colonel. "I was merely remarking

on outlaws in this city, and if I implied that they were Irish
my implication was quite true, unfortunately. Mr. Francis
is too sensitive. My compliments and apologies, sir," and
he bowed to Joseph again, a little too emphatically. "I am
your servant."

Joseph had lifted his head. His face had become sharply
triangular as the muscles in it had tightened like cords. His
nose was flaring, his deep-set eyes were hard glitters from
under his dark-red brows, which had moved down almost
over them, and his pale mouth was a slash of pent rage.
Mr. Montrose also saw that his eyes had flattened, had
taken on the murderer's unblinking intensity, and Mr.
Montrose thought, I was not mistaken. He is dangerous,
and yet, what marvelous control!

A deep and audible exhalation came from Joseph. He
turned from the colonel, who had begun to feel a little chill
alarm, and he went to a chair near the large center table
and sat down. He looked only at Mr. Montrose, who very
slightly nodded. Then Joseph said to Mr. Montrose, ignoring the soldier, "Why were the Irish rioting in New York,
sir?"

"I believe," said Mr. Montrose, "that they did not wish
to fight in this war. They had, perhaps, seen enough of the
misery of war in their own country. Then—they are hungry, and they live in a starving condition in hastily built hovels in Central Park—far up town and far from the city, itself—and in caves, and depend on sustenance and charity
and mercy from the farmers adjacent to Central Park, and
in the Park, itself. They find it very hard, even in these days
of war-necessary labor for the foundries, to earn a living.
No one wants to employ them. It is terrible for a proud and
desperate man, who cannot find work, to watch his parents
or his wife or his little children starving, or begging on the
street for a mere crust of bread. That, Mr. Francis, is the
condition of the Irish in New York, and other cities, in this
Year of Our Lord, 1863, and if there is a logical explanation, beyond senseless bigotry, I fail to find one."

There was the merest rapid flick from Joseph's eye in the
direction of the colonel. He said, and very quietly, "Perhaps they do not find this country worth fighting for, Mr.
Montrose. I do not blame them."

The colonel's hand flew to his sword. Joseph saw it. His
lip lifted in his own derision. But he still looked at Mr.
Montrose as if awaiting a comment. Mr. Montrose

shrugged. He said, "Fools respond to wars. Wise men profit from them—and invent them. Is that not so, Colonel? Have you not said that yourself?"

The colonel's face swelled with engorged blood. "I find no fault in taking a little profit from anything, sir."

"Now we understand each other perfectly!" said Mr. Montrose, with an air of sensible and happy relief. "All else was misunderstanding. We are here, the three of us, to make a profit, for we are pragmatic men. We did not make this war, not even you, Colonel. We are—ah—victims of circumstances beyond our control. None of us loves Mr. Lincoln and his war. Patriotism does not demand blindness and deafness. We may—ah—have larger plans for our country, beyond war. Colonel, will you not join us at this table? I have whiskey, here, and wine, for our delectation."

He pulled forward a large silver tray containing several bottles. The colonel came at once, exuding good-will and fellowship. He even touched Joseph lightly on the shoulder as he sat down. Joseph did not move. He wanted to leave this room, then knew it was absurd and childish, and he was ashamed of himself. The colonel served a purpose, Mr. Montrose and he served a purpose, and girlish outrage should not be permitted to interfere. But his heart continued a sick and murderous thudding in his lean chest and he sweated with the very urgency of his hatred for the soldier, who now represented all the English soldiers he had ever known.

The colonel exclaimed with pleasure at the quality of the whiskey and let Mr. Montrose pour him another glass. He leaned back in his chair. He loosened his tight blue collar. He let his short broad legs splay. He was all boyish frankness. He included the silent Joseph in his artless chatter and laughed almost constantly. Mr. Montrose listened, smiling. There was a locked leather case on his knees, the one he had shown Joseph. He drank carefully, fastidiously, savoring every drop. Joseph drank but a little, knowing that refusal would incite the colonel's scorn again, and fearing his own response to that scorn. The heat heightened in the room. The clamor and roaring and rattling outside became more imminent as the day increased, and the sunlight radiated hotly from every wall of the parlor.

Mr. Montrose's voice became low and confidential. He said to the colonel, "You have done excellently, sir, in the past for Mr. Healey, when we shipped the direst—necessities—to a certain port. We had no trouble, and for that Mr. Healey is very grateful and is prepared to be even more generous. I convey his compliments to you, Colonel."

The colonel's teeth flared and glowed again at this flattery, and Joseph was disgusted. The colonel said, "You must convey my compliments to Mr. Healey and my pleasure in serving him, sir. I deduce this is another shipment similar to the ones before." He added, "Did you say that Mr. Healey is prepared to be even more generous?" His face became eagerly alerted and leaned towards Mr. Montrose.

"Much more generous," said Mr. Montrose, sipping his whiskey. "I might even add that it will take your breath away, sir."

"Ah!" cried the soldier with joy, and he slapped the table. "Then Mr. Healey has finally realized the danger!"

Mr. Montrose arched his brows. "Was it so dangerous, Colonel, to give clearance to the clipper *Isabel* in the port? After all, you are military authority of the port of New York, are you not?"

"The *Isabel*," said the colonel, and now there was the slightest scowl on his low and sweating forehead, "is a commercial vessel operating between Boston and New York, and sails openly, with the tide, day or night. When she takes a different tack, shall we say, it takes the utmost discretion and—consideration—to avoid the Federal patrols. This is not without danger."

"But beyond the limits of the patrols—who believe she is on the way to Boston or other Union ports—there is not much surveillance?"

The colonel again slapped the table vigorously. "You have not heard. The surveillance has become very close, and sleepless, far from the coast. You are not the only ones engaged in—commerce—Mr. Montrose, sir. And different tacks, frequently observed, are usually questioned, and papers beforehand, at the home port, have been minutely examined recently."

He added, "There is perhaps another thing you have not heard. British vessels, leaving this port more or less innocently, have been observed by the Russian Czar's patrols, who are determined that the British not help the Confederacy."

"The Russians have not dared to halt the British vessels?" said Mr. Montrose.

"No. They dare not. The British vessels have the most remarkable—protection. They are very valiant seamen, sir, the British, and I am proud to belong to their race—" He glanced out of the corner of his eye at Joseph, who stirred.

Joseph said, with hard clear precision, "The British, Colonel, are composed of the Celtic races, the Irish, the Scots and the Welsh, who are really one race. The English, on the contrary, are not British. They are mere Anglo-Saxons, who were brought as slaves to England by their masters and slaveowners, the Normans. Have they," he asked, with an air as artless as the colonel's own, "lived down the stigma of slaves as yet?"

The colonel's face enlarged enormously and became purple. Joseph smiled.

He said, "Then there is hope for the Negro, too, that he will live down the stigma of once being a slave. After all, Colonel, he has just to remember the English who were slaves also. And behold what they have accomplished, once becoming free! The Catholic Church, sir, accomplished that!"

Touché, thought Mr. Montrose, with silent enjoyment.

Joseph continued: "I assume, sir, when you speak of the 'British' you mean my fellow Celts? And not Her Germanic Majesty, Queen Victoria's, former bondsmen and slaves?"

"Come, come," said Mr. Montrose, smiling sweetly, "we are not about to begin a discussion of racial origins, are we, sirs? I have read that once the vast majority of us were slaves from the beginning, owned by but a few masters." He gave Joseph a cryptic glance.

"There is nothing I dislike more," said the colonel, with an attempt at a quelling glance, "than the discussion of irrelevancies—"

"Between businessmen," said Mr. Montrose. "Let us continue." He noticed that the colonel was not only angry but sullen. "We were discussing, I think, the slight contretemps between the—ah—Russians and the English."

"The Russians," said the colonel, "have been reporting erratic courses taken by obviously innocent British vessels plying between Union ports. This has led to the outrageous seizure of British vessels by the Federal Government, and some very warm international exchanges between diplomats. The Russians only desire to embarrass the British, for, one day, they will contest for empire."

"And so shall we," said Mr. Montrose. "That is inevitable with empires. Shall we continue? What time can the *Isabel* sail tomorrow?"

"At midnight," said the colonel, who was still sullen. "The usual cargo, I assume?"

Mr. Montrose leaned back in his chair and contemplated the smoke from his cheroot. "We will need more men. There will be sixty very large crates and some two hundred smaller crates. They will be very heavy."

The colonel whistled. His eyes squinted at Mr. Montrose. Mr. Montrose smiled shyly. "This is a first run. If it succeeds there will be larger runs—and more profit for you, Colonel."

The colonel refilled his glass. He swirled the golden contents of it and stared at the liquid. "There are more important personages than I engaged in this, Mr. Montrose. They may not like it."

Mr. Montrose said, "I am aware of those more important men. Nevertheless, we have been chosen this time—by Barbour & Bouchard."

The colonel stared at him. "But Barbour & Bouchard have been—conveying—a far larger cargo from the beginning of the war."

"True. But their operations are increasing. I believe some of their transports have been seized, also, quietly. They have never been prosecuted. They continue." He paused. "Barbour & Bouchard are very powerful men, Colonel. They own senators. Still, they must operate with discretion. The families of Union soldiers must not become indignant. And, though it seems incredible, there are still senators and congressmen and other politicians who are incorruptible. The other conveyers of Barbour & Bouchard have apparently become a little careless. So, we have been approached."

The colonel goggled at him with sudden deep respect and awe. "You," he almost whispered. "And Barbour & Bouchard."

"Let us not name names casually and indiscreetly," said Mr. Montrose. "It is decided? There will be enough loaders tomorrow night?"

"I have never given clearance to that—that—before," said the colonel.

"It is time for you to become more important," said Mr. Montrose. "And to engage in transactions which are more lucrative. You are ready to enjoy the company of very powerful men, who have been giving clearance to various ships, even in New York."

The colonel said, "How are the crates marked?"

"Tools for Boston and Philadelphia and various other ports. They are marked Barbour & Bouchard."

He wrote quickly on a slip of paper. "The wharf," he said. The colonel read it and then Mr. Montrose burned the paper. "You will see that the wharf number has been changed, Colonel."

The colonel was silent. He stared at the ceiling. He seemed deflated. He finally said, "I give clearances to the port. Is it possible that—others—have been clearing, unknown to me?"

"Indeed," said Mr. Montrose. "After all, there are many distinguished men in Washington, with investments. You are about to join them."

"Mr. Healey owns a senator?"

"Two," said Mr. Montrose. "And several congressmen." He smiled tenderly at the colonel.

The colonel said, "Execution is the punishment for clearing such contraband."

"If caught," said Mr. Montrose. "An intelligent man is rarely if ever caught. I am Mr. Montrose of Titusville, and this is Mr. Francis, also of Titusville. Under no circumstances will any other name be mentioned. It is settled, then? There will be enough men to handle the crates, and the *Isabel* will sail tomorrow at midnight, fully cleared. It is not the affair of the military authority to open and examine each and every crate. Crate number thirty-one contains nothing but machine tools, and the crates are openly marked with the name of the respected manufacturers. In short, this is a safer run than for mere food, clothing and the essentials of life. Too, the payment is far greater."

The colonel assumed a serious and even virtuous expression. "It is quite a different matter, sir, to supply innocent women and children with food and covering than gun-running—"

Mr. Montrose lifted a fine hand in warning. "I have said the payment is far greater."

Joseph stared at the colonel's profile with larger disgust.

"How much more?" asked the colonel with blunt avarice.

"Twice as much."

"Not enough."

Mr. Montrose shrugged. He lifted the case from his knees to the table and opened it. It was filled with bills of large denominations and the colonel leaned forward to look at them and his face expressed total greed and delight, and even humble worship. Mr. Montrose slowly removed half the packets of bills—which were tied with colored string—and laid them on the table. "Count them," he said.

There was silence in the room while the colonel counted the bills. His fingers clung to them lovingly; he released the crackling packets with reluctance. His hard mouth trembled with a kind of sexual passion. His fingers began to quiver. Mr. Montrose smiled as the last packet was laid on the table.

"The second half," he said, "will be given to you when the *Isabel* returns safely. Take these with you now, Colonel. I have another case which I am happy to present to you."

He brought another case, empty, from his bedroom and the colonel watched him closely as he laid the money within it, then fastened the straps. He pushed the case towards the colonel. Slowly, the colonel lifted his hands and then let them rest on it tightly as he would rest his hands on the breast of a beloved woman. "I am satisfied," he said, and his voice was hoarse. He looked at the case with the remaining money and his fierce eyes bulged. Then he licked the corner of his lips.

"The extra men," said Mr. Montrose, "will be paid by us. It will not be necessary this time for you or any agent to pay them. This is another safeguard for you, Colonel. So, all the profit is yours."

"I am satisfied," repeated the soldier. His forehead was hugely beaded with moisture.

Mr. Montrose closed the other case. "We hope this will not be the last time you will be satisfied, sir."

Only Joseph saw the merest little flicker run over the colonel's face, and he thought about it. The colonel said with enthusiasm, "I trust not!" He did not wait for Mr. Montrose to refill his glass. He filled it himself and drank it down at once with a flourish, and his face flushed.

"We will meet here again in eight days," said Mr. Montrose. He drank a small glass of wine. "I suggest you return to your rooms at once, Colonel. It is not sensible to remain here any longer."

The colonel stood up, saluted, and laughed a little recklessly. Mr. Montrose opened the door and cautiously glanced up and down the corridor. "Now!" he said. The colonel snatched up his case and ran from the room and Mr. Montrose closed the door after him. He turned to Joseph.

"What do you think of our boisterous soldier, who is so useful to us?"

"I don't trust him," said Joseph. "If possible, I'd put a guard on him."

Mr. Montrose raised his brows. "We have trusted him for nearly three years and have had no occasion to doubt him." He sipped his wine and looked over the brim at Joseph. "Are you not speaking solely from natural dislike, Mr. Francis?"

Joseph considered. He rubbed one dark-red eyebrow with his index finger. "I think not," he said at last. "I never permitted dislike to interfere with business, or expediency. It is just—perhaps I should say intuition. Smile if you will, Mr. Montrose."

But Mr. Montrose did not smile. He looked a little grave. "I have respect for intuition, Mr. Francis. No intelligent man deprecates it. However, we must operate empirically. The colonel has been very valuable to us in the past. There is no reason to think he will not continue to be valuable." He looked at Joseph questioningly, and then when Joseph made no comment he said, "We have no other choice. There is no time. Besides, the colonel is the military authority of the port of New York. What would you do if you were in charge of this, Mr. Francis?"

"I would let the *Isabel* be cleared by the colonel, and then I would not sail. I would wait a few days—after he believed we had already sailed, and then I would sail."

"But he has informers. Come, come. Why should he deprive himself of future profits, Mr. Francis? One betrayal, and he would have cut off his nose to spite his face. I am sure we are not the only ones who use him. One word, and he would get no more money from anyone. The news would spread."

"I don't know," said Joseph. "It is just a feeling I have."

Mr. Montrose studied him again in silence. Then he went to his room and brought out an extra pistol and another box of ammunition. He put them on the table and pushed them towards Joseph. "Load the pistol," he said.

"This is for you. As I said, I do not deprecate intuition though I confess I do not feel it now. I have my own and it has never betrayed me. Nonetheless, I believe you will feel safer with the extra protection."

"I will," said Joseph. He loaded the pistol expertly. "A detestable man," he said. "And a hypocrite. I never trusted a hypocrite." He smiled thinly at Mr. Montrose. "Mr. Healey is often a hypocrite, Mr. Montrose, but he never pretends that you must take him seriously."

"Yes," said Mr. Montrose. "Endearing. It is a joke with him. Remarkable that you should know that."

It was not the compliment that made Joseph again experience an impulse of liking for Mr. Montrose, and even an impulse of trust. This so startled him that he stood with his hand on the ammunition and pondered. He looked up suddenly to see Mr. Montrose gazing at him with that inexplicable affection he had seen before. But Mr. Montrose said, "You have never seen Virginia. It is a beautiful state." He lifted his wine glass and considered it. "It is lovely at this time of year. The locust trees and the honeysuckle are blooming. The hedges and the fields are full of flowers. The lanes are infinitely inviting. The horses stand in the fields and are aquiver with joy, and the young colts race with each other." His voice was tranquil and detached. "Unfortunately, we shall not see all that."

"But, you have seen it?"

Mr. Montrose did not answer. He had a look on his face as if he were not present. At last he said with indifference, "I should like to show you Virginia."

Again Joseph was startled. Of what interest could it be to Mr. Montrose to want to show his associate anything at all? Joseph's long fingers began to beat a tattoo on the gleaming table. He stared at the immaculate narcissi and suddenly thought of his sister. He reached out and touched one shimmering petal.

Joseph heard himself saying, and not without a quick dismay and horror, "I know we do not tell each other our names. But I should like you to know mine."

"It is not necessary," said Mr. Montrose. He stood up and took his case into his bedroom. On the threshold he looked back at Joseph and smiled as an older brother, or a very young father, would smile at him, and between them darted a dizzying sympathy and fellowship. But even then Joseph knew that if he should be unpardonably stupid Mr.

Montrose would be ruthless in dealing with him, and without regret.

"Tonight," said Mr. Montrose, "we are serene gentlemen in New York, whose business has been satisfactorily concluded. Therefore, we shall dine in state in the dining room of this hotel, and we shall then repair to the Academy of Music which will present Chopin, a most delectable composer, and young, and newly celebrated. I trust you favor Chopin?"

"I have never heard any music in my life but Irish ballads," said Joseph. He hesitated. "And the singing of the choir at Mass. And the rowdy music in Mr. Healey's brothels, though I should not call that music."

Mr. Montrose nodded his approval. "Then you have a great pleasure to experience. Chopin appeals to youth as well as to age. I favor him, myself." He looked at Joseph. "Of course, you know of Chopin."

"I have read of him," said Joseph. "He died in 1849 at the age of thirty-nine." His tone was stiff.

"Yes. Alas, that the beautiful and the indispensable die young."

"And the rascals live to a hearty old age."

Mr. Montrose looked indulgently offended. "My dear Mr. Francis, rascals are just as indispensable to this world as good men. They bring vitality and enterprise to what would otherwise be a very dull existence. They bring inventiveness, where there would be only stultification. They bring color. They enliven cities. They have imagination, which most men do not. I have never known a man of distinction and virility and zest who was not, at heart, a sound rascal. They are the true romanticists, the adventurers, the poets. Heaven, I believe, is a duller place for the absence of Lucifer. I am sure he sang the gayest and the naughtiest songs for the edification of the angels. They say he is somber and sullen. I, myself, believe he laughs. After all, contemplating the world with any insight must convince one that it is absurd, and the rascals know it."

This was a new thought for Joseph. But, he said to himself, I cannot laugh. I can't find the world absurd. I find it terrible. He said, "I've had experiences which I did not consider absurd." His voice was again stiff and defensive.

Mr. Montrose looked absently preoccupied. Then he said, "Who has not? It is a great error to believe our experiences are unique and have never been known by others. That is the most dangerous delusion of youth."

I do not always accept what he says, thought Joseph, but he is the only person in my whole life who has ever talked to me, and I to him. Then Joseph understood the reason for the strange liking he felt for Mr. Montrose, and the reluctant sympathy, and the odd if cautious confidence. He also knew that he had omitted his real name not only from the first fear of Mr. Squibbs and his men, but because he had wanted to hide from everyone else also. The fear of Mr. Squibbs had not been realistic for a long time, he realized now, but the mistrust for others had been with him from early childhood. He felt no mistrust for Mr. Montrose and he considered that, too, though he had no illusions about the older man.

"Still," said Mr. Montrose, as if Joseph had been speaking, "it is always discreet to keep one's experiences to one's self. No man has ever been hanged, or laughed at, for discretion."

The dining room was at least as flamboyant as the lobby, and appeared even larger in its blaze of crystal, its glimmer of gilt, its rococo carpet and upholstery. Even the stiff white tablecloths blazed, and the heavy silver and glass sparkled. Here, as it was evening, the gaiety had increased to louder and more feverish laughter and a constant rustle, ululation, tripping and shrillness of eager and excited babble. Here, too, was the same lighthearted music from behind a screen, emphasizing without intrusion the happiness of the diners and their joy in war. The waiters were clad as English footmen, with powdered wigs, scarlet coats and breeches adorned with twinkling brass buttons, ruffled shirts and white silk stockings. The headwaiter, recognizing Mr. Montrose, led him and Joseph to a secluded table near the rose-damask wall where they could see and yet be somewhat secluded. The ladies at the tables were sumptuously clad in colorful velvet, lace, silk and satin, their beautiful half-naked shoulders and breasts rising like Dresden porcelain from their billowing hoops, their hair of many hues and shades elaborately dressed and falling in long ringlets and curls far down their delicate backs, their coiffures glittering with diamonds or daintily entwined with fresh flowers. Flowers, too, stood in vases and bowls on all the tables and the hot scent of them, and the breeze of perfume which constantly swept through the room, and the sweetness of rice powder and cosmetics and the inciting odor of young flesh, almost overpowered the austere Joseph, but Mr. Montrose leaned back negligently in his red plush chair and surveyed and savored it all with a smile of ostensible pleasure. His eyes wandered from one pretty face to another, considering, rejecting, approving, admiring.

Below the music and the vocal confusion and the clatter of fine dinnerware and silver Joseph could hear a rhythmic pounding and faint but insistent music, and then, as the music briefly stopped, the distant clapping of hands. Mr. Montrose said, "There is an officers' ball tonight, and they are dancing with their ladies in the ballroom just above us. Illustrious soldiers and other personages have joined them, from Washington. It is a gala."

"Nothing like a war to inspire a gala," said Joseph.

"Now, now," said Mr. Montrose. "What would you have them do? Be hypocrites and crouch in a dark room, pretending to wail and grieve, and deprive themselves, when they have made, and are making, such a lot of us money?" His face was pleasant but ambiguous. "After all, was this war not planned in London, in 1857, by bankers, and they are all honorable men, as I believe Marcus Antonius said of the murderers of Julius Caesar. Mr. Lincoln said only last week to Congress: 'I have two great enemies, the Southern Army in front of me, and the financial institution in the rear. Of the two, the one in the rear is my greatest foe.'" He idly lit a cheroot and Joseph watched him with his usual intensity.

Mr. Montrose continued, as if he were commenting on the most casually amusing thing: "It is expected that the European bankers, and our own banking gentry, will make four billion dollars out of this war, not a sum to be lightly dismissed."

"If Mr. Lincoln said what he did, and if he knows that this war was planned and finally executed by men who want money and power, why did he war on the Confederacy?"

Mr. Montrose looked at him quizzically. "My dear Mr. Francis, who do you honestly believe rules any nation? The apparent rulers, or the real ones behind the scenes who manipulate a nation's finances for their own benefit? Mr. Lincoln is as helpless as you and I. He can only, unfortunate man, give his people slogans, and slogans, it would appear, are what the people want. I have yet to hear of a nation that ever rejected a war."

He added: "Tomorrow, you will meet some of the gentry I have spoken of, most congenial and tolerant men, who have no nationalistic prejudices at all, and no allegiances even to their own countries, but only to each other and their banking interests. They are the only true cosmopolitans, and they rule us and decide whether we shall live or die. Some are friends of Mr. Healey, but he shyly does not speak of them and what they are doing for him. He is not quite in the modest circumstances you may believe. And all human activity which produces money interests Mr. Healey. Why are you frowning? Do you find this all reprehensible?"

Joseph said, and his voice was somewhat surly, "I have no objection to any man making a lot of money, or any group of men."

Mr. Montrose laughed affectionately. "Then, why do you frown?"

But Joseph could not answer, for he had no answer except a deep and formless uneasiness. "Money," said Mr. Montrose, "as the Bible has remarked, is the answer to all things. Let it be the answer to your conscience, Mr. Francis, for I fear you have one."

Joseph said, and with unusual emotion, "It is not agreeable to me to see these people, in this room, happy that men are dying and the earth destroyed so that they can be prosperous!"

"But," said Mr. Montrose, "you have no objection to keeping Mr. Healey's accounts in the matter of brothels—and other affairs."

"I provoke none of those brothels, nor do I engage in those—other affairs! Mr. Healey's activities are no personal concern of mine."

"So say these people here—that war is not their concern, so long as it is profitable to them."

Joseph was silent, staring down at the table. Then he looked up suddenly and saw Mr. Montrose's expression and could not read it. Yet, he colored.

"Suppose," said Mr. Montrose with a gentle relentlessness, "that some of those brothels came into your own keeping. Would you refuse them?"

Joseph's pale mouth tightened to a slash, but he looked at Mr. Montrose and said without hesitation, "No."

Mr. Montrose shrugged. "There, then. You must not criticise others. We are all men and sinners, are we not? I don't think you truly like sin, Mr. Francis, and would prefer to make a fortune without it. As for myself, I prefer it for what it is, and have freely chosen it. For, after all, what is sin? It is common sense. It is reality. In truth, it is the only reality in the world, and everything else is confusion, lies, hypocrisy, sentimentality, pietistic falsehood and delusion. I suggest that you once came to this conclusion, yourself."

"Yes," said Joseph, and Mr. Montrose detected in him the strange probity that lay under his character. "And I still believe it. But I don't like the means we have to use to get money. I'd prefer to get it in—in—other ways."

"And I enjoy the way it is got, for the way, itself. Ah, I see our green turtle soup is approaching. I will choose the wine." Then he laughed indulgently at Joseph. "There is something Calvinistic in your nature, something Cromwellian: Riches are not to be despised, and if scruples are strangled in the manner of getting them it should be denounced openly and publicly mourned. Ah, now, do not look so murderous. Let us enjoy our soup and listen to the music and ogle the pretty ladies and remember that the worst crime of humanity is hypocrisy. It is the mother of all sins. There is not a man alive, I am certain, who does not wallow in it, knowingly or unknowingly. We must accept ourselves for what we are. That is the secret of a healthy mind and body."

He added, as he picked up a heavy and shining spoon, "Hypocrisy should not be wholly detested. Without it we should have no civilization, nor could men live together for a single hour without killing each other. Other words for it are gentility and tolerance and regard for neighbor, and self-restraint and self-discipline. I might even go so far as to say that without it we should have no churches and no religions."

The great and amorphous uneasiness swelled in Joseph, for he recognized a sophistry here if a sardonic one, but he did not know how to combat it without appearing a puerile fool. He also had a suspicion that Mr. Montrose, without malice, was enjoying himself at his, Joseph's, expense. Joseph tasted his soup, a greenish-brown liquid with bits of turtle meat in it, and decided he did not like it and that he was faintly nauseated. He watched a lively and vivacious swirl of ladies and dashing gentlemen and officers pass the table, and pretended to be interested in them, and Mr. Montrose smilingly and slightly shook his head as if in denial.

Joseph saw this gesture through the corner of his eye and he was mortified at himself. Why was this war of sudden and disturbing interest to him, he who had long ago removed himself from the affairs of other men and the interests of the general world? The war had been in progress, he remembered, for several years, and it had not concerned him in the least nor had he given a single thought to it or conjecture, for he was not involved with mankind except when it was to his personal advantage. Only in that way could he keep himself from being fragmented and dispersed, as other men were, and only in that way could he prevent hurt and injuries, and the absurd frenzies of emotionalism, and the humiliations and defeats such emotionalism precipitated. His indifference to all external things concerning mankind had been his impregnable armor.

He angrily puzzled over his new concern. Then he knew, with such a powerful onslaught of emotion that it shook him. He had seen a young, bloodstained and exhausted young woman, nameless to him, in the window of an Army train, tending the wounded, and he had loved her not only for her beauty but for her devotion and selfless attention to others, and something he had never suspected in himself had been poignantly touched and stricken. I had put her out of my mind, he thought, but I can't forget her, and I can't understand this nor why what she was doing should concern me in the least. She has forced me to be aware of a world I despise and reject, and I should hate her.

He put down his spoon. It touched the merest scrap of folded white paper which had not been there before, and it was close to Mr. Montrose's plate, and Joseph wondered how it had arrived and who had placed it there. Mr. Montrose saw Joseph's eyes directed on the paper and he took it at once, unfolded and read it. He passed it to Joseph and said calmly, "It would seem our plans are changed. We must, unfortunately, leave the concert a little earlier, and this is awkward, for one of my precepts, very valuable, is that one should never attract attention."

Joseph read the slip of paper: "Plans changed. Tonight at midnight, not tomorrow." Mr. Montrose deftly retrieved the paper and carefully burned it with the tip of his cheroot and deposited the ashes into the tray and then stirred them thoroughly. At Joseph's inquiring look he said, "We never question how messages are delivered. It may seem melodramatic to you but melodrama is a natural side of life, however pragmatists may deplore it."

He sighed. "Now I must leave my own message to our banker friends tonight, regretting the delay for a few days. It is a nuisance. You may think I am a little too cautious, Mr. Francis, but delays can be dangerous. We must go to the concert, for the tickets are in my name, and I have the customary seats, and absence would be noted and commented upon. I suggest that we do not converse at the concert, and that I leave a few moments before you, and I will wait and then you will join me." He poured the wine just brought to the table and savored his own glass. "Excellent," he said. "A splendid rosé."

Joseph knew that he must not ask questions. He considered the wild duck placed before him, and its exotic sauce, and took up his knife and fork. The meat was too pungent for his ascetic tastes and the sauce unpleasant. But he had long ago schooled himself to accept food of any kind, remembering his years of starvation. He forced himself to eat, and forced himself to sip at the wine. The hysterically happy babble and laughter all about him was unbearably intrusive, and his deep Irish melancholy, without a reason he could fathom, fell on him again. The music of the distant ballroom enhanced his gloom.

He said, in an effort to disperse it and because something constantly worried him: "The colonel, Mr. Montrose. You mentioned to him that Mr. Healey had chosen me, and therefore implied that he should treat me with consideration. Yet, on our immediate meeting he insulted me, and so insulted Mr. Healey. Would that not show a disregard for Mr. Healey, such as he had never shown before?"

Mr. Montrose drank musingly and gazed at Joseph over his glass. Then he put it down. "That is very astute of you. What conclusions would you draw?"

"That he intends to betray us, as I said before."

Joseph was surprised to see Mr. Montrose's eyes brighten at the thought of danger and he said to himself that though he would never retreat from it if an advantage was involved he would never like it or be pleased at the prospect. But Mr. Montrose, he suspected, loved danger for itself and would even court it, as a wild mistress wooed at extraordinary times, in spite of his concern for caution.

Mr. Montrose said, "You believe he has had a rush of conscience to the head or the heart?"

"No, I don't think he has either. It is something else, and has nothing to do with us personally."

"Um," said Mr. Montrose, and thoughtfully puffed at his cheroot. "That is interesting. You may be wrong, you know, and you may be right. I have considerable respect for your intuitions. I think I will go doubly armed and make some changes by messenger to the docks."

He lifted his glass again. "Is this duck not delightful? Let us enjoy ourselves." He smiled at Joseph and there was a little subtle excitement in his smile and a tensing, catlike, in his body. Then Joseph, with his powerful Irish intuition, understood that in many men there is a suicidal urge, not without delight, and this explained a considerable number of those who worked for Mr. Healey. He, himself, was not among them though he had no love for life as they, themselves, obviously did.

Chapter 19

They left the hotel after dinner, now clad in discreetly dark clothing, and carrying with them leather cases. Joseph, as did Mr. Montrose, wore a pistol holster under his long black coat and in a pocket in the coat he carried the extra pistol. The coachman was waiting for them, as mute as before, and they entered the carriage in silence.

Joseph knew that Mr. Healey owned the clipper, *Isabel,* and that it was his crew aboard, augmented by those Colonel Braithwaite had sent for the night's work. Beyond this his interest did not extend. He sat back on the cushions of the carriage and looked indifferently through the polished windows at the street scenes, the gay seething on Fifth Avenue, under the yellow gas lamplight which lit up the frail green arbors of the new trees and splashed the flagged and brick walks and the cobblestones with flickering amber light and caught a woman's face under a spring bonnet or the flash of a smile or the gleam of a tall silk hat. The streets milled with vehicles of all sorts, filled with ladies and gentlemen on the way to various festivities, and laughter rippled everywhere, and Joseph could hear the crack of whips, the neighing of impatient horses and the rattle of carriages striving to find a passage through the throngs. Every intersection seemed choked with carriages and horses, striving to enter the main stream of Fifth Avenue, and harness glistened under the street lamps and the lacquered carriages, black, dark red, bright blue, green, bore vividly painted scenes on their sides, and every window showed a smiling bobbing head, a waving gloved hand, the movement of a fan, the color of a mantle or a pretty dress. The side streets were less brightly lit, only an occasional uncertain light fluttering down on the heavy and barely moving traffic. Over it all was the pungent smell of drains and dust and heated stone and manure.

Joseph saw something else besides all this gaiety and rapid movement. He saw the little boys, many of them not over five, standing ragged and silent in doorways, dumbly offering wilted bouquets of flowers or baskets of sweetmeats and sundry other cheap articles, or timidly holding out shoeshine boxes, or even begging cups. Many of them were pitted by smallpox, and Joseph saw their haggard childish faces, starved and hopeless and bony, and their feverish and pleading eyes. Among them sat or moved old women in torn shawls, humbly competing with the children for the occasional carelessly thrown penny. The police were everywhere. If a beggar became too desperately importunate he or she was touched smartly by a club and ordered on. Against the dark sky rose the high spires of the churches, the tallest edifices in the city.

The traffic temporarily came to a halt as a number of decently dressed young and old men, poor but clean, moved from a side street carrying placards. Joseph could read them: *LINCOLN, THE DICTATOR! LINCOLN, THE MAN ON HORSEBACK! DOWN WITH WAR! DOWN WITH THE DRAFT! FREE SPEECH! END THE MURDER! BRING HOME OUR BOYS! FREEDOM AND THE RIGHTS OF MAN!*

The police sauntered to the curbs and darkly watched the silent parade of the protesters, ready for incipient riot. But the men moved in a quiet phalanx, looking straight ahead, their bearded faces stern and impassive. They wound their way through masses of horses and carriages and pedestrians. Now their solemn march was broken by jeering whistles, by calls of "Cowards! Traitors!" Some coachmen lifted whips and struck at them. Some spat into their faces. Some reared their horses beside and in front of them. But steadily and peacefully they moved on, across Fifth Avenue and onto another side street.

"Quakers, probably," said Mr. Montrose. "Or perhaps just fathers and sons or husbands. How dare they try to interfere with such a lovely war! Very insolent of them." Flags and bunting hung from every window and near every doorway. Somewhere a roving group of dashingly dressed young men began to sing:

> "When Johnny comes marching home again,
>   hurrah, hurrah!"

"Yes, indeed," said Mr. Montrose.

The young men, half drunk, laughing loudly, pranced in the rear of the silent marchers, taunted them, jeered at them, poked them with canes, made grotesque faces at them, and mimicked them. Those in carriages laughed in appreciation and nodded and waved hands. But the marching men looked straight ahead as if only they were on the streets.

"Futile," said Mr. Montrose, in amusement. The carriage moved on, jostling for space in the traffic.

Horsecars mingled with the carriages and other vehicles, clomping steadily away, lanterns swaying within, and faces peering through the dusty windows at the more affluent parade. Mr. Montrose rolled up a window to shut out the noise which increased as the night increased. He looked sideways at Joseph, wondering at the young man's thoughts, but Joseph's face was hidden in the shadow of his tall respectable silk hat. He sat absolutely still. Occasionally lamplight fell on his gloved hands; they did not move. They were clasped as dead as stone on the head of his Malacca cane. His thin legs were rigid in their black pantaloons. Joseph was thinking: It is nothing to me. It has nothing to do with me.

Joseph had read of halls of music but he had never seen such baroque grandeur, such lavishness of velvet and crystal, such gilt bulging of boxes and such silken brilliant movement as he saw in the Academy of Music tonight. The hall roared with laughter, with voices, with eager banter. Throngs moved down the narrow aisles, the ladies smiling when they recognized friends in the orchestral seats, the men bowing deeply. Everyone glanced up at the crowded boxes filled with women in many-hued Worth dresses, lavishly arrayed gentlemen, feathers, fans, flowers, and constant vivacity. Down in the orchestra pit could be faintly heard the glittering and tentative notes of a harp, the testing run of a violin, the boom of a cello, the rumble of a drum. The whole hall seethed with joyous animation. Programs fluttered; lorgnettes flashed in the light of the immense crystal chandeliers; jewels blazed, tiaras were rings of fire on pretty heads; white bare shoulders were illuminated. The hot hall was smotheringly heavy with the effluvium of perfume and powder and gas. Everyone seemed excited, too noisily elated, too lively.

Mr. Montrose and Joseph were led by an usher with gloves and programs to purple-plush seats midway down the orchestra level. They delicately climbed over the huge hoops of seated ladies, while the gentlemen rose and bowed politely and a word was murmured here and there, "Mr. Montrose, sir. Happy to greet you again. Delightful evening, is it not? No, pray don't apologize. My fault, sir." They looked with curiosity at Joseph, but as Mr. Montrose did not introduce him nor appear to know him they only slightly bowed and turned from him.

Joseph read the program. He looked at the vast stage with its looped purple velvet curtains fringed with gold. It was empty, hardly lit. Two grand pianos stood back to back, waiting. The gaslights, dimmed in front, rose and fell. He looked at his watch. It was seven o'clock. The *Isabel* sailed at midnight. The hubbub all about him faded from his senses. He began to think, frowning. His premonitions were stronger than ever. He thought of his family. Then he glanced up, to evade his thoughts, at a box just above him.

The young lady he had seen through the window of a train sat there, wan and strained in a lilac silk dress with a deep yoke of creamy lace just hardly concealing her breast. Her tawny hair, undressed and without jewels, feathers or flowers, hung down her back. Her beautiful face was set in a pleasant and amiable expression, for she was surrounded by men and women obviously her friends, but her eyes were sunken in dark hollows and her lovely mouth was pale and a little tremulous. She kept touching her lips and brows with a lace kerchief, and her expression, when unwatched, was remote and tragic, and her eyes kept roving in a kind of mute despair. She wore no gems but the dazzle of diamonds and emeralds he had seen on her hand before.

A heavy shock ran through Joseph. He stared up at her. Feeling, perhaps, the focus of his eyes, she looked down at him but her own eyes were blinded with misery and she evidently did not really see him. Someone in the box spoke to her. Joseph could see the soft whiteness of her tilted chin, the pearly perfection of her colorless face, the starlike shadow of the lashes on her cheek, the tender cleft between her young breasts. She was speaking softly and politely, but her weariness was evident. Her round white arms and gloved hands were listless, and her fingers held a large fan of multicolored feathers but did not move it. Suddenly and helplessly, her eyes closed. She leaned back in the chair and apparently sank into a doze, her lips parted like the lips of a child, the lilac silk crumpling and glowing over her collapsed figure.

Then Joseph knew her. He had seen that pallid sadness before, and he remembered. This was Mrs. Tom Hennessey, the wife of the florid senator.

A young gentleman in the box emerged from the dimness behind and carefully laid a silvery mantle over the girl. Some of the ladies leaned forward, and one or two winked and tittered behind their fans. The other gentlemen leaned forward and spoke in concerned voices. The girl slept in her exhaustion, her head thrown back against the purple velvet of her deep chair, her chin raised pathetically.

Mr. Montrose sat next to Joseph but not by the smallest gesture or glance did he convey knowledge of him. However, so acute was he that he felt some disturbance and glanced through the corner of his eye at the younger man. Joseph appeared to be in a state of frozen shock. Mr. Montrose wondered, but did not speak to him. Then he saw that Joseph was staring up at the sleeping girl in the box above, and he was intrigued. A pretty enough piece, there, and a lady, but she was evidently sleeping off too much wine and too much rich food, and had probably danced too late into this morning. Mr. Montrose had no objection to silly frivolous women, but he was surprised that Joseph should be looking up at her so fixedly. He had thought better of the young man.

She seems to be dying, thought Joseph, and the women around her titter and look knowing. Where is her abominable husband? Why is it not possible for me to go to her, to carry her from this place and let her sleep in peace? In some quiet spot where I could sit beside her and watch over her— Away from blood and death and wounds— He looks entranced, thought Mr. Montrose. She must be at least three years older than he. Does he know her? Impossible. She seemed familiar to Mr. Montrose. He had seen her before, at a distance. Then it came to him: Tom Hennessey's wife, and Mr. Montrose could have laughed aloud.

The chandeliers began to dim slowly but steadily, and in laughing protest the roar of voices rose higher. The stage brightened. There were various perfumed flurries in the aisles and smothered mirth as coveys of late arrivals tripped to their seats, exuding fresh warmth, stirring the air with flutters and gestures and ribbons and laces and quick whispers and soft little sounds and coy apologies as they subsided. Joseph watched the stage; his hands gripped the arms of his chair. He said to himself that he was a fool, a puling imbecile, for he had lost control of himself in one devastating moment, and he realized with considerable inward terror that he was not as invulnerable as he had believed and that he, too, could be weak.

Two young men in elaborate clothing and ruffled shirts stepped silently from the wings. They might have been twins, with their thin white faces, large dark eyes, tensed mouths and long dark hair swept over their brows and down over their ears, and they were impeccable, their boots slim and shining. They halted at mid-stage and bowed to the audience, which was just barely quieting and there was a condescending spatter of applause and the ladies patted their gloved hands together graciously. Now the hall was in almost complete darkness and the stage was full of light. The two young pianists seated themselves on their respective benches and glanced over the pianos at each other then lifted their hands and brought their long fingers down on the keys.

Polonaise (Militaire) the program had said. Joseph had not known what to expect for he had never heard great music before, and intense as his imagination was he was still not prepared for the tremendous emotion that took him when the poignant and masculine notes sprang from the instruments. There was a whisper of other instruments under the pianos, but they dominated it, as the sun dominates the light about it, which it has created, itself. From the brief note on the program Joseph understood that the music was the spiritual expression of an oppressed nation which could never be conquered, that it sang of the heart and the indomitable power of the human soul, courageous, unvanquished even in death. It was a sublime victory over the world, and all its meanness and squalid pain and its little passions, and its prison houses and its despair.

Yes, yes, thought Joseph, and he was moved almost beyond bearing, and again he was frightened that he could be moved and involved in anything which did not immediately pertain to him.

Then he felt an unfamiliar exultation, for it seemed to him that if a small nation could still find a voice to express its gallantry and its inextinguishable faith before might then he, Joseph Francis Xavier Armagh, was unthreatened so long as he did not surrender. Like Poland, he too could face God and shout defiance.

Now he forgot the girl sleeping above him and was swept away on the great tidal wave of sound, immersed like a helpless swimmer in pounding billows and sudden crests of light. He heard thunder, then the grave voice of reverence, then sweetness and tenderness, then something which tugged at him like an immeasurable sorrow, forgotten but now awakening. He did not hear the surges of applause between the selections; he just waited for the noise to subside and the music to soar out again, himself dazed, drugged with emotion, in a turmoil of voiceless feeling. He had never heard a nocturne before but now he saw moonlight on the black silk of still water, and stars trailing radiance in their passage. To him this was not music at all. It was a supernal holiness which he struggled to deny, because he feared it, but its beauty held him even as he fought it. Now the pianos swept into the *Largo,* op. 28, no. 20, and the solemn majesty was almost more than he could endure.

Then it was intermission. Mr. Montrose nudged his elbow as the gas chandeliers began to fill the auditorium with illumination. Mr. Montrose then rose and full of murmured regrets he gently edged his way past Joseph and others in their seats and walked slowly and with a musing expression up the aisle, producing a cheroot as he did so. Joseph waited a few moments until the others in the row rose also and edged into the aisle and he followed them in the renewed hubbub of laughter, greetings and happy chatter. A young lady or two looked at him with half-smiles, as if expecting recognition, for they saw he had distinction and height, but he only slightly bowed as he had seen Mr. Montrose do and went up the aisle at a casual pace. But everything appeared unreal to him, disturbed, moved from its place, and without reality, and again he was frightened.

The coachman and the carriage were waiting outside even as the audience spilled in swirling rainbow colors onto the stones for a cooling breath of fresh air. Mr. Montrose was nowhere in sight. Joseph went as inconspicuously as possible to the carriage, and the coachman closed the door behind him. As he expected, Mr. Montrose was already there.

Mr. Montrose said, "I prefer just the piano, and not the embellishments we heard tonight from the other instruments. It makes for a little gaudiness, a little too much emphasis. Still, the pianists are very gifted and were not submerged in the concertos as I was afraid they would be. Chopin has enough intrinsic power to dominate even fretwork and demolish it."

Joseph said, "I never knew it was possible," and Mr. Montrose nodded, not condescendingly but with understanding kindness. He said, "I think you would like Beethoven, or, better still, if I judge you right, Wagner."

The streets were not so crowded now. The carriage began to clatter and clop its way through narrower streets and darker ones, and the houses became smaller and dilapidated with little yellowish glimmers in the windows, and there was a noxious smell and a hollow emptiness and fewer and fewer people. Eventually even these dwindled and what few men there were seemed to skulk and the buildings were blind and the lamplight became feebler and there was an odor which haunted Joseph but which he could not immediately recognize. Finally it came to him. It was the odor of the sea, and Joseph clearly saw an ashen winter morning of snow and wind and black docks and oily water, and felt again the almost forgotten dread and despair and hopelessness. Mr. Montrose reached across Joseph and locked the carriage door without a comment.

At last Joseph could hear the ocean, itself, and he could see distant flickering lanterns moving restlessly, and long deserted streets and bleak and faceless warehouses all about him. The wheels and the horse's hoofs raised noisy echoes in this dark silence and desertion. Mr. Montrose reached under his coat, loosened the flap on his holster, and, seeing this, Joseph also did so. He felt the sudden tightening of his abdominal muscles, the sudden bristling of the hair on the back of his neck, a sudden light cool sweat, and his breath came faster and lighter. He was vexed to see that Mr. Montrose had not quickened at all and that he was completely calm and that he continued to smoke placidly. I may be dead soon, thought Joseph, and so may he, but he appears not to care. Yet, he enjoys every day he lives.

Finally, at the end of this street Joseph could see the black glitter of water and a forest of masts and dully lit piers and wharfs, and he could smell tar and hemp and wet canvas and fish and sodden wood and the stench of the sewers of the city emptying into the sea, and then, on a whiff of wind, strange exotic smells of spice, like ginger or pepper. He saw prowling watchmen with lanterns, great huge brutes of rough men, moving everywhere, and well-armed. The sky was as black as the water, and a cold white moon stared down on the land and the water and sent icy splinters of sharp light over the slow ripples and slower waves. As the carriage rumbled forward several watchmen approached, holding lanterns high, and scowling, but when Mr. Montrose leaned forward so they could see him they touched their caps and retreated. The warehouses appeared to lean closer over the narrow street. The cobbles glistened as if malodorous melted fat had been poured over them, and the wheels of the carriage occasionally slithered. Chill humidity made everything drip as if rain had just halted.

The carriage turned on the docks, past clusters of great and small vessels, some with their sails raised, some with empty masts, and all the ships heaved and bobbed and splashed, and feeble lanterns gleamed from wet decks. There was an air of desertion everywhere. Then Joseph saw, beyond the harbor, out at sea, shifting light and dim shadowy forms of large vessels. "Federal patrols," said Mr. Montrose, as if commenting on nothing significant. An occasional ship spewed black smoke and the smell of burning coal on the air, and at intervals vessels moved away from piers in a quiet that was sinister. Yet Joseph became aware, in spite of the quiet, that here was an intense busyness and commerce, both of war and peace.

The carriage stopped. Joseph saw the bow of a large clipper, and, in the lantern light which fought the darkness on the deck, the name *Isabel*. The sails were already up. Joseph heard, rather than saw, the activity of many men aboard, for figures could hardly be discerned. They were loading huge cartons and crates from this wharf, which was covered rather than open, and larger than other wharfs they had passed. The grating and squealing of iron-wheeled vehicles seemed suddenly very imminent on the dock.

The open doors of the wharf were immense, and were capable of admitting two large teams of horses and their wagons side by side. Dollies and great carts could be seen inside, being heaped with the material to be loaded. Mr. Montrose nodded with satisfaction. "They have worked fast. Another half an hour, and we will be ready."

He was about to get out of the carriage when he saw a military patrol smartly moving on the dock. A young officer approached the carriage and saluted. Mr. Montrose smiled at him genially, and opened the window and showed him the copy of the clearance which Colonel Braithwaite had given him, the original of which was in the hands of the captain on board. "We are going on the clipper to Boston," he said. "Is it a good night for sailing, Captain?"

The captain was obviously a lieutenant, and he saluted again. "A good night, sir," he said. "Are you, and this gentleman, the only passengers?"

"Indeed, yes. Our first journey to Boston. I am afraid it is going to be rigorous." One soldier held up a lantern to scrutinize Joseph. "But," said Mr. Montrose, "as representatives of Barbour & Bouchard, we must do our duty to aid in the war, must we not?"

The young man saluted again, and he moved off with his troop. Mr. Montrose and Joseph left the carriage and now Joseph could hear the booming and echoes of the activity on the wharf, the banging and shrieking of protesting wheels, and the figures of stevedores working rapidly. The wharf inside was nearly empty now except for a few enormous crates at least eight feet high and almost as broad. A wide ramp led up to the lower decks of the clipper, which were dancing lightly on the water. The wharf was lit by many lanterns hanging from the high ceiling or set on waiting crates and boxes. No one challenged or appeared to notice the two men who entered through the door. Joseph was conscious of sharp cold and the intensification of many smells, most of them unpleasant. Flags fluttered from the masts of the *Isabel*. Water slapped, heard even above the activity on the wharf and the decks.

Suddenly a tall young man approached them and Joseph's first thought—from his reading of sea stories—was that here was truly a pirate in the great tradition, a true brigand and murderous adventurer. He was not more than thirty-seven, tall and lean and as lithe as a panther, and he walked with the same grace and economy of movement as did Mr. Montrose. He was obviously the captain, from his uniform and his cap, and he had a narrow dark face, so dark that Joseph at first thought he was either Negro or Indian, and black shining eyes as predatory as an animal's, a great nose and an almost lipless mouth. He had a controlled but reckless air, and he looked at Mr. Montrose with smiling affection and removed his cap. His black hair was thick and curling and unkempt, and he extended a dark thin hand to the other man and he shook Mr. Montrose's hand warmly. He hesitated only a moment, then he put his hands on Mr. Montrose's shoulders in an embracing gesture. In spite of his somewhat casual uniform and his intimation of enormous strength—very daunting—he was obviously a man of breeding as well as deviltry and courage.

"I have news for you!" he exclaimed. Then added, as he saw Joseph, "Mr. Montrose. Great news."

"Excellent, Edmund," said Mr. Montrose. He turned to Joseph, "Edmund, this is my new associate, Joseph Francis. Mr. Francis, Captain Oglethorpe."

Joseph had detected, in the captain's slow speech, the same soft accents he had heard in the voice of Mr. Montrose. The captain bowed ceremoniously. "Happy to have you aboard, Mr. Francis." He gave his hand to Joseph, and his eyes vividly ran over Joseph's face and body like the flash of a knife in lightning. Then Joseph knew that here was a man at least as dangerous as Mr. Montrose and as ruthless if not more so, and he guessed that killing was not beyond him. Yet he had such a gay dark appearance, such a zest, that Joseph was intrigued as well as wary, and he knew that his first impression had been correct. Captain Oglethorpe was, in soul at any rate, a pirate and a brigand, utterly without mercy when necessary, and totally without fear. He carried no weapons, as if his own power were enough for him. Joseph saw that his eyes were restless and mirthful and very intelligent and piercing, and that nothing was unobserved by him. After his brief and in someway frightening survey of Joseph, he turned to Mr. Montrose and nodded.

"I dismissed the extra men fifteen minutes ago," he said. "They were good workers. These remaining are our regular crew. We will leave on the hour, with no delay." He looked with smiling satisfaction—it seemed he was almost always smiling—at the scurrying men. His large white teeth glittered in his dusky face.

"No trouble at all, Edmund?" asked Mr. Montrose.

"None." Joseph noticed that he did not speak to Mr. Montrose with the word "sir." He spoke to the other man as an equal. "The clearance from our friend came here promptly four hours ago."

Mr. Montrose inclined his head. He stood on the littered wharf, out of place here in his elegance. "Mr. Francis, Edmund, has expressed some suspicions of our friend, whom he had not seen before."

"Oh?" said the captain. He turned again to Joseph and again scrutinized him. He said, "May I ask why, sir?"

Joseph said, "I don't know why. There was something about him which made me suspicious. I may have been wrong."

The captain considered. He accepted one of Mr. Montrose's cheroots and lit it with a lucifer, his lively face somewhat thoughtful. He said, "I like first impressions. They are usually true. Still, we have the clearances. There has been only one inspection, crate number thirty-one. It required special tools to open. I invited the military inspector to open others, but he declined. We then went on board for a little refreshment."

He turned again to Joseph. "Was there anything in particular, sir, which alarmed you about our friend?"

"His lack of courtesy to me, a stranger, an employee of Mr. Healey."

The captain raised thick black eyebrows, which met above his nose, and glanced at Mr. Montrose, who nodded. "I never dismiss a man's intuitions," said the captain. He looked at the huge remaining crates. "It may be best to move at once, before midnight."

"Is that possible?"

"I will see. I will go on board again and watch the loading. My men are working very fast but perhaps I can induce them to work even faster." He paused. "Will you and Mr. Francis go to your quarters now, Mr. Montrose? They are comfortable, as you know."

"If you are going aboard again, Edmund, Mr. Francis and I will remain here until the last crate is loaded. I prefer to be easy in my mind. Too, I should like Mr. Francis to become familiar with our—operations."

The captain smiled, as always, saluted and walked with his easy and gliding rapidity to the end of the wharf and then up the ramp to the deck. Joseph, peculiarly sensitive to cold since his childhood, shivered, for the wind rushing in from sea and dock was becoming bitter this early spring evening. But Mr. Montrose smoked pleasantly and watched the men. He looked with interest at the monolithic remaining boxes and crates. "Cannon," he said. "This is a new invention of Barbour & Bouchard, far superior to conventional cannon. It is said they will kill twenty men to the others' five, and can bore through a yard-thick wall of bricks as easily as a knife through bread. Better still, the balls shatter very prettily, and each fragment is as deadly as a bayonet, sharp as a razor. I believe they stole the patent from their British colleague."

"Is the Union receiving the same cannon?" asked Joseph.

"Certainly, my dear Mr. Francis. That was a very naïve question. Munitions makers are the most impartial of men, the most neutral, the most undiscriminating. Their business is profits, and you must have learned by this time that profits are what make civilization possible. Not to mention the arts and the sciences, and amenable politicians."

He smiled at Joseph. "I am sure you have read of that German madman, Karl Marx, a bourgeois and an idealist —the bourgeoisie can afford to be idealists, not having to sweat for a living, they living on profits. Karl Marx is against profits, except for an élite elected by himself. As for others, he is violently against profits, alleging they are the source of exploitation and all human misery. I believe he is also against the industrial revolution, which freed men from the serfdom of powerful rural masters and the overweening aristocracy. But then, theorists like Karl Marx have tremendous respect for the aristocracy and inherited wealth. They are only against new wealth, out of industry. They, in their hearts, fear and despise the working class, no matter how they extol it, as does Karl Marx. The working class threatens such as Karl Marx, and when one is threatened one has a way of coming to terms with the threateners. It is very interesting. At any rate, Karl Marx would prohibit profits on anything. All would belong to the proletariat, he says. But in his heart he means the State, of which he and his kind would be the masters. What a tyranny that would be! He and the aristocracy, together!

"But, I digress. Remove profits and you remove incentive, and barbarism results. It is human nature to work for rewards. Even animals do so. Men are not angels. They will not, unless they are saints or insane, work for anything but their own advantage, and that is sensible. Without rewards the work of the world would come to an end. It is as simple as that. We would be individually grubbing for roots and berries and hunting raw meat, as once we did eons ago. If I were a lawmaker I would insist that every idealist, every lofty bourgeois, work with his hands at a desperate living, in field and mine and factory, before he even wrote a word or uttered one in 'behalf of mankind.'"

Joseph listened intently, now unaware of the activity

about him and the emptying wharf. Much of what he had just heard appeared to him eminently logical, and he could not deny the truth of it. But he said, "There are, though, inequities."

Mr. Montrose shook his head at him indulgently. "Mr. Francis, I never knew of a superior man, an intelligent man, who wanted for bread, and I say this despite the tales of artists in garrets and starveling geniuses. While they are indulging their art it surely would be sensible of them to work for a living also, at least for their daily sustenance."

Joseph thought of his father who had refused to work as a millwright in England, and so had permitted his family to suffer destitution. He had spoken of "right" and "principle." But only men who have independent means can indulge themselves in such nonsense. Men, thought Joseph, like Karl Marx.

He became aware that only two huge boxes remained, to his right, and that the wharf was empty but for himself and Mr. Montrose, and two workmen who were pushing dollies up the ramp. Mr. Montrose had wandered away. He was inspecting, with interest, the innocent proclamations on the crates, and their destination in Boston and in Philadelphia. He was hidden from the doors of the wharf, and smoking idly. Only Joseph was visible from the doors. The lanterns on the ship at the end of the wharf were dancing and hoarse faint calls came from the decks, at a considerable distance. The wind was keener, and the smells of the harbor more insistent. Joseph shivered again. His and Mr. Montrose's leather cases stood aside, near one of the crates, shining brownly in the shifting light, their fine brass locks gleaming like gold, incongruous in that rude open space and on the dirty floor.

He heard a sudden sharp sound of running feet outside, and then in the doorway appeared an Army lieutenant and three civilians, roughly dressed, with bestial faces. Mr. Montrose had heard also, and he thrust his head and half of his body beyond the boxes. Joseph saw that the lieutenant held a double barreled pistol in his gloved hand, and that the civilians held rifles. Joseph became as still and as rigid as stone as he saw three weapons directed at him, and one at the shoulder of Mr. Montrose. Murder had brightened, as if by a superior light, the faces of the lieutenant and his thugs, and every feature shone with an evil radiance.

The lieutenant, a young man with a fair complexion and with waves of golden hair under his cap, said in a clear and quiet voice: "We don't want any trouble. Quick, if you please. Step back from those cases with your arms raised, Mr. Montrose. We want the money in those cases." His air was compact and businesslike and he showed no nervousness.

"The money?" said Joseph, in a bewildered voice.

"No nonsense, please," said the lieutenant in his disciplined accents. "Colonel Braithwaite wants it at once. Your rooms were searched after you left to dine. There was no money case left behind. If you please, sir"—and he stared at Joseph—"kindly kick those cases towards me. We are not jesting. If you do not obey you are dead men."

He glanced swiftly at Mr. Montrose. He said, "Step back, Mr. Montrose, with your arms raised above your head. We know you are armed. But one movement to your pistol and it will be your last. Come, sir. Move quickly. We mean you no personal harm, but we want that money."

Mr. Montrose moved entirely from the shelter of the box with his arms raised. He looked at Joseph, the perfect example of the very young and confused man confronted with imminent violence. But he saw something else. Joseph's face had become hollow, like a skull, and inhumanly dangerous, and his small blue eyes had flattened. The lieutenant was not so perceptive.

"What of the cargo?" asked Mr. Montrose.

The lieutenant, as he was young, could not resist grinning maliciously. "You will not pass the patrols," he said. "We will, sir, take the clearances with us as well as the money."

"Colonel Braithwaite," said Mr. Montrose. It was evident that he was delaying in the hope the captain would appear, and reinforcements, and the lieutenant knew this at once. He laughed shortly. "Do not try to forestall me, please, Mr. Montrose. The colonel leaves for Philadelphia tomorrow. He has been transferred. The cases, sir," he said to Joseph. "The colonel will become impatient."

But the diversion had been enough. The lieutenant had hardly spoken when Joseph rapidly drew and fired his pistol. He had directed the weapon not at the body of the young soldier but precisely at his right thigh. He had fired with total deadliness and care, with not a single tremor or hesitancy, or even a thought.

Before the lieutenant had begun his shocked crumpling to the floor Joseph had swung on the civilians with their rifles and Mr. Montrose had found his pistol. It was evident, in an instant, that the men were aghast at the attack on their leader, that they had expected no resistance, and that they were not prepared to fight to the death. They turned as one man and fled into the night with their rifles. One even dropped his weapon in his flight. It struck the floor of the wharf at the instant the lieutenant dropped, his pistol flying from his hand and clanging and bouncing on the wood.

Chapter 20

Joseph's shot had raised thunderous and bounding echoes in the cavernous depths of the wharf, and the men at the top of the ramp had halted, looking back over their shoulders. They saw at once what had happened and they raced their vehicle into the ship and scattered like mice, shouting.

Captain Oglethorpe suddenly appeared on the ramp, and then he ran down it into the wharf, a black and avenging figure. He reached Mr. Montrose, and he exclaimed, "Clair! Are you hurt?"

"No, no, not in the least, Edmund," said Mr. Montrose and frowned slightly at the other man. "We were attacked by this gentleman here," and he indicated the fallen soldier with a delicate movement of his foot, "and Mr. Francis heroically disposed of him at once. A perfect shot. We were about to be robbed of our funds. Worse, we were about to be robbed of our clearances. Mr. Francis's intuitions were only too true."

He turned to Joseph, smiling calmly. Joseph still held his pistol. He stood over the groaning and bleeding and writhing lieutenant in silent menace. The swaying lantern light showed the soldier's white and sweating face, distorted with pain, and the blood that ran from his injured leg, and it showed his terror. His large blue eyes swiftly roved from face to face. He expected instant death, but he did not speak.

Captain Oglethorpe moved to Joseph's side. His face showed no anger or viciousness, but only interest. He said to Joseph, "Finish him off. We have no time to waste, I see."

A few men were cautiously filtering back into the wharf from the clipper, but they stood warily at a distance, watching and listening intently. Mr. Montrose pursed his lips and considered the groaning soldier. He said at last, "No. There are some questions to which I need the answers. Besides to kill him and leave him here would be, I am afraid, rather difficult to explain on our return, and now indeed we have no time to waste. The patrols may have already been alerted by the other robbers who accompanied our brave military friend. Take him into the ship, Edmund, and stanch his bleeding so he will not die before he has given us some necessary information."

The soldier lay, still writhing, but silent now. The sweat glistened on his face. He gritted his teeth. Death had passed him by, temporarily. But he could still feel its coldness in his flesh.

The captain looked at his distant men, whistled to them and waved his arm, and they came at once. He gave them their orders. They looked down incredulously at the soldier but made no comment. They lifted him, and he suddenly shrieked with agony, but they were indifferent and hurried with him to the ship. The three men on the wharf watched them go in silence. Joseph still held his pistol, and occasionally he glanced swiftly at the doors of the wharf.

"Let me congratulate you, Mr. Francis," said Mr. Montrose. "I could not even detect a movement on your part before you fired." He looked at Joseph consideringly and with a faint smile. "I take it that you did not intend to kill him?"

"No," said Joseph.

"May I ask why not?"

Joseph's face still retained its hollow gauntness, but he drew a deep breath. "I have no objection to killing, if it is necessary. I did not believe it necessary in this instance."

But Mr. Montrose, still smiling faintly, did not entirely believe him. He said, "A most remarkable shot. I could not have done half so well, nor could you, Edmund. It was admirable."

The captain was dissatisfied. "We could have killed him here, taken his body aboard and then dropped him into the sea. What information can you expect from him?"

Mr. Montrose said, "He called me by name. He mentioned Braithwaite, and the search of our rooms for the money. This was well-planned—by our friend. It was to be his last coup, for he is being transferred. Moreover, I suspect he did not love us, and plotted to betray us as well as rob us. No doubt he hoped we would be captured by the patrol or killed by them, beyond the harbor."

The captain nodded reluctantly. "That could well happen, without the clearances. We could, however, if captured, involve Braithwaite in our confessions."

"Be sure he had thought of that, and that is why I need to question our captive."

Joseph was thinking. He had, himself, felt the presence of death. He said, "I do not think that even if we had kept the clearances we would have sailed. That man intended to kill us after robbing us, so that we could not embroil the colonel."

Mr. Montrose considered this, then inclined his head. "That is probably true, Mr. Francis. He wished the clearances not so we would be captured by the patrol out of the harbor but just so there would be no evidence against our gallant colonel. It is well he had no trained soldiers with him, but only ruffians from the gutters of the city whom he could bribe. Had he shot one of us the others would have had the courage, then, to shoot me, and Edmund, but your amazing action, Mr. Francis, startled and frightened them and drove them to panic. Moreover, they had seen their leader fall, and without a leader such animals become mindless. It is well that the soldier was young and could not resist wasting time in baiting us. Otherwise we should now be dead."

In the meantime the final boxes and crates had disappeared with tremendous speed into the clipper. The wharf stood empty, the light was uncertain, and everywhere there were booming echoes. The three men walked quickly towards the ship. "We sail at once," said Edmund Oglethorpe. "We dare not wait until midnight." He looked with friendly curiosity at Joseph, and with some admiration. "I am honored, sir," he said, "to have you aboard my ship, for above all things I like brave men." He put his hand briefly on Joseph's shoulder. "I am grateful that you saved the life of Mr. Montrose, even more than my life."

Mr. Montrose smiled affectionately at the captain. "The soldier knew that when he fired at us it would draw your attention, if you were not already on the wharf, and that would have been the end of you also, Edmund. Still, it was an audacious and courageous thing for him to do, though he had probably watched and waited until we were alone. He was more brave, in this instance, than I suspect he would be on the battlefield. But then, money is a great inspirer."

"On our return, we shall find the colonel," said the captain, as they all walked up the wet and greasy ramp to the deck. He spoke with casualness and almost indifferently.

"Certainly," said Mr. Montrose. Joseph felt a chill touch on the back of his neck. Mr. Montrose continued: "Men like the colonel are not often found on the battlefield. They are much too clever and adroit, so he will not die in battle."

Captain Oglethorpe laughed. "But he will surely die, just the same." Joseph saw the flash of his white teeth in the semidarkness.

Joseph's cabin was small and austere but blessedly warm. One polished porthole stood over the narrow bunk with its clean brown blankets and striped cotton pillow. A lantern swayed gently from the immaculate varnished ceiling, and there was a chair and a low chest. The freshness of sea air and the aromatic odor of wax and soap filled the cabin. Joseph removed his coat and hung it on the wooden wall and placed his few belongings in the chest, and then, for the first time, he trembled.

He was disgusted with himself. He had shot a murderer, who had intended to kill him. Why, then, this girlish quivering? He had slept in Mr. Healey's office rooms with a gun in his hand, twice a month, for years, with the full intention of wounding or killing any robber who intruded. He had practiced to kill. Yet, at the supreme moment his resolve to kill had wavered and he had shot down the soldier instead. Had he thought it not necessary to kill? Was he feckless, a milksop, after all? As a child he had wanted to kill the English and had daydreamed about it. He had wanted to kill those who had truly murdered his mother. What was wrong with him now? If he were on a battlefield he would kill without a second thought. He had been taught: "Never raise a gun unless you intend to shoot, and never shoot unless you intend to kill." He had failed.

But still, in spite of his trembling and self-disgust, he was glad he had not murdered the soldier. This thought increased his revulsion against himself. He rubbed his hands over his face and shivered as he had shivered on the wharf. The next time, he thought, I won't hesitate a single minute. I might have cost us all our lives by my prudishness.

He sat on the edge of the bunk and wondered dismally if he had lost favor with Mr. Montrose and if he had made the one mistake which must be his last, but which would always be remembered against him. Still, Mr. Montrose had not seemed angry. However, he remained an enigma to Joseph, a more impenetrable enigma than ever. I will soon know, Joseph said glumly to himself.

He heard a great flapping far above him, the shouts of men, and then a sliding and swaying, and he knew that the ship was leaving the dock. He knelt on his bunk and looked through the glass. The ship was retreating with almost silent speed through the black water, and anchored masts and other vessels began to flow back. Now the clipper creaked and bowed and rolled a little, and there was the soft sighing of timbers under strain, and a splashing along the sleek hull. She was a fine ship, proud and fast, and Joseph felt he could feel her soul, intrepid and confident. He suddenly remembered the *Irish Queen*, and he recalled that as a child he had thought of her as an old but brave woman, tired, and determined, though longing for death or a safe harbor. This clipper disliked harbors. Joseph smiled reluctantly at his fancifulness, even though he knew that seamen believed that their beloved ships had a being of their own apart from the crew, apart from their owners.

It had been long years since he had last seen the sea and had last been upon a ship, and had last smelled the odors of salt water and tar and rope and wet wood and canvas. All at once he was sharp with memory, and for a few seconds his recollections overwhelmed him.

He compelled himself to look at his smooth, well-kept hands—though they still bore old calluses—and at his fine respectable clothing, and at his handmade boots of gleaming leather, and at his broad cravat with the discreet pearl pin and his cambric shirt. He felt his hair, smooth and no longer ragged. He stood up and went to the chest and looked at his belongings in it, and at the pocketbook which contained a handsome sum of money. He felt at his lean middle for the delicate gold chain which spanned it, and he took out his gold repeater watch and held it to his ear and made it chime its frail fairy notes. It was only half-past eleven, he thought. Now a resolute glow came to him. He was not rich. But he would be rich within the year! He clenched his fist. No more than a year.

Mr. Montrose sat with Captain Oglethorpe in the latter's warm cabin, and they sipped brandy.

"The news, Edmund," said Mr. Montrose. "I know you must go on deck almost immediately. But I must have the news."

"I sent a brave and trustworthy man up near Richmond," said the captain. His smiling lips smiled wider. "To our home, Kentville."

Mr. Montrose considered him. "That brave and trustworthy man was you, dear Edmund."

"Come to think of it, it was," said Edmund, with a vast air of surprise. "After all, I did not want to endanger one of my men, and I wanted no garbled accounts."

"You might have been caught, and killed, as a spy or something."

"I? Dear Clair! Who am I, but a humble returning seaman, a wanderer, a no-account and shiftless man, one who has drifted? One who had only returned from foreign parts recently and had heard only rumors of this war, and just wanted to see his kin again."

"A likely story," said Mr. Montrose. "But you are such a rascal that you probably could deceive General Sherman, himself. I take it you encountered no great difficulties with patrols or bands of Union soldiers, or military occupants?"

"A mite," said the captain. "It was a little chancy a few times, and it took longer than I expected. But I have been a seaman since I was twenty, as you know, and weather does not disturb me, and sleeping in burned houses and abandoned barns, or even in the open, is nothing to an experienced seaman. I haven't forgotten how to ride a horse, and there were horses here and there—"

"Which you stole," said Mr. Montrose.

The captain looked hurt. "To whom do those horses belong? To us or the damned Yankees who really stole them? God damn me if I don't hate them!"

"Did you have to kill very many?"

The captain looked bashful, and grinned. "A few," he admitted. "But what's a Yankee? I did it only when necessary—and when I needed ammunition, or a fresh horse. Your Dad said many times to me, when I was only an ornery young 'un, that a gentleman kills only when he is compelled to do so, and he told you that, too, and I have a great respect for your Dad, even if you never had. After all, he was my uncle, and my own Pa had died when I was small, and he took care of Mama and me and sent me to school, and if he talked too damned much and too piously all the time he had his virtues."

"A true Southern gentleman," said Mr. Montrose. "I know."

The captain looked pained. "You never had any respect for anybody, Clair. Not even for your dainty Mama. You were always a rogue, and you have the audacity to call me a rascal. At least I honored my elders and didn't mock them to their faces, as you did. And I went to church with them, of a Sunday, which you refused to do since you were a shaver of five. There was always something a little flighty about you."

Mr. Montrose nodded. "There's nothing to choose between us, Edmund. We have the same pirate blood, inherited through our saintly Mamas. And what ladies they were! I used to wonder if Mama ever shat. I am sure Daddy believed she did not. But, the news, Edmund, the news."

The captain refilled his glass. The ship was gathering speed and the lantern on the ceiling swayed. "Luane," said Edmund, "never received any of your letters except the first two."

"Daddy confiscated them."

"No," said Edmund. "It was your Mama. All for Luane's good, certainly. It distresses me to remember that you loved your Mama even less than you did your Daddy, and she such a fragile and lovely lady who never raised her voice not even to a slave. No, it was Mama, I regret to confess."

Mr. Montrose's feline face changed. He leaned forward. "You have seen Luane? Quick, you must tell me!"

The captain stared at him then said abruptly, "The Yanks burned down the house, where we both were born, and where your father was born. They burned the fields and the cotton. They drove off the cattle. What they could not take they destroyed—everything. Gardens, hen houses, horses, barns. There's only a chimney or two left, Clair. They burned down everything but the slave quarters. Now even the slaves are gone."

Mr. Montrose's eyes glowed like the eyes of a great cat. "Luane?"

"Luane stayed. She hid your mother in the woods and

when the Yankees went off she brought her into the slave quarters."

"Did they hurt Luane?"

"No. That's a right smart wench, Clair. They never found her. She hid with your mother—for a whole week. She knew what the Yankees did to the slave women, and how they shot the bucks and even the pickaninnies after they drank up your Dad's wine and whiskey. I heard the same stories all over Virginia. Can you imagine a Southerner shooting helpless folks, even black ones?"

"Yes, of course," said Mr. Montrose. "Not as readily as a Yankee, however." He sipped brandy. "You saw Luane."

"Yes. I hollered when I got there, and looked around. Sounded like I was calling the hogs. A mite distressed, you could say. And Luane came out of the slave quarters, and she recognized me and ran to me and shouted out, 'Master Clair! Tell me about Master Clair!' She was fitten to be tied, almost out of her mind. She took me by the arms and shook me and screamed your name over and over. I got right bothered by her hollering, wondering if Yankees were still around, and if you and I hadn't played with her when we were young 'uns together I might have fetched her one, just to shut her up. It was surely Luane, and she doesn't look a day over twenty, and she in her thirties at that."

He shook his head. "A fine wench, still, with those big gray eyes of hers, and a skin like new cream and a mouth —I used to think when I was a stripling—like a dark rose. I would dream at night of bedding her myself, but you got there first, Clair, and she only thirteen. I had dreams of murdering you," and the captain laughed and shook his head again. "Trouble was, your Dad was against white folks messing around with their slaves. He kept slaves, but to give him his due he never abused them, and respected them as human beings with those inalienable rights he was always quoting from the Declaration of Independence, though that proclamation somehow didn't mean he believed in freeing the slaves, or felt it had anything to do with the darkies. Contradictory. No mind, Clair. You will remember that when your Dad found out about you and Luane he carried on as if Luane was his precious only daughter and you a dirty ravisher who should be horsewhipped and hanged. Kind of a simple fellow, your Dad.

Luane was only a slave wench, and you were his only son. He almost had a seizure."

Mr. Montrose smiled unpleasantly. "Perhaps he remembered that Luane was his second cousin, daughter of his cousin, Will, who didn't hold anything against anyone who messed around with the darkies."

"Well, Cousin Will, your cousin Will, not mine, was purely white trash, Clair. Shiftless, no-account bastard. Never had anything but a grubby little farm, and not a slave to call his own. He had no right bedding down with Luane's Mammy, who was owned by your Dad. But he was a right handsome man, Cousin Will, and Luane has his eyes, and his nose, and her Mammy was a pretty wench, herself, a high-yeller as they call them. Luane could pass as white, anywhere."

"I suppose that is a compliment," said Mr. Montrose.

"I reckon it is, Clair, and don't you talk Yankee talk to me. I am a Southern gentleman, sir," and the captain laughed. "Well, I shut up Luane's mouth and so I got the news. Now, you must think kindly of your Dad. Before your son was born your Dad freed Luane, so her child was freeborn, and not a freedman. And now this will make you, I hope, feel even more kindly about your Dad. He loves that grandson of his. He put him in his will. Luane told me."

"I don't even know his name," said Mr. Montrose.

The captain threw back his head and laughed a high and whinnying laugh. "He gave your son his own name, by God! Charles!"

Mr. Montrose stared with numb incredulity and the captain laughed again and slapped his knees.

"Clair," he said, "trouble with you is that you are a very complex man and so how can anyone as stupid as a complex man understand the simpleminded, like your Dad? You think just about everybody has subtle thoughts and such, and is complicated himself. But your Dad's as simple as clean crick water and never had a thought in his head. Why, I knew that when I was six years old. But then I'm not a man of intellect like you, Clair. I could see things right out, but you were always looking for significant shadows and finding your own foolishness instead. Though you didn't think it was foolishness. You thought you were smart."

Mr. Montrose rubbed his fingers through his thick hair. The captain said, grinning wider than ever, "Your boy looks like Luane, though he's yellowheaded like you. Of course, everybody knew he was yours, but nobody ever dared to laugh at your Dad, except you. Not one of his friends would have dared even to smile behind his back. A right brave gentleman, your Dad, and he'd have killed a mocker. Besides, he is proud of the boy. More than he was ever proud of you, at that. Charles was his kin. He looks like a Devereaux, and Luane has Devereaux blood, too. Those folks are prouder than the Devil, himself."

Mr. Montrose was silent. His elegant features expressed nothing.

The captain refilled his cousin's glass, shaking his head as at a huge joke which only he could appreciate. "Luane told me about those two letters she had from you. You didn't know she had been freed. You sent her money. Now, how the hell did you think a darkie pregnant wench, though she looks white, only thirteen-fourteen years old, could run away from her home, and she a slave, and get up North? I tell you, Clair, you intellectual men are right feeble-minded most of the time. True, you weren't even nineteen, yourself, but you should have known better."

"I wrote her we could be married up North," said Mr. Montrose.

"And Luane's got better sense than you have, Clair."

When Mr. Montrose said nothing, the captain went on: "Yes, Luane's got sense. You're a Southerner born. She knew you'd remember that, some day, and that she had been a slave, with nigger blood. You'd remember you're a Devereaux."

"And Luane has Devereaux blood."

The captain smiled triumphantly. "Now there, you surely showed yourself, Clair. You used to laugh at the Devereaux, but they're right in you in spite of everything. Luane knew all about you. She still does. If I didn't know what I know about her I'd swear up and down that she was a lady-born, a high-born lady. There's another thing: She was always devoted to your Ma, especially after the baby was born. You never appreciated your Ma, either. Lady of principles, like your Dad, and better even than a Devereaux in spite of the pirate in the ancestry. Brought up Luane almost like her own kin, though she never showed her true feelings. Only Luane knew."

The captain looked at Mr. Montrose thoughtfully. He also glanced at his watch. "Clair, I'll make it short. Your Ma died, in the slave quarters, with Luane caring for her like a loving daughter, two months ago. Luane wouldn't leave her, not for a minute. And when your Ma was dead Luane dug her grave for her, at the end of what was once the gardens, and wrapped her in one of her own shawls, and mourned her like a daughter." He paused. "Aunt Elinor was a lady, a fine lady, like her sister, my Mama, even if she wasn't any smarter than your Dad. You never could forgive fools, Clair, and yet fools often have dignity."

"What of Luane? How is she living?"

"She's still living in the slave quarters. I gave her money. I brought four hundred dollars with me. I told her you sent it. I said you wanted her to come North, any way she could, and join you. That girl said, 'Tell Master Clair that here's my country and here's my people, and I will never leave them. But I send him my love, and when this war is over I pray he'll come home and live on his own land again.' And she's setting up a garden, and is right thankful for the money and she'll buy a cow or two and horses. You owe me four hundred damn Yankee dollars."

Mr. Montrose rubbed his forehead and bent his head and stared at the floor. "Where is my son?" he asked.

The captain laughed even louder than before. "Your Dad, Clair, is a colonel in the Army of the Confederacy, and where the hell he is now I don't know. But he took your son with him as his personal aide, and I reckon no one in that man's army knows that the boy has any nigger blood in him at all. Luane told him, but I hear he told her, his own Ma, that it was of no account and that God didn't look at a man's color but only at his soul. Luane's right smart and knows better, and I reckon she thinks your boy is as big a fool as his granddad, and don't have any more sense." He stood up. "That Luane's a lady, and a proud lady, and has a high spirit, and she's waiting for you, which I don't think is very clever of her."

He put his hand on Mr. Montrose's shoulder and shook him as if rallying him. "This goddam war won't last forever, Clair. Go back to your own land and your own people. Go back to Luane."

"I can never marry her in Virginia," said Mr. Montrose as if to himself.

"Hell, what's marrying? The wench is waiting for you. If

I had a wench like that waiting for me, damned if I wouldn't go to her even through the whole damned Union Army. I thought I told you: Luane's proud, too. After all, she's a Devereaux even if from the wrong side of the blankets." He pushed Mr. Montrose's shoulder.

"Now, what do we do with the bastard in the brig?"

Mr. Montrose stood up. He looked absent and a little dazed. He said, after a moment, "I will talk with him now. And I want young Francis with me. He's been blooded, as my Dad used to say, after he pushed a bleeding foxtail in my face. I want him to hear what is said."

He looked at his cousin. "Thank you, Edmund. That is all I can say. Thank you." And he held out his hand. He smiled. "You're only an Oglethorpe, but I reckon I admire you."

"Go to hell," said the captain, and laughed his high laugh.

Chapter 21

"You don't dare kill me, an officer of the Union Army," said the young lieutenant. He had sustained only a flesh wound, though a serious one, and had been expertly attended by a trained man on the ship. He lay on the cot in the brig and stared derisively in the lantern light at Mr. Montrose, who sat on the only chair, and then at Joseph, who stood near him with his pistol in his hand.

"You may be due for an unpleasant surprise," said Mr. Montrose with amiability. "Just because the gentleman near you did not kill you does not mean that we shall hesitate now when we are at sea. It was only expediency which preserved your life and made us bring you aboard. Do not try my patience, Mr. ——?"

The soldier spat at him. Joseph aimed the pistol at his temple, and the soldier shrank. He looked up at Joseph's face and saw the hollow danger of it and the flat small eyes and contracted mouth. "You don't dare," he repeated, but it was a trembling question.

"I am losing patience," said Mr. Montrose. "You have heard our questions. Answer them immediately or, sir, you will die before another minute has passed. If you are candid with us we may spare your life. If not, you will be dead and in the sea, as soon as we have passed the patrols."

The soldier was a young man, a very young man, and now he became hysterical both with pain and fear. He began to speak in a rushing and gasping voice. It was almost as Joseph had speculated. Colonel Braithwaite had ordered him to hire ruffians of the city and then, at the right moment, to rob Mr. Montrose on the wharf, take the clearances, and then murder Mr. Montrose, the captain, and Joseph. After that he was to notify the port authorities that he had heard shots, had investigated, and found the three bodies. He was not to go near the ship, but "run for my life," and call for help. The cargo would then be confiscated, after investigation, and the matter closed and labeled "treason." The clipper would also have been confiscated by the government.

In this manner the amenable Colonel Braithwaite would have his huge sum of money before his transfer to Philadelphia, and a malicious man's revenge, over which he would gloat.

Joseph said, "But why 'revenge?' What had our employer, or ourselves, done to him to make him our enemy?"

Mr. Montrose looked at him with immense and unaffected surprise, and seeing this at one quick glance Joseph felt jejune yet confused. "My dear Mr. Francis," the older man gently protested. "Have you not learned as yet that it is not always necessary to injure a man to incur his enmity? In truth, the majority of enemies are made by no effort on a man's part. They are made through envy and malice and the incurable evil which lives in a man's spirit, which makes him by nature the enemy of his fellows, without a single provocation. My deadliest enemy was a man I believed was my best friend, on whom I had conferred favors and disinterested kindnesses, and unsolicited gifts." He reflected, smiling. "I have come to believe that those are provocations enough, and deserving of enmity."

The young soldier, whose face was slimy with sweat and very pale, listened with closed eyes. Mr. Montrose prodded him with a light finger. "But perhaps Colonel Braithwaite had another reason for betraying us."

It appeared he had. The lieutenant was to tell authorities that Colonel Braithwaite's suspicions had been aroused concerning the *Isabel*, and had sent his subordinate to investigate at the last hour. Colonel Braithwaite would maintain that he had given no clearances to the ship, in the event both copies had been found, or if not found that he had been deceived by "tratiors" and gun-runners, and finally becoming uneasy had ordered another investigation. For his perspicacity and prompt action he would be soundly rewarded by the government, and advanced to brigadier general at the least.

Mr. Montrose listened to this without any emotion at all, but Joseph was sickened, and seeing this Mr. Montrose faintly shook his head and smiled. "You will observe that men do not stay bought, Mr. Francis. They need constant bribes, and not only of money, to remain your friends. A bigger reward, a bigger bribe, was open to Colonel Braithwaite, and so he accepted it. Had he not been transferred to Philadelphia but had remained here as port military authority, we could have continued to do business with him."

He said to the soldier, "Aside from the fact that the colonel was your superior officer and gave your orders, how did he suborn you?"

"Two thousand dollars, part of the reward, and the colonel's recommendation that I be made captain." The young man spoke in a dim voice, overcome with pain. He added, "He is also my mother's brother."

Mr. Montrose nodded. "So, he was comparatively safe from blackmail in the future, and bound you with his own perfidy and crimes."

He turned now to Joseph and said, "What do you now suggest, Mr. Francis?"

Joseph's heart gave a great sick leap, and he was silent. The gun was suddenly wet in his hand.

"You promised not to kill me!" cried the soldier and opened his eyes, young blue and terrified eyes large and starting in their sockets.

"I gave you no such promise," said Mr. Montrose. "Well, Mr. Francis? I leave the conclusion in your hands."

Joseph's throat and mouth were as dry as hot stone. He said to Mr. Montrose, "I think I have a more just punishment." He did not know that there was a sound of pleading in his voice. "When we arrive in Virginia his wound will be almost healed. He is in the uniform of a Union officer. We will put him ashore and let him fend for himself."

Mr. Montrose laughed aloud with frank delight. "Excellent!" he exclaimed. "Let him elucidate to our friends in Virginia how a Union officer came to be among them suddenly, in uniform. He will be seized at once for a spy, or if he attempts to explain he will be greeted with happy laughter, and it will seem a mighty joke to our friends. If he is not hanged he will be imprisoned. If he is later rescued by his compatriots, he will not dare to explain to them, nor to mention Colonel Braithwaite. I should love to be present when he tries to rationalize his presence alone in that part of unconquered Virginia, to my people, or when he tries to justify himself to his own friends."

He touched Joseph on the arm. "I greatly admire a man of ingenuity and not merely of force, Mr. Francis."

"You might as well kill me now and have done with it,"

said the soldier in a miserable voice. Mr. Montrose surveyed him kindly. "Young sir, if I were your age I would accept any alternative to death. As you are a thief and a willing murderer, you may go far after all, if your life is spared. So, it is spared. Under other circumstances I would recommend you highly to Mr. Healey."

They heard shouts above and hurrying feet and the captain opened the barred door. "We are being challenged by a patrol boat," he said.

This had happened before and was routine, as the patrols occasionally challenged ships leaving the harbor and examined clearances. The captain looked at the soldier. "Good God," he said, "is he still alive? Now we can't dispose of him before the patrols have released us, and we dare not shoot. Mr. Montrose, you have been careless."

"I think not," said Mr. Montrose. He stood up and fastidiously brushed a cheroot ash from his coat. "We shall leave Mr. Francis with our friend here, with orders to kill if he even opens his mouth. I suggest strangling or smothering, so no sound is heard. You understand, Mr. Francis?"

"Yes," said Joseph, and now his voice was resolute. The soldier had been granted mercy. If he violated that mercy he would die. Joseph doubted that he would prefer execution to life.

The captain dimmed the light of the lantern in the cell, looked searchingly at Joseph, then accompanied Mr. Montrose outside. The door clanged shut and was locked. Joseph sat down in the chair and looked at the soldier. "I will surely kill you if you make a single sound or as much as lift your hand," he said.

There was no porthole in the cell, but Joseph could actually feel the large dark presence of the patrol boat near at hand. He heard the clipper being boarded and the voices of naval men of authority. The clipper had come to a standstill. He and the soldier waited in absolute silence. The soldier had fixed his eyes with fear on Joseph, understanding that this time Joseph would kill him no matter the consequences, and with his bare hands, if he even whispered. The soldier wanted to cry. It had all seemed such a profitable adventure, though dangerous, as explained by his uncle. Money, advancement, honor. Now he was helpless. He suppressed a whimper, and listened acutely to the voices above. He had only one hope: that the authorities would search the ship as sometimes they did. In that event

Joseph would not dare combine murder with high treason. Let the authorities merely approach this cell and he, Joshua Temple, would make a final effort, throw himself on Joseph, and shout, before the other man could kill him.

So the two young men sat or lay in utter quiet, listening intently. No one descended the stairs. No one approached the cell. The soldier lay with clenched fists, looking only at Joseph, waiting, almost praying. Long minutes passed. Then there was laughter, hoarse jesting voices, the sound of a dinghy leaving the clipper, the weighing of anchors, calls of farewell. The soldier became limp. Joseph relaxed a little. The clipper began to move, sighing, gently groaning in her timbers, swaying, the wind thunderous in her sails as they spread themselves under the moon.

Mr. Montrose entered the cell. "We are underway again," he said. "Now, Mr. Francis, we shall have a light supper with the captain, then retire to bed."

The soldier said as he tried to keep from weeping, "Dirty foul traitors!"

The journey took six days for a storm came up which almost wrecked the *Isabel* and made even the stout captain apprehensive. The *Isabel* was overloaded; there was danger of her foundering in blackish green waves which Joseph found unbelievable, so tremendous they were. Mr. Montrose at one point suggested jettisoning some of the cargo but the captain said, "No." He grinned. "I'd rather jettison some of my men."

"You are an incurable romanticist," said Mr. Montrose. "In spite of everything I fear you are devoted to the Confederacy."

The captain's eyes glinted. "There are worse devotions," he said and Mr. Montrose laughed. "I won't repeat that to Mr. Healey who has no devotions to anything but profits."

They landed in hushed darkness at night in a little deserted bay. The keel of the *Isabel* barely escaped coming to rest on a reef under the shallowing water. Everything was silent and seemingly without life when the *Isabel* dropped anchor, but at the very instant the dock, unlighted except for starlight and stormy moonlight, came alive with silent men who, with the help of men aboard, swiftly unloaded her contraband. No one spoke except when absolutely necessary, and then frequently in whispers. Everyone was pressed into service, including the captain, Mr. Montrose, and Joseph. Only the lookouts held their posts, surveying everything through swinging binoculars. The transaction took several hours. Joseph could see only dark figures and sometimes a featureless oval of a face. He felt the unbearable haste and tension, and labored until he was soaking with sweat. The night was humidly hot and breathless and threatening. Lightning sometimes flashed in the black clouds that raced across the moon, hiding and then revealing her. Thunder rumbled. There were brief and drenching showers and the deck became slippery.

For the second time Joseph was aware of war and its impingement on him. He did not find this occasion exciting, though he guessed that many of these reckless men found it so. He also felt that they were dedicated patriots and this seemed absurd to him. They worked and risked their lives, not for profits, but for their beloved Confederacy.

Nothing much of the countryside beyond the rickety dock could be seen, but sometimes the moon revealed a far black emptiness unlit by any lamp or lantern. If people lived in the vicinity their presence was unseen. But Joseph felt a watchfulness in the darkness, an alertness.

At the last Joshua Temple, unspeaking, white-faced, was put ashore. He could walk now, limping. Joseph saw him being forced down the ramp and he heard subdued laughter. At the foot of the ramp and on the dock, the soldier looked back despairingly, but was rudely pushed. He disappeared into the night.

Finally the ramp was pulled aboard, the doors locked. The *Isabel* raised anchor, and silently drifted out to sea, nimble and dancing, her sails filled with moonlight. Joseph experienced a sense of enormous relief, which disgusted him. As if he understood Mr. Montrose said, "There are men who love danger for itself and could not live without it, and search for it. And there are men who do not love danger, but will face it as bravely as the other. I do not know, in all honesty, which I prefer, but if it came to the question of my life I would choose the men who do not seek danger though they will not run from it."

He laughed a little. "I fear I am of the first persuasion, and not the second."

On their return to New York they went to the Fifth Avenue Hotel, and it seemed to Joseph that the near past had

not happened at all. Shortly after their return Mr. Montrose requested his presence at the meeting with the bankers.

Joseph was impressed by their strange anonymity. (He
understood he was not to question or speak, but only to listen.) He heard foreign accents, though all spoke in English
to Mr. Montrose. It was impossible to distinguish among
them, to catch any peculiarity of temperament, or dissent,
eccentricity, or even of individual character. They were
gentlemen, courtly and genial and of the most elaborate
manners, marvelously reserved and polite and attentive,
never disagreeing, never raising a voice. They carried documents and ledgers with them in tooled cases, and drank
wine around the large table in Mr. Montrose's apartment.
When they spoke it was in calm and dispassionate accents,
almost disembodied. There was no emotion, no rancor, no
protest.

Some were Russians, some French, some English, some
German, and others of various races not explained. There
was even a Chinese, and a Japanese, all impeccable and
deferential to each other. It was like a majestic minuet to
Joseph, danced to the clinking music of cold money, and
executed with precision, no eyes brightening or dimming,
no voice lifted in a joke or in mirth. It was business, and
none of them had allegiances or attachments or involvements with any nation, not even their own. It would have
been unseemly to them to have betrayed any human heat
or personal entanglement. It was possible that most of them
were husbands and fathers and sons, but none ever showed
an absent eye or spoke of anything pertaining to his intimate self. Joseph immediately called them "the gray and
deadly men," and did not know why he detested them, or
why he found them the most dangerous of all among the
human species. He noticed that none of them drank whiskey and drank only sparingly of wine. They might have
mutual and intricate business to transact with each other,
but it was most evident to Joseph that none trusted the others.

They talked only of money, the greatest of powers, the
most pragmatic of common denominators. No eye lighted
with humor or friendship or intimacy. It was accepted that
all other things besides money and the power of money
were outside the consideration of intelligent men, and all
the affairs of the world beyond money were trivia to be
considered only in leisure and with urbane and indulgent

smiles, as one entertains himself with the prattle of women or a light and agreeable concerto after dining.

They discussed the War between the States and referred to their notes and documents, as if the death and blood and agony of a fratricidal war—planned long before in London for profit—was only a business maneuver. There were diagrams of profit displayed for when the South was conquered and rich land seized by the North. There was a brief discussion of the movement of industry to the South after the conclusion of the war and the lower wages probable. An Englishman mentioned that England would not be uninterested in the division of land, and that England was heavily invested in the South, and the English bankers would insist on the return of a great interest on the money lent the Confederacy for armaments. The other bankers nodded solemnly. It was only fair, of course. A Russian mentioned, with a cold sharpness in his eye—very ill-bred—that as the North had been protected from England by the Russian Navy the Czar would be distressed if his investments in the North were not given first consideration. A German later spoke of a possible war between Germany and France. "We have investments in Alsace, and the French are not as industrious as the Germans." Two Frenchmen smiled faintly. "We are as intelligent, if perhaps not as industrious, Herr Schultz. But, alas, our countrymen prefer to enjoy life as well as profits." This, for the first time, evoked slight and quickly suppressed murmurs of amusement.

"I think," said one gentleman, "that we can, hopefully, consider the tenets of Karl Marx, who is now in England, in the reorganization of profitable political forces in Germany. We are not unaware of Bismarck. I believe we can manipulate him. Moreover, the Emperor in France— and I honor His Majesty—has been reported to be impressed by the theories of Marx. I have no doubt, therefore, that some—disagreement—can be stimulated between Germany and France in the near future. I am due in London and Berlin and Paris very shortly, and this will all be discussed to the utmost."

An Englishman cleared his throat. "We should prefer that the European press no longer express indignation against Her Majesty, Empress of India."

He was immediately reassured, without any retreat from

neutral accents, that this would be attended to as soon as possible, and the press "informed" in Europe.

Mr. Montrose said, with a deferential inclination of his head to his colleagues, "The United States of America is a new country and not warlike, and this war is not to her liking—"

"My dear Mr. Montrose," said one of the gentlemen, "do you not agree that it is time for your country to embark on empire and become part of the universal monetary plans?"

"Not immediately," said Mr. Montrose. "You must remember that we are mainly, still, an agricultural nation and not an industrial one. Agricultural nations do not engage in wars or disputes to any extent, nor are they particularly interest in the banking business. America is wide and open and we have not as yet fully explored our territory and it may be decades before we can induce the American people to become enthusiastic for wars for profits. The Constitution is also a hindrance. Only Congress can declare war, and Americans are a very recalcitrant people and have suspicion of government, and look on the State with a watchful eye."

"Then, it is the duty of informed men to introduce the theories of Karl Marx into America," said one gentleman. "It is ridiculous that your Washington should be so weak, and government so decentralized, and power left to the individual states. Centralized power, as you know, Mr. Montrose, is the only guarantee of profits and controlled wars, and prosperity. We cannot be too much in haste to introduce the theories and mandates of Karl Marx. Those theories destroy the concept of anything but the centralized power of the State. Once power is concentrated in Washington—admittedly not an immediate prospect—America will take her place as an empire and calculate and instigate wars, for the advantage of all concerned. We all know, from long experience, that progress depends on war."

Did these men, thought Joseph, have anything to do with the conflict between Ireland and England? and a sick coldness spread through him.

"I fear," said Mr. Montrose, "that you will not find Mr. Lincoln very amenable to even the subtlest suggestions after this war."

"Then Mr. Lincoln must be—eliminated," said a gentleman in a cool voice.

Mr. Montrose looked slowly from face to face. "Politicians in Washington have informed Mr. Healey that it is Mr. Lincoln's intention to heal the wounds of this war, to assist the South to recover, to reconcile neighbor with neighbor, to extend the hand of affection to the enemy, and to unite the nation again."

"That is absurd," said one gentleman. "There is too much rich treasure in land and city in the South to allow it to fall again into irresponsible hands. Certainly, your country, sir, will be politically united again, but it is to our interests to keep her spiritually divided, and the animosity between North and South quite alive. That is the only way we can be certain of our profits, otherwise, there might be conjecture—"

"And a comparing of notes," said Mr. Montrose with a most serious face.

The others frowned at him for what they considered levity. "We must not only receive our loans from both North and South," said one, "but the accumulated large interest on those loans. Is it necessary for us to continue to repeat this, sir? These were honorable loans, given in good faith, by us. There are also other agreements which must be honored. If Mr. Lincoln disagrees—he may live, or not live— to regret it."

"He loathes bankers," said another gentleman, in a voice such as a man uses when discussing a revolting and despicable person. "Who does he imagine is financing his war?"

"And financing the Confederacy," said Mr. Montrose with a beautiful smile.

Many cleared their throats as though Mr. Montrose had uttered an embarrassing obscenity. Many appeared to be avoiding a lewd and improper sight, for they discreetly lowered their stony eyelids. To Joseph's surprise Mr. Montrose winked at him over the heads of the bankers, for Joseph was sitting at a quiet distance. That wink partially calmed the hatred and anger and confused turmoil in the young man's mind. The world, again, had briefly intruded upon him and again he had the strength to reject it. Mr. Montrose had found the world preposterous, any involvement in it idiocy, except for profits.

The hours went by and Joseph was witness to incredible conspiracies against mankind, all discussed in voices like the grating of bloodless metal, and at last he thought, An honorable man might sometimes be impelled, in this world, as Aristotle said, to kill himself. I am glad that I am not an honorable man, nor a fool, which is the same thing.

Imperial Russia was mentioned. It was agreed that Russia was not as yet ripe for great wars nor the introduction of Marxist theories which would divide her people. She was especially not ready for revolution, "for," as one gentleman said, "it is impossible to induce revolution in a country where the majority of the populace is poor and only recently released from serfdom. We all know that it takes a certain affluence in a nation, a certain sense of well-being, a certain leisure and idleness and comfort, to be sympathetic to revolution. Intellectuals cannot flourish nor be heard in a nation which is desperately striving to feed itself. They can only flourish and advance theories in a nation with a considerable amount of prosperity, where the main interest of the people is not mere bodily survival, and where discontent and envy can be stimulated. Moreover, the very temperament of the Slavic peoples is averse to the Marxist dogma, unlike Great Britain, France, and Germany, and also the United States. It will take long subversion and I do not think that many of us here will be alive to see it. No, the immediate question now is Bismarck in Germany, and the growing enmity between Germany and France. The situation is extremely interesting."

There was a brief mention of munitions makers all over the world, which Joseph could not entirely follow, but he gathered that the men in this room, and their colleagues, were advancing enormous loans and calculating profits and interest. He thought of Mr. Healey, who was surely not rich enough nor powerful enough to engage these men's attention, and it deeply puzzled him.

Later he questioned Mr. Montrose about this. Mr. Montrose did not reply at once. He lit a cheroot and sipped a little brandy, now that he and Joseph were alone, and then he said, "This was all intended to be relayed to Mr. Healey, not for his own use directly, but for the information of politicians. Mr. Healey owns many politicians. Not only Senator Hennessey, who is one of the most powerful and persuasive, but others. Would it not be dangerous for these men to be seen in the company of the international bankers? There are always inflammatory men, especially among the press, who distrust all government, which is perspicacious of them.

"You will recall a discussion today concerning the dissatisfaction the gentlemen feel for our absurd Constitutional Amendment that only Congress has the power to coin money. They are now trying to influence our government to permit a private Federal Reserve System to coin and issue and control currency, without the consent of Congress or any other governmental agency. What do you think is the purpose of that?"

Joseph shook his head and Mr. Montrose laughed.

"Congress, alone, has the power to declare wars. But wars need financing. It is entirely too risky for the bankers to finance a divided nation, like ours, in a war when Congress guards the public purse and chooses when to coin money. So long as Congress has this power America can not truly engage in important wars. And, if she decides to engage in wars for profit in the future—as all wars are only for profit—she will find herself curbed by Congress and its power not to finance a war. It would be most frustrating, and balk prosperity. So, we must first remove the power of Congress to coin and regulate currency, and give it into private hands which will, in turn, be controlled by international gentlemen such as you have seen today."

Joseph thought about this, his auburn brows pulled together. He said, "Then history is conspiratorial?"

"I believe," said Mr. Montrose, "that it was Mr. Disraeli who mentioned that the man who does not believe in the conspiratorial nature of history is a dunce. He should surely know."

Joseph bent his russet head and thought and Mr. Montrose watched him, far more acutely than the situation appeared to deserve. He watched the play of tightening emotions on that young face, and then the rejection of those emotions. It seemed to him that visible to his eyes only was the powerful corrupting process of a mind and possibly a soul. He pursed his lips as if in a soundless whistle and poured a little more brandy for himself.

Then Joseph said, "Why did Mr. Healey want me to hear all this, without any preparation over a number of years?"

When Mr. Montrose did not reply Joseph looked up at him sharply. He saw that Mr. Montrose was regarding him with a closed and strange expression, partly skeptical, partly affronted, and partly cold. This surprised him. He continued to meet Mr. Montrose's eyes and his own became more and more puzzled. Mr. Montrose finally looked aside.

Why should I believe, even for a moment, that he has the faintest suspicion? he asked himself.

He said, "I never question Mr. Healey's motives, and I advise you to refrain also. He has his reasons. It is sufficient for us to follow them." He felt a vague shame, an emotion long unfamiliar to him, and when he laughed aloud Joseph was both offended and increasingly puzzled.

Chapter 22

"So," said Mr. Montrose to Mr. Healey, "he is not only absolutely brave and ruthless, but is prudent, too. He won't run to danger or recklessness, but he won't avoid them when necessary. I have come to have a great affection for young Joseph Francis Xavier Armagh, and I think you are justified, sir. He can be trusted."

Mr. Healey sat expansively in his study and smoked deeply on his cigar. "I never make a mistake," he said, with happy self-satisfaction. "Minute I saw him on that train I kind of knew. Well, he's coming to see me on a matter of importance, he says. Got in last night from Pittsburgh, and I think he took a trip to Philadelphia, too. So, it all depends—"

Mr. Healey waited for Joseph's appearance, and when the young man entered the study, soberly dressed in black almost to the point of being funereal, Mr. Healey saw that he carried with him a roll of blueprints. Mr. Healey unaccountably sighed, as if in immense relief. "Sit down, sit down, Joseph Francis What!" he exclaimed. "Happy to see you home, boyo. Got good reports about you, too. Handled it well, though you're still a little rough around the edges. Takes time. Sit down, sit down. Brandy? Whiskey?"

"No, Mr. Healey," said Joseph and let his tall lean figure stiffly down into a chair opposite his employer. He was so pale and tense that his freckles seemed to protrude from his high-boned face. "I don't like spirits, as you know."

"Now, that's the only thing I don't like about you, Joe. Never trust a man who don't drink, is my motto. He ain't human. He don't intend, usually, to work with you. In a way, it's kind of an enmity, and for an Irisher it's unnatural."

Joseph smiled whitely. "I haven't time," he said. "When I have time I will drink, perhaps. But I've seen what the

304

poteen does to the Irish, too many times. I don't know why it is, but it is disastrous to them."

"Not to me, it ain't," said Mr. Healey. "If a man can't control himself it's his bad luck, and he don't deserve any sympathy. Some says the drink lets them escape the misery of this here world for a while, and that's good. But when they keep escaping that's the end of 'em. It's up to a man, himself. Well, what is all this?"

For Joseph had laid the blueprints on the desk, though he kept his hand on the roll. He looked at Mr. Healey with a fierce concentration, and he became paler. It was all very well to tell yourself, he thought, that you must have courage—when you are not face to face with the actual situation—but it is quite another when that situation confronts you. In five minutes or so he would either be booted out permanently, or Mr. Healey would understand. Joseph was not too optimistic. He had frequently told himself that he was a fool to consider Mr. Healey, and that he, himself, was a milksop and a weakling and a man of no real resolution and fortitude, willing to gamble everything.

He said, never taking his eyes from Mr. Healey's red face, "First of all, sir, I went to Philadelphia before coming home. I have heard rumors for a long time that the oil in the southern part of the state, just being drilled, is far superior to the oil of Titusville, for it is so far under ground that it is partially refined, and naturally. So, I invested in options." He smiled slightly. "And in consequence I am not exactly solvent any longer."

Mr. Healey nodded. "I heard those rumors, too. Only a couple of wells drilled. A thousand feet or more, sometimes. I didn't invest." He smiled rosily at Joseph. "Should I?"

Joseph hesitated. "I don't know, sir. It's all speculation. You surely have better information than I have."

" 'Course I do," Mr. Healey waved a fat red hand. "But you invested without information, eh?"

Joseph looked at the table. He said, "Mr. Healey, I have to be rich very soon."

"Not something to be ashamed of," said Mr. Healey. "You got your reasons, I reckon. But you should have asked me for advice. Ain't always right to put all your chips on one number. Well, that's for the young, and you're young. Kind of a reckless boyo, ain't you?"

"Necessity sometimes makes a man reckless," said Joseph, and again Mr. Healey nodded. "Happened to me many times," he said. "Sometimes being too damned prudent can cost you all your cakes."

Joseph looked up sharply. Mr. Healey chuckled. "Oh, Mr. Montrose told me all about it. Thought you did the right thing. I don't believe in murder, either, unless it's absolutely necessary. You can get a bad reputation that way, killing," said Mr. Healey, with virtue.

Joseph, without warning, felt an hysterical urge to burst out into wild laughter, but he restrained it. His small blue eyes glinted and sparkled under his auburn brows and Mr. Healey chuckled in appreciation. He said, "Well, so you're bankrupt. You ain't here to ask for a loan again, are you, Irish?"

"No," said Joseph. He looked down at the roll again under his hand. "I don't think it's important, sir, but you don't know my full name."

Mr. Healey shifted his fat bulk in his chair. "I always knew I didn't. Want to tell me what it is?"

"Joseph Francis Xavier Armagh."

This was the first dangerous step. Joseph waited for Mr. Healey to frown, to lean forward, to glower. But to his astonishment Mr. Healey merely leaned back in his creaking chair, blew out a cloud of smoke, and said, "Right sound name, I'm thinking."

"It doesn't matter, sir?"

"Now, boyo, why should it? Do you think for a minute Mr. Montrose is Mr. Montrose? You got better sense than that. You knew all the time the men who work for me don't use their real monikers. Why should I hold it against you that you didn't tell, either?"

"You always seemed to want to know," said Joseph, baffled. The palms of his hands were wet.

"Oh, just curiosity. But you don't go around satisfying curiosity, Joe, without getting yourself in a mighty peck of trouble. Don't tell anybody anything, unless it's necessary, and think on it first."

"I thought this was necessary," said Joseph. "You see, I had to give my full name—on these—and I thought you ought to know."

"Got something to show me?" Mr. Healey leaned forward again with an air of great interest.

Now even Joseph's mouth was deathly pale. "Yes. But first let me explain, sir. I've been watching the wells and the drilling all these years, and the donkey engines, and the wood-burning. And it came to me that as kerosene burns why shouldn't it be burned for fuel, and not just for lamps. I'm not a mechanic, sir, nor an inventor. But I talked it over with Harry Zeff, and he was interested. We went out into the country once, with some kerosene in a pot and we set it afire and we put a pan over the pot and it became steam almost as soon as it boiled."

"No great discovery, that," said Mr. Healey in a tone of indulgence. "The lads at the wells do that all the time."

"But no one has thought of firing engines with it, sir. Any engines, not only donkey engines." He remembered what he had thought then. He had become dizzy with his thoughts. "Kerosene steam engines for industry. It could be used in place of coal and wood. Harry knows a great deal about machinery, now. He helped me draw some rudimentary sketches. I took them to Pittsburgh." He looked at Mr. Healey, but Mr. Healey waited in inscrutable patience, his hands folded across his belly.

"Well," said Joseph, "I found someone there who could put my ideas' and my sketches into patentable order. And I patented it, and it was accepted." His heart was pounding heavily and now there was a painful pulsing in his head. He could not read Mr. Healey's attentive face. "There were other patents, I discovered, along the same lines, but mine was the simplest and the cheapest." He was finding it hard to breathe. Damn him, he thought of Mr. Healey, why doesn't he say something?

Mr. Healey waited, watching the young man's white and haggard face. "Well," he said at last, "go on."

"Last autumn I met, out in the fields, Mr. Jason Handell, the rich oil man who is contending with Rockefeller for the control of the oil industry in Pennsylvania. He owns all the options, well and refineries next to the Park farm, which was sold for only fifty thousand dollars to Jonathan Watson, William F. Hansell, Standish Hanell, Mr. Keen, and Mr. Gillett and Henry E. Rood, who organized their own oil company. Mr. Handell owns just about as much of the land and options and wells in lower Pennsylvania as does Mr. Rockefeller. Mr. Handell's first and only interest is oil, Mr. Healey. He has no other interests and he has a very large oil company."

"So you showed him your patent?" Mr. Healey was most affable.

Joseph's tight face trembled a little. "I did, sir. As I have said, his only interest is oil and the exploitation of oil, and he is a very rich man—"

"Richer than I am," Mr. Healey agreed amiably.

"I—I thought so, sir. And he has the facilities to put inventions into use, as you do not. In fact, inventions utilizing oil are of great interest to him. He—invited me to go to Pittsburgh to discuss—things—more fully with him. I did." Joseph bent his head. He continued. "He told me that it is not as yet feasible to use my patent, as there is a war and the patent must be tested in the field. But he wanted to buy my patent. I said no. If Mr. Handell was truly interested in it, and wanted to buy the patent, it was probably worth much more to me than fifteen thousand dollars for all the rights."

"A right smart sum," said Mr. Healey. "Maybe you should have taken it."

Joseph said, and he was a little less pale now, "No, sir. Mr. Handell wouldn't have given me his time and made me that offer if the patent was worth little or nothing, or was only conjectural. Incidentally, I learned that he did test it, though he never told me, and it was not only workable but heated steam far faster and more efficiently than either wood or coal."

"Who told you that?" said Mr. Healey with bland interest.

Joseph shook his head. "The man who drew up the blueprints for me. I gave him one hundred dollars for the information."

"You should have given him more than that, Joe."

"I intend to, sir. In the future." Joseph paused. He was amazed. Mr. Healey seemed quite at ease and only mildly interested and very calm, an attitude which could only have been termed paternal.

"Mr. Handell," said Joseph, "was the one who suggested I invest in a pipeline for the transportation of oil, which will be built after the war. I did. I am," said Joseph with a wan smile, "pretty well up to my neck in investments, now."

"Handell kind of favors you, eh, Joe?"

Joseph, who was inwardly trembling, considered this. "No," he said at last, "I don't think Mr. Handell favors anybody, sir. They say he is as hard and ruthless, if not more so, as Mr. Rockefeller. Nothing except for a profit.

At any rate, part of the digging for the pipeline is already under way, and the rights are really owned by Samuel Van Syckel of Titusville. But he didn't have all the money he needed. Mr. Handell is lending him the money. It will run to Pithole."

Mr. Healey yawned. "Yes, Irish, I know. I'm invested in it, too. I'm going to build the pumping stations. Got the rights to those pieces of land. Handell's tough. Don't know how you handled him."

"I didn't," said Joseph.

Mr. Healey sat up. "No?" he exclaimed. "He got the better of you, Joe?"

"Not exactly, sir. We were at a stalemate. When he agreed to pay me royalties for my kerosene-driven engine —he says it couldn't be put to practical use at once—I told him when he issued shares he must give you the option of buying at least one-third at the private price. Of the subsidiary which will manufacture and sell the engine."

Mr. Healey's little dark eyes became protuberant. "Irish! what the hell—Did he throw you out and the blueprints with you?"

"No," said Joseph. "I believe you know Mr. Handell, sir. He isn't an impetuous man. He just laughed at me, and asked me why."

"Well, well. Why, Joe? Why consider me at all?"

Joseph looked aside at the gleaming paneled walls. He took a long time to answer and during that pause Mr. Healey began to pass his hand over and over his mouth.

"I—I tried, sir, to forget. What you did for me and for Harry. You took us in when we had nowhere to go. You— you've treated me honestly and decently, sir." Joseph stared at Mr. Healey with a kind of hopeless despair. "I don't know! I just had to do it! Perhaps I'm a fool, but I couldn't go on with it, unless—"

A silence fell in the study and Joseph sat on the edge of his chair, trembling.

Mr. Healey took out his handkerchief. He blew his nose. "Damn this smoke," he said. He put away the handkerchief, and resumed smoking. He studied Joseph.

"Know something, Irish," he said at last, "you sure are a fool. You worked for me honest and square and so don't owe me anything. You repaid me hundreds of times, with your loyalty. I could trust you. So why this, Irish, why this?"

Joseph clasped his hands together on the desk so tightly that the knuckles whitened. He stared down at them. "I haven't an explanation, sir, except that I had to do it." He was freshly amazed. "And I don't know why, either, Mr. Healey, no more than you do!"

"Thought you'd be cheating me, or something, if you didn't?"

Joseph reflected on this. "Yes. I believe that is it. Though it wouldn't be cheating, truly. Say, perhaps, it might have been gratitude—"

"Nothing wrong with gratitude, Irish."

Joseph looked up quickly. "You don't mind, sir, that I didn't tell you at once?"

"Now, let's be reasonable, Joe. It was all up in the air. I'm not in the oil business except for investments and such. Just one of my interests. You got the best man for yourself. But when it came down firm you told me. Well, go on. That's not all of it, is it?"

"No," said Joseph. "Mr. Handell told me to think about it. The one-third, he said, was ridiculous. Besides, I had put in for Harry, too. After all, Harry in a way gave me the original idea— It was a remark he made two years ago, out in the field. So, I thought about it. Then"—and Joseph colored—"I wrote to Mr. Rockefeller. He asked me to come to meet him. I had told him about Mr. Handell's offer and interest—"

"Good," said Mr. Healey. "Play one rascal against another, but watch they don't cuddle up together against you. And then you wrote Mr. Handell that Mr. Rockefeller was interested."

"Yes. So, on this trip I went to Mr. Handell again and told him to make up his mind at once."

"You told Jason Handell that, right to his face, right in his own big offices?" Mr. Healey's face danced with enjoyment and pleasure. "Wonder he didn't kick you out! He's got a mean cold temper."

"He didn't kick me out. He just told me I was an inexperienced, gullible, contemptible, ridiculous greenhorn."

"And you stuck to your guns."

"That I did, Mr. Healey."

Mr. Healey leaned back and laughed aloud. "Trouble with Handell, he ain't Irish. Don't understand how mad we are, I'm thinking. Crazy as loons. Now, he's a man with a mind that don't do anything but churn out dollars. And you just a spalpeen, a young Irisher. I'd like to have seen his face, that I would!"

"It wasn't very pleasant," said Joseph. All his tensed muscles were relaxing. He felt dazed, feeble, but oddly exhilarated, as if delivered from devastating peril.

"I bet it wasn't," said Mr. Healey. "So, how is it now?"

"He will let you buy one-third of the shares at the inside price. And I will give Harry one quarter of my royalties."

Mr. Healey shook his head over and over, as if marveling, as if incredulous. He gazed at Joseph as though at a miracle he did not accept, and could not accept.

Joseph unrolled the blueprints and extracted a sheaf of papers from them. "Here is the agreement I have with Mr. Handell," he said. "We fought over every paragraph."

Mr. Healey accepted the sheaf of papers and read them slowly. Then he put them down. He said, "Sometimes, Irish, I wonder if you got good sense. And then I read this, and I see the sly Irish hand in every line. Tied him up, proper, as the Sassenagh would say. Must be something to that patent of yours. When's he going to pay you anything on it? Got to be a binder, you know."

Joseph let out a long breath. "I said I wouldn't cash his cheque for five thousand dollars until you had looked over the contract and approved of it."

"You've got the cheque?"

"Right here, sir," and Joseph reached into the inside pocket of his coat and pulled out his pocketbook. He gave a slip of paper to Mr. Healey, who pretended to scrutinize it. The warm spring sunlight flowed into the study and Joseph watched Mr. Healey's face and could not read it. He was only conscious of relief, weakening and almost paralyzing relief.

Mr. Healey returned the cheque. He studied Joseph. "What if I'd kicked you out, Joe, after what you told me?"

"I'd have been sorry, sir. But I wouldn't have starved. Mr. Handell offered me a position with him, in Pittsburgh."

"At twice your present salary, eh?"

"Yes."

"And you refused. Joe, you keep me off my feet. One minute I think you're bright and the next I think you're stupid. Can't make up my mind."

"What would you have done, Mr. Healey?" and Joseph smiled for the first time.

Mr. Healey put up two fat defensive palms. Then he dropped them slowly.

"That ain't a question I'm going to answer, Irish," he said.

He put a hand across his desk. "But let's shake on it, Joe. And you cash that cheque and buy your options, and more. No, sir, I'm not going to answer that question of yours. No use thinking back in your life. You just got to go ahead."

He stood up. "Best you get to work." He looked at his watch. "Got to call on Jim Spaulding. All right, Irish. I don't say you're very smart, but sometimes there's better things than being smart. I reckon."

As Joseph went to the door Mr. Healey said, "What do you mean, you'd have been sorry if I'd kicked you out?"

Joseph put his hand on the door, then looked over his shoulder. "I don't know, sir," he answered, and left. Mr. Healey smiled as the door closed and began to hum under his breath.

Mr. James Spaulding sat back in his office chair and regarded Mr. Healey with a plastic face, full of emotional expression—for effect—combining consternation, stupefaction, and absolute stunned amazement. Not all of it was hypocritical.

"Ed," he said, in a low and musical and shaking voice, "you must have lost your wits. I refuse to execute this document until you have had time to consider, to reflect, to judge whether or not you have been under evil coercion and influence—"

"The only evil coercion and influence, Jim, that ever bothers me comes from politicians—and lawyers. Now, don't look as though I stuck a knife in you. You know we know each other too well for foolishness."

"Forgive me!" sang Mr. Spaulding, on the verge of tears. "But, his youth! His inexperience, his—his—I am not impressed!"

He glanced down at the document with loathing, as if it held smelly filth. He let his hands visibly tremble. Mr. Healey was highly amused. "Come on, Jim," he said. "This ain't the op'ry house or a minstrel show. Save the theatrics for the judges and the juries. I know you up and down, as you think you know me. Read that there paper over again, and see what's in it for you, too."

Mr. Spaulding reread a portion. He seemed about to cry.

Mr. Healey chuckled. The two men looked at each other, cynical, without illusion, yet with sardonic affection. Mr. Spaulding then put on an expression of solemn and almost religious dedication, and Mr. Healey kindly refrained from laughing.

"Very well, Ed, if this is what you want I can only respect your wishes." Mr. Spaulding put his hand on the document as if about to swear an oath, and as if the document were the Bible. In truth, he respected it far more.

Chapter 23

Miss Emmy had not been shipped to Senator Hennessey after all. The senator had discreetly refused her, for he had in some subtle way engaged the regard of Mr. Lincoln for his support of the war. He had gone to the President, all candor and concern, and had offered all his wealth and his devotion, and the beset Mr. Lincoln, surrounded by subversion and disaffection, forgot his usual skepticism concerning politicians and had pathetically accepted the powerful senator's offer of friendship and service. It was not his first error, nor was it to be his last. He had regarded the senator's overtures as the mark of a reluctantly persuaded man, for the senator was not of his party but of the conservative Democratic coalition. "I know," he said to the senator, "that you regard us Whigs, or Republicans, as wild radicals and dangerous innovators, and your confession that we are not touches my heart."

"I have my reservations concerning your social radicalism, your Excellency," Tom had confessed with magnanimous splendor, "but in these Dangerous Days are we not all Americans, and must we not all trust our government?"

"My social radicalism, as you call it, Senator," said Mr. Lincoln with wryness, "is only an attempt to overcome certain inequities in the social order, and is also founded on the hope that this war will result not only in our progress and recognition as a Nation, but in national amity, justice, compassion and peace among brothers."

What a damned fool, thought the senator, as he soberly nodded. If such an idiot as he can become President who can not?

"We have no reason to fear each other, North or South," said the President sadly. "We have only to fear our enemies abroad, who wish us to be destroyed. Yet, I believe that no alien will ever drink of our free waters nor tread on our

314

free land. If we are betrayed, we shall be betrayed from within—at the seduction of our foreign enemies."*

So Miss Emmy remained at home in Titusville and Mr. Healey was not displeased. His fondness for the young woman had increased for as the years had advanced so had his desire for variety in women decreased. Miss Emmy, to him, was simultaneously his wife and his daughter. She was a fond habit. He was weary of changes. He had had enough in his youth and early manhood. Now Miss Emmy was to him the favorite cushion for his head, the silent custodian for his shy secret thoughts, the breast of his comfort. He had mentioned her in his will.

Miss Emmy was shrewd and knowing. But her urgent desire for Joseph Armagh had not abated at all. His continued refusal to see her as a delectable and complaisant young woman enraged her. It also insulted her. Did that Irish nobody regard her as beneath him, he with all his pretensions? She would waylay him in the upper and lower halls, languishing, swinging her satin and embroidered hoops, letting him glimpse the expanse of her white breast, beguiling him with her tossed curls and ringlets, coming close to him so he could smell her perfumes—she wafted scented kerchiefs in his face—and dropping her long-lashed eyes at him and then opening them suddenly so he could see their brilliance fixed upon him. She smiled; she sighed; she pined and grieved eloquently when they were alone. She fluttered fans at him and looked archly over their tops. Joseph treated her with cold courtesy, slipped by her, and left her. He would not engage in conversation with her except at the table and in the company of Mr. Healey. While all this was not entirely loyalty it was truly indifference. He thought Miss Emmy a vulgar trollop, and her airs ridiculous, considering who and what she was.

He also could not forget Katherine Hennessey. Never deliberately did he remember her. But he could not forget her tender and beautiful face, her entrancing eyes, her devotion and self-sacrifice, and her exhausted collapse at the concert after probably weeks of attending the wounded and dying. There had been something about her which remained stubbornly in his mind, resisting all his efforts to reject. Perhaps it had been her simplicity, her ardor, her shining-eyed courage, which had reminded him of his mother.

* Actual words of Mr. Lincoln.

He hated himself for remembering. He forced himself to work harder so as to forget. He hated Senator Hennessey for a number of reasons beyond his brutal sensuality, his cruel hypocrisy, his politician's shameless exigency, his greed and grossness. He hated him because he was Katherine Hennessey's husband, and because as a husband he had betrayed her over and over, and had contempt for her. Mr. Healey had laughingly informed Joseph of the senator's tireless exploits with women, and his reputation as a womanizer. He had used his wife's money, as well as his father's, to advance himself, yet, said Mr. Healey with regret, he treated Katherine as if she were a slut and not truly worthy of his respect and consideration. However, he always called her to his side to be photographed with her, the very image of the adoring husband, the family man, the loving father. She always obeyed. She loved him.

For that, sometimes, Joseph despised her. Such a woman surely knew what her husband was. That she permitted him to display himself to her in all his arrogant viciousness was something Joseph could not understand. Was she one of those who enjoyed humiliation, cruelty, assaults on self-respect, brutality? If so, then she was mad and not worthy of anyone's concern or affection. Love, surely, must be turned to hatred by neglect and abuse. That is what Joseph thought, in his youth. He was yet to learn that love endures all things, blindly, helplessly, and cannot help itself. He did not understand even when his most desperate efforts to forget Katherine were always defeated. The sick passion of his love for her tainted everything in his life, and he could not rid himself of it. He saw her face in every carriage, though she was in Washington. He had heard her voice years ago, but he heard it now in every other woman's voice. It had become a shadowy nightmare to him, and he was appalled that he no longer had entire control over his own will and thoughts.

Miss Emmy, the trollop and the drab, held no interest for him. To Joseph, she was a parody of Katherine Hennessey, even if he frequently visited the brothels from which she had come. Her airs and her graces made him loathe her, though they grimly amused him. Sometimes her fine eyes reminded him of Katherine, and he wanted to strike her for this blasphemy. Miss Emmy would see, then, his fierce concentrated look, and thought that it was only, after all, his shyness and his regard for his employer which restrained him. She watched for an opportunity to help him overcome such delicacies.

Haroun Zieff had become Mr. Healey's overseer in the oil fields which he owned, and so Harry no longer slept over the stables but occupied the room he had originally occupied years ago as a waif. But his occupation was not regular. His work often compelled him to remain in or near the fields at night, when a well was ready for "blowing." For the danger and responsibility Mr. Healey paid him thirty-five dollars a week, and a jocular bonus when a well "came in." ("Maybe the old boy thinks I can pray them in," Harry once remarked to Joseph, laughing.)

Joseph had to wait several impatient days before Harry returned from his tours to tell him that all was well, that their employer had not thrown him, Joseph, out, and that everything had been arranged amicably. The two young men sat in Harry's room—the green room—and congratulated each other. Harry had taken up cheroots, which Joseph found annoying, and he had become strong and stocky with a man's muscular and active body, though his dark face was still boyishly impish and his black eyes still glittered with mischief and good nature. Joseph suddenly said, "Now, I know why I thought Captain Oglethorpe looked a little familiar. You and he resemble each other. You're both brigands."

Harry had listened to Joseph's account of the attack on the wharf—though he had not disclosed exactly why he had been there at all with Mr. Montrose. It had been vaguely referred to as a "shipment," but Harry's eyes had sparkled with mirth though the rest of his face remained serious. "You should have killed the bastard," he said.

"Would you have killed the—man, Harry?"

"Of course," said the younger man, as if the question was absurd. "He was going to kill all of you, wasn't he? Isn't your life as good as his own? Or did you think he was more valuable?"

"I'll remember that, the next time."

"Remember that, now," said Harry and now his eyes no longer smiled. "I've found out something: man is a violent animal, no matter what the pure-in-heart say, and nothing will ever change him. I hope not. I've been reading your Darwin. A species that can't fight and protect itself is killed off fast by nature. The old boys in the Bible did a lot of killing in their 'holy' wars, and didn't God once admit to being the God of Battles? Remember that song we're all singing: 'Battle Hymn of the Republic'? Damn me, if it isn't the goriest hymn I ever heard! And all 'to make men free,' it says piously. But all the time it means killing. A man's got to kill when he has to, Joe."

Joseph stood up. "I suppose you're right," he said, and thought of the desperate struggle between the men of his blood and the English, and he thought of his father who would not have killed even to protect his wife and children.

He heard a faint rustling outside the door and smiled a little. Mrs. Murray, the massive troll, was listening again outside the door for any morsel she could gather to be relayed, if important, to Mr. Healey. Her malignance against Joseph had not decreased in these years, but had grown, and was as unrelenting and as sleepless as all evil. Joseph never once had wondered why, for he knew that hatred and enmity and malice are often founded on nothing at all but rise of themselves like sharp stones in a field. He had brought himself to the point where he sometimes teased the woman, suddenly stealing to doors, and throwing them open in her fat and fishlike face. It gave him pleasure to see her furtiveness and hear her flustered mutter that she was "just passing." But she was more wary now. When he flung open the door he could see just the hurrying shadow of her down the hall. It was an early summer evening and the lights had not been lit as yet upstairs, though they fluttered below. Mr. Healey was in his study. Dinner was over. The new warmth of the year, and his growing burden of work, was tiring Joseph. He hesitated after he had closed Harry's door. Mr. Healey, these days, liked him to visit him briefly in the evenings before bedtime, in the study. They talked business, but most of the time they merely sat in genial silence while Mr. Healey studied Joseph and Joseph made a few notes for the next day. He had brought himself, lately, to endure brandy, and even a little whiskey, remembering Mr. Healey's observation. But he was never to like them and always mistrusted them.

He decided to visit the man who had made so much possible for him, and had given him the only lasting kindness of his life. Joseph disliked the gratitude he felt for what Mr. Healey had done, reminding himself that he had given due service in kind. Gratitude involved a man with another man, and that weakened him. But lately it had come to him that Mr. Healey was lonely, as all men are lonely. So he went towards the staircase, yawning a little.

Mr. Healey's bedroom door opened and Miss Emmy appeared on the threshold. The two young people looked at each other. Joseph stepped back, instinctively, and Miss Emmy was obviously startled to see him so close to the door. She stared at him in the warm dusky light, which flowed upwards from below, and suddenly her face flushed and an overpowering emotion ran over it. Never had Joseph appeared to her so desirable, so strong, so virile, so young as she was young, and so full of health and vitality. She stepped impulsively across the threshold, her pale laces and ribbons and satin robe flowing about her, her mass of bright hair curiously agitated, and she flung her arms about his neck, and before he could even lift his hand she had kissed his lips and then pressed her head against his chest, murmuring deeply and wantonly in her smooth throat.

She had not planned her seduction like this, with not only Mrs. Murray in the house, but Bill Strickland in the kitchen, Harry in his room, and Mr. Healey in his study. She had not given danger a single thought, though she was naturally cautious. Joseph's unexpected appearance, the strength of his face so suddenly close to her, the sleek russet gleaming of his thick hair, and his lean figure, had overcome her prudence. She had no plan of drawing him into a room. But her hunger for him, and her desire, and even what love she could feel for anyone, had made her move without a thought, without an inner warning. She clung to him. He had stiffened. He raised his hands to her round arms and grasped them and tried to push her from him, but she clung tighter, and with a kind of uncontrolled passion, rolling her head on his chest. Her heavy perfume sickened him. He said nothing, though she continued to murmur, her breath sometimes hot on his throat, her eyes glimmering up at him like the eyes of a loving and devoted dog.

He felt nothing but disgust and contempt. The heat of her young body, the smoothness of her flesh, her urgent lips, her scent, the brush of her loosened hair against his hands, revolted him. He did not want to hurt her and so stopped himself from hurling her backwards into the room, but more than anything else he was angered that she should want to betray the man who doted on her and had protected her for many years. But at last he knew that he had to do something. He dared not speak for fear of arousing

Mr. Healey below and having him open the study door to see what could clearly be seen at the head of the staircase. He could only thrust. He was amazed at her feverish strength, at the power of her desire, at the avidity of her clutching. He caught her wrists which were crossed behind his neck, and as he did so he felt an iron grasp on his shoulder.

Miss Emmy uttered a faint cry and fell back from Joseph, throwing a hand against her mouth. For Bill Strickland, who had come up from the kitchen by way of the back staircase, had seized Joseph in a hating and gloating grasp, and was now whirling him about to face him, one gigantic fist raised to smash into his face. His own face, never completely human, was distorted with rage and satisfaction and his intention to kill or at least terribly maim. It was the face of a wild animal. The eyes glowed in the semidarkness. A monstrous joy made them flicker, for now this young man, this usurper, this enemy of Master Healey, this contemptuous evader of glances, was in his hands and he meant to destroy him once and for all. Mrs. Murray, over the years, had convinced the mindless creature that Joseph had "his plots" against Mr. Healey, and at the end, some day, he would rob and injure him. And so he had. He was trying to steal Miss Emmy from the Master, and Miss Emmy was Mr. Healey's property, and so Joseph, the hated and suspected, was a thief and a robber.

Joseph was younger but not near as strong as Bill Strickland. He was more lithe, and quicker. He averted his head just as the murderous fist lashed at his face, and the blow passed his ear with a whistling sound and the great clenched hand crashed loudly into the wall. At that instant Joseph freed himself and stepped back. None, not even the paralyzed Miss Emmy, saw Mrs. Murray's head rising from the back staircase, nor the opening of Harry's door.

Joseph's first thought, a prudent one, was to run either back to his room and try to lock the door against this madman, or race down the stairs to the study and the protection of Mr. Healey, for he was not foolhardy and he knew he was no physical match for this enraged and raging beast who had killed many times before, and who surely meant to kill him. But Bill was quicker now. He had whined softly in his throat as his fist had crashed into the wall. However, the pain made him wilder and more terrible. He was on Jo-

seph in an instant, his hands reaching for the young man's
throat. His thumbs sank into Joseph's flesh, and Joseph felt
his breath stopped and the agony of his almost crushed
windpipe. He flailed out, beating his attacker on the
shoulders with his fists, and Bill whined again with ecstatic
delight and pressed Joseph closer to the wall, his blood lust
making him lick his lips.

I am murdered, thought Joseph, as flecks of bloody light
and stars sparkled before him and he struggled to breathe.
Darkness began to close in about him. He felt his body
collapsing, sinking, his knees buckling. Then, just as he
fell to the floor the dreadful pressure on his throat was
released, and his head swam in mingled dusk and shadow.
He knelt there, gasping, clawing at his throat, heaving great
breaths of air, groaning. He did not see Miss Emmy, numb
and stunned, standing in her doorway, nor the figure of
Mrs. Murray, elatedly watching from a distance. He was
concerned only with living.

Then he heard muffled but violent movement. He could
raise his head now and dimly see. And he saw an astonishing sight. He saw the huge figure of Bill Strickland staggering dangerously close to the stairway, and perched on his
back and beating him like a savage monkey—small in comparison with the giant—was Harry Zeff. He rode Bill
Strickland like a jockey, his curly head rising above the
other man's, his sturdy fists rising and falling on face, nose,
ear, forehead, his fingers sometimes clutching a feature and
wrenching it, and sometimes tearing at handfuls of hair.

Joseph pushed himself to his feet, and leaned against the
wall, and watched, incredulous. Strickland tried to free
himself from his torturing and antic burden, whose legs
were wrapped agilely around his trunklike waist. Blood
streamed down Bill's face. He actually danced. Harry
leaned down and bit him savagely in the side of his neck.
That drove Bill to greater madness. He reached behind
him, seized Harry's short legs, tore the youth from his body
and hurled him to the floor. He then raised an immense
boot to kick him in the side of the head.

Joseph forgot his own weakness, the gasping of his
breath, his trembling legs and shaking body. He was on Bill
in an instant. He caught him by the neck just as the foot
came down and smashed harmlessly beside Harry's shrinking head. He had pulled the brute at the very instant before

he could have brought his foot down on Harry, and so Bill
was off balance, and stumbling, with Joseph facing him,
and Joseph still holding him desperately.

Now Bill Strickland's back faced the long stairway and
his heels teetered on the edge of the first step downwards.
He rocked a little, tried to grasp Joseph not only to take
him but to save himself. It was then, for the first time in his
life, that Joseph felt the absolute desire to kill, to demolish,
to destroy, another man, and it was like a sweet if frightful
exultation in him. Kill or be killed! something sang in his
ear. Pure instinct made him loosen Bill for an instant then
pound his fists against the other's broad chest. He punched
with all his strength, with all his desire, evading the grasp-
ing hands of the other man. He kicked at the big knee.
Bill's arms now began to describe great pinwheels in the
empty air. He was fast losing all balance that remained to
him.

Then he uttered a loud hoarse roar of terror. Joseph
pressed him harder. He kicked again. The wheeling arms
became frantic. And then the large heavy body tilted backwards and downwards, lifted into the air as if bouncing,
then fell to the stairs, raised again, bounced, rolled down
the final stairs and crashed with a thunderous sound to the
floor below, the legs and arms sprawling, the head broken.

The study door was flung open, and light gushed into the
hall, and Mr. Healey appeared, a cigar in his hand. "What
the hell!" he shouted. "What is going on here!" He paused,
and saw Bill Strickland silent and bleeding not far from
him on the floor. "Bill!" he shouted. He came into the hall,
walking slowly and carefully, disbelieving, and he stared
down at the obviously dead man from whose lips there was
trickling a thin red stream. "By God," he said, in a soft,
hushed voice. "Jaysus. Bill." He stood there for several
stunned seconds.

Then he looked up. He saw Joseph standing there, gasping, and Harry Zeff, holding Joseph's arm like a younger
brother. He saw Joseph clutching the bannister, his head
bent. But their eyes met in silence. A door softly closed.
Miss Emmy had retreated.

"Did you push him, Joe?" asked Mr. Healey, not loudly,
not accusingly.

"Yes," said Joseph, and his voice was hoarse and ragged.

It was at that moment that Mrs. Murray appeared behind Joseph, and she screamed down at her employer. "Mr.

Healey! This ragamuffin was ahugging and kissing Miss Emmy and trying to pull her into your own bedroom! Your own bedroom, Mister! And Bill here tried to stop him and he threw him down the stairs and murdered him!"

"Is that so?" said Mr. Healey, still in that soft and half-wondering tone. He looked down at the dead man, studying him as if he had never seen him before. Then, ponderously, he began to walk up the stairs, looking again at Joseph's face, looking at him directly, never wavering. He mounted steadily, without haste, without a quickening of breath, and watched only Joseph, who stepped back a little to give him room at the top.

"Now, tell me," he said. Then he glanced at the door and raised his voice a little. "Miss Emmy! You come right out here, fast as you can! Hear me?"

The door opened very reluctantly, and Miss Emmy, white with fright and fear, stood on the threshold, quaking, her hands against her mouth, her eyes fixed on Mr. Healey, dilated and wide. He gave her only a quick look, and turned to Joseph again and repeated: "Now, tell me."

"I told you, sir!" shrieked Mrs. Murray, raising fists as if to pummel Joseph's bent back, for he was spent and had to cling to the bannister, and his head had dropped. "He tried to take Miss Emmy, there, back in your room, dragging her, kind of, and Bill—"

It was Harry who interrupted her frenzied cries. He said to Mr. Healey, "That's a lie, sir. Joe had just left me. Then I wanted to tell him something, and followed him into the hall. And we both saw that man of yours there, that Bill, attacking Miss Emmy and trying to drag her back into her bedroom. Joe jumped him. But Joe isn't that strong, so I jumped Bill, too, right on his back." He held out his blood-stained fingers for Mr. Healey to see. "But he got me, though. He pulled me off his back and tried to stomp me while I lay on the floor, and Joe caught him again and pushed him away, and he went right for Joe's throat—you can see the marks for yourself—and Joe shoved him. And he fell down the stairs. All by himself."

The elfish face was earnest and absolutely sincere, but Mr. Healey was not quite deceived. He was still watching Joseph. "Is it true, son?" he asked.

Joseph said, without lifting his head, "It is true, sir."

"Lies! Liars!" cried Mrs. Murray. "He been after Miss Emmy for a long time! I saw it, myself. He thought he saw his chance tonight, and with you, sir, right down there, in your own house, and he not having any shame nor caring what you done for him, and trying to take your woman and robbing you, and when poor Bill tried to stop him he killed him! I saw it with my own eyes, my own eyes, my—"

"Shut up," said Mr. Healey, with gentleness. He looked at Miss Emmy. "Honey," he said, "who is telling the truth?"

The girl wet her white lips. Her eyes looked hunted. Her glance fled to Mrs. Murray, her gloating enemy, then to Joseph, and then to Harry, and finally back to Mr. Healey who was waiting courteously for her answer. She was an astute girl. Let Mr. Healey suspect for an instant that she had waylaid Joseph and that would be the end of her, for if she agreed with Mrs. Murray the young men would tell the truth. She knew enough by this time of the affection Mr. Healey had for Joseph, and his trust in him, and she did not doubt that he would take Joseph's word before hers, and Mrs. Murray's. There was also Harry, and he was looking at her in a most peculiar and threatening way, his eyes glinting in the half-light, his teeth shining a little between his parted lips.

Miss Emmy shrank. She whimpered. She pushed back her disordered hair. She looked at Mr. Healey. "Mr. Zeff told the truth," she said in a failing little voice. "Bill—he's always been staring at me and I knew he—I always kept away from him. But I—I thought I'd go downstairs and talk to you. I was lonesome. And when I came into the hall, there Bill was, and he put his arms around me and tried to—he tried to drag me back into the room, and he kissed me—" She put her hands over her eyes and sobbed sincerely, and sincerely shuddered.

"Lies! You are all liars!" screamed Mrs. Murray, beside herself with frustration and hate and rage. "Miss Emmy, you stand there and tell Mr. Healey them lies, and you know they're lies, and you know it was this—this man here —who tried to take you, and not poor Bill, who tried to protect you and got killed for it!"

"Shut up," said Mr. Healey in an absent voice. "Now, there's three against one, Miz Murray. Miss Emmy, Joe here, and Harry, and they all tell the same story. What do you think the law would say to that, ma'am? My woman, Joe, and Harry? Everybody knows what I thought about

Bill, and how he kind of lived for me, and they'd know I wouldn't protect his murderer, now, would I?"

"I saw it, I saw it!" Mrs. Murray screeched. "They're all lying! They're all thieves and robbers and killers! And they'll kill you, too, Mr. Healey, one of these days!" She flung herself in the direction of Miss Emmy. "Why don't you tell the truth, you little whore, you no-account little bitch!"

Miss Emmy was staring at Joseph. He was protecting her. He was saving her from what he guessed would probably happen to her if the truth was spoken. Tears gushed into her eyes. She exclaimed to Joseph, "Oh, Mr. Francis, thank you, thank you!"

Mr. Healey made a humming sound. "Well, I reckon that settles it. I got to thinking, lately, that Bill wasn't in good mind. Kind of loco, as they say. Acted up some, sometimes. Well. He was like a brother to me, kind of like a good watchdog. Would've given his life for me. But probably not for anybody else. He must have gone off his head, not thinking, tonight. Poor Bill." He sighed.

Then he swung suddenly to Miss Emmy, and she shrank back. "I always said, and I say it now, that no man, 'cept he's crazy, makes up to a woman unless she's given him encouragement, one way or another, flirting maybe, just out of conceit, not meaning anything, but being just a female." At that he lifted his fat hand and struck Miss Emmy calmly but heavily across the face. "And Bill wasn't all that crazy. He'd been encouraged, and I hope that's all."

But while he spoke he watched Joseph, who had lifted his head. He saw no emotion, no protest, on Joseph's face, but only a faint contemptuous indifference, and he knew all of the truth.

Miss Emmy had fallen against her half-shut door, and had staggered backwards into the room. Recovering herself, she flung herself on the bed and wept. Mr. Healey watched her through the open door, and he sighed. "Damned little bitch," he said. "But reckon there's no real harm in her. Got to remember she's only a woman. Weak vessels, like it says in the Holy Book."

He turned to Mrs. Murray, who had dumbly watched the blow. "Miz Murray," he said, in the kindest voice, "I reckon you'll have to tell the truth, and no prejudice, as the law says. I know you don't like Joe, here. Never did. But that's no call to slander him and try to get him arrested. Miz Murray, I sort of remember Pittsburgh. You remember, too?"

The woman looked at him with sudden stark terror, and she moved back a little. "I got a real good memory, I'm thinking," said Mr. Healey. "Never forget a thing. Now you, Harry, you go for Sheriff Blackwell. He's a real good true friend of mine, and he won't make no fuss. Tell him what happened, and come back with him, and we'll all talk quiet like, with each other. Miss Emmy, too. And you, Miz Murray. Nice and quiet. Keep it in the family. And we'll give poor Bill, down there, a right nice funeral, no expense spared. Poor Bill. Must've lost his head, not thinking, not that he ever really thought. Let him rest in peace. I don't hold no grudge against him."

He nodded to Joseph. "Joe, the marks on your throat are right convincing. Show them to the sheriff."

Joseph's pale lips parted as if he would speak, but Mr. Healey put his hand on his shoulder. "Go lie down awhile, until the sheriff comes. Joe, I don't hold anything against you. A man has to save his life. And I'll remember what you did for Miss Emmy, too."

He looked at Harry. "Better take Joe to his room, before you go for the sheriff. And if you've got some whiskey, give him some, a lot. Looks like he needs it. Don't shake your stupid head, Joe. Do what I tell you."

Harry took Joseph's arm and led him into his room. He went for his bottle of bourbon and poured a large amount in a glass and handed it to Joseph, who was sitting mutely on the bed. "Come on, Joe, drink," he said.

Joseph took the glass. He said, "Do you realize I—?"

"Yes. So you did. But that isn't important. You're the one who's alive, aren't you? And who were you trying to save, anyway? Me. The second time." Harry's dark face widened in a white grin. "Come on, drink. Now, that's better." He was relieved. For Joseph had looked like a dead man, himself, with livid skin and glazed eyes and shaken mouth. Harry had poured a drink in another glass. He caught Joseph's eye and smiled again, and said, "To life! For, by God, that's all there is!"

He raised his glass and laughed, and watched Joseph sip from his own glass and watched the pallor retreat. But Joseph thought, It was his life or mine. The only thing is that I liked to do it. At the very last, I wouldn't have stopped it.

Chapter 24

Another military port authority was soon suborned and it was Joseph, alone now, who managed the gun-running into the South. There were runs not only to Virginia but to North and South Carolina, and danger had enormously increased because of the Union naval blockade which was slowly strangling and starving the South. It was no longer a matter of clearances in New York, and Boston, and heavy bribes, and the danger of first pretending to turn to Northern ports and then slipping out to sea to continue South. It was the infinitely more dangerous task—to be undertaken only in starlit darkness—of evading the naval blockade and sliding silently through it to some remote and half-rotten abandoned dock. Each time the destination changed. But the *Isabel* seemed to move confidently and gracefully under a benign star, and though many other contraband-carrying vessels from the North were regularly seized the *Isabel* was rarely challenged and never apprehended. She was unusually fast, and under the hand of Captain Oglethorpe she danced her way safely from port to port, bravely, at all times, carrying the Union flag on her masts. Still, there were occasions of intense danger and only the wit, courage, effrontery, and skill of the captain surmounted them.

"I consider you, sir, my lucky piece," he said once to Joseph. "My ship has never once been in absolute danger; she has never been seized. Even I have marveled how close we have come to catastrophe, and I believe it was your presence on my ship that saved us. You were born under a lucky star, sir."

"Oh, certainly," said Joseph, thinking of Ireland and the Famine. "I've had nothing but luck all my life. A charmed life. Captain, I am not an adventurer. I do my duty on this ship but I don't enjoy it."

The captain nodded. "Oh, sir, I know that very well.

You are not reckless. I am the only reckless man aboard. My crew is as cautious and as trembling as a woman, and perhaps that is the true reason why we have escaped danger so often."

Then one day Mr. Healey informed Joseph that he was no longer to supervise the contraband-running, which was now taking place at least five times a month and carrying heavier and heavier cargoes. Joseph was relieved, but also dismayed. "You doubt my ability, Mr. Healey, or you don't trust my judgment."

"Boyo," said Mr. Healey, "that's not the reason." He smiled rosily. "Got to protect my investment, that's all. No, you stay at home now. I've got enough other men."

Joseph was still studying law with Mr. Spaulding, whom he had detested more and more through the years. At first indifferent to law he was now interested, for it was a rich caravan to power. There was not a law that did not carry the thumbprint of a politician, and Joseph was finally convinced that money without power was not true security, but was open to rascals and thieves. The power of politics was the greatest power of all, for it was the power to reward and punish for one's own advantage, and to fortify one's self against the rest of humanity and to express detestation of it.

Joseph had induced Mr. Healey to replace Bill Strickland with Harry Zeff. Mr. Healey had shown surprise. "You mean, you want him to drive me around everywhere and saddle and harness-up horses, like a stable boy, and be my servant at my beck and call, for fifteen dollars a week, like Bill? And eat in the kitchen with Miz Murray and sleep over the stables again?"

"No," said Joseph. "I want him to be—what is the military term?—your man at arms, your bodyguard, your guide, your protection, in the fields and in town. You know how it is in Titusville now, overrun with criminals and thieves and adventurers. Harry isn't afraid of anything. Harry's very bright. He knows the oil business better than you, Mr. Healey. He knows it from well-blowing to refinery, to pipeline, to distribution. He has a nose for it. He knows how to save money. And you can trust him with your life, with absolute confidence." Joseph smiled. "For these invaluable services you will pay Harry seventy-five dollars a week, and board and room, and a bonus every five thousand barrels, say of one hundred dollars."   ·

"You're a robber yourself, Irish," said Mr. Healey. "You'll bankrupt me yet."

"And you'll order Mrs. Murray to stop persecuting and brutalizing Liza, one of your maids, Mr. Healey. She is nearly eighteen, and a very nice girl, though you may not have noticed, and an orphan, and shy and timid, and getting to be quite pretty. I am violating no confidences when I tell you that Harry intends to marry her—when he has five thousand dollars."

Mr. Healey shouted, "I'll have no finagling among the help in my house, boyo! It's not a brothel, a bawdy house!"

"Liza, I have said, Mr. Healey, is a very nice girl, and a good and dutiful one, never slovenly nor remiss, always polite and obliging. Harry would no more think of violating her than his own sister, if he had one. But he intends to marry her in time. I hope the time will come soon."

"Maybe you'd like me to finance the wedding," said Mr. Healey, outraged. "My oil-field manager and a kitchen drab!"

Joseph spoke quietly. "Liza is no drab. She is a very sweet and innocent girl and how she endures Mrs. Murray is something I don't know. She could work in other houses, at better pay, but she wants to be near Harry. Mrs. Murray should be warned, and Liza should receive ten dollars a month, instead of four. Mrs. Murray is getting old. The burden is falling heavier and heavier on Liza, now, who is practically in charge of the kitchen and the other hired girls. Mrs. Murray doesn't hesitate to beat Liza occasionally."

"I don't know why it is, maybe I'm senile," said Mr. Healey. "But you got a tongue could wangle anybody. Maybe you kissed the Blarney Stone in Ireland?" He peered at Joseph. "Going in for good works, Irish, as you mellow? Seems I remember the time you wanted to rid yourself of Harry, and told me he wasn't no concern of yours."

"I owe my life to Harry," said Joseph, his face stiff and cold, his sunken eyes almost disappearing as he looked at Mr. Healey, who was smiling at him mockingly. "He owes his life to me. That makes some sort of a—bond—if you want to call it that."

"Thought it wasn't in your nature to accept bonds," said Mr. Healey.

"It isn't," said Joseph. Mr. Healey hummed, smiling.

Sister Elizabeth now wrote to Joseph at his address in Titusville. She invariably thanked him for the money he sent her for the support of the orphanage. She wrote once that because of his regular donations and the kindness of Mrs. Tom Hennessey, and two or three others, St. Agnes's Church had been renovated, and additions to the orphanage built, "so now we can protect and care for twice as many orphans as before, and our Sisters number fifteen. Father is not well, I am sad to say. The sufferings endured in this war have marked him, for he is very tender of heart. We are dreaming of an infirmary—" she added delicately. It was obvious that she had no idea at all of Joseph's source of income, though she assumed he was in the "oil business," and always warned him of danger.

The Battle of Gettysburg had particularly afflicted her. Then had come Generals Grant and Sherman, the Emancipation Proclamation, the Battle of Cold Harbor and the losses the Union had suffered, the burning of Atlanta, and the "bravery" of Farragut at the Battle of Mobile Bay. Then Mr. Lincoln had been re-elected President on November 8, 1864, "though," wrote Sister Elizabeth, "I cannot understand this. Mr. Lincoln always spoke of 'one country, only,' yet the South did not participate in this election, and so, dear Joseph, is that Constitutional and legal? I have heard much of the Constitution, recently, and I confess that it seems an instrument which can be interpreted at will by anyone at all, if one is to read the newspapers. It is very puzzling. It seems much more flexible than the Common Law, though I must admit that I know little of that, either. But there is much hope lately that the war will end soon, for now General Sherman's Army is in Georgia and Tennessee has been invaded. How dreadful is war. Even in Winfield our two hospitals are filled and overflowing with wounded and the dying and the maimed and the blind, and our Sisters do what they can in mercy. One hears such dreadful tales of man's inhumanity to man, which I trust are exaggerated, though remembering the events of my own lifetime I am not truly very sanguine.

"You have expressed displeasure, dear Joseph, over my missal informing you that Sean's Jesuit teachers have been teaching him music, and that he has an angelic voice. As I told you, he sings in the choir, and it is as if the Cherubim are present. When he sings the ballads of Ireland it would almost melt the heart of an Englishman. The Fathers predict a magnificent future for him, either in opera or at concerts, though he is gifted in other ways, also, writing a fine hand, composing poetry which is very soulful, indeed, and being an accomplished pianist and remarkably excellent in all the humanities he is being tauaght. He is, alas, not very proficient in mathematics or botany or biology, the Fathers report, nor overly interested in abstractions or philosophies. This reveals, the Fathers tell me, a very subtle heart, full of sensibility and gentleness. It was once thought he had a vocation, but, alas, this was not so. You expressed the opinion once that you considered him lazy and irresponsible. I am sorry if any of my letters gave you that sad opinion. Sean is of a delicate constitution, one that shrinks from hard realities but is very affectionate and kind and agreeable, and is this not needed in this harsh world? When he is interested he applies himself with zeal, but when he is bored he permits it to become evident. But he is not irresponsible. I am afraid, however, that we must relegate the exigencies of responsibility to more hardy characters—"

Like mine, thought Joseph.

"To characters," the letter continued, "who know no poetry nor the graciousness of living and the beauty—"

Who must support the butterflies, commented Joseph to himself with growing cold rage.

"We cannot all be the same," Sister Elizabeth wrote. "God made diverse natures among men. There are the natures who must toil to the day of their death; it is their nature. And there are natures which are adornments to life, who bring to us the flowers of imagination and love and the arts and music—"

And let us supply their bread and their meat, and feel that they have honored us, Joseph said to himself. Sister, remember? "That doesn't buy any potatoes."

Suddenly he stopped reading the letter and stared into space with a degree of consternation, for he had felt a raw thrust in him like naked hatred for his brother, and he was appalled. He had dedicated his life to the care and protection of Sean, and Regina, and now he felt a loathing repudiation of his brother, a bitter and contemptuous anger. He sat back to consider this, for if he now rejected Sean much of his life had been wasted. Then, as he thought, the face of his dead father floated before him, and he reflected: It is my fear that Sean is like our Dad, who let us starve because he had no fortitude and would not fight for us nor sacrifice one of his "principles" to save our lives.

Now Sister Elizabeth's letter gently hinted that it was her belief that Mary Regina had a vocation. This was so outrageous, so incredible to Joseph, that he skimmed over the silly words.

"You have seen them but once since you left Winfield when you were but a lad of eighteen," Sister Elizabeth wrote, "and that two years ago when you had rooms at the new hotel, the Hospice. Yet daily they grow. Regina grows in grace before the Eyes of Our Lord, a precious Lily, a perfume of Sanctity. She is, I must confess, far more of a scholar than Sean, and appears older, and when they meet at the orphanage it is as if our angel, Mary Regina, is the mother and Sean the beloved child. When Sean expresses impatience that you have not yet provided him 'that fine mansion,' Regina chides him and calls to his memory your solicitude and your love, and your endless labors for your family."

My darling, thought Joseph. He dismissed his brother from his mind, but Regina lingered like a bright and living presence beside him. He thought, Next year, this coming spring, I will remove Sean from those sentimental, dreaming priests, with their arts and their airs and their foolish learning, and teach him how to live. I will take my sister, and she will be mine and not the nuns' with their stupid twaddle of angels and piety and grace. He had the feeling that his brother and his sister were in great danger.

Sister Elizabeth added a postscript: "It is with sadness that I must write you that our dear Katherine Hennessey, who returned to Green Hills when the Confederate troops almost took the capital, is in poor health and seems very distrait and sad, and is inclined to weep. She summons up courage and fortitude to care for her dear child, Bernadette, who is a very vigorous girl and much attached to our dear Mary Regina, who loves all. I often recall that you refused her offer to adopt Mary Regina, and perhaps it is for the best, though our senator would have made an exemplary father. His love for his daughter is very beautiful to see, and he is not ashamed to demonstrate it when he returns to Green Hills, and he has often confessed to me that the condition of his beloved wife is breaking his heart. I visit her as often as I can, which is not too often, as traps are very expensive."

I once thought you a wise woman, Joseph commented to himself. But, my saintly Sister, you are a fool.

He was alarmed when he found that he was thinking of Katherine Hennessey more often than he was thinking of his family, and that there was a sick sinking in him at the thought of her invalidism, and her debauched husband, and her lonely abandonment to the company of a child, and the silent misery of her life. He now suspected that Katherine had not been so obtuse and so feeble-minded that she had not known all about her husband's character, her own humiliation and betrayal, and the contempt in which he held her. When he thought of this Joseph would feel a murderous hatred for the magnificent senator, who had, according to the newspapers, "reconciled Northern Democrats and brought them to the President's side in this dolorous conflict between brothers." I wonder who had given him advance information, thought Joseph, and what that information was.

He questioned Mr. Montrose, who shrugged. "Indications of loot, as I told you before, my dear Francis. Mr. Lincoln has asserted that there will be no looting or degradation of the South when this war is concluded. But others have other plans. Mr. Lincoln is in a very precarious situation."

He added thoughtfully, "There are many who agree with me—and Mr. Lincoln, I have heard, also agrees—that there is much more to this war than ostensibly appears. The South was always proud and independent and believed, with the Founding Fathers, that centralized and powerful government inevitably slides into tyranny. But the North, less proud, less conscious of national tradition, less independent. less manly in many ways, craves the dictator's hand, the tyrant's force, for many of its people have come from nations who were subjected, and dependent on government. It may be, in the future, that it will be the South who will prevent, for many long decades, the collapse of American freedom into Caesarism."

He saw Joseph faintly smiling and he shrugged. "I have no allegiances to any nation or any part of it. I have but one allegiance, and that is to my own freedom, my own stature as a man, and for that I would fight to the death."

"So would I," said Joseph.

One day Mr. Spaulding said to Joseph, whom he was beginning to treat with sly and wary deference, "You do not know the extent of Mr. Healey's—influence. Are you aware, sir, that he owns the controlling interest in four large newspapers, the mortgages, one in Chicago, one in Boston, one in New York, and one in Philadelphia?"

"No," said Joseph, "I did not know." Mr. Spaulding smiled with superb superiority and tossed his mane of dyed hair. "You are not entirely in his confidence, Mr. Francis. Do you know why he owns these newspapers? The people believe what they read. Print is sacred to them. The man who controls such a medium is the most powerful of men, for he controls politicians also. Without Mr. Healey's *Philadelphia Messenger*, Senator Hennessey could never have been appointed as senator by the State Legislature, which, unlike senators, is elected by the people. The State Legislature is quite—respectful—of Mr. Healey. They, many of them, owe their votes to him, as does the governor. Only ten men have been voted into office whom Mr. Healey opposed, and even they are afraid of him now, and court his favor."

"So much, then, for the old aphorism, 'The voice of the People is the voice of God,' " said Joseph.

Mr. Spaulding pursed his lips and averted his eyes as if Joseph had blasphemed. "Well," he said, in unctuous tones, "the Good Lord does expect people to use their common sense and their intelligence."

"Which they don't have," said Joseph.

Mr. Spaulding appeared about to demur, and then he smiled the wide and jovial smile of the politician. "Mr. Francis, if the populace had any intelligence at all the world would not be in its present condition, and there would not be vast opportunities for men like Mr. Healey, and politicians. Therefore, should we not be thankful that human nature never changes and the clever and bold can prosper enormously over the animalistic instincts of their fellowmen?"

Joseph agreed with him, but he did not like Mr. Spaulding in the least and more than suspected that the dislike was mutual.

In the meantime several of his wells had come in abundantly in Titusville, and he increased his leases and his options. To Mr. Healey's surprise and congratulation four of his wells, producing far superior oil to that of Titusville, came in in the southern part of the Commonwealth, and brought immensely greater prices. Joseph received an offer from Mr. Rockefeller, himself, which he rejected. Mr. Handell, in the name of the Handell Oil Company of the United States, sent him a telegram praising him for his "intuition," and then sent him a letter offering him a directorship in the company, which Joseph accepted at once. He then became part of the company, wells and all.

"Pretty handsome, Irish," said Mr. Healey, glowing like a proud father. "Always knew you had brains, and a mighty lot of them. One of these days you'll be leaving me, eh? You've got a right smart lot of money now, and you'll be making more."

"Mr. Healey," said Joseph, "I will leave when you tell me to, and not before."

"Now that," said Mr. Healey, "is right sweet to my ears, boyo, but it ain't very smart, I am thinking." But he glowed again.

He added, "Never thought you were weak enough for gratitude, though."

Joseph said, "You were the first man who gave me any opportunity and did not treat me like a dog. It has nothing to do with gratitude."

"No? What is it then?"

But Joseph, becoming sullen, had no answer. He did not know, himself, what it was that really held him to Mr. Healey. He was to learn a few days later, on a warm April evening in 1865.

Joseph, always indifferent to the war, felt neither relief nor joy when it neared its end, except that a large source of profits was about to be terminated, and abruptly. There were rumors, uttered in hope, that the war might continue in forays for many years, so that the factories could continue to spew out prosperity in the North and the workers in them flourish. To multitudes, the end of the war brought dismay and confusion. It had been exciting and rewarding. Firebrands in Washington shouted for "continuing conflict to the end that every outpost is eliminated!" To concerned constituents they said: "War is not concluded so immediately. We have hopes that the war prosperity will continue, at least for a decade. Moreover, there is the South to be exploited in the event of eventual peace, with all its riches and its land. You can be certain, sir, that the terms of peace will not be gentle. There are opportunities—"

Mr. Spaulding told Joseph of this, laughing richly. "So much for 'holy wars,' " said Joseph, remembering the international bankers he had met in New York, the men who had no allegiances to any race or any country or any ideal.

The lust for justice, for which so many shouted in the newspapers, meant the lust for loot. To the vast majority of Northern Americans the causes of the war, the issues of the war, were as meaningless as Sanskrit, and were as pertinent to them. Only those who mourned their dead whispered, "Why?" To which, as Mr. Spaulding explained, there was only one answer, and that the American people must never know, for the safety of those who truly ruled them.

Though the war continued in sporadic bursts here and there through the desperate South it was known that it had come to an end. Mr. Lincoln said, "We now have the task of the reconciliation of brothers, of binding wounds, of the hand of friendship extended from victor to foe, of lifting up the wounded of both North and South, and of a national mourning for our heroic dead wherever they were born. There shall be no vengeance, for none is needed. There shall be no riches nor plunder for evil men, who batten on the flesh and blood of the helpless. We are one nation, and one nation we will remain until we are destroyed by our Vandals from within."

With that, he sealed his death warrant. The hand that pulled the trigger of the gun which killed him that balmy evening in Washington, in April 1865, might have belonged to an obscure actor. But the power that controlled that hand was not suspected, nor did even the owner of the hand suspect. Political assassins, as Mr. Montrose was to say, have many sponsors, all in accord, and none but they know their names.

Mr. Healey had grown enormously fat through the years, loving his drink and his food with the passion only a full-blooded man can know. He had loved women as well, and still did to a limited extent. He had loved money, but not so much as his physical well-being and his joy in living. To Mr. Healey a day was never drab nor monotonous nor dull nor melancholy nor depressing, no matter the weather.

It was an occasion of infinite interest, private celebration, pleasure, involvement, laughter, and enjoyment. Shrewd about money, he was never cautious about self-gratification. In fact, he viewed money as not just a source of the power to manipulate—though his Irish soul rejoiced in that —but as a means to make life more rapturous, more satisfying. "There's some," he said to Joseph, "that thinks as you grow older that your appetites become less. If they do, you never had them to begin with, Joe. A milky-mouth man loves milk from his birth and dies with the love of it. Sure, and a man can become impotent—happens with lads, too—but a real man never stops loving women. Your stomach can turn on you any time, but that don't stop you from loving your meals and your drinks. Just makes you mad until you can enjoy them again. A man's a man until he dies, but a milksop was never a man. Pure-in-hearts, I call them, and bad cess to them all, and may they have nothing but their damned milk and honey in heaven, too. It's all they deserve. Bet Our Lord dines better."

He peered at Joseph. "You got the capacity, boyo, but you're a Cromwell at heart, and you won't let yourself go. If you ever do—" And his little black eyes, sunken now in folds of red flesh, sparkled. "I hope to be there, that I do! It'll be something to make the angels happy and clap their hands. Reckon they hate the milksops."

His doctor was old-fashioned, and bled him when his head ached too violently and he became dizzy. His doctor also advised him to "use judiciousness in viands." Mr. Healey had never been judicious, except when it came to money. "If I die," he would say, "let me die with my boots on, after a good meal with lots to drink. Hell, is life worth watching everything you put in your mouth, and being what they call 'moderate'? A life of moderation, Joe, is for near-corpses and those who hate living."

"The golden mean," said Joseph. "Aristotle."

"Never heard of him," said Mr. Healey. "If he lived being moderate, he didn't live at all. Maybe he didn't like any part of it. Who wants to live feeling his pulse all the time and calculating his life in the years he has lived and not how he lived?"

Mr. Healey did not die with his boots on. He died almost immediately after an ecstatic romp, naked, in his bed, with Miss Emmy. He had recently concluded a gigantic meal of his favorite food and drink. He died as he had wanted to die, with delicious tastes in his mouth and his body on the soft body of a woman, and happiness in his heart, and aware of his own interpretation of the splendor of life. He died without illness and dwindling and fear, without a doctor at his elbow, without a nurse holding his hand, without pain or agony. He died in the scent of Miss Emmy's perfume, his lips fastened on hers. An artery had burst voluptuously in his brain or his heart, and he never knew it.

It was Miss Emmy's shrieks, as she ran naked into the hall, that aroused Joseph and Harry Zeff and Mrs. Murray, and the maids. Joseph was the first in the bedroom. There lay Mr. Healey, fat and bloated and still rosy, with a smile of total bliss on his mouth, as if he had encountered angels as full-blooded as himself, and as masculine, and had joined their roistering company with shouts of laughter.

"He was a man," said Harry Zeff, as he decently covered Mr. Healey's body with a sheet. Mr. Healey, later the dead recipient of emotional accolades, received none more pungent nor more true.

Chapter 25

Joseph, who had believed that he could never again experience the anguish of human emotion, and that he was removed from the common torments of men, was appalled and distraught over the grief he felt for Mr. Healey. No matter how his disciplined mind fought with sorrow the sorrow kept emerging like a vomiting well of blood, to darken and distort his thoughts, to drown out rationality, to flood over plans and conjectures. He tried to think over his now-threatened future, but it faded before he could consider it in new torrents of grief. He was incredulous to discover how deeply Mr. Healey had intruded into his cold and isolated spirit. He found himself listening for the roaring laughter, the spill of genial obscenities, the robust slamming of doors, the pound of heavy boots. The house appeared to darken, the halls became attenuated, and even the golden warmth of April days became dun. As for the horror that gripped the nation over the assassination of President Lincoln—Joseph never knew it, nor cared.

It was Harry Zeff who arranged for the funeral, and sent for the priest of the little Catholic church. The priest had heard of Mr. Healey. He had not thought of him as a Catholic man, he, the owner of brothels and gambling houses and saloons and the runner of bootleg whiskey. He had never seen Mr. Healey in his church. He had not even thought of him as Irish. (God forbid!) Dubiously, the timid old man surveyed the remains in a long silence. Then he had sighed, and said, "Yes, he was Irish. I can see that. Knew many such as he on the ould sod." So Mr. Healey, though he had died unshriven, was given Christian burial, even if the old priest sincerely doubted that he had died in a state of grace, and certainly he had not received Extreme Unction and was probably laden with sins which would take him an eternity to expiate. "He was a good man,"

Harry told the priest. "He had never turned a sufferer away from his door." The priest sighed again. "That's more than many professed Christians can say," he admitted.

The old priest marveled, in his innocence, at the overflowing of his church by gorgeously clad and very young damsels, handsome middle-aged ladies, florid gentlemen in embroidered waistcoats and ruffles, and sleek lithesome characters in expensive gray and fawn pantaloons—and with high silk hats and rich boots. He could not recall seeing these before and decided they must have come "from distant parts" and certainly not from Titusville. Then, of course, to the priest's stupefaction, the governor arrived, and the splendid senator, Mr. Tom Hennessey, and his lady and their pretty young daughter, and various other politicians, and supercilious gentlemen rumored from New York, Philadelphia, and Boston, all outfitted as the butterfly and all decorous and low-voiced. The obscure little church almost disappeared in a welter of brilliant carriages. There were many newspapermen and photographers. (One noble-looking gentleman wanted to deliver a eulogy from the pulpit, but the priest, recovering a little from his shock and bewilderment, stammeringly refused, and with considerable umbrage. However, he was still shocked. He had considered Mr. Healey only a local sinner and not one of such awesome dimensions.)

Mr. Healey was buried in the little Catholic graveyard near the church, in a fine plot. The undertaker had come from Philadelphia with an entourage. He ordered—after consultation with Mr. Spaulding—a giant cross of marble fully fourteen feet high. Mr. Healey may not have lived as a Catholic Christian, but, as Harry Zeff contentedly remarked, "He was buried as one, and never was there a kinder man." The old priest, whom doubt had begun to plague, was stupefied when Mr. Spaulding gave him a sheaf of money totaling fifteen hundred dollars. "Mr. Healey would like that," he said, with a grandiloquent gesture. The priest had visions of a roast of beef and a statue of the Blessed Mother which would truly honor her and the Poor Box, not to mention two more pews and a new cassock for himself and a month of good meals for the two Sisters of Charity who taught in the tiny church school on the outskirts of Titusville, and something for the Missions. "He never came to see me," the priest mentioned, to which

Harry replied, "He was a very modest and humble man. A Christian."

Joseph did not attend the Requiem Mass. Harry did not press him nor make any comment. Joseph sat alone in the house, with its long booming echoes, and tried to control his grief and his emotions, and their destructive scream in his mind. He had forgotten such sorrow, which he had known when his mother had died and the news of his father's death had been brought to him. Now it came to him again like fresh blood newly spilled, and as terrible, and he knew that sorrow was ageless and vital and part of a man's being. The thought that Mr. Healey was dead was incredible to him, and then the incredulity turned to anguish and a hatred of death, itself. He, himself, he thought in his youth, was invulnerable to death. To him it was a loathsome and humiliating thing.

Two days after the funeral he received a note by hand from Mr. James Spaulding:

The honor of your presence is requested at the office of Mr. Spaulding of Titusville at 2:00 p.m., Thursday, of this week, in connection with various bequests in the matter of the concern of the last will and testament of Mr. Edward Cullen Healey, late and lamented citizen of this fair city.

In spite of his sorrow Joseph's heart gave a great bound. Was it possible that Mr. Healey had remembered him in his will, and if so, why? He was thinking of this when Harry came into his room and showed him a similar letter, and the two young men looked at each other eagerly, ashamed of their hope, yet hoping. "A thousand dollars apiece, I bet!" cried Harry, in a hushed voice, then looked embarrassed. "Discussing it when he's just in his grave!"

"Why should he leave us anything?" said Joseph. When he went to the offices he discovered that all the present thirty-five men who worked for Mr. Healey were in a state of excitement, for they, too, had received the same formal notice. There was not a man who had not been sincerely fond of Mr. Healey, and now they looked at each other in silent query. Only Mr. Montrose was without question, and he kept glancing at Joseph who was as astonished as the others, and he shook his head a little and reproached himself for his former cynicism.

They had all met at Mr. Spaulding's office on the designated day and time, quietly tiptoeing into the room as if a corpse lay there, and seating themselves in a series of small rows of chairs which the lawyer had caused to be set up. It was unusually warm for April and the windows were open and the hills could be seen beyond, over the rooftops, all brilliant gold with new leaves, all bluish shadow and bronze clefts and patches of the deep green of pines and spruces. A nation was in mourning for its murdered President, and flags stood at half-mast and black crepe and bunting hung from every doorway and window, and groups stopped on the streets to talk and to cry vengeance, and newsboys were appearing almost on the hour every hour with fresh headlines in the papers, which were caught up at once by grim-faced men who had, in the past, had nothing but contempt for the dead man.

But no one thought of Mr. Lincoln in Mr. Spaulding's offices, for a fortune lay palpitating there in a sheaf of papers on his desk, and it seemed to many that they had the shine of gold on them. Mr. Spaulding sat like a high priest or at least the Chief Justice of the Supreme Court, behind his desk, gravely clad in black, with a black cravat, his hair decorously smoothed down, his rubbery face set in an expression of solemn sorrow and reverence, his eyes downcast, his hands folded before the papers as if, thought Joseph, he were waiting for the sacred moment to place them as in a monstrance. A faint and mournful scent as of funereal fern emanated from him.

Seeing that all were gathered, Mr. Spaulding let his big head drop as in prayer, or as if overcome and too burdened to speak immediately. All the men decorously waited; not even Mr. Montrose smiled. But Joseph was filled with a wild exasperation. The swine had surely calculated on that ray of sunshine touching his dyed hair in a halo-like glow, for Joseph had caught his sidelong look at the ray just before bending his head, and he had moved a little forward in his big chair to catch it better.

Mr. Spaulding began to speak. It was his grandest hour, for never before had the evidence of so much money lain before him. His voice was like a choir, throbbing and trembling. Now he lifted his eyes, big and hollow and ponderable, full of portentousness and grief, and all at once he looked a very parody of a prophet and Joseph felt an alarming urge to laugh out loud, to shout a ridiculing execration.

"I have here, before me," said Mr. Spaulding, touching the papers with a reverent hand, "the last Will and Testament of my beloved friend, Edward Cullen Healey, who died on the day our even more beloved President died—and perhaps there—there is a portent, a meaning we of feeble intellect and dark understanding cannot penetrate. We can only bow our heads in wonder. We can only Meditate, Reflect, seeking humility, overcome by Awe."

The gathering said not a word. But Joseph thought he heard a ghostly echo of Mr. Healey's boisterous laughter and even, perhaps, a ribald word. Mr. Spaulding took out his scented kerchief and elaborately and slowly wiped brow, then eyes, then blew his nose sonorously. He replaced the kerchief. He began to read again, and every word was like an invocation.

Each man employed in Mr. Healey's offices was to receive a year's full salary in addition to his regular salary, and a bonus of five hundred dollars extra at Christmas, provided he remain for that period at least "in the employ of my major legatee, who inherits my residuary estate." He was also to receive an immediate lump sum of three thousand dollars, "in gratitude for loyal services." Each Christmas he remained in the employ of the "major legatee" he would receive an additional five hundred dollars.

Mr. Montrose received twenty thousand dollars outright, and "a prayer that he serve my major legatee for a period of one year at least." He also received sundry little treasures he had admired in Mr. Healey's house, "notably a Sanger portrait of George Washington." In addition, he received one hundred shares in the Pennsylvania Railroad and "three of the producing wells next to the Parker Farm." "There are no words," Mr. Healey had dictated, "which can convey my affection for Mr. Montrose, who has served me well for over two decades before the date of this Will."

Mr. Healey prayed that Mr. Montrose would find it in his heart to remain with "my major legatee" until his conscience is satisfied that said Major Legatee was fully qualified to continue "without that supreme wisdom, delicacy of tact, perfection of judgment, of which my dear friend, Mr. Montrose is the Proud Possessor."

Joseph glanced at Mr. Montrose who seemed greatly moved. His fine catlike face became very serious, and he looked aside.

Harry Zeff was left the sum of five thousand dollars, and at this Harry let out a loud and involuntary whistle which made everyone jump in his chair. A slight ripple of laughter ran through the room, shaken, unintended, and Mr. Spaulding looked as horrified as a priest might look if the Host were desecrated. He hid the will with his spread hands. He gulped. He implored the ceiling for mercy with uplifted eyes. His jaw trembled; his mouth shook. The sun ray quivered in his hair which, all at once, appeared to rise on his head in a holy breeze.

Harry was immediately thrown into immense embarrassment and confusion, though everyone eyed him with sympathy as well as with smothered mirth. His dusky face was crimson. He cowered in his chair. Even Joseph was amused, and he thought of young Liza.

The unpardonable interruption was ignored by Mr. Spaulding, and after a prolonged delay he began to read again. There were small sums to the girls who worked in his house, a sum of money for a madam he particularly appreciated, ten thousand dollars to St. Francis's Working Boys' Home in Philadelphia, gifts to a seminary, an orphanage in Pittsburgh and—to Joseph's dark amazement—the sum of two thousand dollars for Masses for his unregenerate soul. Mrs. Murray received the sum of one thousand dollars "provided she quits my house and Titusville within ten days" of Mr. Healey's death.

There were other small but pleasant remembrances to friends in various cities. Miss Emmy received an income for life of five thousand dollars a year, an incredible sum, riches.

Joseph had never heard a will read before. When Mr. Spaulding stopped reading he felt a slight sadness, for there had been no mention of his name, no remembrance. It is not the money, he thought. But I believed that we were friends, that he had some regard for me. If he had left me but his watch, a trinket from his chain, a book, a picture— Only recently Mr. Healey had had a daquerreotype taken of himself, and had had it artfully colored, and it stood on his desk. Joseph wondered if Mr. Spaulding would permit him to buy it. He felt the familiar dull aching in his throat. He pushed back his chair, then waited for others to rise, also. There was a smarting in his eyes and a dryness in his mouth.

The small scraping of his chair aroused Mr. Spaulding

from his devout reverie. No one else but Joseph had moved. Joseph subsided. Mr. Spaulding, to his surprise, was fixedly gazing at him as at a wonder, a miracle, a sight not to be believed. He seemed in a state of transport.

Now Mr. Spaulding's voice rose on a radiant crest. "We now come to the Major Legatee mentioned in this last Will and Testament of my beloved friend, Edward Cullen Healey."

Long breaths were taken in the room, except for Joseph, who felt nothing but impatience now, nothing but a desire to leave, to feel his hurt alone, and, he thought vaguely, to run back to the house and steal the daguerreotype. (Surely no one wanted it but himself, and Mr. Spaulding's natural malice would be delighted to refuse any offer from him and cut him with any disappointment and frustration.)

Mr. Spaulding leaned forward in his chair. He had the attention of all, except for Joseph. Then Joseph heard his name—"my dear young friend, my son in all but birth, my countryman, who has so often shown me his affection and loyalty—though he did not know this himself—Joseph Francis Xavier Armagh—"

A deep murmur ran through the office, and every head turned and every eye stared at Joseph, whose mouth opened in a muttered, "What? What?"

Mr. Spaulding rose slowly and majestically, like Neptune rising from the sea, royal sceptre in hand. Mr. Spaulding came from behind his desk. He went weightily down the rows of chairs. He paused beside Joseph. His eyes were filled with shining liquid. He held out his hand, and bowed. "My felicitations, Mr. Francis," he said, "or, I should say, Mr. Armagh."

Joseph was stunned. He had heard nothing but his name and a few other words. He did not want to touch Mr. Spaulding's hand but thinking of that portrait on the desk in Mr. Healey's study he forced himself to take the warm damp fingers. He said, "All I want is that daguerreotype, on his desk, in the gilt frame. I will pay for it—"

At that everyone in the room burst into loud and affectionate laughter. Harry leaned towards Joseph and slapped him heartily on the back, recovering from his own stunned disbelief. Even Mr. Spaulding smiled tenderly, bent down to place his hand gently on Joseph's thin shoulder. Great grins spread from face to face, and Joseph's words were repeated over and over, to renewed laughter.

"All that, and all else too, my dear boy," Mr. Spaulding said. "An Empire. A mountain of gold."

It was indeed. Joseph Francis Xavier Armagh was the Major Legatee of Edward Cullen Healey. Mr. Healey's vast "interests" now belonged to him, "without let or hindrance." Brothels. Refineries. Saloons. Newspaper mortgages. Property in Pittsburgh, Titusville, Boston, New York, Philadelphia. Wells. Endless investments. Enormous sums of money in various banks. A hotel, flourishing, in Philadelphia. Mines. Investments in several lavish hotels in New York, stocks, bonds in countless industries, including munitions and railroads. He was the sole executor, though the assistance of Mr. Spaulding—at a large annual fee— was designated.

"I don't believe it," said Joseph, and he looked about him and the room swam in a shifting mist and the sunlight seemed to dance in the confines of the windows and the blue sky beyond tilted dizzily. He had brilliantly enlarged visions of his brother and sister, of Sister Elizabeth, of Green Hills, and he thought, over and over, that he had lost his mind. Someone was pressing a glass of whiskey against his mouth. He drank it, dumbly. He stared at the head in front of him, and saw every hair on it ensheathed in too-vivid light, and the eyes looking at him were the eyes of a Cyclops. He saw Mr. Montrose's face floating in front of him, dreamlike, wavering. He felt the hard clasp of Harry's hand. His own was cold and sweating. Then he had an awful impulse to burst into tears.

"I don't believe it," he repeated, helplessly, over and over. His hand was shaken by others. He heard voices. He closed his eyes and hid in the darkness for a while.

Chapter 26

Mary Regina Armagh stood in a thick scattering of blood-red oak leaves and surveyed the great white house before her. She said, "But, Joe, it's very big, isn't it, for just three people, and Sean will be going to Harvard. Then, only two will be there."

"Now, Regina," said Joseph in the special voice which was only for her, gentle and firm and paternal, "there will be servants. You know the Hennessey house yonder, with the maids and the butler and the stable boys, and it is only for two, for the senator is rarely there."

The girl lifted her shining regard to her brother. "Can you afford it, Joe? It must be very expensive."

He kept his face grave. "I can afford it, my love. You mustn't trouble yourself. I am no spendthrift."

Regina said, looking down at the autumn-littered earth, "You've worked so hard for us, Joe. You've sacrificed for us and given us all you could, even when it meant depriving yourself. I should hate myself if I thought you built this house for us and it meant worry and more work for you."

"I think," said Sean, "that Joe knows what he's doing. He always did." The lilting voice was touched, in its music, with a faint note of malice. He was as tall as his brother, at nearly nineteen, but sinuous and gracefully swaying in all his motions, and, to Joseph, disgustingly poetic in appearance. He resembled his father, Daniel Armagh, too acutely in appearance, except that he did not have the apparent physical strength even of Daniel. He was pale and smooth of countenance, with his very large light blue eyes beguiling and coaxing—(except when he was with Joseph, and then they became doubtful and a little glaucous)—the most aristocratic and perfect features, a beautiful smiling mouth

347

with fine teeth, and an air of impeccable breeding and elegance. His bright golden hair curled over his smooth forehead, about his ears and down to his nape and it also rose to a tumbling crest high on his head, which Joseph disagreeably called Byronic. To Joseph, Sean did not appear Irish at all—as neither had Daniel Armagh—but pure Anglo-Saxon, and he had to admit to himself that that was at least part of the reason he frequently felt stern towards his brother. But then, were not the Irish—an originally dark Celtic race—heavily mixed also with Scandinavian blood, in particular Norwegian and Danish? Joseph preferred the Irish type mixed with the Spanish, who were excessively proud, dark of hair and eye, coldly combative and brooding. He was also convinced they were more intelligent. Sean did not seem to be intelligent to his brother. He was "light-minded." In short he liked to laugh and sing and be merry—as Daniel Armagh had liked, also, and he was too charming, too pleasant, too gay, too cheerful for Joseph. If Sean ever had a somber thought it was not evident. He loved to live, as had Mr. Healey, but not in Mr. Healey's earthy and robust fashion. Sean's love of life indicated itself in happy jesting, in frequent laughter, in poetry, in music, in art, in tender glances and interest, in delight at the very spectacle of existence. All this Joseph found more than a little reprehensible and trivial and womanish.

Sean also liked to dress, as Joseph called it, "as colorfully as a peacock, at my expense." In short, Sean found all the graceful amenities of life, all its graciousness, all its light and color and symmetry and contour, all its urbane and civilizing elements, endlessly fascinating, endlessly delicious and worthy of worship. He had known the austerity of poverty in the orphanage but had apparently considered it but a dreary interlude which had nothing to do with real life at all, and sometimes he even thought that Joseph had been remiss in not rescuing his family earlier from the ugliness of poverty. (How Joseph could have managed that Sean never considered. It was enough that Joseph had "promised," and had not been able to keep his promise immediately. The realities of life were far from Sean Paul Armagh, and were to remain so.) But he was also very sensitive, "like a silly girl," Joseph would think, and lavish and generous.

It was in Regina that Joseph found a little joy and delight. At barely fourteen she was a woman in mind and soul, though her body was only in puberty. Sean's experiences had been hers, but hers had entered her soul and her ponderings, and she was never to forget them nor their portentousness and dark meaning. This gave her a lovely gravity, a sweetness and depth of temperament worthy of a wise woman, a touching kindness in a word, glance, and deed, a habit of reflection, a love of study, a frequent desire for solitude and contemplation, an earnestness and honesty of outlook which often startled her elders who suddenly forgot she was only a young girl and thereafter talked with her as with an adult. She had lived an immured life, but her mind seemed large and experienced, for she read as Joseph had always read, and with minute attention and awareness. She knew more of life than did Sean, but it distressed her that Joseph's bitter eyes would sometimes fasten on Sean with disgust and even with aversion. Surely dear Joe understood that Sean must be protected and cherished? Surely dear Joe knew that Sean would always be a child? The girl had no memory of her father, but often she thought that Daniel must have been like this, gay and happy and eternally believing in an even brighter tomorrow. At this thought Regina would sigh. What did one do with men who never became men in spirit? Despise them, hate them? Never. One could only enjoy the color and vivacity they brought to life, and never demand anything of them at all but music and beauty.

Like a butterfly, thought Regina. Like a flower. Like birdsong. But were these not valuable also? The world would be infinitely uglier without them, though poor Joe called them parasites. It was unfortunate that they did not possess their own means of sustenance, as did butterflies, flowers and birds, but had to depend on more vigorous others for their existence. If those vigorous others rebelled at parasitism, they were justified, for as Sister Elizabeth had firmly taught, "All tubs must stand on their own bottoms." Regina thought that such as Sean were not made of sturdy wood, but moonlight, and it certainly had no "bottoms!" They could only dance in the air, their wings like rainbows.

Regina knew that Sister Elizabeth had often written Joseph about Sean, with tactful pleadings, though Sister Elizabeth had too much common sense to countenance parasitism or those she called "perpetual whining Poor Souls." But Sister Elizabeth knew the realities of life, and Sean was one of those realities, and so had to be dealt with. She

therefore had written letters to Joseph pleading for Sean—
not that she approved of the youth—but in truth to make
the lives of the brothers a little easier for both. Sean was
Sean, and so he had been born, and not even the direst circumstances would ever be able to change him from a lissome young man to a stern man of business and the dealer
with the iron truths. "Perhaps," Sister Elizabeth had once
said to the young girl, "he will marry a rich woman who
will adore him, and not expect anything from him but love,
pleasing attentions, tenderness and laughter. If Joseph fails
to be tolerant of him it will be tragic for both of them."

For Sister Elizabeth also knew that Joseph had come to
despise and hate the father who had brought his family to
destitution and death.

Regina, then, as subtly and as tactfully as she could,
stood between the two brothers, the grim and resolute Joseph and the bewildered butterfly who could not understand his brother, and so had to take refuge, in defense, in
a light malice, little laughs—and avoidance. Of the two,
Regina pitied Joseph the more, a sentiment which would
not have pleased the sentimental but of which Sister Elizabeth would have approved. She also pitied Sean, so easily
wounded, so easily baffled when others failed to laugh with
him or appreciate his jokes or his beautiful singing voice
and his ardent involvement with beauty.

The three stood near the large white-brick and pillared
house which Joseph had built for his family near the larger
and more ostentatious house of Senator Hennessey. It had
taken nearly two years to build, and it stood on a slight rise
on ten acres of immaculately landscaped grounds, all
groups of trees on plushy grass and gardens and conservatories and summer houses and gazebos. A little brook
flowed on the property, and it, too, had been brought into
order, with primroses planted on its banks, and summer
lilies, and iris and young willows.

The house was ready for its occupants. Much time had
gone into the ordering and choosing of furniture, rugs and
draperies and pictures. Joseph knew that he had no taste
for such things, and so, at the urging of Regina—he could
never deny her anything—had permitted his sister to ask
the aid of the ailing Katherine Hennessey, who loved her.
Katherine, during those months, had come to life with this
new interest, and asked Joseph only how much he desired
to spend, and when he said, "Anything at all, so long as it

is appropriate and the best of its kind," she was delighted and invigorated. Her taste was marvelous, yet not exclusively feminine, except when it came to Regina's rooms. There was not a vista which did not entrance and invite, and this was evident even to Joseph's eyes. He loved to walk about his house, when it was being decorated and furnished, and never interfered, but his own rooms were austere, almost bare, containing only essentials even if those were rich and choice. "Monks' cells," Sean had remarked to Regina. His own quarters' furnishings had been of his choosing, and were airy and beautiful and excelled the taste even of Katherine Hennessey, who admired him and, looking at her young daughter, shyly thought of him as Bernadette's husband. He was so lovable, so kind. Katherine would sigh, remembering a husband who was neither, but whom she could only helplessly love.

She thought Joseph the kindest and most masculine and most admirable of men, for with her he was all consideration and had a way of looking at her which warmed and made her feel a faint stirring of happiness. She did not know that it was because she was cherished and loved by this ironic and gloomy-faced young man, and that her every word, her every gesture, the way she walked, the soft sweetness of her laugh, her glance and her smile, was an occasion for his terrible and brooding adoration, and his even more terrible despair. He had bought the land for his house for the one reason that it was near her own, and that at least he would see her occasionally if only at a distance. He knew that if Katherine ever guessed what he thought of her she would never see him again, and so he was careful. This was not too hard. He had had to be careful all his life.

"Yes," said Joseph today, as he stood with his brother and sister and looked at his blazingly white new house, "it is as Sean says. I know what I am doing, and I always did."

It was autumn and trees roared and crackled in a bright and nimble wind, and the brilliantly green grass was littered with drifts of scarlet, gold and brown and umber. The slate roof of the compact Georgian house shimmered in the sparkling sun. The pillars were snowy and sturdy. The paths were of red gravel. The stables behind awaited horses and carriages. The polished windows gleamed. Brasses glittered. There were swaths of gray, blue, rose, gold, and silver at every window, and the bronze doors were golden in their newness. It now needed only horses for the fine stables and carriages and pony carts for Regina, and servants. Katherine Hennessey was arranging for the servants, a housekeeper, maids, a butler, a cook, and stable boys, and gardeners. In a week from today Joseph and his family would take up their residence. Two years ago he had moved Regina and Sean to his hotel in Titusville. Mr. Healey's house was up for sale. Joseph would spend at least two days a week in Titusville attending to his business, but he would live at the new American Hotel, which he owned.

"I love our house," said Regina, who was clad in the seal jacket and muff and hat which Joseph had bought for her. Her draped silk dress billowed in the sharp and pungent wind. "I shall be happy to live in it with you, Joe, dear." She looked up at him with her deep purplish-blue eyes, and he thought that such beauty was incredible and something, perhaps, to be feared. Her long glossy black curls flowed down her back, far below her waist. Her brow was like the whitest china, never disturbed by a frown. Her features were pale but translucent, as if light not blood passed through them. Her mouth expressed nothing but seriousness, gentle thoughts, and contemplation. My darling, Joseph thought, as always. My dearest darling.

"I hope you are going to let me have the garden you promised," said Sean. "Not one of these ordered and plucked monstrosities. Something free and wild."

"Right in back, where the beehives are, and I hope they sting the hell out of you," said Joseph. But he put his hand on Sean's shoulder, and Sean became still and did not shrug off the hand of which he was afraid. "You can plant all the flowers you want," said Joseph. "There will be a pretty fence to hide them."

"Now, Joe," said Regina, and she took her brother's hand and pressed it and he was weakened and vaguely ashamed. Perhaps, he thought, he was somewhat too hard on Sean, who irritated him to the point of explosion on occasion. He was beginning to realize that Sean feared him—this insulted and puzzled him—and that instead of Sean drawing closer to him he was retreating in smiling silence and nervousness. For whom had he lived, but these two, the brother and sister he had loved and protected with a ferocity that even he sometimes thought of as too intense? He had given them his life, and all the force and strength and power of his life, and had gone hungry, in his youth, so that they would be fed. This house had been built for them, to provide them with luxurious shelter and pleasure. He had stolen for them. Perhaps, in some way, he had killed for them. He had not held his own life as valuable. His life, he had thought since he was thirteen, belonged to Regina and Sean, and not himself. Only they had made it worthy of keeping.

He had fought the world in order to give it to them, tamed, full of gifts and joy and security. As for himself, life had held nothing. He had endured, so that they might have leisure, hope, education, freedom from the terror that had haunted his whole young life. Yet—he was always catching, these days, Sean's large blue eyes fixed on him with a peculiar and even hostile expression, which changed immediately to a smile. Then Sean would say something in jest, or leave the room. Joseph was left with a sensation of furious bereavement, and perplexity. Sometimes he thought: A man gives his life for his family and stops at nothing, and the family is not grateful. Often, it despises. I gave my family not only my life, but all the love and devotion of which I am capable. Do they understand? Or, in a twisted way, do they think they are entitled to all this, for which I labored and gave up my own youth?

It was only when Regina came to him, silently, touching his hand, kissing his cheek, her eyes filled with a mysterious light, that he felt comforted, reassured. He had the strangest feeling that she understood everything he thought in his moments of misery. She would even, at her age, climb on his knee as she had done as a young child and put her arms about his neck and kiss him softly, and hold him as a mother holds a son, protecting him from pain, calling to him that she was there and would not leave him.

Once he asked her with his cold abruptness, "What's wrong with Sean?"

She had thought for a moment, and then she had said, "He is afraid that you think he is foolish, or something, and not serious. He has never told me. It is just something I have felt, Joe. He is truly grateful to you; he knows what you have done for us. But you, in some way, will not let him tell you. He is not strong as you are strong, Joe. You have a very sharp way of speaking. Sean is now a man, not a little boy. You are not his father. Treat him as a respected brother and not one you believe has no wits at all."

"But, he has no wits," said Joseph, and then he smiled.

"He has his own wits," said Regina, and for one of few

times Joseph was impatient with her. A man was a man, or he was not a man. Daniel Armagh had not been a man.

Today, they went back to the Hospice, where they were staying for a few days. Very shortly they would move into the house on Willoughby Road. Sean and Regina would not see Titusville again, in its uproarious venality and noise and vigilantes and confusion and vicious characters. For some reason which Joseph was never to understand Sean had found it exciting, in spite of his delicate airs and elegance. He had taken a great fancy to Mr. Montrose, and Mr. Montrose appeared to have affection for him, something else which vexed and confused Joseph. (Mr. Montrose had left for Virginia a year ago.) Sean, in Titusville, was alert and glowing and interested. He even went out to the oil fields. He would walk the crowded and noisy streets with an air of delight. He had attached himself to Harry Zeff and his young wife, Liza, with happy devotion. (Harry was now, to Joseph, what Mr. Montrose had been to Mr. Healey.) Harry seemed to like him and enjoy his company. He would listen to Sean when he sang Irish ballads, and applaud with enthusiasm.

"Why don't you teach him to be a man in the raw business of life, Harry?" Joseph once asked.

"There are many ways of being a man, Joe," said Harry.

"He's feckless and a milksop."

Harry and Liza had built a house for themselves in Titusville which decorously followed the fashion of old and established residences. They had urged Joseph to stay with them when he was in Titusville, but he preferred the solitude of his hotel. Besides, the distant cries of Harry's infant twin sons annoyed Joseph. Liza had the delusion of the common born: she believed everyone was interested in her offspring and would interrupt Joseph and Harry, when they were in her house, by triumphantly bringing the squalling little boys into Harry's "study." Even Harry, the perpetually good-natured, would have to order her to leave, which made her cry. Joseph liked Liza and remembered her days of brutality in Mr. Healey's house. But she was now comparatively rich, and had nursemaids, and the intrusion was unpardonable.

"Why don't you get married?" Harry Zeff asked his friend.

The very thought was repugnant to Joseph. His old habit of considering his sister and brother intruded on him. "I have seen no woman as yet," he said, "that I would want to marry." He thought of Katherine Hennessey.

Then Harry said, watching him, "You are a multimillionaire now, Joe. Who is going to get your money? Your sister? She will probably marry, herself. Your brother—" And Harry paused, more keenly watching him.

Sean.

Sean would go to Harvard. Then, what would he do? Would Harvard make a responsible man of him, serious, determined to succeed? Would it change his character, make it resolute and strong? Joseph thought, and he was appalled. He knew that men never changed their nature.

The three Armaghs moved into their new house, which now contained its full staff of servants, and were accompanied by Regina's governess, a young lady who had been rigorously convent-trained, and Sean's tutor. (The latter had been chosen from applicants in Boston, a young man named Timothy Dineen, whom Joseph had liked for his serious appearance, his maturity, and his firm understanding of what was important in life, such as fortitude, courage, intelligence, learning, and manliness. Joseph hoped that Timothy would impart some of his principles to Sean but so far the result had not been one for enthusiasm.)

Sister Elizabeth had selected Regina's governess, a Miss Kathleen Faulk, whose mother was known to the old nun. "I want no pieties in this house," Joseph had told the young woman and Timothy from the start. "Keep your holy water, your medals, your crucifixes, your pious literature and your holy pictures, in your own quarters, and do not intrude them elsewhere."

Timothy, who was fearless, and several years younger than Joseph, said, "Mr. Armagh, may I enquire, then, why you chose Catholics for your sister and your brother?"

In spite of himself Joseph gave his hard-lipped smile. "I don't want them to be out of their element—yet. It might confuse them. As for Miss Regina, she is very religious and I never interfere with one's religion. It would make her unhappy to deprive her of what she has always known. Sean —there is muscle in your religion, Mr. Dineen, as well as sentimentality and statues in sickly colors. Endurance. Fearlessness. Respect for authority and education. Masculinity. Awareness of living. Strength. I've known many old priests—" He paused, and Timothy held his own mouth still. "They had what we call fortitude, and faced a Sassenagh with a gun with nothing but their breviaries in their own hands and shouted him down for the sake of a child or a helpless woman."

Again he paused, remembering, and the dark Celtic gloom deepened on his face and the younger man felt a confused pity. "So," said Joseph, "try to put some steel into the backbone of your pupil, Mr. Dineen, and make him a little worthy of the brave men who died for him."

Such as yourself, poor devil, thought young Timothy, who had had the good fortune to be born "lace-curtain" Irish, and whose grandfather had come to America long before the Famine and with a sturdy trade in his hands.

Miss Kathleen Faulk was a pallid fair young woman, very thin but durable, with a large nose and light eyes and an air of competence. She was very tall, much taller than Timothy Dineen, who had a quick but squarish look, solid and compact, obvious muscles and vitality and health, and very deep black eyes and a rolling mass of black hair. He looked like a pugilist, rather than a scholar, and had been taught by the Jesuits and had few illusions left, as he would remark. He wore spectacles on his snubbed nose and his mouth was strong and pink and a little inflexible. Miss Faulk, who earnestly desired to be married, had considered Timothy at once, even though his head did come only to the height of her nostrils, but he continued to show no interest.

Now horses were quartered in the stables, and carriages, traps and buggies, all of the best quality, and exotic plants were already blooming, this chill November day, in the glass conservatories, and warm fires burned on brown, blue, white, rose, and purplish marble hearths all over the big bright house. Joseph had ordered that the servants' quarters under the eaves be made as comfortable and pleasant as possible, and he gave them excellent wages and was courteous to them, and they marveled and were happy and did all they could to please the somber Master on his return from his affairs in Titusville, Pittsburgh, Philadelphia, Boston, New York, and in other cities.

"We must have a party!" said Sean to his sister after they had been installed in their new house for a month and the first snow was falling.

"We must ask Joe," said Regina.

"Joe?" said Sean. "You know what he would say, Ginny. No."

"He knows we can't live alone," said the girl. "He has told me to make friends. I know a lot of the girls in the convent. They would be so pleased to be invited here, with a few of the Sisters."

Sean was aghast. "That ugly mass of tatterdemalions! Joe would give the back of his hand to them, and so would I. I never want to think of that orphanage again. Ginny, you know how I detest their ugliness and poverty and smells—I never could stand them. Their very presence here would depress me beyond describing."

Regina was horrified. She knew that Sean shrank from the sight of suffering, and everything morbid and wretched and unbeautiful, but she had endured the same deprivations and the same unlovely scenes, and thought of the orphanage, now, with compassion and sadness and a hope that she might be able to persuade Joseph to make life there brighter and more bearable.

"They would remind me," said Sean, with real distress, "of all those terrible years we had to spend there, for no fault of our own. And we waited, and waited, all that time, for Joe to keep his promise. I had just about given up hope —He could have done it sooner." He tossed back his golden hair in a gesture of remembered misery and resentment. "He must have wasted a lot of time. He could have done it sooner."

"He could not have done it sooner!" said Regina. "How can you be so cruel, Sean? Sister Elizabeth has told me what Joe suffered, and how he worked for us—" She could not continue for fear of bursting out crying. For one of the rare times in her tranquil life she felt the sharp edge of uncontrollable anger and indignation.

"Very well," said Sean. "I am grateful, and you know it, Ginny, and I don't like the peculiar way you are staring at me now. It is just that I cannot even endure the very thought of those—people. The orphanage. Our party must be made up of better specimens."

"Richer, more fortunate, perhaps?" said Regina and her young voice held its first bitterness, its first contempt, and Sean looked at her uneasily and wondered what had happened to his benign and thoughtful sister and her understanding.

Regina thought: I believed that Sean had the kindest and

tenderest of hearts, and perhaps he has though I don't know any longer. Perhaps he is one of those who cannot bear the sight of ugliness or pain or despair, not out of cruelty or hardness but out of a fear of them and because they offend his eye.

Sean said, "Very well, Ginny, I'm sorry I hurt your feelings. But I can't help what I feel, dear. I never want even to think of that orphanage again, where we were caged like beasts." His melodious voice rose passionately. "Can't you understand, Ginny? I don't care about new friends being richer or more fortunate, as you called them. I just want to know people who are different from those we have known. Is that so heartless, so incomprehensible?"

Regina bent her head and a long black curtain of her hair fell over her face and half hid it. "I will ask Joe," she said. She stood up and left the luxurious breakfast room where she and Sean had been eating, and Sean watched her go, hurt and somewhat perplexed, and with a feeling that his sister had betrayed him. He had always thought of Regina as a young princess, tall and stately and serene, always ready with a look or touch of sympathy, always gazing at her brother with great dark blue eyes which swam with radiance and affection. Now, he thought, it is always Joe, Joe, Joe, as if he were a member of the Trinity, Itself, instead of a rough brute of a man without any of the amenities and with the face of a boulder that has stared at the sky relentlessly for ages. He always frightened me half to death, even at his best. No finer feelings, no subtleties, no eye except for money, money, money.

Sean absently fingered the goldpieces in his own pocket and forgot who had given them to him. Sighing, he went into one of the noble parlors—now called the music room —and sat down at the piano and played to console himself and ease the misery of his own dejection. Soon the delectable notes of Debussy dashed at the gilded paneled walls like bright water, and sparkled in the air and sang like fountains in the sun.

Finally, feeling much happier, Sean's fingers rippled gayly on the board and he threw back his head and sang joyously, hardly conscious of the words but only of the music:

"They're hanging men and women for the wearing of the Green!"

He heard a cough and looked up, smiling, to see Timothy Dineen standing near him. His hands fell from the keys.

"Pretty song, isn't it?" asked Timothy.

Sean began to laugh his light laugh but something in Timothy's face startled him, and again he was baffled. Everyone was very strange this morning.

"I had two uncles who were hanged, and a young aunt," said Timothy, "for that very 'wearing of the green,' in Ireland. Somehow, I don't find it very amusing."

"For God's sake!" cried Sean. "I was just singing! Doesn't a man dare sing in this house?"

But Timothy was staring at the newly falling snow through the velvet-draped windows.

"I don't think your brother would like to hear that song sung so merrily, either," he said. "But come along. You are already half an hour late for your studies." His black eyes contemplated Sean without kindness, and then he turned and went out.

Chapter 27

Katherine Hennessey walked slowly and with considerable feebleness across the vast and whitely shining hall of her house. From large arched windows draped in lace and velvet on each side of the huge bronze doors the lucid light of early morning poured into the hall, and there was softer light streaming down the enormous marble stairs which led to upper floors. Sofas and love seats in rose and gold and blue lined the white-paneled walls, which were traced in silver, and upon orange plants and other exotic flora in their Chinese pots. The air was warm and silky, for this was the middle of May, and the scent of flowering gardens and shrubs and red-bud trees had penetrated into the hall. Beyond the doors fresh new trees lifted their leaves, and they were so young that they appeared wet with gleaming water, and they stirred and glittered in the sun.

A profound and tremulous hope had come to Katherine Hennessey recently, for her husband would run for Governor of the Commonwealth in November, and he would be at home more often, perhaps every weekend and at every holiday, and several consecutive weeks in the year. She had hated Washington and its mud and its teeming people and its predatory politicians, and its dank streets ugly to her, for all their width, and the blank Circles and the ostentatiously large government buildings, and the stench of its Negro slums, and its sewers. The climate had made her ill. The Potomac, to her, was a sluggish and filthy and noxious stream, often covered with fog, and now, to her, the city was a tomb for she still mourned Mr. Lincoln. The houses, the majority of them, had seemed crowded and unattractive, and the wooden and brick walks rough to her feet, and the cobblestones had appeared slimy.

She was quite convinced that Washington had put its own disgusting mark on her husband—poor Tom—and had wearied him to death, and had separated him from his family because of endless and devoted duties. Even in summer, that most awful and impossible summer of Washington, he had had to remain in Washington, toiling for the welfare of the Commonwealth of Pennsylvania and the whole nation, enduring the sodden heat, the stinks, the almost tropical rains and storms, and the pervading mud. Now he would come home. When in Philadelphia—she did not doubt that a grateful Commonwealth would elect him—he would be very near. Perhaps they could have a small house there where she could be with him. He was not young any longer. He was in his late fifties. Here her sorrowful mind would become darkly shifting and confused. In Washington, there had been so many Temptations from Unscrupulous Adventuresses, all preying on defenseless politicians so far from home—so lonely—so homesick— One could not always blame the Gentlemen—one had to hold fast and love and understand, and forgive. One must always console herself that she was the Wife, the Chosen, and must think as little as possible no matter when grief assaulted her and shame and humiliation, and not imagine herself an actual object of contempt, despised, rejected. One must conceal Tears. Katherine was often stringent and harsh in her thoughts of herself. She had frequently, when her pain was too great, gently upbraided her husband, and had wept, and had forgotten that Gentlemen detested tears and fled from them, and that they deserved more consideration from their wives.

Since Senator Hennessey had announced that he was the candidate of his party for the office of governor in the autumn—explaining in luscious tones and with trembling inflections that he wished to be more with his beloved family —Katherine had bewitched herself with the delusion that all she had ever suspected, all she had ever known, of her husband, had been the fantasies of her own hard and obdurate heart, her own abominable hallucinations, her own narrow soul. Why else would dear Tom have given up his labors in Washington as a prominent and popular senator, if not for the desire to return more frequently to the bosom of his family? She had been wrong, wrong, wrong, and wicked and full of evil imaginings, and she spent hours on her knees at home and in church praying for forgiveness and doing penance. She only hoped, humbly, that Tom would forgive her if not soon then before she died. She had appealed to her confessor to inflict more penances on her, and he had looked at her with compassion, and very strangely, and had often lifted her when she had thrown herself at his feet, and had held her shaking gloved hands while thinking thoughts which were not priestly but very much the anger of a knowledgeable man. What did even a priest say to an innocent woman who confessed sins of which she was not guilty? How console her, uplift her? He had finally said, knowing it was the truth but in some way a sophistry on this occasion, that all were guilty before God of monstrous sins, that no one had any merit of his own but only that given to him by the merciful Father, and that peace lay in the knowledge of forgiveness and confession. Sometimes he thought Katherine excessively scrupulous, and had once chided her on this, but her insistence on her sins silenced him. However he had marveled at the besottedness of a woman's devotion to a man so unworthy of any devotion at all, so splendidly vicious, so magnificently and triumphantly wicked and exigent. But love, the priest remembered, was greater than faith and hope, and forgave all things, endured all things, excused all things—and finally blamed itself for the evil of others. If women, thought the priest, would love God as passionately as they loved their betrayers then indeed some Grace might come to this terrible world, for the love of women was far greater than the love of men.

Tonight, thought Katherine Hennessey as she walked slowly and with a slight panting difficulty across the marble to the bronze doors, dearest Tom would be home for his darling daughter's seventeenth birthday celebration. She smiled fondly as she put her thin white hand on the handle of the door. Seventeen. She, herself, had been a wife and mother just before her seventeenth birthday, but young ladies these days were more independent and saucy and had strong minds. Darling Bernadette! She was willful and not always respectful to her elders, but she had such a spirit, such a liveliness, such a way of tossing her long sleek brown curls, such a sparkle of brilliant defiance in her eyes, that one forgave her on the spot. No wonder dear Tom loved his daughter so much. At her age he must have been her masculine replica, and Katherine pondered, with love, on the young Tom she had never known but whom she cherished in Bernadette. I am, thought Katherine, as she pantingly pulled open the bronze door, unworthily blessed.

She was amused at her weakness. I am an old woman, she thought. I am going on thirty-four. That is young no longer. I am beginning to feel the infirmities of age. I must be careful of my health and strength, for my darlings' sakes.

She was going to stroll on the lawns and among the gardens, as her doctor had recommended. She had dutifully taken her iron pills this morning. She had forced herself, as her doctor had ordered, "to partake of Sufficient Nourishment to Invigorate the System and the Frame." But she had become disgustingly and violently ill—as usual—and this caused her fresh feelings of dismay and guilt. So she had again forced herself to drink some milk, weeping, and eat some toast, and to take her pills. Neither she nor her doctor ever once suspected that her suppressed knowledge of the shame, brutality, betrayal, rejection, contempt, and humiliation she had endured since her marriage, and the endless exploitation, had destroyed her health and endurance for all time.

She was at last able to open the heavy door far enough to let her out. She did not know that young Bernadette had come halfway down the stairs to the hall while she had been feebly making her way across it, and had been watching her mother with a mixture of disdain and cynicism and wondering and contemptuous pity. Mama was such a fool, such an old-fashioned elderly woman, such, really, an imbecile. She knew nothing at all about Papa, whom Bernadette loved very much. (She had little affection for her mother, who was so weak and soft and stupid, so determinedly deluded, so devoted, so gentle, so forbearing, so spiritless, so anxious to run, at any time of the day or night, to alleviate someone's distress or hunger or homelessness—even if the person was a stranger. She wasted so much money on that miserable orphanage, and other charities, money which she was spending from what would eventually be her daughter's estate. Bernadette often felt outrage over this, and indignation. So did her father, who agreed with her.)

Bernadette went to one of the windows beside the doors and watched her mother's piteously thin and fragile figure moving with slow difficulty across the lawns. The girl shook her head with amused exasperation. Katherine was dressed in a light blue silk frock, with the new big bustle behind and then draped front—all pearls and embroidery—and she looked like a ridiculous skeleton in it, her feet fumbling under the hem for balance. Katherine's mass of tawny natural waves and ringlets had been caught up in a huge chignon on her delicate head, and Bernadette again felt resentment that her own hair was straight and shining brown and lank, and had to be put up in rags every night to achieve the long fall of sleek tubes which hung down her plump back.

For Bernadette was plump though "pleasingly so, no mere bag of bones," as her father frequently assured her, with a glance at Katherine, who was tall and so desperately frail and thin. Certainly Bernadette had a rounded and mature figure at seventeen, a full and thrusting breast, wide hips, and glossy dimpled arms and legs. Her skin, unlike Katherine's, was faintly golden, another exasperation for it suggested a vulgar exposure to the sun, and Bernadette never exposed herself so. Her round hazel eyes, always sparkling, with short brown lashes, were still another vexation, for her mother had, Bernadette confessed, the most beautiful and changeful eyes she had ever seen, and her father's were light and interesting. Bernadette's face was round—"like a bun," a disrespectful governess had once said—and a little flat in profile, with a small tilted nose, lips too large and red, teeth too large and white, and a chin too aggressive for a woman.

The girl, clad in a morning frock of yellow linen sprigged with tiny roses, fashionably bustled and draped with a moderate simplicity, gave her an air of sprightliness, lively motion, vitality and exuberance, as she watched her mother's progress over the lawns. Now the silly thing was talking to a stable boy, with the deep seriousness and that deep kind smile she always wore when speaking to anybody. Couldn't she ever see how absurd she was, gazing at people like an illuminated saint? No wonder Papa had "associated" with brighter and gayer women! After all, a man can stand so much of a fool, and then he must console himself. Bernadette had not been appalled at the giggling revelations of her schoolmates at St. Amelia's Female Academy in Philadelphia which concerned her father. In many ways, secretly, she was proud of her father's virility and manifest masculinity. At least he was a man, and not a caricature of a woman as her mother was. Bernadette was not deceived that her father was seeking the governorship to be "with my beloved family more often." She knew very well, from reading hints in the newspapers, that Papa was about finished in Washington, and that the State Legislature was no longer in a mood to reappoint him once again. Papa had been entirely too zestful in Washington, though Bernadette never condemned him. She thought him delightful, and justified.

She had her father's own exigency, his expedient way of managing things to his advantage, his own gusto, his own lack of conscience and delicacy, his own unconcern for others, his own absence of illusion, and his own cynicism. She also had his charm, which she used deliberately, and was usually laughing saucily or uttering an impertinent witticism, and she had such perfect health that that health alone drew people to her, forgiving her sallies, her impudence, her arrogant ways. The Sisters at her school had often deplored "dear Bernadette's irreverence," but had loved her, as a whole state had loved her father.

Bernadette, still watching her mother, impatiently pushed aside a strand of her overly fine hair from her forehead—which was too low, too rounded, and freckled. Now what was Mama doing, for Heaven's sake? Katherine, just joined by a gardener's boy, was bending and seriously inspecting the early roses in a flower bed, and from her slight gestures and her expression, she was being gently earnest. Her waist is like a stick, thought Bernadette. She has no bosom, no hips. Her complexion looked ghastly in the sunlight, for all color had long abandoned it except for the deep rose of her mouth. Her hair shimmered like dark gold in the sun, and she was now absently pushing a curling tendril behind one of her ears as she listened to the boy. Her dress was too elaborate for the morning, Bernadette reflected. But she was always dressed as if about to receive guests —and at this hour, too! The light warm breeze was lifting some of the ringlets and waves on Katherine's head and Bernadette thought, with envy, that she, herself, tried to avoid breezes which could unfurl those careful long tubes of brown hair which hung down her back and make them lank and stringy. Mama never wore snoods. Tomorrow, she, Bernadette, at seventeen, would insist on a snood for herself, which would control her hair and make her a mature lady. And she was damned if she was ever going back to St. Amelia's Female Academy! She had had enough of that. She thought of herself, with a thrill of pleasure, being Papa's hostess in Philadelphia, at dinners and soirees and balls. Later, she would have a husband. She was old enough for marriage, for God's sake. She had a man in mind, and all at once her young strong body was hot and trembling.

The man she really desperately loved and desired was Joseph Francis Xavier Armagh, the brother of a girl she tolerated and cultivated assiduously only for one reason. Mary Regina was almost as silly as Mama—and Bernadette resented and envied the other girl's beauty. Regina was sent to no female academy. Her brother kept her at home with a governess to teach her graces and manners, and Timothy Dineen to educate her. Bernadette had long ago discerned Joseph's deep attachment to his sister, and so Bernadette had pursued that sister relentlessly, with sweetness, sometimes even with fawnings, and always with loudly expressed affection and devotion. Regina, who had no love for lavish parties, always accepted Bernadette's invitations, and she had made some friends of her own in Green Hills, girls as quiet and contemplative as herself, and as intelligent.

It was not Joseph's wealth alone which had early attracted the nubile Bernadette, but his very appearance, his air of assurance and power and distinction, his look of ruthlessness, of cold dominance. Sean was like a waving blossom compared with an oak, and Bernadette despised Sean, who was now in Harvard and not doing excellently.

(Bernadette knew almost to the penny how much money it had cost Joseph to get Sean admitted to Harvard. Her father had chuckled about it. "They never want the Irish," he had said, "except for—" And he had rubbed his fingers knowingly together. "Especially not Irish born in Ireland." To Bernadette, second generation American-Irish, the Irish-born were greenhorns and rude and uncouth, except for Joseph Armagh.)

Bernadette had hinted of her attachment to Joseph a year ago, and her father had laughed. "You could do worse, my pet," he had said. "He has even more money than I have, and is a director and a power in many companies, and is no fool, and has a lot of pride, and will go very far, and is deeply involved in politics—I am relying on his support, I must confess, in his newspaper, the *Philadelphia Messenger,* which has great influence. He will never run for anything, himself—one must remember his—er—his—" Tom had paused. One didn't mention brothels to one's daughter. He continued, "With his connections. Some of them not quite gentlemanly. Well, we'll see, later."

It was now "later," in Bernadette's opinion. Mama had been a wife and mother at seventeen. Why, thought Bernadette, I am almost an old maid! I'm not even remotely bespoken. Who wants callow boys, anyway, instead of a man like Joe, who is just like Papa?

Bernadette remembered, with pleasure, that Papa would be coming home tonight for her party. The servants, this afternoon, would begin to deck the huge and glittering house. The lanterns would be hung in the gardens. If the weather remained fair there would be a wooden platform on the back lawns for the musicians and the dancing. There was already a humming and a stir in the servants' quarters and in the kitchen. There would be awnings and tents and candlelight and singing. School friends from Philadelphia were due this afternoon with their chaperones or their Mamas, and every girl who was anybody in Winfield and Green Hills had been invited. Bernadette thought of her gown, which she had selected herself—one of Worth's most beautiful—in New York. It was white satin of a richness like velvet, with loops of tiny silk red roses over the narrow skirt, and roses gathered under the new bustle in the back, and a bodice voluptuously cut to reveal her full golden breasts, and with diamonte tiny buttons, and little flounced sleeves just covering the shoulders. It had been artfully styled to reveal Bernadette's attractions and to conceal her plumpness. Her white silk slippers would have real diamond buckles on them. Her father's gift would be a necklace of fine matched pearls, and her mother's a beautiful diamond bracelet. She would wear long white kid gloves, and roses in her hair. She would be irresistible.

To Joseph Armagh.

Of course, he was the oldest young man to be invited to the party, and he would accompany that foolish Regina. The rest would be "boys," as Mama thought fitting. Polite, nervous "boys" with clammy gloved hands, and some with pimples. Mama really had no sense. She, herself, had married a man old enough to be her father, and she had murmured something about Joseph's "age." Thirteen years difference! How ridiculous. This was strange, too, for Mama was much attached to Joseph, thank God.

Bernadette was the only one who suspected this, for her

disillusioned eyes saw almost everything. But they had not detected Joseph's powerful and unshakable love for her mother. They saw only courtesy and courtliness toward Katherine, and deference, and even a slight overt tenderness. Naturally, he would give all this to a woman of Mama's age, though Mama was only two or three years or so older than he. But men were different from women. Bernadette had almost persuaded herself that Joseph's attentions to her mother, so unnaturally gentle, were for her sake. The girl, ardently pursued by young men even from Boston and New York—brothers of her schoolmates—and young men from Philadelphia and Pittsburgh and Winfield —had no doubt but that she need only lift a finger and Joseph would fall at her feet. She intended to lift that finger tomorrow.

She knew that she amused Joseph with her pertness and her witticisms, which sometimes bordered on his own irony, and that he believed she loved his sister devotedly. She had guessed that at times her effrontery amused him even more, and her liveliness and vitality. With him she was also artless, laughing, coy and flirtatious. She was also, she remembered acutely, very rich and rich men did not marry Cinderellas. Her father was a senator, and he would be governor, and the family had social power in Washington and all over the Commonwealth, and were established —as Joseph's family was not. "Shanty" Irish, Tom Hennessey had once said with indulgence, not knowing that Joseph had applied that term to him on many occasions. "But a good mind, for all that, and some amenities and manners and conduct." He would have preferred that Bernadette had desired Sean, nearer her own age, and very Anglo-Saxon in appearance. "One would never guess he was Irish."

She would advance an idea to her father tonight: She wanted to be tutored by Timothy Dineen, too. "He has taught Regina twice as much as I have learned in Philadelphia. It is only a step for me to the Armaghs' house, and you know how dearly I love Regina, and I would be among my closest friends in Green Hills." She would then encounter Joseph more often in his own house, if her little gambit failed tomorrow. But, how could it fail? Who was he, compared with Bernadette Hennessey, in establishment? She loved him, she told herself with virtue, despite what he was. Such pure love must surely be returned. Besides, her house was far more grand, and she had a lady for a mother.

It would have amused and amazed Bernadette to know that her mother had guessed, even two years ago, that her daughter was infatuated with Joseph Armagh, and that she considered her daughter tender and loving and single-hearted. (She, like Bernadette, thought all the deference, consideration and courtliness extended to her by Joseph was because of a reserved and growing attachment to Bernadette.) Once she had said to her daughter, "Joseph is so strong and dependable and such a gentleman," and she had watched Bernadette's suddenly flushing face with love and understanding. She also thought Bernadette, the dear child, so shy and so young, in spite of the flippancy and the impertinence and the sometimes vicious impatience, and the severe letters from the Sisters. Bernadette could be difficult, Katherine admitted, but that was the fault of her youth which time would ameliorate, and in the meantime her mother must exercise restraint and be indulgent. She could conceive of no man more worthy of her darling than Joseph.

Now, what the hell is she doing? thought Bernadette, watching her mother through the window. Oh, how ridiculous!

For the gardener's boy had picked a white rosebud and was tendering it to Katherine with an awkward bow. Katherine looked at him, smiling. Then she took the rosebud and tucked it in her bodice and was obviously thanking the bumpkin. She bent her beautiful head and sniffed at the rosebud. I shouldn't wonder but that there are tears in her silly eyes, thought Bernadette, highly diverted. But what presumptuousness. I must tell Papa tonight, and how he will laugh—a greenhorn and her old mother, bowing and smiling and scraping to each other. Bernadette was suddenly cross. Had her mother no sense of the proprieties? But then, she was always kissing and hugging the ugliest and most snot-nosed brats at the orphanage, and bringing them gifts. She must have some common blood, thought Bernadette.

Then the girl's attention was caught by something moving briskly through the gates on the graveled road and towards the house. In a moment or two Bernadette saw that it was one of the better hacks of the depot, and that it contained a young lady. Bernadette thought that the woman was probably the mother or the chaperone of one of her own guests due tonight. But where was the guest? Bernadette opened the bronze doors and walked out upon the white steps of the pillared portico.

The lady, assisted by the driver, alighted on the path and Bernadette saw that she was very beautiful and young, and not more than twenty-one, and arrayed lavishly in lavender silk and lace, and that she had marvelous slender ankles and a mass of pale hair under her little tilted hat. Her features, Bernadette could see even from this distance, were small and exquisitely cut, like Dresden, and her gloves were lavender and so was her silk coat and parasol. She was extremely *soignée* and stylish and her figure was lovely in all its proportions, and she was tall. Though she had a controlled air, and was apparently of excellent breeding, there was something agitated about her, and the inquisitive Bernadette was surprised.

Katherine, equally surprised, left the flower bed and went to the stranger, making a soft, self-deprecating gesture with her thin hands. She then motioned towards the house, but the lady—who was regarding Katherine with earnest attention—shook her head slightly. Katherine paused, as if a little baffled. Bernadette could hear their voices, though not their words. Then Katherine was no longer speaking; the wind caught her blue dress and it was as if it had touched the shroud of a dead woman. Bernadette wanted to run to join them but manners had been literally beaten into her by the Sisters, and so she cautiously advanced only to the steps of the portico and strained to hear.

The strange young lady continued to speak, and Bernadette saw that her mother was very still, only her blue dress and her hair blowing a little and that she was, suddenly, dwindled and shrunken in appearance. The young lady's voice rose desperately. "I implore you, Mrs. Hennessey, to be merciful and kind! To understand, to remember that I am a sister-woman in a terrible situation. Not to judge me, or your husband, but only to be kind and compassionate. It was probably most wrong of us—I know it was, and we are guilty, and from my heart I ask your pardon, and even your pity, for one so much younger than yourself. You have a daughter. Consider me as a daughter, too, who comes to you in wretchedness not only pleading for forgiveness, but asking your help."

Then Katherine spoke in a dry and almost inaudible voice: "But—what did he tell you, about me, about himself?" She put her hand to her slight breast in a pathetic gesture.

The young lady's face was running with tears as she leaned towards Katherine. "Only what you know yourself, Mrs. Hennessey, that he intends to leave you when he is elected governor, and that he has asked you for a divorce and you have refused, in spite of my dire situation and my helpless position. Is it possible that you will continue to deny our child his father's name, you who are a mother, yourself? Could any human being be so cruel? I don't believe it, your face is so gentle, so—tender. Tom must have been mistaken. He has told me that you will not let him go, because you want his money, and that you never loved each other, and it was a marriage of convenience, which he has always regretted. But surely you know this, yourself! He prefers, as he has told you, that you sue for the divorce, but, if not, he will be forced to do so, even at the expense of his career, for he has our unborn child to consider. Mrs. Hennessey, I appeal to your womanly heart, your pity, to let him go at once! He does not know I have come to you, but I was driven—I wanted to appeal—"

Katherine rocked vaguely on her heels. She put her hand to her face, as if in bemused wonder, a dream, in incredulity. Her fragile body swayed. Bernadette started down the stairs, only half comprehending. Then Katherine turned, very, very slowly, her hands fumbling helplessly in the air, and she faced the house and took two uncertain steps towards it, her white face blank and without any expression at all. She staggered. She threw up her arms as if drowning, and then she dropped to the shining green grass and lay there, tossed and thrown, a bundle of bodiless blue. The gardener's boy ran to her, and Bernadette began to run. She reached her mother and stood beside her but did not bend or touch her. She looked only at the beautiful young lady who was staring at Katherine, aghast, her hand to her lips.

"Who are you?" she asked of the stranger, and the woman, still looking only at Katherine, said faintly, "I—I am a friend of the senator's—a friend. He wants to leave his wife but she will not let him go." She became aware of the young girl. She looked at Bernadette with stretched green eyes. "Who are you?" she whispered.

"I am the senator's daughter," said Bernadette. "And you are a liar."

When Joseph Armagh entered the great hall of the Hennessey house he saw that Bernadette, disheveled and weeping and swollen of face, was the only one there. The hall had been partially decorated, and then deserted. There was utter silence in the enormous mansion, a sensation that death was already present.

Bernadette, crying wildly, ran to Joseph and flung herself on his chest. His arms rose automatically and held her, and he listened to her incoherent cries with a stunned expression. He listened to her words, finally, with a suddenly sharp attention.

"She lied, she lied!" Bernadette half-screamed. "She is an adventuress—my father—she lied. She killed my mother. I heard it all—"

"Your mother sent for me," said Joseph, still holding the girl, whose morning dress was crumpled and stained.

Bernadette clung to him. "She lied! My father would never do a thing like that—" Her voice became furious, then pleading, as she kept her head rigidly against Joseph's chest. Joseph listened, and as he listened his Gaelic face darkened to bleakness and savagery. He stared over the girl's head as if seeing something unpardonable, something too terrible to be true. The girl continued to pour out her desperate words, her gasping accusations, her defense of her father, her anguish over her mother, and Joseph, all at once, was aware of her youth, her misery, her wildness and hysteria. He put his hand on the head that lay on his chest, and his face blackened more and more.

"Hush, hush," he said. "Where is your father?"

Bernadette shrieked, "She won't see him! He doesn't dare go into her room! The priest is here—Extreme Unction—and the doctor's with her! To say such things about my father! To think my mother believed them—Oh, my poor mother!" The long tube-like curls had long ago lost their roundness. Bernadette's fine lank hair swathed her like a brown veil, and numerous tendrils on her cheeks and forehead were wet with sweat and tears. Her face was not only swollen, but blotched with red, and she seemed almost beside herself with frenzy, rage and grief and hate. She took Joseph by the arms and shook him and looked at him with starting hazel eyes veined heavily with scarlet, and almost mad in appearance, and dripping.

"My mother doesn't believe him! He tried and tried—She won't have him in her room. He wanted to go in, and she screamed—It was terrible. My poor father! So many enemies—It isn't fair—you've got to tell her—the doctor won't let him in. Oh, my God, Joseph, help me, help me, I don't know what to do! I—I went in, and she wanted to kiss and hold me—I couldn't, I couldn't—I was so afraid—"

Joseph took his own handkerchief and wiped the girl's streaming face and eyes and she sobbed brokenly and clutched him again and convulsively clung to him. He looked about for servants, for someone who would take this weeping child away and comfort her, but every door was shut. The gas chandelier had been lit. Its stark light shown down on the cold white marble of the hall. The stairs were empty. There was no sound. The pictures on the walls gazed at him; the silk of the sofas and love seats gleamed. The pots of little trees and plants seemed wilted. Joseph began to stroke Bernadette's tangled hair gently and absently, and after a while Bernadette stopped screaming and only sobbed, huddling herself tightly against him. He had seen two carriages outside, but it was as if no one was here but himself and Bernadette.

Then a discreet maid's head slyly popped from behind a distant door and Joseph said, "Damn you! Come here and help Miss Bernadette, you slut!" The woman emerged, her eyes sliding, her tongue licking the corners of her lips. She touched her dry eyelids with her white apron. "I didn't want to intrude, sir," she whined. Her face was full of that evil enjoyment which the inferior feel when the superior are in distress. She glanced at Bernadette without favor, and then she assumed a compassionate expression and put her hand on the girl's shoulder.

"Come with me, Miss Bernadette, dear, do," she said. "You must rest."

Bernadette tore herself from Joseph and shook the woman's hand from her and showed her teeth like a wolf. "Get away from me!" she cried. "Get away!"

She seized Joseph again, looking up at him, frantic and distraught. "Don't leave me, Joe, don't leave me!"

Where was that bastard of a father of hers, that he was not with her to comfort and help her?

"I won't leave you," he said. "But your mother sent for me, an hour ago. Where is your father?"

"In his room. I don't know—in his room. He can't stand it—he doesn't know what to do—"

I bet, thought Joseph, and he felt again that powerful urge to kill.

He took Bernadette to a sofa and forced her to sit upon it. She dropped her head to her knees and her arms swung helplessly beside her head. He looked at the avidly staring maid. "Stay with Miss Bernadette," he said. "Don't leave her for a moment." He paused. "Which is Mrs. Hennessey's bedroom upstairs?" With pity he looked down at Bernadette, so agonized, so broken, her arms swinging close to the floor, her long hair hanging about her, her face hidden, her voice keening lamentations and despair.

"Second door to your left, on the floor above," said the maid, and she approached Bernadette cautiously, as if fearing the girl would leap at her throat. She sat down on the edge of the sofa beside the girl and folded her hands in her apron and looked up at Joseph with total emptiness. Her face assumed a hypocritical expression and she sighed. The gaslight glared down pitilessly, and there was still no sound. Yet here was a house which had begun to prepare for a party. Who had sent the guests away? How could there be such abandonment here? Bernadette's wailing sobs echoed through the vast hall. The rich have no friends, thought Joseph. But then, who does?

Joseph went to the wide marble staircase with its gilded bannister and it wound above him. He reached another wide long hall, the white floor partially covered with an Oriental runner; landscapes, excellently painted, hung on the walls. Sofas lined one side. Heavy carved doors of polished wood stood shut before Joseph. At first he did not see Tom Hennessey sitting with his head in his hands on a love seat, the very portrait of despair, nor the priest beside him who looked only ahead as if the other man was not there at all. Here the light of the chandelier was not so vivid, and the hall wavered in half-shadow. When he finally saw the two men Joseph stopped and he looked at Tom Hennessey and a ball of fire and acid stuck in his throat and his vision jerked with the intensity of his hatred.

The priest saw him and rose, a strong middle-aged man recently come to Winfield to the new St. Leo's Church. He held out his hand and said briefly, "Father Scanlon. And you are Mr. Armagh for whom Mrs. Hennessey is asking?"

"Yes," said Joseph and shook hands with the priest. "How is Mrs. Hennessey?"

The priest glanced at the senator who cowered lower on his seat, and he said, "She has received the Last Rites." His grave calm eyes studied Joseph. "It is not expected that she will—live."

He went before Joseph and opened a door and then stood aside. He had seen Joseph's expression when he had looked at the senator and he had sighed inwardly. Joseph entered a dimly lit bedroom large and wide, with three arched windows draped in golden silk and with a white marble fireplace in which a small fire burned. It was a beautiful room, spacious and silent, with only one gaslight burning on one wall, and turned low, and Joseph was aware of muted colors, green and rose and gray. In the center of the room stood a richly canopied bed, and in that bed lay Katherine Hennessey gazing at nothing, and her doctor sat beside her and held his hand on her pulse.

Her tawny hair was spread out on her white silken pillows like a glowing wave, and her white face was absolutely still, and she appeared already dead to Joseph as he slowly approached her. But she felt his presence. Her eyes, dulled now and empty, faintly brightened, and she whispered his name. He bent over her in silence and with a sick and ferocious sorrow, and she moved her free hand and he took it. It was as cold as death. He said, "I came, Katherine," and it was the first time he had ever used her name and he said it not with restraint now but with all the power of his love for her. The faint brightness in her eyes increased. She turned her head to the doctor and whispered, "Alone, please." The satin coverlet covered her to her throat, but she shivered in the warm air, her slight body hardly lifting the quilt.

The doctor stood up, shaking his head dolefully at Joseph, and he murmured, "Only a minute or two." There was a smell in the room of flowers and spirits of ammonia and some other acrid odor of useless medicines. The doctor left and Joseph knelt beside the bed, and Katherine held his hand as if only he could keep her alive, and the iciness of her fingers recalled the touch of his dying mother. The little fire hissed and sparked and threw up reddish lights onto the hearth, and a summer wind hummed softly against the closed windows.

Katherine's dying face was the face of a girl, a suffering and tortured girl, and her lips were gray and her nose was pinched and the nostrils moved in and out as she tried for her last breaths. She did not look away from Joseph, whose head was so near hers, but her eyes probed into his earnestly, hopefully, pleadingly.

"Yes?" said Joseph. "Yes, dear. What is it?"

"Bernadette," she whispered. "My little girl, my child. She loves you, Joseph, and I know you love her and that you have just been waiting to speak—" Her throat almost closed, and she panted and struggled, her chin jutting out.

Joseph knelt very still beside the bed and looked at her and his hand tightened about hers to give her strength, to keep her for a while. Her words entered his mind slowly, and with only a dull astonishment.

"Take her, keep her," said the expiring woman. "She will be—safe—with you, my dear. Take her away—so innocent —so young—Joseph? Promise me?"

"Yes, Katherine," he said. The gaslight rose and fell in a slight draft of air. The pallor of Katherine's face shone in it like marble, itself. "I promise."

She sighed deeply. Her eyes still held his in that pathetic hope and certitude, and she tried to smile. Then she sighed again, and closed her eyes.

He knelt there, watching her, holding her hand, and he did not see the doctor return with the priest and did not hear the beginning of the Litany for the Dying. He did not see Tom Hennessey standing in the doorway, shrinking, not daring to enter. He saw only Katherine's face, becoming smaller and smaller, but quiet now and with growing peace. He did not see the great golden Crucifix that stood over the bed. Nothing existed, had being, but Katherine Hennessey.

Only he heard her final faint breath. He still knelt, not moving. Her hand was flaccid in his. Then he dropped his head so it lay beside Katherine's and he closed his eyes and the awful ripping of grief tore him apart, and he felt that he, too, had died. His cheek touched hers and slowly he turned his head and touched her fallen flesh with his lips.

"Go forth, Christian soul," the priest intoned, and Joseph was again on the ship beside his mother, and there was nothing at all anywhere but anguish and darkness and pain.

Later, when he went slowly down the stairs to the hall, feeling his way with his feet like an old man, he found Tom Hennessey sitting beside his daughter and holding her in his arms and comforting her, and Bernadette had clenched her young arms about her father's neck and she was sobbing against his chest.

"It isn't true, my darling," said the senator. "It was all lies. The woman tried to make me leave your mother—she was mad and infatuated—I tried to drive her away—I wrote her a foolish letter because I pitied her—I confess I was a little drunk—My darling, your blessed mother had always been delicate, her heart, but she understood—She understood. You mustn't grieve. It is for the best—an end to her suffering—" His voice had never been so deep and so resonant and so rich, and Bernadette's sobs lessened.

Then the senator saw Joseph near him, silent and watching, and the eyes of the men met and neither spoke. For a long time their eyes held each other. At last Joseph, hardly making a sound, left the hall, opened the door and went out into the warm summer night and closed the door after him. But the senator stared at the door for a considerable space, for never had a man ever looked at him like that before.

Chapter 28

Mr. James Spaulding was old but his avidly sympathetic eyes under their heavy lids were as bright and malignant and smiling as ever, and his hair as flagrantly dyed. The rubbery texture of his features—now wrinkled and somewhat collapsed—had become even more mobile and seemed almost in constant motion, with the pursing and pushing out of lips, with the wrinkling of forehead and heavy cheeks and the sniffing and twitching of nose. His ears were larger and pushed out his hair which was now poetically near his shoulders. He affected the long soberly rich coat of Prince Albert, and the striped trousers and the subdued cravat and the big pearl pin, and his boots were narrow and polished.

He was very rich, for he not only received a handsome "stipend" from the estate of Mr. Healey, as had been designated in the will, but Joseph was careful to give him gifts also, for, as Mr. Healey had jovially warned him, "You've got to keep on buying your friends, Joe, no matter how loyal and true they seem to be. You can buy them with services, but there's no substitute for cash. There's one thing sure: You can't buy them with protestations of love and appreciation and sweet words. No nourishment in them." So Joseph continued to buy Mr. Spaulding and had had no reason to complain of the return in faithfulness and attention to his interests. They did not trust nor like each other, for Mr. Spaulding had also detected the peculiar probity that lay below the immense large rascalities of Joseph's manipulations, and Mr. Spaulding never trusted anyone who was not as great a scoundrel as he was, himself.

Joseph had doubled what he had inherited from Mr. Healey and was well on the way to tripling it. "Midas touch," said Mr. Spaulding with admiration. "Luck of the Irish, as Ed used to say. But you've got to have no conscience," he would add with virtue. He now feared Joseph, he who had never feared a man before and this increased both his respect and his dislike. He could not understand why Joseph had not joined the company of voracious and malevolent men who had looted the prostrate South. He also could not understand the hatred Joseph felt for Thaddeus Stevens of Pennsylvania, ruler of the Republican House of Representatives, and once a vicious enemy of the conciliatory and grief-stricken Abraham Lincoln who had only desired the healing of fratricidal wounds.

It was Stevens who had proclaimed, concerning the beleaguered South: "I have never desired bloody punishment to any great extent, but there are punishments quite as appalling and longer remembered than death! They are more advisable, because they will reach a greater number. Strip a proud people of their bloated estates, reduce them to a level with plain Republicans, send them forth to slave labor and teach their children to enter the workshops—and you will thus humble the proud traitors." He advocated that Congress carve up "the damned rebel provinces," and fill them with settlers from the North—"as though," Joseph said, thinking of Ireland, "the whole South were a conquered foreign land." Stevens tried to force Congress to divide up into tiny thirty-five acre farms, the great plantations of the South, and sell them to freedmen at ten dollars an acre. "I should like to see the Southern whites," said Stevens, "be forced to return to their origins in the British Isles! Or perhaps to France."

Joseph said to Mr. Spaulding, "He is a low-born dog, and he is full of secret hatred of himself, which is to be expected." But Joseph was also thinking of the Irish estates which had been seized by the English and sold to Scots and Englishmen, and the former owners of the farms driven out, starving, onto the highways and byways with their wives and children and old parents. Mr. Spaulding confessed, himself, that he could not understand the virulence of Stevens, who was one of the foremost in the persecution and attempted impeachment of President Andrew Johnson, who had mildly attempted to carry out the merciful plans of the murdered Lincoln. "I can," said Joseph, who had read *Das Kapital*, by Karl Marx, and who remembered his conversations with Mr. Montrose. "He hates himself, for he knows what he is, and to escape the effects of this hatred he hates others, particularly those of finer parentage and tradition." He found little to choose between the Communist Manifesto of Karl Marx of 1848 and Thaddeus Stevens's convictions. "Though Marx," he would reflect, "came of better blood and breeding."

Thaddeus Stevens, in his blood lust, longed for vengeful power over the helpless. Mr. Spaulding remembered that Joseph had come to him and had said, "Find out as much as you can about Stevens, his hidden background, his earlier life, any congress with women, his ambitions, his private affairs." For Stevens, to Joseph, had become the epitome of the English conqueror, without mercy or justice or compassion.

Mr. Spaulding had sedulously carried out his mission. No one knew exactly what had happened—not even Joseph himself knew completely—but Stevens, on the very crest of his triumphant hatred, died suddenly on a sweltering August day in 1868 in Washington, and to the last he was voracious and brutal of lip, and Napoleonic in posture. Yet the evil that had lived in him lived after him, and the Radical Acts set up by Radical Republicans in the North almost destroyed the fallen South, and almost mortally divided a precariously united nation.

It was not the last time that Joseph had put his power for or against a politician. The time had now come, he had decided, to destroy the man he most despised in the world, a man who, though he had not belonged to Stevens's party, had assiduously supported him with a view to loot in the South and had voted with him to impeach President Johnson. Joseph, to increase his power, had become an American citizen. He had arranged a meeting with Mr. Spaulding this warm August day, and he would soon arrive at Mr. Spaulding's offices with his secretary, Timothy Dineen.

Mr. Spaulding had often complained to himself that Joseph was "secretive," and did not often ask the advice of wiser and older heads—like Mr. Spaulding's—and bought and manipulated without apparently consulting anyone. So Mr. Spaulding did not know that Joseph had bought vast acreages in Virginia, at a very low price, and had sold them to Mr. Montrose—Clair Devereaux—for an even lower price. There was just a simple notation in Joseph's personal books: *Investment in Virginia—large loss*. Mr. Spaulding wondered at this, for Joseph was probably the only man who had sustained losses in the South. It was dangerous now, in the North, to be a Democrat, so Joseph had become a Democrat, and when Mr. Spaulding had incredulously protested Joseph had said, "I despise Whigs." To Joseph the whole tragedy of the country had become a conflict between England and Ireland. Had this been pointed out to him by an astute philosopher he would have jeered with derisive laughter, for, as he frequently said, he had no allegiances, no country he loved, and all nations were for exploitation. Only Mr. Healey would have known and understood. Mr. Spaulding knew all the villainies of men, but little of the deep and passionate and subterranean origin of their motives.

So, as Mr. Spaulding awaited the arrival of his client, he read last night's editions of the *Philadelphia Messenger,* the largest newspaper in Pennsylvania. The *Philadelphia Messenger* pointed out, with pride, that it was Mr. Joseph Armagh who had investigated young Jay Gould—"the audacious Wall Street financier"—and had brought to the attention of President Grant that Mr. Gould had "cornered the fifteen million dollars in gold in the nation, in circulation, and had thus forced up its price." Mr. Armagh had also informed the President that it was the President's own brother-in-law who had been the Spy in the White House, and in Washington, and had so conspired with Mr. Gould. As a result of this manipulation the whole country's currency had been shaken, and the whole financial structure. "But Mr. Armagh's enlightenment of the President caused the Treasury to move in and sell government gold, thus saving the country, which might have been ruined." Unfortunately, the paper continued, Mr. Gould's government contacts informed him in time, and he sold at once—at an enormous profit. Other plotters, less in touch with Washington, fell into bankruptcy.

"Are the bankers our rulers, or are our elected officials?" demanded the newspaper in wrath. Joseph, on reading this, had laughed out loud and with contempt at such naïveté. His banker friends, whom he frequently met in New York, and who came from other countries to meet with him, had given him the information concerning Jay Gould. "For," as they said, "America is not prosperous enough for looting as yet. That will come later—we do not know how much later—with the establishment of a private banking institute in America, which will have the power to coin money, and not Congress: a Federal Reserve System. This can come only in the form of an amendment to your Constitution."

It was only in New York City, these past few years, and in some other Northern cities of the New England States—notably Massachusetts—where it was completely safe to be a Democrat. And the Democrats, being only human, found looting quite easy for men of no conscience and inspired only by greed and the lust for power. In theft and rapacity they made even the Radical Republicans look like country shopkeepers. In two years alone the organization of William M. Tweed and a few others of his Tammany conspirators stole seventy-five million dollars from the depressed city of New York, and their total thievery from 1865 to 1871 was estimated by investigators to be in the neighborhood of two hundred millions. Tweed threatened contractors doing business with New York so efficiently that they added one hundred percent to their bills to the city, and returned the overcharge to the Tweed Ring. As a result, in one case alone, New York paid nearly two million dollars for plastering one lone city building, and over a million and a half for some thirty-five tables and chairs. Tweed, of course, was a director of the Erie Railroad, together with one Fisk and Jay Gould, and suborned politicians and judges and even many in the legislature.

This was done with such aplomb, such grace and geniality, such loving laughter, that the miserable inhabitants of New York felt only love for their exploiters, and even adoration, for did these not, close to Election Day, supply them with bread and food and money and beer and whiskey and coal and other gifts for their votes? The fact that if the Tweed Ring had not robbed them in the first place they could have bought these things, and more, for themselves, never entered their simple minds, or, if some man pointed this fact out to them they became infuriated.

Once Joseph had read, "If the people are robbed, oppressed and exploited, if they are driven to wars and calamities and panics and destitution, they, themselves, are the guilty, for they are stupid beyond imagining and look no further than their voracious bellies."

An informed electorate, who would elect only just men no matter their financial power or lack of it, was an impossible dream. Mankind adores its betrayers, and murders its saviors. Joseph did not intend to be a savior of America,

and he often found himself thinking, "The lumpen proletariat, which has no reason for existing at all!"

It was with a sort of brutal vengeance, then, that he had,
as director of two railroads, approved the most appalling
retaliations on the Molly Maguires, the desperate and striking Irish railroad workers in Pennsylvania. If the Molly
Maguires did not murder and fight as violently as did their
oppressors, if they, the Irish, succumbed merely for food,
then they deserved what they received. I found a way,
thought Joseph. Let them find a way, too. For this reason
he had not entirely detested the Tweed Ring. They were
Irish who had refused to remain despised and destitute, and
had looted as they had been looted. He had informed on
Jay Gould and his fellow conspirators not because he, himself, found them reprehensible but because they had threatened his own profits.

But the *Philadelphia Messenger* and the Pittsburgh
newspapers fawned on Joseph Francis Xavier Armagh, and
imputed to him the most immaculate motives and patriotism—"though he had been born in Ireland"—and wondered aloud why he had not sought public office for himself,
"for the sake of his adopted country." (The newspapers quoted a member of the President's Cabinet who had
said, with rage, "You can't use tact with a congressman!
They are all thieves and open to bribery, as we all know.
You must take a stick and hit him on the snout!" The people, of course, had not listened.) Joseph had smiled darkly
when he had read these effusions the night before he came
for consultation with Mr. Spaulding. He, himself, had been
among the bribers of eager congressmen for the sake of his
railroads. (A railroad construction company, Credit Mobi-
lier, had stolen twenty-four million dollars from the U.S.
Treasury, and this had been accomplished with the aid of a
congressman. The congressman had suborned his own colleagues in Congress by giving them free stock in several
railroads, which paid over six hundred percent in dividends
a year.)

Public office was not for Joseph Armagh. It was more
profitable to manipulate the government from outside rather from within. He was to teach his son, Rory, this most salient fact. "The American people beg to be seduced," he
told Rory. "Why should we refuse their love? This is as
true in your day as it was in mine."

When Rory mentioned that an Irishman, Sheriff James

O'Brien, had taken the Tweed Ring's secret accounts to the *New York Times,* which published them in 1871, it was the end of the Ring. The Ring, Rory reminded his father, had tried to bribe the intrepid newspaper with five million dollars not to publish the accounts, but had failed. The newspaper had aroused the desperate New Yorkers and Tweed was put in prison. (Tweed later escaped to Spain, in the guise of a sailor, but even there the newspaper followed him and this resulted in his identification and arrest. He died in a New York prison in 1878.)

Joseph then said to his son, Rory: "We must, of course, always remember the Fourth Estate, as Edmund Burke called the press. I admit that if they, together, ever exposed the government and its thieves—and us—that would be the end. But we have ways of suborning and buying the press, too. Not all of them, certainly, but a number. For we can buy newspapers, and publish what we will." He laughed and said, "Rory, you have probably observed that the newspapers often speak of 'a changing world.' But the world never changes. It is always the same—the eater and the eaten. As your Church told you when you were a child, it is Original Sin, and thank God for it. It has made us rich and powerful." He thought of the Panic of 1873-76, which had, by forcing out small railroaders, made vast fortunes for the Vanderbilts—and himself.

On this hot and golden, dry and rustling August day, Mr. Spaulding read the laudatory effusions of the newspapers concerning Joseph Armagh, and smiled downwards and rubbed his oily and elastic nose, and waited for his client. He wondered how much Joseph would give him this time, and for what.

Joseph arrived with Timothy Dineen before noon, for he had been out in the oil fields since early morning accompanied by his manager, Harry Zeff. (The Armagh Enterprises now had impressive offices in Philadelphia, and that city was Harry's headquarters, and his assistants were the younger men who had been Mr. Healey's "associates," plus clerks and lawyers to the number of over two hundred.)

Mr. Spaulding was all love and heartiness on greeting the young man, and full of solicitude and little tender cries and congratulations. He patted and plucked, though he knew very well that Joseph detested intimacies or even the touch of others.

"Sit down, dear boy, do!" exclaimed Mr. Spaulding. He ignored Timothy who abhorred him. Joseph sat down in a deep red leather chair and Timothy stood near him as though guarding him, his black eyes studying Mr. Spaulding as if he expected him to produce a knife or another lethal instrument. "Brandy, Joe? Whiskey? Wine? I have them all!"

"Nothing," said Joseph. He looked worn yet more potent than ever, and his leanness had increased rather than diminished with his prosperity. He had learned not to despise fine clothing, and his long coat and trousers of black silky broadcloth were expertly tailored if not magnificent, and his vest was not embroidered and his linen was plain white. His black cravat was thin and tied in a bow rather than folded, and a black pearl held its knot. His boots were elegant, though now dusty from the fields. His russet hair was still thick and vital but it had faded, here and there, to shadows of incipient gray. He was clean-shaven as always, and was not following the fashion for mustaches and beards and heavy sideburns. His face was still bony and taut, almost fleshless, his arched nose thinner than ever, his mouth still a closed blade. But his small blue eyes had gained a fixed power over the years and sometimes glittered between his auburn lashes when he was angry or annoyed. There were only a few men who admired the appearance of Joseph Armagh, but women found him fascinating and his cold indifference to the majority only increased their infatuation.

Mr. Spaulding cleared his throat and glanced at Timothy. "Mr. Dineen?"

"Whiskey," said Timothy. His short strong body was broad now with good living, but his muscles were firm and active and his black hair was abundant and carefully waved.

"Whiskey it is!" cried Mr. Spaulding in delight, as if Timothy had given him extraordinary pleasure. "What a warm day it is, to be sure. Yes, indeedy. We expect cooler days at this time in August." He smiled expansively and lovingly as he poured whiskey and soda into a tall glass for Timothy, and extended it to him, making a leg, thought Timothy who took the glass without an expression of thanks.

Mr. Spaulding sat down and beamed at Joseph. "I have been reading all about you in the papers, dear boy! 'Amazing entrepreneur! Associate of the great New York Wall Street Financier, Mr. Jay Regan—the Goulds—the Fisks! Proud that he is a citizen of this mighty Commonwealth! Railroads, mining, oil, milling, building, financial baron!' "

"Not to mention my brothels," said Joseph, "nor my rum-running from the South into my Northern distilleries."

Mr. Spaulding held up tender palms. "They are services deeply appreciated if not publicly approved," he chuckled. "Do you not serve humanity intimately as well as industrially and financially? This is not to be deplored, no matter the blue noses."

"Nor my gun-running here and there, in Mexico and abroad," said Joseph, as if Mr. Spaulding had not spoken. The older man chuckled again, but now his eyes were wary. Joseph was baiting him. He said, "We must make a living at anything that comes to our hands."

"Such as looting the South of its cotton," said Joseph. "Well, I was not guilty of that."

Mr. Spaulding sighed. "I didn't make an enormous profit, Joseph, though others did. It was enough, but not enormous. Besides, had I anything to do with Reconstruction? No."

Joseph said, "Harry Zeff tells me your recent reports to him are well in order. I haven't much time. I am taking the two o'clock to Winfield. I have a mission for you." He paused. He did not move even a finger, yet he gave the appearance of ruthless quickening. "I want you to send me, post haste, a full report on Governor Tom Hennessey. Everything you have, know of accurately, and from your files, which Mr. Healey began and enlarged. No matter how small—I want it. I should like a brief sketch of his father, too."

A hot and brilliant silence fell in the large offices, which smelled of warm leather and wax and lemon oil. Mr. Spaulding had folded his hands on his desk. He regarded Joseph intently. His smile had disappeared but his eyes were brighter and the heavy lids lower.

Then Mr. Spaulding said—Joseph's eyes had suddenly frightened him—"Your father-in-law." His voice, usually so fruity and full of tremolos, was flat and expressionless.

"My father-in-law."

"The grandfather of your two children."

"The grandfather of my two children."

Timothy shifted on his neat feet and drank deeply of his

whiskey. There was a sudden shrill singing of cicadas soaring through the open windows. The hills beyond, though still green, showed a tarnishing here and there where hot yellow dust had settled on them, and all at once the traffic on the street was very imminent in the room.

"The governor is running again for office this autumn," said Mr. Spaulding, who was becoming unnerved. "Has what you desire anything to do with that?"

"Yes," said Joseph. His quiet hands, clasped on his knee —long and thin and well-shaped—did not stir.

"But," suggested Mr. Spaulding, and now he licked a corner of his lips with a wet and darting tongue, "more than that?"

"More than that." Then the laconic Joseph said, "I want him absolutely ruined. Stripped. Dishonored. Prison, if possible, though I doubt we can arrange that. He's been too sly and has had too much help to cover up."

Mr. Spaulding leaned back in his chair. He was never shocked at anything, and even this did not startle him. But he was curious.

"It might rebound on you, Joe," he said. "Your father-in-law."

"How can it?" said Joseph. "I control quite a number of newspapers, especially those in Pennsylvania. I have influence in New York, too. But even if some muckraking sheet blares it out, how can it hurt me?" He gave a faint smile.

"I am not running for public office. I am not a politician who can be hurt by public opinion, or votes. There is nothing anyone can do to me, either the people or the government. I am entirely too rich. My affairs are—respectable. I am a director of the big Handell Oil Company, and director of many other companies. I am invulnerable. A word or two to influential politicians—" He raised one hand briefly. "I think we could even keep it out of the newspapers entirely. We will give him a chance to submit or be publicly crucified. He has only to renounce any desire to be governor again—and accede to the loss of his fortune, to the extent we can manage. I will be the one to give him that advice."

"He will never know who did it," said Mr. Spaulding.

"I intend to inform him, when it is done," said Joseph.

Mr. Spaulding caught his breath. He had guessed long ago that Joseph hated his father-in-law, but he had thought it a conflict of temperament. Governor Hennessey had been

overwhelmingly pleased by his daughter's choice of a husband. Her wedding had drawn dignitaries from all over the
Commonwealth, and Washington, and two foreign ambassadors had been present. The wedd ng had taken place in
Philadelphia in the governor's house—his own, not the
Commonwealth's—and it was still mentioned frequently
among society, and even in New York. It had been so lavish, so ostentatious, that one or two small newspapers had
protested "this extravagance in the midst of a Panic—people starving—strikers being murdered by the railroaders—
miners being shot down in their own little shacks before
their wives and children. The display must invite the anger
of Providence." Mr. Jay Regan, Mr. Fisk, and Mr. Gould
had been there, with their resplendent wives and the ladies'
jewels. The little daring newspapers had mentioned Mr.
Gould in particular, and his cornering of the gold currency,
but it had not known of Joseph's part in the defeat of the
larger conspiracy to ruin the country.

"You will inform him," said Mr. Spaulding in a thoughtful tone, remembering everything. "Of course, Joseph, it is
not my affair, but we have been friends since you were a
youth and I first taught you law at our dear Ed Healey's
behest. May I ask why?"

"No," said Joseph, and saw Katherine Hennessey's face.

Mr. Spaulding sighed. He stirred some papers on his
desk. His eyelids blinked rapidly. He said, in a subdued
voice, "Mrs. Armagh—even if she never guesses the—the
—diablo ex machina, as it were—will be very hurt, for she
was always devoted to her father, and he to her."

Joseph smiled with grimness. "Mr. Spaulding," he said,
"you feel no commiseration for Mrs. Armagh, though you
have known her from childhood. You are merely curious. I
don't intend to satisfy your curiosity. As for Mrs. Armagh
being distressed, I doubt it. She has never been pleased that
her father saw fit to marry a girl not much older than herself, a few months after we were married. A girl, I might
recall to you, who already had an ambiguous child less
than a year old."

"There was no scandal, Joseph."

"Of course not. I saw to that, and so did Hennessey. He
adopted the boy. Very kind of him, was it not?" He
thought of the day Katherine Hennessey had died, and the
young woman who had come to her with her pleas. The
young lady, it was later discovered—but not publicly—had

been the daughter of a congressman, and a powerful one also. On her marriage to Tom Hennessey the newspapers had declared that she was "a young widow, relict of one of our heroic officers who later died as a result of his wounds and left her with an afflicted little boy." (The affliction was the fact that he "had never seen his young father.")

Joseph felt no hatred for Elizabeth Hennessey, the new young wife. She, too, had been a victim of the senator's lies, cruelties, seductions, and betrayal. Her father must have had considerable power in the White House, Joseph had thought when the marriage had taken place. He later discovered that the congressman had been a relative of the President, and one much favored by him.

Bernadette had never forgiven her father. She had proclaimed that it was "a dishonor to my mother," for she had recognized the newspaper photograph of the young lady immediately when the engagement was announced. She remembered that her father had stigmatized the girl as a trollop, a strumpet of the streets, an adventuress, but Elizabeth was none of these things. She was the daughter of a notable congressman, and Bernadette, always conscious of class, had found that unpardonable. This, and the fact that her adored father had displaced her in his affections, was the real reason for her outrage. The "dishonor" to her mother meant nothing at all, for Mama had been a fool, though a sweet and tender one. But Bernadette, to her utmost surprise, discovered that she had loved her mother a little and she was desolate for months. (There was also the reality of the little boy, named Courtney, the name of Tom's father. Bernadette had hoped to have that name for her own son.) Her father, in short, had "betrayed" her, Bernadette, long before her mother had died of her grief and shock, and had loved someone else more than he had loved his daughter, and he had lied to her, vilifying the girl he later married.

"One of these days!" Bernadette had sobbed to her husband, "I will tell Lizzie exactly what my father said about her, to me!"

"She probably knows what your father is, my love," Joseph had replied. This remark had precipitated Bernadette's quick and flaming anger in defense of her father, who had had the ill luck to marry two stupid women. However, her defense did not decrease her wrath against Tom Hennessey. Joseph had not cared enough to wonder at this or talk to his wife concerning her inconsistencies. He did not care enough for Bernadette to console or soothe her, either. The emotions of women were of no interest to him, and if they displayed them in his presence he was bored and vexed, as one is annoyed by an insistent and not exceedingly intelligent child, or a pampered pet. He found no intellectual satisfaction in conversing with women—he was almost convinced they had no intellects—except for Regina, his sister.

A silence had again fallen in Mr. Spaulding's office. He was still avid with curiosity. He felt no commiseration for Governor Hennessey and what this would all mean to him. Joseph Armagh was stronger than the governor. Joseph Armagh would destroy the governor, for his own reasons, which were not known to Mr. Spaulding. The weaker, as usual, would go down. That was the law of nature and why should man quarrel with it? It was not even a matter of morality, or, coming down to it, legality.

"It may take time, Joseph," said Mr. Spaulding.

"Time is money," said Joseph. "The more time the less money. Paradox, isn't it?"

Mr. Spaulding understood. "Say, about six weeks before the elections?"

"No. He must withdraw his candidacy as soon as possible. That is the first step." He made a motion as if to rise, and Mr. Spaulding said with haste, "I will attend to it as soon as possible. The information goes, as usual, to your house in Green Hills, and not your office?"

"Yes," said Joseph, and stood up and Timothy put down his empty glass.

Mr. Spaulding rose and the two men looked at each other over the desk. "Jim," said Joseph, "you have been loyal and most helpful to me through these years since Mr. Healey died. In appreciation—your birthday is next week, isn't it?—you will receive a small token from me. This will not be part of the payment upon receipt of the evidence I have requested." His voice was a rich parody of Mr. Spaulding's but the latter did not notice.

"Joseph," said Mr. Spaulding, with real emotion, "you are too kind."

The astute and intellectual Timothy Dineen—who was also a pragmatic and courageous man—never deceived himself that he had Joseph Armagh's full and unrestrained confidence. In the matter of business, it was true, Joseph trusted him and never questioned him. But he never spoke of his own feelings or his own reasons for doing anything, nor approached Timothy beyond the ordinary hedges of friendship and mutual respect. Timothy often guessed a number of things, intuitive as all the Irish, but he was never really positive. Joseph came as close as possible to regarding any other human being as a confidant when with Harry Zeff, but even here there was some reservation of self, some refusal of commitment, some detachment, some restraint. Never was there true bonhomie, total relaxation, positive warmth, towards even Harry, yet Timothy understood that both men would have risked their lives for each other and that Harry would not only have risked his life but would have given it without a thought, and that he loved Joseph more than he did even his Liza and his children.

"The trouble with poor old Joe," Harry once said to Timothy, "is that he believes no one honestly and completely cares about him, except his sister Regina, and I think he has his doubts there, too. He was so broken about Mr. Healey's death because it came to him that Mr. Healey had greatly cared for him. I think he felt a little appalled at that," and Harry had smiled wryly. "It disarranged his conclusions about people for a time, and Joe doesn't like his neat conclusions getting untidy, or disordered. It takes too much time to resettle them. I think he finally decided, in the interests of neatness and reason, that Mr. Healey had some affection for him, and he had no other heirs, and so—" Harry had spread out his dusky hands expressively.

"I often wonder why he married Mrs. Armagh," Timothy had said. "He certainly has no sound attachment to her. That's obvious to anybody."

"I've wondered, too," said Harry. "It was a big surprise to me. Joe isn't the marrying kind. I don't think he ever cared about a woman in his life, except as a frequent necessity. Yes, there is his sister, of course, but she's hardly a woman to him." Harry had given Timothy a quick and covert glance, but Timothy had only nodded.

"Sometimes I'm sorry for Mrs. Armagh," said Timothy, "though she's a lady hard to be sorry for, with that temper and that cynicism of hers, and her skeptical outlook and her—well, her real malice for people. Yet, she loves him to distraction. In comparison, her children are nothing to her."

"Well," said Harry, "he's rich and strong, and women

love that, and he's handsome in a hard sort of way. Must appeal to women. I'm sorry for Mrs. Joe, too."

Timothy, this hot August afternoon, after leaving Mr. Spaulding, was riding back to Winfield in Joseph's private railroad coach, which had once belonged to Mr. Healey. He sat at a table going over his papers. Joseph sat in a chair near the large windows and looked out through them, but Timothy knew he was not seeing anything of the hot landscape, all gold and green and russet and purple and blue, which was moving rapidly beyond them. What did men like Joseph Armagh think, when they were alone, or when they forgot their companions? Timothy was not so stupid as to believe that Joseph thought exclusively of money and power, as other people averred with malignance and envy. Mr. Armagh was a man, and in spite of himself he had a man's emotions and a man's blood and a man's thoughts. He was not a machine, not an abstraction. The life force of humanity could burst through rock. Even when held down it seethed underneath in the darkness, waiting the day of explosion.

Did Joseph think of his brother, Sean? Timothy remembered the day when Joseph had received a letter from Sean, the last letter he was to receive from the laughing and heedless and finally rebellious young man. Sean had left Harvard without even a farewell to his teachers or fellow students. Sean had not cared in the least for them, or for dull disciplined learning, or the law Joseph had insisted he study. Sean wanted to sing, to laugh with joyous companions, to drink until he fell unconscious—but still singing—to play happy music, and beautiful music, and, as he had told Joseph, to live. Timothy had once heard them raging at each other.

"You are a gray stone!" Sean had shouted. "You aren't a man, a human being at all! What do you know of life and loving, of pain—lovely deep pain down in your heart—of turmoil in your soul, if you have one? What do you know of deprivation and grief and hunger and anguish? You know nothing, nothing, but your damned money, and making more of it, no matter how, and the hell with everything and everybody else!"

Sean, in his wild passion and his sense of personal injury, had not noticed the sudden terribleness of Joseph's face, and the clenching of his lips. He had cried on:

"What do you know of loneliness, and loss of hope? You

rarely if ever came to see me in the orphanage! Yes, I was told you were 'working,' for God's sake, and had no money to visit me! That's a lie! You could have spared some of your money to come, and tell me that you thought about me and cared about me. But, you didn't. There I was, stuck in the mud of that damned orphanage, among sniveling nuns and dirty brats, with no beauty and no pleasure and no anticipations—and there you were off, forgetting me, and Regina, and not giving us a thought—just making your damned money! And what has it done for you, pray? Nothing. You can't even enjoy it!"

Joseph had not answered. His face became even more terrible, and Sean became even more frantic about his "wrongs."

"You must have hated us! Yes, you've provided for us, and it must have killed you, almost. You deserted us when we needed you most, as little children. And for what? Just for money. Once, when I was nine I had the pneumonia. You never came. It was nothing to you. You probably hoped I'd die."

Joseph had stood up then, and Timothy had seen a long and awful trembling along his body. Joseph had lifted his hand and had struck Sean wordlessly but savagely across the face, and then had left the room. Sean had whimpered. Then, holding his flaming cheek, he had collapsed into a chair and had wailed aloud in self-pity, and then noticing the quiet Timothy had pleaded with him for compassion. Timothy listened, and then he had said almost gently, "You are a dog, a selfish swine, and you don't deserve one more thought from your brother. Go on and play. That is about all you are worth, and at your age, too, for Christ's sake!"

That was the last time Timothy saw Sean Armagh. Sean returned to Harvard the next day, after the Christmas holidays. It was the final year at Harvard, and Sean had left the university in the spring, and had disappeared. Only Timothy, sent there to investigate, noticed that Sean had been careful to take with him everything of value in his handsome room, which Joseph had bought for him, and his best clothing and his fine luggage.

It took several months to find Sean, and Timothy led the search. He was finally discovered, gloriously disheveled, golden-haired, drunk and soiled, laughing and drinking and joking and singing in the saloons of Boston. Sometimes he was accompanied by a fiddler. Sometimes there was an ancient piano which he could make thunder and ring and clamor and dance at will. He played and he sang for a handful of pennies, for beer and whiskey, for free lunch, for applause, for camaraderie, the spurious friendship of the saloons, the spurious warmth and companionship and admiration. In a few months he was penniless and ragged.

"We can't let him starve," said Joseph, with that terrible look on his face when his brother was mentioned. "We can't give him any money in any amount, either. He would just throw it away on his fellow ruffians, and drunkards and ne'er-do-wells."

"Let him starve," Timothy had said with unusual feeling and Joseph had glanced up at him sharply, had studied him, and then had slightly smiled.

"No," he said. "We can't let him starve. I don't know why, but we can't. Perhaps it is because his sister wouldn't like it. Does he have a rooming house? Well, see that he gets ten dollars a week. Tell one of my boys in Boston to give it to him, Tim."

But two years ago Sean had disappeared. He had not been found since. No one knew, or professed not to know. He might have been murdered, been injured or died and buried in potter's field. The hospitals were canvassed, the poor houses, the refuges for such as Sean. He was not there. At each disappointment, at each ending of hope, Regina said nothing though her face became more and more translucent and lovely and ethereal, and she was more attentive to Joseph.

"He is like my father," said Joseph. Regina bent and pressed her cheek to her brother's, and Joseph had taken her hand like a child and Timothy had marveled again. He had known then, without any doubt, that Regina Armagh had her brother's complete love and confidence and absolute trust, and that she knew the import of his thoughts if not the thoughts themselves, and that for him she had the tenderest love and an almost saintlike compassion, and knew all about him and sorrowed over him.

Joseph never spoke now of his brother. He never searched for him. Had Sean come to him, begging for forgiveness, Joseph would have helped him. But he would never forgive Sean. Sean was as dead to him as if he had seen him in his grave. He would never forget. Regina must have guessed this for she did not speak of Sean to Joseph, but only to Timothy, and sometimes she would put her hands over her face and cry.

Was Joseph, today, as the train roared in its passage, thinking of any of this? Timothy asked himself. He did not know. Joseph's harsh profile was illuminated by the falling sun. He neither smoked nor drank. He rarely attended social events in Green Hills or Philadelphia or New York or Boston, or in other cities, unless they were connected with business. He had a wife he did not love but who occasionally amused or beguiled him a little, and sometimes even made him laugh when she teased him or cajoled him. Perhaps he had some fondness for her. She was not pretty, but she was charming in a lively and hoydenish way, and she had a sharp and diverting tongue. She filled the house with her loud Irish voice, her laughter and her gusto, and her admonitions to servants and to children.

Rory and Ann Marie, the twins, were nearly five years old. Did Joseph love his children? He was sedulous about them and often spoke to his wife about her carelessness concerning them. They were denied nothing, and Timothy thought this unfortunate. The young should be deprived frequently, as a matter of discipline. Perhaps Joseph was fond of them, but would give them nothing more than fondness. He was, perhaps, as Harry Zeff had said, afraid to love, suspicious of love, and cynical above all things. And, thought Timothy, who can blame him, remembering Sean? Love betrayed, if it did not descend into hatred, became wariness and indifference and doubt, fearful of fresh hurt. Except for his sister, Joseph Armagh was joyless. Timothy suspected that there had been little joy in his life at any time, and he found himself intensely pitying this deserted and silent man, this man who had nothing, with the exception of his sister, to live for. Perhaps he had once had something for which to live but it was now gone.

Yet, he was driven. That was obvious. It is inertia, thought Timothy. But Timothy did not know that it was a vengeance on a world which had denied to Joseph Armagh the ornaments that make life, and had brutalized and had rejected him, and had taken from him the only valuable things in existence: faith, hope, and love.

Chapter 29

Governor Hennessey had given half his interest in his house to his daughter as a wedding gift when she married Joseph Armagh. ("It was his wife's, not his, anyway," Joseph had remarked.) When she was twenty-one she inherited half of her mother's estate. The other half had gone to Tom, who was already married to the congressman's daughter.

So Joseph now lived in the great and beautiful mansion at which he had once stared, on an early April evening, many years ago. The governor rarely visited that house. He and Joseph had nothing to say to each other, though Tom chatted heartily in the presence of his son-in-law, to cover Joseph's silences. He told his daughter that he "adored" his grandchildren, though they somewhat subdued his picture of himself—in their presence—as an ageless gallant. He was now in his sixties, and as vain and sensual and ambitious as always. His young wife came with him on his visits to Green Hills, but it was most evident that she and Bernadette would never be friends and would only tolerate each other. Elizabeth was, intrinsically, a kind and composed young woman, and very intelligent, and she had long forgiven—though not forgotten—her husband's betrayal of her. But more than anything else he loved his little son, Courtney, whom he had "adopted" as the orphaned child of a dead hero. This further inflamed Bernadette's jealousy, and when the child was present she either ignored him or shouted at him pettishly and ordered him to behave himself. She was not so stringent with her own children, and forgave them their selfishness and their tendency to quarrel loudly with each other, and to answer her insolently.

"This is a new day for children," she would tell Joseph. "We give them more liberties now, and more freedom, and understand them better, and do not constrain them so much as our parents did us—you and me, Joseph."

Joseph would think of his laughing and singing father, who had been like a child to him, and he would think of his mother, who had died in such agony and fear for her children, and with such desperate love. He said to his wife, "You are quite right, my love." Bernadette, who had heard an ambiguous note in her husband's voice, had looked at him piercingly. "Well," she said, "you must surely remember how your father punished you severely for the slightest thing, and how your mother never showed you affection and was always correcting you."

Joseph never told her. It would be beyond her comprehension. To Bernadette, Joseph had been a "poor Irish lad," who had come to America with his mother and his brother and sister, and had made a fortune by his own efforts, and also by the will of Mr. Healey. She was never curious about Joseph's dead parents. She was never curious about his past life, for Bernadette lived in the present. But she was desperately jealous of Regina, who lived in this house, and hated her and longed for her to marry and go away "and leave me in peace with my darling," she would think. She had been complacent about Sean. She had never liked him though handsome men usually attracted her. When she looked at the regal Regina she would say in herself, "Shanty Irish!" and it would console her. Once Regina was out of this house that would be the end of the "other Armaghs."

She was endlessly giving parties to introduce Regina to eligible young men, who became infatuated with her at first sight—and with her brother's money. She forced Regina to go with her to Joseph's new house in Philadelphia, where he often stayed for weeks now, and there she would have balls and dinners and soirees for Regina. She, herself, had once been pursued by young men. Regina was endlessly pursued. But Regina smilingly rejected all ardent overtures, though with kindness. Her dark beauty was a radiance which attracted both men and women, young and old. She had but to put on a gown and it was a glowing robe on her lovely figure. Joseph had given her a magnificent sapphire necklace, bracelets and ring, and pins for her black hair,

but they were no more brilliant and shining than her blue
eyes between those odd golden lashes. Her arms were long
and white and round. She was overly tall for a woman,
Bernadette would think, but she had a grace that no other
woman seemed to possess.

"She is an awful old maid, with no sensibilities!" Bernadette would complain to Joseph. "I am afraid poor Regina
is very stupid. She hardly ever speaks, and if she does she is
so grave it makes me ill. Doesn't she ever intend to marry?
How dreadful, if true," but Bernadette did not believe that
Regina would not marry.

Joseph said, "Let the girl alone, for God's sake, Bernadette. You are a shrew sometimes, I'm thinking."

"She is no girl!" Bernadette snapped, her hazel eyes
flashing with jealousy. "She is twenty-three years old, the
same age I am!" When Joseph did not answer, Bernadette
threw up her arms and round eyes in elaborate despair.

"Why don't you help me to get Regina married? Have
you no affection for your sister? Do you want to see her
dry up in old maidhood, and sit by the chimney corner?"

"Regina prefers her life as it is, perhaps," said Joseph,
and remembered a day when Regina was eighteen and had
told him she loved him but now must go away. He tried to
forget that day, and there had been no more said about it,
but fear lived in him like a brazen snake, tense and coiled.
When Bernadette spoke of Regina marrying it was not an
annoyance to him. Even marriage, and the separation
which marriage would bring between brother and sister,
was preferable to—that. Anything under God's evil sun
was preferable to—that. He therefore began to be somewhat of an ally of Bernadette's, to her comfort. He, too,
began to look for a husband for Regina. But Regina did
not marry.

Bernadette, who was as cynical about religion as she was
about everything else with the exception of Joseph, made
Novenas earnestly for the marriage of Regina. If Regina
would marry, she would pray, she would learn to love her.
Surely the Blessed Mother did not like it that she hated
Regina, though it was not, of course, "my fault." So Bernadette wheedled the saints and God and His Blessed Mother,
to get Regina out of her house.

"What have you got against marriage?" she once asked
Regina.

"Why, nothing at all, dear Bernadette," said Regina, surprised, her sweet clear voice amused. "I think it is a holy estate, as the Church teaches."

"Why don't you enter it then?" demanded Bernadette. "Everybody thinks it so odd that you are still unmarried, at your age. Why can't you fall in love?"

But I am in love, thought Regina, and tears filled her eyes. My heart is dying with love. My spirit is filled with love. I think of nothing—but my love.

She said, and her voice was low and searching, "You do love Joseph, don't you, Bernadette? Truly and eternally love him?"

"Can you ask that? Dare you ask that!" cried Bernadette, and those round full eyes glittered with emotion and anger. "I love him more than anything in the world. Everything else in the world is nothing to me, compared with Joseph."

"I know," said Regina, and knew that the time had finally come and she could go in peace. "Always remember that, dear Bernadette. Hold fast to my brother. He needs love more than anything in this world, and he has had so little. Help him. Comfort him."

This was very strange to the vociferous Bernadette, and she actually became unusually still and stared at Regina. "What are you talking about? 'Comfort, help him.' Do I do anything else, by the Saints? He is my life. There's nothing else. Why should he need comfort or help? I'm here, am I not?"

"Yes, dear," said Regina, and bent her head and kissed Bernadette on that round, low, and freckled forehead, and Bernadette was freshly startled. She put up her hand aimlessly to the smooth brown chignon of her hair, wondering. Her figure was quite matronly now, but still pleasing, and she wore elaborately draped skirts to give her height, and was always scintillating with bracelets and earrings and jeweled combs, and she was always moving with verve. She thought Regina a poor thing in her simple frocks and her simple way of dressing all that splendid, glossy black hair. Regina had no more life than a wax doll. She had a thin aquiline nose, too, and not a charming tilted one like Bernadette's. Why, thought Bernadette in exasperation, does everyone think she is so beautiful? She does have a presence, and a wonderful complexion, but no spirit.

Two days after Joseph had returned to Green Hills from

Titusville, Regina went to her brother's rooms in the great and echoing mansion, the rooms which had once been Governor Hennessey's. He had had the ornate and baroque furniture removed, and the embroidered draperies and the lace, and had replaced them with fine utilitarian tables and chairs and sofas and plain rich rugs and straight draperies at the windows, and no gimcracks or ornaments except for several valuable paintings which hung on dimly painted walls. Bernadette rarely went into those rooms, for they depressed her. All those books, that big mahogany desk, that stark narrow bed—it was like the den of a poor man. She, herself, occupied her mother's rooms, and had embellished them to her own filigreed taste, which leaned towards gilt and velvet and silk and strong color. Her mother's canopied bed was a fountain of Venetian lace, all falls and swoops and rufflings, over bright pink, and the subdued rugs had been removed for Chinese rugs in the most vehement shades. Every corner was crowded with whatnots heaped with figurines and other trifles, and every spindly table overflowed with them.

I have always been a stranger in this house, thought Regina, as she climbed the stairs to her brother's rooms. I have never had a home except in the orphanage. She was whitely resolute tonight, but her throat and breast hurt with almost incredible pain, and she prayed under her breath, and it seemed to her that her lungs were locked and she could not breathe. A cool sweat had broken out over her face and her body, and she could feel the dampness in her armpits and over her neck and back and in her palms. Her heart was beating with tremendous force, and she gasped as she climbed those wide marble stairs and the lighted chandelier burned her eyes. She prayed, "Oh, dear Lord, help me, help me." But there was no response and she felt a dragging coldness in her middle and a weakening of her legs under her brown linen frock with its high neck and long sleeves. Her wonderful hair fell down her back in waves and billows and flowed with her movements. "Help me to make Joe understand, dear Blessed Mother," Regina prayed. "Help him to know that I must go to my Love, to the only marriage I desire and have ever desired, since I was a child."

Her eyes and head began to swim and she paused at the top of the stairs, and struggled for breath. She thought of her brother and the pain she was about to inflict upon him, and she cringed at the thought, and put her hands over her face, shaking her head slowly from side to side. She was trembling so strongly that she had to brace her hand, finally, against the wall to keep from falling. Of what was she afraid? Her brother's sorrow, and only she knew how violent his sorrow could be though it was silent. She thought of Sean, and cringed again. Sean had left him and now she must leave him, never to see him again except as a shadow, a formless image. She would hear his voice, but she would not see the years gray and shrink him. Her most pressing misery was that it was very probable that Joseph's voice would never again be heard by her, and that she would not even see his shadow. Joseph's anger was total, and Joseph never forgave nor forgot.

"Help him," she prayed aloud. "I must do this thing, and he must know. Help him." Regina had never known fear before, and it had the taste of cold iron in her mouth. She had never known such grief and it was overwhelming. She had endured the destitution of her earlier life with tranquillity and without complaint, for it had seemed a life of the utmost richness to her and not deprivation and hunger. She had never fully understood Sean's revolt, nor his rebellions and impatience. Grief and fear were not familiars of hers, and she felt terror at their presence now in her mind and spirit. They were shattering. They assaulted her, and almost turned her away. Then, after a while, she felt new strength and resolution and went to Joseph's door and knocked at it.

Dinner was long over. Rory and his twin, Ann Marie, were in their nursery. The servants had gone to their quarters. Where was Bernadette? No doubt in her bedroom, carefully and anxiously applying various cosmetics to her round somewhat flat young face, or brushing that long fall of straight brown hair, or trying on some new gowns. Joseph never spent his evenings in companionship with his wife. Regina hesitated. She had a new thought. Surely Joseph loved his wife or he would never have married her. Joseph was not easily moved nor persuaded. He did everything with cold deliberation. He had wanted to marry Bernadette, and he had married her. There was nothing else.

Surely he loves her, thought Regina and heard her brother calling to her to enter.

Joseph knew her knock and so he was putting aside his book when she entered and his saturnine face showed a lightening and a pleasure no other person ever evoked. It was almost a lover's smile, with a far blue glinting under his auburn brows. He stood up to greet his sister, tall and concave of body, and severely dressed even in the privacy of his own rooms. No one had ever seen him disheveled, not even his wife, and he was always compact and brittle in appearance, with the wiry strength of his countrymen. "Regina," he said, and took her by the hand and sat her down in a dark leather chair near his. He turned down his reading lamp a little so it would not shine in her eyes.

Regina dreaded to begin what she must say, so she said, instead, "What are you reading, Joe?"

"Law," he said. "I'm always reading law." He thought of what Cicero had said: "Politicians are not born. They are excreted." It was hardly a quotation to mention to a young lady, but he smiled again. "I find it invaluable in politics. How do you know what law it is profitable to break unless you know there is such a law?"

She did not smile, as he had expected. He sat down opposite her. "Joe," she said, "I wish you were not always trying to give the impression of being a villain. You know you are not."

He liked to joke with Regina. However, he saw that she was serious and distressed. "I'm glad you have a good opinion of me, Regina." She looked down at the hands she had folded in her lap.

"Joe, dear, to the end of my life I will always have a good opinion of you, no matter—"

He was instantly alert. "No matter—what?"

She bent her head a little and so he could only see her white forehead and the arch of her nose, and he wondered, with sudden alarm, if this immured girl had the slightest idea of what he was. She was more his hostess than was the somewhat rowdy Bernadette, for she had more poise and graciousness and natural good breeding, and so she had met scores of his acquaintances, among them some of the most vicious and expedient of politicians and entrepreneurs. She had met the men who worked for him and who managed his countless enterprises and all their ramifications. He had never concealed from her the manipulations he undertook to have certain politicians brought to public attention, nominated and then elected, though he had been careful not to let her know the cynicism of those manipulations and why he supported those men with money and publicity in his newspapers. He had thought that she believed that this was the way of politics and that the "best men" were always chosen. She had met all these not only in the house in Green Hills but in Philadelphia and in his town house in New York, and in Boston. Yet he had been convinced that the very innocence of his sister prevented her from knowing the truth, and guessing what rascals bowed over her hand.

He suddenly thought of Tom Hennessey, and he stared at Regina sharply and repeated, "No matter—what?"

"I meant to say," the girl answered very quietly, "even if you stopped loving me, as your sister."

He was relieved, yet he had the feeling that she had been evasive. Now she looked up at him straightly and he saw that there were tears in her eyes.

"For God's sake, Regina!" he said. "Why should I ever stop loving you?"

"Promise?" she said, like a child, and tried to smile.

"I promise." But his uneasiness increased.

"Even if I leave you, Joe?"

He did not answer her immediately. His eyes fixed themselves upon her intently and for the first time she saw something in them that frightened her. But he spoke calmly enough. "Why should you leave me? Are you thinking of marrying, Regina?"

"In a way," she replied, and he could hardly hear her, for she had averted her head again. "The only marriage I ever wanted."

He stood up as if goaded to his feet, but he said nothing, and only watched her. She put out her hand to him but he would not see it.

"Oh, Joe," she said, and it was a cry of pain. "I know I promised you that I wouldn't speak of it again—when I was about eighteen. I have tried, Joe, I have tried with all my strength, to put it—aside. But it has grown stronger and more demanding all through these years, and now I can't resist it any longer. I must go. To the Carmelite Order, in Maryland. I must go at once. Oh, Joe, don't look at me like that! I can't bear it. You must know that I've wanted this all my life, ever since I could remember, even as a very young child in the orphanage. When I first spoke of it to you you said I was too young to know my own mind, and that I must see the world, and, Joe"—the tears were heavier in her eyes than before—"I can't bear this world. I can't bear it. Once you said to me, 'A sane and intelligent man finds this world horrifying, mad,' and it's quite true. I don't want to be part of it, Joe. I can't be part of it any longer."

She stood up in agitation and stood before him and he looked down at her with an expression that terrified her. But she swallowed her rising fear, and clasped her hands tightly before her and her face implored him to understand.

"What do you know of living?" he asked in a voice of such immense disgust that she took a step backwards. "A convent girl. You may be twenty-three, but you are like a schoolgirl still. I've taken you to Europe, and to dozens of cities here, but they made no impression on you. You never saw them, did you?"

"Yes, I saw them, Joe."

"If you had seen them you'd have wanted them. But the nuns blinded you, made a fool and a dolt out of you, deceived you, seduced you into nonsense and superstition and medieval fantasies, filled your mind with idiotic dreams and visions and myths. Destroyed you, my sister."

But she was shaking her beautiful head slowly. "No, that is not true. No one even suggested to me that I had a vocation—"

But Joseph had burst into harsh and raucous laughter. "A vocation, by God! A vocation for what? Prison? Isolation? Endless witless prayers? Sacrifices? For what? For whom? To what end? What purpose?"

She had a wild thought, even in the midst of her fear, that he was like a man desperately and agonizingly fighting for his life, his very life. He was even gasping in quick pants, and clenching and unclenching his hands. She could hardly recognize his face.

He went on in the most cruel voice she had ever heard: "It was all wasted on you, all that I—You know nothing at all. You never had to struggle for anything, or work for anything. You've lived in luxury since you were thirteen years old, the luxury I provided for you. It probably has palled on you, so you turn to mysteries and occult imaginings, out of sheer idleness! What have I denied you? I gave you and—" He stopped a moment and his gasping was louder than ever. "I gave you my life, and all there was in it. I thought I also gave you reality, the enlightenment, the education, which a sensible woman should have. I gave you the world I fought for, and now you come to me with vaporings and girlish simperings and little coynesses and tell me that it was all for nothing, that you don't want what I have given you. You want, you say, stone cold floors on which to kneel and pray your stupid vain prayers, and confess sins that you never committed, and hide behind screens so that no one will ever see you. You want to hide. Yes, you want to hide!"

"Joe," she said, but he waved her fiercely into silence again.

"From what are you hiding, Regina? The world, you will say. But the world has never abused you as it abused me. It never showed you its real face, as it showed me. You know nothing, you fool, you know nothing! And in your stupidity you indulge yourself in romantic illusions of a cloistered life, where all is white lilies and incense, and pretty statues and imbecile serenity and pious music—and those doltish prayers! You are bored. Why don't you marry, as all women marry, and have children and live the life other women live with contentment?"

Regina's chin dropped to her chest and Joseph, in his furious rage, hated her as one hates a betrayer. The crown of her black head shimmered in the lamplight. She was very still, standing there in her brown linen frock which, all at once, looked like a habit to him, loathsome and ugly beyond anything he had ever seen. He wanted to hit Regina, to strike her to the floor, and as he felt the impulse he also felt a squeezing of intolerable anguish in himself, a disintegrating grief. It was also familiar, and because it brought memories of two other women he stammered roughly, "I'd rather see you in your coffin! I'd rather see you dead!"

She heard the torment in his voice, the despair, the frantic suffering, and she looked up and her face was full of compassion and love as well as fear.

"Joe, you don't understand. I love—I want to serve, if only with prayers. I love—Joe."

"Love what?" he exclaimed, with another ruthless gesture. "What God? What witlessness is that? There is no God, you damned fool of a maudlin woman! There is nothing to serve, nothing to pray to, nothing that hears, nothing that has mercy. I know. My father lies in potter's field, in an unmarked grave, and my mother's bones lie in the sea—for all their prayers and all their faith and all their charity. I saw hundreds die of the Famine, men, women, children, infants, old grandmothers—lying in the ditches of the roadways, biting their hands in their last convulsions of hunger. Did your God hear, or care, or send His angels to feed those innocents? Those of us who survived were turned away from the ports of this country, either to return to Ireland to starve to death or wander like vagabonds on vagabond ships hoping for harbor, for a crust of bread—literally, a crust of bread.

"Oh, you irrational fool! You don't know anything of this world! Where do you suppose a lot of my money comes from? From conspiratorial wars, from planned wars. Have you ever been in a hospital for wounded or dying soldiers, younger than yourself? Have you tended them and bound up their wounds? What do you know of this accursed world? I tell you it is hell, and the slaughter of the innocents goes on every day, in every nation. And no God cares, no God helps, no God hears. And that, by Christ, is what you want to serve—a lie, a superstition, a myth, a monumental hoax and fraud, something that never existed and does not exist!"

Then Regina said, in that brownly gleaming room which echoed with shouting, "It is for such a world that I must pray, and serve with my prayers. Why do you execrate God for the wickedness of man? Man has his choices. If he chooses evil that is free will and not even God will, or can, interfere. I know you have no faith, dear Joe. It would be useless for me to try to convince you—for who can speak of the knowledge of the heart and the soul? It is only there. I have pity for this world. You think I know nothing." Her mouth trembled but her eyes held his resolutely. "But I know too much, Joe. Who am I to reproach you, who did all things for your family? I don't think even God reproaches you—too much. In a way, Joe, your whole life has been a prayer—for those who did not deserve such a sacrifice—Sean and me. No, no. We did not deserve it. I doubt anyone deserves such selflessness."

Joseph was taken aback, even in his fury and contempt and rage. He forced himself to stop panting. He could not stop the hard roar of his heart, but he spoke with reasonable quiet, "If you think and believe that, how can you bring yourself to want to leave me, desert me, betray me, for a nothingness, for a lie, for emptiness?"

"I'm not really leaving you, Joe, nor deserting nor betraying you. You will never be outside my prayers, my love. I will only love you more deeply, and be even more grateful to you. You will always be in my thoughts, for, in this world, you are the only dear thing to me."

She stood before him, tall and slender and lovely, her face very pale, her beautiful eyes shining and now unafraid, and he had a sudden abhorrent vision of all that glory immured behind stone walls, and that voice raised only mutedly in prayer, and that soft flesh lying on stone in an ecstatic prostration before—insanity. He felt an almost voluptuous sense of horror and revulsion, and it showed in his expression and again Regina took a step backward with renewed fear.

"I will not let you go. I won't let you destroy yourself," he said.

"I will not be destroying myself. I will be saving myself, Joe."

But now she could only helplessly shake her head, over and over, as if she had no control of her own movements. He watched her and he wanted to take her in his arms and hold her savagely and he also wanted to kill her.

She finally said, "I wanted you to understand how I feel, dear Joe. I knew it would cause you grief and make you angry. But I thought you'd understand, a little, about my own happiness, for there is no happiness for me in this world and never will be. I must go where there is peace and prayer and penance. It is all I want; there is nothing else. If you understood, even that little, you would say, 'Go, my sister. Everyone must find happiness, or at least peace, in his own way.'"

"Happiness!" he exclaimed, with new and overpowering disgust. "What fool talks of happiness? There never was such a thing except for hypocrites and liars and the mad. There never was any peace, and never will there be in this world, and this world is all we know and all we'll ever know. We must make our own compromises with it, and accept it. But you want to run from it! If that isn't weakness and cowardice I'd like to know what it is."

Again she shook her head hopelessly. She could not speak of the great love in her soul, her great and humble acceptance and joy in that acceptance, for it would only infuriate her brother more. She said at last, "I must go, dearest Joe. I have already made the arrangements. I leave tomorrow night. I did not tell you before, because I was afraid—afraid of my own vacillation—that you would persuade me—But nothing can turn me aside, now. Nothing. Not even you, Joe."

She looked at him but he only stared at her with raw hate, a man betrayed and, he thought, betrayed with malice and smug satisfaction. He thought of Sean who had accused him with a cruelty surpassing his own, and had deserted him. So he said in so quiet a voice that Regina could hardly hear him, "Go, and go to hell, you slut. Go, the both of you. You weren't worth a year of my life. You weren't worth even one hour—either of you."

"I know. Only I know, Joe," said Regina, and walked silently from the room. He watched her go. He had thought he had known all the desolation it was possible for a man to endure, but this was the worst of all. Now he would not put out his hand to stop his sister, even if he could have stopped her. She had become as dead to him as her brother, and as hateful.

Regina went to her own room and knelt on her prie-dieu before the Crucifix on the wall, and she cried silently and tried to pray but there was only pain in her now and a last remembrance of her brother's face.

Bernadette had been aroused in her room by the loud exclamations and shouts of her husband and had tiptoed into the long warm hall to listen. She had heard most of the conversation between Joseph and Regina, and she had felt a huge leap of exultation. Now she would be rid of that simpleton, Regina, and Joseph would finally realize that he had no one in the world but his wife, faithful, devoted, endlessly loving.

Joseph did not appear the next day at all. When Regina, weeping, confided in Bernadette that she must go, and why, Bernadette made large dry eyes of sympathy and uttered the most tender words of encouragement and gave Regina the warmest embraces. "Of course I understand, love!" she cried. "I never knew anyone who had a vocation before, but I understand! You can't resist it. It would be a sin to resist. Don't worry about Joe. I will console him, and he'll come to accept it all, himself."

So Regina was comforted and never knew she had been comforted by a young woman who despised her and was glad to see the last of her, and that her consolations had been false and hypocritical. The girl left in more peace than she had believed possible, clinging for a last moment to Bernadette, who accompanied her to the depot with her small luggage. She already looks like a nun, the dunce, thought Bernadette, as she murmured against Regina's cheek and uttered the most extravagant promises, with elation in her heart and the deepest relief.

When Joseph finally appeared the day after Regina had left Bernadette was all indignation against Regina, and sympathy, but he looked at her and said, "We will not speak of her again, if you please."

Chapter 30

Joseph received an interesting letter from Mr. Spaulding one cool September day, addressed to the house in Green Hills. After its effusions of friendship and attachment, it said, with the utmost delicacy:

Our friends accepted the contribution to the Party with grateful astonishment for your unequaled generosity, which, they declared, demonstrates your concern for the Commonwealth and her weal. They will at once attend to the other matters which I earnestly brought to their attention, and trust you will be gratified at the result.

After loving inquiries concerning Joseph's family, Mr. Spaulding added the following: *I should not be surprised if a mutual friend visited you almost immediately. If so, extend to him my obedient regard.*

Joseph immediately destroyed the letter. But he sat and considered the import with black and vengeful satisfaction. He needed that satisfaction for his life had become barely tolerable since Regina's "desertion," which was now but one piece with Sean's cruel accusations and flight. He felt alone as he had never felt alone in all his life before, and had some sentimentalist archly pointed out to him his wealth, his wife and his children, he would have burst out laughing and the sound would not have been pleasant. He had never before thought of using his family as a source of revenge, but in these days he thought of it constantly. Often, in the past, he had contemplated suicide, but only as a random if acute and very brief impulse. Now it intruded several times a day, and with it a passing but enticing sense of relief. He knew at last that a man should find his motivation for living in himself and not for others who could and would betray without any hesitation at all, and even with malevolence.

Some men lived for their country, some for some incredible God, some for their families. But Joseph had come to realize that all these were externals and had no identity with a man's own identity, except, possibly, he would think with wryness, that God who had—or the myth of Him— seduced his sister from her brother's house. That, to Joseph, was the utmost madness and the utmost secret betrayal of one's integrity. No abstract had verity in man's immediacy of needs and hungers and survival. Call this animalism, if you wish, Joseph would think. But what is there in man's history—except for a few demented saints who never knew the world anyway—but animalism? He had come to hate himself in that he had deprived his own youth of any joy or adventure or investigation into available pleasures, for his family. He wondered, sometimes, if he had not been a little mad, himself, in regarding his own existence as valuable only as it related to Regina and Sean, and that, in his personal individual self it was worthless. He would often think of Mr. Healey, who had lived only for himself and so had found life interesting, exciting, and rewarding, and had died in bliss. Mr. Healey had not died in sorrow, and not with black vengeance in his soul. Mr. Healey had never dedicated his life and his labor to others, had never considered others more meritorious than himself or more deserving, or that they should be served first before he was served. Consequently he had never been betrayed—he had never given others an advantage over him—and had never found a need to hate nor been provoked to hatred. So, by first thinking of himself and serving himself, he could be kind and often just and solicitous to others. In short, Mr. Healey had had self-esteem, which was an entirely different thing from pride, for which Joseph had never wanted.

A man who lived for "others" killed the only thing which was valid in a man—his own consciousness of himself and his own identity. Self-obliteration was a crime against life. Joseph now held Sean and Regina as adversaries who had destroyed him, one with selfish cruelty, the other by finding Someone who needed her more than her brother.

"I do not understand you these days," Bernadette complained. "You were never a fatuous husband or father at any time, nor attentive to me as are other husbands to their wives. Do you not know that I love you dearly, and need you and your strength and comfort? You avoid me; you rarely speak, never smile. Who else do I have but you?"

For an instant this shook Joseph out of his black thoughts and meditations. It was with harsh pity that he said to Bernadette: "Don't be a fool! Live for yourself, not for me or anyone else! You have—yourself. That is more important than your husband or your children. Never be dependent on anyone for anything. That is disastrous."

Bernadette was taken aback, and she stared, her eyes filling with tears. "What does a woman have but her family—her husband?"

Joseph had made a short but distracted gesture. "Think what that did to your mother," he said, and left his wife, who, for the first time in her young life felt the coldness of desolation, the terrible bleakness of it. Not even her father's "defection," as she called it, had stricken her like this. Her emotions, except for her passion for Joseph, were more or less superficial and explosive and short-lived, and could easily be placated or deflected. Now she wept as a woman and not as a child.

Governor Tom Hennessey sent a brief telegram to his son-in-law. EXPECT ME IN GREEN HILLS ON THURSDAY INST FOR BUSINESS CONSULTATION. On reading this telegram Joseph smiled a little in exultation. He informed Bernadette who was aroused out of her own doldrums since that last conversation with her husband. "We shall have a party!" she explained. But Joseph said, "My love, let us first find out how long your father can remain with us. He may have to leave for Philadelphia almost at once."

A carriage was sent to the depot for the governor, and Bernadette was in it. She would talk to Papa privately before arriving back home, and he would, no doubt, explain to her exactly what Joseph had meant and how she could overcome it.

But the governor was unusually taciturn with his daughter. He seemed pale and preoccupied, and there were deep clefts in his usually robust and florid face, and his eyes appeared turned inwards and haunted. He mumbled, "My darling, your husband is not a leisurely gallant nor dilettante nor idler. He has problems, like myself. Like myself," he added, and looked at Bernadette impatiently, willing her to stop her chatter. "Did you think he has nothing to do but dance attendance on you and play with your children? A man's life is apart from these, and greater than these, though this may offend you and your vanity." He patted Bernadette's small gloved hands, for she was about to cry.

"Surely you remember what Byron said: 'Man's love is of his life apart. 'Tis woman's whole existence.' It is quite true, and women should remember that and not prattle and complain."

"I only want him to love me," Bernadette said, gulping down a sob.

"I am sure he does," said her father, and hoped to God that was somewhat true. "Why else would he have married you? He was rich in his own right, richer than I ever dreamed. He did not marry you for money." (What the hell had he married the girl for? the governor asked himself, who had never been deceived that Joseph had felt any grand passion for Bernadette.)

He went immediately to Joseph's rooms, and into the large room which Joseph now used as a study and which had once been the governor's flamboyant bedroom. Joseph met him there with a quiet word and an offer of an immediate drink, which the governor accepted with gratitude. "A large whiskey," he said. "Perhaps you'd better have one, too. I have bad news."

Joseph had never been an accomplished actor at any time. He thought, How did a man arrange his face so that it expressed apprehension—even if no apprehension was felt—and what did he put in his voice? Joseph saw Mr. Montrose's expressive countenance, and so made his own a passable facsimile of concern and attentive solicitude. He tried for Mr. Montrose's flexibility of voice, and said, "Have you, then? Then we must talk about it. Now. I hope it does not concern any punitive coming legislation against the alleged atrocities of the railroaders? Don't they understand that men do not run railroads so that the Molly Maguires and their fellow strikers and anarchists may live luxuriously, with no profits to the men who have risked everything? And who had the brains to create railroads in the first place?"

The governor said, and for the first time he smiled cynically, "Haven't I, at your suggestion, Joe, expressed my solicitude many times for those wretches—and so got their votes—and managed to defeat any legislation which would help them?"

"So you have," said Joseph. "What it is to be a politician! I am glad I am not one. Lying is not exactly my forte."

The governor, sitting in the only comfortable chair in the

stark study, narrowed his eyes at Joseph. Tom Hennessey was no fool. He had never liked Joseph, and had always suspected him without the slightest reason—objectively. All Joseph's later politeness and political help had not overcome Tom's memory of that night when Joseph had looked at him in the hall of this house after Katherine had died. Bernadette had told her father that Katherine had asked for Joseph. Tom always wondered why. Had it been something about Bernadette? Had Joseph already hinted so much to Katherine? Yet he had looked at Bernadette's father as if he wanted to kill him, and with such hatred, too. Of course, Katherine could have babbled to Joseph before she died—Tom had come to that conclusion. Katherine had always been a dim-witted fool. Tonight, Tom dismissed the unlamented Katherine from his thoughts.

"I'll make it brief," he said, and his voice was rough with renewed agitation and now with open anger and despair. "I was informed, yesterday, by our Party that I would not receive the nomination this year. Yet, only a month ago I was assured of it by the State Chairman, himself. Who else?"

Joseph had seated himself nearby in the growing dusk of the room. The early autumn gardens outside sent up a poignant strong scent of mowed grass, chrysanthemums, late lilies and roses and crisping leaves. It was still falling daylight outside. Here it was becoming dim and shadowy, for great trees loomed outside and their tops brushed against the windows. Joseph, unusual for him, had mixed himself a whiskey and soda, and he carefully sipped at it and looked at the floor, as if pondering.

He said, "Now, why should they do that? What do they have against you?"

Tom put down his glass with a thump on a nearby table. "Nothing!" he shouted. "Haven't I done everything they suggested? Haven't I followed all their directives? I've served the Party well by God! Now they turn on me." He breathed heavily. "I've even done some things—well, they were profitable for all concerned, but I took on the possible danger, myself. They profited more than I did."

Joseph shook his head. "I'm not a politician, Tom. I don't know the ways and the reasons of politicians."

Tom laughed cynically. "Oh, Joe. Don't be so humble.

You know damned well you are one of the big political powers in this Commonwealth. Just tell those bastards to change their minds at once or they'll hear from you. It is as simple as that. They wouldn't dare cross you."

"I have heard hints," said Joseph, "that they'd prefer a younger man. Hancock, for one. After all, you aren't young any longer, Tom. And, you've made your fortune. They take all that into consideration."

Tom studied him. Joseph's air was entirely too disinterested. He had never been one to shilly-shally like this, to Tom's knowledge. It was not in character.

"Joe," said the governor quietly.

He's an astute bastard, thought Joseph, and I am no actor. I am not even a good liar. He thought. Then he looked at Tom with an expression he hoped was concerned and disarming. "All right, Tom. What do you want me to do?"

"I've told you. Tell them to change their minds—or no more funds, no more bribery."

"I don't bribe," said Joseph. "I send only small gifts of appreciation. No one has any evidence of me bribing anyone."

"You took care of that, you and your Philadelphia lawyers," said Tom, with mounting anger. He saw Joseph shrug his thin shoulders. He saw Joseph smile at him faintly.

"Very well," said Joseph. "I will write them tonight. I hope it will help to change their minds."

"Telegraph," said Tom Hennessey. "I hear they intend to nominate Hancock on Monday. There's no time for writing."

"Very well," Joseph repeated. He went to his desk and wrote for a few moments in his angular tight script. He brought the paper to Tom, who put on spectacles to read it.

ALL CONTRIBUTIONS RECENTLY MADE ARE TO BE USED AS PREVIOUSLY DESIGNATED IN BEHALF OF THE CANDIDATE HERETOFORE CHOSEN. JOSEPH ARMAGH.

Tom Hennessey scrutinized it. He wished it could have been warmer, more explicit, and that it had mentioned his name or referred directly to him. Then he saw that this might not be prudent. He said, with some surprise, "I see you have already made a large contribution."

"Yes, very large. In August. After all, are you not the perennial candidate?"

"When you made that contribution you had no idea about—Hancock?"

Joseph stood up. He looked at Tom with glittering blue eyes full of cold umbrage, and Tom was so frightened that he sat up in his chair and stared. Joseph said, "When did they mention Hancock to you?"

Tom's full face, so sensual and brutal, trembled. "Monday, Joe." When Joseph did not speak he cried, "Joe, I'm sorry! I am almost out of my mind. I see bogies everywhere. When will you send that telegram?" His hands had become wet and cold.

"At once," said Joseph, and went to the bell rope. His whole attitude expressed rigid offense, and Tom was alarmed again. It would be fatal to antagonize Joseph Armagh, to whom he greatly owed his past elections. Tom said, with an attempt at a placating smile, rueful and affectionate, "Yes, I see bogies everywhere. Probably in Bernadette and your children, too, and Elizabeth!" He tried to laugh. Then as relief flowed through him he laughed again, with real heartiness, and took up his drink.

"That telegram will settle it," he said.

"I hope so," said Joseph. A maid came into the room and Joseph directed that she give the telegraph message to a groom, who was to take it to the depot at once. When the maid had left Tom said, his voice breaking, "I can't tell you what this means to me, Joe, and how grateful I am. I tell you, I've been on the verge of apoplexy since Monday. I have scarcely slept or eaten."

Joseph considered him with those small hidden eyes which were so inexplicable. "Then you must make up for it tonight," he said. "In the Bosom of your Family."

Joseph was unusually pleasant and amiable to Tom Hennessey at the dinner table that night, and Bernadette marveled, for she had never seen her husband so kind to her father before, nor so—almost—intimate. There had always been a reserve in Joseph towards Tom Hennessey, but now it appeared to have disappeared. She begged her father to remain "for a little festivity."

Tom, enormously relieved, flushed with wine and food, consented. Bernadette immediately began plans for a dinner party and a ball. "Very sudden," she said. "But everybody will come. I will have the invitations delivered by hand tomorrow. Everbody will be so pleased." Her round hazel eyes danced at Joseph with infinite love. Whatever her father's hasty visit had portended Joseph had settled it, and dear Papa was so relaxed now, so comforted. He sat there as if this house still belonged to him, and in a way, reflected Bernadette, with warm pleasure, it still did in spite of Elizabeth and that brat, and Mama's last instructions.

Joseph thought, Let the swine enjoy himself now and in the next days. It will be the last time. The condemned man's final meal. He smiled at Tom and directed a maid to give his father-in-law more wine. Tom's light eyes sparkled with satisfaction.

Joseph waited. One week. Two weeks. As he waited he inwardly grew colder, and felt his own impatient exultation. He was not surprised that on the morning of the fifteenth day he received a telegram from his father-in-law: WILL ARRIVE TONIGHT AT FIVE. MUST SEE YOU ALONE, AT ONCE.

Joseph crushed the telegram in his hand and smiled. He went to see Bernadette who was having her breakfast, as usual, in bed, her coverlet covered with jars of cosmetics, and perfumes, combs and brushes, mirrors, crumbs and lace handkerchiefs. It was not often that Joseph came here during the day, and hardly more often at night, and Bernadette's flat faintly golden face flushed and shone with joy. Her maid was laying out her morning attire, and a small fire burned to offset the early chill, though the day was brilliantly blue and sparkling outside. Bernadette's curling rags were concealed by a lace cap with ribbons and she wore a bed jacket of blue silk and lace, and her plump arms lifted themselves eagerly to Joseph for a kiss.

He was not sorry for his wife and what she would soon know. Bernadette, in her way, was as pragmatic as he and much more earthy and very practical. She loved her father still, and she would be greatly grieved, and I, thought Joseph, don't care a damn. He stood by the bedside and one of his hands was held by Bernadette and she was chattering, her hazel eyes darting and flashing with life and laughter, and Joseph thought how immediate she was and how her plans rarely ran beyond the day and the pleasures of it. He gathered she was going to tea with some friends in Green Hills, and her malicious and tripping tongue tore the reputations, the wits, the motives, and the lives of all her friends apart, and with the utmost gaiety. Joseph found himself listening. She could make him laugh with her jokes and sallies and her witticisms, for none of them were kind and all of them struck very accurately on their intended targets. He could not remember Bernadette speaking gently and kindly of anyone, except her father. She found her own children boring and annoying and had, thought Joseph, a hard hand on her in spite of her prattle about "the modern method of bringing up Our Precious Little Angels."

He neither loved her nor hated her. He did not like nor dislike her. Therefore he could almost always be temperate and detached with her, with no emotion whatsoever except occasional tedium. She might have been, to him, a dog of the household of which he was not fond and yet did not resent. Occasionally he found her body enticing, but he wanted no more children. He cared for Rory and Ann Marie hardly more than he cared for their mother, but since Regina's desertion he had begun to consider Rory and even to listen to the childish remarks of Rory's twin sister, Ann Marie.

Joseph's aloofness increased rather than decreased Bernadette's devouring passion for him. She thought it genteel and aristocratic, unlike her life-loving and very coarse father. He rarely kissed her and then only when in bed with her, and then he would not remain in her arms to sleep but left her in silence. She could not quarrel with him because of his indifference to her, which she had persuaded herself was masculine strength. ("Dear Joseph is too deep for facile expressions and protestations and all the other trivialities.") Because he was too uninterested in women, Bernadette would think, she had no occasion for jealousy when he was often away for weeks at a time, and even when in Green Hills he usually remained only two days out of a week. She never knew that he preferred the expensive trollops of Philadelphia and New York to his wife, and that he was the "protector" of a beauty, a successful young actress in the latter city, an Irish girl with a delectable face and figure and a glorious singing voice. Joseph took no effort to conceal his adulteries from his wife nor did he flaunt them. He did not care if she guessed. It was nothing to him, as Bernadette was nothing to him. Once he had felt a faint compassion for her on the night of her mother's death, because she was young and abandoned and wet with tears and sweat, and frantic, but he felt no pity for her now, and never the slightest tenderness. Had she discovered any of his affairs and if she had reproached him he would not have been angered or ashamed. He would have said to her, "What is it to you? What are you to me?"

She was aware of Joseph as she had never been aware of anyone before, and she had noticed how even more gaunt he had become since "that horrible Regina left here like a thief in the night." His face had become more taut, his eyes more secret, and the shadow of gray more pronounced in his thick russet hair. The planes of his face were sharp and angular, the hollows under his cheekbones deeper, his complexion paler. But he never spoke of Regina as he never spoke of Sean. It was as if they had not lived at all.

He said to her when her chatter slowed a little, "I have a telegram from your father, Bernadette. He is making an unexpected visit to me, tonight, on business. He will arrive at five."

Bernadette's face gleamed with delight, and her white teeth flared. "Oh, how wonderful, and he was only here a short time ago! I must send my regrets to Bertha Holleye, about the tea—"

"No," said Joseph. "That would be rude, wouldn't it?" He looked about the crowded gaudy room which had once been Katherine's, and he remembered the night of her death. "Go to your tea. Your father will be here only an hour or so before you return. I think he has some very important news for me."

Bernadette flapped a little fat hand. "Oh, he wants to tell you he has been nominated again! Is that such news? But, I suppose it will call for a party for our friends, to celebrate, as usual." She looked up at Joseph and there was something about him which vaguely disturbed her. "There's nothing wrong with Papa, is there, Joe?"

Joseph said, "Why should there be anything wrong?"

"Well, then, is it about your business—all your business matters?"

Joseph looked down into her adoring eyes. "I wouldn't be surprised in the least," he said. "I am pretty sure it is my business."

"There's nothing wrong with that, either, is there, Joe?"

Like all the rich who had never known destitution or privation money was a tender and emotional thing with her, and wealth something to guard with all the resources of one's mind and vigilance against anything or anyone which could diminish it by a penny. So Bernadette stared at Joseph with those round and somewhat bulging eyes and she no longer smiled.

"Not a thing wrong with my business, my pet," said Joseph.

He looked at her curiously.

"You are a very rich woman yourself, Bernadette, in your own right. And you are getting richer. Why should you worry about my affairs?"

"No one is ever rich enough!" she said, with passionate emphasis, and slapped her breakfast tray so all the china jumped. "Papa once said you were the richest man in Pennsylvania. That isn't enough. I want you to be the richest man in the country!" Then she laughed. "Rich as Mr. Gould, Mr. Fisk and Mr. Vanderbilt and Mr. Morgan and Mr. Regan, and all the rest. Richer."

Joseph's eyes narrowed so that there was only a glint between his lashes.

"And what would that buy you?" he asked, with greater curiosity. "More jewels, more Worth gowns, more journeys to Europe, more horses, carriages, houses, servants?"

"Just to have it," said Bernadette. "That's all. Just to have it."

"But why?"

She was fondly exasperated and took his hand again. "Joe, why do you keep on making money?"

"Just to have it," he mimicked her, and then when she laughed he did not smile but left the room. She lay back on her pillows, oddly and namelessly dismayed. He had looked at her as at an enemy, or as if he had hated her or thought her ridiculous. Bernadette was not very subtle, though she was acute. She chewed thoughtfully on a little jam-covered biscuit. Then she said to herself: Don't be absurd. Joe loves me. But he is very strange. I don't always understand him. He has not been the same since that Regina went away. A new thought came to Bernadette and she sat up quickly. Would Joseph have cared that much if it had been herself who had left, she, the mother of his children?

She saw Joseph's face again. Her love tried to blind and dazzle her. But she rarely lied to herself as she lied to others. She said aloud, "No, he wouldn't have cared that much." Again she felt that bleak desolation which had wounded her before.

When the maid came to take away the tray Bernadette slapped her smartly on the cheek then burst into tears.

All the household knew Joseph's moods, though he invariably seemed restrained, silent, never raising his voice, never speaking roughly or too quickly, never complaining. But the strength of his personality was such that he projected his mental climate without a word or a glance. So the great house was unusually quiet this day. The children stayed with their governess, the aging Miss Faulk, and Timothy Dineen found it necessary to consult with someone on a certain matter and so left the house in a trap, and the servants moved softly and spoke in subdued voices. The white mansion stood in the crisp bright air of autumn under its fading trees and every window was bright, but it seemed to be abandoned. The red calla lilies, the chrysanthemums in their beds, the very late roses, bent in the shining wind, but there was no other movement outside, and no sign of any groom or gardener's boy. The only sound was the dry crackling of dying leaves and then the sudden screech of a bluejay or the shattering sound of a delayed woodpecker against a trunk, or the distant stamping of a horse in its stall. Bernadette, looking dejected, had gone to her tea.

Joseph waited in his rooms. Never had time crept so slowly on sluggish feet. He kept glancing at his watch. Twenty after five. Twenty-five after. Half-past five. He heard hoofs and wheels and he stood up and looked through the window and saw the glittering black family victoria moving through the gates, drawn by two absolutely white horses. Joseph opened a cabinet, then, and laid out whiskey and glasses and soda and rang the bell for the butler. "Governor Hennessey's luggage should be taken to his room but I should like to confer with him as soon as possible, in my study."

He rearranged the neatness of his plain white cuffs, and then his cravat, and rubbed his hands over his thick hair. He looked tall and black and deadly in the quiet room. There was an ice-cold exultation in him. He had destroyed worthier men than Governor Hennessey in his surge to power and money, but he had done it with no animosity at all, no feeling of vengeance or triumph. It was only business. But this was vengeance indeed, a personal vendetta, a focusing of loathing and enmity and hate long in the gestation, long in the gathering. The arrogant and swaggering governor, seemingly invulnerable, had become vulnerable and had been destroyed.

Joseph made himself sit down and open a book. He heard the butler greeting the governor, heard Tom Hennessey's mumbled reply—he who never mumbled—and then heard the quick but stumbling footsteps up the stairs and down the long hall to Joseph's rooms. The governor appeared on the threshold and Joseph rose, his face shut and without expression.

Tom Hennessey, large, overfleshed, flamboyant and impressive, now appeared disheveled and soiled, hasty and sweaty. All his color was gone. His face was like cracked plaster, quivering, his sensual mouth hanging loose, his chin uncertain, his forehead glazed and wet. Always immaculate, "the glass of fashion," he seemed unbuttoned and roughened now. There was a wild agitation about him, a trembling uncertainty, a desperate upheaval. His light eyes, always cynical and domineering, now had a distraught and leaping shine. His longish brown and gray hair, usually carefully combed and cajoled into waves, hung over his cheeks and neck and forehead, tangled and ungroomed.

Joseph said, "How are you, Tom? Was your train late?"

The governor walked unsteadily into the room. He looked about him, as if he had never seen this room or this man before, and did not know where he was. He took an aimless step or two, towards the windows, back again, then to one side. He stood at last behind a chair and gripped its back and looked at Joseph, and his breath was grating and noisy in the sunlit room.

"They have ruined me," he said, and his voice was thick and unsure.

Joseph saw that his eyes were deeply bloodshot as if he had been drinking. His cheeks puffed out and in as he breathed. He did not look away from Joseph. He repeated, "They have ruined me."

"Who?" said Joseph and came closer to his father-in-law.

The governor raised one formidable forefinger, and then it wobbled and drooped and his hand fell to his side. "I will find out, and I will cut their throats," he said with the utmost malignancy. His eyes jumped. "They haven't finished with me yet."

"Please sit down, Tom," said Joseph and hoped that he was conveying solicitude. He took his father-in-law's shivering big arm and forced him into the chair he had been clutching. "Let me get you a drink. Then you must tell me about it."

"A drink," said the governor, and he croaked as if choking. "That's all I have been doing for two days and two nights. But give me a drink, and a large one," and he coughed, strangling. He tried to drop his exhausted head against the back of the chair but he was so distracted that it immediately bounced forward and he clenched his fists on the arms of the chair and his breathing was very loud and audible. "God damn them," he said. "Oh, my God, curse them! But I'm not finished with them yet! No one ever got the better of Tom Hennessey!"

Joseph put a glass half full of whiskey into the large white hand with its rings and its polished nails. Tom drank deeply, gluttonously, as if the glass held the elixir of life and strength. He inhaled raucously. His heavy shoulders visibly shook. He looked at the glass. Then he glanced up at Joseph with his reddened eyes, like the eyes of a tormented bull, and he said, "You haven't heard?"

"No," said Joseph. "I haven't even seen any newspapers this past week. I've had too much work here in Green Hills. But, what is wrong? Who has ruined you?"

The governor became still. He looked up at Joseph and those eyes fixed themselves on the younger man as if he had suddenly sensed something direful, something not quite in focus or apparent. He watched Joseph as he said, "You must know that though the Party gave out the idea that they were going to nominate me after all, they didn't. Day before yesterday they told me finally it was going to be Hancock."

Joseph frowned. He sat on the edge of his desk and considered his boots. He compressed his lips, slightly shook his head. He said, "They did not tell me."

"Not you? Not the biggest contributor to the Party? Not you who named the five state senators last year, and got them elected? They never told you, wrote you, telegraphed you?" The governor sat upright in his chair, and panted, but did not look away.

"No," said Joseph, "they never told me."

Now he turned his face to Tom and Tom saw his fierce concentrated eyes, his implacable face, the blade of his mouth and the white tension of his nose, and he misinterpreted them. He said, "I don't understand it. You, of all people." His voice was broken and rusty. "My son-in-law." He drank again, took the glass from his thick mouth and groaned. "But, you can do something, even now."

"What do you suggest, Tom?"

"Threaten them. It isn't too late." Then his face sagged. "Yes, it is too late." He put down his glass with a crash on the desk and rubbed his hands over and over his shaken face as if he were washing it. "It's too late. I forgot. There's worse."

His shoulder heaved under his creased fawn coat. He bent his face in his rubbing hands and Joseph thought he was weeping. All the strong muscles and the fat of the great body visibly shrank, as though disintegrating. Now he was no longer the buoyant and commanding governor of the Commonwealth, the former colorful senator of the United States of America, the owner of enormous wealth and power. He was a shattered old man, wrecked, thrown down, dismantled, full of bewilderment and despair and an agony he had never known before in his life, and a sense of demented incredulity.

He felt another glass being pressed against the back of one of the massaging and aimless hands. He started. Then he reached for the glass and fumbled it to his lips and the liquid went partly into his mouth and partly down his chin, dribbling. Joseph watched him and the quiet ferocity of his face deepened. He said, "You haven't told me. What is 'worse'?"

The awful eyes, robbed of all human anguish, disbelief, and torture, glared at Joseph. The large features were convulsed, misshapen. "Worse!" he said. "They—know everything. It isn't just Washington, though that's bad enough in their hypocritical eyes. Oh, God help me, God help me! Since I was governor—Joe, you know yourself. You profited. The state contracts, roads, bridges, right of ways, government buildings. All of it. Yes, I profited, too. But they did, more than I. More than even you. I did what they told me to. I obeyed every suggestion. I never objected. I was their man, wasn't I?" His eyes enlarged on Joseph, blood flecked, mad. "Do you know what they told me yesterday? That I was, in my way, the head of a Tweed Ring, here in this Commonwealth! They dared to tell me that! Who profited most? They did! Do you hear me, they did!"

"Yes," said Joseph. "But, can you prove it?"

"Prove it!" shouted the governor in a roaring voice. "Of course I can—"

He stared at Joseph.

"Can you? How?"

"The contractors—"

"The contractors are men making a living, and they can be intimidated by politicians as you know only too well, Tom. Do you think they will confess to the influence and the threats and the promises that were brought to bear on them? And so hang themselves, or at least be forced into bankruptcy and litigation and prosecution? And, perhaps, even be murdered? We all know what politicians are, don't we, Tom?"

He regarded the governor with gravity. "But I'm sure our friends told you that, yesterday, didn't they?"

Tom's big fingers smoothed themselves over and over the empty glass. He licked the drops of whiskey on his mouth. He was shaking as if struck by a powerful wind. "Yes," he whispered, "they did, that. But I thought you would help me."

Joseph sighed. "I'm no Samson, Tom, and neither are you. We can make an effort to show who really profited. I have a battery of lawyers in Philadelphia and they are ferrets. They could find out—though they'd put themselves in physical peril, as they'd know. We can appeal to the Attorney General, himself. We can appeal to muckrakers and zealous reformers in the Commonwealth. I can print accusations in my newspapers, and screaming editorials. And, what will it amount to? If your—friends—are indicted, so will you be, Tom. So will I. We're all in it together, robbing the people. That's what they'd call it, wouldn't they? And it would be the truth."

He smiled a little. "The other Party would be out of its mind with delight—if we told them. We could testify under promised immunity. State's evidence. Corruption, malfeasance, theft, graft, spoils, intimidation of contractors to the state, looting, exploitation of labor, inferior materials at the highest prices, subornation, perjury. Everything. Of course, we could plead, ourselves, that we were intimidated, threatened. Do you think the people would believe it? You, the rich governor, I the financier and what not? Come, Tom."

"I don't care—" whispered the desperate governor.

"I see. Something like from *Macbeth*: 'I am one, my

liege,' who am so incensed—or something—concerning the world that 'I am reckless what I do to spite the world.' Tom, do you want to go to jail? Or, at the very least, to be dishonored and outcast, forever? Do you think the other Party will take you to its bosom in gratitude? We all know the worth of politicians' gratitude, don't we?"

The blood-hazed eyes did not leave him. But a maddened speculation had begun to gleam in them. Tom said in a clearer voice, "You do not know it all, Joe. They have told me I have to make 'recompense.' That I must return 'the money' to the Commonwealth. With interest, with 'judicial and righteous penalties.' They told me. It will take almost all the money I have, all my investments. Everything. They have even shown me documents from Washington—They have even—forged—documents showing the source of the Hennessey money. Blackbirding. Things like that. Only part of the money, they told me, will be returned to the Commonwealth. The rest—"

"Is for them?"

"Yes."

"They were that bold?"

But Tom Hennessey did not reply. He was studying Joseph as he had never studied friend nor enemy before, with all the concentration and power of his intellect, which was not small, and all his intuition, all his Irish subtlety. Still watching with the complete focusing of his mind he said, "Yes, Joe. That bold. Something, somebody, is behind it. They wouldn't be that bold without orders."

Joseph looked deeply into the eyes below him. He said, "They can't take everything. They won't take everything. You still have Katherine's money. You still have your wife's money. It is enough to keep you in modest circumstances, in your house in Philadelphia. Anything is preferable to scandal, exposure, indictment, prosecution, jail. Isn't it? Anything is preferable to living in fear, isn't it? In the end you'd be better off financially by not fighting these—atrocious—demands. Do you realize how much lawyers would demand? They'd reduce you to poverty, Tom. I know lawyers."

"You are asking me to do nothing at all?" Tom was slowly rising from his chair, clutching the arms and back. "You are asking me to do that?"

"I am advising you," said Joseph.

"And—you will do nothing—to help me?"

Neither of the two men saw Bernadette, all black velvet and lace and bangles and veiled hat and gloves, on the threshold. She had just appeared. She had run happily up the stairs to greet her father, and her face still held the fading remnants of a smile, the mouth half-open and up-turned, the eyes flashing, the hand outheld. But she had come upon her husband and her father, confronting each other, and the sharp Bernadette had suddenly known that here was not a friendly family discussion but two adversaries. She felt the hatred in the room, the feral smell of deadly enmity. She had known instantly that one of these men was maddened beyond endurance, and the other was the maddener, ruthless and terrible. She had heard their last words. Her hand slowly fell to her side and she had a sensation of giddiness and terror.

She could hardly recognize her father in this broken man, whose potency was dwindling before her eyes, whose hair was disheveled, whose clothes were soiled and untidy, whose head was bent like the head of a dying bull stopped in his charge. She could not recognize her husband in this lean stiff man with the vindictive smile, the narrowed eyes, the contracted muscles held as if about to strike. She put her hand to her mouth, an unusually feeble gesture for Bernadette.

"I will do nothing to help you," said Joseph in the softest voice. "Not even if your life depended on it."

Tom Hennessey pondered on that. He looked about him vaguely, and now Bernadette could see his inflamed and bloody eyes which did not see her at all. Tom put his hand to his head. He licked his lips.

"What did you say?" he muttered.

"Nothing to help you. Not to save your life, Tom."

Tom put his hands to his throat and moved his big head. He gasped. He did not look away from Joseph. There was now a deep crimson flush on his forehead, a rising of thickened veins in his neck.

"Why?" he asked.

"Katherine," said Joseph.

"Katherine," Tom repeated, in a dull low tone. "Katherine. What had she to do with you?"

"Nothing. It was what you did to Katherine."

Tom's gaze fixed itself with renewed intensity on Joseph. The crimson flush was deepening. He slowly raised his right hand and pointed at Joseph.

"Now I remember," he said, and his voice was very choked. "You were a lad. You—you had been looking at this house. I knew I'd remember sometime. A dirty shanty Irisher. That's all you were, all you are. You wanted this house. Shanty Irish. A beggar. You plotted it all. From the beginning. You—took my daughter. It was all part of it. All part of it. Dirty shanty Irish." He stopped and groaned and panted. He said, "Katherine. Yes, I remember. You were always— It was Katherine. You waited a long time, Irish."

"I waited a long time," said Joseph. "But Katherine never knew. On the night she died she asked me to marry your daughter. It was her wish. And so I did."

Tom saw his face and for the first time in his life he shuddered before another man. He lifted his arms and clenched his fists. He staggered towards Joseph beating his hands impotently, blindly, in the air. He fell forward, stumbling, reeling. Bernadette uttered a thin shriek. Tom fell upon Joseph, still flailing. Then, instinctively, for he felt the older man sagging and collapsing, Joseph caught him in his arms, staggered himself a moment, then held Tom Hennessey, fallen against his chest, arms hanging.

It was then that Joseph saw Bernadette. He did not care what she had heard or what she had seen. He said to her, "Help me to put your father in a chair."

But Tom was unconscious now. He slipped out of the chair in which they put him, Bernadette all the while crying and half-screaming and slapping her gloved hands together in distraction. Tom lay on the floor between them with a suffused face, breathing stertorously, his eyes half open.

"You killed my father!" Bernadette shrieked. "What did you do to my father?"

"Ring for someone," said Joseph. "Send for a doctor, and some of the grooms and we'll put your father to bed."

His voice was cold and neutral. Bernadette stopped her crying. She stared at her husband, blinking, big tears on her smooth golden cheeks.

"I heard," she said. "You never cared anything about me, did you?"

"No," said Joseph, though he again felt a dim pity for her, "I never did. But there is nothing we can do about it now, is there?"

The doctor, and other doctors summoned from Philadelphia and even Pittsburgh, said that the governor had had a stroke, that his whole left side was paralyzed, that he would probably never speak again nor leave his bed. It was possible that he would not be fully aware or conscious of his surroundings from this time on, and must have constant nursing. He could not be moved. His life depended on it.

Bernadette, pale and quiet, said, "This is my father's house. He will stay in it as long as he lives, and I will never leave him. Send for his wife—and her child."

So Tom Hennessey had returned to his house and would remain there until he died. Joseph found a profound irony in this. He could even laugh quietly to himself at the irony. He was all courtesy to the grief-stricken Elizabeth, whom Bernadette hated. Elizabeth's little boy, Courtney, joined Rory and Ann Marie in the nursery.

Bernadette wanted to say to Elizabeth, to wound her, "My husband killed your husband," but her helpless and now devastated love for Joseph prevented her. No matter what Joseph did, to her, to anyone else, her besottedness was not shaken though she now feared him. Her mother: Had Joseph really loved her mother? Yes, it was so. She, Bernadette, must live with that all her life.

Joseph's newspaper in Philadelphia expressed its sorrow for "the stricken governor," and prayed for his recovery.

When Tom Hennessey died two years later—after an existence which had held no awareness of love or hatred or money or influence or power or even living—he was eulogized in the press as "the greatest and most humane Governor this Commonwealth has ever known. The defender of the weak, the upholder of the workingman, the staunch fighter for the Right, for Progress, the hater of corruption and exploitation, the patriot, the farsighted politician who had Dreams of a nobler America—this was Governor Thomas Hennessey, who was stricken down at the height of his struggle for the Nation. We grieve with his family. We pray for his soul."

Tom was buried beside his wife, who had loved him.

Chapter 31

While in New York Joseph's friends said to him during a discreet meeting: "It would be impolitic for any of us, except you, Mr. Armagh, to approach Senator Enfield Bassett personally. The cartoonists are too favorable to him and he has only to lift a finger for them to lampoon anyone who tries—er—to talk reasonably to him. He did it with the more obstreperous of the Greenbackers, though they had to be careful there, considering that both the conservative Democrats and the more moderate Republicans opposed them."

"I remember," said Joseph. "The radical Republicans joined with the Greenbackers, but we soon eliminated them from politics."

"We didn't," said a gentleman from Austria-Hungary, smiling. "We were entirely against the gold standard for America, and helped your innocent President Lincoln to issue greenbacks to pay for his war, though there was no solid currency behind them. We had our hopes, then, that your government would continue to issue fiat money instead of gold currency—for that is the sure way to—reorganize—a country."

"Make it available for loot," said Joseph, who was not always deferential to his colleagues. "Money by government fiat, not backed by gold and silver, inevitably bankrupts a country, doesn't it? But I thought you gentlemen were in accord that America was not yet ripe for total looting and for the introduction of Marxist Socialistic principles." He smiled at them with what they had long ago called his "tiger smile." "I am afraid," he said, "that you will have to wait a considerable time before America goes off the gold standard again, becomes Socialistic, and therefore ripe not only for looting but for conquest if not by arms then by bankers. Yes—a considerable time before

430

America becomes the slave of the Elite. Perhaps, however, your sons—"

"We have no time limits," said another gentleman. "We are patient." Another gentleman said, "Republics never survive, for their people do not like freedom but prefer to be led and guided and flattered and seduced into slavery by a benevolent, or not so benevolent, despot. They want to worship Caesar. So, American republicanism will inevitably die and become a democracy, and then decline, as Aristotle said, into a despotism. We can only work quietly and diligently for that day, for it is our nature," and he laughed a little. "No sensible man can endure to see fools voting in a free election, and deciding a nation's destiny for themselves. It goes against reason and right government. It is the highest and most distorted absurdity."

"Still," said Joseph, "the people became militant against President Grant who was considering a third term, and called him 'Caesar.' "

"We have said," said a gentleman from Russia, "that America is not ripe at this time either for democracy and her child, despotism. But the time will come. We will succeed in persuading your government to go off the gold standard and issue greenbacks by fiat. One way is through wars, but we have other methods, as you know, Mr. Armagh. Revolution, for instance, persuading the people that they are oppressed, and inciting incendiarism."

"Catilina did that," said Joseph. "It seems to me that he was slaughtered."

"He was before his time," said a gentleman from England. "Forty years later he would have succeeded. Now, in your country, we have only to turn your conservative Democrats into radicals, a hard task, but we may succeed. In defense, your radical Republican Party will have to become more conservative. This will confuse the people. But we have spoken many times of this before. The problem of Senator Bassett now confronts us."

Joseph thought of the time, only four years ago, when the strikers against the Baltimore & Ohio Railroad in Maryland had desperately rebelled against a reduction in their miserable pay of ten percent. On July 20, 1877, the governor had called out the 6th Maryland Militia, who marched to the railroad station, fired on the strikers and their wives and children and killed twelve people. But the strike had spread to Pittsburgh, where the Pennsylvania

Railroad had also cut wages. Governor Hennessey had ordered out the militia and there fifty-eight strikers, and soldiers, had died in furious pitched battles, and millions of dollars' worth of railroad property had been destroyed. But the Great Strike, born of the terrible depression of 1877, and nourished by starvation and wretchedly small wages, spread all over the country. President Rutherford Hayes had finally halted it, but not until the railroad barons had been forced to concede a little and had reduced a working day from fourteen hours to twelve and had made it possible for the workers to afford enough bread for their children, and meat once or twice a month. Joseph remembered that a large number of the strikers had been Irishmen, the Molly Maguires, fresh from the "ould sod," who had found the railroaders little different from their English landlords. However, they had been seduced by the slogan that in America there was no difference between races and religions, and that a man could practice his faith in peace. Perhaps their disillusion had fired their desperate rioting and not only the incredibly low wages. Joseph smiled grimly, and his colleagues, who thought him a capricious man and not entirely "solid," saw that smile though they were unaware of the reason. Joseph thought: There are other ways of revenge than rioting and striking.

He said, "Our new President, Mr. James Garfield, has said that he will institute new reforms in this country."

The others exchanged discreet glances. Mr. Jay Regan, the New York financier, said gently, "I am sure he can be dissuaded by intelligent and reasonable argument."

"Or, if not, he can be assassinated," said Joseph, and laughed his disagreeable laugh. "Like Mr. Lincoln." He saw their coldly affronted faces, and laughed again. "Gentlemen," he said, "I am not against judicious murder, as you know. But we were speaking of Senator Bassett. He is a Republican, but not a radical like our Reconstruction fanatics and our shouting congressmen and senators, therefore the conservative Democrats also voted with him in considerable numbers. The President likes him, and consults him. They may be hatching schemes deleterious to us. That is what you fear, isn't it?"

"True," said Mr. Regan, and shifted his heavy belly in his chair and lit a cigar. "Gentlemen," he said to the others, "Mr. Armagh and I are Americans, and so we are blunt and prefer to nail a subject down and not dance a minuet or a waltz about it."

"Your politics," said a German, "are your own, at this point, Mr. Regan. But we do know that Senator Bassett is leading the coalition against foreign contract labor, and trying to force through an Alien Contract Labor bill, which will prohibit the importation of cheap labor from Europe to work in your mills and mines and factories. The senator is listening too much to the criminal unions in America, and to sobbing sympathizers, and to 'reformers.' And other senators, and congressmen, too, are listening to Senator Bassett and his mobs. We all know that if alien labor is halted American labor will become arrogant and overweening and demand impossible wages and conditions, and that will be the end of the American progress and wealth. You will not be able to compete in foreign markets. Our own profits will be fearfully diminished. Besides"—and he looked at the Americans—"does not America need more and more immigrants? Think of your vast Territories to the West, lacking cities and factories and industry. Must they be deprived of people, of growth?"

"You touch my heart," said Joseph.

This was the sort of remark, uttered with quiet irony, that disturbed his colleagues, even Mr. Regan, who had a great affection for him.

"It has been the experience of America," said Joseph, "that alien labor does not move West in any quantity, but huddles in the warrens of the Eastern cities. Which, of course, is our plan in any event. If they moved West to open the Territories, who would work in our mills, mines, and factories? Gentlemen, let us be rough and honest, and not use sanctimonious words. We want alien labor because it is very cheap, and because American labor is demanding the right to live, too. That is intolerable to us. Let us proceed from that honest premise."

He saw secret cold eyes, calculating, but he knew he was safe from them. His knowledge made him invulnerable. Besides, Mr. Regan, the Morgans, the Fisks, the Belmonts, the Vanderbilts, the Goulds, might all be American villains but they had an American sense of humor also, and not an overpowering affection for their European colleagues. They would plot with them, but they would always have some peculiar sardonic reservation. They would plan to destroy

American freedom and establish themselves as the Elite—as the others planned for their own countries—but they would do it with urbanity and self-mocking hypocrisy. It would all be the same in the end, but the means were gayer and not icily cynical and bloodless. The words of Mr. Vanderbilt, "The hell with the public," would prevail, but the public would well know the sentiments of their coming rulers, and their present ones, and might even smile at their raucous effrontery. It was the deadly men, who spoke in low tones of "human rights" and "compassionate considerations"—while they methodically looted, and endlessly plotted against human freedom and human dignity—who were execrable.

But, thought Joseph, would a nation prefer a jovial executioner to a solemn one? He thought it very likely that America would. His experience with politicians had so convinced him. Well, America chose her own politicians, not on the basis of worth and honor and manliness and probity, but on their smiles, their public good-nature, their appearance, the people's own emotionalism, their own excited delusions. Joseph thought of his son, Rory, handsome, enchanting, humorous, gay, and witty—a born equivocator and of course, a politician. "Always lie, always be charming," Joseph had told his son. "Americans adore delightful pitchmen." Rory was not quite nine, but he was extremely intelligent, an attribute Joseph was later to tell him not to display before the American electorate. "Americans suspect too much intellect," he would say. "They prefer a glittering clown. You must learn to kiss babies and have a throb in your throat, and if you can have tears in your eyes and a smile on your lips simultaneously the public will go mad over you."

"If Senator Bassett succeeds in getting the Alien Contract Labor bill passed," said Mr. Regan, "it will be the end of American expansion, and the end of profits. Labor, if in short supply, can enforce impossible demands. It is as simple as that. So, Senator Bassett must be—persuaded. Other senators hold him in the highest regard."

"So Senator Bassett must lose that regard," said Joseph. "What skeleton does he have in his closet?"

"None that we can find, and we have sought," said Mr. Regan. "He has led a life of the utmost virtue." The others smiled bleakly. "He has never taken graft. He has never had a mistress. When he was congressman he refused the spoils. He is not a rich man. He owns farms and pays his workers high wages, incredible wages. His wife is a Southern lady—"

"That ought to be enough to swing the radical Republicans away from him," said Joseph. (That was another sort of remark of which his colleagues disapproved.) "Can't we bring it up that due to his wife the senator never helped loot the South the way the Reconstruction boys did?"

Mr. Regan coughed a little, but his eyes, ambushed under his thick brown brows, twinkled. "Unfortunately, the conservative Democrats and the conservative Republicans have noted that fact with approval."

Joseph said with politeness, "Has anyone considered murdering him?"

Mr. Regan laughed. "That would only inflame those who are with him, Joseph. Well, it seems in your pocket, my boy. We have decided that you, who have never been conspicuous, should try to persuade the senator. You have shown more discretion than others of us."

"I gather," said Joseph, "that Senator Bassett is well informed about the labor situation in America. He cried for the impeachment of the Governors of Maryland and Pennsylvania, who brought out the militia against the railroad workers. He is no tyro, no radical. We can't bribe him. We can't threaten him with 'exposure.' Or," he added in a meditative voice, "can we?"

"I think we have told you that there is nothing. He is a mountain of the Christian virtues."

"There is always something," said Joseph. "I will set my men to work at once." He looked at the men around the great oval table and saw their intent eyes. "There is no man alive, gentlemen, who does not have something to conceal, large or small. If small, then it can be blown up to gigantic proportions. It is easy to make even a saint into a mountebank, a deceiver, a betrayer of the people, if one is clever enough. I think my men are very clever."

Four weeks later Joseph went to Washington, which he called "a white ship on a sea of mud and fog." He hated its smells of sewers, its heat, its spiritual atmosphere of corruption and slyness and expediency and spoils. Grand avenues were being laid out, and Joseph reflected that similar avenues in France had led to the easy looting and insurrections and assassinations by the Parisian mobs, for no walls

or turnings had impeded them, nor had soldiers any means
of ambush. We don't, thought Joseph, as yet have a Rousseau or a Mirabeau or a Robespierre, nor are we as yet infected by communes as were the French revolutionaries
and their rich leaders. But, thanks to my friends, we will
most likely have them in the future, in the lifetime of my
sons or my sons' sons.

Joseph detested Washington, which amused his friends,
for was he not part of its corruption, venality, and spoils?
Had he not used senators and congressmen with cynicism?
They did not know of his ambiguous probity, for he was
hardly aware of it, himself. For instance, he had not rushed
eagerly to invest heavily in munitions during the Franco-
Prussian War, in which his friends had made combined bil-
lions. He had liked neither combatants, though at one time
he had heartily hated Bismarck, who had been infected by
Socialism. Yet, were not his friends plotting to infuse
Marxism into all nations for their destruction and bankruptcy, so that they could be silently conquered and ruled
by the Elite? When something could not be reconciled in
his mind he suppressed it as irrelevant.

He had rooms in the Lafayette Hotel, a modest hostelry,
for at all times, unlike some of the more flamboyant entrepreneurs, he avoided ostentation and the public eye. His
tastes were austere. He did not like gleaming carriages and
fine horses. So his invisibility was not strategy but nature.
That it immeasurably helped him did not occur to him,
though it did to his colleagues. However, politicians usually
knew when he was in town, and some were anticipatory
and some were uneasy. Senator Bassett was a resolute man,
but he was disturbed at the news. When Joseph Armagh
appeared hides had a habit of becoming raw—or were
groomed to glossiness. Senator Bassett doubted that if he
should encounter Joseph he would be groomed, though he
did not know Joseph personally. Joseph's presence, in itself,
was ominous, as the senator's friends had informed him.

"He is one of the prime movers against the Alien Contract Labor bill," the senator was told. "He moves quietly
and without overt noise, but he is there just the same."

"I will wait," said the senator. "My God, how I hate
these behind-the-scenes politicians! They are worse than
the elected ones, for they control too many of us. I thank
God that senators are appointed by State Legislatures and
so never have to run for office like the unfortunate con-

gressmen. I hope senators are never elected by direct vote of the people, for the people are volatile and can easily be misled by a smile or a wink or a few coppers in their hands, and, above all, by grandiose promises."

"Joe Armagh is one of the chief promoters of a Constitutional Amendment to elect senators by direct vote of the people, and to stop their appointment by State Legislators only."

"Not in my lifetime, I hope," said the senator, in a stern voice. "We'd be redundant, then, which is probably the whole plot anyway. And we'd be the creatures of the politicians just as the congressmen are."

Senator Enfield Bassett was from Massachusetts. He was a small but compact man with a great head, too large for his frame. He gave the impression, in spite of his stature, of considerable strength of body and mind. He had a big and vital face, kind and very intelligent and eloquent, and was forty-five years old. He did not wear a beard but only a very curly mustache which he vainly tried to straighten with wax. His hair, somewhat short, had that tendency also, and he lavishly used oil on it. His eyes were beautiful, large, black, and expressive, with long silken lashes. There was something about them, however, which disturbed his friends. They were never known to harden or grow too intent or piercing, but always shone with humor. His nose was not conspicuous, though his mouth was unusually generous, and he had fine white teeth. If there was a slight inclination to the rococo in his attire his friends loved him for it. They knew that this did not extend to rococo judgments, but that always he was balanced, thoughtful, sincere and moderate. Above all things he was adamant against the exploitation of American labor, its agonies, its unjust oppression and misery—and against the importation of alien labor which was willing to work for almost nothing in its wretchedness and so cripple American labor.

"I am not against Europeans," he would say, "for are we not all Europeans? But I am against the importation of foreign labor which is brought here in cattle boats, sick and starving and diseased, not to be succored and helped by 'compassionate' owners—and do they not act like owners? —but to be driven into our mills and factories and mines like beasts, there to work until they die on their feet—and then are buried in unknown graves. They are confined behind stockades, with no access to the world outside those stockades. Their wives and their children are pressed into service. Their lot is terrible, unconscionable, not to be endured in any Christian nation. Their fate is far worse here than in their native countries. At least there they had a little land. What have they here? Nothing but servitude. They never see a copper of their earnings. It goes to company stores for their meager needs.

"The time has come, my friends, when we must practice what we preach. We say we are a free nation. But, are those who are imported here like cattle free? We must stop such importation. Henceforth those who come to our shores must be free men, willing to assume the responsibilities of freedom, proud men with trades and with skills, and not mute creatures willing to work to their deaths for a little bread and unmarked graves. Thank God we have abolished open slavery. Let us now abolish covert slavery. No entrepreneur must henceforth be permitted to import desperate men for his own profits, to the detriment of our own people, who demand a decent wage and a decent shelter."

"Progress," said his opponents. "Shall we close the doors to our country to the wretched, the serfs, the meek?"

Senator Bassett knew who "owned" those politicians. No man owned him. It had been, in its way, a miracle that he had been selected by his State Legislature for his office. "An oversight," he would say wryly. "They must have just come from church."

This was the man of integrity that Joseph Armagh had arrived to suborn.

He did nothing overt. He asked two senators to extend an invitation to Senator Bassett to meet him, "in the interests of mutual concern." The invitation was extended. Senator Bassett believed in the aphorism that a man should know his enemy, the better to judge him and to overcome him. So he agreed to have dinner with Joseph in the privacy of the latter's rooms. It was a day of intense heat, July 1, 1881, tropical, dripping with moisture though the sun shone and there had been no rain; fetid, stinking of sewage, fouled dust, horse droppings, stagnant water, and rotting vegetation, and other smells which could not be defined but were rank. The hotel was not situated in a fashionable quarter and the bricked street was narrow and, as usual in Washington, blowing with scattered filth in a hot wind. Across the street stood endless rows of what Joseph called "terrace houses," from his memory of the towns in Ireland, that is, attached houses of a dull reddish stone with tiny smeared windows and painted doorways on flagged or wooden walks. The windows of Joseph's rooms were open and the curtains blew in and out and the velvet draperies were dusty. There was constant traffic; the rattle of steel-rimmed wheels invaded the rooms and the clopping of horses and the barking of stray dogs.

The rooms were small, plushy and very hot, and some of the crowded furniture was of horsehair, and the rugs were cheap. The senator observed this with some surprise. This hotel seemed hardly the place for one like Joseph Armagh and for a moment the senator thought that this must be secretiveness. Then he studied his host and saw his good but austere clothing and decided that this atmosphere was more to Joseph's taste than grandeur, and for some reason he was more alarmed than before. Ascetics were not as easily moved as grandiloquent men; they tended to fanaticism and were often less than human in their emotions. Too, they frequently lacked conscience, could not be bribed easily, and, if they had humor it was usually wry and acrid, and without pity.

Yet when Joseph turned to him with a formal greeting and an expression of gratitude that the senator had kindly vouchsafed to accept his invitation, Senator Bassett saw something in his fleshless face that touched him. Here was a man who had known infinite pain and sorrow and cruelty and rejection, and as the senator had suffered these himself he recognized them. He also remembered that a French poet had said, "In this world the heart either breaks or turns to stone." Joseph's had probably turned to stone, and now the senator felt oppressed and despondent. There was nothing so relentless as a man who had endured all the evil that the world can inflict, and who had turned against the world.

"I have ordered ham and a bird for you, Senator," said Joseph, "and beer and plum pudding. I hope it is all to your taste."

"You are very kind," said the senator with new surprise. "They are my favorite victuals." He was about to ask how Joseph knew that, and then he remembered, with a fresh rise of alarm, that Joseph had probably learned a great deal about him and such minute inspection was not flattering and could be dangerous. It had also had a purpose. The senator well understood that Joseph was here to try to persuade him to retract on his support of the Alien Contract Labor bill, for the withdrawal of such support would endanger its passage.

"I am gratified," said Joseph, in the stilted and formal tone he had used since the senator had arrived. "I, myself, eat sparingly, and this heat ruins any appetite at all. I wonder why you senators remain here in the summer, and especially as a holiday is almost at hand."

"We have work to do, very pressing work," said the senator. He sat down at the laid round rable with its clean but cheap linen and tarnished silver. "I don't like Washington, myself, but I am here to serve my country." The old and pompous words sounded, in the senator's strong yet musical voice, not hypocritical but sincere. "Against its enemies internal and external."

Joseph could study a man without giving any indication of such acute study and he soon knew that the senator was a man of absolute rectitude and not a political liar, and therefore he was out of place in this city and an anomaly. He also knew that the senator knew why he was here, and that the senator had accepted his invitation not because of his power alone but for his own judgment of Joseph's formidable weapons. Joseph's hidden scrutiny scanned the senator's face, lingered on the mouth and the large soft eyes of a deep liquid black and on the determinedly curly hair and mustache which were, in this heat, rebelling against oil and wax. He felt the faintest qualm, something he had not felt for years, and he crushed it. He had nothing against the senator personally. He knew this man had been very poor, almost as poor as himself, and that what he had —mortgaged though it was—had been bought with earned money and not through loot and bribes.

Joseph's own dinner consisted of a dish of thin broth and a slice of cold meat and bread, and tea. He ate absently. The senator, though becoming more wary every moment, ate with heartiness and commented on his colleagues with kind amusement and did not name them. He was witty. When he laughed his laugh was higher than the usual man's laughter, and ran to the suggestion of a cry at the end. The beer refreshed him and he drank it copiously.

"I heard," said Joseph, "that you are really a farmer. I, myself, was born in the country. In Ireland."

"Ah, we have a number of congressmen who are Irish," said the senator. "Yes, I am a farmer, born on a farm. I own four hundred acres of land in Massachusetts and another five hundred in New York State. Four tenant farmers. Now," he added, with a sparkle of those unusually fine black eyes, "when I say I 'own' those acres I mean I have title to them but the banks really own them. I am paying them off, with high interest. I was born in Massachusetts, but my wife was born in Georgia. I met her here in Washington when I was a congressman, and her father a senator. He felt she was stooping pretty low to marry me," and he laughed. "I have," he continued with pride, "a very pretty daughter who is marrying into a fine family in Boston. A very fine family. In September."

It suddenly occurred to Joseph that the senator's artless recital was very like the very young Harry Zeff's recital on the platform of the depot in Wheatfield so long ago. Again that sick qualm came to him, and again he crushed it down.

"So your wife is a Southern belle," said Joseph, with an attempt at jocosity.

The senator laid down his fork and looked at him. "Yes," he said. "A beautiful lady still." His heart had begun a curious sharp beating. His judgment of men was very astute and he knew that such men as Joseph Armagh are not given to jocoseness or pleasantries. Yet Joseph's face was unreadable. He had hardly touched his meal.

The senator said, and he was somewhat breathless, "I know you are here on business, Mr. Armagh. How can I serve you?"

"You are not my senator," said Joseph, with much courtesy, "but you indeed can help me. I am a direct man. You probably know that I am here to discuss the Alien Contract Labor bill which you instigated and are now trying to push through the Senate. And I know that you have a number of your colleagues with you, for they highly respect you and would oblige you, even if they have, perhaps, some reservations about that bill."

The senator said, "Yes, they had reservations in the beginning. They do not have them now. They will vote with me out of conviction and not out of personal respect or friendship for me. I would not have it otherwise."

"Spoken like a man of integrity," said Joseph. "I prefer to deal with honest men—who are usually reasonable into the bargain."

The senator struck a lucifer on the sole of his shoe and

lit his cigar with hands that visibly trembled. "Mr. Armagh," he said, "I have heard all the arguments against that bill. I have considered them all. This is not a whim on my part, an emotional excitement. I have studied foreign contract labor for a long time, and have been outraged at the treatment accorded those poor creatures who, because they are forced to accept abnominably low wages, keep American labor out of work. Did you know that some of your—friends—hired Chinese laborers to work on the railroads for twenty-four dollars a month, and then charged them for clothing and boots so that they had nothing left to feed or shelter themselves, except for barely enough to keep them alive? And a kennel in which to sleep? We have Hungarians, Bulgarians, Austrians, Poles, Germans, and God knows what else constantly being imported to replace what is alleged to be 'high cost American labor,' and to subdue the struggling unions, and these poor souls hardly fare better than the unfortunate Chinese, who died to the man.

"There is no use to speak of conscience to your friends, Mr. Armagh. They tell me that these desperate men, and their families, are better off in America than in their own countries. They know it is a lie. Those men are lured here with promises which are never fulfilled, of course. We treat mongrel dogs better than these, Mr. Armagh, and I am sure that you know it. We have ostensibly outlawed slavery for black men. We now have slavery for white men. At least most of the owners of black men regarded them as valuable property, and fed and clothed and sheltered them with some adequacy, and had physicians for them. But these white slaves do not have these. Ah!" exclaimed the senator with passion, "I do not know how those friends of yours can sleep of a night, Mr. Armagh, or how they can compose their immortal souls when they die!"

Joseph stared at him and smiled grimly. "I have never known anyone's sleep to be disturbed, Senator, or their immortal souls either, if there is plenty of money to hand.

"Now, you have spoken of the wretchedness of the foreign labor we have brought here. At least these people have their passage paid." His hollow face had begun to darken and the senator watched him. "They had not had to watch their countrymen die in ditches from hunger, or their families. There was always some bread, some cheese, some cabbage, some shelter, no matter how sparse, no matter how poor. They never knew real Famine. I, Senator, did. I arrived here as a lad of thirteen with a young brother and a newborn sister to care for, and for what I received I paid for, with my own earnings. I had no job to go to, no shelter prepared. I was not a man. I was a child. And I was turned away from your free ports, Senator, until by some compassionate intervention I was allowed to enter, with my family.

"I have worked all my life, at any work I could find to do, since I was scarcely thirteen, and supported a family. I starved, Senator, starved more painfully than do your foreign labor, for which you have so much pity. And I never grumbled. There were no senators to succor me, to plead the cause of the desperate and starving Irish who wanted to come here just to work. We were despised and rejected, everywhere we went. We were refused work, until we had to lie and say we were not Irish, not 'Romans.' No one cared that we suffered the consumption in this brave free land of yours, Senator, and died in our own blood, and wanted for bread and clothing. We were not permitted to work! We were not permitted to live. Yet, somehow we lived. Somehow tens of thousands, hundreds of thousands of us, fought our way out of the trap of our existence with our own hands and brains and courage. We asked no quarter; we were given none.

"Now, Senator, were we more fortunate in the beginning than your foreign labor?"

So, that's what it is, thought the senator with a great inner bound of understanding and compassion. He will take revenge on the world that did that to him.

"This world killed my parents," said Joseph. "They were murdered just as surely as if they had been shot. Well, it is not important, is it? The fact remains that alien contract labor, brought here on free passage—as we were not—has the same opportunities, or lack of them, which I had. Most of them are men, but I was a child. You will say they have families with them. So did I. Let them do as I did. Let them work as I did. They are not feebler than I was. Eventually, if they are determined, they will break free—as I did."

The senator said, in the gentlest voice, "In other words, you want them to suffer as you did. Knowing the bitterness of hunger and exploitation—you would have them endure that, too?"

Joseph said, "Are they better than I?"

He made an abrupt gesture. "But I am afraid that we are digressing. Foreign labor is necessary for the expansion of America, so we must have it."

"I agree," said the senator. "But let us pay them decent wages and give them a decent opportunity. Let us help the unions to succeed in demanding adequate money for our American labor, too. The whole point is that foreign labor, willing to work for almost nothing, is depriving American labor of work and starving it to death. Do I need to remind you of the railroad strikes and the murder of the strikers, and even of their wives? If that is necessary for 'the expansion of America' then I say—let us not expand!"

"It is said," Joseph remarked, "that you cannot bake bread without killing the yeast."

The senator pushed his chair from the table with a gesture of despair. "I love epigrams. The trouble is that they are seldom generous or pitiful. We are talking of men, Mr. Armagh, not of yeast. Until more labor is needed we must not have foreign labor brought here in cattle boats. When it is needed, they must be paid a decent wage."

He added, "You speak of prejudice, Mr. Armagh, against the Irish. There is prejudice against these poor people also. Because they are what they are they are treated as less than human by our own citizens. That, too, must be rectified. There is no room among honorable men for prejudice against other men for the fault—if you want to call it that—of their birth. Prejudice would be laughable if it were not so heinous, so evil. You, above all, should understand that."

But Joseph said "We are not men who ask without rewarding. I suppose you know that?"

The senator had become pale, and now all the kind humor had left his face. He said, "Yes, Mr. Armagh. I know. Do I not know! If my colleagues showed any signs of shame they could be forgiven, perhaps, for human failings and human greed. But they are not ashamed. They will vote against the best interests of their country—for money —and smugly swagger over it, and look for more. They are hired whores, Mr. Armagh. They are worse than whores."

Joseph could not help smiling. "But, like whores, they receive their pay. Come now, Senator. We are not offering bribes or anything so vulgar as that. We should be just grateful to buy what you could offer, for an excellent price."

"To withdraw my support from the Alien Contract Labor bill—which I instigated—and take my colleagues with me?"

"Exactly. It is a small matter."

"The answer, of course, is no, sir."

"There is no argument that can persuade you even to consider the matter?"

"No. I have heard all the arguments. I have rejected them all for months. I am truly astonished that your friends should try again, for they have approached me before." He stared intensely at Joseph. "Do you not know that what you have said, what you have offered, is a criminal offense against the dignity of the Senate, that you have attempted to bribe me and so have opened yourself to prosecution?"

"I know that, Senator. But you have no proof."

"And besides," said the senator with immense bitterness, "it would only amuse some number of my colleagues, honorable men all!"

He added, "But I have hope that this bill will pass. The President is with me. We have a seemingly quiet and amiable Chief Executive, but he is a man of principle and has plans which he has confided but to a few, and I am proud that I am one of them."

"I have heard of President Garfield's convictions," said Joseph. "I think he is ill-advised."

The rooms had become hotter. The brown walls radiated the raw and burning sunlight. Dust swirled on the windowsills in little dust devils. The sound of the traffic was louder in this room as the two men regarded each other in a pregnant silence. Then the senator said, "What do your people want?"

Joseph smiled his tight and bitter smile. "What does any man, in his heart, really want? Power. Hypocrites scream ideologies and slogans to gain it over the gullible and what I like to call the 'pure-in-hearts.' But my—friends—have no ideologies though they will solemnly use those of others if it serves them. They are men of many interests, politicians, merchant chiefs, mineowners, industrialists, bankers, railroaders, oilmen, shipbuilders and owners, munitions makers, men of inherited wealth, men of illustrious family both here and abroad, princes, if you will. Landowners. They have several things in common: None is devoted to his particular country. None cares about the people's welfare in any nation. All are avaricious beyond the avarice of the general public to comprehend. All are sublime egotists. All are enemies of what you would call freedom, Senator. They want to rule, each in his own sphere, cooperating with the others. They want to be the Elite, with absolute authority over the lives and deaths and destinies of the world. At heart, they are all Robespierres, Dantons, Mirabeaus. Jacobins."

The senator stared at him fixedly, for he had heard the irony and contempt under Joseph's words. He thought for a few moments and then said, "Jacobins. Yes. Revolutions never rise from the working people, the farmers, the petty shopkeepers. They rise from the bored and overfed bourgeoisie, the men who already rule, the so-called intellectuals, the affluent restless whose souls are empty of any spiritual value but lust for cold violence. In all history no despot ever rose from what is called 'the people.' Despots rise from the depraved radicals, who hate their fellowman though they soothe him with soft words and flatteries and pretend to be his friend. You see, Mr. Armagh, I know my history, too."

"Then," said Joseph, "you also know, as the Renaissance Italians knew, that politics and moral ethics never mix. Politics and ethics are a contradiction in terms. An honest politician is either a hypocrite—or he is doomed."

The senator stood up. He reached to a chair and picked up his tall silk black hat. He held it in his hands and studied it, and his expression was both grave and suffering. He said, almost inaudibly, "I still have hope that my countrymen will elect good men and not thieves and liars and exigent rascals and soft flatterers and potential looters."

He looked at Joseph. "I think I have said all that needs to be said I will not abandon my position. I cannot, in conscience."

Joseph stood up also. Now he held a sheaf of papers in his hand. "Then, Senator, I trust you will have a conscience concerning several people in these notations. Please read them."

The senator took the papers. He began to read them, still standing. His face slowly grayed, became ghastly, though no feature moved. But drops of sweat appeared on his forehead and rolled down his cheeks like tears. Joseph watched him. Finally he could watch him no longer and he went to a window with a taste like dead dust in his mouth. He clenched his hands on the gritty sills and stared down sightlessly at the traffic. The silence behind him became weighted, as if inhabited by a corpse. He at last heard a rustling and knew that the papers had been replaced on the table. Still, he could not turn.

The senator said in a dry whisper, "Who knows of this besides you?"

"Only one other, Senator. In full. The information was gathered separately by a dozen trained men who have no interest in you, and do not know the whole story. I have not shown these papers to my—friends. I preferred to show them only to you."

"What do you intend to do with that information, Mr. Armagh?"

Joseph slowly turned from the windows. His eyes felt scorched. He saw that the senator appeared to have dwindled, shrunk, and that he had the aspect of a man already dead.

"Senator," said Joseph, "if you do not withdraw your influence from the Alien Contract Labor bill I intend to give that information to the newspapers—and to several of your colleagues. I am sorry. You know there is no libel involved. You know the facts in these papers are true."

The senator fumbled for the chair he had left and now he fell in it. His head drooped. He said, hardly above a whisper, "We are in new days. It is no longer heinous—or repulsive—to have had a mulatto grandmother, who was a slave in South Carolina. She was a gracious lady, and was educated by her mistress, and tutors. In turn, she educated the children of her mistress, who had freed her. At last her mistress gave her a large sum of money and helped her to come North, to Canada. But, you know all that. She married a Canadian farmer of some substance—it is related here, why do I repeat it? They moved to Massachusetts. I knew her well. She was until her death the dearest thing in my life."

He looked up at Joseph now with eyes wide and haggard. "She taught me that nothing is so important as liberty, and that even liberty is not valuable unless it is accompanied by honor and responsibility. She taught me that no man worthy of the name can call himself a man unless he has integrity."

Joseph looked aside. "Then it does not matter if the news comes out that you had a grandmother of so many virtues, does it?"

The senator said, "We have quite a number of Negro congressmen in Washington these days, Mr. Armagh. No one despises them, or insults them—"

Joseph then knew that the senator had not heard his remark. He said, "But your wife, the lovely Southern belle from Georgia—she does not know, does she? And your daughter, who is to marry the Boston scion of a fine family —Mr. Gray Arbuthnot, isn't it?—he does not know? Perhaps they will not be so broad-minded as your senatorial colleagues, Senator, and I am afraid that they, too, will suddenly lose their tolerance, and not support you. I have noticed that 'tolerance' has a way of vanishing when a man's own future is at stake if he pursues it. There is something else, also. Your enemies will conclude that your passion for the welfare of the American workingman, and your opposition to the importation of foreign labor, rises from the fact that you are the descendant of a slave, and so have a slave's sensitivity to the 'enslavement' of others. Do not think men are kind, Senator. They are devils."

The senator was still staring at Joseph and his lustrous black eyes shimmered as if with tears.

"My colleagues, in the Senate, are conservative Democrats and the more moderate of Republicans. They will not turn from me."

"They will. When did a man ever support anyone held up to public aversion or ridicule, no matter how innocent or good? None, to my knowledge. Each of your friends will think of his own political future. He will not jeopardize it for you, my dear sir. Certainly, we all palpitate in the North about 'the rise of the Negro.' It is fashionable. But it is abstract. Coming down to facts is quite another thing, as the liberals well know, and the Whigs. Many of your conservative Democratic friends are from the South, you will recall, and so are your 'more moderate' Republicans. Publicly, they will utter soft words, but in reality they will run from you."

He added, "And what will your wife think? How will she endure the humiliation? Do you think Mr. Arbuthnot will marry a girl descended from a Negro slave? Think on it, Senator. For, it is stated here, your wife does not know your history, nor your daughter."

The senator's head fell on his chest. He said in a broken voice, "You have said it. Men are devils."

"True, Senator. You have only to tell your colleagues that on further reflection you are not supporting the Alien Contract Labor bill any longer, and all this information will be destroyed. No one will ever know. I give you my word of honor."

The senator gave a groan of anguished laughter. "I have only to abandon my principles, desert my convictions, give up all that makes life endurable to a man!"

"Think of it as protecting your wife and your daughter, Senator."

The senator, a very sensitive and subtle man, heard something strange in Joseph's voice, and he looked up quickly. "Ah, so you gave up much, perhaps, to protect others, Mr. Armagh? Others you loved?"

For an instant—so fleeting that the senator thought he had not seen correctly—Joseph's face was formidable. But Joseph's voice was reasonable and easy when he spoke. "Perhaps, Senator. I can tell you this: No one is worth a man's life, a man's sacrifice."

The senator stood up. He looked down at the papers. He wet his gray lips with the tip of his tongue. After several long moments he said, "It is possible that you are right, sir. I am coming to the conclusion that this world is really hell."

He put his hat above a face that had shriveled and become old and sunken. "I will think on all this," he said.

"You have to six o'clock tomorrow night, Senator. Send me word. If I do not hear from you—"

The senator nodded. An unfathomable look of resolution filled his eyes. "I have until tomorrow night, to six o'clock, to tell you that I withdraw—or do not withdraw. Yes. You will hear from me."

He turned towards the door, and his step was slow and feeble. Joseph went quickly to the door and opened it. The senator stood on the threshold. He turned his head with what appeared to be a heavy effort and looked Joseph in the face. "Mr. Armagh," he said, "may God have mercy on you, for you are not a bad man. No, you are not a bad man. So, it is all the worse for you."

Joseph's eyelids almost covered his small blue eyes. "I am what this world made of me, Senator. But is that not true of everyone?"

"No," said the senator. "No. That is not true. We have our choices."

Joseph watched him walk uncertainly, as if drunk, down the long, hot and narrow hall with its shut doors and smells. Then the senator, reaching blindly for a handrail, crept down the stairs. Joseph shut the door.

He stood for a long time in the middle of his dusty blowing room. He looked at the fragments of the dinner he had eaten with the senator, at the dirty dishes and the soiled glasses. His eye touched the empty hearth. Suddenly he shivered, as if cold. He took the sheaf of papers and dropped them into the fireplace. He knelt and struck a lucifer. He set fire to the papers. They were thick and resistant. He lit more lucifers. The room filled with a smell of smoke and sulphur. The papers caught more freely. Now they burned as if with jubilation, and pieces of black paper flew up the chimney. Those in the fireplace curled into long black worms, then disintegrated. Joseph took a poker and demolished what was left. As always, he had not been able to resist innocence.

He sat on his narrow heels and said to himself, You are a fool, of course. You don't even know why you did the thing you have just done. What is that man to me? One politician more or less. I acted in my own worst interests. How am I going to explain this thing to my associates? I dare not tell them what I've done. They'd laugh me out of existence, and then move to destroy me. This is a fine situation!

He looked at the black ashes and all at once something tight in him loosened. No one knew he had had this information except Timothy Dineen, who had gathered the reports of other investigators and had drawn them into one concise report. Joseph had only told his colleagues that he had "some information which might persuade Senator Bassett. I can try, at the very least. I think he will listen to reason." He would have to tell them that the senator, at the last, had not listened to reason at all. Joseph shrugged. The rest lay with their new plots, which he doubted would be efficacious with a man like the senator.

He already knew what the senator's decision would be. He would not withdraw, for then he could not live with himself. Joseph stood up, restlessly. There was no train out of Washington tonight, or he would have left. He would have to stay in this abominable white and corrupt city, full of stenches and evil, until tomorrow.

Joseph went to a Brahms concert that night but the music could not distract him as usual. He saw Senator Bassett's face everywhere in the orchestra seats and in the boxes. Once he thought, If I knew where he lived I'd go to see him tonight and tell him— Tell him what? Of the destruction of the "information"? Would that console a man so wounded now? Would he be reassured that no other enemy would unearth the story sometime in the future? Could he live with that knowledge, the fear, the haunting dread? He did not fear for himself. He had the most appalling fear of all— that the truth would destroy those he loved.

Love, thought Joseph. Like all things else it was a lie and a delusion, a crippling and a betrayal. No wonder it was so celebrated: It was so rare, so beyond the nature of man that it struck him into marveling as would a miracle. Only those were safe who never loved and did not love. They were safe from the world of men.

He walked back to his hotel in the midnight heat of the city. The bricked or cobbled or muddy streets were crowded with vehicles, loud with laughter and the steel rattle of wheels and the clomping of horses' hoofs. He saw the faces of politicians, rotund, flushed, jovial—he had met them often and knew them. They waved at friends from rich victorias and coaches, and smiled and smiled and smiled. They never stop working, thought Joseph. They are sleepless predators.

The fetid tropical heat did not lessen. It was worse in Joseph's rooms. He tossed and dozed and had nightmares. Once he dreamt that he was on a little skiff and he saw his mother's hand stretching up to him from black waters. But when he reached for it it sank again, and he heard a moaning. He awoke, sweating, just as the blue-green light of the predawn appeared. Then he got up and washed.

When he was listlessly eating a meager breakfast a messenger arrived at his door with a letter. He opened it and saw it was from Senator Bassett. For a moment or two he squeezed his dry and scalded eyes together before he read. Then he stiffened. The senator had written:

You have asked me to withdraw at the price of not destroying those who are dearest to me. There is but one way

*I can withdraw that will not lacerate my conscience so that
I cannot rest in peace. When you have received this I will
have gone the way of all flesh. But with my dying breath I
can only say this to you: I have laid a curse on you and
none of those you cherish will ever prosper or fulfil your
dreams and your hopes.*

It was not signed beyond the initial "B."

Joseph stood up abruptly. He thought he was smothering. There was an enormous chill all through his body, and
an awful sickening. Everything became cloudy about him.
The walls and the ceilings of the room became mist, ruf-
fling and flowing, dissolving. He felt faint. He had to reach
for a chair, and he fell into it, the paper falling from his
hands. He put his hands over his face and shuddered.

It was not the dreadful curse of the self-immolated man
which disturbed him, for he was not superstitious. He believed neither in curses nor in blessings. It was something
else. He had killed a phenomenon: an honest man. After a
long while he thought, But then, an honest man is ludicrous. He has no place in this world, and never had such a
place. In a way, if all honest men died this would be a
peaceful world, for there would be no transient disturb-
ances and agitations, no foolish hopes, no dedicated and
fruitless efforts doomed from the beginning, no crusades
fated to be destroyed, no lofty eloquence.

He was in the railroad station among the seething
throngs when President Garfield was shot, not thirty feet
from him.

A few months later the Alien Contract Labor bill was
passed by both the Senate and the House. "We owe this,"
said one senator, "to the labors of our beloved Senator Enfield Bassett, who gave all his selfless energies to the passing
of this bill. He died as an overladen horse dies, harnessed
and pulling with all his strength, and it was an honorable
death. The burdens of Public Office often kill. We consider
Senator Bassett as much a martyr to his country's weal as
President Garfield who died on September 19th, after a
desperate fight for his life over many weeks."

Joseph Armagh did not believe political assassinations
were "random things, brewed up from insane minds and
disordered intellects," as some newspapers averred concerning President Garfield. The hand on the trigger might
have been "random," and the mind and intellect "insane

and disordered." But the men behind the assassin were not random or insane or disordered. They knew why and what they did.

Chapter 32

Joseph Armagh said to his son, Rory: "You are not doing exceptionally well in mathematics, at your school. But I notice that you excel in history and English and German and French, Latin and literature." He smiled at the boy. "So, I am pleased with you. However, you will have to be more proficient in mathematics to get into Harvard." He laughed. "For an intellectual you are singularly healthy and sane and pragmatic."

"I know enough about mathematics to think I should get an increase in my allowance," said Rory with his beguiling and impudent smile. "I get only two dollars more than does Kevin."

"A dollar is a dollar, and it is a lot of money. Three dollars a week for a lad of fifteen is sufficient. Kevin buys his own pets out of his one dollar a week, and is very serious for a spalpeen only nine years old."

Rory was tall and slender and moved lithely and quickly, with his grandfather, Daniel Armagh's, grace but with his father's strength and economy of movement. He was exceedingly handsome, with a buoyant and energetic air, which he had inherited from his mother. He was also courtly and gallant, even at his young age, and was always ready with a pungent joke. He had Joseph's once-russet hair, but his curled, endearingly—to the ladies and young girls—over his forehead, about his ears and almost down to his nape. But the russet was brighter than Joseph's had ever been, with a more pronounced reddish tinge, and was vital and coarse. He had a big well-shaped nose with a slight tilt at the tip, and a smiling mouth, also well-shaped, and large white teeth. His eyes, under red-gold brows, were light blue and mocking and usually mirthful, though frequently touched with good-humored cynicism. Like Joseph's, his cheekbones were broad, his chin determined. He gave off an almost visible aura of gusto and health and joy in life, and exceptional intelligence. His pink lower lip had a sensual thickness to it.

He was also exigent, in a charming and coaxing way, though he could also be brutal when necessary. He appeared more mature than his age. Unlike other very handsome youths he was always curious, always searching for new knowledge, new insights, and he found humanity uproariously funny. Except for his father. He knew, even at fifteen, almost all there was to know about Joseph and had acquired his knowledge in many avid and devious ways and from scores of other men and from the newspapers, and from his mother, and he found his father endlessly fascinating. Joseph was the only creature Rory feared, and perhaps loved. Young as he was, he was not a virgin, nor had been since he was fourteen. Girls, and even older women, were as attracted to him as he was attracted to them, and even from his earliest youth he was gayly licentious and did not care who knew it. He was as brave as his father, but unlike Joseph he loved danger and the excitement of it. He would be, many said with conviction, an extraordinary man, not only because of his appearance and his ability to fascinate men as well as women, but because of his intellectual qualities, his eloquent and manly speaking voice, and his flair for smiling sarcasm.

He was already a politician in the small world he still occupied. Though he was sometimes suspected by his school fellows to be "bookish," he led them. He rode a horse like a centaur, played tennis magnificently, and could climb like a monkey, for he was fearless. At times he was even rowdy.

His twin sister, Ann Marie, did not resemble him in the slightest. She was a slender, rather thin, and quiet girl, somewhat tall and of so flat a figure that her mother constantly wailed over it. Once as noisy as her brother, she was now inclined to silence, probably, Joseph thought, because her mother "never stopped talking." She had fine straight and light brown hair, which she dressed simply as befitting a schoolgirl of fifteen, an oval face with a clear pale complexion, large sherry-brown eyes, a small nose and controlled mouth resembling her father's. Her mother had convinced her, when she had been still very young, that she possessed no beauty but was "very plain," so the girl wore clothes without distinction and which were often drab. But Joseph, once becoming aware of her, saw that she had the austere elegance so much admired by the Irish, and it startled him, for his children were fourteen years old before he was actually conscious of their being and their identities.

For, to him, Rory and Ann Marie had been "Bernadette's children," or the grandchildren of the loathed Tom Hennessey. As such he had little interest in them and less affection, beyond an indulgent vague fondness when he saw them playing or listened to their arguments. He had often forgotten their existence, and sometimes, hearing their distant voices, he had wondered who possessed them. He paid their bills at preparatory (boarding) schools in Boston and Philadelphia, but as Timothy Dineen wrote out the cheques for all expenses and Joseph merely signed them, he was hardly aware even of this. To Joseph Armagh, his "family" had meant his parents, and then his brother and sister. Bernadette's "family" was something else again and not part of himself as Sean and Regina had been. On more than one occasion, when someone queried about the welfare of his family, he had absently but sincerely seemed surprised and had replied, "I have no family." He finally discovered that others looked at him, then, in a sidelong and speculative fashion, which was more than a little unpleasant, and so he was careful now in his answers and, while he never demonstrated enthusiasm, he would say, "My family is well, thank you," and change the subject impatiently.

He never visited his children at their schools, nor had he shown any interest in their progress. As he was not very often in Green Hills it would sometimes be months before he saw his children. He did see them at Christmas and Easter, and found their presence boring and avoided them. It was as if his profound devotion to his brother and sister, his total engrossment with them, had depleted the vital reserves of love in himself and since Sean and Regina had "deserted" him he was more than ever detached from other human beings, and absolutely indifferent. The spring of his affections was filled with stones.

Bernadette's adoration and love for him had become fanatically obsessive since she had learned that he cared nothing for her and had married her only at her dying mother's deluded request. She had her father's tenacity of purpose: she would win Joseph's love no matter how long it would take, and she dedicated herself to his interest and his well-being and served him with a slavishness that everyone knew, and even pitied, because Joseph was not conscious of it at all. He only knew that Bernadette was no longer insistent with him or demanding. He was not grateful for this blessing, nor did he care. The less he saw of his wife the more contented he was. He appreciated her as a fine housekeeper and an excellent hostess, and that was all he desired of her. He had not approached her sexually since his younger son, Kevin, had been born. He had not wanted another child; he held Bernadette to blame for Kevin, and so he had avoided her since that time.

He was not cruel nor harsh with her. She simply was absent from his mind, and when he was away from Green Hills he never thought of her at all. Had she died he would have felt no regret. He rarely conversed with her, and since Kevin's birth she could no longer amuse him or make him give his grudging laugh. Sometimes he appeared startled, as if wondering who she was, when she entered a room.

Bernadette, though not a stupid woman, still did not know the extent of his uninterest in her. She had the romantic notion that selfless and passionate love would eventually reach him, and as she was optimistic by nature she was infrequently discouraged. On those rare occasions she would ask herself in despair: What do I see in him? Why do I love him with all my heart and soul? He is not handsome in the accepted fashion. His voice is cold and short. He is not suave nor considerate. He shows me no tenderness. He looks at me blankly. Yet, how I love him, how I adore him! I would die for him.

The mystery of love never occurred to her, and so she suffered deeply and intensely because her love was not requited. However, she never gave up hope. There was much that was superficial in her and so she did not know that it was sufficient for love to serve, however despised or unnoticed. But Joseph's mere presence in her house was enough to give her a piteous joy. When he asked something of her—as he would ask a servant—she was ecstatic. Her adoration surrounded him like a bubble.

His indifference to her children did not disturb her as once it had done in a faint fashion. The fewer those whom Joseph cared about the more she was pleased. She was jealous of Timothy Dineen, and was elated when James Spaulding died and Timothy had been dispatched to take his place in Titusville and in Joseph's interest in the northwest section of the Commonwealth and in Ohio and in Chicago. (There were eight lawyers working under Timo-

thy in Titusville, and a very large office force.) Joseph had
a new and handsome secretary, one Charles Devereaux, a
brilliant lawyer, a man of his own age who, Bernadette
dimly knew, was from "somewhere in Virginia." Charles
had enormous responsibilities, of which Bernadette did not
even try to guess. She was passionately jealous of him, for
he accompanied Joseph everywhere and lived in this house
when Joseph was in Green Hills, and there seemed, to Bernadette, too much affection between them and too much attachment. It was only when Charles was present that Joseph really laughed or exhibited the slightest animation.
Sometimes she complained petulantly to Joseph about this,
saying that he preferred the company of his secretary-asso-
ciate to the presence of his wife and children, but Joseph
never answered, and so Bernadette came to hate Charles.
His exceptional and almost beautiful appearance would
have attracted her under other circumstances, but now she
thought of him as an enemy who had "stolen" affection
rightfully belonging to "the family." As for Harry Zeff and
his Liza, they never came to Green Hills. Bernadette had
made it very obvious that she despised the presence of
"that Arab" and "his servant girl," and found them offensive and an insult to herself. "One of these days," she said
significantly, to Joseph, nodding her head wisely as if she
had secret information, "that Harry will betray you. But
you never listen to me."

It gave her enormous satisfaction when her children
were old enough to attend boarding schools in Boston and
Philadelphia. The potential rivals were eliminated. She
would effusively declare her love for them, and how she
missed them, to sympathetic friends, but she was happy
they were gone and was even happier when they visited
friends during the summer holidays. In short, if she could
have imprisoned Joseph in the great white mansion in
Green Hills she would have been overjoyed, and would
have been content not to have seen anyone else herself, for
all her gregarious disposition.

She had made herself so cutting and vicious to Elizabeth
Hennessey that Elizabeth had bought the house that Joseph
had built for his family and had removed herself and her
son. Sometimes Bernadette wondered why Elizabeth remained in Green Hills at all. Of course, Joseph "managed"
Mrs. Hennessey's affairs, as a kindness to the widow whose
husband he had destroyed, Bernadette conceded. But he

could have done that as well if she had gone back to her
native Philadelphia. Elizabeth was rarely invited to the
Hennessey house except at Christmas and on New Year's
Day, and Courtney, her son, attended the same school in
Boston as did Rory. Bernadette did not see her half brother
more than once a year and had no interest in him. He was,
in her opinion, a "poor thing" contrasted with the resplendent Rory.

Bernadette had lost the charm of youth, and was now a
very plump matron heavily encased in restraining whalebone, with a large bosom and larger hips, but always extremely fashionable and overdressed. Never very pretty,
her round flattish face had acquired a double chin and her
original golden tint of complexion had become engorged.
She had nothing left now but her fine and sparkling hazel
eyes. She wore her thin brown hair, which was modishly
cut short in the latest fashion, elaborately and painfully
curled all over her blunt head. She also dipped into the
paint pots and not always discreetly. But her vivacity and
energy, if sometimes a little forced now, still pleased her
many friends if her growing overbearing manner and auto-
cratic and malicious judgments did not. She was the leader
of society in Green Hills, as due the wife of so powerful
and distinguished and dangerous a husband, and was also
feared in Philadelphia and other cities. Now, as she would
contentedly and proudly assert, she could "mingle" at ease
with the Belmonts, the Goulds, the Fisks, the Regans and
Morgans and others in New York, and there was none who
could belittle or snub her. Her jewels rivaled the jewels of
any other woman. She favored Worth as her dressmaker,
and her millinery was superb. When, once a year or so, she
insisted on accompanying Joseph to Europe—her only insistence these days—she had a French maid with her and
so many trunks and bags that an extra stateroom had to be
engaged besides the one she occupied and the one Joseph
used. Joseph became reconciled to her presence. As always,
she was a perfect hostess to his colleagues.

Once she had said to Joseph, "No one now ever seems to
care we are Irish." She had said this with smugness and
with a triumphant toss of her curled head. She did not understand why Joseph had given her his fierce and concentrated look which lasted several minutes, and why she had
felt so abashed and so bewildered. She had not detected the
rage and contempt in his eyes, nor the hatred that had

caused a blue fire under his brows. She only knew that in some fashion she had offended him, and so had fawned humbly upon him. He had not spoken to her for several days after that.

Then when her children were fifteen years old she received the most wounding and most crushing experience of her life.

In 1875 Joseph had visited Mr. Montrose—whom he now knew as Clair Devereaux—in Virginia. The beautiful new plantation house had impressed Joseph and so had the flourishing fields of cotton and the herds of cattle and the fine horses. "Without your help in the purchase of the adjoining property I'd now be the usual bankrupt Southern plantation owner—thanks to Yankee carpetbaggers and sundry other scalawags," Clair had said, shaking Joseph's hand warmly and with deep affection. Then he had added, "This is my dear wife, Luane, whom I married in Pittsburgh two years ago."

Joseph thought that Luane Devereaux was one of the most beautiful women he had ever met. He saw her wonderful gray eyes, her masses of black hair, her full rosy mouth and her lovely body. He knew, now, the history of the Devereaux's. Ostensibly, in Virginia, she was Clair's concubine and servant. Later he met their son, Charles, who had been wounded in the war which had killed his grandfather. Joseph was astonished at his resemblance to his father, for he had Clair's curling yellow hair and subtle face and height, though he had inherited his mother's eyes. Charles, at that time, had been graduated from Harvard Law School and was practicing in Boston. He had married a Boston girl of good family.

Charles had given Joseph a challenging look on the first meeting, but Joseph had ignored it and had thought Charles somewhat of a fool. Later, he changed his opinion. He met Charles three times after that, and slowly Charles came to trust him and no longer challenged him with his cold gray eyes. Charles became very successful, and a partner in his firm in Boston. When Mr. Spaulding had died of old age and infirmities Joseph had offered Charles his place, at a very large salary. Charles had hesitated, and then had said to Joseph bluntly, "I assume my—history— won't be broadcast in Titusville?"

Joseph said, "Don't be a damned idiot. I am not offering

you this because I have had long association with your father, and admire him. I am offering it because I think you are competent. If I've been mistaken I'll boot you out without any ceremony at all."

Charles had understood that Joseph had deliberately misunderstood him. He also knew that his "history" was meaningless to Joseph, though he did not discount the fact that Joseph could be very dangerous indeed if necessary. So Charles, who had inherited his own father's intrepid love for danger, and knew all about Joseph, had accepted the offer. He had an impressive house in Titusville where he lived with his wife and consulted with Timothy Dineen, but he traveled with Joseph and was his "confidential legal adviser" and associate. He was a fanatical Southerner and often amused Joseph with his derision for Northerners and "Yankee expediency." He was exigent, himself, and lacked all scruples when it came to Joseph's interests.

In 1880 Clair and Luane Devereaux had died of the flux and Joseph had attended their funeral. He had said nothing when Clair had been buried in the Devereaux family plot and Luane had been buried among former slaves. But he saw Charles's face. He said to Charles: "What does it matter where a man's bones are buried? My father's grave is unknown. My mother's bones lie in the sea. At least your mother has a resting place and a tombstone. Who is more fortunate, you or I?" From that time on Charles gave Joseph his unrestrained loyalty.

Charles saw everything, understood everything, and said nothing in the years he served Joseph Armagh. Sometimes Joseph's ambiguous probity amused him. He knew about Senator Bassett. He had helped to gather the information about the unfortunate man. Like his father, Charles was indifferent to the sources of income or how that income was obtained. Still, it wryly touched him that Joseph had destroyed all evidence against the senator.

It was a never-ending source of cynical and inner hilarity to Joseph that Charles had a slight aversion for Harry Zeff, and sometimes, like Bernadette, referred to him as "the Arab," though he truly admired Harry's genius for organization and management, and learned from him and was politely deferential to him. To Joseph, the spectacle of humanity was absurd and its pretensions laughable. When Harry said of Charles, with some admiration, "That's a mean Southern bastard," Harry did not understand why Joseph's small eyes glittered with merriment. "You'd think," Harry said, "that no one born north of the Mason-Dixon line had any right to call himself human. Or claim to be an intelligent gentleman." Joseph had replied, "If the history of every man in this world were known, back to our forefathers, none of us would have reason for any pride at all." Harry had smiled and had not answered this. He knew too well the pride of Joseph Armagh, and so Harry had his own souce of secret laughter.

It was on one warm June day, brilliant with sun and suffused with the fragrance of roses, that Joseph became really aware of his children.

He and Charles were in Green Hills for a few days. Joseph was at his desk in his rooms and Charles was standing by a window looking over the glistening green grass and the flowers and the long lawns and trees. He suddenly said, "They are fine young people. I wish I had children of my own."

Joseph had looked up impatiently. "What?" he said.

"Your children," said Charles. "Rory looks like one of those Greek gods we hear about, and the girl is delicate and graceful. A lady."

Joseph stood up and went to the window and looked out. Anything that caught the attention of Charles Devereaux must be remarkable, for Charles, like himself, was usually uninterested in others and considered few worthy enough to deserve a remark.

Rory and Ann Marie were walking side by side over the long lawns in the sun. There was a deep affection between them. They were holding hands like very young lovers, and their heads were bent and they were evidently talking seriously. Rory's reddish head was bright in the sunlight, and seemed haloed with color, and he walked like a dancer with poise and economy and ease. His handsome boy's face was absorbed and attentive. He was somewhat of a dandy and wore the latest fashions, which became him. Ann Marie walked beside him, with a faintly timid air and lightness, her blue dress clinging to her slight but proud figure, her brown hair shining, her pale face gentle and quiet. She kept glancing at her brother very soberly, and occasionally she nodded.

For the first time Joseph was thoroughly and completely aware of them, and that they were his children, and that they were personable and human and had a poignant air of youth and identity. They were also beautiful and in some way moving. Joseph leaned on the marble windowsill and stared at his children and then said to himself, in reluctant and even angry wonder: My children! Suddenly they were no longer Bernadette's, but his own. They were not the grandchildren of Tom Hennessey, but the grandchildren of Daniel and Moira Armagh, and they had their blood and their flesh.

I know nothing about them, thought Joseph, with renewed wonder though without regret. They were like a revelation to him, for they had destiny also.

At some distance behind them Kevin ambled, his stocky child's body, broad and strong, possessed of the awkwardness of childhood. He had a dark square face with hard facial bones, very resolute and grave. It was the gravity that redeemed it from pugnacity. His deep brown hair was a mass of curls. His dark brown eyes were examining something he held in his hands, and he was intent upon it. Joseph had never noticed it before: Kevin resembled Moira Armagh's father, a sturdy and compact Irishman who would never compromise with anything, not even with his God, a quietly belligerent man of daunting pride and self-respect.

Joseph, at the window today, did not know he was smiling as he looked down at his children. He did not know, until somewhat later, that love for them had come to him on that June day and that finally they were his own and part of himself, and that he had acquired another family.

On Rory's fifteenth birthday Joseph said to him, trying to smile, "I am going to make you President of the United States of America." Rory looked at his father with impudent thoughtfulness and said, "You'll try damned hard anyway, Pa. And I'll try with you." Then Joseph knew that his son would do anything to please him, and he had felt sharp pain and a sudden blank confusion.

Rory asked, "Why should that be important to you, Pa?"

Joseph had considered, and Rory watched him and saw the darkening of his face and the tightening of his mouth. Joseph said, "I could never explain it to you, I am afraid. I have too many memories." Rory had nodded, as if he understood in entirety.

For Ann Marie Joseph had acquired a special tenderness. She had a simplicity of character which both frightened and touched him. It was not Regina's simplicity, which had been full of knowledge, but a limpid simplicity that knew nothing of evil and so denied it. For Kevin Joseph now had a rough and rollicking affection, and he sometimes called Kevin "you old man. I think you were born with a beard." Rory acquired learning with ease and insouciance, but Kevin labored earnestly and grubbily.

When Joseph learned that his children had always loved him he was both ashamed and remorseful, and was sometimes incredulous. But, there it was. He had done nothing to gain their love, and yet they had given it to him as they had not given it to their mother who had indulged them and then had pettishly resented them because they had not lived up to the "new theories" she had acquired from reading Horace Mann's effusions. They did not respond as Horace Mann had alleged children would respond to certain methods. It finally came to Bernadette that they thought their mother somewhat silly, and as Bernadette was not silly in the least she had been outraged.

She had always been glad when they were absent, so she could think of no one but Joseph. A year after the day Joseph had secretly acknowledged his children as his own she had learned that he loved them. For that she never forgave them. Her jealousy crushed and almost demolished her. It wounded her in her deepest places. Without an effort they had gained Joseph's love, and she, who gave her life to him, was rejected. She became distraught. She regretted that she had ever given birth to them. They were her rivals, her enemies. To please Joseph she pretended solicitude and affection for them. They had stolen from her, she believed, what was rightfully hers.

To Bernadette the most grievous day of her life occurred when she had complained to Joseph of Ann Marie's "ugliness," and had said, "I doubt the girl will ever make a good marriage, with her lack of beauty and presence. Dear me, she is not in the least charming. She has no style at all."

Joseph had turned on her with so vindictive a face and with such a savage look that she had recoiled.

He said, "Let my children alone. I warn you, let my children alone."

Bernadette, abandoned, felt the first profound prostration she had ever experienced. She had been forced to take to her bed, she who was never ill. For days she lay in her darkened room, unable to weep, and could only stare dryeyed at the painted ceiling. She could not even speak. She felt that she was dying, and actually longed for death.

When she recovered a little she had aged. Her grief was more endurable but heavy with sorrow. However, she had courage. It is just a matter of time, she would tell herself. They will soon be married and gone, and I will be alone with Joseph, and he will finally know that he has no one but me. We are not getting younger. Some day he will understand and love me, and I can only wait for that.

She knew, by now, his many infidelities. She knew of the woman he loved. But, she was his wife, and a wife's position was impregnable, upheld by God and society and all legal sanctions. Even Joseph Armagh could not forever ignore these. Now there remained to her, in her clutching despair, only her husband and herself.

Chapter 33

One of his classmates said to Rory Armagh: "Your father is only an Irish whoremaster."

Rory replied: "And your grandfather was a pious Puritan blackbirder, who baptised miserable savages and blessed them then spirited them into slavery, though it was against the law. Nothing like a few prayers on the way to the bank!"

"Hah!" said the other youth. "At least my father doesn't sleep with his mother-in-law."

Rory, the good-tempered and genial, had then almost beaten his opponent to death with a wild savagery he had never displayed before in all his vigorous life. He was immediately expelled, and returned to Green Hills, and his father, in Philadelphia, received a formal letter from the schoolmaster:

I regret to inform you, sir, that your son, Rory Daniel Armagh, has been expelled from this school because of a violent and unprovoked attack he made on young Mr. Anthony Masters during recess on April 12 inst., in the Yard. Mr. Masters has been confined to the infirmary with sundry lacerations and bruises and a broken arm and a Concussion, and his condition is serious. It is not believed he will be able to return to his classes for several weeks. Mr. Burney Masters, of Boston, who is a revered and distinguished member of Boston Society, is much incensed over this brutal punishment inflicted on his son and is considering legal action. It is only due to my importunities and beseechings that he is delaying such action and has it under advisement with his lawyers, of the notable concern of McDermott, Lindsay, Hòrace and Witherspoon. I have the good repute of Our School to consider, and this dastardly attack will hardly enhance the Reputation of our Institution, and there will be Discussions among Parents which will rebound upon the School. This is said because so many of our graduates have gone on to careers of distinction in Public Affairs and business, and never before has there been such an Incident.

It is unfortunate that young Mr. Armagh has been expelled only two months prior to his graduation from the School, but he invoked this disastrous contretemps and no one else. I regret that we cannot recommend him, as projected, to Harvard University, nor to Yale or Princeton, or any other Institution of repute and learning, despite Mr. Armagh's scholastic record which heretofore led all others. No one deplores this Event more than do I, Your ob'ent Servant, Geoffrey L. D. Armstead.*

Joseph returned at once to Green Hills with Charles Devereaux in a cold fury both against his son and Mr. Armstead, who was no favorite of his. Joseph said, on the train, "That damned supercilious old bastard! Prim-lipped Puritan and pecksniffer! I had to pay twice the fee to get that damned Rory enrolled at that school, among the Genteel Scions of Boston and New York and Philadelphia, to quote Armstead, and now see what he does! Ruins and disgraces himself, and humiliates me."

Charles said, "Let us hear Rory's story from himself. I know of Armstead. He would appear at Harvard when I was there, at teas and such, with his wife, who is a mean little brown hen of a woman, though of such Noble Ancestry, as she would confess, herself. They make a fine pair."

"Of course, I know that Rory is a favorite of yours," said Joseph, with an angry glance at his secretary. "If he had murdered young Masters you'd find some excuse for him." He ran his lean fingers through his thick russet and white hair, and the implacable expression which everyone feared settled on his face. "What can we do to ruin Armstead?"

Charles gave this long consideration. "He is not a businessman. Inherited wealth, old family, sound investments, married into a rich family of the same calibre. No political background, and doesn't mingle with politicians. Of course, there is always something, as we've found out in the past. But that would take time, and Rory is only seven weeks away from graduation, so we must get to work at once to have him reinstated. The only thing we can do—if it is at all possible—is to put pressure on Mr. Burney Masters, the father, to force his son to apologize publicly to Rory and withdraw his charges, and get Rory reinstated at once. Armstead could never refuse Mr. Masters. Masters is an alumnus of that school and has a large scholarship running."

"Burney Masters," said Joseph, frowning. "Didn't he run against the Irish Mayor of Boston and lose?"

Charles smiled. He took out his notebook and pencil. "So he did. And isn't the mayor a friend of yours? Didn't you contribute to his campaign? It seems, if I remember correctly, that Mr. Masters ran on a Reform Platform and said some unkind things about the Boston Irish during the campaign. Not that that will do us any good, however. It was a miracle that the present mayor was elected under the circumstances. The mayor is hardly one who can put pressure on Mr. Armstead, who despises him. I believe the feeling is mutual."

Charles leaned back in his comfortable chair in Joseph's private coach and closed his clever gray eyes and thought for a considerable time. Joseph waited. Then Charles said "Ah!" in a deep and contented voice.

"Mr. Armagh, I do believe there is something. You will remember that all odds were with Mr. Masters for his election over the present mayor. Mr. Masters conducted a strong and determined campaign, and is an eloquent speaker, and put a lot of money of his own into that campaign, and had the backing of all the Beacon Street élégantes and gentry. The present mayor was too florid—and too Irish—to be very effective, except among his own, and his way of dancing a little jig and singing an Irish ballad or two on the platform did not enhance his repute among the Proper Bostonians, though his own enthusiastically applauded him. Mr. Masters not only led, according to the Boston newspapers, but his dignity and presence, as they called it, 'boded well for an administration which would not be soiled and corrupt as the previous one was, but one of which Bostonians could be proud and vindicated as citizens of an honorable city.'

"Then," concluded Charles, "something happened during the last three weeks of the campaign. Mr. Masters made fewer and fewer public appearances. His speeches were weaker and more restrained, and less pejorative. He seemed to have lost steam. He made no appearance at all during the last week, and refused newspaper interviews except for one mild plea for his election. His posters disappeared. His people made no more house-to-house calls. There were no more bulletins on Major Issues. Now, that is very interesting. I wonder what happened to Mr. Masters?"

"I wondered at the time, myself," said Joseph, sitting up and looking at Charles with interest. "I asked Old Syrup, as we called him, and he only smiled that peculiar Sphinx-like smile the Irish can assume when they have 'something under their nose' which they prefer not to make public. So, he had something on Masters, something lethal. It must have been very good. Charles, send him a telegram in my name tonight and take a letter from me to him tomorrow."

"He's a wily character," said Charles. "He wants to be governor, and he won't do anything, even for you, which will jeopardize that."

"But I know something very lethal, myself, about Old Syrup," said Joseph, with great satisfaction. "If he wants to be governor he had better not antagonize me. I think we have concluded the problem. In the meantime I will deal with Rory."

"With fairness and restraint, I hope," said Charles. This time Joseph smiled a little.

The two men were met by a wailing Bernadette who exclaimed at once, "Your son! He has disgraced us forever! And I was such friends with Emma Masters, who leads Boston society, and we were received almost everywhere in Boston! The Armsteads were gracious to us, too, on more than one occasion, and were most civil. Now, we will be outcasts in Boston, humiliated and ignored and snubbed, all due to your son's extravagant temper and viciousness and violence—attacking a refined young gentleman like young Masters!"

Only Charles saw that she felt considerable secret elation over this episode, for she believed that Rory would no longer be so loved by his father, and therefore would no longer be her rival. Joseph glared at her and said, "Refined young gentlemen do not provoke attacks. I will be in my study. Send Rory to me at once."

"If you do not punish him severely you will be lacking in your Duty, Joe," said Bernadette, a little dismayed at Joseph's reception of her complaint. "To think he would have been graduated from that distinguished school in June, with honors, and now he will not graduate, he will be accepted only in the lowest establishments and will not be admitted to Harvard, and he has ruined his future!"

"Send Rory to me," said Joseph, and left her abruptly. Charles accompanied him. By the time they had reached Joseph's rooms Joseph was again in an icy rage against his son, for he had had to leave important business in Philadelphia. Joseph did not like intrigues for intrigue's sake, and only indulged in them when absolutely necessary.

Rory, immaculately dressed as always, and resplendently handsome in spite of an impressive black eye, came at once to the study. His high color was a little subdued. He wore a curious expression of reserve and tightness, like his father's, but Charles had never seen this before on the lad's face, usually so open and twinkling and mirthful.

Joseph let him stand before him like a penitent. "So," he said, "my son is a boisterous and murderous hooligan, is he? Without any thought at all he tries to destroy his own future, which has already cost his father a pretty penny, sir. What have you to say for yourself?"

Rory said, and his cynical blue eyes were averted, "He insulted—you—Pa."

Charles stood behind Joseph's chair, and he tried to catch the seventeen-year-old youth's eye, but failed. There was a heavy sullenness on Rory's usually merry mouth, and a secretiveness.

"Now," said Joseph, "that's a very fine sentiment, I am thinking, protecting your father's honor. Look here, Rory, I have never concealed my activities from you. I have told you many times that businessmen are not concerned with legal or illegal activities, so long as they don't engage the attention—too keenly—of the law, and even then that can be surmounted. Business is business, as it has been said over and over. It has no particular ethics. It has only one standard: Will something succeed or not? We are not the Salvation Army or Morality Troops. We deal with a hard and exigent world, and so have to be hard and exigent too, if we are not to be bankrupts. I've told you this often, and I thought you understood."

He paused and looked at Rory. But Rory, with rare stubbornness, was staring at his feet. He did not look defiant in an immature way, or rebellious as many youths appear when castigated by a father. He had the appearance of someone who is protecting something, or someone. However, only Charles noticed this, and not Joseph, who was growing coldly angry again.

Rory said, "He called you—names."

Joseph's thin mouth tightened even more. "Rory, I have been called every name you can imagine, and many more. Some I have deserved; some I have not. It is of no importance to me and should not be of importance to you. I thought you understood that. You will be called names, too, in the future. If you are sensitive to name-calling then you had better settle for a clerkship in one of my offices, or teach in some obscure little school, or open a shop. Now, Rory let us put this nonsense aside. I will do what I can to get you reinstated. I think it is possible."

"My marks," said Rory, without looking at his father, "are high enough so that I don't need to return to that school. I excelled in all the curriculum. I didn't even have to take the last examination; my record stood for itself. Old Armstead knows that. He is only being malicious, because he hates you, Pa, and me—because we are Irish. He'd do anything to frustrate you. You will remember how he opposed my entry into his damned stupid school." Now the boy flushed and he looked at his father with an anger equaling Joseph's own. "I resent it that you had to pay double to get me enrolled there!"

"Who told you that?" asked Joseph sharply.

"Old Armstead, himself, with that spittle-satisfaction of his, four days ago."

Joseph and Charles exchanged a glance.

"If I can't make my way with my own endowments in any damned school or college I don't want it!" exclaimed Rory, his face deepening in color. "I won't be mortified any longer!"

Joseph's tone was gentler when he spoke. "You have to face the facts of life, Rory, and I don't like it that you are beginning to sound Noble. Endure humiliations, but bide your time for your revenge, and never forget. The day will always come when you can repay. I know. But once a man begins to feel Noble he is already defeated. If he won't fight, then he'd better tuck his tail between his legs and slink away. That's the law of life, and who are you to defy it?"

Charles said, "Every man has to endure belittlement for one thing or another, Rory. He has to make his compromises, though without weakness. If he can conceal something about himself which is injurious, then he should do so. If he has nothing really deadly to be ashamed of, but it is said that he has, then he should fight."

Rory was extremely fond of Charles, but now he said to him with bitterness, "That is all very well for you, Charles, but you are a Devereaux of Virginia and no one could ever unjustly point a finger at your parents, or yourself."

There was a sudden long silence. Charles looked again at Joseph who shook his head peremptorily. But Charles drew a deep breath and said, "You are wrong, Rory. I am a Negro."

Rory flung up his head and gaped at Charles, his mouth opening. "What!" he cried incredulously.

Charles nodded, with a beautiful and amiable smile. "My mother was also a Devereaux, by blood, but she was born a slave, and she bore me, an illegitimate darkie, to my father."

Rory stared wide-eyed at Charles's yellow hair, sharp features and gray eyes. He looked stunned.

"Rory," said Charles, "if someone asked me if I were a Negro I would say yes. I feel no disgrace, no inferiority. But it is my affair, my secret if you will have it so. It is no business of anyone else's. Before, say—Divinity—there is no color, no race. There are only Men. But the world doesn't know that, and so a man often has to protect himself from undeserved malice and cruelty. He keeps any harmful secret to himself."

Joseph was moved as he had rarely been moved before. That the proud Charles Devereaux should risk telling a seventeen-year-old youth such a dangerous secret told Joseph more than anything else of Charles's loyalty to him and his attachment to his family. Joseph was not a man for gestures, but he put his hand briefly on Charles's arm.

Rory was still staring at Charles, and now the stony hardness of his young and vital face softened. "By golly," he said, almost in a whisper. He thought. Then he said, "I guess I'm not the man you are, Charles." However, the secretiveness had returned to his eyes, and Charles saw it.

"I reckon," Charles said, "that young Masters didn't only call your father an Irish something-or-other, but said something else about him."

"Yes," said Rory, after a long pause.

"It can't be very important," said Joseph, still touched. "What was it, Rory?"

Rory was silent. He was staring at his boots again and the heavy flush had come back to his face.

"Well?" demanded Joseph with impatience.

"I can't tell you, Pa."

"Is it that disgraceful?" Joseph was smiling again.

"To me, it is," said Rory.

"My God, lad, don't be a fool. You know what I am. I've never pretended to be anything different from what I am. I never hide anything, though I don't shout it to the skies. I'm not concerned with people's opinion of me, nor should you be."

"Suppose, Mr. Armagh," Charles intervened, "that we let Rory have his own little secret. Later, he'll laugh at it. Every man is entitled to one little secret of his own, isn't that so, Rory?"

"Maybe Pa doesn't want this to be known, or talked about," said Rory and he looked at his father with such poignant love that Charles was shaken. But Joseph was curious and did not notice the emotion in his son's eyes.

"If young Masters knew it, then everybody knows it," said Joseph.

"But, it is a lie!" Rory cried out. "A dirty lie! I couldn't let a lie like that pass, before the whole school!"

Something dangerous flickered between Joseph's eyelashes. He considered his son. The truth did not occur to him. He had been most careful, most discreet, in one single area of his life, more completely secretive than ever before, and he did not think of that one area now for he believed that only he and one other knew about it.

He said, "I hope you aren't turning into a dainty milksop, Rory. Lies are told by the thousands about me. It doesn't matter; I don't care. But what was this particular lie that so inflames you? We can settle it between ourselves."

A look of complete despair, but of increased stubbornness, fell over Rory's face. He shook his head. "I can't, I won't, tell you, Pa."

Joseph stood up so suddenly, and with so ferocious a face, that even Charles fell back. Joseph said in a quiet but terrible voice, "Don't defy me, you young jackanapes. Don't tell me you 'can't' or 'won't.' I'll not have that impudence from you, that lack of respect, that insult. Out with it!"

Charles had recovered himself. He said, "Mr. Armagh,

suppose you let Rory tell me what it is, between us two, and let me be the judge? Would that satisfy you, Rory?"

But Rory was shaking his head. "I'd never repeat it to anyone!"

Joseph hit his son fiercely across the face, the way he had hit his brother, Sean. But, unlike Sean, Rory did not collapse, did not burst into tears, did not turn away. He rocked on his heels for a moment, then straightened himself, and looked at his father steadily, almost expressionless. The mark of Joseph's hand flared out on his cheek.

Regret was not a common emotion for Joseph, but all at once, as he stared at his son he felt regret and a kind of deep shame. The boy was fearlessly confronting him in silence. He would endure any punishment to protect his father, and Joseph suddenly understood that and his regret deepened to remorse. Charles stood in silence, a little aghast.

But Joseph said, in his grudging tone, "All, right, then, you wretched young spalpeen, you can keep your damned silly secret, and be damned to you, if your secret is so precious. Who cares about it? I thought you had more sense, and more manhood, than to be affected by lies. I never was. I have accepted humiliations you haven't heard of yet —and bided my time. There was only one thing I could never have accepted, and that would have been a filthiness against my parents, my father or my mother."

Rory looked aside. He did not speak. Charles saw that his cheek was quivering. Joseph tried to smile. "There is very little, my son, that would be a real calumny against me. So, take it with more ease than you did this time. Very well. You may go."

Rory bowed shortly to his father and then to Charles. It was at Charles that he looked directly, and it was with great respect and a glint of admiration. Then he left the room, walking stiffly, his head held high, his shoulders squared. When he had gone Joseph shook his head and laughed his grating laugh.

"It seems that no matter what I've told him, and let him know, about myself, he still is squeamish. I don't like that, Charles."

"He has courage, and that is a rare virtue," said Charles. "He is like a rock. He won't give way; he won't crumble. It's not so much a matter of rectitude, but of honor."

Joseph was pleased. But he shrugged. "There's no place

for honor in this world," he said. "My father never understood that, and so he perished. Well, then. Let us get on with the matter of the Honorable Mr. Masters." He looked at Charles. "Yes, the lad has courage, hasn't he? I hope it is the right kind. What do you think young Masters said about me, Charles?"

But Charles did not know. However, he wondered how Anthony Masters had come by his knowledge. Someone had been indiscreet. Charles did not know that it was Bernadette who had babbled to her "dear friend, Emma Masters," in a moment of wine-induced lachrymose confidence, and the meek pious Emma, always avid for tidbits which could injure others, had told her husband, and her son had overheard. Like all well-kept secrets, it had been simple to discover. Bernadette did not even remember that hazy evening and the false sympathy of which she had been the victim. Had she remembered she would have been terrified of Joseph's knowing, but that was the only thing that was important about the matter. Besides, she would have thought, Joseph's infidelities were well known. One more was insignificant, though this was the most unbearable of all. She had discovered it when she was the least aware of discovering anything.

The affair of Mr. Burney Masters was absurdly easy for Charles to conclude, far easier than many others he had concluded. He did it with almost immediate dispatch.

"Old Syrup," the Mayor of Boston, was happy to receive a communication from his dear friend, Joseph Armagh—"We got to stick together, us Irish, for damn me if anyone else will ever stick with us"—which implied that if it was his Honor's desire to be governor Mr. Armagh would oblige him with a breath-taking campaign contribution, or, better still, if he desired to be a senator Mr. Armagh was on the most amiable terms with many of the Massachusetts members of the legislature. In fact, Mr. Armagh's influence in Washington, itself, was stupendous.

"Old Syrup" enthusiastically hated the Brahmins of Boston who had tried to defeat him, had humiliated him and despised him during his struggling and desperate political career, and had exploited him and starved him in their manufactories and mills in his earliest youth. He gave Charles Devereaux a quick and friendly vignette of those days, as they sat together drinking brandy and smoking cigars in the mayor's lavish offices in City Hall. His first young wife had died of "the consumption" for lack of food and warmth and adequate shelter. During her funeral Mass the church had been invaded by street vandals—inflamed by their masters—and her very poor wooden coffin had been befouled, as well as the Host. The priest had been beaten unconscious, and the mourners scattered with blows. "Even the little colleens."

"I tell you, sir," said the mayor to Charles Devereaux, "not even the darkies in the South was ever treated the way us Irish was treated in this country, I am thinking. You're a Southerner, sir? I heard it in your voice. Slaveowners, eh? But you took care of them. You've got to be oppressed, Mr. Devereaux sir, or your people oppressed, to know what it's like." He looked at Charles's patrician face and fine clothing with a sort of belligerence. "But, you don't know, do you?"

"I have some imagination, your Honor," said Charles, with a smile.

"Well, your Dad and your Mum was probably rich plantation owners. Don't matter. I don't hold grudges. Well, not many, anyway. We Irish got long memories. We don't forget easy. Well. So Joe wants to put a hard hand on Burney Masters, does he?"

Charles had laid a thick sheaf of gold banknotes on the desk at the very beginning, and in some admirable fashion they had disappeared as if into blank air. Nothing was said about them, out of respect, not even a word of thanks.

Mr. Burney Masters, about four years ago, had been caught in *flagrante delicto* with a pretty young shoeshine lad only twelve years old. "Right there, in his own garden, on Beacon Hill," said the fat mayor, with glowing satisfaction and many chuckles. "I'd bin havin' him watched for a long time. He had that sweet pursy look that men like him have, that lovin' look. I'd met his kind before. You wouldn't think it now, sir, but I was a good-lookin' lad, meself, and was approached by the Masters, many the time. Right in the mills. They got the certain look: Anxious. Tender. Lookin' out for your interests. Always talkin' concern, and the like, and helpin' a lad out, advance himself. Soft gentle hands. Writin' letters to the newspapers, deplorin'-like 'exploited labor.' Gettin' themselves a reputation for Good Deeds. Sufferin' for The People. Good causes. Whigs. Busy like bees, protestin'. Now, I don't say every man like that is what Masters is, but a hell of a lot of them are. They don't care much for the wimmin, and the girls. Just lads." The mayor shook his huge head deploringly. "Scholars, a lot of them. Some of them write books, exposin' one thing or another. Gives me pleasure, sometimes, to expose 'em, too."

It seems that the shoeshine lad was not the only one. There was also a very young handyman in the Masters' household who, with a little urging, revealed considerable data concerning himself and other boys and Mr. Burney Masters. "So," said the mayor, leaning back in his chair, "we had him. A word or two. And that's how he lost the election. Well, glad to mention it to Mr. Masters, in Joe's behalf, and that Rory of his. Consider it settled."

It was. Within a few days Rory was back at his school. Young Anthony Masters, from his infirmary bed, confessed he had "unbearably provoked" Rory by "defaming his father." "Something," Mr. Armstead said virtuously, "no manly youth could endure, and certainly no gentleman. We are sad that it led to bad temper and violence, but One can Understand. The Age of Chivalry and Honor has not yet departed."

Rory, resentful inwardly but smiling outwardly, was graduated with honors in June. He did not know how it had all come about but he knew his father was potent. He would have preferred to have beaten young Anthony Masters all over again, but, because of Joseph, Rory restrained himself and kept his eyes fixed ahead, though Anthony stood beside him.

Rory was valedictorian of his class, something he had earned himself, and something he did not owe his father. He and Joseph were both proud, and even Bernadette shed a few public tears and almost forgave Rory for his father's love. In September Rory entered Harvard. He was to graduate four years later *summa cum laude.*

Chapter 34

Joseph Armagh never knew exactly when he had become conscious of Elizabeth Hennessey as a desirable woman. He did not ask himself, for he was no tyro at physical attraction, nor did women as people ever occur to him, except for his mother and Regina, and, perhaps, Sister Elizabeth, long since dead. When he became aware of Elizabeth his own daughter, Ann Marie, was only six years old and Kevin had just been born.

Elizabeth, four years older than Bernadette, had come to live in the Hennessey house with her son, Courtney, after the senator had suffered his stroke. Though Bernadette had constantly maligned her and her "poor thing" of a son, and had resented her presence, Joseph was indifferently aware that Elizabeth was a reserved woman with beautiful manners. She was also very pretty in a cool aristocratic way which did not particularly appeal to him. He preferred stupid romping women of zest and laughter and animal ebullience who made no demands on him and who were easily forgotten. In any event he would not have, deliberately, noticed the widow of Tom Hennessey. Anyone connected with the senator held only aversion for him, including Bernadette, and, at that time, his own children. He had offered to manage Elizabeth's affairs from his own office. That had been a matter of courtesy. He had expected her to refuse. But she had accepted.

She had a rather cold face, somewhat neutral, with a slight thin nose that occasionally had a pinched expression, a still and dimly colored mouth, and large greenish eyes flecked with gold. Her blond hair was smooth and fine but too pale to be striking. She was too slender, as well as tall, to be in fashion, yet she dressed with rich and quiet style, hardly noticeable. Her slender hands were always ringless except for her wedding ring, which she had removed lately.

478

She looked at the world with unruffled interest and acceptance, and apparently had no attachment to anyone except her son, Courtney, and even with him she was aloof.

Her son was very like her in appearance, manner, and silent movement. It was not for many years that Joseph learned that Courtney and Rory were deeply fond of each other, and that there was between them a sort of David and Jonathan affection. Certainly no two youths were ever so dissimilar in temperament, outlook, and ambitions, for Courtney, though intelligent, according to Rory, was a poor scholar and rather languid and inactive. Joseph did not notice, for a long while, that Courtney and his mother had a strange way of communicating without language. A mere exchange between those two pairs of green eyes, a slight smile, the slightest gesture of a hand, and they understood each other perfectly. But before Joseph saw this he had thought Elizabeth and her son to be strangers, uninterested in each other, and only elaborately polite when together.

Courtney, according to the disdainful Bernadette, was not only a "poor thing," because he was so pallid in contrast to Rory, but he "ailed," she would say with contempt. Certainly Joseph vaguely noticed that the boy appeared to be at home too often when he, himself, arrived in Green Hills, and there had to be a tutor during the summer months for him if he were to advance in his classes in the school in Boston which Rory attended.

Rory, himself, often tutored Courtney, and would sometimes mockingly call him "Uncle Courtney," which, for some peculiar reason was a source of mild hilarity to the boys. It was the only time Joseph ever heard the older boy laugh outright, and the only time he would show some animation such as striking Rory affectionately on the shoulder with his bony fist, and calling Rory "you fat Irish hooligan." Courtney, himself, was thin almost to emaciation, and Bernadette scornfully reported him as "playing with his food, and we have the best cooks in town." The presence of Elizabeth and her son in this house finally hotly infuriated Bernadette, who found Elizabeth's calm and lack of responsiveness "unnatural." Though Courtney was her half brother she could not endure him. When she learned that he wrote "poems," she nodded her head and said sagely "Well, that's to be expected, isn't it?" as if the writing of poems was somehow unmanly and depraved. She never learned that Rory also wrote poetry, though not with the fineness and delicacy of Courtney's.

It was when Courtney was about seven years old that Joseph became aware of Elizabeth Hennessey for the first time, beyond the mere fact of her quiet presence at the dining table or in passing her in the wide marble halls of the Hennessey mansion. Sometimes she would nod to him in her passage, but she rarely spoke. She was apparently as indifferent to him as he was to her and noticed him about as much.

There were very large and elaborate and expensive conservatories in the rear of the Hennessey house, and attached to it, so that one walked down a short hall into boskiness and fragrance and exotic foliage and flowers at any time of the year. It was the one spot in the mansion that really attracted Joseph, and he often spent time in the conservatories, silently watching the assiduous gardeners or sitting in a corner content to breathe in the humid and perfumed air. Sometimes he did ask the name of a flower or a particularly spectacular plant. It never failed to interest him that when the winter snows lay heavily on the ground and on the roofs the flowers bloomed in their tropical splendor as if eternal summer lay about them, and volcanic lakes.

One day before the Christmas holidays Joseph strolled into the conservatories. It was a gloomy day of thick gray snow falling outside, and a wind that grumbled and howled in the chimneys, and dark. The conservatories were particularly fragrant just now and with the scent of roses and lilies in forced bloom, and there was also a fugitive scent of almond from somewhere and a breathing of warm fecund earth. Gaslights flickered and illuminated the broad glass windows against which the snow hissed and the wind battered.

Joseph thought himself alone, for this was the dinner hour of the gardeners and their day's work was done. He saw before him the long aisles between the plants and the rainbow colors of flowers, and prepared to wander among them. Then he heard another door open from another section of the house, a rapid tattoo of footsteps, and then Bernadette's loud, and now somewhat shrill voice railing in outraged anger. "Elizabeth! How dare you cut my white rosebuds! You know very well that they are for our Christmas Day dinner! Such effrontery, not even to ask me! Such

—such impudence!" It was the voice she used to servants. Joseph stopped, half-hidden behind a huge tubbed plant which stood on the floor.

Joseph heard a rustle of silk and then he saw Elizabeth's pale blond head rising between two aisles at his left, and at some distance. The gaslight fluttered on her white face. She said in a voice that was particularly lovely yet without real intonation, and certainly without emotion, "I am sorry, Bernadette. I wanted to ask you but you were upstairs with a headache and I didn't want to disturb you. I've only cut half a dozen, and there are so many dozens left. Courtney is in bed with that awful cold of his, and he does like white roses so, and I thought I'd cut these few for him."

Bernadette never learned that a restrained voice meant dignity and control of strong feeling or good manners, especially in women. She thought such a voice was servile, fit only for servants, and that the possessor was timid, humble, inferior, and worthy only of abuse and peremptory correction. Or worse still, afraid of her. In all these years with Elizabeth in her house she had not learned to the contrary.

"Oh, you wanted them for that sickly, miserable son of yours, did you?" Bernadette shouted with coarse derision. Now Joseph could see her, in her scarlet velvet dress which was too small for her slightly obese figure, her curled head bobbing with hateful emphasis, her plump flat face distorted with contempt and ridicule. "He's always abed like a consumptive girl in a decline! Now, let me tell you something, Elizabeth Hennessey! This is *my* house, and *I* am mistress here, and you and your son are here only by my sufferance and good nature and regard for my father, and from this time hence you are to *ask* me for any favor, for any flowers, for any decisions, and not have the impertinence to do what you will without regard for my station!" She snorted. "And yours. If you have any, which you do not."

She had never spoken so to Elizabeth like this before, and before this her voice had always been, if not polite or considerate, or least a little courteous though forced. Her spiteful remarks about Courtney and Elizabeth had never been in their presence, but only to Joseph and her friends.

Elizabeth stood there in silence before this virago whose dislike and hatred and resentment had suddenly broken forth from any controls she had heretofore kept over them for the sake of vague decency in the presence of others.

"I want to tell you something else too, my woman!" Bernadette continued to shout. "I've wanted to tell you this for a long time and only refrained out of respect for my father. He never could endure you." Her face was gloating with elation and joy that she could finally vent her stifled loathing on Elizabeth. It actually shone in the gaslight. Her mouth spread in a grin of delight and her eyes glittered with glee at the thought that she was wounding and injuring Elizabeth. "He was forced to marry you and adopt your brat, because your father had more political power than he did! But I want you to know that no one really believed you were the widow of a war hero, and that Courtney is his son, miss! You were probably a wanton woman and don't even know the paternity of your son. You, with your namby-pamby ways and graces and pretensions of being a lady—you who cohabited with a man to whom you were not married and God knows how many other men! Don't you know you are the laughingstock of half a dozen cities, not to mention Green Hills? You are absolutely shameless. You go among respectable people of propriety and reputation as if you deserved to be in their company, and not on the streets where you really belong, and only the fact that you are my father's widow prevents my friends from drawing aside their skirts when you appear. You are hardly more than a strumpet, and everybody knows it!"

Elizabeth's face had changed. It had become rigid and immobile. She said, in her chilly voice, "You have forgotten. Your father left me his share in this house, and your mother left you her share. I pay my portion here, and my son's expenses." She fixed the panting Bernadette with her great green eyes. "I will not reply to your filthy insinuations, which are worthy of you, Bernadette, for you are a vulgar and cruel woman. You are without sensibilities or ordinary decency, and if you are avoided by your family it is your own fault."

"What!" screamed Bernadette, advancing a few more paces towards Elizabeth.

"Don't come any nearer me," said Elizabeth, and now her face and voice were charged with passion. "I warn you. Don't come nearer."

Joseph, to his amused amazement, saw the desire to kill

on Elizabeth's face, and with it her desperate fight for control over her unbelievable rage.

"I want you out of this house, my house, tomorrow!" shrieked Bernadette. "Bag and baggage, out of my house!"

"This is my house, too, and I will leave it when I desire, and not before." Elizabeth's voice was louder but still under control. She held the roses tightly. "These, too, are my flowers, as well as yours, and I will cut them when I will, and not defer to you at any time, from this day forward."

Bernadette raised her arm, her first clenched, and she advanced directly in front of Elizabeth, and her face was evil with rage. But Elizabeth caught that arm in mid-air, as the fist was descending on her, and with a gesture of full loathing and disgust she flung Bernadette from her with such strength that Bernadette staggered, tried to get her balance, fell against the plants near her, then fell heavily to the floor. Instantly she yelled like a banshee, and she uttered imprecations that Joseph had not believed she knew. They were full of foul words and gaspings.

Elizabeth looked down at her, then turned with dignity and scorn and moved up the aisles towards Joseph. She saw him for the first time, and stopped abruptly, and scarlet waves ran over her white face. Her green eyes were blazing with an ardor and anger he never guessed she was capable of, and her mouth was parted.

Bernadette was still howling threats on the floor, and struggling to rise. Joseph smiled at Elizabeth. "I am glad you said that, and did that," he said. "I've been wanting to do the same for a long time. But after all, I am a man, and that would be improper, wouldn't it?"

She stared at him. Bernadette was on her feet now, and she too stared down the aisle at her husband, her mouth slavering, tears on her cheeks. But she had stopped her shrieks. There was something here that terrified her, though she had not heard Joseph's remark which had been almost inaudible except to Elizabeth.

Joseph stood aside for Elizabeth to pass. She still held her roses. She began to move past him, then, without volition halted when they were only inches apart. She looked up into his ascetic face, and at a mirth in his small eyes she had never seen before. The pale gray silk over her high and beautiful breast trembled. Her eyes did not drop or falter, but now there was a film of tears over their greenness, which Joseph saw now was not a deep emerald green but a pale green like brook water which reflects grass. For the first time, looking down at her, she became a desirable woman to him, and not only a desirable woman but a woman of mind and high pride and spirit and self-respect —a truly womanly woman, such as his mother had been, and his sister, and Sister Elizabeth.

"Don't leave," said Joseph to her.

She gave him the very shadow of a smile. "I don't intend to," she replied, and he laughed a little and bowed to her as she went on her way.

Joseph watched her go. The gray silk dress fitted her slender figure as smoothly as a skin to where it broke, over her hips, into drapes and folds that fell classically to her feet. At the doorway she paused and glanced over her shoulder at Joseph and he could not understand her expression. He did not know until much later that she had loved him for several years.

Now Bernadette was at his side, clutching him, weeping, crying out her fury at Elizabeth. He pushed her away, and she stood and looked at him with fear and suffering.

"You spoke and acted like a slut, with no self-discipline at all, and no shame," he said, and his voice was harsh and brutal. "I heard it all, so don't lie as usual. Until you mend your manners, and treat Elizabeth with consideration you must not speak to me. I don't like fishwives." He added, "You owe Elizabeth an apology. I suppose it is useless to ask you for that, but you can show it in some fashion if that is possible for you."

He left her then as if she had been an abominably bumptious servant, and Bernadette was left alone to cry in a lonely desolation that had nothing to do with Elizabeth. From that night on she held her tongue in the presence of the other woman, never again spoke to her directly but only obliquely, and was expansively polite to her when Joseph was in Green Hills.

Six months later Elizabeth bought Joseph's first house from him and left the Hennessey mansion with her son. A month after that they became lovers.

It had happened without premeditation, and without Joseph being conscious that he loved Elizabeth Hennessey. He had almost forgotten that night in the conservatory, except that his aversion for Bernadette had increased.

As he handled Elizabeth's extensive affairs in his offices

in Philadelphia himself, for it was a private matter, he was approached one day with a fine offer for some property she owned in the city. He decided he would consult with her rather than conclude it himself, as usual, for it involved a respectable sum. He left for Green Hills the next evening, and Elizabeth met him at the door of her house herself, and not a servant. She looked at him mutely, and then her smooth cheeks flushed and she stood aside and let him into the hall.

Then she said, "Would you like a glass of wine, Joseph? Have you dined?"

It was late, and the servants were abed on the fourth floor, and the summer twilight still lingered in the west in a lake of pure serene jade.

"To tell you the truth, Elizabeth," he said, with honest surprise, "I don't know if I have 'dined' or not. I didn't come in my own coach, but on a regular train, for my coach is being repaired. I am staying only overnight. I have business to conduct with you."

She knew at once that he had not gone as yet to the Hennessey house, and she felt a curious and breathless excitement, an excitement she had forgotten had ever existed for her. She said, "Let us go into the morning room and I will see what there is in the pantry, for I dislike disturbing servants who have worked hard all the day."

This consideration for servants or others was unique to Joseph. He followed her into the morning room which he had remembered had been furnished in Bernadette's flamboyant taste, all carved and gilt furniture and heavy silken draperies. Now it seemed larger for the scale of furniture was smaller and it was simple but gleaming, dove gray and blue with a touch of pink, and the French windows were open to the rose-filled gardens. There was a scent here not only of the roses but of lilies and fresh grass and wind and air. (Bernadette believed that the "night air" was dangerous and so very little entered the Hennessey mansion even during the summer.) Elizabeth painted in water colors, and the gray silk walls bloomed with bright tints of wild flowers and ferns and water in narrow wood frames, something again unique to Joseph who was accustomed to enormous gilded frames for pictures. He studied them while he waited for his hostess, and was impressed by her austere taste which was so like his own. He felt the usual tightness in his neck and shoulders loosening, and the compression in his chest easing. The house was silent, yet filled with breezes and he could hear the fluttering of new leaves on the trees.

Elizabeth returned with a large silver platter on which there was a cold bird, wine, a salad, brown bread and butter, and a glass of yellow custard. She set out the small oval table with white linen and bright silver. She did not speak. This, in itself, was refreshing to Joseph who heard nothing but voices all day long, everywhere. He studied Elizabeth, in her white frock sprinkled with small violets and green leaves, her pale blond hair glimmering in the candlelight, her face composed as always, and as delicately reserved. Her waist, he noticed, was very slender, her breast daintily swelling, her hands capable and swift and very graceful. She had a profile which seemed to have been carved by a marble knife.

He had not known hunger for a long time. Nor had his relish for food increased. Yet, all at once, he felt hungry, and he sat down at the table and Elizabeth sat near him, her hands in her lap, watching him. He did not know of the passion in her eyes, and that the supposedly resting hands were tightly held together. When he did glance up at her she gave him her cool smile and still said nothing. The house was full of the soft sighing of the wind and the scent of the gardens and the whisper of trees. There was nothing else.

She poured two glasses of wine, one for herself and one for Joseph. He had never liked wine. He suddenly found this wine delicious, and as suddenly intoxicating. He leaned back in his chair and for the first time looked fully into Elizabeth's face.

He started to speak, and then all at once he felt a desire for Elizabeth he had never felt for any other woman, a desire so hot and so intense and so tender that he did not recognize it for what it was. He could only think how womanly she was, how intelligent her face, how exquisite her white throat, how fine her chin and her nose, and how clearly green her eyes. It seemed incredible to him that such a woman, so patrician, could have loved the gross Tom Hennessey.

As Elizabeth gazed at him calmly she knew, surely and completely, that he loved her if he did not know it yet himself, and that it was possible he had loved her for a considerable time. She knew all about Joseph. Tom Hennessey had told her, with ridicule and envy, and she had learned much since she had gone to live in the Hennessey house. Now she said to herself,.But what I felt for Tom is nothing compared with what I feel for this man, and have felt for a long time. That was only girlish infatuation. This is love, the love of a mature woman for a man. This is the man I have always wanted.

She looked at his hands, his face, his eyes, his graying russet hair, the spare strength of his body, and she felt the power in him, a different kind of power than that which Tom had possessed. It was a fine-honed power, and invulnerable. She remembered what Tom had said of him and something turned away in her, as at a spoken lewdness. Tom, like his daughter, had been a liar. She felt no betrayal of Bernadette, no shrinking, no considerations for any propriety or custom or social stringencies. Bernadette did not exist for her.

They sipped wine together in the deep and eloquent silence, and listened to the night sounds outside, and the sudden hoot of an owl and the sleepy cry of a bird. The tension in the room increased, became sweetly unbearable, and all things in the room had an enormous imminence as though they possessed a life of their own. The candlelight had a consciousness, and its golden shadows were alive.

Then Elizabeth simply stood up, and Joseph slowly rose also. Elizabeth gave him her hand, like a child. She blew out the candles, and a soft darkness filled the room. Hand in hand, like young lovers, they went up to her bedroom together.

When Joseph awakened in the morning, just as the blue-gray dawn stood at the windows, and he saw Elizabeth beside him in her white bed, his first sensation was of a peace he had never known before, a fulfillment, an astonished contentment. He saw her pale hair on the pillows, her mysterious sleeping face, the girlish mounds of her breasts. He had never done this with any other woman before, but he gently took a long strand of her hair and kissed it. It was warm and fragrant against his mouth. He kissed her shoulder.

She moved and went into his arms and she said, "I love you."

But he could not answer that in turn because he had never told a woman he loved her. It was three months before he could say it without feeling absurd and without embarrassment, and then he knew it was true. For the first time in his life he knew joy without fear, joy to the uttermost, joy without skepticism or wariness or doubt. He knew what it was to love a woman, not only with sexual ecstasy but with his mind and his whole self. He never believed it was possible.

Three months later he said to her in the small but expensive hotel where they often met in New York, "I will divorce Bernadette, and we will be married."

Elizabeth said, "You have three children, one only a toddler, and we are Catholics, and I have a son also, and we have duties."

For the first time Joseph was angry with her. He said roughly, "You don't mind committing adultery with me, and I believe that is against the Church, too."

Elizabeth looked at him seriously and said, "In some way, I don't think either of us is committing adultery. Our marriages were adulterous, and that is the worst kind."

He said still roughly, "What about Tom Hennessey? You wanted him, didn't you?"

She smiled a smile he had never seen before, full of mischief and light. "I was young, and he seduced me. But I seduced you. In some fashion that is quite different!"

"That may be logical," said Joseph, "but it is hardly theological."

The months and the years that followed seemed to him incredible in their wonder and strange ease and lightness. He had always felt old, cramped, constricted, and now he knew what it was to feel young, released and almost free. It was an ambiguous feeling touched with vulnerability and even with a little fear at times, as if he were no longer his own man, his own fortress, his own invincibility, sufficient unto himself.

He had never known what it was to trust fully in all his life, but he trusted Elizabeth and this often disturbed him. After all, she was a woman, he would think for the first years; she was another human being and mankind was capricious, changeable, inclined to treachery. Then as time passed he felt less apprehensive in trusting Elizabeth, and came to trust her fully and without any reserve at all. She was that paradox to him: An intelligent woman. He found himself not only talking humorously to her and even with a little heavy banter—which surprised him as a new language —but confiding some of the aspects of his enterprises with her, though hardly all.

He was also surprised by her subtlety, by her quickness of perception, her common sense, her sudden insights, her shrewd grasp of intricate matters, and her comments. She never pretended to be revolted by some of the things he told her, nor did she appear to believe that she should be revolted. She would listen with gravity, and if she had reservations she would voice them, and, to his delight, he sometimes found them practical.

Once he said to her, "There are times when I can hardly believe you are a woman!" To which Elizabeth would reply wryly, "I never believed that intelligence was a matter of sex, though that is the delusion of many."

On one occasion he said to her, "Elizabeth, you are a great gentleman," and she smiled. She thought to herself, My darling, you are the man I have been waiting for all my life. How fortunate it is that we both knew at last.

Elizabeth was an endless and fascinating discovery to Joseph. She had, he would tell her, a thousand faces. She was a thousand different women. She shared his love for music. Her own knowledge of the art was necessarily more formal, for she had been taught at her schools, but she too discovered different men in Joseph. His perception, his engrossment with it when she accompanied him to the Academy of Music in New York, touched her almost to tears, and she marveled. His library, filled with the books he was constantly buying, and reading, commanded her respect and admiration. He had had little formal education, as he had often told her, but he was in all ways an extremely educated man and not the "money-grubbing brute" her father had called him. He had, she discovered, a sensitivity that he carefully kept within the core of him, as though it were a shameful secret and an entry for enemies. Bernadette had once jeeringly told her of Sean and Regina, and Elizabeth guessed that Joseph would never forgive nor forget nor recover from his sorrow.

She gave him, once more, a motivation for living. He found himself enjoying life, reluctantly, and finding pleasure where he had never known it lived. His entry into her world of the mind and the spirit was cautious, half-retreating, dubious, sometimes sardonic, but he entered just the same and found it absorbing. Finally his impulses to suicide became fewer and fewer, and at last he felt the urge but once or twice a year, when he was away from Elizabeth for longer than he desired. He was still gloomy and distant with others, still suspicious and contemptuous and reserved, but he was less apt to be so as the years passed, and his first impression of strangers was less automatically condemning.

It was probably Elizabeth—unknown to both of them—who had made him see his children for the first time, or rather her influence over him. She had often told him of her affection for them, particularly Ann Marie who was very like her, but he had dismissed this as womanish sentimentality. However unconscious it was, however, Elizabeth had succeeded in gentling him to some extent. He only knew that he loved her and that without her life would blacken for him again.

Bernadette, who had long suspected her husband of infidelities—she had received many arch hints from her friends in Philadelphia and New York—did not discover Joseph's liaison with Elizabeth until five years after it began.

She often went to New York with a woman friend or two to shop, and they remained overnight in the Fifth Avenue Hotel, where Joseph maintained a large suite. She loved the uproar of the city, and the stench and smoke from soft-coal fires and industry did not disturb her, and she had favorite shops and jewelers which she visited. She usually went to New York when Joseph was absent from Green Hills, for when he was "at home" she could not bear to be away.

She was strolling happily with a friend, and gossiping, when they arrived at an intersection roaring and shrilling with traffic. They waited for a break in the crowds and wagons and carriages, and as they did so Bernadette desultorily glanced to her right and saw a closed carriage almost within touching distance of her gloved hand. Then she stood, stiff and motionless, staring, disbelieving, feeling a jolt in her breast like a deadly blow.

There sat in the carriage, waiting, Joseph and Elizabeth. They were laughing, and Bernadette thought dimly, I have never seen him laugh like that. Elizabeth's usually composed face was incandescent with laughter below the violet silk of her bonnet, and she looked impossibly beautiful and vivacious, her cheeks pink, her green eyes scintillating. Joseph was holding her hand and apparently teasing her. Suddenly he lifted her hand to his lips and kissed it, and she pretended to be shocked, and laughed again. Her face was the face of a woman rapturously in love, and Joseph's face, for all its sternness and lines, was the face of a lover. It was a face totally unfamiliar to Bernadette in its absorption. Never had he seemed so almost gay and insouciant.

"Do let us move on," said Bernadette's friend beside her. "I declare, you seem rooted to the walk, dear." Numbly, moving as uncertainly as an old woman, and stumbling under her brown merino skirt, Bernadette obeyed. She felt feeble, drained as if bleeding to death, dazed, broken. Her vital parts seemed to be disintegrating, dropping away from her, and a sickness and anguish she had never known before lumbered in her breast. Her friend mercifully was chattering on, and Bernadette, her eyes swimming in a mist of agony, looked back over her shoulder. The carriage had crossed the intersection, and had halted at the doorway of the small and expensive hotel on the corner. Joseph and Elizabeth were alighting from the carriage. Bernadette saw Elizabeth's violet watered-silk suit with its lace ruffles and bustle, her velvet slippers, and the violets pinned on her breast. Joseph was gallantly, if a little stiffly, assisting her, and very briefly he held her in his arms as she stepped down. She looked up at him, her face tremulous with love and desire, and he looked down at her as he held her. Then they entered the hotel together.

"Fie," said Bernadette's friend, very crossly. "What is wrong now, dear? You look like death. Here are my smelling salts, but let us move to the shop window. People are staring at us. Are you faint? Well, it is very warm for autumn, isn't it?"

Through the haze of her enormous suffering Bernadette heard herself say, "I thought I saw—someone—I knew, going into that hotel. He—he looked like Joseph. Perhaps he is staying here, which is very unusual. Would you mind if I inquired?"

"Not at all," said her friend, who had suddenly spied an intriguing hat in a window. "I'll go in this shop and wait for you. But why should you think your husband is here? Aren't his offices in Philadelphia?"

"He has interests in New York, too," said Bernadette. There was such a great and crushing pain in her throat. She left her friend and entered the hotel. It was a small rich lobby, which hinted of discreet money and even more discreet privacy. A manager and a clerk, in Prince Albert coats, were standing at the counter and Bernadette, conscious all at once both of her new infirmity and her plumpness, went to them. They courteously watched her approach, and with curiosity, for ladies did not enter hotels unaccompanied, and Bernadette was obviously a lady even if a little dowdy in spite of the Worth suit and the light sable boa on her shoulders, and her expensive black velvet millinery and her jewels.

Her throat and mouth were as dry and parched as hot summer stone. She tried to wet lips that felt swollen and thick, and tried to smile. "Pardon me," she said, "but I thought I saw my—my brother—enter just now with his—wife. I—I didn't know they were in town."

"The name, madam?" asked the manager, who had a beautiful set of whiskers.

"Uh," said Bernadette. "Mr. Armagh."

The manager consulted the book on the counter, and looked through his pince-nez. He shook his head regretfully. "The name seems familiar," he said. "But there are no Mr. and Mrs. Armagh registered. Are you certain you saw them enter, madam?" He looked at her with eyes at once glaucous and secret.

"Yes. I am sure. Just a moment ago. Please," said Bernadette and gave him a heart-breaking smile. "Oh, please."

The manager regarded her for a long moment, then closed the book. "I am sorry madam. You must have been mistaken."

"But—the lady and the gentleman who just entered—"

The manager said, "You must be mistaken, madam. No one has entered here for the past half hour."

Bernadette stared at him and he stared back, like a basilisk. Then Bernadette turned and left the lobby and went out into the street again and looked about her with glazed eyes and did not, for several minutes, know where she was or why she was here. People jostled her. One or two swore at her. She saw and heard nothing. Her arm was taken, and her friend said, "The hat wasn't in the least becoming. Bernadette! What is wrong with you? Are you ill?"

"Yes," Bernadette whispered, and looked at her friend with such blind and tortured eyes that the other woman was appalled and frightened. "I want to go to the hotel. I—I must lie down. I may have had a seizure of some sort."

She did not return to Green Hills for two days. She

could not move from her bed. Her friend called a physician who feared that she had had a stroke.

If Joseph had died she could not have suffered more torment, more consuming grief, more anguished incredulity. His other infidelities, though they had humiliated her, had not been too difficult to condone. Gentlemen were gentlemen, as her own father had taught her through his own conduct. But gentlemen, though they might frolic with other women occasionally, and find them agreeable, still loved their wives, and did not love the other ladies. They were only passing pleasures, passing interests. So they were not very important, certainly not important enough to threaten a wife.

But Bernadette had seen Elizabeth's and Joseph's faces, and she knew they were in love and now in some way she guessed they had been lovers for a long time. This was no passing frivolity of Joseph's. He was not "toying" with Elizabeth. He loved her. She, in turn, had given him glances of adoration. They had entered the hotel engrossed only with each other, she clinging to him, his head bent to listen to what she was saying.

Once Bernadette thought, Incest! Of course it was incest, it was vile, it was intolerable, it was filthy beyond imagining. A man and the woman who was his father-in-law's widow. It was not to be borne. Abhorrent.

But Bernadette knew she had to bear it. With the powerful instinct of love, she understood that a single word from her to Joseph would cause him to leave her finally, and forever, and that she would never see him again. A word to Elizabeth, and it would be the same. Nothing could part them, not public outrage, not public condemnation, nor probably any legal sanctions, or society's horror. Bernadette knew that out of some primeval knowledge. She began to live in terror that her own temper, her own sorrow and pain, would cause her inadvertently to speak, and so she watched all her words with Joseph.

She avoided Elizabeth, and though they were neighbors both contrived not to see each other more than once or twice a year, and if they saw each other in distant gardens they affected not to be aware. This was not hard. They had scarcely encountered each other over the past few years, and then had exchanged only a cold word or two. Now Bernadette fled into her house at the mere far flick of a skirt on lawns, which might be Elizabeth's. "Ah, God," she would whisper to herself, "if it had been anyone, anyone at all, but that woman! I might have borne it."

Bernadette had known hatred before for Elizabeth. Now she hated her with so powerful a hatred that it was like a fire in her, never extinguished. For her husband she could only helplessly feel an enlargement of her love, and her continued determination to have him love her in return. At last she persuaded herself that as Elizabeth was a "light woman" Joseph would eventually grow tired of her. Strumpets did not engage the affections of gentlemen for an excessive period of time.

To the end of her life she would say, "My husband never even glanced at another woman but me. He was most devoted, always. As for myself, I lived for no one else. We were all the world to each other. Our life together was an idyl."

Chapter 35

One day when Joseph and Charles Devereaux had finished a long conference with Harry Zeff in Philadelphia
Harry slipped a note into Charles's hand with a wink. It
asked Charles to come back into Harry's office as soon as
possible, confidentially. It took Charles an hour to arrange
this, and Harry smiled with relief and nodded. Though he
was hardly fifty, his hair was a glossy riot of white curls
which made the swarthiness of his face much more striking, but he had not lost his cherubic look of mischief and
humor. He had grown stout with good living, satisfaction
with life, the love and adoration of Liza and the affection
of his children. Nor did the fact that he was now twice a
millionaire distress him.

"How you stay so young," he said to Charles. "You're
almost Joe's age but you don't look more than thirty-five.
Not dyeing your hair, are you, Charlie?"

"Hardly," said Charles, seating his elegant body into the
chair opposite Harry. Harry's offices were lavish with leather, fine pictures on the paneled walls, rich carpets, and a
fire chuckling on the black marble hearth this cold and
snowy winter day. Harry leaned back in his chair and
puffed on his big cigar and put his thumbs in the armholes
of his vest. "You look like the damned swollen capitalistic
plutocrat the Populist newspapers are always cartooning
and shouting about," Charles remarked. "Striped trousers
and black silk embroidered vest and long black coat—all of
it, and big belly too. 'Wall Street Exploiter of the Poor and
Oppressed.' That's you, Harry."

Harry laughed. "I suppose," he said, "there are people in
this country who have been as poor as I have been, but
there's none who has been poorer. The next step would
have been starvation—to death. Funny how so many howl-
ers about the poor have never known poverty or struggle or

hard work or misery or hunger. I'd like to give them a taste of it, that I would, as Joe would say."

But there was no bitterness in his lustrous black eyes and his red-lipped smile. Harry could endure even Populists and Socialists with a merry gaiety, as rather immature and ignorant frothers who did not know the nature of man nor the true predicament of mankind, or were malcontents who had too little intelligence to grasp reality, too few natural endowments and too little energy for anything but envy. "If a man's a failure," Harry would say, "he thinks that entitles him to tell the government how to run the country." (Harry, himself, did not care much for the government, because he understood it, but he had a jovial contempt for those who hated it only on vague principle and without a practical reason.)

"It seems we have a problem," he said to Charles, and now he looked as serious as it was possible for him to be. "You've hèard of Sean, Joe's brother, who disappeared somewhere in the slums of Boston a long time ago?"

"Yes," said Charles. "It is also my job to destroy, unread, the twice-yearly letters Joe receives from his sister. He won't even give the poor woman the satisfaction of knowing that at least he saw them, by returning them to her."

Harry frowned at the tip of his cigar. "Well, you know Joe, Charles."

"Indeed I do," said Charles. "He never forgives nor forgets. Look what he did to Handell of the Handell Oil Company a few years ago. Cornered all the stock and threw Handell out, almost a bankrupt."

"Um," said Harry. "I know. But you've got to remember that Handell tried a little fast trickery on Joe, in the matter of Joe's invention of the kerosene fueling for industrial machinery. It wasn't a big sum, as money goes, but it was still considerable. Joe never accepts treachery in the jolly way it is thought up—just a prank between friends, of course. Maybe that's because he has little sense of humor, eh?"

Charles's seamed face colored a trifle. "Look here, Harry, you know how I feel about Joe. I know how my father felt. To my father Joe was another son, and Joe took a huge loss in buying the land next to my father's and selling it to him for half the price the Yankee scalawags were asking." He smiled. "On the coat of arms of the Devereaux's is the inscription, 'We remember friend and foe.'"

"Well, that's burned in on Joe's soul, too," said Harry. "Perhaps Joe was a little hard on old Handell, but Handell knew Joe very well and he had no sense doing what he did. Had he stolen from Joe frankly and impudently it might have been another matter, but it was done slyly and meanly, and then denied. Well, we aren't discussing Handell, who's dead now anyway. It's Sean Paul Armagh, Joe's brother."

"Dead, too?"

Harry scratched his fat chin. "No. But I have yesterday's Boston paper here and you can read it for yourself." He grumbled, "Damn it, why didn't the fool keep his mouth shut?"

Charles took the newspaper. Prominently featured on the second page under the headline GREAT SUCCESS FOR TENOR, SINGER OF IRISH BALLADS! was a photograph of a slight, rather pretty middle-aged man with a charming deprecatory smile and thin fair hair, alleged to be Sean Paul. The lively story then went on to explain that Mr. Paul had sung for many years "in various of our public establishments which cater to the workingmen who drink beer and liquors—a somewhat deplorable habit of those of that class;" and then had come to the attention of a kindly gentleman whom Mr. Paul designated only as "Mr. Harry," who had, to quote Mr. Paul, "rescued me from penury and failure and assisted and encouraged me, with money and consolations beyond a mere expression of gratitude." It was "Mr. Harry" who had had him taught formal music and voice, "in various musical establishments and under the best of teachers, two of operatic fame," and had then "launched me on the road to success."

The success, at first, had meant only minor musical halls in Boston which the Irish favored. It had, however, been more than enough to sustain Mr. Paul. He had also sung on many occasions in other New England towns, "and enthralled the devotees of Irish songs with his musical genius and his magnificent and poignant voice, moving all to tears and rapture." However, under the aegis of "Mr. Harry" Mr. Paul had increased his repertoire to include not only Irish ballads but "the songs of all the people," and "exquisite operatic selections, rendered with deep feeling and tender passion." Now, exclaimed the report in superlatives, "Mr. Paul has been enaged by the Academy of Music in New York and in Chicago and Philadelphia and other cities, for a series of concerts, all of which are now oversubscribed. His accompanist is—"

Charles laid down the paper and looked at Harry with suppressed amusement. "I gather," he said, "that you are the enigmatic benefactor of Sean Armagh, the modest gentleman who avoids the limelight."

"How could you have possibly guessed," said Harry, with more gloom than Charles had ever seen before. "Well, damn it, I was in Boston, and I like beer and I went to a pub, as Joe calls saloons, and there was Sean singing like an angel—and not drinking. Like a damned angel. He looks like one, too. That's a bad photograph. He reeks with charm and softness and ingratiation, and all of it's sincere. Every man jack there was crying in his beer, and I cried too. Voice like a soaring sweet horn, or maybe it's a flute. Never could tell the difference between instruments. But it rang back from the walls and the ceiling, and no one moved except to wipe his eyes and sob a little." Harry paused. "I knew I had to help him."

"Why didn't you tell Joe? Wouldn't he have been glad to know his brother had a little success then, such as it was?"

"My God," said Harry, with emotion. "Joe had been preparing his brother to help him in The Armagh Enterprises for ages, for years. When Sean was at home in Green Hills, Joe would drag him away from the piano and wouldn't let him sing. Sean was going to be a shrewd businessman, that he was, to quote Joe's exact words again, right here with his brother. That's what Joe had been working for all his life—making sure his brother would be a multimillionaire entrepreneur like himself. He forced Sean almost through Harvard. Sean despised it. I think he was just bewildered, myself. He had no more taste for this business than a simpering schoolgirl, and that was my first impression of him anyway.

"I believe they had a—disagreement," Harry said judiciously, giving a slight cough. "There was some rumor they came to blows. It goes back a long time. Joe's not a man who confides in anybody, but one day he did tell me that his father was what he called a 'ne'er-do-well,' who liked to sing in pubs, too, and treat one and all with his last handful of shillings, and he let his farm be taken for taxes, and he came to America and died before his family arrived.

"In any event I knew that Joe would hate his brother

more than ever for doing what their 'feckless' father—another phrase of Joe's—did in the old country. Any reminder of his father had a way of almost driving him out of his mind. I think that is what makes him so adamant and infuriated when he encounters any weakness or softness or lack of interest in good solid success—like his."

"I see, " said Charles.

"Well, perhaps you do, and perhaps you don't," said Harry, shaking his head. "You've got to be in Joe's position, with his memories and his starving years and his struggles and the persecutions he endured because he is Irish. Yes, sir, you've got to know what real bloody persecution means. You've got to know what your own people suffered."

He sighed. "Everything he did was for his family. He never really lived for himself. Though he was a good one for advising others to do that! He just lived for Sean and Regina. It's only lately that he seems to have become a little more human—over the past fifteen years or so. I guess there's a woman behind it all," and Harry's eyes became secret. " 'Find the woman.' Isn't that what they say? Anyway, I'm glad of it. First time he's ever looked happy, and I've known him since I was under fifteen. That's a long time for a man to be miserable."

Charles spoke with unusual gentleness. "And you are afraid that Joe will blow up when he finds out about his brother, as he will very soon?"

"Look," said Harry, "I've known Joe since we were boys together. He saved my life. I saved his. I'd give my life for him, and he knows it. But he can't stand deceit. He can't stand treachery. He won't stand underhandedness. That's not his way. He's got his own code of honor. He'll think I deceived him, diddled him, had a joke at his expense, betrayed him."

"For rescuing his brother?"

"Charles, if I'd told him in the beginning he'd have raised hell with me. He might have thrown me out. I was a rich man by then. I could have gone on without Joe. I have interests, too. Joe couldn't have hurt me. It was just the thought of him throwing me out, putting me out of his life forever, never speaking to me again, never looking at me, that gave me nightmares."

"He's done dozens of things that weren't ethical," said

Charles, "and many more that were illegal. Why should he cavil at what you've done, out of compassion for his brother?"

Harry shook his head dismally. "You don't understand. He did those things to other businessmen. It was dog eat dog. But he won't take treachery or slyness from anyone he has trusted to some extent."

Charles mused. "I suppose it never occurred to him that his brother and sister had the right to live their own lives?"

Harry sighed again. "I guess you don't understand."

"I understand all right," said Charles. "You're in a good hot pickle, Harry." He scrutinized the unhappy man. "If you know his fancy lady, why not confide in her, very fast? You think she has a lot of influence over him."

Harry's dusky face sharpened and came alive with anger. "Don't call her a 'fancy lady!' " he shouted. "I know her. I saw him with her several times. She is a great lady!"

"Well, ask her advice. And you'd better be quick about it, Harry. He sometimes looks at the Boston papers when he has time."

"Um," said Harry, but a little hope had come into his eyes. He chewed his cigar.

"At any rate," said Charles, "Sean isn't using his surname. Joe might overlook the whole thing, not recognizing his brother."

"You forget," said Harry. "He's going to sing soon in Philadelphia and New York, and Joe won't miss the posters. He's always going to concerts. He has his own boxes now. Once he's seen Sean on the stage, singing his heart out, bang goes Harry out the front door, probably half dead, too. Why didn't that damned Sean keep his mouth shut and not mention me in the papers? He'll probably talk the same way in New York and Philadelphia, too."

"Well, they call that gratitude," said Charles. "Better consult that lady, Harry." He stood up and looked down at Harry. "Sometimes, in this naughty world, a candle lighted in the darkness gets smashed, contrary to Shakespeare. I wish I knew more how to help, but I don't."

"You've given me an idea," said Harry, and tore up the newspaper and put it into his wastebasket.

Elizabeth, when Harry called upon her, knew at once from his manner that he had more than guessed at the liaison between her and Joseph Armagh. She knew Harry well, liked his Liza and himself, and had admiration for both and the utmost courtesy. Still, his almost boyish awkwardness at approaching her now made her color a little, then she resumed her dignity and listened with her special attentiveness. At last she said, "Yes, I understand, Harry. I also understand Joseph, and your predicament. I will do my very best." She paused. "I am to be in New York next Tuesday. I will do my best." She smiled at the stout relieved man. "It was so kind, so good of you, Harry, so compassionate. Compassion is a rare thing in this world. I am sure we can bring Joseph to respect it and not condemn it. He isn't quite as formidable as—as he once was. At least I like to believe that."

Harry was depressed again, thinking of an episode only two weeks ago. Joseph had shown no signs of "softening." However, it had been a business matter—

There was a blizzard in New York the next Tuesday, almost as severe as the Great Blizzard of '88 a few years before, and Elizabeth's rooms in the quiet small hotel were warm with lamplight and firelight. She had dressed carefully in Joseph's favorite color which matched the pale green of her eyes, and the long gown, with its tight bodice and draped bustle, twinkled with brilliant buttons. She ignored style in the dressing of her hair, and it was arranged in smooth light yellow wings about her calm face and knotted in a large chignon at her nape. She wore the emeralds he had given her, which she never wore in Green Hills. She had, over the years, improved his appreciation for food, which always remained simple, however, and so there was roast chicken with savory dressing and a hearty soup and salad, a rosé wine, plain pastries and a great deal of tea. His consumption of tea always surprised her. In addition she had perfumed herself with a violet scent, his favorite, though she never guessed why he preferred it.

"You never grow older, my darling," he said to her, after he had removed his snowy greatcoat and hat and gloves and had kissed her with that curious reticence of his.

"Yes, I do very well for an old lady of forty-four," said Elizabeth in her tranquil voice. "But then, when one is in love, and loves, one never grows old. I have a letter from Courtney, by the way. He hopes to be graduated from Harvard next June, with Rory. I hope so, too. You know Rory." She smiled. "But how is Ann Marie? Has she recovered from her chill?"

"Bernadette's still trying to marry her off," said Joseph, sitting down in his accustomed comfortable chair near the fire and holding out his cold lean hands to the blaze. "She is having a ball for the girl in March, on her twenty-first birthday, and Ann Marie is already cringing." He thought about his daughter, who had considerable resemblance to Regina, but thank God—if there was one—she had no inclination to the religious life. Joseph had not permitted his children to attend any schools but secular ones. "Her chill? I didn't know she'd had one, but then I haven't been in Green Hills for nearly three weeks."

It was one of Elizabeth's sadnesses that she did not see Ann Marie very often, for she believed in respecting the wishes of parents and knew that Bernadette had protested Ann Marie's visits to her house. Too, it made life less harassed for the young woman, who had much to endure from a mother who disliked her and thought her "another poor thing, like Courtney Hennessey." To Bernadette gentle and retiring people, no matter their intellect or accomplishments, were to be despised for "lacking character." The Armaghs, she would think, lacked character except, of course, for Joseph. Even the splendid Rory and his light inclination to be a rogue hardly inspired her affection, though she basked when compliments concerning him were made to her. "He is a *true* Hennessey," she would say, with meaning.

"Bernadette didn't write you?" asked Elizabeth.

Joseph shrugged. "Probably. I never read her letters. Charles does, and replies politely." He watched Elizabeth arrange the round table for their dining near the fire. A hotel servant could do that but she liked to preside and prepare for Joseph and he watched her with a love that had not diminished with the years but had grown more solid and rooted. In her turn, as she worked, Elizabeth gave him glances full of tenderness. The once russet hair was now heavily inlaid with whitening gray but the somber face never changed except to smile more frequently than ever before in his life. He said, "Elizabeth, I have to go again to Geneva in April. Come with me."

"But doesn't Bernadette—usually go with you?"

"Yes. I am ending that. Come with me."

Elizabeth hesitated. She thought of Sean. She did not want to annoy Joseph just now so she said, "Please let me think about it Joseph. I always liked Geneva."

He was very pleased. "Then," he said, "it is decided." He had the sharp eyes of love. "Have you been to see your doctor? Your color has not improved and you seem thinner."

"He says it is my age," replied Elizabeth. She knew her hands were almost transparent now and that an unusual weariness had been her almost constant companion during the past six months. "No consumption, if that is worrying you, Joseph. After all years do tell, you know. He could find nothing wrong, my doctor."

"Forty-four is not a great age," said Joseph, and an intense sick alarm came to him such as he had not felt since his mother had become moribund on the ship, and it dried his mouth and throat and made him cough and reach for his glass of wine. "Anemia, perhaps? All you ladies are always having anemia."

What if Elizabeth was removed from his life? His old strong impulse to suicide surged into him as it always did when he was personally threatened or melancholy. Life without Elizabeth would be intolerable, for she was as entwined with his life as the roots of twin trees had become entangled. She was all the joy he had ever known, all the peace and wonder and delight. Sometimes they would sit like this for hours, he reading his books or newspapers and she reading also, and they would not speak, but the companionship was like one heart, one body, content, rich, contained. He lived, he would think, only for these occasions with Elizabeth.

"I have had three chills this winter," said Elizabeth, "and I am not young any longer. That is probably the trouble. Perhaps I need a change, such as Geneva," and she smiled at him over her wineglass. "How wonderful it would be to travel in Europe with you, Joseph," and now she gave the matter sincere thought. He reached over the table and touched her hand and his small blue eyes were the eyes of a shy youth.

Then she spoke with much animation. "I have just received notice that Sean Paul, the glorious Irish tenor, is coming to New York in three weeks for a recital at the Academy of Music. I do hope, dear Joseph, that you will be able to take me."

Her smile was still serene but her heart began to beat quickly. Joseph's austere face changed, darkened. "Sean

Paul?" he said, lingering over the name. "I never heard of him."

"He isn't young. Possibly near my own age. But he is quite celebrated in Boston, I hear. He sings Irish ballads, and operatic selections, and people are quite mad about him. He has always preferred quiet private recitals but has now been induced to give pleasure to wider audiences. I do believe I have the leaflet announcing his New York recital with me!" She rose with a rustle of green silk and disappeared into her bedroom and Joseph waited with a slowly gathering heavy anger. Nonsense, he said to himself. It couldn't be the—same. Sean had probably died of intoxication, in some nameless gutter, and good riddance to him. Then with the anger came pain and the old sense of loss and despair.

Elizabeth returned with the leaflet which featured Sean's photograph, and she gave it to Joseph. He did not at first read the lyrical announcements, the quotations from music critics. He looked at the shy smiling photograph and knew that this was his brother. Feeling giddy and unreal, he then read the quotations. Again he stared at the photograph. Sean. It was truly Sean. He could not understand his emotions now, but there was a weak slackening in him, a faintness, and his eyes blurred. He put the leaflet on the table but he still stared at it and Elizabeth watched him with trepidation.

He became aware that a long silence had come between him and Elizabeth. He looked at her now and saw her waiting and anticipatory smile. He said, "You never saw my brother, Sean?"

"No." Now she assumed an expression of perplexity. "I only saw Regina once or twice, but not Sean." She put her hands suddenly over her mouth and pretended astonished delight and incredulousness. "Oh, Joseph! Is this wonderful singer, this marvelous Irish tenor, your brother, Sean? Oh, I can't bear it! How proud you must be! How elated!" She leaned across the table and took his hand and her face shone with genuine pleasure.

He made the preliminary motion of discarding her hand, so immeasurable was his enigmatic and complicated rage. But she clung to it, and he looked into her eyes and he knew he could not reject Elizabeth even with the slightest gesture.

"Yes," he said. "He is my brother. But it is a long story."

"Tell me about it," she said.

But how could he tell her of the years she could not possibly understand? He looked again into those green eyes, and knew that he was wrong. She could understand. In short hard sentences he told her, and she never spoke nor moved, and only watched him, the light in her eyes quickening, misting, or growing tender as he talked. He had told her something of all this before, but not with such emotion, such detail. He had not spoken much, either, of his brother and sister, dismissing them only with contempt.

When he had finished, Elizabeth said, "But, don't you see, Joseph? You have succeeded with Sean after all. Without the education he had received he wouldn't have known anything, really. Education, though often despised in youth, makes its importance emphatic in maturity. It makes for discrimination. Had Sean been uneducated, ignorant, he would never have understood more than saloon singing, or had any aspirations beyond that. But he knew there was something else: excellence. That you gave to him. That should be your pride and your comfort."

He said nothing. He was staring at the fire now, gloomier than ever, and as unreadable. But she knew she had reached him, for she knew everything about him. She said, very softly, "You have told me many times that your father sang in the pubs in Ireland and wasted what little he had in beer and whiskey for others, and was concerned only with the pleasure and happiness he gave—to the neglect of his family. There is something in that story, dear Joseph, that is not entirely complete. He was a joy to his friends and your mother, who loved him. Sometimes I believe in fate. If it was fated for him to die as he did, and your mother, too, then it could not have been avoided, taking into consideration the circumstances of their lives."

"Don't talk like a fool," said Joseph, with a roughness towards her she had never seen before. "Weren't we taught as children that there is such a thing as free will? Yes, and it is true, I am thinking. My father chose his life. Unfortunately he chose the lives of his wife and children, too."

He saw that Elizabeth had become very white and that she was shrinking a little. He could not bear to hurt her in the slightest. He took her hand again and pressed it strongly in his palms and tried to smile. "Forgive me," he said, and that was the first time in his life that he had ever said those words, and he paused to recall them with astonishment. "I wouldn't hurt you for the world, Elizabeth."

Elizabeth thought, "He is wounded, and almost slain," and I wonder if he ever did "rise and fight again." Yes, perhaps. But not with the same profound intensity, not with the same dedication. She moved her hand in his, and her fingers clung to his hand.

"We were talking of Sean, dear Joseph, and no one else. He succeeded, thanks to you, and only because of you, where your father failed. You gave him character, persistence, determination. How proud you must be, should be, my dearest."

"Why the hell hasn't he written to me?" asked Joseph, and Elizabeth knew she was succeeding and closed her eyes for a moment.

"Perhaps he was ashamed, remembering all you have done for him. Perhaps he knew you would remember your father, and his singing, and he didn't want to anger you more than you were already angered. You are quite an inexorable character, you know, my dear, and I have a feeling you always frightened your family."

"Hah," said Joseph. He took up the leaflet again and studied it. He turned it over: "My dear benefactor, one whom I shall call Mr. Harry, came to my assistance when I most needed it. To him, then, and to a relative I do not care to name at this time, I owe my success and the adulations I have received. I dedicate my New York recital to them, as I do all my prayers."

Joseph rose suddenly, and his face was one Elizabeth had never seen before and she was aghast. He said in a terrible voice, "Harry Zeff. He did this behind my back. He never came to me and said, 'Your brother has been found and needs your help.' No. He preferred to wait to mortify me with my brother's—success. Gloating. Throwing it into my face that he could do more for Sean than I could! Laughing at me—behind my back. Why? Why? I made his fortune for him. But, what could I ever expect but ingratitude and slyness and treachery? And a murderous envy?"

Elizabeth stood up also, trembling. She put her hand on his arm and for the first time he pushed that hand aside. He was aglow with rage and humiliation.

"This is the end—for Harry," he said in that frightening voice.

Elizabeth said, "Will you listen to me for one moment, Joseph? If you do not, then we must not meet again, even if I die of it. I could not bear to see you."

Even in his monstrous rage he heard her, and knew that she meant it, and he stood still and waited, his hands clenched.

"Do you honestly believe," said Elizabeth, in a marveling voice, "that Harry Zeff would ever do anything to mortify or injure you, or gloat over you? Gloat over you! My God, Joseph! I don't believe it, that you should think so. Why, you must be out of your mind! But Harry knows you, and fears you. He knows what you had planned for Sean. He knows how Sean—deserted—you. He knows what you must have suffered. Please try to understand, though I doubt you ever understood anyone in your life, even me, who loves you.

"Yes, he helped Sean. He believed in Sean. He encouraged Sean to make the most of his voice, and paid for it, himself. Did you ever ask yourself why? It is because Harry loves you, Joseph. He didn't want that part of your life to be defeated, to have come to nothing. Sean has made a wonderful success. He owes that mostly to you. Harry only helped him to achieve it and enhance what you had already given."

Joseph heard her. Then when she had finished he glowered so that his eyes disappeared. "Now, then," he said, "how do you know all this, Elizabeth, about Harry and my brother? Have I been led up the garden path?"

Elizabeth put her hands tightly over her face for a moment. When she dropped her hands she looked thinner and more exhausted than before and Joseph saw it and the awful alarm returned to him. "Please sit down, Joseph," she said, and her tone was so quiet he could hardly hear her. He sat down, rigidly, perched on his chair and Elizabeth sat down also.

She knew that Joseph could bear only the truth, and that even if the truth destroyed him he must have it. There was nothing else to do and so she told him the complete story, with candor and in that newly exhausted voice full of pleading and love. When she had finished she lay back in her chair with closed eyes as if she were asleep or had fainted.

Joseph looked at her face and it was for her that he felt compassion. He knelt down beside her and took her in his arms and kissed her forehead and her cheek, and then she was clinging to him, crying. "Why is it," she wept, "that you reject love and tenderness so? Oh, I know, my dearest. Your life has been so dreadful, so barren, and you have known betrayal and misery. You are wary now, and who can blame you? Harry would have told you, but he was afraid, for you are no gentle character, my darling. You struck fear in your brother, too, and in Regina, though you perhaps never knew it. Do you know how frightful it is to have others fear you?"

He said, "Elizabeth, are you afraid of me?"

She put her wet cheek against his, and her arms about his neck. "No, my love. I do not have any fear of you. You see, I know all about you and with love and understanding everything else is nothing. Isn't that what St. Paul said? Yes."

A few days later Joseph walked into Harry Zeff's offices and said with what for him passed as a genial smile, "By the way, my brother, Sean, is singing in New York on Friday and Saturday. I know you don't like music very much, you heathen, but I should like to have you and Liza join me in New York, at the Fifth Avenue Hotel, as my guests. I have a box at the Academy of Music, and I insist you be there. After all, it isn't every day that a man has a famous Irish tenor as a brother, is it? After the recital we'll have a gala."

Harry slowly stood up, his black eyes fixed on Joseph. He could not speak. He could only extend his hand and Joseph took it. Joseph said, in a very soft voice, "You son of a bitch. You sentimental son of a bitch, Harry."

Chapter 36

Rory and Courtney walked in Harvard Yard together in the gold and gilt of the April sun and the flowering of forsythia. Rory said, "I always thought Pa was joking when he told me he'd make me President of the United States some day. I joked with him. I told him that, of course, he would probably do that. You know Pa. He climbs mountains where other men climb anthills. But a man has to face facts. There is no more possibility of a Catholic becoming President in this country than a Negro. Well, anyway, we're going to law school, and Pa isn't young any longer, and if we make a success in The Armagh Enterprises that will be enough for Pa. I hope," added Rory.

Courtney said, with that neutral serenity so like his mother's, "Don't be too sure, Rory. What your father wants, your father gets, one way or another. Isn't he talking even now of you starting your political career as a congressman? Or do you think he just jabbers? Incidentally, men like your father never grow old. Titian, I believe, painted his most famous painting, *The Assumption*, when he was ninety-one years old, and da Vinci was full steam ahead in his middle-age. It's only the young who babble, 'sound and fury—signifying nothing.' "

"All right, old man," said Rory. He pondered, frowning, as he kicked a small stone from his path. "You know what I'd like to do? Teach."

"You're out of your mind," said Courtney, awed. He stopped. "Anyone less likely to be a teacher, or want to be, than you?"

"Well," said Rory, "there's a lot of farce and lies and hypocrisy in this world, and real absurdity, and nonsense, and I suppose there always has been. We need an Aristophanes every generation to show it all up. A real farce. Of course, it's tragic, too. But people don't realize the tragedy: the hilarity of human existence. I've thought about enlightening the younger generation about that. How to laugh—Hogarthian laughter. If possible."

"It isn't," said Courtney. "People—everybody—take themselves too seriously. Each generation thinks it will save the world, make a new Utopia, a new order. It ends up in the same Dismal Swamp."

"It shouldn't."

"But it does. Because human nature never changes. It's the one immutable in the world. It's a mess. When a full human being appears he gets crucified or laughed out of public life, or damned or ridiculed, and then everybody forgets him and goes on in the same happy stupid way. You haven't forgot your history, have you?"

"A people who forget their history are doomed to repeat it, as Aristotle said. Why isn't it possible for a people to remember their history and then avoid future mistakes, Courtney?"

"They are too stupid," said Courtney. "And they listen to politicians."

"Then you don't believe that each generation is more intelligent than the last?"

"Of course it isn't. Where are our great men, Rory? This generation has no Michelangelos, no Ciceros, no da Vincis, no Socrateses, no Platos. We're a dull drab industrial civilization, without inspiration or real joy or creativeness. It's all machines, and worship of machines. Like Karl Marx. He loves machines. He thinks they are the new Dispensation. He screams against 'business' but he's the real patron saint of business."

They reached a low gray wall of stone and sat on it, smoking. Banks of bright gold forsythia rose behind them. The sky was like pale blue porcelain against which trees—filled with a tawny haze of buds—stretched their newly flexible branches. The old gray façades of the distant buildings were showing the fresh green of young ivy. The air was warm but nimble, the grass shyly lush and fragrant and dotted with dandelions and buttercups and tiny white daisies. There was a sea wind, nostalgic and exciting. The young men on the wall smoked peacefully and looked about them and were young with the young world. Courtney glanced idly up at the sky to see the delicately shining crescent of a new moon just rising in the east.

He was really wondering about Rory and his dual na-

ture, which had always intrigued him. Rory could change
from a rascal, with the rascal's joyously incredulous smile
and arched eyebrows, to glum sobriety. He was at once a
cynic, immune to sentimentality, and then, in an instant, he
was almost naïve. He could laugh heartlessly at the predicament of a classmate, and then the next moment he would
lend him money, give him advice and help him. He could
be ruthless and exploitative with a prostitute, and then,
without warning, he would give the woman twice as much
as she had asked and show her solicitude. He could lie
amiably and readily, without shame or compunction, and
then endanger himself with the absolute truth and show
disgust with liars. He could be cruel and indifferent and
shortly afterwards full of pity and kindness to the one and
the same person. Was all this caprice, Courtney would
think, the capriciousness of a very volatile and alert man,
or was neither manifestation sincere? He finally came to
the conclusion—though not always without doubts—that
Rory was truly dual. For that somewhat thick red lower
lip, sensual like his grandfather's, could tighten into austerity with the ascetic's rejection of sensuality. But whether he
was the dedicated scholar or the thorough-going scoundrel,
the protector of the weak or the derider of weakness, he
was honest as of the moment. This very startling versatility,
this changefulness, created a fascinating individual which,
combined with his splendor of appearance and obvious potency, made him irresistible to both men and women.
Though he seemed never to be the same—like a flashing
dragonfly in the sun—there was a basic immutability in his
character over which his attitudes and emotions merely
scintillated. That stable quality, Courtney thought, is something men would reckon with in the future, to their bewilderment, and possibly to their discomfiture. Rory might be
Gemini, but he was also himself, mysterious and unknowable, like his father. Courtney and Rory might be closer
than brothers, trusting each other beyond the trust they
gave anyone else, but even the subtle Courtney never fully
guessed the personality of the other. However, Courtney
had the wry conviction that Rory understood him, completely, and that Rory was never deceived as to the nature
of anyone else.

To those whom Rory cared little about—or those he had
decided to hoodwink—he was apparently light-hearted,
gay, generous, good-natured, humorous, witty, broadly tol-

erant and careless. To those closer to him he sometimes
showed his intrepid character, his adamant ruthlessness, his
staunch strange rectitude, his powerful determination, and
his exigency. Once Courtney said to him, "You wear many
masks," to which Rory replied, "But they are all me." "It
must be tiring," said Courtney. Rory had laughed. "No, it
is always interesting. I never know what I am going to do
next."

Courtney doubted that. There was a certain deliberation
in what Rory always did, a certain calculation. However,
one could always rely upon his loyalty, once given. He
might say to a friend, "You've been a damned fool and deserve your punishment," but he would always help the
friend to evade that punishment, cursing him meanwhile
and publicly excoriating him. To the discriminating
Courtney, Rory's hearty good-fellowship with the most improbable people—low mountebanks, sly reprobates, villains,
rogues, unkempt and noisy ne'er-do-wells, drunkards, fail-
ures, ragtag and bobtail, and the stupidly insistent—seemed
incredible and unworthy of him. For, within an hour or so
Rory could be found disputing with professors in the most
learned fashion and obtuseness and in the most elegant and
impeccable phrases, and showing a fastidiousness in
thought and argument beyond the range of most young
men of his age. But Courtney had known very few politicians. He did not guess Rory was a born politician for quite
a considerable time.

Rory was all placid youthfulness today when he and
Courtney sat on the wall and swung their legs and smoked
and idly contemplated their fellows walking in the Yard.
There was nothing on Rory's vivid face which revealed his
capacity for thought and reflection. He seemed a rather colorful and beefy young man with nothing on his mind but
girls and whiskey and athletics and adventures, and spending unearned money. His thick thatch of red-gold hair
shimmered in the frail sunlight. His handsome face was relaxed. His light blue eyes wandered with apparently no
thought.

Then Rory said, "I thought you and Ann Marie would
be openly engaged by this time. Or, has she changed her
mind?"

"She's afraid to speak to her mother about it," said
Courtney, and he frowned. "She knows how your mother

hates my mother, and me. Ann Marie is a very timid girl, you know."

"I never noticed it," said Rory, remembering the vigorous way Ann Marie would pull his hair when they were in the nursery. He smiled. "I thought it would be announced on our twenty-first birthday, but it wasn't. I've talked to her, as you suggested, but she actually quails at the idea of speaking to Ma."

Then he scowled and looked down at the grass. He had never been unaware of the liaison between his father and "Aunt" Elizabeth. But he loved both, and approved of the affair which had gone on over the years. Ma was impossible. Rory did not blame his father. However, he understood his twin sister's fear of approaching their mother on the subject of an engagement to Courtney Hennessey.

"I talked to my mother, about six months ago," said Courtney. Rory stared at him, surprised, raising his bronze eyebrows. "I thought she'd faint," Courtney continued. "She was very agitated. She said it was 'impossible,' and she wouldn't tell me why. Do you have an idea?"

Rory considered this. "No, I don't. There is no impediment to the marriage that I can conceive of. You are the son of Everett Wickersham, your mother's first husband, and you were only adopted by my grandfather. No consanguinity to the last degree. So, that can't be it. Your mother—likes—my father. There shouldn't be any objection there. And Ann Marie and I love your mother. So, why should Aunt Elizabeth be 'faint' at the very suggestion?"

"I don't know," said Courtney, feeling miserable in the fresh sunshine.

"Suppose I speak to Pa?" said Rory. "He has no patience with foolishness. He likes you, too."

"I should not like any disagreements in the family," said Courtney. "I am not exactly 'family' in the meaning of the word, though I was adopted by Tom Hennessey. I am not really your 'uncle,' or Bernadette's brother, except by courtesy of adoption, which means nothing. I do know, though, that my mother was very disturbed at the idea and turned very white and became upset. She told me I must put it out of my mind." Courtney grimaced. "I've wanted to marry Ann Marie since I was ten years old!" He thought again, despondently. "Since I spoke to Ma she seems to have failed in health. She is growing thin and nervous. She keeps looking at me, as if she is about to burst out crying. I just don't understand. She loves Ann Marie like a daughter—which is more than you can say for your own mother." He looked bitterly at Rory.

Rory shrugged, tranquilly. "Oh, I know Ma. Maybe Aunt Elizabeth is afraid of my mother and doesn't want her to come down on Ann Marie too hard. Hatred is a very stupid thing, unless you can make it work for you," added Rory, the politician.

"How can we make the hatred between your mother and mine 'work' for us?" asked Courtney.

"Let me think about it," said Rory. "Maybe I can get Pa on your side. He doesn't give a hoot for Ma's feelings or opinions." He said it without rancor.

"I only know this," said Courtney. "I love your sister, and I am going to marry her even if we have to elope. But she cries at the thought. But I think I've just about persuaded her. She talks of the 'family.' So long as we have you on our side, Rory, and eventually my mother, why should we care?"

To his surprise Rory did not answer for a moment. Then Rory said, "There must be something. Anyway, as Napoleon said, the difficult we can do immediately. The impossible takes just a little longer. I'll find out."

But Courtney, the controlled and usually serene, felt something ominous in the air, something not to be grasped, something hidden. He was not a young man of moods, like Rory, and not given to premonitions. However, there it was: something threatening and terrible, beyond his comprehension. He tried to fix his attention on Ann Marie, her gentle pale face, her large light brown eyes like sherry, her smooth brown hair, her abashed little mannerisms, her quiet timidity, her radiant and sudden smile. He felt a sharp powerful emotion which shook him. He loved Ann Marie. Nothing, not family or anything else, would keep him from his love. There was nothing beyond it.

"What's the matter?" asked Rory. "You look like death."

"It's getting chilly," said Courtney, as the warmth heightened. He tried to divert himself. "How are you and Maggie Chisholm getting along?"

"Her Dad won't have her marry a Catholic," said Rory, smiling with humor. "Nor an Irisher. I'm beyond the pale.

Her Dad has a nose like a fox, and sniffs. When I go to see her he acts as if she had dragged something smelly from the gutter into the house. Old Boston. But, we're going to be married." Rory never confided in anyone, not even in Courtney. He smiled, Courtney thought, like a Cheshire cat, secret and knowing. And contented. I wish, thought Courtney, that I was as sure of everything as he is.

"You can't be married in the Church," said Courtney, "unless Maggie agrees to it and brings up your children as Catholics."

"Who says anything about the Church?" said Rory, with a magnificent gesture. "I'd marry Maggie before a Muslim priest, if it came to that. Or a justice of the peace."

"Heretic," said Courtney. They heard the bells ring for dinner and slid from the wall and made their way towards Memorial Hall in the last warm rays of the sun. They locked their arms together, both aware of the deep affection between them and the trust. Courtney's premonitions receded. He acquired something of Rory's confidence in life: After all, what force was strong enough to divide those who loved each other?

After dinner, and whistling happily, Rory went to call on Miss Marjorie Chisholm on Beacon Hill. Her mother was dead and the female head of the small family was a romantic and loving aunt who favored Rory and would be discreet about his forbidden visits. Marjorie's father dined at this time every week with his grim mother some distance away.

The Chisholms were fairly rich and very much in social power in Boston, claiming some lateral descent from Paul Revere. Rory found their old rosebrick house narrow and dark and somewhat "poor," for he was accustomed to the grandeur of his mother's house and the immense drawing rooms and domed painted ceilings and gilt and marble and fountains and statues and expensive paintings and silk walls. Here, in the Chisholm house, the windows were tall slits prim and recessed, like a spinster's mouth, the doors thick but narrow with a stained-glass fanlike window over the front entrance, the roofs of steeply pitched slate, and the shutters painted brown. It rose abruptly from the bricked street, was close to its neighbors, with a dank garden in the rear. The furniture, to Rory, was gloomy and dull, with brass pulls and dark velvet seats and glimmering tops to the tables. There were no enormous and glittering chandeliers as there were in the Hennessey house, but muted lamps of brass and china, filled with kerosene, for Mr. Chisholm did not "believe" in gas and certainly not in the new electricity which some of the more "advanced and thriftless" houses were already boasting. Once Rory had shown, with pride, some photographs of his mother's house to young Marjorie, who had studied them with an inscrutable face. She finally said, "It looks very grand—but a little formidable. What in Heaven's name do you and your family do in that gigantic place?"

Rory said, "When Ma's there it doesn't seem so 'gigantic.' She's everywhere."

"It seems bigger than the 'cottages' in Newport," said Marjorie. "And I always thought they were—vast." She did not add, "And somewhat tasteless."

Maggie was tiny. Her head scarcely reached to Rory's shoulder, and she had a dainty little figure, delightfully doll-like. She was dark and vivacious and gay, with great black eyes almost constantly full of laughter, long black lashes and thick black brows, and black hair from which glistening ringlets were always escaping and framing her olive-tinted small and pointed face. She dressed exquisitely but demurely, and she could dance as expertly as Rory and played tennis almost as competently as did Rory, himself. She had a dark crimson mouth, with very white little teeth, and she also had a most endearing if a tenderly mocking smile. She was quite the belle of Boston, and she was nineteen years old, and intelligent and sprightly and extremely witty as well as kind. She had fallen in love with Rory Armagh the moment she had met him, and as she had an iron will under all that gay and effervescent exterior she had decided, within five minutes, that she would marry him. It took Rory a month to decide that for himself.

Mr. Albert Chisholm had felt contempt for Rory on the very first meeting, for he knew all about Joseph Armagh. He was an upright man because he had never been tempted to be anything else, and had never known poverty or anxiety. To Mr. Chisholm, Rory was not only an undesirable suitor for his only daughter because of his, Rory's, father and his "nefarious enterprises and engagements in Despicable Politics," but because of Rory, himself. He thought Rory too "light-minded," too "undependable," too careless, too brash. But then, he would say to his daughter with disdain, he was Irish and everyone knew what the Irish "were." No man of propriety or position had anything to do with them, or admitted them to his house. They were born without conscience or compunction or morals or firmness of character. They "pushed" themselves, even worse than did the Jews, and tried to invade decent society which had a Duty to morality and to the country.

"Yet, Daddy, your trusted secretary is a Jew," said Marjorie.

"My dear girl, Bernard is *entirely* different from the average Jew! Surely you must have seen that for yourself. But this young Armagh—he is typical of the Irish. No, he must never enter this house again. I forbid you to see him."

Naturally, Marjorie saw Rory at least twice and sometimes even three times a week. They were now at the stage where they were seriously discussing an elopement.

"You think your Pa is against us," said Rory. "But it would be nothing compared to what my own Pa would say, my sweetheart. He'd look once at your Pa, with his white sideburns and mustache and his air of smelling something foul all the time, and he'd laugh at him. Now, Pa has no religion, but let someone say anything about the 'Papists' and he'll have that man's lights and livers. And Pa mistrusts men like your father. He calls them hypocrites and names I wouldn't repeat to your darling innocent ears—he's met too many of them in his lifetime. And demolished too many of them. Not out of resentment for the superior way they've acted towards him, but just because he knew what they were and despised them."

Marjorie had a temper, and loyalty. She flared up and bridled and her pretty dark face flushed. "Sir, just *what* is my Daddy?"

"Oh, come on, Maggie. I'm not trying to offend you. I'm just saying what my Pa would think of yours. Pa eats men like your progenitor alive, for breakfast. Pa's no easy boy. He's got a back stiffer than your father's. In fact, your Pa is a willow branch compared to Pa. Besides, Pa wants me to marry an heiress, rich in her own right, someone whose father is powerful internationally, like himself, who is known, to quote him."

"Somebody flamboyant and vulgar!" cried young Marjorie.

"Well, not exactly," said Rory, admiring the fire in the big black eyes. "A lady, too. Not a Back Bay girl of a family that doesn't have much influence in Washington, for instance. And my Pa would think your father's money mere wooden nickels."

"Indeed!" exclaimed Marjorie, her little rounded breast heaving. "Perhaps you had better, sir, start searching for that American princess of yours and leave this insignificant Bostonian chit alone!"

"I happen to love 'this insignificant Bostonian chit,'" said Rory, and took her in his long strong arms and kissed her soundly, and she became weak and trembling. "Ah, love," said Rory, "what does it matter what they think?"

She nestled her head against his shoulder, and clung to him, her ringlets brushing his mouth. But she was also practical. "You have your law school to go through," she said, in a shaking voice. "Years! I'll be old, old, and so will you."

"We'll elope, quietly, to some other state, and no one will know, and when I've been graduated we'll tell them all to go to hell."

"But we wouldn't be able to—to—" and Marjorie blushed furiously and dropped her eyes.

"Sleep together?" said Rory kindly, kissing her again. "Of course we will! I have it all figured out. I will get a small apartment in Cambridge and we can meet there without anyone knowing. And you needn't worry about any— consequences. I know how to protect you." His mouth parted hers and sought, and she thought she would faint. She pulled her lips from his.

Marjorie was very red now. But she pressed her head against the region where she imagined his heart to be and murmured, "Ah, Rory, Rory." Her little body was wincing with inexplicable thrills, and she was at once ashamed and hungry.

Tonight they had decided to take Aunt Emma into their confidence. If she refused to be an accomplice she would at least not mention anything to her brother. She adored young Maggie, and was very fond of Rory, and she was always reminding them to be "prudent." She thought this clandestine romance very exciting, for she had had none in her own life, and she was by nature romantic. She was always reading "French" novels, which her brother found reprehensible, and which she was always trying to hide from him. She was as small as Marjorie, but very fat and rosy and sweet of face, and somewhat untidy and overelaborate in dress, and she could never seem to arrange her brown-gray hair neatly. It was always spilling down her neck and about her ears, and she was always thrusting hairpins into it, and laughing. There had never been any suitor in her years as a girl and a young woman—she was not fifty—but she frequently hinted at some tragic love affair, and would sigh over it with moist eyes, and murmur something about "Papa," and Marjorie would hug and kiss and console her. She feared her brother, Albert, and could not understand why Marjorie did not fear him, too. Marjorie feared nobody and nothing, except at times she feared losing Rory. She found his duality of nature infinitely fascinating, but she also mistrusted it, for a new Rory was always being presented to her and she had her family's firmness of disposition and constancy, except when she was angry, which was quite often. Once she had roundly shouted at her father, "We need new blood in this effete family!" "But not Irish blood," her father had replied. He never let her know it but Marjorie could daunt him, as could her dearly loved dead mother, and when Marjorie's eyes flashed like this and her face was fiery, he became weak with longing and grief. Marjorie did not guess, until much later, that her father would forgive her anything.

After kissing Rory with enthusiasm Marjorie led him into the "back room," as Aunt Emma called it, though it was a small sitting room for the family. No one, of course, ever used the dark chill double parlors except when guests were present. Marjorie's aunt was knitting placidly, an endless pile of gray wool which was never completed. She looked at Rory and her face became rosy and pretty and she accepted his kiss like a loving mother and told him, as always, that he was "the handsomest young spark I have ever seen." He had brought her a bouquet of daffodils and narcissi—none of which would grow in Albert's wet dank garden—and had delicately refrained from bringing Marjorie the same. This was a politician's deft gesture, and Marjorie grinned wickedly. "Oh, my dear," said Aunt Emma, sniffing the bouquet and then lifting damp eyes to Rory. "How did you know they are my favorites, the bright blossoms of spring?"

If Rory winced at her old-fashioned and melodramatic expression he did not show it. He said, with gallantry, "Why, dear Aunt Emma, they remind me of you." She looked at him coquettishly, and almost cried, and gave them to Marjorie to put into a vase for her. The girl returned with them and put them on a round table covered with a dark red velvet cloth and immediately the rich but drab room took on radiance and Miss Chisholm stared at them, overcome with sentimentality. "Ah me," she sighed. "They remind me of—" She touched her eyes with her handkerchief. She always wore black silk, summer and winter, as if in constant mourning. Marjorie squeezed her hand and winked at Rory.

He leaned towards the lady, all earnestness, gravity and boyish sincerity. The light blue eyes were the eyes of a very young boy and his somewhat fleshy and highly colored face was very serious. This caught Aunt Emma's attention immediately. She had never seen him look so beguiling, so trustful, so pleading.

"You know, Aunt Emma," he said, "that Maggie and I love each other, don't you?"

"Indeed, my dear, I do know." Miss Chisholm sighed again, deeply, reverberatingly. It was the sort of romantic tragedy on which she doted. She thought her niece and Rory another Juliet and Romeo.

"But," she added, her kind voice trembling, "Albert will never permit you to marry."

"However," said Rory, watching her, and now taking her short fat hand, "we do intend to marry. Almost immediately. We are going to elope."

"Oh, oh!" cried Miss Chisholm, seeing Romeo and Juliet marrying surreptitiously in some dark, candlelighted cave with only monks for witnesses, "Albert will simply never countenance that!"

Rory gave Marjorie a look and she bit her lip. "Countenance that or not, that is what we are going to do, Aunt Emma." He patted her hand. Reluctantly, she removed it. Her eyes were full of tears. "But Rory, I have heard from Marjorie, herself, that your own father would be so opposed, too!"

"There comes a time when children must think for themselves—if they love each other," said Rory. "For what is more than love?"

As this was Miss Chisholm's own sentiment, she hesitated and for an instant girlish delight shone on her face. But she was not a New Englander for nothing. She said, "But Marjorie will have no money until she is twenty-one, and even then she will not get it if she insists on marrying someone to whom her father objects. Then she will have to wait until she is thirty."

"I know," said Rory. As he had never known poverty he said, "We don't mind being poor, Aunt Emma, for a little while, until I am graduated from law school—"

"Three years," said Miss Chisholm, the New Englander dominant in her now. "And Rory, do you have anything but your allowance from your father?"

Rory had always thought his father unduly penurious and suspicious of students' profligacy, and so his allowance was only fifty dollars a month. "It's enough for skylarking," Joseph had said.

"I have an allowance of thirty dollars a month, just for pin money," said Marjorie. She looked at Rory with a look he could not fully interpret. "Aunt Emma, we don't intend to tell anyone, but you. I will go on living here at home, and Rory—"

Miss Chisholm was excessively shocked. She looked from Marjorie to Rory, and then back to Rory again. Her face was quite white. "But, my dears! You intend to *deceive* your poor parents, not tell them—"

"What else can we do?" asked Marjorie now, blinking her eyes at her aunt. "We don't like it, but we have no choice." Her aunt had fallen back in her chair horrified.

"So—so deceiving, my dear children! So disrespectful! So disobedient! It would be best to tell them, keep your consciences in good order, live together openly in the sight of God and man—"

"On eighty dollars a month?" asked Rory. "We might not even have that, if we tell the old gentlemen. We might be cut off with nothing, and I wouldn't put it past my Pa to haul me out of law school, either, and set me to work at slave labor, for nothing, in one of his damned offices. As a lesson. Then Maggie and I would be parted"—he paused and looked at Miss Chisholm, weighing her—"for eternity."

Miss Chisholm quivered inwardly, shuddered deliciously, closed her eyes and let her head fall back in grief. "Like myself," she whispered.

"O God," Marjorie's naughty mouth formed the words soundlessly.

"So," said Rory, "we can only necessarily—deceive our Pas until I am graduated from law school. Then we can be bold, and tell all the world."

Miss Chisholm recovered and became Bostonian again. "Still," she said, opening her eyes and they were a little sharp now, "your father, Rory, might never forgive you, and then you'd have to wait until Marjorie is thirty for her money. Your father is a very rich man, Rory. A prudent young man thinks of—inheritances. He does not lightly reject them." Romeo and Juliet wistfully faded into limbo. "I do love you, Rory, but I'd feel very sad if Marjorie married a penniless—"

"I'd inherit from my mother," said Rory, speaking with outward assurance but with no assurance within. He knew how besotted his mother was. She would do as Joseph told her, not out of fear for him but only to please him.

"She is very rich, Rory, in her own right?"

"Rolling in it," said Rory. "She inherited gobs from her mother, and her father. She owns our—mansion—in Green Hills, in Pennsylvania. You must have seen photographs of it. It frequently appears in the newspapers when Mama gives a soiree or something, for Personages. Presidents have been our guests. My grandfather was a senator, you know, and then Governor of Pennsylvania for several terms." He knew his Miss Chisholms.

"Yes, yes, dear, I know. And you are your Mama's favorite child?"

"Absolutely," said Rory, with never a droop of his eyelids. "Denies me nothing."

"Then," said Miss Chisholm, "you must tell your Mama at once. No doubt she will come to your rescue." She spoke briskly and smiled with happiness.

The sharpness of the remark caught Rory without an immediate response. Then he sighed, dropped his head, looked mournful. "Mama," he said, "is absolutely terrified of my father. She is in very poor health. An annoyed word from him would crush her, perhaps destroy her." He saw his mother's short obese body and engorged complexion and snapping eyes, and visualized her as a drooping flower. It almost made him laugh out loud. "But she has told me secretly of her will. I—I receive—though I pray that her health will improve and that God will spare her for many years to her devoted family—three-quarters of her fortune.

Some"—and now Rory let his wide blue eyes wander to a musing distance—"fifteen million dollars."

"Fifteen million dollars," whispered Miss Chisholm. She calculated interest. "It is invested, secure?"

"Good as gold," said Rory. He resolutely would not look at Marjorie and the black mischief in her eyes. "Mama doesn't believe in using even the interest on interest, not to speak of capital, which is sacred."

"She is in poor health, you say?" said Miss Chisholm in a sad voice.

"Very poor. Heart, I believe."

"You damned liar," mouthed Marjorie at Rory, for she had finally cornered his eye.

"But if she discovers you deceived her—three years from now?"

Rory gave a sigh that was almost a dry sob. "I doubt she will ever know," he said in the politician's rich and unctuous voice. He partly covered his eyes with his hand. "The doctors give us little hope. For her long survival."

Miss Chisholm moistened her lips and considered, though her face was full of maternal sympathy for the rascally young man. Fifteen million dollars, at four percent, in a short time—Possibly more, with the investments. Mr. Chisholm's fortune was much less than that, much less. And dear Rory was so intelligent. Any law firm would be overjoyed to have him grace its staff. One had only to be discreet— How unfortunate that he was Irish, and a Papist! Were he not dear Albert would approve the match instantly. He would strut like a peacock, and boast in his genteel way.

Rory's face was still partly hidden by his hand and Miss Chisholm wanted to comfort him. She did touch his strong broad knee with the tips of her fingers, gently. How sad to know one's dear Mama was on the edge of her grave and none could save her! Fifteen million dollars. The lamplight made the scoundrel's head glow in red-gold. Marjorie sat primly in her chair, her eyes downcast, but the dimples rioting in her cheeks.

"What can I do for you dear children?" asked Miss Chisholm. (Albert, later, would "come around." Fifteen million dollars, with interest at four percent, was not to be despised.)

Marjorie said, "We are going to elope, perhaps day after

tomorrow, dearest Aunt Emma. Then we are going—" She paused. It would be indelicate to mention that Rory had already rented three furnished rooms in Cambridge. "We will be—away, for perhaps three days. It is Rory's spring vacation. Then he must visit his parents, of course. I should like you, dearest Aunt, to tell Papa that I am visiting Annabelle Towers, in Philadelphia."

"Can't you tell him yourself, my cherub?"

"I intend to. But you could mention to Papa that I received an invitation this morning, and then later I will speak to him."

"But Marjorie, that would be a fib!"

Miss Chisholm was shocked, she who was always equivocating, in fear, before her redoubtable brother. Marjorie sighed, as if dejected. "What else can we do?" she murmured. "We love each other."

"I see," said Miss Chisholm, already formulating the "fib" in her mind. "And then you will return home, Marjorie, and Rory will go to his parents. You will live apart— oh my dear children!—for three long years! How will you bear it, married in the sight of God but not in the sight of men!"

Then she thought again of the fifteen million dollars and the poor Mama in a dying condition, poor sweet lady. It might be only a few short months.

"We will bear it," said Rory, with a very noble expression, which constituents would later learn to trust and admire. "After all, everything can be borne for Love. Didn't St. Paul say it was the greatest of all, more than faith and hope?"

This appeal to Miss Chisholm's favorite saint quite undid her. She put her handkerchief to her eyes and cried a little. Never once did it occur to her that these plotters would hold any assignation before it was safe to do so. They would be married, but they would live in chastity, pure and untouched, bearing all things for love's sake, trusting in their Heavenly Father—and in fifteen million dollars, something intractable remarked in Miss Chisholm's really pragmatic mind.

She said with sorrow, "I did so plan, all Marjorie's life, on a beautiful wedding, in the church in which she was baptised. Rory, you are a Roman—forgive me, dear, I did not intend to offend you—but will your Church approve? I understand that—"

Rory said, "We will find a minister. Aunt Emma, what are trappings where Love is concerned?"

But Miss Chisholm was about to suggest that the young lovers wait until poor dear Mama—But ah, that would be most uncouth and cruel. She said, "You don't mind being married by a Protestant minister, Rory?"

Rory almost said, "I'd be happy to be married before Satan, if it was to Maggie," but he rather had the thought that this would be too much for Miss Chisholm, who had weakened. He said, with a grand gesture, "Is not even a minister a Man of God? Who can deny that?"

Miss Chisholm was not quite certain that she liked the "even," but did not comment. "But I will not see my dearest niece married!"

"I will bring you my bouquet," said Marjorie, kissing her.

They were married before a Presbyterian minister two days later, in Connecticut, in a small obscure village where the name of Armagh meant nothing, but the fifty dollars Rory gave the astounded minister quite shook the threadbare poor old man and made tears come into his eyes. This young couple was dressed so modestly and plainly. It was obvious this was a great sacrifice, and he said so to Rory, with a timid smile.

"Think nothing of it," said Rory, and then when Marjorie pinched his arm warningly he added, "It is the happiest occasion of my life, and I have been saving my money for a long time for it."

They returned to Cambridge discreetly and hid themselves in the dingy three rooms Rory had rented for twenty dollars a month. They had few if any amenities, but they were ecstatic. Then Marjorie said, "Are we really married, Rory? I mean, in the eyes of your Church?"

Rory hesitated for but an instant, then he said, "Married? Of course we are married! Don't be an idiot, Maggie. Here, let me unbutton your dress. How beautiful your little shoulders are—and what is this I see? Now, now, aren't we married?"

Never again was Rory to know such happiness as he knew in those three rooms in the poor section of Cambridge. He was to remember that to the day he died, and his last conscious thought was, "Maggie, O dear little Maggie! My God, my darling Maggie!"

Chapter 37

"Whatever I engage in," Mr. Carnegie had once told Joseph, "I must push inordinately." He had smiled at the younger man. "We are Celts together, are we not? We understand each other. The Anglo-Saxons are no match for us."

Joseph had laughed his rough and grating laugh. "Do you remember, sir, what Samuel Pepys said in his Diary of 1661: 'But, good God! What an age is this and what a world is this! That a man cannot live without playing the knave, and dissimulation.'"

Mr. Carnegie had tilted his cigar and had studied Joseph. "Um. Well, Joseph, did we make this world? We have to come to terms with it, and I, my lad, have no quarrel with it. I met it fairly on the field, and I won. Or, aren't you satisfied that you won, too?"

Joseph said, "I have no quarrel with the world, either. I played on its fields and I won, more or less fairly."

"There is one thing," said Mr. Carnegie, "if a mon plays fairly he will niver win. That is the way of the world, my bairn."

He thought, Here is a man, a fanatic, who once had a stern goal in life, but has now forgotten it. But fanaticism is its own motive power, and so he will continue. Is that not true of us all? Who can tell what gods, or what devils, drive us?

He took a liking to Joseph out of his Celtish soul. He had built his steel plant on the Monongahela River after the enormous Bessemer mills of England. He said to Joseph, "This may seem to you a small beginning in America, laddie, but I advise you to invest in it." So Joseph had invested. By 1890 his investment had increased fiftyfold. By 1895 his wealth received respect from the most powerful in

Europe and in America, even though before he had been rich by general standards. Mr. Carnegie had said that the vast gaining of money was "the worst species of idolatry," with hardly a twinkle of his icy blue eyes. He stayed in his castle in Scotland, where Joseph visited him from time to time, and pretended a carelessness concerning his steel empire in America which he ruled from afar. The little Scotsman had a genius for money, and Joseph had already learned that such a genius is not acquired but is inbred. "There's many a mon," said Mr. Carnegie to Joseph, "who works all his life, with intelligence and industry, and acquires niver a sovereign, and other men, with a flick of a wrist get everything. Now, I'm a wee Presbyterian, and so I believe in predestination. A mon's a fool or a wise man by the willing of the Almighty, and we should not quarrel. Let us thank Him that He made us clever."

"By dint of hard work," said Joseph, who knew Mr. Carnegie's history.

"Ah, and that we did, too, and nae doot about it," said Mr. Carnegie. "I have niver been one to underrate hard work. But ye must hae a mind for it, too, laddie."

He thought to himself, And a bitterness besides, and do I not have it, too? Without bitterness a man canna succeed. "I am nae optimist," he said, with caution, when he had advised Joseph about investments. "I just judge. Many's the optimist who niver had fifty dollars, and niver will, because they are optimists. Pessimism hae saved mony a mon from bankruptcy. By the way, laddie, I dinna care for your friends."

"They care for you," said Joseph, smiling. "They think you a mighty man."

"Now, is that not strange? I am no assassin."

Joseph had not replied to that, for he knew too much. But he was to remember that conversation in desperate later times in his life. "A mon," said Mr. Carnegie, "can be hanged for a little murder, but for big murders he will receive applause." He winked at Joseph. "Or, he will be famous. At the least he will be exonerated. His masters will niver be known. They are too braw for that."

"You are speaking of a coup d'état," said Joseph.

"All political murders are coups d'état," said Mr. Carnegie, and had smiled a little at Joseph's somber expression. "There was niver a king or an emperor or a president murdered by a little caprice or temper of a little man, and that ye know, laddie."

And there are other murders, thought Joseph.

He had a strange dream. He lay in a warm bed in his discreet hotel with Elizabeth Hennessey, and was surfeited with peace and contentment. He slept dreamlessly for a while. Then he found himself in a green-blue twilight in a place he did not know, nor did it seem to be furnished or have any background. He saw Senator Enfield Bassett, a man of honor and sadness, and his lustrous black eyes were filled with sorrow as he looked at Joseph.

"I would, if I could," he said, "withdraw the curse I laid upon you, but it is not possible. When the wronged curse, or the innocent die, it falls upon the guilty living and no one can remove it. May God have mercy upon you, for I am prohibited from mercy."

Elizabeth started awake, disturbed by Joseph's choking cry, and woke him in turn. The hot dawn of a summer morning had painted gold on the dusty windows of the bedroom. Joseph sat up abruptly, sweating and livid, and stared at Elizabeth as if he did not know her or know where he was. Even his eyelids were matted and his hair, risen like a mane, framed his gaunt face in mingled faded russet and white streaks. "My dearest, what is it?" Elizabeth exclaimed, alarmed, and took his arm. Her shoulders and breasts were like sunstruck marble in the early light and her pale hair streamed about her.

"Nothing. Nothing. It was only a dream," he muttered, and lay down again. But she saw that he was staring fixedly at the ceiling, and remembering. "Only a nightmare," he added. "About someone—who has been dead a long time. I don't know why I should dream about him; I haven't thought of him for years." He tried to smile at her fear-filled eyes and anxious expression. "Nothing at all." But he looked again at the ceiling with that fixed look.

She lay down beside him, quietly, his wet hand in hers. She could feel the bounding of his pulse and the tremor of his fingers. "I haven't thought of him for years," Joseph repeated. He tried to laugh. "I never harmed him, or at least I wouldn't have harmed him. I destroyed all evidence against him."

"But why, then, should you be upset?"

Joseph sat up again and wiped his forehead with the

edge of the sheet. He said, "He wrote me a note. He said he had laid a curse upon me—and mine. I haven't even thought of that for fourteen years, or more. I'm not 'upset,' dear. I'm not superstitious." He paused, patted her shoulder. "It was a nightmare. I thought he came to me and said he would withdraw his 'curse,' but couldn't. That was all. A stupid dream."

The room was already hot, the increasing light striking through the heavy lace curtains, but Elizabeth felt cold. She said, "It was so long ago and nothing has happened to you—or yours—has it? There is no accounting for dreams." She rang the bell for coffee and rolls and smiled at Joseph, then rose and put on her white peignoir, throwing back her damp hair. "I am not superstitious, either," she said.

She picked up a gold-backed brush from the dressing table and began to smooth her hair. Her smiling eyes met Joseph's in the mirror. She saw that he did not return her smile and that he was abstracted. "He's dead, you say," she said. "What did he die of?"

"He killed himself."

Elizabeth's hand stopped and her fingers felt cold again. She put down the brush. Joseph said, as if speaking to himself, "A man like that has no business in politics. If he can't stand the bells and the soot he should stay off the trains."

"You mean," said Elizabeth, "that politics are no place for an honest man."

"Did I say he was honest?" asked Joseph, vexed with himself that he had even mentioned Senator Bassett. He put on his dressing gown, and his face was gloomy. "I think our coffee and rolls have arrived. I'll open the door."

They did not speak of this again, but Elizabeth was never to forget that hot morning in New York. Two hours later Joseph went to Boston to see his son, Rory.

"Now," he said, "I am all for hard work and ambition, and that you have, boyo. But why elect to attend summer classes and rush through law school like a fire engine?"

Rory's amiable blue eyes had a little secrecy about them. But then he made himself look frankly at his father as they sat together in his humid room. Joseph was not deceived. "Why should I waste three years?" asked Rory. "I can do it in two. Isn't life for living? If I want to start to live a little sooner, what's wrong with that, Pa?"

"I thought you were going to spend the summer on Long

Island with those friends of yours, sailing and boating and what not, as you've been doing the past two years. They're important to cultivate, too."

"I'd rather go on," said Rory.

"Giving up all those sports you're mad about? Come on, Rory, out with it."

"I'm going on twenty-two," said the young man. "I can't see myself in school until I am twenty-five or so. I told you, Pa: I want to start living as soon as possible."

"And you think being one of my stable of lawyers will be 'living'?"

Rory's eyes shifted. "If you want me, Pa."

Joseph frowned. "You're being evasive. I never had time to live. I don't want that to happen to you." He was astonished at his own words. He looked at the signet ring on his finger which Elizabeth had given him, but he was not thinking of his mistress. "I would be the last to advise you to trifle with time and waste it, for I know how valuable it is. But on the way I'd like to know that you have been——"

"Enjoying myself?" Rory was deeply touched. He drew his chair closer to his father's, and they smiled at each other. "Pa, you've made life easy for your family. Don't think we are ungrateful, Ann Marie and me, and even that black bear of a Kevin. Black Irish. You deserve having us off your hands as soon as possible." He thought of his sister, and hesitated. Joseph said quickly, "Well, what is it? Don't try to hide things from me, Rory. I always find out, you know. You've tried it in the past."

"Ann Marie," said Rory. He stood up and put his big hands in his pockets and started to walk up and down the room, not slouching, but with a fast loping stride that was at once strong and graceful.

"The hell," said Joseph. "What about Ann Marie?" He loved his sons dearly, and in particular Rory, but Ann Marie was his darling. "She's been looking languid lately and I've thought about it, but her mother says she is well and just moons about. Is there something wrong?"

Rory stood at the window and looked out. Well, he had promised Courtney and now if ever was the time, seeing Pa was in a soft mood, very rare with him. He said, "She wants to get married."

"What's wrong with that?" asked Joseph. "Does her mother know? Who's the man? Somebody impossible, perhaps?" He sat up in his chair.

"Somebody I'd consider very eligible," said Rory. He could feel the heat and color in his fresh face, and he waited for it to subside for he would rather have been drawn and quartered than to let his father know that he knew about him and Elizabeth.

"One of your Harvard jackanapes with no money, and no family? Come on, Rory, speak up."

"He has money, and comes of a good family," said Rory, and had to smile. Now he turned from the window. "Perhaps you wouldn't think so, yourself, but I do." He looked at his father and he tensed. "It's Courtney. Courtney Hennessey. Our adopted uncle," and he laughed a little.

He was prepared for his father to frown, to consider, perhaps even to object for a moment or two, for men really did not want their daughters to marry. But he was not prepared for the fierce change on Joseph's face, and he could not read it, and was aghast. Did the old man consider that his mistress' son was no match for Ann Marie? Yet, he had always shown Courtney an offhand kindness and even some distant consideration and affection.

Then Joseph said in so soft a voice—though his eyes were appalling—that Rory could hardly hear him. "You are out of your mind! Courtney Hennessey."

They stared across the room at each other, and Joseph's face was a pallid shine in the shadow. There was a blue spark jumping in his deep-set eyes. He looked at Rory with an air of rigid shock.

O God, thought Rory. What's the matter with him? What's wrong with Courtney? He said, "Pa, what's wrong with Courtney? I know that—I know that Ma hates his mother and him, and I don't know why, but then Ma hates practically everybody. You wouldn't let her objections stand in the way of Ann Marie and Courtney, would you? Ann Marie's no kid any longer, Pa. She has a right to her life."

But Joseph hardly heard him. He began to speak, then gasped. He thought of Elizabeth. It came to him with stunning power that Rory, of course, believed the general story that Courtney was the son of a deceased military hero, and not, in fact, his real uncle. What in God's Name can I say? thought the stricken man. Elizabeth. Why hasn't the truth been told long before this? Ann Marie, my child, my little girl. Bernadette. I know her. This will be a fine rich and vindictive joke to her, a final triumph over Elizabeth. He began to speak again and was forced to cough. "Has—anyone told your mother yet?"

At least he's not raging, as he can! thought Rory, a little encouraged. He came back to his chair and regarded his father seriously, and then was more alarmed as he saw the jolting shock was increasing on Joseph's face. "No, Pa. *She doesn't know*—yet. Courtney has been pressing her to tell Ma, but she's afraid. Ann Marie's such a mouse. We call girls like her 'mice,' here in Harvard. You know. Soft and gentle and retiring, with nothing much to say for themselves, and always avoiding unpleasantnesses, and you know how unpleasant Ma can be."

But Joseph merely stared at him blindly, desperately looking for a way out of this dilemma, a way that would be no shame to Elizabeth and no cruelty to Ann Marie. But, what was the way but the truth?

Then Joseph cursed aloud, and Rory, who thought that he knew every obscenity and invective known to the English-speaking world learned that there were others, also. He had heard his father swear before, yet never had he heard him use such foul words, and with such cold passion too. Rory was very perceptive. He knew that his father was cursing not with rage but with a sort of helpless despair and pain.

Joseph finally stopped that rough hoarse stream of vilenesses, and became fully aware of Rory again. He said, "I can only say this: It is impossible. There is an—impediment. Go to any priest and ask him."

"Courtney did," said Rory. "The priest had to look it up. He had his doubts for a while, but then he said that as Courtney was no in-law, really, but only the adopted son of my grandfather, the real son of a stranger—" Rory stopped, for his father even in his fixed silence was more formidable than the young man had ever seen him. Something took Rory by the throat.

"I said," Joseph repeated, "that there is an impediment."

"But what? If there is, Ann Marie and Courtney ought to know. If some Church authorities object—well, there are always other resources, and we aren't all that pious, either, are we?" He thought of Maggie, waiting for him in those three wonderful shabby rooms.

Joseph stood up. He was only in his early fifties but all at once, to Rory, he appeared old, even broken, and weakened, and this alarmed the young man more than ever. A raging Joseph was to be greatly feared, but he could be faced, as Rory had discovered before, and he could even be reasonable when his cold rage subsided. At least, sometimes. But this man was not raging. He was turning now and Rory saw his face, almost pleading and completely devastated.

"I should have been told before," he said, and Rory knew that he was speaking only to himself. "I might have stopped it in the beginning." He looked at Rory with an expression in his eyes which Rory had never seen. "Believe me, Rory, there is truly an impediment. I can't tell you, but there is. You must tell Courtney—"

"What?" said Rory. "What shall I tell Courtney—and Ann Marie?"

When Joseph did not immediately reply Rory went on, "I promised Courtney I would try for him. I promised to find out—if there was something. But I can't go to him with a foolish vagueness. I have to have facts—or something."

Joseph still did not speak. Then Rory's mind began to whirl. How long had Pa known "Aunt" Elizabeth? How long had the liaison been in existence? Before he married his, Rory's, mother? No. He would have married Elizabeth. Courtney was no brother, thank God. But, what was he? Then Rory's thoughts came to a black dead halt and he and his father looked at each other without words.

Joseph saw his son's widening shocked eyes. He nodded, and turned away. Rory stood up and said quietly, "My God. So that's it. All that coverup, all those years. Why?"

"Don't be a fool," said Joseph. "There were too many to consider. Mrs. Hennessey. Courtney, himself. Your grandfather's—position. But your mother and I—we always knew. Women, before you were born, were not automatically absolved even when they married the man— It may be different in these days. It wasn't, then. Mrs. Hennessey was not a strumpet, but she would have been branded so, marriage later or not. She had been seduced and deceived by a scoundrel, God damn his soul."

Rory went and stood beside his father. He had the queerest desire to console Joseph, though why he should console him he did not know. Certainly Courtney and Ann Marie were the miserable ones, the wronged ones, and not Joseph Armagh.

"What in hell am I going to tell Courtney?" Rory said in a wretched voice. He added, "I need a drink." He went to a fine walnut cabinet and brought out a bottle of whiskey which bore the seal of The Armagh Enterprises, and he twisted the cork with a desperate viciousness as if he were wringing someone's neck. He knew that Joseph did not approve of "young men in college" having whiskey in their rooms and "drinking themselves blind on the poteen," and he, Rory, had heretofore been discreet. He looked over his shoulder at Joseph and said, "I think you need one too, Pa."

"That I do," said Joseph, and now his old almost obliterated brogue came back in his voice. "Several, I am thinking." He almost fell into his chair. Rory put a fine engraved glass into his hand, then stood before his father. They both drank deeply, as if dying of thirst. Rory looked down into the glass. He said, "There were the old Pharoahs—they married their sisters. It went on for centuries, dynasty after dynasty. It was accepted. It was even the law. Courtney—he's only half an uncle," and Rory tried for a small and dismal laugh. "He needn't know. Ann Marie needn't know. There aren't any inherited diseases in the family that I heard of. Pa, I don't find the idea repulsive. No one would ever know."

"You've forgotten your mother," said Joseph. "She knows. She's denied Courtney's blood tie often to me, because she hates Elizabeth and would have her a trollop if she could. But—she knows well enough. And, she'd tell Ann Marie at once, with pleasure, to hurt Elizabeth. And Courtney. And me."

"I don't think—" Rory began, and then actually blushed and seeing this Joseph was faintly and ironically amused. He thought of the day he had struck Rory, only a few years ago, and he knew now, with a sudden enlightenment, that Rory had not wanted to "shame" his father by letting him know that he knew of him and Elizabeth, and that others knew, also. He reached out and awkwardly touched his son's hanging hand, then withdrew it in embarrassment. He was a stranger to such gestures.

"How she found out I don't know," said Joseph. "But she did. I can see it in her face when she speaks of Elizabeth. She would kill her if she dared. It doesn't concern me. Your mother knows that I married her, not for money, not after seduction, but for a reason I prefer to keep to myself. It happened a long time ago. I am entirely indifferent to what your mother wants, and I was always indifferent to her. I never deceived her about my feelings, so I am not guilty of anything but marrying her. Perhaps I should not have done so. But I did. I don't regret it now. I have my children."

"Pa," Rory began. Then he saw that his father was merely being factual and not sentimental. Joseph continued. "It was to protect Elizabeth that I took as many precautions as I could, and not to protect your mother. Perhaps I should feel sorry for your mother, and sometimes I think I do, but that is of no importance either. The important thing is the impediment which stands in the way of Courtney and Ann Marie. It is not only an impediment, it is highly illegal, and punishable by law, and be sure your mother would see to that! You and your Pharaohs. I can see that you are a born lawyer."

But Rory did not smile. Not asking, he refilled their glasses and they drank again. Even little Marjorie was temporarily forgotten in this extremity. "What shall I tell Courtney?" Rory asked, wincing inside.

"Suppose his mother could be persuaded to tell him the truth? I'd rather he wouldn't tell Ann Marie though."

"He'd hate his mother, and his father. His father! My grandfather! Isn't that the damnedest thing?"

"I doubt he'd hate his mother," but Joseph thought, with a sick wrench, of Elizabeth, and the deep love between her and her son. "Perhaps she can explain it so that he will understand. Don't you tell him, though, for God's sake. The fewer people he thinks know about this the better he will eventually feel."

"Courtney's already told her about Ann Marie, and wanting to marry her," said Rory. Joseph looked up, freshly shocked. "And Aunt Elizabeth, he said, got damned agitated and became sick, and thin, and told him it was 'impossible.' She wouldn't talk about it any longer to him."

So, that is what has been hurting my love, thought Joseph.

"I'll suggest to Elizabeth that she tell Courtney," said Joseph. "You had better tell him to visit her in a few days. Give me a week. I hear he is staying the summer with you at law school. I never thought he'd been an extraordinary lawyer, but I suppose you two can't be separated."

For the first time Rory showed bitterness. "It seems there

is something more between Courtney and me than mere 'friendship,' " he said. "Well, nothing can be changed now. It's a terrible mess." He suddenly remembered Marjorie and swore under his breath. "I have to write a note to somebody, and send it, if you'll excuse me. I'm breaking an engagement. I want to be with you for a little longer, Pa. Let's go out to dinner together."

Joseph had frequently suggested dinner with his son in the past but sometimes Rory had not been very enthusiastic, and never had he invited his father before. Joseph looked at his son again and Rory returned the look, then all at once they simultaneously extended their hands to each other and shook them.

"And for an encore, let us go hear your Uncle Sean on his last recital of the season," said Joseph. "I haven't seen him since he returned from Europe two months ago. Why doesn't he get married, or something?"

But Rory knew, if Joseph did not, and Rory went to write his note to Marjorie. His young mind was full of misery.

Chapter 38

Courtney Hennessey arrived home in Green Hills very early in the morning, after his mother had written him briefly that she had *something of grave importance to impart to you, my dear*. It was not like his mother to use stilted language to him, nor to be so completely reticent, as if she feared eavesdroppers or was afraid to put the matter on paper, or, perhaps, had not the courage to write what must be said. There had always been complete confidence between mother and son, for they were much alike and not only in appearance, and trusted each other as they had never trusted anyone else. So Courtney, as he swung down from the train at half-past six of a warm July morning at the depot in Winfield, and looked about him for a family carriage, was more disturbed than his tranquil expression showed. It could not be money, he thought. His mother was a rich woman, and Uncle Joseph managed her affairs. (Courtney, unlike the prescient and inquisitive Rory, had no idea of the liaison between his mother and Joseph.) It might be her health, and alarm sharpened in Courtney as he recalled her somewhat frail appearance and sudden silences during his last spring holiday.

The carriage was waiting for him, and a coachman, yawning, in the sweet bright light of the July morning. Even though it was very early passengers were already waiting for the trains to Pittsburgh and Philadelphia and New York, yawning also, and standing over their luggage. The coachman helped Courtney with his bags, and the young man then sat in the open carriage and was driven from the depot to Green Hills. He liked homecoming. He liked the warm open country and the quiet roads and the thick green trees and the passing over covered bridges and the shine of green water reflecting back the green shadows above them. He liked the glimpses of farmhouses, once the

town was behind, the white fences, the red barns, the cattle
going into the fields, the smoke lifting from tight chimneys,
the barking of farm dogs and the clucking of fowl. He
liked to hear the hailing between farmer and farmer, to see
furrows plowed with the golden sun, the scent of earth and
hedgerow and growing corn, the rows of green cabbages,
the rising of yellow wheat, and, above all, hear the soft silence only enhanced by the peaceful sounds that sometimes
filled it. Boston was charming and narrow and Old World-
ish with its attached houses and bricked walks shaded by
elms and maples, and New York was exciting and magnificent, and he knew London and Paris and Rome and Athens. But something was lacking in cities for all their air of
vitality and movement and noise; there was a sterility about
them, a strange absence, in spite of parks and streams and
rivers in their midst. It was only in the country, anywhere,
that a man felt true identity and was part of something.

Courtney took off his hat and let the warming wind ruffle the hair that was so like his mother's, pale, fine and
thick. He had her features, but whereas hers were like porcelain his were sharp and keener, and his green eyes, unlike
hers, had no sadness or determined quietude. He had her
slenderness and height, but his was taut. As he sat in the
carriage with the sun on his head and face he thought of
Ann Marie, and smiled. So long as there was little Ann
Marie nothing very evil could be in the news he would
soon hear—unless it was news that his mother was dying.
He said to the coachman, "How is Mrs. Hennessey, Sam?"

The coachman yawned again and replied, "Well, sir, she
seemed well enough, until about a week ago, and now she
seems troubled, in a way, sir. Absent, as it were."

"Troubled." "Absent." That was a new description of his
mother, thought Courtney. All at once he wanted the
horses to run faster and not dawdle peacefully on the dusty
road. The shine on the land was less tranquil to Courtney
now, and he was irritated when they had to halt so that a
placid and slow-moving procession of cattle could cross the
road. The farm boy looked at him without interest, and a
dog snapped at the heels of the horses and scolded them.
They went on, and soon they were rolling down Willoughby Road, past quiet mansions still unstirring, and then turning in the drive of what once was the Armagh house but
which now belonged to Elizabeth Hennessey. Courtney had
only faint memories of once living in that "titanic white

mausoleum," as he called the house where Ann Marie
lived, and nearly all were disagreeable due to Bernadette,
the daughter of his adoptive father. He had never liked her,
but he had never understood the constant animosity she
had for him, as if she detested the sight of him and his
mother. He saw her very rarely in these years, but when he
encountered her she did not try to conceal her hostile
hatred—yes, it was hatred. He knew that.

She is likely to have a seizure when she knows about
Ann Marie and me, he thought, and not without pleasure
though with a little apprehension about the girl he loved.
Ann Marie was of age; she could marry whom she desired;
Uncle Joseph liked him, and had shown him many indulgent kindnesses when he had visited Rory in Boston. No
doubt it will please him, too, to vex Bernadette, thought
Courtney of his brother-in-law, whom he called "Uncle,"
out of respect for his greater age. It always startled Courtney when he heard Joseph called by his Christian name, as
if it were an impertinent familiarity, and this amused him
as it amused him when Rory referred to Joseph affectionately as "the old man," or "Pa." Courtney knew very well
that though Rory loved his father as he loved no one else
but his Maggie, he was also profoundly afraid of him, as
were Ann Marie and Kevin. Courtney frowned anxiously,
thinking of Ann Marie, her shy timidity, her instinctive re-
treats from a hard face or a rough word, her desire to placate and restore harmony. Yes, her mother would not be
gentle to her, very soon—as if she was ever gentle! thought
Courtney, and for the first time his indifference towards
Bernadette, his adopted sister, turned to active aversion.
His mother once had told him that Bernadette had, at one
time, "been considered quite pretty and very lively and full
of wit and spirit, and very stylish," but Courtney, remembering Bernadette as of today, could hardly believe that
that stout body, straining against whalebone and steel, that
sallow face engorged on the wide flat cheeks with apoplec-
tic red, the nose that seemed too small in all that flesh, and
the big malicious mouth, could have been appealing. Even
her fine hazel eyes, sparkling in amber and gold and shadows of green flecked with brown, had been overwhelmed
by facial corpulence and held nothing kind or amused in
them, but only a steadfast malevolence. She was only about
forty-one or so, but her hair was dyed a bright chestnut
brown and was lifted high over her face in the wide and

towering new pompadour, giving her a gross expression. She was still quick of movement, in spite of her obesity, but she had a tendency to waddle, an ugly contrast to Elizabeth's smooth grace of walk and posture. She also used heavy scent, even in summer, when heavy scents could be sickening and oppressive, and her face never took on any sweetness or pleasure except when she saw her husband.

At these times Courtney—the only one—would feel some pity for her.

It was still not quite half-past seven, but as he got out of the carriage Courtney, glancing up at the windows of his mother's rooms, saw that the draperies had been drawn aside and the lace curtains were blowing gently in the silken breeze. His mother usually breakfasted no earlier than half-past eight, or even later, in bed. The fact that she was obviously awake and up at this hour disturbed him even more than before. He went into the house very quickly, to be met by a maid who told him that his mother was waiting for him in the breakfast room. At least, he thought, tossing his hat in the general direction of a hall chair, and then walking down the long white hall to the rear, his mother was well enough to rise and eat downstairs. So, it must be something else.

The breakfast room, octagon in shape, was serene in pale yellow and green, and the table was already laid and the gold silk of the curtains was moving in the light warm wind. His mother sat at her place, palely beautiful as always, in her green morning dress, her hair hanging down her back and caught at the nape by a green ribbon. She looks like a girl, thought Courtney, cheered, as he bent to kiss her. She patted his cheek, and then saw his hands and said, "Oh, you are all soot, my dear. Do wash, and I will wait and just drink a little coffee before you come back."

"I was worried about you," said Courtney, "so didn't stop to wash."

Now for the first time he saw the violet shadows under her eyes, her unusual pallor, the tight little lines about her mouth. She glanced away. "I am quite well, Courtney. Do come back soon." Her voice was low and yes, it was "troubled." Her proud shoulders sagged as if she were very tired and had spent some sleepless nights. Courtney rushed up to his rooms and washed, took off his brown suit and replaced it with a light gray one, smoothed his hair, and ran downstairs again. He had just reached the foot of the stairs when a sick premonition, without a name, struck him. He stopped, his hand on the newel post, in the sunlit silence of the hall. He remembered that Ann Marie was "soon" going to "speak" to her mother. He had made her promise, in his last letter—which announced his arrival in Green Hills very shortly—that she would not "speak" until he was beside her to give her courage.

He had also asked her, in his letter, to meet him on horseback "at our usual place." That would be in about three hours. The thought of seeing Ann Marie very soon gave him courage, too, and he went back to the breakfast room. His mother sat as if in a dazed trance, a cup of untouched coffee in her hand, her eyes fixed on the table on which steamed covered dishes of silver. With the clarity of new fear Courtney could see every detail about his mother, and even the tiny rose pattern on the white china plates and the glitter of the silverware. He sat down, and his mother started, for she had not heard him enter.

"News of any kind," she said, "can always wait for a contented digestion, can't it?"

"It depends," said Courtney. "If it is bad news, yes. Good news, no." He watched her intently from under his yellow lashes.

"I don't know," said Elizabeth, in a subdued voice, "whether or not the news is 'bad,' or not. It may be—for you, my dear. I don't know. You are young, and the young can rebound." She helped him to creamed eggs and hot toast and poured coffee for him, and he saw how translucent her fine hands were. He also noticed, for the first time, that she was not wearing her wedding ring. There was no line indicating that it had ever been there. When had she removed it? Then he breathed deeply, with passionate relief. She was going to be married! He smiled. Dear Mama. He was happy for her, knowing her loneliness. He only hoped the man was worthy, and not some mountebank or blackguard looking for her money.

He ate a hearty breakfast, and urged his mother to eat also. She attempted to, and failed. She kept watching her son, and he saw this, and smiled to himself again. She was hesitating to speak. She said, "I miss you so much this summer, dear, since you decided to rush through law school with Rory." Ah, thought Courtney, she is delicately leading up to the revelation, and paving the way.

"I can't leave him there alone in Boston," said Courtney.

"God knows what he'd be up to without my supervision. The girls are mad for him, and Boston is full of unmarried girls, and he would most likely get into mischief."

"Rory may seem impulsive," said Elizabeth, "but he really isn't. He's a very calculating young man. I don't mean that unkindly, for I am very fond of Rory, and he amuses me. I mean that whatever he does is well thought out beforehand. He studies all the advantages, all the risks, before he makes a move, and never speaks of it first. That is what makes people think he is impetuous—it just seems sudden to them, though it is not."

Courtney thought of Marjorie Chisholm. Rory rarely spoke of her lately, and then only casually: "Who? Oh, Maggie. I think I'm going to see her this afternoon, if I can get this tort out of the way first. Yes, she's very well." That was all. Courtney knew a great deal about Rory, but there was also much he did not know. He was beginning to wonder if Rory was losing interest in Marjorie, and abandoning the thought of marrying her. He often went off for hours two or three times a week and blandly never mentioned where he had been, and Courtney suspected another girl had taken his interest. Poor Maggie Chisholm.

"You make him sound cold-blooded," said Courtney to his mother. "Or mistrustful."

"I think Rory is two persons, all in one," said Elizabeth, trying to smile. "Yes, he is cold-blooded, but he is also warm and generous. Yes, he is mistrustful, but he is also as confiding as a puppy. Rory keeps his own counsel. He will show the face he wants to show, but not the others. Yes, others. I have the feeling, and always did, that he has both rectitude and ruthlessness, that he will stop at nothing to gain his ends, and yet at times something will make him stop. He always courteously listens, rarely disagrees, though I suspect that at times he is full of disagreement. He is a very complex young man, full of paradoxes. A rascal, if you will, one hour, and an upright and immovable man the next."

Courtney was surprised at his mother's subtlety and perceptiveness. He said, "Yes, Rory is all that. Argus-eyed, and every eye watching, aware. He sometimes looks like a candid English schoolboy, years younger than he is, and all naïveté and innocence, and that isn't really put on. It is one of his ways. He is feeling like that—at the moment. There is no resemblance between him and his twin sister, Ann Marie. In fact, I feel Rory is twins, all in himself!"

They both thought of Ann Marie. Courtney drank a little coffee. His heart had begun to beat fast. It was time that he should again speak to his mother, and when Elizabeth saw his face she became weak and frightened. But, at least he would be the one to open the subject and not herself, and perhaps she could avert the final revelation.

"Mother," he said, putting down his cup and turning his face resolutely to her, "I talked to you about Ann Marie quite a long time ago, but you became so agitated and repeated so often that it was 'impossible,' that I let the matter drop temporarily. After all, I was still in school. And I was afraid that I would make you ill, you were so disturbed. Mother, what have you against Ann Marie?"

Elizabeth clenched her hands together in her lap and her green eyes fixed themselves bravely on her son. "Courtney, I do have a reason—to object. I told you it was a most important reason. My dear, you are the only child I have. I would not have you make a mistake. There is bad blood in the Hennesseys."

"You married one," said Courtney. "He wasn't so bad. In fact, he was a kind old codger, treated me like a son. Couldn't have been a better father, and I only adopted. I think he cared more about me than he did about his real child, Bernadette. If you felt that way about the Hennesseys—and you once told me you had known the senator for a long time before you married him in Washington—why did you marry him?"

"I loved him," said Elizabeth and bent her head.

"Did I hear past tense? Don't you still care about him, even if he is dead?"

"No. I see now it was only infatuation. Courtney, he was indeed kind and loving to you, better than most—real—fathers. But he was a bad man, Courtney, and I must confess that to you. A very bad man. In fact, he was really—criminal. It is too long a story to tell you. Bernadette is no better than her father was. She is even an evil woman, in many respects. Yes, the Hennesseys have bad blood. I don't want you even to think——" O God, would this be enough, please?

"In short," said Courtney, after a moment or two, "you are telling me that it would be too much for you if I married Ann Marie."

"Yes," she whispered. She looked up at him and saw the determined pallor on his face. "There is also the impediment."

"Mother," he said, holding to patience, "there is no consanguinity, and that you know. I have discussed this matter with priests. One was doubtful. The other was sure it would be perfectly all right. Bernadette and I have no blood relationship. I am not really Ann Marie's 'uncle.' I am the son of Everett Wickersham, and though I am grateful that the senator thought enough of me to adopt me and give me his name I now wish to God that you had let it be, and let me retain my real name."

Elizabeth squeezed her white, paper-thin eyelids together in extreme pain.

"Even if there is a technical impediment, and the Church objected, I should still marry Ann Marie," said Courtney, with firm gentleness.

"But would Ann Marie?" asked his mother, opening her exhausted eyes again.

"I've discussed it with her. Mother, we are very much in love. She says she will marry me. And nothing is going to stop us. I don't care if her parents throw her out. I doubt Uncle Joseph would, though. Still, it doesn't matter. You can throw me out, too, if you want to. I have money of my own, which the senator was kind enough to leave me. But, I am going to marry that girl and as soon as possible, even if the sky falls in."

"Have you thought of the legal side of it?" asked Elizabeth, feeling that it was no use at all, and there would be no last minute mercy for her.

"Of course, Mother! I am studying law, you know, and am taught by lawyers, and I asked about it, and they thought even the question was absurd. There is no legal impediment to our marriage."

Elizabeth pushed herself to her feet and moved feebly to one of the windows and looked out. She said, "You can't marry Ann Marie, Courtney. I can't bear— The very thought—"

"I thought you loved her," said Courtney, with bitterness.

"I do," said Elizabeth, so faintly that he hardly could hear her. She put her hand against the side of the window to support her, for she felt she would fall. "But, there is her mother—the Hennesseys."

"She also has another inheritance," said Courtney. "You once told me that her grandmother was a lady, a beautiful person, though you only saw her once."

Elizabeth remembered that disastrous day, twenty-three years ago. "So she was, Katherine," she said. "A very wronged woman, who was destroyed by her husband. But all the Hennessey blood has come out in Bernadette, and it is in her children, too. Rory has much of it. Would you care for children like Bernadette, Courtney?"

"No. But there is the Wickersham side, too, have you forgotten? And your side, Mother. I think we will be too much for the 'Hennessey blood.' "

His mother was silent. Was she really so thin and he had not noticed before, and so delicate in appearance? She still had not turned to him. She was clutching the side of the window. Then she was speaking again. "Joseph Armagh would not permit it. I know."

Courtney stood up. "You are mistaken, Mother. Rory and I have discussed all this. He knows his father has some affection for me. He believes there will be no objection from that quarter. And even if there is, it doesn't matter. Mother, I am soon leaving to meet Ann Marie, and we are going at once to her mother and tell her."

Elizabeth turned so swiftly from the window that she tottered, and had to catch a curtain to support her, and her face and eyes were so filled with horror and fear that Courtney was shocked. She cried, "You must stop her! She mustn't tell Bernadette! I know Bernadette! I know what she will say to that poor girl, and it will kill her!" She pressed her hands to her breast like one pleading for her own life. "Courtney, in God's Name, just tell Ann Marie that for several reasons—reasons—you cannot marry her. Tell her as gently as possible, and then leave her and never see her again. You are both young. You will both forget." Her eyes were stretched and full of agonized tears.

He stood and looked at her in silence, and now the dread premonition he had felt months ago returned to him, confusing and torturing him. But he also saw his mother's frantic despair, her overwhelming suffering, her fear.

He said, "Is that what you wanted to tell me, Mother, that I can't marry Ann Marie? Is that why you called me home?"

She nodded, unable to speak, but her eyes were imploring, begging him to agree and not ask anything else. Finally she could say in a broken voice, "I—I felt—that you hadn't given up, that you were still determined to marry that child. So, I sent for you. I knew it had to be stopped at once—"

"Give me one sound reason why I should not marry her, and what I should tell her. That is all I ask, Mother. A sound reason, and not an emotional or superstitious one. If I consider it sound, then I promise you I will give it full consideration, and perhaps act on it. But if it is not sound, then—" He spread out his hands eloquently.

"Believe me, dear Courtney, it is sound."

"Then, tell me!" he cried, overcome with wild impatience. "I am not a child! I am a man!"

"I can't tell you," she said, and her lips twisted in suffering. "If I could, I would. But you must believe me."

He shook his head in an equal despair. "Mother, you aren't making sense. There is no 'sound' reason. The only one would be if I were really Ann Marie's uncle."

Elizabeth fumbled for her chair, blindly, and fell into it. She leaned her elbows on the table and covered her face with her hands. Courtney stood and looked down at her. He felt suddenly paralyzed. The paralysis was making his lips thick and without feeling, his throat dry and parched. He could hardly breathe. He tried to move his head, to throw off this choking, this vomitous feeling in his stomach, this melting of his body. He could not look away from his mother. He heard her weeping. It seemed the most desolate sound he had ever heard, and yet he was filled with a madness of anger and torment.

Gardeners were mowing the lawn outside and the breeze brought in the fragrance of fresh-cut grass, and a boy was whistling, and the trees were rustling, and a distant dog barked and someone called, laughing, outside. But in this room was a deadly silence, the silence that follows a murder, an ugly pent silence, and it was enhanced by the light and the scent from beyond the windows.

"You should have told me, long ago," he said, and thought he would vomit right there. "You shouldn't have let it go so long. You should have told me, before it reached this point."

His mother groaned from behind her sheltering hands, "How was I to know it would come to this? I hoped you would forget, after I spoke to you before."

"So the senator was really my father?"

"Yes." He could hardly hear her.

"And I was born before he married you?"

She could only bow her head. He hated her now, yet he both loved and pitied her as he had never done before. He wanted to denounce her, and he wanted to comfort her. He strangled a little and coughed, and the black desolation rose to his face, his lips and his eyes like deathly water, and he was drowning.

"And Bernadette is really my sister? God, if that isn't a frightful joke! Odious Bernadette! Mother, she knows, too?"

"Yes," Elizabeth murmured. "She does."

"Who else?"

"Joseph Armagh."

"They are the only ones?"

She nodded again, her face still covered. She could speak a little more clearly, though her voice was still muffled and faint. "Bernadette was told—what everyone else believes— but she knew right from the first that you are the son of her father. She has denied this to me, repeatedly, trying to humiliate me. But, she knows the truth. And she would like to throw it into Ann Marie's face, that poor child, to hurt her, and us."

"You should have told me, years ago."

Elizabeth dropped her hands and he saw the red marks on her wet white face and her deepening agony. She said, "Why should I have? To brand you, to make you feel ashamed, as a child? To make you despise your mother? What purpose would that have served? If you had not wanted to marry Ann Marie you should never have known, Courtney. Can you tell me one reason why I should have told you 'years ago'?" A dim astonishment stood in her eyes.

"No," he said after a moment, "there was no reason to tell me, until now." He looked at his watch. "I must go soon to meet Ann Marie. Somehow, I must tell her—something. I can't tell her the truth." He now looked as broken and exhausted as his mother.

Elizabeth came to distraught life. "You must tell Ann Marie not to speak to her mother—about any of this! For the girl's sake. I know Bernadette!"

"Yes," he said. He began to turn away, but compassion took him, and he went to his mother and bent and kissed her wet cheek. She clung to him and groaned. "I wish I had never been born," she said. "I wish I were dead. I would have died to save you from this, my son."

Ann Marie had been blissful when she received Courtney's letter that he would arrive on a certain day and that he would speak to his mother, but that he would accompany her when Ann Marie "spoke" to hers. Before that, he would meet Ann Marie in the woods and they would "take our usual ride" in the open country. The "usual ride" consisted of a bridle path some half mile distant from Willoughby Road, away from low-hanging limbs and up and down a moderate hill. The time of meeting was to be half-past ten.

Bernadette only knew that when Courtney was at home her daughter occasionally met him for an excursion on horseback. That had begun when the girl had been only eight and Courtney nine, and had continued. Courtney had many influential friends of "family" in Green Hills, and these friends were male and to Bernadette, much as she hated her brother and resented him as part of the "seduction" Elizabeth had practiced on "my poor weak father," Courtney had his social uses. He introduced Ann Marie to his friends, and so the excessively shy girl had a number of suitors who were attracted by her gentle demeanor, her sudden sweet smile which had a certain fascination, her beautiful tawny eyes with their changing lights, and even the awkward youthfulness of her thin body which refused curves and so gave her an air of early nubility. Bernadette might deride her for her "boyish" appearance and bewail the fact that Ann Marie "had no style at all," but young men found this very appearance beguiling as it hinted of perpetual youth and delicate virginity. Ann Marie's light brown hair, fine and shining, refused to curl no matter how hot the irons were which were applied to it, and the curlers. It had a way of falling from pins and rolling down over her shoulders like an amber veil, which the young men also found endearing.

She had had many proposals, but had refused them all, and when Bernadette berated her she would answer nothing. She knew her mother disliked her, and she had no real fondness for Bernadette, but she respected her and was terrified of her. Bernadette had slapped her but a few times in her life, and when she was much younger, but had Bernadette used any other weapon in cruelty to her daughter except the cruelty of her tongue, she could not have inspired in the girl any greater fear of her. "But why?" asked Courtney several times. "What can your mother really do to you?"

"I don't know," Ann Marie would answer in misery, twisting her thin hands together. "It is as if there is something hidden in Mama, which could explode and destroy if she were pushed far enough, and I am afraid of it." Courtney thought this ridiculous. He knew all about Bernadette and disliked her immensely, but after all she was a woman and a mother and he could not imagine her becoming really violent in a disgusting way, though once or twice he had seen a look on her face which made him understand, in a small measure, why Ann Marie could fear her. It was an elated, almost gleeful, expression, full of hate and malice, and there would be a certain glitter in her eyes which Courtney had felt was not entirely sane. He had the aversion and mysterious apprehension of the utterly sane for those who could lose control and were not capable, at those times, of any control at all. It was like an elemental force, beyond human reason or harnessing.

Understanding, therefore, both Bernadette and the retiring and extremely shy and vulnerable Ann Marie, Courtney had written the girl that she must wait for him to go with her to Bernadette and announce their intention of marrying. Once he had believed that he should not be present, but when he had urged Ann Marie to confront her mother the girl had exhibited so much real terror, such inexplicable terror—to him—that he could only soothe her and advise her to "wait."

Ann Marie had awakened early. The depot was more than three miles away but with the keenness of love she was certain that she could hear the howling of the train as it brought Courtney to Winfield. She sat up in bed, and hugged her body with her thin young arms and smiled with joy and anticipation. Then she threw aside the silken sheets and went to the window which faced the house where Courtney lived, and she sat beside it, watching and waiting, sometimes shivering with delight and a real ecstasy of love, sometimes feeling fear at the thought of facing her mother later. But Courtney would be beside her, holding her hand. They would face Mama down. After all, she, Ann Marie, was past twenty-one and so her own mistress, and darling Papa liked Courtney, and it would all be settled today. She would meet him in the woods, as usual, and they would ride a little, then return to this house and confront Mama. After all, as Courtney said, what could Mama really *do?* But all at once Ann Marie was cold and trembling.

I am a mouse, she thought with regret. That is what the boys call me; Rory told me, but he did not intend to be unkind. He wanted me to be less shy. But no one knows that I never wanted anyone, or loved anyone, but Courtney, from the time we were children together. Dear Courtney, with his wonderful green eyes which could be so quietly merry and then so icily stern, and with his air of strength and indomitable courage. With Courtney she would be safe forever, and no longer afraid of people, no longer shy, no longer frightened, no longer conscious of secret malice and the sly cruelty which lived in everyone—except, of course, Courtney. And, perhaps, Aunt Elizabeth. She adored her twin Rory, but he was too complex for her understanding, too protean, too, she believed, capricious. At one moment he would be affectionate and thoughtful of her, and the next he would be impatient and teasing. He bewildered her and when Rory saw this he would laugh outright at her, but with good nature and renewed teasing. Rory feared no one, except Papa, and why he should fear Papa was not to be understood. She, Ann Marie, had found him the most considerate and loving of fathers, at least for a long time. It was possible, though Ann Marie did not know it, that she was the only one in her father's world who did not fear him and walk cautiously about him. Even Kevin, the "black Irish" as Joseph called him, was wary of Papa, in spite of his dark and bearish appearance and his obvious and explicit strength, his square and pugnacious face which challenged everyone in a gentlemanly way, and his quiet firm manners and rocklike simplicity. Ann Marie had discovered that Kevin ignored Bernadette and her frequent tantrums, and was not disturbed by them in the least and seemed honestly unaware of them. In consequence Bernadette could not intimidate him and could only fume.

Ann Marie was glad that Kevin, seventeen years old, was at home just now, and would be for another week when he would leave for Long Island and his "boating friends," as Papa called them with contempt. Kevin, rarely demonstrative, always compact and apparently living in himself, never afraid, seeming even stronger than his splendid brother, Rory, loved his sister and she loved him dearly in return. For the first time Ann Marie thought of Kevin as an ally, after she and Courtney had faced her mother with the news of their engagement. They could even ask him to be present, looming by their side like a dark but invincible presence.

Then Ann Marie was ashamed. No wonder Rory teased her, and Courtney smiled at her sometimes with affectionate surprise at her shyness, and no wonder Kevin would shrug as if she were amusing! They all knew she was a cowardly mouse, a really poor thing, always retreating from others, always blushing if a stranger spoke to her, always shivering inside at shadows, always hiding. She was a woman. She behaved like an infant girl. She had no fortitude at all, and none of the calm strength of dear Aunt Elizabeth. Why was she always so frightened, always on the run? No one had ever really hurt her in her twenty-one years. The nuns at her school had been kind and gentle to her. Her brothers and her father loved her and sheltered her. Mama, it is true, had a hard and sometimes alarming manner, and she always knew where to wound, and was always excitedly happy when she found a target for her malice. But Mama was the only one, and Mama, as Courtney had said, was only a woman after all.

Ann Marie glanced at her boudoir clock at her bedside. It was nearly half-past seven, this bright July day. Eagerly, she looked through her window. The Hennessey carriage was rolling up the driveway to the portecochere, and there was Courtney, getting out of the carriage. The girl strained at the window, her heart beating with joy and ecstasy at the distant view of her lover, his head shining palely in the sun. She could hardly bear her rapture. She wanted to run from the house, even in her nightgown, and go to Courtney and throw her arms about his neck and kiss him, and let him hold her tightly as he had done before. She closed her eyes, quickening with delight, with longing, with abysmal passion. When she opened her eyes Courtney was no longer there, and the carriage was going back to the stables.

She did not deserve Courtney, she, only a mouse. She must have courage. What a disgrace she would be to Courtney in his professional life, and his social meetings, if she shrank from everyone and hid herself as was her custom! He would be mortified forever and come to despise her. He had told her it was not hard to be courageous, and that she must cultivate some assertion or she would suffer lifelong wretchedness. Today, she would not wait for Courtney to be beside her when she told Mama. She would begin to lose her cowardice today. When she met Courtney, as arranged, she would tell him, with superb serenity, that she had already told her mother, and he would be proud of her. She stood up, in her thin silken nightgown and looked at herself resolutely in the mirror, and she thought she saw a certain firmness there, a certain maturity, in spite of the shadowy morning image of a girl seeming much younger than her actual years, with abashed eyes and a way of averting her head, letting her hair veil her from open revelation.

There is only Courtney, she thought, as she turned away. Nothing can ever separate us, except death. We love each other. I am going to be worthy of his love.

Her mother breakfasted in bed at nine, luxuriously and with petulant sounds. No one ever intruded upon her there, except Papa, who rarely intruded. Ann Marie, with her new resolution, decided to intrude. Let her heart beat furiously as it did now, and her breath become painful, and her flesh weak. It did not matter. She must begin to be brave.

She bathed, brushed her long hair carefully, braided it and tied it severely with a ribbon at her nape, then put on her brown riding habit and boots. She knew she looked best in this plain and austere garb, with the jaunty brown derby on her head, and her gloves on her hands. Her awkwardness became elegance, and she was not unaware of this. She took off her hat and gloves and went down to the ornate breakfast room with its tiled floor and center fountain with goldfish swimming in the bubbling bowl, and its rounded ceiling depicting nymphs and satyrs and secret leafy bowers and little pools of water. The big windows were open on the hot gardens, all scarlet and rose and yellow, and long lawns. The heat of the day was rising. To Ann Marie it was all a vivid sight, rapturously vivid, everything outlined with radiance and a shimmer of holiday and joy. How beautiful the world was, how ecstatic, how significant and heavy with love and delight. How marvelous it was to be young and quivering with anticipation and conscious of one's body, even to the feel of a cuff against a thin wrist. Where could sadness be in this world, what dissonance?

The maid informed her that Kevin had already had his breakfast and was out riding. Ann Marie, who had given a thought to having Kevin present when she went to her mother, was at first disappointed, and then resolute. Yes, the time had come for her to be brave. She put her hat and gloves on an empty chair. There was a shaking in her middle but she forced herself to eat and to drink coffee. She glanced very often at the watch pinned to her lapel. Nine o'clock. She would wait until Mama had finished her breakfast. That would be at least half-past nine. The maid said, "Mrs. Armagh had a telegram this morning, Miss Ann Marie. Mr. Armagh will be home tonight at eight."

"Oh, how wonderful, Alice," said Ann Marie. She was blissful again. It would be a family gala, in spite of Mama. Fortified by Courtney, Kevin, and her father, what could harm or frighten her? Once one had courage nothing could terrify. In two hours she would be in Courtney's arms, laughing happily and incoherently, her lips against his neck, safe with him, forever rescued and secure. They would ride together in the hot day, talking of their future together as they always did. They would live in a little townhouse in Boston while Courtney completed his studies. Ann Marie closed her eyes, unable to endure the bright gold of her happiness. She said a little prayer of gratitude within herself. When she opened her eyes the morning, the furnishings of the room, the shine of the windows, were almost too much to bear, so brilliant were they, so tender, so promising. Mama, of course, would not suffer a small wedding. After the Nuptial Mass crowds would gather here on the lawns, and there would be lanterns and dancing and music and laughter, and she, Ann Marie, in white silk and lace and with a bridal veil, would dance with Courtney and there would be no one else in the world at all. Perhaps August the tenth. That would give Mama plenty of time. No doubt she would manage a Papal Blessing, too. Ann Marie smiled, and the maid who served her thought, Why, she is really a very pretty young lady!

Ann Marie's favorite dog, a white setter, stole into the breakfast room, which was forbidden to him, and the girl slyly fed him bits of buttered toast and a strip of bacon, while the maid frowned, disapproving. Ann Marie said, "How did he get into the house, this monstrous creature?" She patted him affectionately and he put a paw on her knee and begged for more tidbits. "Alice, do bring him some more toast." Her voice shook with her joy, and her throat trembled with it. She bent and hugged the dog, and kissed his snowy head and she laughed, and the maid thought, What's come over her this morning? She looks all shiny.

Ann Marie said, "Alice, would you ask Mrs. Armagh's maid if I may see my mother? It is very important."

While she waited Ann Marie paled and the trembling returned and she sat up rigidly in her chair and told herself over and over that she must be brave. For one cowardly moment she hoped that her mother would refuse to see her "at this hour." Then she castigated herself. There was no time like the present. If her mother did not want to see her now she would go to her anyway, and demand to talk to her. The maid returned and said that Mrs. Armagh would see her daughter, though she felt unwell today. No wonder, thought Ann Marie. She eats too much at dinner. Mama ate enormously, voluptuously, passionately, as if there were some hunger in herself that could not be appeased, and drank quantities of wine so that her face became glazed and her temper vicious. Ann Marie sighed. She did not understand her mother at all.

It was time. Ann Marie stood up, put on her hat and gloves and grasped her crop. She said to the maid, "Alice, will you ask the stable boys to put on Missy's saddle for me, as I want to ride in half an hour?"

She went into the great white marble hall, trying to control the sudden pounding of her heart, and she ran up the white stairs admonishing herself. When she reached the top to catch her breath she felt a sudden hard chill, a darkening of everything. Then she went firmly down the upper hall to her mother's rooms, and there was a cold sweat on her forehead and between her shoulder blades, and fear had returned to her. It was as if a ghost was walking beside her, whose face was invisible.

Chapter 39

Bernadette was still in bed, a mounded figure in pink silk and lace, her hair in curlers, her flat round face reddened with food, her eyes hostile and vindictive as she looked at her daughter. But she smiled, the flesh heavily moving on its bones. As usual the coverlet was sprinkled with the crumbs of her breakfast, and a few coffee stains. She was still chewing a small creamy pastry and her lips were richly smeared, glossy with fat.

"What on earth is so important, at this hour?" she asked, and reached for her coffee cup, at which she drank thirstily. She licked her fingers and wiped them on the satin brocade cover. "Annie, I wish you wouldn't wear a riding habit so often. It looks so mannish." She called Ann Marie "Annie" because it humiliated the girl and derided her, as if she were an inconsequential servant impudently climbing up from the kitchen. She sighed gustily. "Of course, with your figure all prettiness is wasted, unless the bosom is padded with handkerchiefs."

"Mama," said Ann Marie, and sat on the edge of a gilt chair near her mother. Bernadette saw that the girl was internally agitated, and she stared at her, at her fine pale face, long and slim, and at the sherry-colored eyes and tightly braided hair. She looks, in some way, like my mother, thought Bernadette.

"Mama, I must talk to you," said Ann Marie. There was a white line on her upper lip and Bernadette, who never missed anything, saw it.

"Talk, then," said Bernadette, and yawned vastly.

"I've wanted to talk to you about this for a long time," said Ann Marie, beginning to sweat in her habit yet feeling cold. Her voice trembled.

"About what?" said Bernadette. She laboriously lifted herself on the pillows and squinted at her daughter. "What is the matter with you? You seem about to faint. Is your news so terrible?" She laughed derisively. "What could happen to you here in Green Hills, you moping about the house and riding and gardening, like a withered spinster? At your age. I was a married woman at that age, with children. Of course, we can't expect that of you. Perhaps you want to go into a nunnery, like your addle-headed aunt, Regina."

She looked at Ann Marie's hands. She said, "Hasn't anyone told you that you do not wear riding gloves in the house? Take them off."

The big gaudy room was full of hot sun and a hotter breeze. Ann Marie looked at the hovering maid, avid for gossip. "I'd like to be alone with you, Mama," said the girl.

Bernadette was immediately interested. She waved her fat arm at the maid and dismissed her, and the woman left reluctantly. Bernadette reached for another pastry, examined it, frowned, bit it tentatively, then devoured it, making smacking noises almost sexual in the hot quiet. "Go on," she said to her daughter, who was looking down at her hands, now bare.

Ann Marie said in a low voice, "I am going to be engaged, Mama. Today."

Bernadette sat up in a flurry. "No!" she exclaimed. "Is it possible? Who, for Heaven's sake? Robert Lindley, who has been haunting this house, or Gerald Simpson, or Samuel Herbert or Gordon Hamilton?" Her eyes were elated, glinting, opened. "Robert Lindley!" she cried. "When did he propose and why didn't you tell me? He is a great catch —for someone like you, Annie, a great catch!"

She marveled. This stick of an ugly girl, who never touched the paint pots for her lips or curled her hair or showed interest in clothes and had no social graces! Who would want her? But then, men were peculiar. They had the oddest tastes.

O, God, thought Ann Marie. Please help me. Her lips felt cold and damp. She said, "None of them, Mama. It is someone else."

"Well, tell me!" shouted Bernadette. "Must I drag it from you? Or is it someone impossible, someone without a penny or family, who will disgrace us?" Her face darkened to crimson, and animosity danced in her eyes.

"Ma, it is someone of family, and money," said Ann

Marie. Had the sun been clouded? Why was it so chilly in here, this hot day?

"Good! Excellent! What is his name? For God's sake, girl, speak up."

"Someone I have loved all my life," said Ann Marie, and heard herself stammering. She looked at her mother now, imploring, hoping for kindness and mercy and affection. "Mama, it is someone you do not like. But we love each other. No matter what happens, we are going to be married. We have talked of this for three years."

Bernadette was angry. "I can't imagine myself disliking any young man of family and money! What's wrong with you? I am just amazed that such a gentleman would want you—if he does—and it's not all your vaporish imagination, Annie. You've talked of it for three years, and never told me? Is that respectful to your mother? Or does his mother object to the match?" Her anger deepened. "If he is independent, what does it matter if his mother objects? Your father is a match for anybody."

"I know," said Ann Marie. "And I feel that Papa will not object. He likes the young man. But, you don't, Mama. That is why I am here now, to tell you."

Bernadette swore, as roughly as her father had sworn. "If you don't tell me at once, my girl, I will lose my mind. Why are you so secretive? I hate secretive people, but you were always sly. Speak up!"

A thick numbness rose in Ann Marie's throat, and she was terrified. Her mother looked so—imminent. So fat, so gross, so threatening. Be brave, she said in herself. What can happen to me, except her rage? She can't kill me. Don't be such a mouse, Ann Marie, such a quaking fool.

She tried to meet Bernadette's eyes.

The room dimmed all about her. Her lips were cracking. Her bones felt as if they were breaking, one by one. "It's Courtney," she whispered.

"Who?" said Bernadette. She craned forward, as though suddenly deafened, her big breasts spilling over her belly.

"Courtney, Mama."

Bernadette could only stare at her daughter. The dark blood began to recede from her face, leaving it like wet dough. Her eyes sank in her fat so they were hardly visible. Her lips turned livid. She began to heave as if smothering, her fat body shaking. Heavy clefts appeared about her mouth, and in her forehead. Her nose became very white, sunken between her cheeks.

"Are you out of your mind?" she asked, and her voice was hoarse. "Your uncle! You must be demented." She looked sick.

"Mama," said Ann Marie, and then stopped. Her mother's aspect of shock, of incredulity, frightened her even more. She at last could say, "I know you don't like him, or Aunt Elizabeth. But we love each other. We are going to be married." It was out now, and she tried to look at her mother but Bernadette's appearance was growing more dreadful every moment. "It doesn't matter what anyone can say," the girl continued through her parched throat. "We are going to be married."

Bernadette let herself sink slowly back onto her pillows, but her eyes never left her daughter's face. She studied her. She said, "I think the law will have something to say about that." She was incredulous again, and now her easy rage was loosed within her. "What are you talking about, you idiot! He is your uncle!"

"Not really, Mama." Why was her own voice so weak, so placating, like a child's? "Just my adoptive uncle. There is no impediment to our marriage. He is only the adopted son of my grandfather. I know you've resented him all these years, because your father adopted him. It—it was not kind. He had nothing to do with it."

But Bernadette was still staring at her as at something that could not be believed. She seemed to have lost speech, she who was usually so voluble.

Then an evil spark began to grow in the depths of her eyes, and she sucked her lips in and out and watched her daughter, and the glazed look she wore after dinner at night spread over her face, but crackled now, webbed, like old china.

"Does Elizabeth Hennessey know about this?" she asked, and Ann Marie did not recognize that voice for a hideous elation lay under it, a breathless excitement, a secret and almost uncontrollable jubilation. It fascinated Ann Marie, even while her fear grew.

"No, Mama. But Courtney is here this morning, and he is going to tell her." She hesitated. "He wanted to come here with me, later, to tell you, too."

Bernadette spoke softly and viciously, and looked at a distance. "He will never dare to come here again. So, he is going to tell his mother, is he? I should like to be there when he does!"

Ann Marie felt herself draining, withering away. "Mama," she said, "we don't care what others will say. We are going to be married." (If she could only stop that dreadful vibration in her legs and arms!)

"Oh, I don't think you are, I really don't think so," said Bernadette and now she turned her jumping eyes on her daughter again. "I don't think the law would like it."

"Mama, you said that before. What has the law got to do with it? There is no legal impediment, and Courtney now thinks there is no religious one, either."

"Oh, he does, does he?" Again Bernadette was smiling and exultant. "So, he doesn't know, does he? I hope his mother is telling him right at this minute. I've waited a long time for revenge on that trollop, and now it has come. That trollop, who seduced my father into marriage to give her brat his name, and mine! Let her suffer now as she has made me suffer, she and that precious son of hers."

Ann Marie stood up, and held to the back of her chair. "Mama, I am meeting Courtney soon."

Bernadette, again staring at her, licked the corner of her lips and a speculative and gloating look filled her eyes so that they sparkled as they had done in her youth. She seemed, for all her stare, to be coming to a decision. Then she said, "How far has this gone, my girl? How far beyond kissing and hand-holding?"

Ann Marie's pale face turned scarlet and her face quivered. "Mama," she said. Watching her closely for a moment Bernadette began to nod her big head over and over.

"Very well. You are not a strumpet like his mother." What shall I do? she asked herself. Let her go and have him tell her, himself, ashamed and degraded? She tasted the thought and smiled. But she could not wait for later developments, and to hear it from the mouth of this silly chit. She studied Ann Marie. The maternal instinct was not entirely stifled in her though she disliked the girl and was jealous of Joseph's love for her. Well, she would have a little revenge on Joseph, too, when he saw his daughter's grief. It was a mother's place to warn and enlighten her daughter, she thought with sudden virtue, and made her face grieved and even a little sympathetic.

"Sit down, Annie," she said. "You will need support when I tell you what you must know. Sit down, I say. Don't

stand there gaping like a dying fish. There, that's better."
The girl sat again on the edge of the chair, her feet planted
firmly as if preparing for flight.

Bernadette folded her hands together like one about to
pray and rested them on one fat knee. "We all thought to
spare that Hennessey woman, for the sake of her child, and
her own good name. We were wrong. We should have blazoned out the truth from the very beginning, so my daughter would not have come to this pass."

"What, Mama?" the girl whispered. She leaned forward.

"That Courtney Hennessey is indeed your uncle, my
brother, my half brother, if you will. His father was your
grandfather—my father. Now, what have you to say to
that, Miss?"

She waited, brutal eyes fixed on her daughter. Ann
Marie did not move for a full minute, but her young face
grew gray. Then she put her hand to her cheek as if it had
been struck violently. Her tawny eyes had widened,
dimmed.

"I—I don't—" she began, then coughed.

Bernadette waited until the strangling sound stopped.
Pity was not completely dead in her. After all, this was her
daughter, and now her old smoldering anger against Elizabeth deepened into fury.

"You mean you don't believe it, Ann Marie?" She
reached out and put her hand on the habit of the girl. "Yes,
I agree it is frightful, but it is true. Your father knows. I
think that is why he is coming home tonight—to help you.
Courtney Hennessey had no name before my father gave
him his, and he was born a year before my father married
his mother. She had political influence. She forced him. We
held our peace for the sake of my father's reputation. After
all, he was a senator, and scandal would have ruined him."
Now her fury blazed out. "She seduced him while my poor
mother was still alive! She tried to make my father leave
my mother! She came to this house, this very house, and
broke my mother's heart so she died that night. I was there.
I heard it all. She was already in a delicate condition, the
drab."

She began to cry, snuffling, and the tears were sincere
and acid with hatred. "Will there be no end to the misery
that woman has caused this family? First my father, then
my mother, then me, and now my daughter." She thought
of Joseph, and her tears came faster, but of Joseph and

Elizabeth she dared not, even now, speak. "I wish she were dead."

I don't believe it, I don't believe it, Ann Marie was thinking almost prayerfully. Dear God, it can't be true, can it? Mama is lying to me; she is always lying. But why would she say such things?

Bernadette lifted her streaming face and gazed at her daughter and there was genuine sorrow on it, if only a little, as well as fury. "Ann Marie, my dear child, you have been as wronged as your grandparents were wronged, and I, and I was only seventeen when it happened—when she killed my mother. She took my mother from me, and then my father, and all she had to offer was a brat born out of wedlock!"

Ann Marie stood up, that stunned gray look deepening on her face. Then, very slowly, horror brimmed her eyes and she shuddered and she held her cheeks with her hands as if mortally stricken.

"We almost eloped—last Easter," she muttered, and shuddered again.

"And that would have been incest," said Bernadette. "Thank God you were spared that, and this family, and all the shame and notoriety. No decent man would have married you after an incestuous marriage had been annulled. You would be worse in his eyes than a doxy. A doxy like Elizabeth Hennessey."

Ann Marie's face now expressed nothing at all but a dazed absent-mindedness. She put on her gloves and took up her crop. She looked about her at the room, and she could smell coffee and toast and bacon and heavy scent and heat and hot wool and hot silk, and her stomach turned over. She went quickly towards the door. "Where are you going?" Bernadette cried after her.

"I don't know," the girl said, in a dim voice. "I really don't know." She stopped at the door like one bemused in a strange place, and uncertain where to go next. Her profile was as sharp as white stone. Then she had gone. Bernadette called after her and got out of bed in a sweltering flurry of lace and silk, but Ann Marie had disappeared.

Kevin was in the stables when his sister approached at a stumbling run, her habit skirt dragging unheeded in the dust, her hat askew on her head, her face agape and blank. Kevin had just returned from his ride. "Hey!" he called to his sister. "What is all the hurry?"

But Ann Marie, as if she did not see or hear him, was stammering to a stable boy. "Is my horse—Missy—is my horse ready?" She had begun to pant. Her nostrils were dilated and her eyes had a crazed expression. Kevin was suddenly frightened. He had never seen Ann Marie like this before, so distracted, so quietly frantic, so ghastly of color. He put his hand on her arm. She appeared not to be conscious of his presence. Her slight breast was rising and falling rapidly, as if she had been running for miles.

"Ann Marie!" he almost shouted in her ear. She started away from him then, and cringed, but she did not look at him. The stable boy was bringing her horse and offering his hand to assist her. She sprang up into the saddle and Kevin was aghast at her face. He watched her wheel the horse and race off, her skirt billowing in the breeze she created.

He said to the stable boy, "Quick! Bring out my horse again."

Ann Marie was only a distant little cloud of dust now. Kevin leaped into his saddle and galloped after his sister, and he knew the first real fear of his somewhat stolid young life. Something had happened to his sister, and she had seemed out of her mind.

Courtney Hennessey, riding to meet Ann Marie, had given long and wretched thought to what he must tell the girl. He held back his own pain, which would devour him if he let it, so that he could concentrate on the alleviation of pain in Ann Marie. He could only tell her the oldest story, or lie, of all, that he was interested in another girl now, whom he had met in Boston, and that he knew, at last, that his love for Ann Marie had been the love of a brother for a sister, and not real attachment. Banal, banal, he cursed to himself. Perhaps he could say that it would be "years" before they could marry, and that she must not wait for him, and then he would quit law school and go abroad, he would not write to Ann Marie. He might even stay longer, until his acute grief and despair subsided. He might try to convince her he was a scoundrel, unfit to touch her hand. Very melodramatic, he told himself with contempt.

He could clearly see her stricken face, her suffering eyes, and hear her stammered questions. He knew that above anyone else in the world, even her father, she loved him, clung to him like a child. He tried to tell himself that she was young, that his long absence would cure her of him, that she would meet some other man. But as for the truth, he could never tell her that. He knew how fastidious she was, how revolted she would be, how appalled. There was also his mother to consider who should not be shamed at this time in her life.

It seemed incredible to him, and nightmarish, that he was in fact a true Hennessey, and not only by adoption. He had loved his father, but now he hated him. One conscienceless man could destroy numerous innocent lives in one heedless and lustful moment. Tom Hennessey had done this, to his wives, his son, his granddaughter. God knows how many others he had injured during his career. Hundreds, thousands, perhaps. Courtney knew much about politicians, and much about his father.

He did not see the warm quiet pasturage he rode over, nor the green leaves of trees so brilliant that they appeared newly varnished, nor did he see the quail rising at his passage nor the way the grass bent and glistened nor the little pools of red and yellow and white wild flowers among the trees and in small hollows, nor did he hear the rustle of any wing or the cry of any bird. The hills beyond were radiant in the sun, green and violet and purple, and the small river that ran from them through the pastures trembled and rippled in silver splashed with blue and lemon shadows. Distant white farmhouses stood in an air so pure that they seemed built of shining marble, their red roofs glowing in the light. But Courtney saw none of this. It was irrelevant to his pain and had no meaning for him. The polished blue sky had no consolation; its very luster was a mockery, and alien. One small part of his consciousness remarked in bitter wonder why the world should be so lovely and the thoughts and circumstances of man so terrible, as if man were a dark intruder and rejected by every leaf and sound and petal, not only with contempt but with laughter and indifference.

Now the green earth began to rise as the horse climbed up the side of the low hill towards the woods at its summit, and the sun heated Courtney's face and shoulders and he felt nothing but the black coldness in himself. His head was bent. Over and over he considered various stories he should tell Ann Marie, and all of them were full of bathos and insincerity and sounded cruel. But, like his mother, she should be protected from the truth. Any lie was better than that. He could see her face, so poignant, so trustful, so timid, so fearful of hurt, so anxious to please. It was not a beautiful young face, but it had more than beauty for it was without malice or slyness and above all it was not stained by life. It had a certain angelic and dispassionate quality, without human experience to mark it. He could see her eyes, sherry eyes full of clarity and brightness, reflecting back her thoughts which were never murky. Now he must throw misery into that face and quench those eyes and he did not see as yet how he could do it. How could such a soul and such a face have been born of Bernadette and Joseph Armagh, and how could she, by God, have been descended from Tom Hennessey?

Once Tom Hennessey had said of his dead wife, Katherine: "She was most unfortunate. She was a born fool." He had said this to Elizabeth in the hearing of her son and Elizabeth had not replied, to Courtney's memory, for he had been very young then. Now Courtney wondered about Katherine Hennessey and he considered that it was very possible that the young Ann Marie, in her innocence and trust, must resemble her grandmother, who had apparently not been able to stand fast in the world in which she had found herself and had had no protection. For such as Katherine and Ann Marie the world was a savage strange place full of monsters, and inevitably they were destroyed.

He reached the top of the hill and it lay in a luminous silence with the deep low woods just beyond. Here and there on the rough ground lay small stones and small boulders and between them grew tiny pink flowers and green leaves, frail with life, and Courtney thought again of Ann Marie. They grew there in gentle courage, but he knew that their roots were feeble and once plucked they died almost immediately. He looked about him and he was all alone and below him lay the shining land from which, he knew now, every man was exiled and had been exiled since the beginning of time. The Garden was not really for man. His natural home was crepuscular and shadowy, full of stealthy footsteps, thorny ways and the glimpse of deadly enemies from behind every rock. It was a place of ambush, and flashes of distant fire and the rattling and roar of dead and blasted trees, and earth on which nothing living could grow and have its being. Man's natural habitat was hell, and not this world. Its voice was clangor and discord and shouts of hate, the thunder of arms and death, and its random illumination was lightning. No wonder that everything innocent ran from man as from a Fury, knowing it had been condemned, by an inexplicable God, to be dominated by this liar and this murderer for no fault of its own. Courtney was a skeptic, but now he found his spirit in revolt against a God who could have perpetrated the race which was a blasphemy and a curse under the sun. It was easier to believe in Lucifer than in a God, and much more credible.

He knew that these thoughts came from the necessity to wound and destroy something innocent and good, but they seemed all the more filled with verity for that.

The woods were deep and meshed and filled with old dead leaves and moss and vines, and some of the trees were virgin timber with low boughs tangled together. No sound came from the woods, and nothing except a scent of fecund decay and a cool aromatic breath of dampness. The trail Courtney and Ann Marie took bypassed the woods and wound about them, and then descended again to the land below. Sometimes Ann Marie would bring a basket for mushrooms growing in the woods, or arbutus in the spring, or glossy chestnuts in the autumn. Courtney bent his head almost to his horses's neck as if the weight of pain was too heavy for him. Nothing that his mother had told him had lessened his love for Ann Marie. In fact, it was heightened for now it was forbidden and he knew that never again would he come up this hill and never know again what he had known before.

He heard the swift pounding of hoofs rising from the other trail which led up the hill and his heart pounded with torment in answer. He thought he heard following hoofs, but dismissed the idea as an echo. Then all at once Ann Marie and her young mare burst up before him, as if jumping from the ground, and Courtney tried to smile and he lifted his hand.

But Ann Marie reined in her horse so suddenly that the mare half-reared then fell back, whinnying in indignation. Ann Marie sat straight and high in her saddle, and her habit was lifted by a light wind, but she had lost her hat. She sat there and looked at Courtney and then he said to himself with a kind of terror, She knows. He saw her face, convulsed, frightfully white and sunken, and he saw the horror in her eyes and the leaping despair and the agony. She looked down upon him and seemed to recognize him as something not of her world, not of her life, but threatening and indescribably catastrophic. It was a disastrous face that confronted Courtney.

"Ann Marie!" he cried, and spurred his horse to approach her. But she swung her mare about and in an instant she had plunged wildly into the woods, the terrified mare crashing and stumbling, rising and falling in the uneven terrain. Before Courtney could even reach the edge of the woods the girl and the horse had disappeared, leaving only echoes behind them, and smashing sounds.

She will be hurt in there, she will die in there, thought Courtney, and got off his horse and his legs shook under him. He could feel the blood driving to his heart, and cold sweat rushed out over him, and everything took on the sharp brightness and sharp shadows of nightmare and dread. He heard a shout; he hardly heard it as he ran for the woods, and then he heard his name called, and he halted. Kevin, on his own horse, had arrived. Kevin swung down and flung aside his reins, and ran to the other young man.

"Where the hell is she? Where's Ann Marie?" he shouted. "I followed her up here. She was riding like mad!"

Even then Courtney could take thought. He said, "She just rode up, and then—then her mare bolted into the woods. She didn't say a word. Nothing."

"Jesus," said Kevin, and they both listened for a moment to the distant breaking and tearing sounds. Kevin's face was horrified and desperately alarmed. Big though he was, and somewhat clumsy when in a house, he ran with Courtney to the woods and they pounded into them, and were immediately drenched with dank coolness and dimness. Kevin lurched like a great black bear, native to this element, apparently lumbering but moving with sure speed, dodging tree trunks and low hanging limbs, sometimes sinking into small natural pits, jumping over stones, wading through old pungent leaves, pushing aside brush, leaping over fallen trunks, and arousing, in his passage, cries of dismay and panic from the hidden creatures who had been stricken into voice and movement by this impetuous intrusion. Courtney, who had considered himself more agile than this bulky youth, found himself panting behind him, falling once in a while, tearing his clothing on brambles and thorns, bruising and ripping his flesh, staggering against an unseen trunk in the dimness, spraining muscles in his ankles and legs, and panting and sobbing aloud.

Kevin wasted no breath on shouts and calls. His eyes followed the crushed path of his sister's horse, and the branches which still swayed after her flight. He heard Courtney behind him but did not look back. He was like a battering ram in that green and sullen dimness, that twilight of entwined trees. He splattered through a little rill, and then ran faster, as if gaining new strength and Courtney almost lost him.

The smell of the woods, disturbed and aroused for the first time in years, flowed about the young men, acrid, bitter with fungus, and the effluvia of many things which had died in those hidden places and under those wet black leaves and in that watery moss. Something was shrilling and screaming at a distance, and Kevin stopped a moment to listen, and then ran in that direction, with Courtney fast upon him. Now Kevin's strength and speed increased. He plunged into thickets instead of pulling them aside with his hands, which were now bleeding. He stopped only once to call, "Ann Marie! Where are you!" Only the awful shrilling answered him, a disembodied plea, and Courtney came abreast of him and he saw the young man's broad and deadly white face like a ghost in the duskiness and the fear in his dark brown and starting eyes. "It's her horse," he said to Courtney. And he ran on again, with Courtney at his heels.

Then Kevin stopped so suddenly that Courtney fell against that big brown back, started to fall and had to catch the heavy muscular arm of the youth. There was a hot anguish in his right ankle, as if it were broken and his shoes were filled with water. He looked over Kevin's shoulder, and then it was as if everything deafened about him, and died.

Missy, the mare, lay sprawled near a tree, which she had struck, her legs threshing the air, her long neck outstretched, her teeth glimmering in torture, her eyes rolled up. And near her lay the broken body of Ann Marie, almost lost in that obscurity, for her habit was nearly the color of it, and she did not move nor utter the slightest cry. Kevin saw all this. He saw that the writhing mare's hoofs would soon strike his sister and he ran to her and huddled down and pulled her free and safe. She was like a flaccid doll in his hands, her hair tumbled about her in a brown veil, her arms hanging loosely. Her habit was shredded and ripped.

"O God, no," said Courtney aloud, and ran to Kevin, who was gently lowering his sister to the ground again. The fearful shrilling of the mare was louder; her screams sent wing echoes through the woods, and answering cries. The two young men bent over Ann Marie and Courtney brushed her hair from her face and for the first time he saw that the hair on her skull was matted and black and streaming with blood.

They knelt on their hands and knees above the girl, their breath loud and raucous in the cool dusk. They could see her girl's face, still and closed and shut, the tawny lashes on her white cheeks, blood beginning to darken her forehead and temples. Courtney fumbled for her pulse, and then he burst out into the first tears he had shed since he had been a child. "She is alive," he said. "We can't move her. Kevin, run down to the house and bring people up here to help us." His voice was so quiet in contrast with his tears and his expression, then Kevin looked quickly at him. "We'll need a carriage and a door and blankets, and send someone for a doctor so he'll be there when we bring her down."

"Tell me again," said Kevin, and he looked at Courtney with such a face that the other man flinched. "What happened to my sister?"

"I don't know. We always met there. We were to meet this morning. She had arrived just before you. She said nothing at all to me, though I spoke to her." Courtney caught his breath, let it out slowly. "Then the mare turned —she must have been frightened by something, skittish, she was always skittish, and she ran into the woods with Ann Marie. That is all. You came right at once."

"I saw her in the stables," said Kevin, and he spoke precisely through his big white clenched teeth. "Something was wrong with her. It was as if she had seen or heard something—in the house, or had been told something. Do you know?"

Courtney cursed furiously. "Damn you, go for help, for doctors! Why are you just kneeling there and staring at me? I know nothing, except that her horse bolted. Get along now, or she'll die here. I'll stay. For Christ's sake, can't you see she's badly hurt, you glowering idiot? Do you want her to die while you jabber away?"

"I'll find out," said Kevin, in an ominous voice. "I don't believe that horse bolted. I believe Ann Marie deliberately spurred her into these woods, for just this very thing." He jumped to his feet and ran off the way he had gone and Courtney could hear the noisy slogging of his running feet.

Now Courtney was alone with the unconscious girl, whose head was bedded in a heap of moss. She did not move. She lay as if already dead, so small, so rumpled, so silent and so still, so battered and torn and bleeding. The horse shrilled and screamed nearby and Courtney cried out in total anguish. "For God's sake, be quiet, Missy! For God's sake!" But the horse threshed and shrieked and rolled in her own agony, her burnished brown hide streaming with blood.

Courtney wanted more than anything else to lift Ann Marie in his arms, to hold that bloody little head against his chest, to speak and kiss and comfort. But he was afraid to cause more damage. He could only squat and lean over the girl whom he loved so devastatingly and with such terrible longing. He lifted one of her little slack hands. It was cold and lifeless. He pressed it against his mouth, his cheek, and he murmured, "Ann, Ann Marie. O God, what is wrong, my darling? Why did you do this? Who drove you to this?" He smoothed her fingers over and over, hoping for a little warmth, for a little response, but that ivory silence did not stir nor those eyes open. Shadows filtered over her face, which was diminishing, slackening. The lips parted, but not to speak. Courtney listened for her breath, his ear close to her mouth, his hand on her wrist. The breath was short and light, the pulse like a frantic thread. The long aureate lashes lay unmoving on her cheeks. Her young breast hardly rose or fell.

"Who did this to you, Ann Marie?" said Courtney. "Who could have driven you to this? For you knew didn't you? Someone told you. Who, my love, who, my dearest love?"

Then he knew. There was no one else who could have told the girl the truth but her mother, Bernadette. Her father was not due until tonight. There was no one else but Bernadette. Ann Marie had "spoken" to her mother after all, in spite of warnings.

She was like a child lying there in the woods, stricken and alone, thrown down, abandoned, mortally hurt, seeming to sink deeper, moment by moment, into the black leaves which were her bed. Courtney bent his head and touched her cheek with his own and he cried as he had never cried before, and something burned and shifted and lusted in him and he knew the deepest and most murderous hatred he would ever know.

He heard his own voice, stammering, mumbling aloud, "How could anyone do such a thing to this child? How could anyone be so monstrous? Who had the hate to kill like this, ruthless, gleeful, deliberate? Didn't that woman know what you really are, my darling, a defenseless little girl, harmless, wanting only to love and be loved? O my God, Ann Marie, how I love you! Don't die, my darling. Here I am, Courtney. Don't leave me, little love. I never wanted anything in the world but you, Ann Marie. Do you hear me? Don't die, don't leave me. If I can only see you sometimes—it'll be enough. Enough for my whole life."

His incoherent words mingled with the screaming of the dying mare, and the flutter and chatter in the trees. His voice rose, senselessly, frenzied. "Ann Marie! Where are you? Come back, come back to me! Don't leave me."

His shaking hands smoothed her hair, felt her blood on his fingers. She was growing cold. He took off his jacket and covered her, tucking the collar under her chin gently like a father. He rubbed her hands, held them between his sweating palms.

He did not know the precise moment when she opened her eyes and looked at him clearly, knowing him, but when he finally realized through the red haze of his grief that she was conscious he thought he would collapse with joy. He saw that she was even smiling a little, her white lips curving in the sweet smile he had always loved.

"Courtney?" she said.

He held her hands tighter. He bent over her more closely. He looked into her eyes. "Ann Marie?" he whispered.

"Oh, Courtney," she said, like a child, but not like a child who knew her world had been destroyed about her. "Where am I? What are we doing here?" Her voice was feeble but steady and bewildered. She tried to look about her then winced with pain, and moaned. But she turned to Courtney again. "What happened to me, Courtney?"

She did not remember. Concussion, thought Courtney, and was grateful. "Missy bolted. Don't move, love. Kevin has gone for help."

Her child's forehead was gently wrinkling in a frown.

"Missy? Bolted? She never did that before. I don't remember even riding her. I don't remember—"

"It doesn't matter, Ann Marie. Nothing matters but that you are alive. Help will soon be here. Kevin's gone for it."

"Kevin? How did he know we were here?" She sounded girlishly interested.

"He—he decided to join us. Don't worry about it, dear. It isn't important. I'm here with you. You'll be all right, my love, all right."

She looked at him trustfully. Her hands were a little warmer. He bent over her again and he kissed her softly on her mouth, and her chill lips moved in response, and her fingers tightened on his own. Her eyes were so clear, so unharmed, and even in that duskiness he could see himself reflected in the amber of them as he had so seen himself many times before. "Dear Courtney," she said. "I love you, Courtney."

Then he saw a strange thing happen. He saw his reflection retreating, moving backwards, becoming smaller and smaller in the iris of those steady eyes. Now he was but the tiniest of faces in that iris, and that face dwindled and wavered and then became a shapeless speck, and then was gone.

"Ann Marie!" he said.

But she was looking at him starkly now and with full knowledge, and without a movement or a change of expression she uttered the most awful groan, and it seemed to rise not from her lips or throat but from some vital part in her body. She closed her eyes and murmured, "Mama told me." She was silent.

He called her name frantically over and over, but she did not respond and he did not know if she heard him or had fallen unconscious again. There was nothing now but the screams of the tormented horse and the frightened response from the trees and the effluvia of decay and the fungus smell and a faint creaking among the trees, and a growing dimness in which all things were dissolving.

Courtney lay down beside the girl and held her hand and he wished he could die there with her or that neither of them need ever again know what they had learned this day, but would awaken as if from a nightmare they had dreamed together.

Part 2

RORY DANIEL ARMAGH

For they eat the bread of wickedness, and drink the wine of violence.

—*Proverbs* 4:17

Chapter 1

The nightmare would never end. Courtney and Kevin and Elizabeth sat in a small parlor at the rear of the drawing rooms in the Armagh house, in a silence too heavy to break even by a sigh or a murmur. It was nearly midnight and the air was almost hot and had not cooled with the coming of darkness and there was a prowling sound of heated thunder in the hills but no lightning, no moon, no stars. Elizabeth was leaning back in a chair, her white face tilted towards the ceiling, her eyes closed in exhaustion, her green and brown print frock seemingly too large for her body, her pale hair disheveled. Kevin sat in ponderous black immobility, his dark curls almost on end, his olive-tinted face shut and clenched, his dark eyes staring before him. There were deep scratches on his hands and cheeks from the thorns he had encountered, and the blood was dried on them, and he had not removed his torn brown suit and his boots were still muddy and leafmold still clung to them. Courtney sat near his mother, as quiet as she, and his face even paler with bluish shadows under his cheekbones.

The small parlor was gay with the vivid colors Bernadette loved, all intense blues and scarlets and yellows, the domed ceiling painted with dancing lambs and shepherdesses in an impossible meadow of verdigris green filled with daisies. The lamps were lighted. The room was incongruous tonight, with the three silent figures within it in varicolored chairs, their motionless feet on a Chinese rug of jade and primrose and azure. Little porcelain figures danced on little round gilt tables, and an ormolu clock chimed happily on the white marble mantel, and festive and coquettish figures frolicked in paintings on the yellow silk walls and the scent of late roses blew in through the opened french windows.

575

Three physicians were upstairs in Ann Marie's room, and her father was with them, and Bernadette was under sedation in her gaudy bedroom, and the hours passed one by one. Occasionally a maid came in with fresh tea and cinnamon toast and to remove cups which had not been touched. Famous physicians had been summoned from Philadelphia, Boston and New York, by telegram, and would be arriving tomorrow. In the meanwhile Ann Marie was almost moribund. Everyone in the little parlor started and trembled at any nearby sound or distant voice, terrified to receive fatal news, hoping that Ann Marie still lived, that there was a chance for her life.

The climb down the hill had been part of the continuing nightmare, with Ann Marie laid on a door covered by blankets and herself wrapped in them, and with Kevin and Courtney riding behind. Courtney remembered, with a shudder, how Kevin had returned to him with a rifle in his hand and had efficiently and mercifully put an end to the suffering of Ann Marie's horse. He had done it without a glance of regret or sadness; it was a task to be done and so must be done. The shot had clamored through the surly green gloom of the woods, but Ann Marie had not heard it. Then had begun the descent down the hill to the waiting victoria with a covered door hastily removed from the house, the men ready to lay the unconscious girl upon it, the men who had carefully carried her from the stubborn forest.

Courtney knew that Kevin must be told, for otherwise catastrophe would result. Courtney knew all about Joseph Armagh, and of what he was capable and he guessed what he would do when he discovered who had sent Ann Marie plunging to her very probable death. Bernadette, the mother, must be warned. Her husband must never know her part in this disaster, if only for Elizabeth's sake. What had happened to Ann Marie did indeed demand vengeance, but it most not be the sort of vengeance Joseph Armagh could inflict, for Ann Marie might live and she must not be the cause of violence between her parents and the things which Joseph would undoubtedly do. And, there would be scandal. So, Kevin had to know in order to induce his mother to keep silent. Courtney doubted that Kevin and Rory had a great love for Bernadette, but they must be protected as much as possible, for they were young and had a future, and Bernadette would not hesitate even at injuring her sons

—as she had destroyed her daughter—to inflict torment on her husband and avenge herself on Elizabeth.

So, as the dolorous procession wound down the hill Courtney put his hand on the neck of Kevin's horse, and Kevin turned his bleak square face to the other man and his dark eyes were cold and hostile. "Are you ready to tell me?" he asked.

So Courtney told him as tersely and as emotionlessly as possible, and in very few words. "There is no doubt your mother told Ann Marie, though I had warned her to wait until I was with her. I didn't know then anything about the truth; I just wanted to be beside Ann Marie when your mother was told that we—that we—were going to be—married."

Kevin had listened without any expression on his broad face. When Courtney had revealed his own blood relationship to Kevin the younger man's eyes had flickered and widened and he had stared at Courtney intently, but had said nothing. If he thought anything at all about Courtney's reddened and mortified look he did not show it. They rode on slowly, when Courtney had finished, and Kevin had looked straight ahead.

"We must learn our own story, that no one said anything to Ann Marie, and that her horse had been frightened by something—a rabbit, a squirrel, a distant hunter's shot—whatever—and had bolted into the woods. We both saw it. That is our story."

Kevin had nodded briefly and the strong hard jaw became harder and his somewhat heavy lips had tightened. He had said, at last, "But what if Ann Marie becomes conscious, and tells him?"

"I don't think she will," said Courtney, and he bent his head. "She is too kind, too gentle, too understanding. She would not hurt either of her parents, not even if she died for it."

Then Kevin said, "I'm sorry. I'm damned sorry, Courtney." He had looked then at his young uncle and with awkward commiseration. They had not spoken again. But when the house had been reached, a house in waiting noisy turmoil, Kevin had gone to his mother and had taken her forcibly upstairs while she wailed and wept, and had pushed her to her room and had shut the door. He did not come downstairs for a long time. When he did he had grown older and his look was closed and compact and he had greeted Elizabeth, when she came into the house, with mature kindness and courtesy. He had answered all her anxious questions with such steadiness and surety that Courtney, who could not speak, could only admire him for his new manhood and his manifest strength of character.

Elizabeth found an occasion to whisper to her son, "Ann Marie—she never knew, you never had the opportunity to tell her?"

"No," said Courtney, and looked at her directly and she believed him. "I had no chance. Her horse bolted before I could say a word."

"Then we have had a reprieve," said his mother, and she had begun to cry. "The poor child, the poor little girl. How fortunate for everyone that Kevin had decided to meet you with her, to ask you something about Rory. Is anything wrong with Rory?"

Courtney only shook his head, and then they had begun their long vigil. Joseph had been met at the depot by Kevin, and Joseph had entered the house and had gone immediately upstairs to Ann Marie and her doctors who were fighting for her life. Silent at last, Bernadette slept a drugged sleep.

The great gilt and teakwood clock in the hall chimed half-past twelve. The thunderous prowling in the hills came no nearer, did not retreat, but the heat of the night intensified. No one in that room had eaten a dinner, and none had been offered by the housekeeper or cook. It was as if everything had withdrawn, in that house, to one room on the second floor. The huge glittering chandelier in the hall looked down on desertion.

Then they all heard slow steps on the marble stairs and Courtney and Kevin stood up and the two young men clenched their hands and stared at the door, afraid to go into the corridor that led to the hall, and afraid not to. Then Joseph appeared in the doorway and they saw his face, grown old with anxiety and fear and dread, and his hair which appeared to be a ragged patch of tangled russet and whitish gray. But his eyes were more alive than any of those present had seen them before. It was as if a fire burned behind their bitter and starting blue, and his wide thin mouth curved inwards.

It was at Elizabeth that he looked first, and she slowly

rose and said, "Joseph? How is Ann Marie?" Her own eyes were strained and brilliantly green in the lamplight, and her mouth shook.

He said to her in a rusty voice, "She is alive, but that is all. She has not regained consciousness. They are afraid her skull is fractured and that she is bleeding internally. No bones were broken, except for her left arm. One doctor has left; the others will remain until the specialists arrive tomorrow. She will have nurses then, too. They have been sent for." He paused. "We can only hope that she will survive the first shock."

Elizabeth sat down abruptly, for she was weak and worn, but the two young men faced Joseph in silence and it was at them that he now looked and the bluish fire in his eyes brightened ominously. He said to Kevin, "I should like to hear your story again."

It took all Kevin's will power not to glance at Courtney. The clear darkness of his face had turned sallow during these hours. He said, "I told you, Pa, on the way home from the depot, but I will tell you again. I met Ann Marie at the stables. I had just returned from a gallop. She said that she was going to meet Courtney in their 'usual place,' and that he had arrived that morning. There was something I wanted to ask Courtney—about Rory—and I asked Ann Marie if she would mind my coming for a few minutes, and she said that of course I could come." Here Kevin decided a little improvisation might help and he made himself smile quickly. "I knew I wasn't very welcome, but I went, just the same. She rode just ahead of me up the hill. I don't think I was twenty feet behind. I—I noticed that Missy seemed a little nervous, but Ann Marie said she was always skittish the first few minutes or so.

"Ann Marie raced ahead as we came near the top of the hill. I reached the top just in time to see her rein in Missy in front of Courtney's horse, and then—I don't know just what happened. Perhaps it was a rabbit, or a squirrel. I did think I heard a gun go off on the other side of the hill. But Missy reared up and whinnied—you know how unpredictable horses are—"

"No, I don't," said Joseph. He was watching his son's face with an eagle's predatory concentration, watching for the slightest sign of a falsehood, embarrassment, or obvious elaboration, and Kevin felt the sweat start out between his shoulder blades, for he knew his father and his ability to fathom the minds of others. "But, go on," said Joseph.

"I think Ann Marie cried out, or something, but the horse was too much for her though she's had her two years. Anyway, the horse circled on her hind legs, dropped down, and bolted for the woods. Courtney and I ran after her. We found Ann Marie, and Courtney stayed with her while I went for help. That's all, Pa."

Joseph regarded his son in impassive silence, his eyes moved over the youth's face, studying every line, every feature, peering into his eyes, his own face darkening as that relentless probing went on moment by moment and there was only the sound of the distant thunder and the disturbed muttering of the trees outside.

"And that's all?" he said finally. "You have told me everything?"

It was hard for Kevin to dissemble and to lie, for he had had no occasion in his life before to do so. He did not have Rory's style and flair and color and easy ability to deceive and tease and evade with a look of artlessness. His face was visibly wet now, but he forced himself to speak, to choose every word. He wrinkled his forehead. He pretended to be examining his memory while that thin and implacable man waited in a terrible silence.

Then Kevin spread out his hands and shook his head. "I can't think of another thing, Pa. I'm not good at describing things, I know, or giving them drama, but that is truly all that happened." And now he pretended at weary exasperation. "Pa, we are the ones who saw it all, Courtney and I, and spent those hours with Ann Marie before you arrived home! We've had hell beaten out of us, and I don't understand why this inquisition!"

But Joseph slowly looked away from Kevin and turned to Elizabeth. His voice changed to the sharpened ears of the young men. He said, "Elizabeth, you had something to tell Courtney this morning, didn't you? I asked you to do it. Did you tell him?"

Elizabeth's eyes were a momentary green flash at her son and then she said sadly, "Yes. I told him. At breakfast." She stopped. "We agreed that he would tell Ann Marie some story that would not be the truth, but would hurt her as little as possible."

"What story?" said Kevin, with an air of rejuvenated interest. "Is there a secret?"

"Be quiet," said Joseph. Now he turned to Courtney and Courtney was horrified to see the powerful and senseless hatred in Joseph's eyes, the coldly violent force of his expression. "What were you going to tell my daughter," he asked, and his voice was harsh and menacing.

Courtney could not understand why this heightened concentration should be directed on him, this sudden deadly passion, and for the first time he could completely understand why so many potent men had cowered before this man. But after his first stunned reaction Courtney stood up tall and straight in hauteur, and he answered:

"I hadn't made up my mind which story would hurt her the least. Frankly, I've never dreaded anything so much in my life. You must remember, Uncle Joseph, that this was a stunning revelation to me, that I love Ann Marie, that it had shaken my whole life, all my hopes, apart. It was like an earthquake—it was like death, itself. I know you are thinking of Ann Marie, and what it would mean to her, but she was not alone, Uncle Joseph. I'd like you to remember that."

Kevin drew nearer. He put on an avid look and leaned forward like a youth dying to be informed. But when Joseph gave him a fierce glance he drew back a step.

"Now," said Joseph, "tell me what happened."

"I have nothing to add to Kevin's account, not a word. Ann Marie just rode up, her horse reared, made a circle on her hind legs, whinnied, and bolted into the woods. Ann Marie and I didn't exchange a single word, not one, though I think I greeted her. I can't remember. It all happened so suddenly. It was all so fast that I didn't immediately see Kevin right behind her on his own horse. There is nothing else."

"So, my daughter never knew?"

"No. Not to my knowledge. Who was there to tell her but me?"

"There was her mother," said Joseph, and he saw the young men exchange a glance.

Courtney swallowed through a dry throat. He said, after apparently giving the matter consideration, "Ann Marie and I had agreed that she would not tell her mother—about us wanting to marry—unless I was with her. I have no reason to believe that Ann Marie broke that agreement. When she rode up to me, and before Missy reared and bolted, she was as always—glad to see me, eager to talk—" He could not go on. The face of Ann Marie stood before him as he had seen it this disastrous morning when she had confronted him with terror and revulsion and anguish. He bent his head.

"You are sure she did not know?"

"I am sure," said Courtney, when he could speak again. "I'd have known at once."

Joseph put his hands on his hips, a gesture alien to the American-born, and so curiously foreign. But he looked hard into Courtney's face and he said with precision, "I think you are both lying. You are trying to protect—somebody."

Elizabeth cried, "Why would my son, and yours, lie, Joseph? What makes you think they are lying?" She was standing again and her face was like white fire in the extremity of deep indignation.

Joseph's eyes went to her face and he contemplated her in silence, but his own face changed subtly. "Perhaps, Elizabeth," he said, "they have been lying to you, too."

Kevin broke in. "What is all this about? What was Ann Marie going to be told? What is the mystery?"

He was not prepared for his father's answer. He expected Joseph not to reply, or to turn away. But Joseph's eyes were again fixed on the youth's face and were again terrible. "No one told you that Courtney and Ann Marie could not marry? No one ever told you that Courtney is your blood uncle, your half uncle, if you will, the brother of your mother?"

"No!" exclaimed Kevin, giving a great start and making his eyes bulge. "For God's sake! I thought—I thought he was adopted by my grandfather!" He turned to Courtney and affected to give him sharp consideration and speculative conjecture. "I thought his father's name was Wickersham."

Elizabeth's drawn face had deeply flushed. She turned aside, her head raised in proud defensiveness and suffering. Hell, thought Kevin, I'm sorry to have to do this to her, but my parents and my family are more to me than Elizabeth Hennessey and old Grandpa.

Joseph said, watching her, and now there was a darkness

of shame and regret on his face: "I'm sorry, Elizabeth. But I have to know the truth. My daughter is upstairs, probably dying, and I want to know who told her the thing which almost killed her, and drove her to this."

Elizabeth turned slowly to him and audibly caught her breath and her eyes were green stone. "You were always too imaginative, Joseph," she said, and her voice was cold and steady, as if she were speaking to a servant, and he heard it and something roiled in him, galling and sickened. "I think Ann Marie has more strength than you give her credit for, and I believe that even if she had been told she would have accepted it."

They regarded each other now in silence and Joseph thought, She will never forgive me, my Elizabeth. It will never again be the same between us—if there will ever be anything.

Elizabeth was thinking this also, and now added to her weariness and anxiety and sympathy was an enormous pain and withdrawal, a regret that something beautiful had been shattered and even if repaired would be cracked and subtly disfigured.

"You might not have humiliated my mother, before your son," said Courtney, feeling deep rage. "Would you like to give it to the newspapers, too? Shall I summon them for you in the morning—or have you already told your doctors who can spread my mother's secret far and wide?"

"Courtney," said Elizabeth. "Courtney, take me home. Please. I feel we are unwelcome here."

"I will take you home," said Joseph.

"You will not," said Courtney. "She is my mother. What have you to do with her anyway? She came here to a house where she is hated by your wife, and is insulted, by you, and she came only because she loved Ann Marie like a mother and because she thought she might be able to help —help with your wife. My sister! God damn it, my sister! The very thought is hateful to me, do you know that, Mr. Armagh? Do you know how much I despise your wife, and now despise you?" The young man's face was blazing with the fervor of his rage and his new hate. "And your wife has had the audacity, over all the years I can remember, to be insulting, ungracious, cruel, contemptible, and vulgar to my mother! She who isn't good enough to wipe my mother's feet with her bare hands! But still my mother came to this disgusting house, again to be shamed and insulted, again to be told that her presence here is unwanted. Mother, let us go."

So, thought Joseph, whose face had turned a dark crimson, there is one thing he does not know, and now he felt remorse—an emotion so strange to him that it startled him, for the last time he had felt such a thing had been when confronting Senator Bassett. Courtney had taken his mother's arm, and she was drawing her lacy shawl over her shoulders, and Kevin was watching and listening admiringly.

Joseph went and stood before Elizabeth and faced her, and she could not look away though her eyes were full of tears and her lip trembled.

"I will take you home, Elizabeth," he said. "Courtney, no doubt, would like to stay here for a little while for any news of Ann Marie. Elizabeth?"

"No," said Courtney. But he saw, with astonishment, that his mother and Joseph were seeing only each other, and as one who loved, himself, he knew the expressions of love, and he was aghast. He stepped back, his hands moving in a gesture of sharp repudiation, and his mouth felt suddenly scalded. He thought he would be sick. He had never seen his mother's face like this, helpless, melting, for all her pride; he saw her tears. And he saw her bow her head. He wanted to kill Joseph when Joseph gently took Elizabeth's arm and led her towards the door and looked down at her with all the solicitude and tenderness of a lover, a lover asking forgiveness and expecting it as a matter of course.

Kevin had seen all this, too, and his black eyebrows had shot upwards, intrigued, amazed, and then more than a little amused in spite of all that had happened that day. So, that was the way it was, was it? He felt no condemnation for his father, no embarrassment. He was young and even his apprehension for his sister was forgotten for a few moments while he chuckled inwardly and shook his head and wondered if his mother knew. No doubt she did. No doubt that partially explained her hatred for Elizabeth. Poor old Ma. Well, compared with Aunt Elizabeth she was only a fishwife, loud, noisy, vindictive, coarse and lashing of tongue, and full of boisterous malicious laughter and exaggerated gossip, always hoping for an evil story concerning friends, always deprecating, always exercising her rowdy wit on anyone she disliked—and she disliked practically everyone (including her children) except Pa. The thought of his father as the lover of a woman made Kevin chuckle inwardly again. Even such as Joseph Armagh could be held in the hands of a woman. Let that be a lesson to you, my bucko, Kevin told himself. If a woman can do that to Pa, above all men, then what could a woman do to you, eh?

He became conscious of Courtney, who had sat down again, his elbows on his knees, his face in his hands. Poor old Courtney, what shocks he had had today. Discovering Ma was his sister—he had always disliked her. Knowing what he must tell Ann Marie, and he in love with her. Then, the tragedy that had almost killed Ann Marie—of course Ma had told her: he had known that almost at once, or at least he had known that dear old Ma had done something to the girl. Then Courtney had had to tell him. Now, that was a noble old boy, Courtney. Protect Ma, who was like a rhinoceros. Talk about Sir Galahads: Old Court had the strength of twenty, not ten. Protect the whole Armagh family.

If anything, Kevin felt more affection and admiration for his father than he had done before. He sat down near Courtney and said, "I am going to have a drink, and I think you need one, too, and then I'll tell one of the damned maids to bring us some sandwiches and coffee."

"No," said Courtney, from behind his hands, but Kevin whistled and pulled the bell rope. "Please yourself," he said. "There isn't a funeral in this house, but even at funerals they eat baked meats, or something. You've never been to an Irish wake."

Courtney dropped his hands. His face looked dull and lifeless and his pale hair was disordered, and his eyes had a defeated expression in them. But he said, "Yes, I've been to Irish wakes. You forget I'm Irish, too. I'm a Hennessey by birth as well as by name, and I wish to God I could wipe that out." A ripple of shadowy anger ran over his features, and a new bitterness, and a sorrow that he could not express.

He did drink the brandy that was brought to him and Kevin, and a little color took the pallor from his cheeks, and he even ate half a sandwich and drank some coffee. In the meantime he listened to every sound. Eventually he heard Joseph come back—it was a long time to Courtney—and go upstairs again.

When Courtney returned home, after hearing from a maid that Ann Marie was still "resting," and that there had been no change, he did not look for his mother. He saw a light under her door, and he felt the heat in his face. He went to his room and threw himself on his bed and a blessed numbness came to him. He never knew whether he slept or not but at least the agony had retreated, and had become mercifully unreal for a little while.

But Joseph sat by his daughter, watching the faces of the physicians who ministered to her, seeing the long brown braids on her pillow, the hollow remoteness of her young profile, the arm in its sling, the bandage on her head where her hair had been shaved. He listened for her breathing. Occasionally she moaned.

It was almost dawn when—as if in a vision that stood before him in unwavering light—he saw the face of Senator Bassett and remembered the curse that unfortunate man had laid upon the family and person of Joseph Armagh, and remembered his own dream.

It was ridiculous, even to remember. It was, this superstition, fit only for old wives in chimney corners, cackling of banshees and the little people and omens and visitations, and moldy curses. But Joseph sat by his daughter and he thought of Senator Bassett whom he had murdered as surely as any assassin.

Chapter 2

There was not a night that Elizabeth Hennessey did not sit upstairs at her bedroom window and watch the Armagh house. It was January now, and the lawns and the trees were filled up with snow and there was a wide desolation on the sky near sunset, when a lavender shadow ran over the whiteness of the earth and the steepled spruces and the pines stood black against a coldly sparkling orange west. No sleigh bells scattered thin music in the silence, chimneys cept for the upper servants' quarters, and no movement could be seen at black windows, and no coming or going. No sleigh bells scattered thin music in the silence, chimneys smoked but desultorily; the roofs were marble under the moon. The New Year came and went, and there were no yellow opened doors, no laughter, no guests, no ball as usual.

For Joseph and Bernadette had taken their daughter, Ann Marie, to Europe the last of September for a hopeless round of celebrated neurologists in Geneva, Paris, Rome and London, and brain specialists. Kevin and Rory were at their university, and did not come home for the holidays. Courtney had accompanied Joseph and Bernadette during their desperate hegira until Bernadette had more than made it plain that he was unwanted and unwelcome. He was now in Amalfi and gave his mother no indication of when he would return. Elizabeth guessed that he knew of her liaison with Joseph Armagh, and that in some way, in his grief-stricken misery and confusion, he blamed her for his birth, Ann Marie's condition, and the final humiliation of her affair. Some day, she knew, when his grief was less, he would see more clearly. In the meantime she had to be satisfied with his brief cold notes to which she replied with maternal warmth and love.

It was Rory who kept her informed of the family, from

letters from his mother. Joseph's letters to her were abrupt
with sorrow and despair, and she knew she must not reply
to them. Ann Marie could walk now, feed herself, help a
nurse to dress and bathe her, but beyond that she had been
reduced to the intelligence of a child of less than three, and
had no memory of her past life, no memory of Elizabeth
and Courtney Hennessey, and did not remember her brothers from visit to visit. She had lost the years of her education
and her experience. The only clue that sometimes heartened the family was an awful and unremitting fear of
horses and terror of even a small copse of trees. But as the
months passed these fears began to abate so that the
parents were able to take her, without a blindfold, into a
carriage. So, the last hope was dwindling out, and Joseph
was trying to reconcile himself to the fact that his shy and
timid young daughter would remain an infant for the rest
of her life. Once only he wrote to Elizabeth: "It were better if she had died, for though her bodily health has been
restored and she is becoming quite plump, her mental fac-
ulties do not increase. The only consolation I have is that
she is seemingly contented, as she was as a very young
child, and laughs and plays as that child, and is docile and
affectionate, and above all, happy with the innocence of
childhood. Her lineaments and color are those of a young
child. Who knows but what this is kinder to her than maturity, and growing old and bitter and disillusioned and sad,
and full of the fears of maturity? At least she will never
know these, never know loss or discontent or wretchedness.
She is in the Limbo about which we were taught by the
priests, that is, in a state of 'natural' happiness where there
is no darkness, no fright, no longing, but only affection and
kind words and care."

Rory wrote Elizabeth that the family expected to return
in the spring with Ann Marie. Doctors had strongly urged
that the girl be placed in "a comfortable retreat with those
other unfortunates who had been born in that condition,
where she will receive professional solicitude and taught
simple tasks and be among her own kind." Bernadette had
eagerly agreed, thinking of the melancholy presence of her
daughter in her house, with attendant nurses and constant
comings and goings of physicians, and "disruptions," as
Rory quoted his mother. But Joseph had refused. His
daughter would live and die in her home.

Elizabeth, against her will, sympathized with Bernadette.

It was all very well for Joseph, who was rarely in Green Hills, except for an occasional weekend and holidays. His would not be the daily depression of the sight of nurses and the bulletins of physicians. He would not have to see Ann Marie daily, and remember her as she was. He would not have to deal with recalcitrant servants, who resented the darkening presence of an invalid and the special meals and the authority of bustling nurses, who could be arrogant. All this would be the province of the gregarious, lively and active Bernadette, who hated responsibility and especially hated the very sight and smell of illness either in herself or others. If Ann Marie, in her present state, were deeply attached to her parents, the matter would be different, but Elizabeth gathered that she was equally happy with nurses and servants abroad, did not miss anyone who did not appear as usual, and hardly recognized Bernadette or Joseph. Once Joseph had had to be in London for three weeks—he had taken Rory with him—and when he went to Ann Marie on his return the girl had not recognized him at all, and had been shy with him for nearly a week. That, thought Elizabeth, must have been devastating.

Is he punishing Bernadette for what he suspects, but does not know? Elizabeth would ask herself. Is he punishing her because Bernadette was never fond of the poor child, and is this his revenge? Even Elizabeth who knew him better than anyone else in the world could not answer her own questions. When she thought of Ann Marie it was like thinking of the dead, for the girl was now no longer a young adult, and could no longer take her place with the living. What lived in Ann Marie was not the thinking and speculating and wondering soul, alive to experience and joy, and even sorrow. It was a simple, natural, animal spirit which would never grow older, never develop, never know love, never miss anyone, never rejoice.

Sometimes Elizabeth thought: Is Ann Marie's brain permanently damaged, or is she in retreat from life and will not return to it? There were some gentle people who once cruelly injured could no longer face existence as it was, and is, and develop loss of memory or fly back into a childhood which was less painful, less agonizing, less demanding of acceptance. Once again on that rose-island full of unending sunlight they would never return. No one could answer Elizabeth's conjectures, for no one knew. Had Bernadette driven her daughter back into those infantile days—because the present and the future were too direful to face for one like Ann Marie—or had it all been truly an "accident"? Bernadette would not speak, of course, if she knew anything at all, and Courtney and Kevin had been explicit enough and their stories had never varied. Yet Elizabeth, highly intuitive, had the strangest conviction that both the young men had not spoken of an enlightening incident. She remembered that Courtney had said that Ann Marie had regained consciousness briefly in the woods, had recognized him and had spoken to him, had asked where she was and how she had come to be there, and had told him that she loved him. Yet, later, when Elizabeth had asked him to repeat that to her he had looked at her with green eyes newly chill and remote and had said, "Mother, you must have imagined it, or mistaken what I said. I only said that she opened her eyes once; whether she knew me or not I don't know. She immediately lapsed into a coma again." So, Courtney, who never lied, had lied to his mother. The reason could only be guessed by intuition, and intuition could be wrong. At any rate the strong deep bond between mother and son had been destroyed. Whether or not it would regrow was only a conjecture. The loss was greater to Elizabeth than the thought of Ann Marie, who at least did not know pain and would never know it in the future.

In the meantime Elizabeth watched the slow and desolate winter days come and go, and at last the clear cold light of February, the dark storms of March. Spring always comes, she would comfort herself, though it is not the springs we knew in our past. Life is not really renewed. It only rises from dead leaves of sorrow and loss and suffering, and it is stained by them so that each new spring brings its own sad remembrance, its old yearning, its old spasms of pain, and is dimmed inexorably so that the last spring is full of shadows and without color, without meaning, and the farewell is without regret. The best hope given to man in the Bible was, "In the grave there is no remembrance."

Elizabeth's own house was as silent and deserted as the Armagh house, for no longer were there joyous anticipations of meeting Joseph in New York, no laughing excursions with him, no long talks before a comforting fire, no lying with him in a warm bed entwined like two trees, no morning sight of his face, no leaping of the heart at the sound of his voice. Only in love is there a real springtime, she would sadly reflect. Only love makes us immortal and immune to living; only in love is there youth and hope. Without it, we are blasted trees in an ashy forest where nothing moves or has a significant being, and where there is no sunset and no rising of the sun, but only a smoky twilight. Elizabeth did not go to New York for concerts and the theater or for shopping. She was not the sort to make friends readily, or keep them close to her, for she was essentially dependent upon men and had little regard for women as confidantes or companions. So she sat in her deserted house and watched the weeks go by, and lived only for the spring when Joseph would return. In the meantime her own life was in abeyance.

Would she and Joseph ever know again the profound intimacy of trust, of love given with abandon? Or would the memory of that hot disastrous night slide in the midst of their love like a doubting traitor? It doesn't matter, Elizabeth would think. So long as he is within sight and sound, nothing will matter to me. Is it only women who are abject in love? We can forgive everything, even betrayal, even insult and neglect and unfounded accusations. Men are more to us than women are to men, I seem to remember, and that is probably our curse. I try to feel pride and I can only wallow in my longing to see him again. Had I mortified him as he mortified me he would never look at me all the rest of my life, but all I desire is embracing him once more. When he took me home that night I could think of nothing but asking him to love me for forgiving him. But then, suppose it had been my own child and not Ann Marie? I remember that, and that is my own excuse to myself, for I love and so am without self-respect and am willing to condone. Joseph, Joseph!

In early January Joseph cabled his son Rory: MEET ME IN LONDON ON THE 17TH THIS MONTH.

Damn, thought Rory. Has some doctor given him some new hope? No, that is not like the Old Man. It is something else. Pa is one of the kind that doesn't "hope," and I'll give him credit for that. He's too realistic.

He said to his wife, Marjorie: "I have to leave you for a while, my love, for my father is asking me to go to him in London." Marjorie said, with spirit, "Take me with you. I'd like to meet your father. Yes, dear, I know. You still have your education to complete and you are Papa's puppet and are afraid to let him know that you are married to a descendant—lateral—of Paul Revere. It would lower the tone of your family." She added pensively, "I wonder what Daddy would think of all this. I really do."

"Maggie, don't be a shrew."

Marjorie smiled sweetly. "That is always a crushing answer of a man, isn't it? It's supposed to make a wife grovel." She threw herself into his arms and cried, "Rory, Rory! Just don't stop loving me! Just go to your father and remember I am here, waiting. Rory, I'd die for you. And isn't that something I should be ashamed of? Never mind. Kiss me."

"You women demand too much," said Rory, indulgent to her for loving him. "We have affairs, and all you can think of is kissing."

"And love," said Marjorie. "Didn't St. Paul say that was above faith and hope? Never mind. One of these days you men will learn the truth of that—if you don't destroy the world first."

"Oh, we are very predatory beasts, like all males," said Rory, and went to London.

Rory knew that nothing could be so dank, dark, cold, and miserable as England in winter, so wet and depressing, so foggy and smoky, with every chimney pot thickly and turgidly spewing out black soot and the stench of coal gas, and with a sky hardly lighter. However, he liked sea journeys and the ship was comfortable and luxurious—Rory had hounded "old" Charlie Devereaux for first class fare, something which Joseph did not approve of for "profligates." So Rory had a fine stateroom all to himself, his breakfast in bed, and a chair on the sheltered portion of the promenade deck. He had also taken his lawbooks with him, for he had no intention of falling back in his strenuous classes, and some books of poetry and history. Like his father, he read intensively and constantly, something which surprised strangers who did not reconcile "bookishness" with such an easy, amiable and articulate, and above all, such a handsome and vigorous young man who was always ready to engage in any sport and had a reputation as a womanizer. Rory did not usually like books concerning politics, though he liked politics itself, but his father had said with that saturnine smile of his, "No matter. It is more important to learn about the people who control politicians and the events of a nation, and decide its destiny." Rory had already met a few in New York. He kept his opinions to himself.

Rory was not a young man who particularly admired modesty and the modest. "Why hide something if you have something superior to show?" he would say. So he had contrived that the captain of the ship knew that he was on board and he was immediately invited to the captain's table, the captain a Scotsman with a bright red beard and mustaches and hair, even to the hair growing out of his ears. He also had pointed blue eyes, like drills, Rory commented to himself, and a big Semitic nose, and his name was MacAfee, and he was gallant to the ladies at his table and brusk with the men. He decided he did not like Rory's sort, brash, smiling too much, too rich, too friendly. However, on the third day out he was not so certain in his dour Scots' mind that Rory was lightheaded, spoiled and a little stupid, and by the fifth day—though his original dislike had not abated—he thought the bucko was in some way in need of watching, "though it's hard to put a finger on it," he confided to his first mate, who was also Scots. "Smiles like a bloody bright sun in the morning, smiles all the time, jests —that he does—and walks like a dancer, but there's some'at that makes a mon's hackles rise."

"He's Irish," said the second mate.

"That he is," said the captain, scowling, and tugging at his red beard. "And a Papist, no doot. But we must remember, laddie, that he is a Celt like us, for a' that." He scowled again. "I know all aboot his Dada, and that's a blasted one, but he's a director of this line. A shame it is."

Rory hardly liked Captain MacAfee better than the captain liked him, but Rory was not a man who cultivated dislike and grudges and prejudices as a matter of course. It was too time-consuming, when there were more interesting things to notice and enjoy, particularly the company of a very young lady who sat at his left hand and who was accompanied by a strict middle-aged lady with an enormous bosom glittering with jet, a face like a partly domesticated harpy with a suspicious mind and dark little eyes "like a snake's," the jovial Rory remarked to himself. Rory learned almost at once that the interesting young girl was Miss Claudia Worthington, and that she was the daughter of the Ambassador from the United States of America to the Court of Her Majesty, Queen Victoria—the Court of St. James's. She had had a bad "chill" in the winter and had just recovered, but was not returning to her finishing school in New York, where she was in her last term, but was going to "Papa and Mama" in London "for the summer, and journeys to Devon and Paris." Miss Lucy Kirby, the formidable harpy, was her chaperone and had been her governess, and was also her personal attendant.

It was Miss Kirby's opinion that Miss Claudia was a "chatterbox," and that it was very ill-bred of her to take to a stranger even if he sat next to her at the captain's table, and that the stranger was no doubt a scoundrel—to judge from his somewhat flamboyant clothing, his unreserved and "too familiar manners," and his way of laughing very heartily and showing all his big white teeth. He was entirely too facile, too cheerful, to be a gentleman. Even when Miss Kirby heard who he was she had tossed her head forbiddingly. Rory did not rise in her estimation. It was not hard in America to acquire vast fortunes—if one had no scruples, and Joseph Armagh, it was usually hinted in some unfriendly newspapers, was not distinguished for scruples and "bought and sold politicians like horses at a horse fair." The fact that her employer, the Honorable Stephen Worthington, was not distinguished for his scruples, either, but— the *New York Times* had openly declared—had "bought" his ambassadorship, did not lessen him in Miss Kirby's regard. After all, he had a Position. Besides, he paid her generously and his wife was a lady. It came to Miss Kirby eventually that the ambassador knew Joseph Armagh very well, indeed, and met him frequently in Washington, though when at home in his mansion on Fifth Avenue in New York he had a way of talking about Mr. Armagh which implied good-tempered contempt and more than a little fear. Miss Kirby, who was no idiot, had learned that the contempt was assumed in order to hide the more baleful emotion, and so she had come to the conclusion that Mr. Armagh was a monster and should be ridden out of the country on a rail, after being thoroughly tarred and feathered. And this was his son who sat so at ease and rallied Miss Claudia mirthfully, and teased her! It was hardly to be borne.

Claudia was only sixteen, but a knowledgeable and sophisticated sixteen, for she knew the value of position and money. Rory thought her affected at first, or even not very well-bred, for there was a certain exaggeration of gentility and ceremony about her. She wore gloves at all times, and took them off only at the table, to reveal hands which were not at all elegant or even pretty, and had large knuckles and hard angles. But Rory saw almost at once that she was not conscious of the imperfections of her hands, and that she wore gloves all the time as the mark of a lady who also had a Position. She was a tall girl with a body too slight for her beauty but with hips that needed no padding to exceed normal expansion and be in high hour-glass style, and Rory suspected that her legs would be heavy in proportion also. He also suspected that the young bosom had been assisted with certain artifices which gave it more importance for a girl of sixteen, and therefore nubile, and with a very slender waist which he was certain a man could embrace with two hands without trouble. He liked thin waists in girls, though he knew this was often obtained only at the cost of painful whalebone and tight laces.

Rory adored pretty women. Even his passionate love for Marjorie, his wife, had not dimmed his appreciation of the other sex, nor would he have rejected overtures of an amatory nature from any delectable female. He knew his own nature well, but did not feel that he was being false to Marjorie. He loved Marjorie and he would never love anyone else, he told himself, and in a curious way this was quite true. Yet a little frolicking with a charmer of a bent like his own would not harm his devotion to Marjorie, and would certainly not diminish his joy in her. He had never had any real intention of remaining totally faithful to Marjorie— though this decision was, for the first few months, not in his conscious thoughts.

His first impression of Claudia Worthington was that she was not in the least pretty or enticing, but "foreign" in appearance, and he was not sure that he liked "foreignness" in women. She had an angular face with broad cheekbones and deep hollows under them, a straight somewhat arrogant nose, a very broad pink mouth, and tilted eyes which made him think of them as "Oriental." They were of an unusual color, dark, greenish brown. Her eyebrows were abnormally thick and black and almost met at the bridge of her nose, and were tilted also. She had a strong and obstinate chin with a dimple. Her neck was not sweet and tender, as a girl's should be, but had a tint of sallowness in it, and visible cords. Her hair was chestnut brown, thick and shining as the hide of a well-kept animal, coarse and heavy and plentiful, and so needed no "rats" or switches to make it rise impressively high in the new pompadour over her somewhat low dark forehead, and the two long curls that fell from it over her shoulders were "real" also. She dressed with instinctive taste, and not with that tendency of young girls to elaborate on current fashion. Her dresses were rich but decorous, her belts broad but restrained, her shoes daintily narrow, her coats marvelously cut, her jewels becoming to a girl that age. She wore little gold buttons in her ears and almost always just a short string of finely matched pearls, and a pearl ring on her finger surrounded with opals.

For diversion, for flirtatious episodes no matter how innocent, Rory preferred blatant women as did his father, but for an entirely different reason. Joseph's preference rose from a desire to regard a woman as only an object for necessary and immediate pleasure, and then to forget her, allowing her no part in his life, and not even a memory. But Rory liked blatant women because they were usually full of fun, health, zest, and common sense, and never "clung" to a man demanding more than he was prepared to give.

Rory decided at once that Claudia was not a blatant girl, and right after that that she was not pretty in a way he liked, and that she had a manner of opening her eyes very wide that might have been engaging in a lovelier girl but was only just a hard stare in Claudia, and not an attractive one at that, and, with the heavy brows above them—too low over them—they gave her a rather scowling look even when the lips below them were smiling. She is a sullen piece, Rory had thought the first day, and had decided to ignore her.

Then, at dinner, he was startled. It was not that she wore anything unusual. The mauve silk gown with its pearl-beaded bodice decorated with a jeweled watch was stylish enough and enhanced her figure. It was something else. He found he could hardly look away from this unpretty girl, with the pouting pink underlip and the very unprovocative profile. Just when he had decided that she was quite ordinary in appearance, he found himself thinking, Why, she is exotic, captivating, unusual! The next instant she was only a schoolgirl on holiday again, chattering about something inconsequential in her rather light and immature voice, a voice quite infantile. She had a mannerism of hurrying too fast in her speech so that her words ran together, then catching her breath in a rush. Sometimes her voice was inaudible, though her lips continued to move rapidly.

It was this quality of hers—to appear commonplace at one moment then inordinately esoteric the next—without a feature changing—which was entrancing. She used no overt arts to attract, no learned coquettishness. Rory had heard of charm, and he thought Marjorie exquisite, but now he saw that there was an irresistible attribute that was really charm in its full meaning and had nothing whatsoever to do with beauty or any endearing possession of the owner, or any grace of character or anything that can be learned and successfully imitated. At these moments Claudia's very deficiencies of conventional beauty only enhanced that magnetism so that the observer was left feverishly wondering what it was about her that was so striking, so fascinating, so able to hold the eye that one could not turn away. Her expression, her eyes, her smile, her manner? It was none of these. It was something intrinsic and explicit, and if the girl knew that she had it she seemed unaware.

But Rory soon saw that the captain and two other gentlemen at the table were as caught by this indefinable but powerful thing as he was, and that they were as fascinated as he and doubtless as bewildered. It was not simply a sexual thing in itself, nor did it imply sexuality. It was only there, as fearful a weapon as any woman could possess, and enchanting. It was mysterious, even when the person possessing it was not in the least mysterious.

In the days that followed Rory tried to fathom the secret of bonafide charm, but it was not to be known, nor analyzed. The girl's character was not impressive for depth, intellect or kindness or sympathy or perceptiveness. It was, in fact, somewhat shallow, without flair or passion or subtlety. But there was in it, too, a hardness, a perverse decisiveness, a self-absorbed egotism, which should have been repellent. There was a hint of greed and exigency in it also. Yet, Rory would think, what is it she has? When she turned that charm upon him—consciously or unconsciously—she appeared the most adorable creature in the world, desirable above all other women, and he felt giddy. Now he could understand the masculine fools who gave up thrones, honor, family, tradition, and pride for women like this.

But Rory wanted something more in a woman than even this intimidating yet resistless charm. He walked every morning and evening on the promenade deck with Claudia, who found him delightful, as she told Miss Kirby with defiance, Rory huddled in coats and Claudia in furs, and Miss Kirby trailing them like a truculent and silently protesting grenadier in brown tweeds and a sable boa. Rory, the politician, knew that it was necessary to cultivate everyone of any importance, and Claudia was important, and even though after the fifth day she bored him almost to open yawning and flight, he was gallant to her. She chattered, and it was usually only about herself, her clothes, the people she knew, her school, her friends, her family, her "distinguished" father, what he had said to the Queen and what Her Majesty had said to him, her coming presentation to the Queen, in feathers and white silk, how the Princess of Wales had admired her mother's Christmas gown and jewels, horses, dogs, her pet cat, and her dull lessons, which Miss Kirby presided over every morning after breakfast. If Rory tried to introduce another subject, such as books or travel, she would glance at him impatiently and say, in a light petulant voice, "Really? Don't you think Paris too advertised? Did I tell you what Angela Small, the minx, said to me before I took ill? It was too, too malicious."

But Rory noticed that she never failed to mention the financial position of anyone she spoke of, or quoted, or their social eminence. If she had ever had a poetic thought, or had ever been aware of the world of nature and beauty about her, it was not evident. Music? She liked Gilbert and Sullivan, of course, everybody did. Opera was dull. (She used that word for everything that did not catch her interest or was irrelevant to her.) Her world was herself, foremost. All things and people orbited about her. She accepted this fact with complacency, and never questioned it. So long as Rory did not look directly at her he was unaware of her charm, her mysterious magic and fascination. Then she was only a school miss who was ineffably dull herself, and somewhat stupid, self-engrossed, incapable of forming good judgment about others except when it served her own interests, and materialistic to a degree which even the materialistic Rory found repulsive. It was only when he looked at her that he was undone and shaken, though his intrinsic dislike for her did not lessen. In truth, it increased, for her attraction for him made him dislike himself, also, and hurt his own egotism. He began little maneuvers to avoid her, but she was there at lunch and dinner, and she could always find him for walks, and so at last he said to himself, Why, this silly little thing is actually pursuing me! His male pride was tickled, but he wished that she had some authentic intelligence and did not prattle clichés she had been taught in her school and in her society, and that she had just one original thought occasionally.

At the farewell party given by the captain just before arrival in Southampton, Claudia appeared in rose-lace and satin and was so compelling that hardly a man could keep his eyes from her, and Rory thought, She is the most beautiful thing in the world, yet she hasn't a single beautiful feature and not the ghost of a brain in her head! She was delighted that people believed her to be at least eighteen, and delighted to inform them that she hadn't yet "come out." But then she would say, she would be seventeen in two months.

Claudia and Miss Kirby were met at Southampton by two of the ambassador's attachés. Claudia graciously introduced them to Rory, and mentioned that his dear Papa was the famous Joseph Armagh, and Rory was invited to accompany the party in their special coach to London. But Rory had had, for the present, quite enough of Miss Worthington, for all her charm, and hastily excused himself and disappeared. In some way, as he sat in the first class carriage on the sooty train to London, he felt that he had escaped, and he thought of Marjorie who had intelligence, wit and perception, and a lovely depth of character, and sympathy. The train was cold, but the thought of Marjorie warmed him, and he took out his writing case and wrote her a letter on the spot. It was very fervent and Marjorie was overjoyed when she received it, though she blushed at some of the innuendoes.

Rory avoided Claudia and her party at the great and thunderous and smoky station in London, and found himself a hack and was on his way to the somber if luxurious hotel at which Joseph usually stayed in the city. As Rory feared, it was dank and rainy and dark in London, and a foggy mist brooded over it, and black umbrellas glistened everywhere on the milling streets and the omnibuses splashed through puddles and there was the pervading stink of coal gas. Even the shoplights looked dim and dreary.

The hotel was huge and old, ponderous and comfortable, and, thank God, there was a large fire in the fireplace in the lobby and so the interior was just a little warmer than it was outside. Everything was dark crimson and mahogany and looking-glasses framed in old gilt, and everything was hushed as if in a cathedral. But there were bowls of daffodils on the tables and some narcissi, grown in hothouses no doubt, thought the chilled Rory. He went up to the usual Armagh suite on the third floor in the gilded and creaking elevator which was raised and lowered by ropes. (No effete electricity here!) Why did his father choose this hotel, when there were a few gayer ones in London? He never knew that when Joseph entered this lobby he was really fleeing from a leaking thatched hut in Ireland, and that he had just escaped murderous enemies on the black highways outside.

The suite was enormous, and thank God again, filled with firelight and lamplight and blessedly warm. Rory knew that his father could not bear the cold, but he did not know why. He could only be grateful. He saw at once that Joseph had grown much older, and was thinner than ever, though controlled as usual. The broad stripes of whitish-gray in his thick russet hair had widened. He greeted his son as though he had seen him but the day before. But Rory said, "How is Ann Marie? Is she, and Ma, with you?"

"They are in a sanitorium in Paris," said Joseph. "Ann Marie? She is the same. Rosy and healthy, flourishing." He paused. He looked down. "She will never recover her mind. We are reconciled to that now." His closed face did not change but there was a sinking about his mouth. "I am here for only a few days, Rory. On business. It is time that you were introduced to—the men who matter."

"The ones I met in New York?"

"No. You saw only the Americans. Now you will meet the international—" He stopped. Then he repeated, "The men who matter." He explained no further. They had a sumptuous dinner in their private dining room but Rory noticed that his father ate very little. But then, he always did. He hardly touched the wine, which Rory drank with gusto, his ruddy face becoming even more ruddy. From time to time his father studied him acutely if not openly. The fires crackled; the scent of roast beef and Yorkshire pudding and kidney pie was comforting.

Rory liked to make his father smile and forget his somberness. So in his lively and amusing way he told him about Claudia. "The ambassador's daughter?" said Joseph, showing some interest. "A chit, you say? The ambassador. That sod."

It was rare for Joseph to utter obscenities, and Rory was immediately interested. "I thought he was an old friend of yours, Pa."

"Friend? I have no friends," said Joseph. He studied his still-filled wineglass. "Except, perhaps, for Harry Zeff and Charles Devereaux. I have—acquaintances. I recommended Steve to certain people, and the President. He owes me a lot."

"If you have such a low opinion of him why did you recommend him?" asked the inquisitive Rory.

Joseph looked at him with pent impatience. "Haven't you learned yet, from all that I have already told you, that politics is entirely removed from personalities, boyo? Do you think I, and the men I know, go about recommending good men of character and integrity? Don't be a fool, Rory, and disappoint me. Such men would not serve our purposes in the least. We pick the men who will serve us. The ambassador has power in the other party, too, for he is a rich man though not a man I'd want to see in the company of my daughter." The darkness deepened on his face as he thought of Ann Marie. "Nor with a young son of mine, either. He can help, when you run for congressman, a few years from now."

Surfeited, drowsy, comfortable, Rory leaned back in his chair and his pale blue eyes were apparently candid. "Pa," he said, "why do you want me to be a congressman, then a senator, perhaps, a governor, or, as you used to say, President of the United States of America?" He smiled as at some happy jest, but his father gave him one of his fierce glances and Rory no longer smiled.

"I thought I told you," said Joseph, in slow but emphatic words. "The country that would not accept me and my family, the country which rejected me, the country which despised me—it will accept my sons as representatives, senators, or whatever. That will be my—" He stopped, sipped a little wine.

Rory was uneasy. "But you are accepted now, Pa. It was a long time ago."

"It will never be 'a long time ago,'" said Joseph, and his long thin fingers clenched into a fist on the table. "We Irish have long memories."

And black ones, too, thought Rory, who had no black memories and no memory of pain at all. He knew his father's history, for Joseph had told him often enough. But, thought Rory, it is the history of many immigrants to America, Jews, Catholics, hopeful poor Protestants, laborers from eastern Europe. They did not retain "black memories." They were only thankful to be in America. Rory's bronze brows drew together in thought. It was possible that they did not possess the unrelenting pride of the Irish, or the sensibilities of the Irish. Well, I don't, thought Rory, who was proud of his race and had encountered only a few insults in his protected life, and had found even those hilarious.

"Tell me again about that girl, Claudia," said Joseph, and Rory was startled. It seemed a puerile request from his indomitable father, and even a little unworthy of him. But Rory rarely questioned his father, for Joseph had his reasons. So Rory talked merrily of Claudia Worthington, and did not notice that Joseph was watching him closely and that occasionally he drew in his mouth as if deeply thinking. Sometimes he smiled, and always he watched as Rory, a little drunk now, gave a very colorful picture of the young lady, and tried to describe her fascinating and elusive quality.

"You were impressed with her then, I am thinking," said Joseph.

Rory considered. "She is not pretty, and then she is suddenly beautiful," he said. "But she isn't quite seventeen. One of these days she may be a remarkable woman, though she hasn't the brains of a gnat."

"Brains aren't necessary in a woman," said Joseph. "In fact, they are detrimental. You should have accepted their offer of the private coach."

"Why?"

"Damn it!" said Joseph. "Do I have to spell every word out for you, you young idiot?"

The dining room was hot now and full of the scent of food and wine and spring flowers. But all at once Rory was cold, even shivering, with a sick premonition.

Joseph stood and Rory stared up at him. Joseph said, "I thought I taught you that you must never let a single opportunity go by, but always make use of the smallest. The ambassador's daughter is not a small opportunity. Remember that."

What the hell does he mean? thought Rory. Does he want me to squire her about London? I can do that without too much effort, and perhaps a little enjoyment. I am willing, as Barkis said.

But Rory saw his father's eyes fixed intently on him and he knew that Joseph was thinking of something else, and plotting. "The ambassador's wife," said Joseph, "is distantly related to the British Royal House. Keep that in mind. The ambassador is giving a ball very soon for his daughter's debut, I understand. She will be presented. She will inherit, from her mother, a considerable fortune, and from her father even more, and she is their only child. She has uncles with broad powers in Washington and London and Berlin and Rome. Never let yourself forget that. We have, of course, been invited to the ball."

As if Rory's stunned staring was too much for him Joseph abruptly left the dining room. Rory remained, leaning far back in his chair. He refilled his wineglass. He looked about him vaguely, frowning. He knew well enough now what his father meant.

Suddenly he wanted to see Marjorie, to hold her in his arms, to kiss and fondle her, to smell the lily scent of her bright black hair, to hear her mocking voice, to touch her breast, to look into her eyes. Maggie, Maggie, he thought. Nothing can ever separate us, my impudent darling. My little Maggie. It was the wine, of course, but his eyes filled with tears, and he shivered from head to foot though the fire blazed up, and for the first time in his life he knew the full meaning of fear.

Chapter 3

"This," said Joseph, "is where the Committee for Foreign Studies meets regularly, in London."

Rory knew all about the international Committee for Foreign Studies, for he had seen its discreet American quarters from the outside, on Fifth Avenue in New York. Nothing proclaimed its presence. His father had shown him one day. "Here," he had said, "and in their quarters in other capitals, lives the real power of the world, and here it is decided what the world will do."

"Without benefit of elections and the people's will, of course," Rory had said. His father had looked at him sharply and with disgust. "Don't be a fool, Rory," he had said. "Sometimes you sound like a child. Elections and the people's will, for God's sake! When were they ever of any consequence?"

"I believe," Rory had answered, "that once they did exist in Athens and Rome and Jerusalem and Alexandria, and perhaps in America and Britain, too."

Joseph had actually laughed. "And for how long, may I ask, boyo? Don't be a fool," he had repeated. "I expect much of you, you spalpeen, in spite of your innocent questions which aren't innocent at all. Stop teasing me. You are wasting my time."

For all his scrutiny, which was formidable, he had not noticed that the lower lids of Rory's eyes had relaxed, widened, artlessly, like a child's eyes, and he did not know that when this happened Rory was reserving his opinion, which could be as immutable as his own, and as dangerous, and as secret.

Rory knew that the Committee for Foreign Studies had some three hundred members in nearly every country in the world, all bankers or industrialists, politicians and financiers, and that they had meeting places in every capital

and that those meetings were discreet and unostentatious
and that the general public was unaware of them. The
meeting place in London was an old and decorous mansion
of gray stone and ostensibly owned by a British banker who
lived alone and was reputed to be a bachelor by his neighbors. None of these men sought publicity, and lived private
lives which were known for philanthropy and quiet reserved living with their families. All had "private" fortunes,
or let it be casually known that they were engaged in the
professions, dabbled occasionally and mildly in politics,
and art, or did "a little banking, the family name, you
know." Many of them had sons in government, industry,
the Navy or the Army, or in the professions. Some of them
were openly known as impressive financiers, especially in
America where the possession of wealth was regarded as
akin to holiness, and in Zurich, where the same opinion
prevailed. But none really knew what they were, except
themselves.

They controlled interests in almost all the important
newspapers in the world, appointed writers for those newspapers, and editors, directed editorial policy. They were the
real owners of publishing houses, of magazines, of all the
media that guided public information. They were the ones
who really appointed the Cabinets of Presidents, and the
Ministers to government in nearly all other countries. They
controlled elections, built up their candidates, financed
them, everywhere in the world. Any presumptuous or intrepid man who did not meet with their approval was lampooned in the press, discreetly libeled, or "exposed." The
politicians, themselves, were often quite unaware of who
had advanced or destroyed them. Even Presidents did not
always know. Kings and emperors sometimes were vaguely
aware of the momentous shadow that hung over their
thrones and decided the destinies of their nations, and
many were quite convinced that should they denounce that
shadow they would be exiled, or perhaps even assassinated.
The grip on events was not iron, but it was equally pervasive and persuasive, as soft and silent as mist which concealed invincible armies. They were never quoted in the
press concerning politics or wars or other policies. There
was never any public opinion except through their manni-
kins, who were excellently chosen for their popularity with
the people. It was possible that only Popes knew who and
what they were, for the Vatican, too, had listening posts in

every capital, but by a peculiar coincidence if a Pope hinted of what he knew an anti-clerical movement began in chosen countries and the Pope found himself in quite a desperate situation. An open exposure, an open encyclical, could result not only in anti-clerical convulsions in various countries, and exiles of the Religious, but bloodshed and terror. It had happened several times in the past and the Popes were aware of it. It had happened in France in 1794. It had recently happened in France again. It had happened in Germany and in South American countries lately, and now was threatening Spain and Portugal. The gentlemen had many weapons and never hesitated to use them, on kings, emperors, princes, Popes and Presidents. Sometimes it needed but one emphatic event. Sometimes it needed coups d'état. But whatever was needed was ruthlessly and invincibly employed, not only as a punishment but as a warning to others. Revolution was one of their weapons, and "popular uprisings," and incendiarisms and attacks on the forces of law and order.

Rory knew all about this Invisible Government which decided the destinies of nations, their survival or their obliteration, for his father had told him. Moreover, he had taken Political Science in college, which, while it did not reveal the enemies of mankind and their peace and security, hinted at it. "The world really exists on money and on nothing else," a professor had told his students. "This is a fact of human existence which must be acknowledged, however we might wish to protest. Some call manifestations of it commerce. Some call it politics. Some call it 'spontaneous movements of the People.' Some call it 'revolutionary change of governments.' Some call it holy wars in behalf of freedom. But all these things are implacably plotted by the men who really rule us, and not our ostensible elected administrations. It is a matter of money. Even the most unworldly of idealists comes face to face with that fact eventually. If he can be used he will be financed. He then deludes himself that 'worthy and compassionate persons, or whatever,' have come to his aid in the Name of the People. If he does not meet with approval, if he honestly believes that there should be some other motivation for the energies of man besides simple greed—if he believes that the nature of man can be exalted to heroic proportions—then he is destroyed by public laughter and public ignominy and it is suggested that he is insane. If he is an authentic hero his fate is much worse: obscurity. His name will never be mentioned in the public means of communication. What he writes and says will never again be known by the people. He is consigned to Limbo."

Well, Rory had thought, they tried that with Christ throughout the centuries, but they didn't accomplish it. They probably never will. Of course, they have used the name of Christ during whole eras, and were regarded as Christian Gentlemen, but even that trick didn't succeed. Well, not too often, anyway. Rory was careful not to let his conclusions be known by his father, though he more than suspected that Joseph despised the men with whom he was associated. Rory was more indulgently inclined to regard them, not as hateful, but as assassins who could be defeated at their own games. His father could have told him differently, but Rory had never confided his ideas to him, for he had youth's arrogance and assurance of being clever and omniscient. Rory was even convinced that in some ways these formidable men were ridiculous.

His facile opinions were more than a little shaken during the meeting in London. He was never to be quite the same in his conclusions, and he aged during those hours. Still, he did not tell his father. He was afraid that Joseph might be angered against him, or even worse, consider him an ignorant fool. No one else in the world had ever had the influence over Rory that Joseph had, not even Marjorie. If he had spoken to Joseph, after those hours in the meeting place of the Committee for Foreign Studies, his own life would have been entirely different. His death might have convulsed the world. Or, it might have led to nothing. The public, as always through the endless centuries, preferred the satisfactions of its bellies and its titillations and womanish emotions, and its warm little comforts, to thought and investigation. The men of the Invisible Government were wiser in their understanding of human nature than were the men who cheerfully believed that humanity could be advanced, could be totally human. "Give a dog a bone and he will happily crunch on it and never know what is going on about him," Rory was to hear that day in London. "Nor will he care." They supplied the bones, as Rory finally understood, and the good men who protested were blown into silence by hurricanes of public-induced laughter, or were assassinated.

The Invisible Government controlled public opinion

over assassinations. They sometimes made the murdered man a hero—and attributed to him opinions which only confirmed their own powers. All that he had wished to warn his people against was obliterated in a rose shower of sentimentality, or was perverted against those who had stood with him in fighting the enemies of his country.

This Rory learned on the January day he met the dangerous men in London and began to understand them. They did not speak of "assassinations," for they were delicate gentlemen, and decorous. But the implications were there. They did not speak of controlling governments. They spoke of "information" and "guidance" to rulers.

The men Rory had met in Washington and New York were rambunctious and shameless, and they had American open exigency, and had laughed over it. But the men he met in London were entirely different, and there were no Americans among them. Moreover, they had no sense of humor. Money, Rory was to discover, was not humorous in the least. It was the most serious thing in the world beyond any God man had ever dreamed of or had known.

Joseph had introduced Rory as "my son, of whom I have told you before." He looked at Rory, and not without pride, though he hoped that his colleagues would not consider him too showy, too ornate, too handsome, and too young, and possibly superficial. For Rory lit up the immense dark room like a rocket in the English dusk, the gas chandelier shining down and glinting on his red-gold hair, his ruddy face and his wide amiable smile. There was a fireplace at each end of the dank room with its long oval table shining like dulled satin in the gloom, and about that table sat some score or more men who scrutinized him with uniformly impassive faces.

They were, of course, not the same men Joseph had met so long ago, when he had been younger than Rory, himself, except for half a dozen who had been fairly young then. But these were their sons, or their immediate successors. To Joseph, their faces had not changed at all. They all appeared circumspect, gray, compact, merciless and deadly, their eyes barely alive in their cold faces yet all-seeing. They were all without race or racial identification. The gentleman from London was nearly the twin of the gentleman from St. Petersburg and the gentleman from Stockholm could hardly be told apart from the gentleman from Paris. None of them were fashionably dressed. All had quiet hands with faintly polished nails, and few wore rings. Anonymity was their garment, their desire, their uniform. Each wore, in his black tie, a single large pearl, and Rory thought, looking at them, I bet they bought those pins by the gross at Cartier's. They might have all been forty, or all eighty, though none was wrinkled or flabby or fat or crumpled.

But Rory, all at once, stopped smiling easily from one man to the other. They did not frighten or disconcert him. They did not make him flinch in himself, or feel too young or brash. They did not embarrass him. It was that he felt he had never encountered so much concentrated force in all his life before, such a gathering of intense and solid power. It was inhuman to him, and for that reason to be watched and considered. Evil, if human, could be guarded against, armed against. But these men were not even evil, he thought. They were, as Nietzsche had said, beyond good and evil. They existed. They were amoral, not immoral. They probably have steel guts, he thought, and not normal bowels.

As he looked slowly from one to the other his lower eyelids relaxed, widened, giving him that artless boyish look which had sometimes annoyed Joseph. Joseph glanced about the table, feeling warmth in his face, expecting genteel rejecting eyes which delivered their opinion that Rory was indeed too young, too shallow, too colorful, for their taste and acceptance. Rory looked like a schoolboy! He leaned forward in his chair, his arms casually folded on the table, mildly observing. He might, Joseph thought with humiliation, be some jejune youth optimistically facing schoolmasters and hoping, by charm and smiles, to change a rigorous judgment. His genial gaze moved from one man to another, pleasantly, indeed with a sort of foolish expectation, thought Joseph, who wished to God he had waited a few more years.

Then he noticed that every man was looking only at Rory and that a shadow of movement had touched them as if they had straightened in their chairs. The slightest of smiles lifted every colorless lip. It was impossible to say who was the leader in this organization, but a gentleman looked at Joseph almost kindly and said, "He will do very well, I think. Indeed yes, I think he will do very well. Welcome among us, Mr. Rory Armagh."

"They are all bastards," Joseph had told his son. "They

are, without doubt, the wickedest men on earth, though I am sure they would be astonished to hear they were wicked. They might even be outraged. Many, I am sure, even believe in God and support churches, and this is no hypocrisy on their part. I remember what Disraeli, the Prime Minister of England, said about them, with some surprise, 'The world is governed by very different personages from what is imagined by those who are *not* behind the scenes!' I believe he had a little success, for a time, in opposing them, but it was no use. It is like opposing Mount Everest."

"But they didn't assassinate him," Rory had said.

"No. Perhaps, being a brilliant and astute man, he discovered too much about them, which his heirs, and his Monarch, might have made public. I believe I heard something about that, years ago. I also heard he was an enormous cynic—and who can blame him? Had he exposed them, do you think the people would have listened?"

Rory had thought. Then he had said: "You are one of the richest men in America, Pa. Perhaps those bastards served your purpose once, but now you don't need them. Why not get out?"

"You don't resign from a club like that," Joseph had said, with a twitch of his mouth. "To use another metaphor, I have a tiger by the tail, and you know what happens to a man who lets go the tail."

"But you want me to know them, and for them to know me?"

Joseph had considered him a few moments. "Yes. They can make you, Rory. They can make you President of the United States of America, though you'd never see a hand of them anywhere, or hear one of their voices, or catch a glimpse of them. And—they could destroy you, too, and no one would ever know who did it." He really smiled then. "Don't be afraid of that, though. I, like Disraeli, know too much about them."

"And all I'd have to do is serve them like a good little valet? Is that it, Pa? An obedient little servant. Never questioning. Running about with a silver salver."

Then Joseph's face had become bleak. "Aren't we all servants in one way or another? Don't be a fool, Rory." There were those who were always silenced by Joseph's ambiguous remarks, or confused by them, but Rory was not among them, a fact which Joseph did not as yet know.

"You should never have joined them in the first place, Pa."

"Idiot," Joseph had replied, and he was smiling again. "Without them I'd really not be what I am. And what I am is what I have lived for, all the days of my life."

Now, as Rory sat among the men of whom his father had told him, he understood completely what his father had meant: That it was very probable that they did not consider themselves in the least wicked or reprehensible or evil or amoral. They had looked upon the world and made that world their own. They were a criminal conspiracy, but they did not regard themselves as either criminal or conspirators. They were businessmen, realists. What gave them power was, in their eyes, virtuous and righteous and reasonable, for who was more worthy than themselves to control and manipulate the world of men? Someone had to rule, and who better than men of intellect, money, strength, and unemotional judgment?

But what could they do, thought Rory now as he listened with youthful deference to the gentlemen about the table, if the tens, hundreds, of millions of people opposed them? Call out their mercenaries in every country in the world, their armies, their navies, which they control? Could they slaughter a whole planet? But there was no danger of that, of the corrupted people rebelling, for the people never learned or knew the names of their enemies, of those who ordered wars or their cessation, of those who threw down or raised up governments, of those who inflated or devalued money, who decided who was to live and who to die or be exiled. In fact, the people would not care under any circumstances so long as their tiny pleasures and tiny needs were met. It was such an ancient story: bread and circuses. Benevolent despotism accompanied by an entertaining show of elections and plebiscites—which meant nothing at all.

For Rory, listening, understood that these men *did* consider themselves benevolent, and that they were convinced that their aims were for the benefit of mankind in general. The gentleman from Zurich, with an eye to informing this young man, spoke in a soft and even compassionate voice. Had not the world from the very beginning been torn into bloody fragments by ambitious petty rulers, tyrants, politicians, emperors, national factions, chauvinism, and other gaudy barbarisms? That was because the world had always been ruled by passions and emotions, and never by reason and discipline. "Once we are in full power," said the gentleman, "working together, collaborating together, all over the world, then will we have a true millennium of general prosperity and absolute peace. Once we control governments, without dispute, their currencies and their people, their schools, universities and churches, the earth will know its first tranquillity."

The others nodded their grave approval. Why, the sons of bitches believe they are Messiahs! thought Rory, and smiled and smiled his resplendent smile, and nodded when it seemed the occasion to nod. The tremendous individualism which was his as an Irishman listened and thought under the bright cover of his amiability. He knew that his father had heard this same story thousands of times, and that he had derided it in himself, and to his son only. "There's many a murderer," Joseph had said, "who believed he was doing his victim a favor, and probably convinced that victim, too. And there's many a thief, individual or government, who persuaded their victims that by depriving them of their money through taxes or other confiscations they were advancing the 'public good,' or removing a source of corruption. Yet all the time they are driven only by the lust for supreme power, the lust to elevate themselves over their fellowmen, to become supermen, the Elite. You have to hate your brother a lot to come to that conclusion, I am thinking."

Rory, relaxed, free, deferential and boyish, listened, not with the black inner rage which had been his father's, but with intensity of purpose and an immense if amused contempt. He did not underestimate them. He knew their power. All at once, and for the first time, he felt a surge of ambition for the destiny his father had decided for him. He loved a fight. In his youth and strength and pride he felt equal in potency to any of these men, for he had blood in his veins and not bankers' ink, and he had been told that he had eloquence both in speaking and writing. From nowhere came the memory of what he had been taught in random religious lessons concerning the Revelations of St. John, who had prophesied these men and had written that one day they would rule the world entirely, and that none could buy or sell without their permission, "both small and great, rich and poor, free or bond." Was it the mark of the Beast, that men would have to wear on their foreheads? Rory could not remember, and his smile became more respectful and even a little tender.

Because Rory was a superb actor, which his father was not, he could control the very glinting of his eyes and could hide twitches of muscles or the slightest facial expression. They had never fully liked or accepted Joseph, because of his irony and sardonic remarks at the gravest and more portentous moments. They did not like men who made sallies against what was accepted as sacred. Joseph had served them, and they had served him, but their trust was not complete. Looking at his son there was not one there who did not conclude that Rory was their "man" for the future, young, personable, ambitious, materialistic, and a fine politician. They knew he was acting; they were not deceived. They knew he was trying to impress them, and they felt kindly towards him for that. He was a young man without illusions. Under their tutelage and perhaps under his father's, he would be theirs. Rory knew what they were thinking, and he thought, Why, they are only human after all, damn their black souls!

Rory also knew that he must never tell his father his real opinion of his associates, for Joseph was no hypocrite, no dissembler, and no actor, and it was possible that at some time, in a fit of revulsion, he might inadvertently convey to them his son's true convictions. That would be fatal. Rory was not overly patriotic, as were other young men of his age, nor was he fervent in his belief that America was the noblest, most pure, most righteous, most free, most benign of any nation of the past or present. He had listened to too many politicians, the mouthpieces of these men. He knew that America was on the road to empire, and that she had already begun to flex her muscles and test the edge of her sword. But, after all, she was his country. Too, no son of a bitch was ever going to tell Rory Armagh what to do. Rory was no humanitarian, no defender of the public weal, but he revolted at the thought of being the serf of these creatures, and his children serfs also, their convictions formed in their schools and by their religious and political leaders, who were in their pay or dared not reveal the face of the enemy. The complete enslavement of humanity not only in their daily work and rounds but in their souls and their minds—which was the more terrible—made Rory's Irish spirit glow like an internal core of fire ready to burst into a conflagration.

To obtain what they had plotted for so long, from grandfather to father to son, they must first throw the world into chaos, dismantle governments, incite violence and fury among the mindless masses, cause enfeebling wars which would weaken any nation ready to contest with them, raise up tyrants who would subdue the people, destroy the validity of nations' currencies. Then, in the general catastrophe they could exert their unbelievable power and assume command.

Not by any coarse or rude or cynical word did they convey all this to Rory, but with an air of judicious virtue and impregnable confidence. They did not say, "We shall have the damned world on its knees to us." They said, "It is time that men of experience, culture, intellect and justice exert their influence for a Better World for Everyone, under one government and one Constitution. We are already busy in The Hague—" I bet, thought Rory, and gave them his soft respectful look. Joseph watched him and for the first time wondered if he really knew anything about this shining son of his, and if he had ever guessed his thoughts.

There was wine on the table and hard English biscuits and the decanter was passed from man to man, and the silver salver also, for they would not permit a servant who might eavesdrop on conversations which affected the life and death of a planet. The wine was excellent. Rory mutely toasted the French gentleman, who first looked surprised, then smiled palely, and nodded. The English gentlemen, for there were several here, would have preferred sherry but they drank the wine with an air of condescension—who drank table wine except at dinner? Rory felt hilarious. They made more tiny little mouths over the wine than they did over their infamous plots.

The rainy dusk outside deepened and there was a hiss of hail at the tall draped windows and the fires flared up in orange spurts. The gentlemen got down to the business of America, as well as of the world in general. "Your Scardo Society," the gentleman from Russia said to Joseph. "Is it progressing?"

"We now have an equal number of Democrats and Republicans in it, and a few Populists and Socialist-Farmers."

The gentleman from Russia nodded. "It goes well, then."

"But Gospodin," said the French gentleman, "how goes it in Russia?"

"Still not ready," said the Russian gentleman, with a rueful air. "But soon. Our young Lenin is coming along splendidly. He was doing very well at Samara as a barrister. His polemic writings are attracting wide attention among disaffected Russian youth. Not too long ago he went to meet Zasulich, Axelrod, and Plekhanov, and the Marxist Osvobozhdenie Truda (Deliverance of Labor.) As you know, he was exiled in 1897 to the Yenisei Province in Siberia. He recently married a good comrade, Natasha Krupskaya, and has finished his great work, *The Development of Capitalism in Russia,* which we will soon contrive to have published. The Russian Czar is very lenient." The gentleman smiled. "Yes, we have great hopes for Vladimir Ilyich Ulyanov. He is our best theoretician against the falsifiers of Marx."

Dear little proletarian, thought Rory. Dear little aristocrat.

Now they turned in earnest to the subject of America.

"I thought," said the gentleman from Zurich, "that we had succeeded very well in America, in 1894, when your Congress enacted a 2 percent Federal income tax on incomes over $4000 a year. As a beginning—of the control of the people's property. Yet, Herr Armagh, it was permitted by one of your old fools, Senator Sherman, to call it 'communism, socialism, devilism,' and another of your old fools, Joseph Choate, the dean of the New York Bar, dared to proclaim to the United States Supreme Court that the tax 'was a communist march on private property'—"

"Well, isn't it?" said Joseph. It was the sort of remark, reflected Rory, for which Pa was probably famous here, and he saw the other gentlemen's faint frowns. The gentleman from Zurich delicately cleared his throat.

"That is beside the point, Herr Armagh. We have discussed this question, and the debacle, a few times before, and we discuss it now because of the urgency of the occasion. Your Supreme Court declared, on May 20, 1895, that the income tax was un-Constitutional. You have never told us fully what you did about it."

"I told you all I knew," said Joseph, in an irascible tone which was clearly out of place in this genteel gathering. "I talked confidentially with old Justice John Harlan before the decision was rendered, and he delivered his opinion to the Court that their final decision was 'a monstrous, wicked injustice to the many for the benefit of the favored few.' We had newspapers denounce the Court's decision. We arranged for a young man you all know, William Jennings Bryan, to give his famous proclamation: 'You shall not press down upon the brow of labor this crown of thorns, you shall not crucify mankind upon a cross of gold.' While this did not refer directly to the income tax, it was understood to be so. In fact, we got him nominated for President, free silver or no, to expand the currency, about which most of my countrymen are dubious. You must admit that all this is no mean advance in America, which is suspicious of the tax-gatherer, the demagogue and enthusiastic innovators of all kinds, not to mention tinkerers with the currency."

"Yes, yes," said the gentleman from Germany, with impatience. "But Americans are still in favor of the gold standard, and a country with a gold standard is not easily—"

"Have a little patience," said Joseph. "Rome wasn't built in a day, to coin a new aphorism."

"But we are not immortal," said an English gentleman, who could not forget that Joseph was Irish. "Your newspapers, Mr. Armagh, are entirely too powerful, still, in America, and in the main they oppose our ultimate plans—which they cannot guess at as yet. Still, something has alerted them. Someone. Marcus Alonzo Hanna—he is an ambiguous man, whose measure we have not yet determined. He is a powerful Republican industrial millionaire, yet he forced many of his associates to sign intimate working agreements between them and labor. Who has alerted him to us? He helped to defeat Bryan, and was the force that elected your present President, Mr. McKinley. Did he not make speeches, and made Mr. McKinley make speeches, that American currency was 'in danger'? Who gave him that information, Mr. Armagh, which we believed had been discussed only in the midst of absolute secrecy?"

"Damned if I know," said Joseph, with more irascibility. "I know he is adamant on the subject of the gold standard, but his man, McKinley, once voted with the free silverites when he was in Congress. If he has changed his mind, Hanna changed it for him. Hanna honestly believes that freedom can only survive on a gold standard, and, as we know, he is quite right."

He looked at his friends. "Do you suggest that Hanna meet with an accident?"

His tone was derisive, but Rory saw the faces of the other men. They don't like Papa, thought Rory, with enjoyment. And my Papa is quite a man, yes sir, he is quite a man.

"You must not think—though you believe you have evidence to the contrary—that all Americans are soft sheep," said Joseph. "I know it sounds incredible to you, but we do have a few men of integrity yet in the government, and in the country. They are aware, if only by instinct, of what is 'behind the scenes,' as Disraeli called it. We can't murder them all, can we?"

There was a thick black silence in the room, and now all the faces, despite the flickering chandelier, seemed to float, disembodied, in the gloom. Then a gentleman said in a pained voice, "Mr. Armagh. We know you come of a violent race, but we are not violent men. I am sure none here has ever lifted his hand against anyone. What we do is by way of reason, persuasion, public opinion, the press—whatever comes to our hands."

What philanthropists! thought Rory, bending forward as if to listen with greater concentration.

Joseph was assuring his colleagues that a Federal income tax was "certain to come in America in the near future," and also a Federal Reserve System, a private organization controlled by these gentlemen (a new Amendment to the Constitution, which would take from Congress the power to coin money). On the agenda was also the discussion of direct election by "the people" of United States Senators. The gentlemen nodded in approval, but appeared dissatisfied. "Only an American war can rapidly bring these things about," said one.

I see it now, thought Rory. This meeting is just a resumé for my exclusive education, for all these things have been long in discussion. I should be flattered. They appear, though, to be telling a lot, but in fact they are not as yet telling me very much. They want to see how I take it before I become a Member in Good Standing.

A Spanish gentleman looked at Joseph and said, "I liked your editorial in your newspapers, Senor Armagh, concerning Cuba: 'Blood on the roadsides, blood in the fields, blood on the doorsteps, blood, blood, blood! Is there no nation wise enough, brave enough, and strong enough to restore peace in this blood-smitten land?' Very telling, though not in the least subtle. But appealing, I gather, to American innocence and simplicity?"

"I don't deserve credit for those editorials," said Joseph. "We just quoted the *New York World*'s editorial in an issue of 1896. But Americans are really in sympathy with the insurrectos of Cuba, against Spanish rule, innocence and simplicity or not. With the help of the press. Pulitzer's newspaper, *World*, and Hearst's *New York Journal*, speak of nothing but 'Cuban blood' now. Some of their 'extras' are even printed in red ink. Teddy Roosevelt is a wonderful help, too. He foams at Spain in almost every speech. He is an authentic internationalist."

"Unfortunately, Mr. McKinley is President, and Mr. Roosevelt is only Assistant Navy Secretary," said the French gentleman, and there was another silence. Rory felt it weighing on him, but no one spoke of Mr. Roosevelt again.

"I think we have done a good job in Hawaii, too," said Joseph. "We have not been idle in America, gentlemen, though you often imply that. American sugar planters and Marines have been inflamed through our efforts against Queen Liliuokalani, and are now asking the President to annex Hawaii. I often have conversations with my good friend, Captain Alfred T. Mahan of the U. S. Navy, of whom I have spoken before, and he agrees with me that America must expand beyond her borders. Cuba and Hawaii are only the beginning, he assured me. He told me that we Americans will have to 'decide the most important question confronting us, whether Eastern or Western civilization is to dominate throughout the earth and to control its future.' He is certainly our man, if he knows it or not." He glanced at the Russian gentleman. "You, or us?"

The Russian gentleman smiled gently. "As you know, Gospodin, it is neither. It is only us, together." Rory smiled gently also. They do insist on spelling it all out for me, he thought, in case Pa hasn't told me enough in the last couple of years. But it is nice of them. I really do appreciate it. So, they were advancing a war in Cuba, against Spain, were they? How were they going to manage that? Mr. McKinley was not a warmonger, but a peaceable man. What was done would have to be catastrophic, to plunge an already hysterical America into war. Rory's pale blue eyes narrowed, and then he saw his father watching him for his reactions to what he had already heard, and he gave that gentle smile again and let his eyelids relax and he looked hardly twenty years old.

When they were in their carriage returning to the hotel Joseph said—for Rory, the voluble, was uncharacteristically quiet—"What do you think of all that, my bucko?"

"You've told me a lot about them before, Pa. But now I've seen them. A couple are not much older than I am, yet they all look old. Is it the portrait of Dorian Gray in reverse? Are they young somewhere else?"

"Don't be frivolous," said Joseph, who knew his son was not. "I've told you: The majority of them are Good Christian Gentlemen, with quiet secluded homes and devoted families. If you asked them just what they are they would answer that they are a fraternal organization engaged in the business of consolidating the world under one government in the name of peace and tranquillity and orderly society. Call—us—a mutual aid organization, too."

"They are advancing their cause of a world-central government at The Hague, too, aren't they?" said Rory. Joseph gave him a sharp look, and then it softened into pride.

"You are not as puerile as I thought you," he said, and touched his son on the shoulder. "But then, I don't think I ever did."

"You are quite right, Pa," said Rory, after a moment. "They are, in fact, sons of bitches." He looked genial again. "I don't think they liked some of your remarks, and I don't think they entirely trust you, which is regrettable, isn't it?"

"Just don't talk so much," said Joseph, and frowned. "Mens lives have hung on their tongues. Make no mistake: These men are the real rulers of the world, as I've told you before. They didn't give you their names today, but eventually they will. Yes, they will."

Chapter 4

Joseph and Rory went to the ambassador's ball, in the American Embassy, a huge gray and gloomy building which was, however, adequately heated—for which Rory was grateful. There was no man present, he thought, who looked as distinguished as his father in his formal clothing, and he noticed that the gorgeously clad ladies noticed that fact also. Was it his detached and impassive look, his air of restrained strength, his dispassionate conversation, his cold courtesy? Rory had no answer, but his eyes followed Joseph with admiration.

The ladies all appeared beautiful in their Paris gowns and jewels, the gentlemen all courtly and gallant. The music and lights were gay, the fires big, the refreshments lavish, the wine pouring like a red or white river into glittering glasses, the chandeliers blazing. There was such an atmosphere of amiability, sophisticated intellect and generous good-will that Rory was delighted. Here there were no stern and concentrated faces, no whisper of international evil, no plots, no soft-spoken conspiracies—yet Rory knew that they were here in person. He heard French and German spoken all about him, and other tongues, all lilting and vivacious.

The American Ambassador, his Excellency, Mr. Stephen Worthington, was the gayest and most vivacious of all, and he had, Rory observed, his daughter's magnetism. He was always surrounded by swirling groups, sparkling and flattering. His lady was a dun little person in a dim gray gown, and had a way of seeking corners.

His Excellency had Claudia's exotic appearance, heavier in him and at moments repellent, for his features were grosser. His dark chestnut hair was long and carefully waved, his mustache discreet and aristocratic, his height graceful, his changeful eyes dancing with affection and pleasure in the company about him. His voice was modulated, with an acquired English accent which never slipped, and his laughter was a rich sound and full. It was evident that he was very popular. He greeted everyone as if his or her presence was the one he had been waiting for for a long time, and he was delighted to see the dear one again. Rory studied him at a distance. He wondered if he were as stupid and shallow as Claudia, and as pettily self-absorbed, and as exigent, and greedy. After half an hour's contemplation of his host Rory came to the conclusion that he was, indeed, but that he had learned to conceal these unappetizing traits in the name of diplomacy and advancement. The eyes, in spite of the constant smiles and open laughter and suetty chuckles, had a cold calculation in them, and a watchfulness. Here, too, was an execrable man, for he would agree to anything which would be to his advantage, no matter how venal.

Claudia, of course, was there, in girlish gauze and white silk with a slim diamond necklace and a diamond bracelet, all in the best of taste and not ostentatious. Rory danced with her, and tried to avoid looking at her directly, for then he was disarmed and fascinated, over and over attempting to fathom her elusive charm. She chattered breathlessly, as she danced, pointing out "distinguished persons," and hardly uttering a sentence when she did not mention "dear Papa," and what this noted gentleman had said of Papa and what Papa had said to him, and how Papa was so graciously received by all the European monarchs, and how attached Her Majesty, Queen Victoria, was to him, she who did not particularly care for Americans. Why, only a year ago she had come out from her widowed seclusion to be present here at a ball, and she stayed all of fifteen minutes! "Remarkable," said Rory, trying not to look at her, and trying to concentrate only on that silly infantile voice which was sometimes inaudible in its breathlessness. She smelled of jasmine, and forever after Rory hated that scent. He thought of Marjorie, and her naughty bantering, and her telling little jokes, and ached.

Rory loved parties, for he by nature was gregarious like his mother, and he loved the sight of pretty women, and he loved wine and whiskey and caviar and rich dishes and shine and glitter and the flash of silver or gold slippers, and music and lights and fires. But by ten o'clock he found he was mysteriously fatigued. It was this damned English climate, he thought, which made his back ache like this, and made him feel an elderly rheumatoid condition. He danced with a multitude of ladies, young and old, even his shy and frightened hostess. He was gallant, dashing, handsome. Younger feminine eyes followed him, and so did older eyes, lovingly. He was witty, bright, courtly. He hardly seemed American, thought many, forgiving him. Gentlemen found him surprisingly adroit and informed and intelligent. He had surreptitiously visited the one small table which held "vulgar" whiskey, and he had visited it several times. He felt the need for it, though Joseph had often warned him that "the creature" was direful for Irishmen. He had, on too many rueful occasions, conceded the truth of this. But what was one to do after that meeting of the Committee for Foreign Studies, two days ago, and this accursed climate, and this ball, and that stupid little Claudia who insistently found him after every dance he danced with another lady?

Joseph, who never missed anything, was quite aware that his son was visiting, too often, that secluded and a little shameful table with the whiskey. He also noticed that Miss Claudia was pursuing him with girlish ardor. He also saw that Rory was dexterously trying to avoid her, and he frowned.

He waited until the next morning when Rory was painfully sober and keeping his eyes sedulously away from the sight of the covered silver dishes filled with broiled kidneys, hot ham, bacon, eggs, trout, pasties, and other English breakfast delicacies. Rory drank black coffee only, and played with a buttered crumpet, and his color was not very florid today.

Joseph said in a cold voice, "Go on with you, boyo. Have a hair of the dog that bit you. It's the only cure."

Rory rose like a suddenly animated spring and shot to the cabinet where he poured himself a small glass of whiskey. He drank it like a man dying of thirst, and said "Ah!" in a deep and grateful voice. His eyes watered, but his color began to return. It was sleeting outside, and very dark, for all it was nearly noon. "This damned climate," said Rory, and dabbed at his eyes.

"No worse than Boston, or New York, at this time of year," said Joseph. "Well? Do you feel better? I've told you all about the poteen and what it does to us."

"Is that why you don't drink it, Pa?" asked Rory, with more courage than usual when with his father. "Or are you afraid that if you do drink it you might be offguard—"

"Against what?" Joseph's voice was deadly.

"Nothing," said Rory. "That is, I mean, someone might take advantage of you."

"No one ever did, except my father," said Joseph. "No one ever will." His narrow face with the bony cheekbones tightened, as it always did when he mentioned Danny Armagh. "I don't drink much, except a little brandy or wine, because I don't like it, boyo. I never acquired a taste for it. Why make your palate and stomach suffer?"

"I drink it for effect," said Rory.

"And that's the worst reason of all," said Joseph. "No man should look for escape."

"Paraphrasing Patrick Henry," said Rory, with recklessness, "is life so dear and reality so sweet that they must be purchased at the price of moderation?"

Joseph could not help smiling. "You do have the Irish tongue on you, I admit. Sit down, Rory. Unless you want another drink."

"I do," said Rory fervently, and poured another two fingers. After that he sat down and could consider the steaming silver dishes without too much disfavor. He helped himself to a strip of bacon and a spoonful of broiled kidneys and discovered that they did not nauseate him this time. He could even relish them a little.

"Distasteful as reality often is," said Joseph, "we have to face it."

Now he is going to suggest something really disagreeable and appalling, thought Rory and blinked at his father rosily.

"The ambassador and I had a few minutes of conversation last night, before you almost disgraced yourself and had to be helped to our carriage by two footmen," said Joseph. "A very interesting conversation."

I bet, thought Rory, but he looked at Joseph with genuine affection.

"We came to the conclusion—after observing a few incidents—that a marriage will be arranged between you and Miss Worthington, say a year or so from now."

Rory became very still. The fork lay in his hand without moving. The heavy eyes were fixed. Rory felt sick again. "I don't like her," he said. "She's foolish and silly and without brains, and she bores me to death. I wouldn't marry her if she was the last woman on earth."

Joseph leaned back in his chair, but he was tense. "I knew you'd say that, bucko. What does all that matter? Are you looking for hearts and flowers, for God's sake? Are you romantic?" and he looked as if he wished to spit. "Romance, and love, are for children and imbecile young girls, not for intelligent adults. Do you think I loved your mother, or found her intelligent and full of witty conversation? Men don't consider these things when they are planning on an advantageous marriage. Only adolescent Americans want what they call 'love.' No wonder marriage is in such a bad state in America, with all that moonlight and roses and summer breezes! They're a bad foundation for a judicious marriage, with advantages."

"You can't marry a woman who revolts you," said Rory.

"Does she that? I saw you staring at her as if she were a basilisk," said Joseph. "When she danced with someone else you still stared after her."

"I couldn't help it," said Rory. "She's got that damned something or other—I don't know. But I can't stand the girl, honestly. To be honest again, it wouldn't be fair to her, either."

The sleet hissed against the windows, the air darkened, the wind rose, and the fire rose also. Joseph considered his son. Then he said, "But you are going to marry her just the same, Rory. That does not mean you have to be faithful to her. There are other women."

"Suppose you wanted to marry one of them?" asked Rory.

For the first time that Rory could recall Joseph looked away from a direct confrontation. He stared at the windows. "You don't," he said. "Not unless you want to throw your career away. Or the lady is unwilling. Or there are—impediments."

So, Aunt Elizabeth was "unwilling," thought Rory, and felt compassion for his father.

"It is settled, then," said Joseph. "You will marry Miss Claudia within two years."

Rory's facial muscles bulged about his full-lipped mouth. He played with his fork. He said, "I want to marry someone else. We—we are practically engaged."

Joseph stood up abruptly. "Who, for Christ's sake, you idiot?"

"A girl I met in Boston. A wonderful girl, intelligent, dear, beautiful, kind, and generally adorable," said Rory. "A girl of a rich Boston family, who'd grace our name, to use an old fashioned expression."

"Who?" repeated Joseph, and his voice was pouncing.

"You don't know her, Pa," said Rory, and now he was frightened. That damned whiskey. It could surely betray a man. "It really isn't official. I—I am just playing with the thought. A lovely girl. You'd like her." He had an idea. "Her father opposes the alliance."

Joseph's face blackened. "He does that, does he? One of those Boston Brahmins who despises the Irish, and Papists?"

"I think I'm bringing him around," said Rory.

"You mean you are humiliating yourself—you, the son of Joseph Armagh?" Joseph's look was dangerous. "A Boston chit, a miss with dainty little manners! Money, you say? How much?"

"Not as much as we have. Her father is a member of an old Boston law firm. His father, and grandfather, established it. He is quite wealthy. No money problems there."

Joseph slowly sat down. His voice was too quiet. "Have you spoken for the lady already?"

"No."

"Have I met her father?"

Rory hesitated. "I don't know. Perhaps."

"I know them all. I must have met him, if he's a lawyer —and rich. Now, listen to me, boyo. The day you become engaged to Miss Claudia Worthington I will give you two million dollars. The day you marry her you will receive ten million. Can your Boston chit match that?"

Rory was silent.

"If you reject Miss Claudia," said Joseph, "and listen to me carefully: You will not be my son any longer. You will receive nothing more from me, living or dead. Is that perfectly clear?"

O God, thought Rory, thinking of his fifty dollars a month and Marjorie's thirty and of the dreary little flat in Cambridge which was his heaven. He said, trying to smile, "Claudia is only sixteen. Well, nearly seventeen. We'll have a year or so to consider, won't we?"

"True. In the meantime you will not see the Boston lady any longer—unless she is willing to oblige you, outside of marriage. Some of these Boston ladies are quite—ardent—

let us say, for all their hoity-toity manners and 'family.' "
Joseph smiled unpleasantly.

Rory said, "I still have to complete law school."

"Who says you do not? In fact, I insist on it. When you
pass the bar the marriage will take place." Joseph slapped
the table with an air of finality. "It is settled, then, though it
was settled last night between Steve and me. A most suit-
able marriage, and the girl is obviously infatuated with you,
though I cannot tell why." Joseph invited Rory to smile
with him, and Rory finally succeeded in doing so. His back,
or something, was aching like a fever in him, or as if broken. Just let me finish law school, he thought. That's all I
want. Then the hell with everything else, and I'll have my
Maggie.

I'll find out, thought Joseph. I'll set Charles on this at
once, and a few other of my men. We've got to stop it before it becomes serious. He was not too vexed with his son,
whom everyone had admired last night. Young men get in
the damnedest difficulties, especially when they are full-
blooded like Rory, and there are always women waiting for
them like vultures. Let the boy have his fun, so long as he
understands that it is not to be serious. For some reason Joseph felt an icy and vindictive satisfaction in the thought of
the jilted Boston Brahmin's daughter. It was time, God
knew, it was time. Now he was even proud. The son of an
Irish immigrant would reject the daughter of a Boston
scion! He, Joseph, had waited a long time.

Maggie, thought Rory. He also thought of the ominous
men he had met, and he remembered how he had planned,
in the future, to circumvent them. He dropped his aching
head in his hands and was nauseated again. But he was by
nature optimistic. He had a year, perhaps two years, and
who knew what would happen in that time?

He stood up in his morning flannel robe and went to the
roaring fire. "It's damned cold in here," he said, and stirred
up the coals and rubbed his muscular arms. The chimney
pots of London boiled out their black smoke and the air
was full of their gassy stench. It seemed to invade Rory's
whole being as well as his nose, and his courage sank.

What would his father say, and do, when he discovered
that his son was already married? Rory did not underestimate Joseph. He knew his father would stop at nothing.
The only solution, then, was not to let him even be suspicious, and to wait until he, Rory, had passed his bar exami-

nations. Rory saw the men of the Committee for Foreign Studies, and he felt that he had committed an act of absolute betrayal, though he could not understand why at this agitated moment.

Chapter 5

For the first time in his life, as he crossed the tumultuous and angry gray Atlantic on his way home, Rory Armagh felt the need of a confidant. It was not so much the thought of the bankers and giant financiers—including some noblemen—whom he had met in Europe, which so disturbed him, but the implications and ramifications of their growing power. He remembered that the Committee for Foreign Studies was mainly an American establishment, with a branch in England, and that the Committee was only part of a whole, under different names in different nations and with different nationalities. In America, there were at least five generals who were members of the Committee. The vast interlocking organizations, with their one aim and their one mind, were what was so appalling to Rory, and their brotherhood control of politicians. Where had he heard: "In hell, there are no disputes"?

This whole apparatus had begun with the League of Just Men, of which Karl Marx had been a member, but the apparatus was not Communistic or Socialistic or Monarchist or democratic or anything else. They merely used these political ideologies as weapons against mankind, to confuse it and tame it and enslave it. They were not involved in philosophies or metaphysics or ideals or any other of the intellectual toys with which so-called intelligent men beguiled themselves and persuaded themselves of their mentality. They were above politics as such. Let the rabble pretend happily that it had influence on its government, so long as that rabble never guessed who indeed ruled their government! It was their very dispassionate ruthlessness and almost inhuman drive which admittedly frightened—yet stirred up—Rory Armagh. It was indeed beyond good and evil, and had nothing to do with normal ambition, of which Rory possessed more than the average measure. Why, he thought, the bastards would destroy their own countries, their own families, their own sons, to get what they want!

Rory could understand passion and vehemence and downright wickedness and human plotting and deviltry and treachery and lies and thefts, and even murders. But he could not understand the men he had met in America and abroad, and so they challenged the very blood in his body, his very humanity.

Somberly and jerkily walking the tilting decks of the ship, he recalled some of the things he had heard in London: "We must now have prudently scheduled wars all over the world, for they will be more and more necessary to absorb the products of our growing industrial and technological society. Without them we will have a glut of products—and a glut of populations—leading to stagnation, poverty, and natural crises, which could well undermine our ultimate objectives. In short, wars and inflation can proceed only under planned auspices which uncontrolled disorders jeopardize.

"The middle class, in all nations, as we know, must be eliminated, for they tend to stimulate and encourage and invent chaotic liberty. They stand in the way of our Plan."

Rory knew what the Plan was: Wars, confiscatory taxes to destroy the middle class, inflation and national debt. When these became unbearable even the most docile population had the propensity for rebellion. It was then that the anonymous plotters came into their own and seized ultimate power, in the name of law and order.

"Without a Federal income tax in America our objectives remain uncertain there, and frustrated. We must, all over the world, have entire control over the people's money. Such taxes are necessary for wars and inflation and the mechanization of humanity, the dependence of humanity on what we shall decide to give it. Without war, we cannot have a planned society, anywhere in the world. We are succeeding, without war and only through taxes, in the Scandinavian countries, but that is not possible in such immense countries like America and Russia, where revolutionary tactics, peaceful or violent, are absolutely necessary, and which need to be financed through taxation."

Rory's only confidant now was his father, who was also his teacher, however wry and derisive in his remarks concerning his colleagues. Rory no longer asked Joseph why he belonged to the Committee for Foreign Studies, and the infamous Scardo Society in America, composed of intellectual radicals. For he knew that in a distorted way this was Joseph's revenge on a world which had so frightfully abused him as a child and youth, and, worst of all, had forced him to deny his very intrinsic identity. This had been an assault not only on his physical survival but on his spirit. Was this true also of the other men? Rory did not know.

Sometimes Rory asked himself: Doesn't our own government know? If they do not, then they are fools. If they do know, they are traitors. Which is worse?

His other confidant, besides his father, who had warned him not to speak to anyone of what he had superficially learned in London, was Courtney Hennessey, in whom he had usually confided more than in anyone else, even Marjorie. But Courtney was immured in Amalfi, damn him! and even if he were not he must never know what Rory already knew. However, he would have been a "comfort." His normality, his cool common sense, his lack of hysteria and impulsiveness, would have been soothing to Rory, might even have given him some assurance that the normal people far outnumbered the villains—which Rory frequently doubted anyway.

As the days passed on the ship Rory's usually easy and imperturbable mind was greatly disturbed, thrown into disorder, conjecture, and apprehension. On the one hand his natural cynicism made him shrug, for did not mindless men deserve any fate plotted for them? On the other hand was his natural rebellion, born of his Irish nature, against any group of men who would "guide," as they called it, the free human soul. That was the province of religion, and guidance there meant discipline and elevation of the spirit beyond its own mean instincts. But the "guidance" of the anonymous men meant serfdom, not for the advancement of men but for their human disintegration and reduction to animalism.

Rory was not an idealist; he did not believe that man could be better than he already was, for the nature of man was immutable except through religion, and even there the mutability was precarious and unstable. But at least in a more or less free society a man had a choice—to a limited extent—and to Rory that freedom of choice was precious. To be a rascal or not to be a rascal, to be responsible or irresponsible, to be good or evil: That ability to choose made man more than a beast even if his choice was disastrous. His mind was his own. Admittedly, sometimes the choices of men made for an uneasy and changeful society, but that was preferable to the hell of monotony where men had no choices and were duly fed, bred, put to planned activity, deprived of decisions concerning their lives and their recreation, and fell to the status of domestic creatures.

There had been little vexation, little change, little anxiety, in Rory's life so far, no alarms except for the catastrophe to his sister, little brooding or melancholy, little *Weltschmerz* or *Weltanschauung*. Now, to his mortification, he felt that he had lived in a silky nest, his only aspirations to be successful, to pursue pretty women, to dance and cavort and make himself generally agreeable—for he liked the world very much indeed. He had always disliked gloomy men, though, paradoxically, he had liked gloomy poetry. He disliked scholars, but was scholarly himself, in a very objective way. He had a fine mind, analytical and cool and, reasonable, but it had never been much engaged in subjectivities, which he had usually suspected. "I am no Jesuit," he would tell Courtney. Naturally without illusion, he had been tolerant of the world of men.

But during these days at sea that equable nature, that laughing skeptical nature, came fully into its second duality, which had heretofore not been dominant. He discovered crevices, hidden caverns, deep rivers, dark and somber places, silences and ponderings, in himself, and was not happy over it. For they forced him to be aware, not only of Rory Armagh and his immediate concerns and ambitions, but of the world he lived in, and to be as responsible to that world as it was possible for him to be. He knew, without any doubt at all, that he must keep this new and frightening awareness to himself, and from his father, who, he suspected, had his own dark places.

He began to drink, not only at the table in the great dining room on the ship, but in his stateroom. He began to brood, and all the deep melancholy of the Irish mysticism invaded him. But when he appeared on the decks and in the public rooms there was none gayer, more voluble, more full of jokes and twinklings and laughter, than Rory Armagh. None of this was simulated, but was genuine as of the moment. Yet his character became more and more firmly knitted, and much of the amiable embroidery of it was slowly but steadily discarded from the fabric. He felt this change in himself, and was not certain he liked it. He knew the potentialities for this change had always been in him, but he had kept them under control until now.

He discovered a complaisant and fairly well-known young actress on board, accompanied by an enormous amount of trunks and a personal maid, and within four days he had found himself happily admitted to her bed. They drank champagne together, and laughed, and romped, and for hours, sometimes, Rory could forget the "deadly quiet men," as his father had called them, and what he was nebulously deciding to do about them in the future. Never once, as he lay entangled with the pretty young actress, did he feel that he was unfaithful to Marjorie. Marjorie lived on a different plateau in his life. In New York, he said a loving and joyful farewell to the actress and proceeded to Boston and to Marjorie.

His mind had been taken up with its unique glooms and dismays and horrors on the ship, with the exception of the hours of interlude with the actress, and so he had not given too much thought to his predicament concerning Marjorie. Indeed, the predicament was really his father. He never once considered giving up his young wife, whom he adored. Now, as he entered the miserable little flat in Cambridge this new problem asserted itself with black anxiety.

Marjorie was waiting for him, for he had sent her a telegram from New York. She had lit fires and filled the dun rooms with hothouse flowers, from her father's own conservatory. She had arranged a fine dinner. When Rory saw her he felt a blaze of emotion in himself, delight, joy, peace, and wholeness. Her neat little figure, so trim and without a sign of fussiness, was clad in a white silk shirtwaist, very severe, even with cufflinks, and buttoned down the front with little pearls, and a black silk skirt. Her dark pompadour kept breaking out into tendrils about her saucy little face, with the smooth olive cheeks just touched with apricot, and her black eyes were huge and dancing. She threw herself into his arms and he caught the scent of lemon verbena, and the fragrance of her young body. He swung her up in his arms and danced about the rooms with her and she kissed him and laughed and protested, and clung to him.

Immediately he forgot everything, or at least all he feared stood at a somber distance in his mind, not permitted to invade this beatitude of being with Marjorie. He must tell her all about his journey, whom he met, what he said and did—and, after a pause—how was his father?

He evaded the answers for a while during which he triumphantly waved a long blue velvet box under Marjorie's little nose. While she jumped and struggled for it, and her mass of curls fell down her back, and she shouted, he laughed and settled the answers to her questions in his mind.

It seemed that Joseph, to give his son an idea of the comforting feeling of wealth, had presented him with a cheque for two thousand pounds. Stunned by all these riches, Rory had gone shopping for a trinket for Marjorie on Bond Street. His first impulse was to spend it all on the trinket, but his natural prudence, hidden under all that generous outpouring of humor and laissez-faire, advised him that he might need some of that money in Boston, too. So he had spent one thousand juicy pounds on a beautiful opal and diamond necklace for Marjorie, with a pair of earrings to match. Capturing the box at last Marjorie opened it eagerly and screamed with delighted shock at the magnificence, and her little fingers trembled and her eyes glowed as she fastened the jewelry at neck and ears. Rory watched her with such an inner bulging of his heart that his eyes filled with moisture.

"Where on earth did you get the money?" cried Marjorie. "You must have stolen it!"

"Hard though it may be to believe, Papa gave it to me," said Rory. Marjorie's face went blank. She looked at him slowly. "Oh, Rory, you told him then?" Her own eyes became moist with relief.

"Yes, I told him—in a way," said Rory. "I had to break it easy to the old boy. I told him that I was practically engaged to a chit of a Bostonian girl, of fairly good family, and of some mediocre intelligence, and sometimes pretty."

"Rory, behave yourself. You must tell me. What did he say?"

"Well, my love, he reminded me I have to finish law school. I didn't tell him we were already married." Rory paused. "That would have been a little too much at that time for him to digest. So, I let it rest there."

Marjorie's black eyes sharpened on him. "Just what does that mean, rascal?"

"It means that we get him used to the idea that we have —plans."

"Fiddlesticks! I know you, Rory. You are hiding something."

Rory spread out his hands disarmingly and nothing could have been more candid and boyish than those light blue eyes. "You wrong me, sweetheart, you really do. I have told you all there is. I did tell Pa that your father was a distinguished lawyer in Boston, and he asked if he knew him and I said I didn't know. I didn't mention names. I thought it best; let him mull over what I'd already told him."

Marjorie stood on tiptoe to kiss his mouth warmly. "Rory, you never exactly lie, but often you don't exactly not lie, either. You are a very wily Irishman. You tell people what you want them to know, and not a word more or less, and let them make of it what they will. Even me."

"You don't trust me," said Rory, with an air of injury.

"Of course I don't! Do you think I am a fool? Never mind, my pet. Do let me see what I look like in the crown jewels." She ran to a dusty mirror and preened in the low lamplight and firelight, and the gems glistened and sparkled in a very satisfactory fashion. "But how shall I explain them to Papa?" she asked.

"Hide them. Wear them just for me," said Rory, and took her hand and led her into the tiny bedroom, while she protested very mildly and mentioned roasting beef.

Marjorie completely forgot to ask Rory what the business had entailed in London, which was just as well because Rory could never have told her.

When he returned to his rooms at Harvard he found a telegram waiting for him, which had been delivered just that day. He read it over and over, disbelievingly, aghast. He actually trembled. Then he sent his father a cable: UNCLE SEAN DIED THIS MORNING. CABLE FUNERAL ARRANGEMENTS.

Chapter 6

Sean Armagh, who had continued his "professional name" of Sean Paul during his concerts and recitals, kept a suite of rooms in a Boston hotel for when he was present there, which was often. "For here it was, in this Athens of the West, where I was discovered," he would say, with a soft theatrical gesture of his thin white hand. It was not hard for him to fill his eyes with tears at will, for he was by nature emotional, and people in Boston were always touched. It was a large suite of several rooms in an old but grand hotel full of gilt and rose damask and marble stairways, and he occupied it with his business manager, Mr. Herbert Hayes, a large portly man of much presence and much brown hair and much jewelry, about forty-four years old, also a bachelor. Though considerably younger than Sean he treated Sean as if he were a child, and a not very intelligent child, and bullied him, was proud of him, and loved him. He arranged everything for his client, and Sean had nothing to do but practice and sing and enrapture audiences, and read billets-doux from ladies. (Sean, however, knew to the penny how much he had in the banks, and grew pettish over any offer that did not meet with his approval.)

Joseph, not having had the advantage of an academic education, nor having ever resided in a college dormitory, nor having ever been a member of a fraternity, did not know what was "wrong" with Sean. Rory and Kevin, his sons, did and without any doubt and with such sly chucklings and lewd winks. "It was being brought up by all those nuns," said Kevin, "and never seeing any other men but priests who were cowed by the Sisters anyway."

"I think," Rory had once remarked, "that Pa's character was such that a character like Sean's sort of got crushed in any encounter. Not that Uncle Sean had a character of much strength, anyway, or much resolution of manliness. Rice pudding with custard could describe Uncle Sean's spirit, to be charitable. Pa once did remark that our sweet singing uncle was 'womanish,' and it upset him, but he made excuses that his brother was an 'artist.' Uncle's petulant little ways were excused under the same copy-book heading. 'At least,' Pa would say, 'he made something of himself with his singing and talent, which is more than could have been said about our father, whom he much resembles.' Pa must have loved his Dada once; he wouldn't have been so bitter about him if he hadn't. When Uncle Sean succeeded that made Pa forgive both his Dada and our nightingale uncle. But he has never found out about him, which is just as well. I doubt that Pa would have known what it meant, anyway."

Joseph would have known. He had read too widely and too largely not to have understood if it had been put before him in plain words. But his natural Irish prudity in part insulated him from recognizing what was "wrong" with his brother. Moreover, he thought such activities not only unmentionable even when among men, but esoteric and inexplicable, and probably engaged in "only by foreigners." He never once suspected homosexualism among any of his colleagues or acquaintances, not even when it was blatant, and he certainly would not have believed it existed in his own family. He might tell Sean to "be a man," as he did whenever he encountered him, and did not know that it was impossible for Sean to "be a man." Had he understood, Rory would sometimes think, he would probably have murdered Uncle Jenny Lind.

Sean had tried to attach himself to Harry Zeff, out of both gratitude and love, but Harry had soon suspected and had abruptly removed himself as benefactor and friend. Thereafter had followed several "love affairs" between Sean and the new friends he made among the camp followers of the arts. He had finally settled on one love, his manager for a number of years, Herbert Hayes, who was also of his persuasion. It was Herbert who had taught Sean to be discreet, and not to throw his arms affectionately about other men in public—even when the gesture was comparatively innocent—and not to mention his aversion to the ladies but, on the contrary, to pretend to be a gallant and a womanizer, "like your brother." Herbert, too, had taught him to hint of an unrequited or deceased love, whom he could never forget and to whose memory he was still devoted and loyal. This was not hard for Sean to do, for he was an actor as well as a singer by birth. Herbert let him wear exotic clothing, for that was more or less expected of an artist, but he never let it get effeminate.

Herbert was masculine in appearance, in manner, in dress, in voice and gesture. He loved Sean Armagh with a jealous and devastating love, and served him like a lover. Sean's interests were his interests. He had no others. He was a very competent pianist, himself, and so worked with Sean at his practice. He picked every accompanist. He arranged all tours and was so shrewd that Sean never accepted a fee lower than the most recent one, and usually it was higher. Herbert, it was, who gave newspaper interviews, or sat vigilantly near Sean when Sean gave them. Herbert arranged the repertoire. Herbert wrote the brochures. Herbert bullied concert hall managers and accompanists. Herbert arranged the lighting, and coached Sean in the most effective postures. Not being a fool, in spite of his love for Sean, he had demanded, and had got, a very sizable salary and occasional lavish gifts, and traveled always with his client. They both loved luxury, though Sean did not care much for paying for it, being under the impression that all hotel suites should be donated by "the management."

Herbert arranged for the constant singing teachers and listened to them with the acuteness of a bird listening for a worm in the ground. He also arranged that those teachers would not have his and Sean's propensities.

Rory and Kevin often idly sought "reasons for Unkie's conduct," and all of them were, of course, fallacious: Too much feminine company in youth; a too strong and dominant brother; the lack of a father in his childhood and youth; his early orphaned condition and his early dependence on women. A too gentle character, too soft, too weak, too bending, too unable to resist perversions. Too unworldly. Too easily influenced by evil men whom he encountered, who intimidated him. The fact that his "condition" was intrinsic to him, had been his from birth, would have been disbelieved by his young nephews, who alternately pitied or despised him. They might laugh at him between themselves but they were scrupulous in pretending, when with Sean, to believe him entirely average or what they considered average. That, to Sean, his propensity for his own sex seemed quite normal, would have inspired the utmost incredulity in Rory and Kevin, in spite of their academic sophistication. Sometimes Sean was repulsive to them and they kept a wary distance from him. As a person, he was liked by them, with his gentle manners, his high musical voice, his air of eternal youthfulness, his hatred for the violent word or gesture, and, curiously, his bland innocence. They preferred to blame Herbert Hayes, and they loathed him, which was eminently unfair.

The general public did not know about Sean's "conduct" for Herbert was sedulous about this, knowing the calamitous consequences, legal and public, if it should become generally known. It disturbed him that Sean's nephews appeared to know, but they would certainly not betray their own uncle. His one terror was that Joseph Armagh might learn of his brother's aberration. He had met Joseph on many occasions, in dressing rooms and in hotel suites, and Joseph affrighted him, for he knew that here was a man of no compromises, no deviations, and of an absolutely rigid character, and that to him a man like Sean would have appeared totally criminal, worthy of exposure and exile, if not death. Joseph's powerful personality overwhelmed Herbert Hayes, the direct fierceness of his eye made him quail. He mentioned this once to Sean, and Sean had sighed gently, assumed a pathetic expression, bowed his head and had murmured, "True. True. You have no true conception, dear Herbert, of the agonies of my young childhood, which Joe inflicted upon me, the abandonment, the heartless indifference, while he pursued money for his own aggrandizement and importance. He detested everyone, and was not happy unless all those about him flinched when he entered a room. Ah, if my poor sister were only here! She could tell you a sorry tale of Joseph's abuse of us when we were mere babes."

He had persuaded himself that all this was true, long before he had fallen with tears and cries of emotion upon Joseph's chest when Joseph had first visited him to offer congratulations on his success. The girlish malice he had felt for Joseph, the deep envy and resentment of his potency, his quality of manhood, had inspired in Sean a hidden hatred he disguised in the form of contempt. "It is my sensitivity," he would say to Herbert, "the sensibilities of a born artist, which were so affronted by my brother's very person and temperament. I know it is wrong, but how can I change my nature?" He would look at his friend, pleading for absolution, his light eyes swimming in liquid. "Joe is so coarse, so unfeeling, not able to experience true human attachment and the spirit of sacrifice. A gross man, I am afraid."

Had Sean heard anyone call him a liar he would have been—almost—genuinely horrified. For he had pushed from his remembrance all that he knew of his brother and that brother's desperate struggle for the younger members of his family. To acknowledge that struggle, to express gratitude, to feel any pity or understanding at all, would have lowered Sean in his own estimation. Maligning Joseph, he could acquire self-esteem and elevate himself above his feared brother.

Rory had guessed this a few years ago, and for his uncle he felt good-tempered derision and amused tolerance. He also thought Sean pitiable, as well as revolting. But Joseph had appeared to believe that it was Rory's "duty" to be loyal to his family, and so he repeatedly asked both his sons to visit their uncle when he was in Boston. But Sean was not asked to Green Hills more than once, for Bernadette had made it plain that she thought him detestable, and had resented him. She was not aware of his propensities, and had never heard of such things, but some uneasy revulsion stirred in her when she saw Sean. She thought him very ladylike and pretentious and affected, though she kept this opinion from Joseph. Sean, in his turn, had hated her anew, remembering his earlier impression of her as a "loud, bouncing woman."

It had been Herbert Hayes who, from prison, had sent Rory the telegram announcing Sean's death. For Herbert had murdered him. Sean had fallen wildly in love with a new young accompanist, and had told Herbert of his passion, and had asked Herbert to remain as his business manager but to cut "all ties of affection with me." Herbert, betrayed, desperate, crushed and then made nearly insane, had simply strangled the man to whom he had given so much and with such devotion and dedication, and then had called the police.

All this Rory discovered from the police, themselves, when he went to his uncle's suite. They were callously locking up all the dainty treasures with which Sean traveled, and they were not deferential to the stunned young man but cynically, and half-laughing, gave him full information. "Yes, yes, I know what my uncle was," said Rory, looking about him dazedly. "Poor Herbert. I suppose he will be hanged. I wonder what the hell I am going to tell my father."

The newspapers solved his problem in large black head-lines, in Boston and New York and Philadelphia and Washington, and other large cities. They were most discreet, and coyly so, but a knowledgeable person could guess at once the import of their insinuations. Rory kept the newspapers for his father, who had cabled he would return to America at once to take charge of matters, and the funeral. In the meantime, out of pity, Rory visited Herbert in prison where he was awaiting indictment, and he found him whitely calm and despairing. He was piteously grateful for Rory's visit. "After all, I went out of my mind and killed your uncle, such a genius, such a spirit, such a voice. I can't tell you why. I prefer to bury the secret with me." Rory mentioned that he knew many fine lawyers in Boston, but Herbert shook his head and looked like death. "I want to die, too," he said. "Your uncle was my whole life, and now I have nothing left."

But Rory got a good lawyer for him. He read the newspapers with dismay and thought of Albert Chisholm and what he would say to his daughter about "that Armagh family." Mr. Chisholm would have no illusions though he would delicately refrain from enlightening Marjorie, of course.

Joseph took the fastest liner out of Southampton for New York almost immediately. He was alone and isolated, for neither Harry Zeff nor Charles Devereaux had accompanied him to Europe this time on the dismal hegira in behalf of Ann Marie, and they were needed by The Armagh Enterprises. The journey was like a more ghastly repetition of his first journey to America, to Joseph, with the boiling and livid seas, the harsh winds, the sleet, the snowstorms, and the wailing of the horns in the fogs. He shivered in his warm and luxurious stateroom. He tried to keep from thinking. Rory's cable had not informed him of the manner of Sean's death, and he assumed it was "a weakness of the lungs," from which Sean had always suffered. It was, he thought, one of the plagues that harassed the Irish. He tried to read. It was hopeless. He had felt misery behind him, and misery waited for him, and fresh sorrow and loss. But he would not let himself think.

Rory met him in New York, alone. The young man

thought this best. When Joseph immediately demanded of him the cause of Sean's death Rory replied, "Let us get out of this hack and into the hotel. I have the newspapers for you." Snow and wind lashed the windows of the cab, and Joseph, with a sense of calamity, could only stare at Rory's set face and could only think how much older the young man seemed. Rory did say that all funeral arrangements had been left in abeyance awaiting Joseph's return. "Good," said Joseph. He thought of Sean, not as the middle-aged singer of much acclaim and success, but as little Sean with the light and petulant eyes and the lovely childish voice, and his eyes felt dry and parched. "It is as it was only yesterday, himself singing in the steerage to lighten our mother's pain and wretchedness," he said to Rory, who was surprised at this sentimentality on the part of his father. His voice had actually taken on a lilting brogue, as if he were a child again. He shook his head, somberly, and kept wetting his lips. "The priest bought him an apple on the docks of New York, where no one wanted us, and he'd never eaten an apple, they all rotting in Ireland along with the potatoes. I shall never forget how he ate it, poor little spalpeen, licking every morsel and every drop of juice." He sighed shortly. "He was too long without the apples of existence, too long, I am thinking. He was always frail."

Rory considerately looked through the snow-lashed window, and now his regret was for his father and not for his murdered uncle. Harry Zeff had had many quiet conversations with Rory on the subject of Joseph, for Harry had been determined that Rory would not be another Sean to blacken his father's life with ingratitude and girlish cruelty. "I knew your Dad when we were boys together," he would keep repeating. "I know what Joe suffered for his family. I know what Sean's running away meant to him, and I know what it meant to him when Sean finally accomplished something by himself. He was as proud as a peacock." He had looked at Rory then. "I read something once, a Turkish poet or something, your father was always giving me books to read though I never wanted them. Omar Something. How can I remember? It was about a man forgiving God, and not the other way around."

Rory had quoted:

"O Thou Who man of baser earth didst make,
    And e'en with Paradise devised the snake,

For all the sin wherewith the face of man
Is blackened, Man's forgiveness give—and take."

"Yes, yes," Harry had said, nodding with contentment. "That is it. The old Turks understood, didn't they? Joe's got a lot to forgive God for, and don't you be forgetting it, as Joe himself would say."

When Rory and Joseph reached Delmonico's, Rory said, "It's very cold and you are tired, Pa. You need a drink." Joseph scowled at him. "I seem to remember that on every gloomy occasion you reach for the bottle, Rory. Well, then, let's have it."

The steam pipes clanked desolately but Rory had ordered a fire, remembering how cold affected his father. He mixed a hot toddy for Joseph and Joseph said, "Where do they get lemons here this time of the year," and Rory said, "Why, from Florida, by fast train. These are new days, Pa, very modern and fast."

Joseph drank gingerly, and then with a sudden thirst Rory had never seen him exhibit before. When he appeared to be relaxing, and warming, Rory said, "I won't beat about the bush. I thought you ought to see some of the newspapers from Boston, and some from the yellow press in New York, before you go to Boston to arrange for the funeral and bring Uncle Sean to the family plot in Green Hills."

"Why should I see the newspapers?" demanded Joseph. "What is all this mystery? Well, let me have the damned things."

So Rory gave his father a sheaf of headlines and shouting print, and made himself another drink and prudently absented himself for a while in the next room. He heard no sound but the turning of pages, except for one exclamation, "Oh, my God!" Rory winced, and wished he had brought the whiskey bottle with him into this room. The hell with you, Uncle Jenny Lind, he addressed the dead man, grimly. It wasn't enough that you once kicked him in the teeth, but you had to do this thing to him, too.

Rory saw the sudden welling of the fire as Joseph savagely thrust the papers into it. But Joseph did not call him immediately. For Joseph was thinking again of Senator Bassett. He was not thinking of the explicit scandal which had fallen upon his family. He could only see the face of the man he had destroyed, and he saw that face in the bright coals on the hearth, and he heard, again, the dead voice and reread the last letter the unfortunate man had ever written.

After a long time Joseph called his son and Rory went back into the darkening room. "I think," said Joseph, "I need another of your infernal drinks." But when the silent Rory gave it to him he only held it in his hand and stared at the fire, and his face had become stark and pallid, and occasionally he shivered.

Sean was buried in the family plot with its huge obelisk, and he was buried quietly, and the innocent priest said, "—this sad and famous victim of an insensate act on the part of a madman. We can only mourn the loss of so magnificent a treasure— We can only condole with those who grieve, and remind them—"

The snow fell on the bronze casket and into the black and waiting grave, and those who had been invited to accompany the father and the two sons exchanged looks which were meekly malicious, except for Harry Zeff and Charles Devereaux and Timothy Dineen, who stood with Joseph like a bodyguard and let the snow fall on their uncovered heads. The handful of earth and the holy water also fell, and Joseph did not turn away but looked at his brother's coffin and nothing at all showed on his ravaged face.

Two days later, without even seeing Elizabeth, he returned to Europe. Before his trial, Herbert Hayes hanged himself in his cell.

Chapter 7

After his uncle's funeral, and his and Kevin's return to Harvard, Rory was taken by a profound depression which he had never known before. He had heard of "black Irish moods" but had thought them only invented by the poetic Irish to explain the melancholy experienced at times by all men. He could not shake off his depression, though he attempted to find the cause. Even Marjorie, with her mocking jokes and ardent love, could not alleviate it much.

Rory found himself studying the newspapers and trying to "read between the lines." But everything seemed tranquil in an America of rising prosperity and hope, despite the screaming politicians and that segment of the press known as "yellow." America rejoiced in her freedom. She was the Mecca of a whole envious world. She was at once naïve, ebullient, happy, rich, expanding, innocent, gay, and emotional, caring more for news of the British Royal Family than for the speeches of her President. Americans adored William Jennings Bryan and laughed happily at cartoons lampooning him. Their opinions are like froth, thought Rory. Their emotions are equally turbulent and shallow. Yet under that froth there appeared to be a serene and tranquil current, flowing steadily to Utopia and its golden towers, where every man would own his own "cot," to quote a newspaper, his own land and his own destiny.

Rory had still been in Europe when, on January 25, 1898, the little American battleship, *Maine,* entered Havana Harbor to the alleged joy of both the Spanish government and the Cuban insurrectos. Everyone pretended that this had happened by invitation of the government, though it was not for a considerable time that it became known it was at a secret request of the American Consul General, for reasons never quite divulged. The Spanish commander of the port personally visited the battleship, accompanied by cases of rare Spanish sherry as a gift, and he invited the officer-crew to a bullfight. The President of the United States said that the visit of the *Maine* to Cuba was "simply an act of international courtesy."

But Joseph had told Rory that the "friendly act" was to protect American citizens resident in Cuba, "or perhaps to use them for certain reasons." It was also to protect American property if the interior revolution reached Havana. Joseph did not expound on the "certain reasons" for the presence of the *Maine*. But Rory began to watch the newspapers. Sometimes he derided himself. He was looking for bogeymen, for traitors under beds, for conspirators. Feeling the power and pulse of America now that he was home it seemed amusingly incredible to him that any conspiracy of anonymous men meeting in St. Petersburg, London, Paris, Rome, Berlin, Vienna, or anywhere else, could truly gain an international ascendancy over his country, and destroy her for their own ambitions. Was it possible that his father had actually taken them seriously? Of course, they were powerful, for they were financiers and could manipulate the currencies of Europe—but how could they possibly manipulate America's currency, and her politics and her government? Even the "robber barons" of America were too American to permit such a thing. Rory had heard them laugh in New York at "our European trolls." It had been the laughter of strong and humorous men, men who appeared at national celebrations of the Fourth of July, to give fervent speeches on patriotism and "the glory of our beloved and invulnerable and peaceful country." There were, as they often remarked, "two oceans girding and guarding our shores from foreign ambition and foreign attack." The Monroe Doctrine was a revered document, third only in the esteem of Americans after the Declaration of Independence and the Constitution. It was impregnable.

Wars? Confiscatory taxation? Inflation? National "emergencies"? They were as remote from America as Arcturus. They were European aberrations, a disease of old and decadent countries, and would never invade the healthy tissues of the American body politic, for all its innocent flamboyance and noise and fireworks and denunciations and excitements and roaring emotions, and other irrationalities.

Kevin was a freshman at Harvard, and he and Rory often met in little quiet restaurants in Boston. Kevin was young, but he was as tall if not taller than his brother, and he was a "black Irish bear," as his mother often said. But there was something about Kevin which was not juvenile or collegiate, something steadfast, immovable, and rational, without emotional overtones or rashness. Kevin was not a "talker." It had long been Rory's opinion that Kevin knew more about Ann Marie's "accident" than he would ever tell, and nothing could force him to tell. When Kevin appeared his presence was not just the presence of another very young man, awkward, uncertain, gawky or defensive. He was simply there, and he was felt almost tangibly. Between the two brothers was a deep and unspoken love and trust, yet it was rare when they confided in each other and had never, as yet, been totally frank. "Baring one's soul" was just not the Armagh way of life, and it would not have occurred to Rory to disobey Joseph and ask Kevin his opinion of what his brother had seen and heard in London, and in New York. If anything, Rory was even more secretive than his brother, who had a reputation for it. If either had encountered a grave trouble they would have gone to the other for assistance, without offering any explanation at all, nor being expected to offer such accounting. They had their father's innate dignity and his contempt for emotionalism of any sort. "Like a damned woman whimpering into her pillow," Joseph would say of any man he knew who could not control his feelings, or desired to display them. "Or taking off your trousers and underdrawers in public. Have they no self-respect? They want everyone to quiver with sympathy for them, and love them, for God's sake!"

This was the attitude of the Armagh brothers also, who had pride if no "sensibilities," as Bernadette called it.

Kevin was a good student if an uninspired one. He worked hard, as Rory had never had to work, yet he was as retentive as Rory. He sweated and labored over his books. His papers were adequately prepared, if pedestrian. Rocklike, bulky, strong, he was admired on the track and in the field. No one knew what Kevin thought though Rory came the nearest to guessing. Kevin was pragmatic. Kevin was realistic. Kevin was never haunted by bogeymen or nightmares. Kevin was forthright and blunt, and no sweet-sayer, and he often had manners which were stigmatized as rude or boorish. It was just that Kevin had no time for fools or for the little niceties and frivolities. "What are you saving your time for, then?" Rory had once rallied him. "For me," Kevin had replied, at fifteen. On taking thought, later,

Rory acknowledged that that was an eminently sensible remark. There were absolutely no affectations in Kevin, no pretensions, no hypocrisies. He had had many more fist-fights in his life at eighteen than Rory ever had had, and he had fought efficiently and without passion and without rancor. "He is like my Grandda," Joseph had once remarked. "There was no stopping that black Irish bull when he had set his mind on something."

The trouble was that no one, as yet, knew exactly if Kevin had set his mind on anything, not even Rory, though it was expected that he would go on to law school and then into politics, as his father had decreed. Kevin was no conversationalist. Whatever he thought was his own, and his mind was not to be invaded. His dark eyes were keen but not lively, sharp but not sparkling, and never seemed to smile. His large blunt head sat firmly on his short neck and wide shoulders, and he looked at the world not boldly but with an entire lack of wariness. If he sometimes asked a question, and the person became evasive, he immediately changed the subject. Whether or not that hinted at a lack of interest in others no one ever knew, except Rory, who knew it for an amazing sensitivity which Kevin kept hidden, and a deep respect for the privacy of others.

Rory and Kevin met for dinner at a grubby little Boston restaurant on February 10th. Both were inclined to frugality and to complain of their father's parsimony, and Rory was careful with the remainder of the money Joseph had given him. "Count your pennies and the pounds will take care of themselves," Joseph would say, and his sons agreed with him, for all their complaints.

The restaurant was really a saloon, or a pub, as Joseph would have called it, and the beer was excellent and so were the roast beef sandwiches, pickled pigs' feet, ham, pork sausages, potato salad, rye bread, tongue, and baked beans. Here healthy young men from the colleges, who had penny-pinching fathers of great wealth, could drink and dine heartily and smoke or even spit on the sawdust-covered floors, and tell their lewd jokes and roar joyously at each other, and boast of their sexual successes, mostly fictitious. The young ladies of Boston were often offensively unattainable, and the brothels—most of them owned by The Armagh Enterprises—were expensive. It was a favorite spot for both Rory and Kevin, and they could sit far back in semi-shadow and talk at a greasy wooden table, and rarely be accosted. It was known that their father owned the saloon, as he did many others in Boston, and there was an aura, therefore, about the two brothers which they would have protested had they guessed. Didn't they have to pay as much as anyone else? Did Pa let them have credit? No. Their only distinction was that the Irish bartenders insulted them more than they did others, and loudly called them "shanty Irish," and pretended to ignore them.

Rory gave Kevin the news of that part of the family still in Europe, for the death of their uncle had prevented confidences before. They did not speak of Sean. Had he been murdered by robbers or an offended husband they would have talked of him. But now he had been consigned to the discreet Limbo of the Armaghs, and so did not exist any longer except in their gloomy memories. A tinny piano—Sean had once played and sang here long ago—covered their intermittent conversation. Rory, the voluble, did not find Kevin's short remarks and long silences oppressive. There was an empathy flowing between them which needed few words. Kevin had guessed at once, tonight, that Rory was preoccupied—a rare thing for him—and even somber, and he waited for either Rory to speak or not to speak. The big dim gaslights flickered in their dirty globes and it was cold and dank in the saloon, but the beer was good and both the young men had fully filled their stomachs. The portrait of the naked lady over the bar seemed exceptionally ruddy and exceptionally fat, and beamed at the diners and drinkers below her in a most benevolent mood.

Rory bent his handsome red-gold head over his beer mug and seemed to be tracing with his eyes the lacy patterns on the sides. He said, "I was only away for a little while but it seemed months. What a hole London is! But it's got a feeling of power which we don't have even in New York or Washington—a feeling of empire, of puissance, as the old boys used to call it. A kind of—throbbing—all over. But the 'merry men of England' have long gone, thanks to Cromwell and Victoria, and the Cavalier spirit is dead. If it ever existed."

Kevin waited. Rory glanced up at him swiftly with those apparently candid eyes of his. He said, "I heard something about us sending a battleship to Havana, while I was in London. Hear about it, yourself?"

"Sure," said Kevin. "We're getting ready to take over Cuba. And other loot."

Rory was enormously startled and taken aback. His brother had spoken so casually, as of a self-evident reality. His strong voice had been dispassionate and even indifferent.

"For God's sake, why?"

Kevin shrugged his heavy bull-like shoulders. "Guess we want a war."

"Why?" Rory almost shouted. He was still shaken.

Kevin shrugged again. "Who knows? I suppose we are on our way."

"To what?"

"To being like other countries."

"What the hell does that mean?"

"Come on, Rory. You know. Empire. And something else, too."

Rory's chest tightened. "What do you mean by 'something else'?"

Kevin frowned, and his big dark face became lowering. "How could I know, or you, or anybody else? Except Pa, perhaps. You just get a smell of it. A sort of feeling, fog, in the air. I've been studying some—things."

"What?"

"Hey, you are shouting. I've been reading about the Morgans, the Regans, the Fisks, the Goulds, the Vanderbilts—all the rest. Running back and forth to their houses in London and Paris and Vienna and on the Riviera. Lot of activity lately. It's reported in the newspapers—galas, weddings, fiestas, international society. The thing is I don't believe it. They always did it, but this time I don't believe it's so damned innocent."

Rory was stupefied. Kevin gave him a glowering smile. "Didn't you meet some of them in London?"

Rory nodded, unable to speak. "And they were all marrying their daughters off to European nobility, and such," said Kevin. "Selling the girls like heifers. Well. But it's something else, too, more important. I have a prof, or I should say I did have one. They let him out in January. He talked about the international bankers one period. Just a little. But I knew; it all snapped into place, what I've been reading in the papers. I don't know why he was kicked out. Or maybe I do."

A deep coldness settled in Rory's interior. Suddenly his brother no longer looked impassive and young, but worldly and weightily disgusted, and more adult than himself, who was six years older.

"Who do you think has been stirring up those insurrectos in Cuba?" asked Kevin. "They live better than American farmers in the backwoods live. Who made those poor peasants suddenly conscious that they were 'oppressed'? It isn't race or religion that divides them from the Spaniards; they are the same people, with a little mixture of Indian, probably. Who's kicking up shit in Cuba now?"

"Who?"

"Us, of course. For some damned reason or other. Do you think the cane-cutters in Cuba are now suddenly all fired up about 'liberty' and 'the rights of man'? Why, they can't even read, for Christ's sake. All the poor devils want is peace and guitars and romance and girls and wine and dancing. Food's almost for the asking, and they don't need houses like ours, and heat. But all at once they are talking about 'liberation.' You're the heir, Rory. Now you tell me why?"

But I can't, thought Rory. He was chilled inside and out, and shivered.

He said at last, "What do you mean, I am the heir?"

Kevin smiled darkly. "You are the older son. You are almost out of law school. You'll be the first in politics. You've just come back from Europe. Pa sent for you. I'm not going to ask you why and expect you to tell me the truth. You said it was something about Ann Marie, and I didn't believe it for a minute, for she wasn't in England. Rory, I may be only eighteen, but there's no milk on my chin. Pa never told me much, if anything, but I can almost read his mind. You just have to listen, not with your ears, but with another sense— Oh, hell, I can't explain it, can't prove it. It's just there."

He drank some beer. "I read everything Mark Hanna says to the newspapers. And everything the President says. They hint. Maybe that's all they dare to do. Incidentally, I don't like our grinning Teddy Bear, Roosevelt, Assistant Navy Secretary. I just read that he ordered Commodore Dewey to get ready to attack Manila, eight thousand miles from here."

"Hey, Irish, gonna sit there all night, and not drinking?" a bartender shouted at them. "Think we run this pub on talk?"

"Shut up, Barney," said Kevin, waving his hand. "But

send us more beer." His hand was massive, like a hod-carrier's, and his young face was suddenly massive too. " 'My country,' " he said, " 'may she always be right. But my country, right or wrong.' " He stared at Rory and now the dark iris of his eyes was surrounded by a glistening whiteness. "So long as she is my country, and not somebody else's."

Rory's lips felt without muscle or strength. "Who else's could she be, Kevin?"

Once again that heavy shrug. "Well, they are talking about a World Court in The Hague just now, aren't they? or maybe Pa didn't mention it. Maybe you forgot to read the newspapers about it. Maybe the English newspapers didn't think it was important. Or something."

Now he smiled widely and cynically at Rory and his big wolflike teeth, as white as snow, flashed in the gaslight "I'm just Little Brother. I don't know a thing. Let's drink up this slop and get out of here. I've got an early class tomorrow."

On the night of February 15th the battleship *Maine* was blown up in Havana Harbor. Over two hundred American officers and crew were killed. No one ever discovered who or what had caused this disaster, but it was enough for the enthusiastic warmongers throughout the country, and their bought press to demand war. No one was quite certain who was the "enemy," but after a little thought it was decided it was Spain. Later it was decided that a submarine mine, applied outside the ship, might be the cause, or again, it was argued, its munitions magazine had been exploded inside. Who was guilty? No one ever knew. Assistant Secretary of the Navy Theodore Roosevelt vehemently shouted that he was "convinced" that the disaster in Havana Harbor was not an accident, but the rescued captain of the ship, Mr. Charles D. Sigsbee, urged patience and calm until an investigation was concluded. Mr. Roosevelt almost lost his mind with rage. In the meantime the Spanish government expressed its horror, and went into mourning for the American dead. The government in Madrid made conciliation offers over and over, in despair, in an attempt to avoid a war, but Assistant Secretary of the Navy Roosevelt screamed for "vengeance."

President McKinley was a prudent man, and not a warmonger. He begged the country to wait for the official investigation. "It is possible," he said, "that agents pro-vocateurs are responsible for this, and not the Spanish government. I have heard whispers, and I have heard rumors—" By these words he signed his death warrant.

Mr. Roosevelt was beside himself. He said of the Pres-ident, "He has no more backbone than a chocolate eclair. Do you know what that white-livered cur up in the White House has done? He has prepared *two* messages, one for war and one for peace, and he doesn't know which one to send in!"

So, they have moved, thought Rory Armagh, reading all this in the newspapers. It was not a nightmare after all. I was not frightening myself in the dark. What I heard in London was no gibberish of little plotters. It is the begin-ning of their Plan.

In the meantime the President, despite Mr. Roosevelt and his friend, Captain Mahan, asked the American people to retain their senses and not be misled "by those who would lead us into a war which I have heard—though it may be only a rumor, a rumor—is the overture to a series of wars to entangle our country in foreign adventures. What the purpose is I do not entirely know; I can only sur-mise. Let us remember what George Washington implored us to do, to have peaceful relations with all countries but foreign entanglements with none."

"White-livered cur!" shouted Mr. Roosevelt.

The pressure on the President via the press and Mr. Roosevelt became insupportable. He pleaded over and over that as America was only just emerging into new prosperity she should mind her own business and be judicious and balanced. But it was hopeless. The hysterical and enthusi-astic masses, led by vociferous editorials in the yellow press, demanded war against Spain, though none was quite certain why there should be such a war. So, despairing, faintly aware of the powerful forces against him from a watching Europe and New York, he succumbed. On April 11, 1898, the President, broken-hearted, frightened, sent in his war message. On May 1 Commodore George Dewey steamed into Manila Bay, in command of America's Asiat-ic Squadron, and sank all the Spanish warships that were there—eight thousand miles away.

The Spanish government in Cuba, and the insurrectos themselves, were dumb with astonishment and incredulity. They heard that Mr. Roosevelt had joyously declared that the war was "in behalf of American interests." What those interests were no one was quite sure—except for the men in Washington and New York, in London and Berlin and Paris and Rome and Vienna and St. Petersburg. They called a quiet and exultant meeting, and shook hands, and said little or nothing at all.

In June the American forces, singing, though they knew not why they sang, landed at Daiquirí, Cuba, with a loss of two men who had drowned. In July the miserable Spanish forces at San Juan Hill, Santiago, and at El Caney, were overwhelmed. On July 3 Admiral Cervera's Spanish fleet, commanded by disbelieving officers, tried to escape from Santiago and were destroyed by American warships, ordered there days before. The invading Americans, on July 17, captured Santiago, and the Spaniards surrendered.

On July 26 the Spanish government in Madrid asked for the terms of surrender, and an armistice was signed in Paris on August 12. It was no sooner signed than the news arrived that American forces had taken Manila, the Philippines, and Puerto Rico in the Caribbean Sea—there had been no resistance at all.

"How do you like the *Journal*'s War?" cried the *New York Journal* with exultant delight, and the American people roared happily in answer. From London the American Ambassador congratulated his friend, Theodore Roosevelt, in an exuberant letter. "It has been a splendid little war!" he declared.

America had acquired many overseas bases now. President McKinley was not pleased. He thought of Theodore Roosevelt and his friend, Captain Mahan, and he had many other thoughts. It was unfortunate that he put some of them on paper and sent them to alleged friends he had considered sympathetic. They found thoughtful resting places on faraway desks in various cities in Europe.

Rory Armagh had lost interest long before the signing of the peace treaty in Paris. For his brother, Kevin, had died in the "splendid little war," killed in Santiago on board the American battleship, *Texas,* on July 28.

Chapter 8

At the beginning of spring vacation Kevin had said to his brother, "I'm not going back to Green Hills this summer. I'm not going to my usual stint in Philadelphia in Pa's offices, either. I've got a job for the *Boston Gazette,* doing feature articles on the war."

"You?" said Rory, disbelieving. Kevin had smiled. "You may think I'm just a plodder, and I am. But I can write factually. I may not be inspired or hysterical, but I can write objectively. So, the paper hired me, and I'm off to the wars to report. I think it'll be over, soon."

"You are looking for excitement," Rory had accused him, dismayed, thinking of their father. Kevin laughed. "Know anybody less excitable than me? No, I'm looking for something."

"What?" But Kevin had shrugged his big heavy shoulders, which were so effective on the football field. Kevin was "deep," as Joseph would say. He never revealed anything he did not want to reveal, about himself or anyone else, so Rory knew there was no use in pressing him. But Rory thought of what the faceless men had said in London: "We cannot have nationalism and sovereign states, which divide and disperse our interests. We must work for a world Socialistic empire, which we will be able to control without tedious distractions of independent political entities and their internal and external quarrels."

"In short," Joseph had ironically told his son, "they will plunder the people of the world through heavy taxation in every country, then 'benevolently' return to the subdued masses part of that revenue in 'gifts,' 'aids,' 'social justice,' 'sharing,' all the people's money anyway—for which the cowed populace will be humbly grateful and become obedient and conforming. No, I won't tell you anything more. But you will learn as we go along, and accept it all." He

654

had stared a moment, thoughtfully, at Rory. "We will have to see if you are reliable."

"Pa," Rory had said, "you are not really one of them."

Joseph had looked away. "That may be your opinion, Rory. I am as interested as they are in power." He remembered what Mr. Montrose had told him so long ago, in his early youth, that Marxism was not a "movement" for the liberation and rule of the "proletariat," but a conspiracy of those who called themselves the "Elite," and whose aim was despotism.

Rory was to wonder to the end of his life if young Kevin had had any insight about these things, and to remember his conversation with him in that cold February of 1898.

When Joseph and Bernadette and Ann Marie returned in early April it was Rory's miserable and unwanted task— undertaken with some wincing and resentment—to inform his parents that Kevin had already left America as a correspondent for the *Boston Gazette*. Joseph was predictably angered, and Bernadette threw up her fat arms and cried, "How ungrateful, how stupid, how like Kevin, to do this to his father! In the middle of term, too."

To Rory's surprise Joseph had suddenly smiled his saturnine smile. "Well, he may learn something. I always thought he was 'deep.'" He had looked sharply at Rory. "I hope you didn't—shall we say—gossip with him about London?"

Rory was offended. He said, "Pa, I'd like to talk to you in private," and they had gone upstairs to Joseph's rooms and Rory had told his father of his last real conversation with Kevin. Joseph had listened with that intensity of his, and then had nodded his head, even pridefully. "We have a good one, there," he had remarked. "I always thought it. Did you suspect that there was a touch of the knight errant in Kevin?"

"No. There never was. He is absolutely practical and disillusioned, Pa."

"Good," Joseph had said. "But to think the spalpeen used my name with that damned paper to get that job! Well, at least it shows he has enterprise and impudence. We won't need to worry, then. No harm will come to him. It's not as if he had enlisted."

Kevin's articles began to appear in the newspaper almost weekly. To his family's surprise there was a kind of surly jocularity in them, a cold underlying cynicism, as well as practical reporting. They contained no ebullient patriotism, no hero-singing, no excitement or jubilation about "our war of liberation." They were totally dispassionate, which did not entirely please the sponsor. Then the articles stopped the latter part of June. Joseph, frowning, put enquiries in motion. He discovered that Kevin was no longer in the vicinity of Cuba. The newspaper asserted that, at his own desire, he had gone to the Philippines, "somewhere," and had written that he wished to be an "observer" on a battleship. The *Gazette* believed that the battleship's name was *Texas*, and expressed its hope that it would soon be in possession of "dispatches."

The next dispatch was a telegram from the Admiral of the American Fleet at Santiago that Mr. Kevin Armagh had died as the result of a "random wild shot, coming from the enemy," which had reached Kevin "by a freak or ordinance of God," for it had not been directed at anyone or anything in particular. Standing in the great marble hall of his house, with the telegram in his hand, Joseph felt the atavistic Celt stirring in himself, a Celt who did not believe in the random or coincidental, but who believed in Fate. He stood in that hall, silent, motionless, for a long time before he went upstairs to inform his wife of the death of their son. He held himself stiff and climbed slowly, like an old haughty man who knew he was dying.

If Bernadette had a favorite, in spite of her "sharp Irish tongue like knives," it had been Kevin, who had protected her from the supreme disaster only a year ago, and who, though always looking at her with his dark eyes devoid of any illusions or deep affection, had often appeared to understand her. Her raw humor of girlhood had become harsh and full of raillery, but Kevin had laughed in appreciation as no one else seemed to do these days. He had often, in the past three or four years, even joined her in joking extravagance and had actually teased her out of bad tempers. When she would become roughly hysterical in the presence of Joseph—who had a sardonic way of baiting her, knowing her love for him—it was Kevin who had given her warning winks and slight shakes of the head, and had quieted her. As much as it was possible for her to love any of her children she loved Kevin.

It was late on a very hot thirtieth of July, and Bernadette, whose corpulence was a heavy burden in the heat, had been napping before her lonely interlude with a bottle and a glass, and then dinner. She sat up in her bed in her darkened room as Joseph came in, sweating in her pink silk and lace nightgown, her graying brown hair wet about her face and straggling on her mountainous shoulders. Her face, round and puffed with fat, was crimson and steamy, her once-fine eyes sunken in flesh and dazed with sleep, her nose and chins oily. Her huge breasts pushed against the fragile silklike udders, and she smelled of expensive perfume and perspiration and talcum powder, and hot obesity. "What, what?" she mumbled.

Joseph knew where she kept her secret bottles, for a vengeful maid, discharged by Bernadette, had told him of her mistress' generous tipples in the evening. Joseph knew that his wife was now frequently drunk before dinner, but he cared no more for that than he did for anything else concerning the desperate Bernadette. Still without speaking and while Bernadette stared after him, slowly coming to full consciousness and blinking rapidly, he went to the little French cabinet near a far wall, lifted the lid and took out a bottle of Irish whiskey and a sticky glass. She watched, and the crimson on her cheeks deepened and a fresh burst of sweat poured out upon her and stained the nightgown darkly. She watched him, numbly, as he poured a good measure of the whiskey into the glass. Only her eyes moved when he came to the bed and put the glass in her hand. "Drink it," he said. "I think you are going to need it."

How did he find out? Bernadette asked herself, mortified and heartbroken. It must have been that damned Charlotte, with the sly mouth. "I don't think I want it," she mumbled, dropping her eyes with mingled shame and wretchedness. "It's too warm."

"Drink it," Joseph repeated.

For the first time she became aware of what he had done. Startled fully awake now, she looked up at him, her eyes as wide as possible in all that flesh. She knew at once that he had not done this in mockery and contempt, as he had done other things when he had discovered certain secrets of hers, and had exposed them. Then, to her stunned amazement, as she held the glass reluctantly in her bloated hand, he actually drew a white and gold chair near to the bed and sat down in it, and she saw his face completely for the first time and she saw that it was the color of the whitish-gray in the russet of his hair and that his wide thin lips were as blue as huckleberries, and that every muscle in his face was as flat and stiff as ivory.

A horrible feeling of impending disaster hit Bernadette. He was going to leave her. He was going to divorce her so he could marry that shameless Elizabeth Hennessey. He had given her the whiskey because as a last kindness to her he was softening the effects of his assault upon her very soul. "No, no," she groaned, her lips feeling thick and lifeless. "Oh, no."

"Drink it," he said, and he was looking at her now not with his usual distant aversion, his murderous indifference, his open loathing, but with an expression she had seen but once before, when she had been little more than a child on the night her mother had died, and he had held her in the hall below and had tried to comfort her. She burst into tears, then afraid that he might newly despise her, she drank hurriedly, gasped, choked, drank again. He took the glass from her and put it on her bedside table, which was cluttered with lace handkerchiefs, bottles of perfume, a little dish of lozenges, a porcelain figure or two, and two or three rings. The heat of the room, with its closed draperies, was like the core of a burning coal and sickening with scent and the odor of a large wet body.

The heat of the day had been too hot for Bernadette's usual enormous meals, and she had eaten only a roll and coffee for breakfast, and the strong whiskey immediately spread through her vitals, hot, yes, but comforting—consoling—deadening, bringing with it a mendacious courage and fortitude, all of which she had needed for the many years of her life with Joseph Armagh. She panted, looking at him with eyes like a mortally stricken and humble animal dying before a hunter, and said, "You are going away. Tell me."

"I am not going away, Bernadette," he said, almost gently. He could not look at her eyes, so tortured, so pleading, so despairing—no, he could not look at them now. "It's just—I have bad news. It just arrived. Kevin—"

Oh, God be thanked, he is not going to leave me! something cried joyously in Bernadette, and a glow came over her face. She put out her hand impulsively to her husband, and he actually took it, wet and swollen though it was, with deep fat dimples where the knuckles should have been, and he held it in spite of an almost incontrollable revulsion. Then she remembered his last word. "Kevin? What about Kevin?" The glow was in her heart, too. He was not going to leave her. He would still be her husband. "Kevin?" she repeated.

He had seen the glow and had accurately guessed its origin, but he could not detest her now or repulse her. "I've had a telegram," he said, and he felt the hoarseness and dryness in his throat. "Kevin—he was on a battleship, *Texas*, at Santiago, as an observer for his newspaper. He was—shot. On July twenty-eighth. I've had a telegram, from the admiral." He felt her heavy hand slowly grow cold in his and saw her stupefied face, her thick dropped mouth, her empty eyes. She was trying to speak, coughed, mumbled, but did not look away from him. "He," she could say at last in a voice so faint he could hardly hear her, "he wasn't a soldier. And, isn't the war over?"

"Yes," said Joseph. There was still no real feeling in him, no real awareness of the news he was telling, only a shocked stillness such as a soldier might feel when the steel entered him and the pain had not yet begun. The pain would inevitably begin, he knew, for pain was an old familiar and he knew all its nuances, its stealthy approaches, its sudden overwhelming anguishes, its sudden incredulity and savage rebellion. But as yet it was only creeping in the darkness toward him on silent feet, letting its victim try to gather resisting but hopeless strength. "But, he was killed," said Joseph to his wife.

"Kevin," whispered Bernadette, stunned, incredulous as he was. "But he is only eighteen years old! It can't have happened to Kevin—he is only eighteen years old."

Joseph could not speak. He had expected conventional weeping from the dramatic Bernadette, and he had expected to be forced to console her. But the stunned and awful shock in her eyes stunned him also, for now he knew that she loved her son, and he squeezed his own parched eyelids together and heard the first crackling of the enemy's approach to him.

Then Bernadette screamed, tore her hand from Joseph's and clapped both her hands with a frightening noise to her cheeks. She screamed over and over, and her maid, in the next room, came running, aghast. "Send for the doctor," Joseph told her. "Mr. Kevin has been killed—in the war.

Send for the doctor immediately." He was barely heard above that tearing sound Bernadette was helplessly making, her eyes wild and bulging, vivid as fire with pain.

The doctor came—Joseph had not left his wife and had tried to calm her—and Bernadette was given a generous sedative. Only when it began to affect her did she cease her broken shrieking, her animal-like cries, her threshings on the bed, her calls upon God and her favorite Saints, her pleas to her husband that it must be a mistake, the war was over, it was some other mother's son; who would shoot Kevin, and why? and it was a nightmare, an error, the prank of an enemy, a wrong dispatch. Joseph must— must—. He had held her back on her pillows, had tried to give her more whiskey, but she had struck the glass fiercely from his hand and then had clutched him like a drowning woman, rolling her head on his shoulder, pushing him away for a moment as if he had attacked her and she was defending herself, then clutching him again and rolling her head on his shoulder and writhing against him.

The doctor, the maid and Joseph waited beside her bed and slowly the screaming, that fearful screaming—hoarse and broken—had finally stopped. Bernadette lay on her pillows, drenched in her own sweat, a disheveled but pathetic lump of flesh in her stained pink silk, panting and muttering. Then, for the first time, she had begun to cry, and the doctor nodded with sympathetic satisfaction. Joseph held her hand, and it was quiet at last, though trembling. She saw only her husband.

"There is a curse on us," she whimpered, and her eyes widened with horror. "Ann Marie. Your brother, Sean. Kevin. In one year, Joe, in one year. Who will be next? There is a curse on us. A curse on this family."

Then her eyes closed and she fell asleep and instantly snored under the drug. The doctor said, with pity, "She should sleep for several hours. I am leaving these pills, for later, when she wakes up. It is best to keep her under sedation for a few days. I will return tonight."

There were things to be done before the pain took over entirely. There was a telegram to Rory, to Charles Devereaux, to Timothy Dineen, to Harry Zeff. There were telegrams to Washington requesting the return of the body of Kevin Armagh, to be buried in the family plot. There were telegrams to senators, and other politicians. There were orders to the domestic staff in the house that no news-paper reporters were to be admitted. There was a message to the priest to come later to console Mrs. Joseph Armagh. There were so many arrangements to be made—before the relentless and terrible enemy pounced, bringing with it an absolute helplessness. The dire panoply of death began.

After he had completed what he must do Joseph went to his daughter's rooms, the once pretty girlish rooms she had decorated herself, so sunlit and fresh in color, so simple and charming. They were none of these now. They had been converted into a hospital center, plain, functional, cleared of all but absolute necessities. One room held the three beds of the three constant nurses, and their parapher-nalia. What had been the nursery but which had later been converted into a sitting room for Ann Marie, was a nursery again, filled with childish toys and other playthings, bright with nursery pictures on the walls and a table at which Ann Marie now ate all her meals, for no longer would the rooms downstairs know her and no longer would she run down those marble stairs. She would be assisted down them in the mornings for a short ride with a nurse or two, and then would be taken upstairs for her babyish naps, her bland meals. She would be tucked into bed at night, a nurse singing lullabies beside her, and she would sleep. Did she dream, ever? Joseph would ask himself. Were they the dreams of an infant, or the dreams of a woman? Sometimes she awakened, wailing, and all in the upper rooms heard that sorrowful sound, and shuddered, and waited until she was soothed and pacified into sobbing sleep again. Some-times the sobbing was the weeping of a bereaved woman who could never be comforted, the weeping of a woman who asked only to die. On hearing that Joseph would think: I don't know how it is possible, but I believe she knew. Yes, I believe she knew. I believe that when she sleeps, sometimes, she knows again and can't bear it.

The sun was still blazing, but low in the sky and redden-ing it, when Joseph went into those rooms which Berna-dette rarely entered. Ann Marie had eaten her bread and milk and fruit pudding and had drunk her mug of cocoa, and was now sitting where she always sat, near the window, in a white-padded hospital chair. For she was frequently and serenely incontinent, like a young child, and with as lit-tle shame, and as naturally. She was dressed for the night in a white plain dimity nightgown and a flowered wrapper, and her long soft brown hair had been braided into tight silky braids on her shoulders and her face was the face of a pampered, loved, and contented child. Her slim body had reverted to the outlines of babyhood, also, so that she was plump and rosy and dimpled as she had been at the age of three. Her legs and arms and hands and feet were immature again, her face was flushed and round, her lips full and pink, her flesh shining, her eyes innocently questing and shyly smiling—those lovely sherry-colored eyes with their long aureate lashes. She had never had what Bernadette had called "a proper bust," and now what she had had was merged in the general softness of her child's body.

"It is not often that we encounter such a reversion," the doctors had told Joseph in Switzerland and in Paris, "but it is not unknown. It is as if some deep unconscious will had decreed that childhood is safe and must never end, and that the soul must never know maturity again." A number of them had looked curiously at Joseph. "Has she had an unbearable shock to her sensibilities, some grief, some catastrophe, which makes present reality untenable to her, and unendurable?" To which Joseph had said, "No. She had only an accident."

They had told Joseph that she might remain in this state to the end of a possible long life, full of infant health, or she might retreat even further into immaturity and finally be unable to leave her bed, and then she would die of inanition and atrophy. They did not know. They had advised institutions, but Joseph had refused. His daughter would live and die in her own home, as she would wish, herself. She would have nurses, and nursemaids to attend her and to play with her. She would never be unhappy or frustrated or reduced to tears. She would be a child for all her life, most probably, but she would be a happy child.

"There are worse fates," said one of the doctors, shrugging.

Now Joseph sat beside her and took one of her soft little hands and said to her, as he always said, "Who am I, Ann Marie?"

"Papa," she said with triumph, and smiled that radiant smile of hers, affectionate and confiding. It was a nightly game.

He looked into her eyes, and saw the healthily glistening whites of them. the lashes, the bright irises. He always looked deeply into them, hoping hopelessly for some sign of the soul of Ann Marie in them, some shadowy hint that the spirit had not left forever. But it was the infant Ann Marie who looked back at him trustfully, the child in her cradle, the child in her nursery bed. So much for the theory of growing and maturing souls, he thought, as he had thought a thousand bitter times before. So much for immortal souls, gaining knowledge and wisdom and awareness. What Ann Marie had learned in twenty-three years was gone, irradicated, blotted out, as if it had never been there at all.

There was a cloth doll in her lap, and now she took it in her arms and hugged it and uttered a gleeful little sound. "Kiss Pudgy," she told her father, and he dutifully kissed it, and closed his eyes against both the endless pain of his daughter's spiritual death and the pain that was threatening him. He said, "Ann Marie, do you remember Kevin?"

She looked at him obediently. Only her voice was the voice of the woman she had been, clear, hesitant, hoping to please. "Kevin? Kevin?" She shook her head and pouted as if she had been rebuked.

"Never mind, dear," said her father, and passed his dry hands over his drier face, which felt scorched. He took up the doll again and shook it at her playfully and she laughed and snatched it from him, and hugged it again. "My Pudgy," she said. "You can't have her, Papa." The nurse, the younger one, was sitting nearby in her white clothing, knitting, and she smiled as if at the prattlings of a child and said, "We were very good tonight, Mr. Armagh." She had heard the news of Kevin's death, but as Mr. Armagh, who terrified everyone, had not spoken of it she did not speak of it or offer her condolences. "We took our bath nicely, and tomorrow we'll go for a little walk, won't we, Ann Marie?"

"And see the flowers," said Ann Marie, nodding. "The flowers. And the trees."

She looked through the windows at the far distant house where Elizabeth lived. It could only have been Joseph's imagination—but was there a faint darkening and yearning on her full rosy face, a tightening into womanhood for an instant, a despair? He leaned forward, hoping and fearing both, but the haunting had gone and the placid serenity had returned. But his heart was jumping. He stood up and kissed his daughter good night, and left her, for there was so much to be done, so very much to be done and there was no time for pain as yet.

He went into his wife's rooms again, and the sun was setting in scarlet majesty and the grounds about the house were peaceful and filled with shifting shadows of hot gilt and purple, and the tops of the trees were dancing in liquid gold. Joseph paused to look at all that which he owned, and the enemy crept nearer. "A curse on the family," Bernadette had wept. "There is a curse on us. Ann Marie, Sean, and now Kevin. A curse on us."

The ancient Celt, the Druid tree-worshiper, the Celt who had known mysteries and occult darknesses, stirred in Joseph again like a man awakening from centuries of sleep. Nonsense, he thought, and there was a movement of sickness in him, a dread. The Bassetts were eliminated all the time, and the executioners never lost an hour of healthy sleep nor suffered one twinge. He thought of the faceless men in all the nations who planned and destroyed as a matter of course and expediency, with no qualms, no stirrings of primeval spirit, no atavistic incantations against pursuing vengeance. They were realists.

Bernadette slept, stupefied, mouth open and drooling, and Joseph sat beside her and did not hear the muted dinner bell and did not go downstairs. He watched his wife until the room was dark and her maid began to light a lamp here and there. Then the pain came. Later, for the first time in his life, he deliberately got drunk.

Chapter 9

Joseph had enough powerful influence to have Kevin's body shipped back to Green Hills as speedily as possible, in the sealed bronze casket he had ordered. Accompanying it were two captains of the American Fleet off Santiago, and a company of sailors in full dress. There was a note of condolence from the admiral: *It was indeed a random shot from one of the retreating Spanish men-of-war, though all had surrendered. The bullet, which was extracted, was of the manufacture of Barbour & Bouchard, the American munitions makers. Of course, we know that munitions makers sell to all customers—my deepest condolences and regrets. Young Mr. Armagh endeared himself to us with his honesty, courage, intelligence and consideration—*

A random shot. It was no more than that. The Celt, the ancient Celt, stirred in Joseph again, the Celt of occult mysteries, of bloody vengeance, of Fate, of elves and fairies and screams in the night. Of banshees wailing under the moon, and misty bogs and green lakes as still as glass and hills of vapor. Kevin was part of that also. Joseph said to himself, over and over, Nonsense. It was an accident—as Ann Marie's was an accident.

As Kevin had not been a soldier or a sailor there could be no military funeral in late August, but the captains and the sailors were there, and one of the sailors rendered Taps in the Armagh family plot in Green Hills with the tall marble obelisk looking down enigmatically. There would be a small marble cross on Kevin's grave, as there was on Sean's grave. The black earth waited, and the funeral—private—took place during a hot dark day full of thunderous threat. Joseph stood with Bernadette, who was swathed in black veiling, and his son Rory whose full jovial face was set and somber, and his henchmen, Charles and Timothy and Harry, and watched his younger son's coffin lowered into

665

the ground to the murmurous prayers of the priest. A crowd of reporters, kept back by police, stood at a distance snapping photographs. Kevin was a hero. Though only a civilian, an observer, he had "braved" danger to report honestly to his countrymen, and so was a hero. There were rumors of the Congressional Medal of Honor, given posthumously. (It eventually arrived and was mounted in Kevin's room at home.)

"Not all who die in the service of their Country wear a uniform," said the priest. "There are Heroes who serve as nobly—" Joseph thought of Senator Bassett. Bernadette was weeping and swaying beside him, and he put his arm about her absently. Once, in her grief she had said recently to him, "The Armaghs brought disaster to the Hennesseys!" Then she had abjectly apologized and almost groveled before her husband.

"You are all I have left," Joseph said to Rory the night of the funeral. "So all you do must be for us." He had never seen Rory cry before, not even as a child, but Rory broke down and wept like a woman, his face in his hands. "What is it?" Joseph asked, but not with contempt. Rory did not answer. The ancient Celt was stirring in Rory also, but he could not have explained it logically. There was only a dark confusion within him, a far clashing, a sound like footsteps in the night, a breath that could not be identified; but also a certitude, a terror, a dread. He wanted to run to Marjorie, the sane and lovingly mocking, and be held in her arms, for Marjorie knew no turmoils and was full of common sense.

So was Elizabeth Hennessey who, if Catholic, was also Anglo-Saxon. Her reticence had kept her from going to the Armagh house during the period of mourning, though she ached for Joseph. She had sent flowers from her conservatory. She had written notes of condolence to Bernadette, and to her lover. She had not been invited to the funeral. She thought of Kevin, the big dark young man who was so solid and sensible and kind. Why was it that the best died and the evil lived and flourished? It was an old mystery, not to be explained. But, in truth, Elizabeth did not believe in mysteries. She went to Kevin's raw grave the next day and said to him, "Godspeed, my dear, Godspeed," though she did not believe in the incantation.

There had been no message from Joseph for a long time. Elizabeth waited. There was nothing else she could do. If a woman was helplessly and hopelessly in love with a man like Joseph Armagh she could not be even delicately aggressive or suggestive; she could not intrude, demand, accuse. She could only wait, and sit at her window and wonder if Joseph were still in his house or had left for Philadelphia, Chicago, New York, Boston, or other cities. There was no word from him. Is it over? she asked herself, and felt that she could not endure existence if that were so. She had seen photographs in the newspapers of Joseph tenderly enclosing his wife in his arms at the funeral, and then leading her into the carriage, she collapsed against him. Men were sentimental, unlike women. Perhaps the death of his son had made him turn diligently and remorsefully to his wife; it was just like a man. Men loved the heroic and self-denying role, even if it destroyed them. In many ways they were serious actors, and adored dramatics. Often they did not know they were acting. It was that part of masculine nature which Elizabeth feared and distrusted. That part surely played its own role in wars, for men were romanticists and always, thought Elizabeth with wry sadness, on parade. No true woman had ever written a marching song nor had yearned to blow a bugle or sound a drum. No woman, really, had ever put "duty" above love, unless she had loved only a little. Women knew the forces of life and what impelled them; men could only write poetry. Women lived. Men struck postures.

In the second week of September Joseph came to Elizabeth. She held out her arms mutely to him, wise enough not to cry, not to ask, not to reproach, not even to console. She took him to her bed, almost without speaking, and held him close and kissed him and said nothing. She lay in his arms and felt his love and his grief and his anguish, and touched him gently—and still said nothing. She had the wisdom of a woman completely in love, asking only to give. It was enough for her that he had returned to her. There was nothing else.

It was almost dawn when he said to her abruptly, "I asked you before, Elizabeth. Do you believe in curses?"

"No," she said at once. "If you are speaking of family calamities—they happen to all families, without curses, sooner or later. I believe in a merciful God. He would not permit any of His children to curse His other children. 'Vengeance is mine,' sayeth the Lord. 'I will repay.' "

That's what I am afraid of, thought Joseph, the wry

Celt, who did not believe in God. He tried to smile at Elizabeth in the blue-gray light of dawn. "Don't become mystical with me, Lizzie. There is no occult 'vengeance.' "

Then, why did you ask? Elizabeth asked him silently. But she only kissed him gently. She said to him, "I am not superstitious, and neither are you, my darling."

They did not speak of their families. Joseph asked nothing about Courtney. Elizabeth held Joseph in her arms and felt she was holding her whole world. But a man with a woman did not feel that. This she knew. It was enough for her that she loved and was loved in return, but a man never gave his whole heart to love and that was a fact with which no wise woman ever quarreled.

Joseph, in Philadelphia, read the reports gathered by Charles Devereaux and his investigators regarding his son, Rory, and he felt a cold outraged anger. That damned young swine, secretive, wily. Why had he married the girl? To be sure, she was of a notable and aristocratic family, of much wealth and position. But why had he married her and so jeopardized his future?

"I feel that Rory has done himself well," said Charles, looking at Joseph with curiously remote gray eyes. "Marjorie Chisholm has an impeccable background. They married in secret because of possible opposition by their families. I am not going to question Rory's reasons for fearing you would oppose the marriage. I know the reasons of Mr. Albert Chisholm. I think the marriage should be revealed. It will not do Rory harm. It might, indeed, do him a lot of good—married to the daughter of a distinguished family, of Boston."

"You wouldn't understand," said Joseph. "He is going to marry the daughter of the ambassador, Claudia Worthington, who is related to the British Royal Family."

Charles said, "No, I don't understand," but he did. He, too, was partly of an oppressed race who longed for both justification and retribution.

"Write for an appointment for me with Mr. Albert Chisholm, confidentially," said Joseph. "In the meantime, talk to the minister who married them, and the town clerk who recorded the marriage. You know what to do, Charles."

Unfortunately Charles did. He did not like it nor did he approve of it. But, he was the son of his father and there were other things to consider besides emotionalism and what men called "love."'

Mr. Albert Chisholm, upon receiving Charles's cool and businesslike letter, thought to himself, No doubt that scoundrel, Armagh, is going to plead with me to allow a marriage between his son and Marjorie. I will soon put him in his place. That night he called his daughter to him and said, "Marjorie, my dear, are you ever seeing that young— Armagh, is his name? I truly hope not. You know I forbade you to see him again or to answer his letters and his impudent importunities."

Marjorie's smooth olive face became very still. "Why do you ask, Papa?"

The letter had been very confidential, from Charles, and Albert was too sensible a man, and knew too much of the Armagh power, to be indiscreet. So he said, "I have noticed that you never accept the invitations of highly eligible young men, my dear child. So I have feared you are still thinking of that rascal's son."

Marjorie dropped her eyes demurely. "I go nowhere with Mr. Armagh," she said, and this was quite true. "I am afraid that other young men do not interest me, as yet. They seem so callow—compared with you, Papa."

Mr. Chisholm bridled with pride and happiness, but he shook his finger archly at his pretty little daughter. "But Papa cannot remain forever with you, my love. You must really consider marriage. After all, you are going on twenty-one—in eight months."

She suddenly sat on his knee and began to cry, and he was taken aback. He said, as he smoothed her thick glossy curls, "My dearest child, I did not mean to make you unhappy. Marjorie, I would do anything in the world to give you happiness, in the measure allowed to human beings. You must never forget that."

She put her small round arms about his neck and cried even harder and cursed Rory inwardly for his insistence on secrecy. She could no longer bear the deception on her father. She looked at him tearfully. "Even if I wanted to marry Rory, Papa?"

He stiffened, and hesitated, then said with resolution, "I pray, my child, it will never come to that. But, if it does, I will swallow my pride and permit it. But do not think rashly, Marjorie. Your whole future depends on one decision."

Marjorie cuddled in his lap like a kitten, thinking

furiously. Then, without any warning at all, a terrible premonition came to her, of desolation and abandonment. It was silly. She was Rory's wife. It is true that his brother had been killed in the war, but nothing evil could ever happen to her Rory, nothing could ever separate them. Nothing.

Chapter 10

Mr. Albert Chisholm had decided exactly how he would receive the swaggering and impudent Irishman, Mr. Joseph Armagh. He would sit calmly in his office, behind the desk which had belonged to his grandfather, with the silver bowl made by his distant relative, Paul Revere, filled with fresh flowers—it was late September and the flowers were bronze and gold—and he would receive Mr. Armagh with calm dignity and courtesy and offer him a cigar. He would speak in quiet and modulated accents—these Irish were so loud and noisy and obstinate—and so Mr. Armagh would know that for the first time in his life he had encountered an authentic gentleman. Mr. Chisholm had given orders to his secretaries. They would conduct Mr. Armagh at once to his inner sanctuary, with discretion and soft footsteps, and would not converse with him.

Mr. Chisholm had a whole lifetime of decorum, proper behavior, and patrician clichés behind him, so he would not need to strive confusedly for these things. They were automatic. He wore his frock coat and striped trousers and stiff winged collar and black cravat with the pearl pin, and discreet gold cufflinks, and his gray mustache was neatly cut and waxed and his light eyes were calm. The day was cool and so a small fire burned in brisk orange on his black marble hearth, and behind him loomed his immense law library, all beautifully bound in gold, crimson, and dark blue leather, and the carpet on the floor was a true Aubusson, and the wood that showed was polished to a rich mahogany. The furniture was all black leather, and burnished, and the aromatic scent of the chrysanthemums mingled with the scent of lemon oil polish and beeswax and burning cannel coal. His clean windows looked out on the street, with dark red draperies framing them. All in all, he thought, it was very impressive, and though he was one of the three partners of the firm his grandfather had established he had many young and ambitious lawyers "under" him, who did most of the work now. (They, being brash and young, called him "Grandpa" behind his back and had little respect for his legal knowledge. "Grandpa stuck with the Law," they would say derisively, whereas anyone of intelligence knew that the Law was to be manipulated by clever men in behalf of affluent clients. They had increased the business, and Mr. Chisholm believed it was all due to him.)

A secretary put his head into the room and announced Mr. Armagh. Mr. Chisholm rose in a stately fashion and waited. In a few moments, he feared, the big room would be roaring with a rude Irish voice, barroom expletives, shouting and what not. Mr. Chisholm had asked for a brass spittoon that morning, and one stood near the visitor's chair, across from the desk, for no doubt Mr. Armagh was an ardent tobacco-chewer and spitter. Mr. Chisholm had thought of a newspaper under the spittoon, but that would be rude, he had finally decreed. He had sighed. He had already decided that if Mr. Armagh was really desirous of his son marrying Marjorie, and if the young people, unfortunately, were as eager, he might be persuaded to take the matter under advisement, however it offended his standards and his hopes for Marjorie, who had been the belle of all the cotillions and whose debut had been mentioned in the New York and Philadelphia newspapers. But he winced at the thought of Marjorie belonging to such a family, and having all her delicate sensibilities constantly outraged.

Joseph entered the office and the secretary closed the door softly behind him. Mr. Chisholm gaped. He could not believe it. Here was one not at all like the Irish Boston Mayors, such as Old Syrup, and sundry other politicians whom the fastidious Mr. Chisholm had long deplored. Here was a tall, lean man impeccably dressed in dark well-tailored clothing, his linen immaculate and beyond reproach, his few pieces of jewelry in excellent taste, his boots narrow and quietly polished. But it was Joseph's ascetic face which fixed Mr. Chisholm's attention, that reserved, emotionless face, clean-shaven, stark and—yes!—aristocratic. The mingled russet and white of his hair had been expertly barbered, neither too long nor too short, and his expression was both controlled and formidable, and those eyes were the eyes of a most intelligent and immovable man. Something tight loosened in Mr. Chisholm. Was it possible that this immigrant Irishman was a *gentleman?* Scots-Irish, perhaps, with a background of Covenanters? Mr. Chisholm had such in his own family.

"Mr. Armagh, I presume?" said Mr. Chisholm in a carefully subdued voice and held out his hand. Mr. Armagh took that hand briefly. It was long and slender, Mr. Chisholm noted, and very strong and dry. Mr. Chisholm had not intended to say this but he did: "I was most distressed to hear of your son's death, ah, in the line of duty, Mr. Armagh."

"Thank you," said Joseph. His voice, Mr. Chisholm thought, might be a little too melodious, with a certain lilt notable in the Irish, but it was the voice of a *gentleman!* Neither too emphatic nor dull, and very controlled. "Please sit down, Mr. Armagh," said Mr. Chisholm, a little shaken. Why, compared with this man, Rory Armagh, the son, was a hod-carrier! Still, blood told. The mother, perhaps, was a vulgar woman, and that explained Rory's skeptical wide laughter, vibrant coloring, vitality, and the cynical smile he bestowed on everybody, and his way of lightly mocking his elders. Still, blood told, and Mr. Armagh was evidently a man of "blood." Mr. Chisholm felt his vitals quiver with relief. Mr. Armagh was also very, very powerful, and very, very rich. There might be a compromise— It was rumored that some of the Irish were descended from kings; landed gentry. Joseph had seated himself, one long lean leg over the knee of the other, and he was looking at Mr. Chisholm, still not seated, with a most penetrating regard.

"Brandy, Mr. Armagh?" asked Mr. Chisholm, gesturing to a small cabinet nearby.

"No, thank you. I don't drink," said Joseph. Well! An Irishman who did not drink! Mr. Chisholm drank discreetly, such as brandy and the best of wines, but he respected men who did not drink. "A cigar?" suggested Mr. Chisholm, more and more shaken.

"No, thank you. I don't smoke."

Mr. Chisholm was an expert on picking out plebeians who affected to aristocratic restraints, and he knew that Joseph was not affected in his rejection of brandy and cigars. He simply did not care for them.

"I know you are a very busy lawyer," said Joseph, who was studying Mr. Chisholm acutely. "So I will take up as little of your time as possible." He had come swiftly to the conclusion that Mr. Chisholm was not very intelligent, but was a gentleman and a slight ditherer, and a kind and somewhat hesitant man. Under other circumstances Joseph would have been inclined to look favorably upon him and think that Rory had not made too bad a choice in a family. He glanced quickly at a silver-framed photograph of Miss Marjorie Chisholm on Mr. Chisholm's desk. A lovely child, with a fine bright face and mischievous eyes and a wide brow and a tangle of black curls: No one could quarrel with such a beauty.

He bent and opened his dispatch case and brought out a sheaf of documents and laid them on Mr. Chisholm's desk. "I have discovered, as no doubt you have, sir, that documents and evidence are much more telling than conversation, and save a lot of time. May I suggest that you read these?"

Mr. Chisholm gaped again, and sat down slowly and then put on his pince-nez. He began to read. Joseph did not watch him. He looked about the room and thought how much this resembled his own rooms at Green Hills. However, there was no aura of power here, just meticulous and boring law, ponderous and dusty. Yes, a ditherer, poor bastard.

There was an ormolu clock on the mantelpiece, and its soft tick became louder and louder in the complete quiet of the room, and the small noise of the fire was the noise of an approaching holocaust. Joseph began to watch Mr. Chisholm's face. Moment by moment, as he quietly turned page after page, his coloring dwindled, became very pale, then absolutely white, and his facial muscles sagged and twitched, and his eyes drooped, and a thin double-chin began to hang under the real one, like dewlaps. Suddenly, he was an old and diminished man, and his mustache quivered, and he sank deeper and deeper into his chair. His hands began to tremble, then increased to a palsy. His lips, under that pathetically groomed mustache, became purplish gray, and jerked. Joseph frowned. He had hoped not to encounter this. He had thought to face a very quietly pompous man of much composure and resolution, who would agree with him, or at least listen to his arguments. But Mr. Chisholm was looking broken and disintegrated. Joseph suddenly remembered what his father had said: "Gentlemen do not fight. They come to an agreement." Joseph had laughed at that, even when he had been only twelve. He had always laughed at it—until now. Had he known fully about Mr. Chisholm his approach would have been different. Damn Charles. Charles was a gentleman. He should have warned his employer.

Mr. Chisholm slowly turned the last page. He looked at Joseph. Joseph had expected stricken and terrified eyes, but Mr. Chisholm's were wounded and unafraid.

"So," Mr. Chisholm said, "my daughter is married to your son, Rory. I forbade her to see him. I knew nothing but catastrophe could result. I was quite correct. Mr. Armagh—it was not necessary for you to threaten me, and Marjorie."

Joseph sat forward. "I did not know with whom I had to deal, Mr. Chisholm, or my approach would have been different. Let me be brief. I have other plans for my son. He is all I have left. He must make a name for himself. Your daughter cannot give him that name."

Mr. Chisholm said, as if he had not heard Joseph: "If Marjorie, and I, do not give our consent to the annulment of this marriage you will shame my dear daughter as not being married at all—she was underage—and the minister was 'deceived.' In fact, the minister was a fraud, and not a duly ordained minister. The town clerk who recorded the marriage was deceived also. He never recorded the marriage. All records have been destroyed in that little village. There is no record. Therefore, Marjorie has been guilty of fornication with your son. You know these are all lies, Mr. Armagh. You have used your influence. If Marjorie, and I, give our consent to a legal annulment, quietly suppressed so that no one will know, there will be no reprisals. Am I correct, Mr. Armagh?"

"You are correct, sir," said Joseph.

"If we do not agree"—and Mr. Chisholm was taken by a violent spell of coughing—"you will ruin me. You have done your research very well, sir. It is quite true that the Panic of '93 forced me into debt, and I have not recovered my finances. You own my paper at the banks. You will demand payment on that paper. That will reduce me to penury. I thought my bankers—were gentlemen."

Joseph said, "Bankers are never gentlemen."

Mr. Chisholm nodded. "I know that now. I see terrible ramifications— My ancestors fought for America— No matter. That will bore you. Sir, if Marjorie quietly seeks an annulment of this fatal marriage, and it is granted without publicity, you will withdraw your threats against my daughter, and me?"

"Yes," said Joseph, and he stood up and went to the windows and looked out.

"And if we inform your son, Rory, you will still take reprisals?"

"Yes," said Joseph. "He must never know. Your daughter must just tell him the marriage is over, for her own reasons."

Mr. Chisholm reflected. "You love your son, and I love my daughter. I was willing that this marriage continue. But you are not. Mr. Armagh, on second thought, I am desirous that my daughter should not be connected with you. With you, sir. Even through your son. She would not be able to bear it. She was brought up in an honorable family—"

Joseph swung to him so sharply that Mr. Chisholm coiled. "So was I," said Joseph. "An honorable, God-fearing, decent, land-owning family. A family, a nation, a religion, ancient in history. But, sir, we were destroyed as ruthlessly as Russian serfs are destroyed by their masters. We were hunted down like animals, like vermin, for no reason at all but that we wanted to be free, as a nation, and to practice our religion. That was quite a heinous crime, wasn't it? To be free is to be condemned. To seek freedom is to be a criminal. To revolt against oppressors is to die. Yes, I know that. Your own ancestors left England for just the same thing. But you have forgotten. Your ancestors were poor driven English yeomen, who wanted nothing but peace and to serve their religion. This they were denied, as my people were denied. So they emigrated—here.

"Long before your ancestors were a distinct people, sir, the Irish were an ancient proud race. We were never slaves, as you Anglo-Saxons were, and never, by God, shall we be slaves!"

Mr. Chisholm sat back in his chair and stared and his thoughts were jumbled. Then, still looking at Joseph he said, "You are taking revenge."

Joseph returned to his chair and sat down. "You are very subtle, Mr. Chisholm."

"I never knew I was," said Mr. Chisholm, almost with humility. "But this I know now: There will be no peace or civilization in this world until we forget our wrongs and live and work together as men, and not avengers."

"That will be the Millennium," said Joseph, and he smiled. "Do we not all have reason to be avengers?"

"I do not," said Mr. Chisholm, and believed it. He felt humble and sick and ashamed, and, odd to say, he felt compassion for Joseph Armagh.

Then, thought Joseph, you have no spirit.

"So long as we hold hatred for anyone," said Mr. Chisholm, marveling at his new thoughts, "we are not men at all. We are beasts. It is against the dignity of men that we should hate. It is against the ordinances of God."

You are a naïve fool, thought Joseph, with some pity. You do not know what is going on in the least. If I told you you would drop dead of horror and despair. Perhaps your God is merciful. He will never let you know. But Mr. Chisholm was looking at him strangely.

"Mr. Armagh, you have no religion at all, have you?"

Joseph was silent for a moment or two, then he said, "No. I do not. I have not believed in anything since I was a young child. The world taught me that, sir."

Mr. Chisholm nodded. "I so suspected. Mr. Armagh, one of these days you will be driven to the edge."

He stood up. He was stately again, but not with an offensive stateliness. He said, "Mr. Armagh, what you wish will be consummated. You may rest assured of that. I am not impressed by your threats against me and my daughter. I wish it ended. I hope never to see you again."

Then Joseph said, "I wish I had known your kind when I was a child, sir. We might have come to the same conclusion." His face was full of regret, and yet he was coldly amused.

He left then and Mr. Chisholm watched him go. Again, he was swamped in pity, and again he was humbled. God forgive us, he thought, for what we do to each other.

Mr. Chisholm said to his daughter, Marjorie, in his study at home: "He will not only destroy us, my love, but he will destroy his son, Rory, also, unless we agree to this. It is for you to choose."

"You mean, Papa, that you are willing to do as I choose?" asked Marjorie. She had not cried at all. She had sat near her father in his study, with his confidential secretary and personal lawyer, Bernard Levine, just behind her, listening. Bernard had been hopelessly in love with Marjorie for a number of years; he was a slight young man with a quiet intelligent face, brown eyes and hair, who listened more than he spoke.

"I mean exactly that, my love," said Mr. Chisholm. "No matter the result, it is yours to say and only yours," and he thought how much she resembled her mother as she sat before him in her blue serge suit and shirtwaist and neat little buttoned boots, her black curls vehemently bursting from her pompadour, her small face quickly changing with her emotions and her black eyes eloquent but disciplined. He had called her and Bernard into his study that night, and had simply given his daughter the papers Joseph had left with him. Only once she had exclaimed uncontrollably, and that was at the revelation of her marriage to Rory. "Oh, Papa!" she had cried, in a tone of deep remorse and affection. "I am so sorry that I deceived you. But it was for Rory's sake. His father—"

"I know all about Mr. Armagh," said Mr. Chisholm, with sadness. "I wish we had known each other earlier." This was so enigmatic to Marjorie that she had stared at him and wondered.

Now he had given her the choice, to destroy him, and perhaps Rory, to save her marriage. She doubted that Joseph would "destroy" Rory, his only remaining son, and in a way his only remaining child, out of disappointed ambition and his famous anger. He was not so womanishly capricious, as Rory had often remarked. His first rages, Rory had told her, were later modified by pragmatism and his own brand of reason. But still, Rory had not cared to risk that rage by revealing his marriage. Marjorie felt cold and sick and wild with anguish. Surely it was all a nightmare. She was now being asked to give up Rory, never to see Rory again, to permit the destruction of her marriage. Rory, Rory. She became incredulous.

"He, Mr. Armagh, would not do what he threatened to do, Papa!" She clenched her little hands on her knee. "Why, he loves Rory, and Rory loves him! Rory is all he has!"

Mr. Chisholm noted, with sorrow, that Rory, not himself, was first in her thoughts.

"I am afraid, my dear, that he would do exactly that." Mr. Chisholm turned to Bernard. "You saw Mr. Armagh in my office today. You know, from reading the newspapers and the hints in them, what Mr. Armagh is. Bernard, do you think that in this instance he would—er—mellow, come to terms, to acceptance?"

Bernard hesitated. It tore him apart, he thought, to see Marjorie so agonized, for all her calm. But he said, "From what I know of Mr. Armagh, and his history—the man has fascinated me for a long time for some reason, and I have read almost everything concerning him—yes, I think he would do that. I read, on the occasion of his brother's murder, that he had, for many years, abandoned that brother before their reconciliation because Mr. Sean Paul did not rise to his standards, and ambitions. There is also a rumor that he has a sister in a convent, whom he ignores. That may be only hearsay. And there has been gossip, newly revived, that he was the cause of the death of his father-in-law, long ago. I understand that he has ruined many men, in pursuit of his goals. That part is no mere gossip, or hearsay. It is a fact. He has stated in these papers before us that he has 'other plans' for his son. I think we can safely say that if those plans are thwarted that he will do as he has threatened. I never heard that he threatened anyone without carrying it out. There is a great deal about Mr. Armagh that I know from my long reading about him."

"Just in newspapers, and magazines, Bernie?" asked Marjorie, and now she was paling even more and she was more tense.

"No. There was something about international bankers which I read recently. Mr. Armagh is a director of many large banks in the United States, so it is safe to say that he is in close touch with the bankers of America, and Europe. It was all in a—book. I hear it was suppressed, later, just when it began to be sold in quantity. I don't know if Mr. Armagh is one of them, but he is certainly entangled with them." He looked at Mr. Chisholm, sitting in ashen misery in his leather chair. Mr. Chisholm looked disbelieving.

"Bernard, what you are hinting, it is not to be believed!"

Bernard shrugged his shoulders, a gesture Mr. Chisholm disliked, and spread out his hands in a "foreign" gesture which Mr. Chisolm disliked even more. "I read, just today, in the *Boston Gazette*—a newspaper you do not care for, sir—that our government is in deep debt to the bankers for this past war, and that the U. S. Supreme Court will soon declare the Federal income tax un-Constitutional again. The war, though short, cost several billion dollars. The bankers in New York hold the government's paper. In an interview with Mr. Morgan he declares that the only way to be 'solvent' is to have a permanent Federal income tax. In short, if we are to have wars—though he did not say that, of course—the people must be taxed for them. No taxes, no wars. I also read a privately circulated leaflet that there is something called a Scardo Society, formed of prominent American politicians and industrialists, who have already decided that wars are necessary for prosperity, in this increasingly industrial age."

He shrugged again. "There have been many hints of these things in the New York newspapers, too. Whatever is going on, sir, is being kept very secret, and those who even slightly suspect are being ridiculed or ignored or suppressed. I don't know, sir. It is certainly very sinister." Again he spread out his hands. "I do know that reviewers in the newspapers ridiculed and violently attacked that book I mentioned, and called the writer a believer in bogeymen. There was a curious similarity in the attacks."

Mr. Chisholm sat in profound and shaken thought, and Marjorie thought, Oh, Rory, Rory! Nothing must part us, Rory, never, never. The great cry in her swelled to her eyes, eyes dry and aching, and there was a choking in her throat. She was filled with desolation, rebellion, hatred, despair.

Mr. Chisholm came out of his shock, shaking his head. "I am glad I am no longer young, and have no sons," he said. "For the first time in my life I have a fear for my country. Still, I can hardly believe it. I am sure we will never have a Federal income tax on individuals; I am sure we will have no more wars. The Hague repeatedly says so— No matter. We must solve our own problem. Marjorie, my dear?"

"I cannot believe a man can be so monstrous as to threaten a harmless gentleman like you, Papa, and a harmless girl like myself—and his own son! His own son!"

Mr. Chisholm could not bear to look at his beloved daughter, so pale, her face quivering, her eyes strained and huge with suffering, and so tense on the edge of her chair. Her mouth, usually smiling with mischief and affection and wit, was the mouth of a tormented woman, pleading for reassurance. No, after one glance, Mr. Chisholm could not bear to look at his Marjorie, and now he hated Joseph Armagh with the first real hatred of his life. His thin hands clenched on the arms of his chair. He understood, now, why it was some men would kill, something which had made him incredulous before. Only madmen, only the deranged, the illiterate, the low-born, the ignorant and stupid and animalistic, killed, he had once thought. Now he could understand. The blood swelled into Mr. Chisholm's withered throat and engorged it. His face turned scarlet and broke into sweat.

But he said calmly enough, "I am afraid he means what he says, Marjorie. I should not like to put him to the test. As for yourself, I was not young when I married your mother; I am old enough to be your grandfather, my love. I do not fear for myself, for how much longer will I live? I will always have a little sustenance. But I do fear for you, my daughter. He would, indeed, ruin you, and your—your —husband." He hated Rory now, who had taken Marjorie into this frightful situation, who had put her under threat from an evil man.

"Bernard, what do you say?"

Bernard looked down on his clasped hands. "I agree with you, sir. We dare not take the risk. If Marjorie wants this marriage to continue she has only to say so. I am sure, in spite of what—he—says in those papers, that the legality of the marriage can be proved. It may be difficult. It may take years. But I think a court test, and a summoning of witnesses, would bring out the truth. After all, perjury is still a crime and highly punishable. Marjorie has her marriage certificate, with the names of witnesses, the town clerk, the minister. Not all of them would be able to lie in a court with conviction. Too, sir, you have a name."

Hope flared in Marjorie's tormented young face and a glow filled her eyes. Now Bernard could not look at her any longer either.

"I don't think, however, that we should forget Rory Armagh, himself," continued Bernard. "He is not the character his father is. The pressure which would be put upon him might be unsupportable. From what I have heard of him, in certain places in Boston, he might remember his father's money, and that he is the heir—"

"No, no!" cried Marjorie, swinging to him eagerly. "He has just this last year at law school! Then he would tell his father, upon his graduation, that he is already married! That is our agreement. Rory loves me. He will never give me up, willingly, and I would be willing to put my life on that."

Bernard said, "But his father has threatened him, too, and his father is known to keep his threats. Nothing would stop him—to separate you and Rory. His father has enough influence so that Rory would never gain entrance to a law firm of any repute, anywhere. If he set himself up as an independent attorney—he would find few clients. Sir," he said to Mr. Chisholm, "would you, yourself, risk taking young Mr. Armagh into your firm, in face of his father's opposition?"

Mr. Chisholm thought. He thought of his partners, his associates. He became small in his chair. "No, I wouldn't dare that," he said finally. "No, I wouldn't dare. Nor would my partners permit it."

"But I have money, Papa," said Marjorie. "It won't be long before I am twenty-one. It is in your hands to permit me to have Mama's money at that time."

Mr. Chisholm's color, in his wrinkled pale face, became ghastly. He averted his head. "Marjorie, I must confess something to you. I—I had control of your mother's money, for she trusted me. During the Panic, a few years ago, I put up her money as collateral for debts, for borrowing— It is not lost. In a few years, I hope, I am sure to recover the full worth of my investments, and I will return the money to your—inheritance. But Mr. Armagh has threatened to make that impossible—he owns my paper, from the banks—"

He put his hands over his face. "Forgive me, my child," he said, and his voice broke.

Marjorie was on her knees beside him, embracing him, kissing him frantically. "Oh, Papa! Oh, Papa, it doesn't matter! I don't care! Please, Papa, look at me. I love you, Papa. It doesn't matter at all." She was freshly terrified.

"In a few years—your inheritance will be intact, with interest," said Mr. Chisholm, and he sat in Marjorie's arms like an old child, his head on her shoulder. "You would never have known, my love, if this had not happened."

"It is all my fault," said poor Marjorie. "If I hadn't married Rory when I did, we should not be in this nightmare. Forgive me, Papa. If you can, forgive me. Oh, how could I have brought this down on you, threatened by a low and wicked man, you a gentleman, my father! I hate myself. I despise myself. I wish I were dead." Now, for the first time, sitting on her heels, she burst into tears. She dropped her head on her father's knees and groaned.

"My darling," said Mr. Chisholm. "Don't reproach yourself. Your grandfather, your mother's father, opposed our marriage, too. I never did know why. But we married, just the same, and I never regretted it, and the old gentleman came around nicely." He paused. "But I don't think Armagh will do that." He lifted Marjorie's face in tender hands and kissed her over and over. "Hush, my love. I can't bear to hear—those sounds— Hush, my love. You are young. There will be a way— You are young."

Bernard waited, suffering with them, until Mr. Chisholm put Marjorie back in her chair. He said, "Mr. Armagh has mentioned, in these papers, that Marjorie was underage and did not have her father's written consent when she 'allegedly,' he says, married his son. And that, apparently, the marriage has not been consummated." Bernard coughed. "It says in these papers that Rory Armagh and Marjorie Chisholm have never—cohabited."

He looked at Mr. Chisholm. "So, we have a small choice. Marjorie can sue for annulment of her marriage, which was never—consummated, very quietly, in New Hampshire. No names will be mentioned, in the press, says Mr. Armagh. It will be secretly arranged. Very delicate, very refined, of Mr. Armagh, isn't it?" Bernard's mouth twisted with disgust. "That is to save, he says, Miss Marjorie Chisholm's reputation and any future marriage she might consummate. I think," said Bernard, "he has shown this 'generosity' in order to avoid a court suit to maintain the marriage, which might—though it is a small chance— be decided in Marjorie's favor. In spite of all his power. Then, too, I think he wants to avoid an open confrontation in the courts, with the resultant notoriety and scandal. Mr. Armagh, I have read, is a man who cherishes his privacy above all else."

Marjorie sat in her chair, listening. Her face was very calm, very quiet, though the big tears rolled down her cheeks without stopping. She seemed unaware of them. Then she said in a voice without any emotion at all, "I will seek the annulment. Papa, you must arrange it."

"My child," said her father, and could have cried.

"I am not going to think about it," said Marjorie. "At

least, not yet. I am your daughter, Papa, and I hope I have a little of your courage, and fortitude. I won't think about anything, yet."

Joseph had not mentioned anything in the papers about the secret little flat in Cambridge, but Marjorie had no doubt that he knew. Why had he refrained from speaking of it? To expedite the annulment of her marriage, for lack of consummation? That was, surely, true. She thought of that blissful little place, which had always seemed so full of light to her in spite of its dinginess, and she felt something break and shatter in her. Never to go there again, and cook and wait for Rory. Never to see Rory again, never to hear his voice, feel his kisses, lie in that sagging bed with him, in his arms. She squeezed her eyes shut against the anguish. No, she must not think of that, yet. Otherwise she would die, lose her mind, betray her father. Oh, Rory, Rory, she said in herself, don't suffer too much, my Rory. She could see his face, his smiling sensual mouth, his eyes, his bright coloring; she could hear his voice.

"I will write to Rory tonight," she said, and her voice had never been so calm. "It will be easier than telling him. I don't think I could trust myself, if I did. No, I could not."

She would never tell her father of that little flat in Cambridge. She must let him believe that the marriage had never been consummated. Were he to know he would insist the marriage be maintained, for he was an honorable man.

She wrote to Rory that night, her young face drawn and wizened and dry:

I have come to the conclusion, after a lot of thought, my dear, that our marriage was doomed from the start. We both deceived our fathers, and so invited calamity. I am not going to lie and say that I have not had a considerable affection for you, but I must confess to you now that that affection has been steadily declining. I have tried to revive it, but have failed. Therefore, I will seek an annulment— No one need know that we had that flat in Cambridge. In mercy, my dear Rory, I hope you will not put me to mortification by appearing in any court and contesting me and my word. I should be forever shamed and would not be able to take up my life again, as I must. We were full of folly, and our hopes were childish. I will remember you with affection, as a dear friend, as a brother. It was a mistake, from the beginning. We can only go on from this place, and I will remember you ever, with kindness. I am returning the jewelry you gave me, for I cannot keep it in all conscience, now that my love I had for you—or what I thought was love—no longer exists. Please do not try to see me. Please do not write. Nothing can change my resolution. If ever you loved me, please heed my wishes, and cause me no more pain.

She went to the dark little flat that day and laid the letter and the jewelry on the pillow of the bed. Then she broke down. She flung herself on the bed and hugged the pillows to her desolate young heart and lay, stricken and silent, for a long time, trying to get strength to leave this place forever. She found a tie Rory had left behind, a worn tie, and she took it with her and left the flat and never looked back.

When Rory read the letter he said to himself, "It is a lie. It is all a lie."

Only two days ago he and Marjorie had lain in this bed, clenched together in a joyful and passionate ecstasy of love, and Marjorie had cried over and over, "Never leave me, Rory, never leave me! Take an oath, Rory, that you will never leave me! I should die, Rory, if I never saw you again!"

His Marjorie, his love, his darling, his little bright wife with her mischief and dimples and intelligent wit and laughter, his Marjorie who never lied: But she was lying now. In some way that old bastard, her father, had found out about them, had forced her to write this letter to her husband, had threatened her. Well, he, Rory, was not going to let this happen to him and Marjorie, no matter what it cost.

For six months, thereafter, he stormed the Chisholm house, the door resolutely unopened for him. For six months he wrote wild accusatory letters to Mr. Chisholm, letters full of despair and denunciation, of hatred and threats. He wrote to Marjorie every day. His letters were returned unopened. He tried to waylay her, but he never saw her. He grew thinner and paler, and his bright coloring diminished. He thought of enlisting his father's help. The Armaghs, he thought vengefully, were more than a match for that old soft-spoken Pecksniff of a Chisholm.

Then one day he received a sealed packet which informed him that the marriage between one Marjorie Jane Chisholm and one Rory Daniel Armagh. had been annulled in a small obscure court in New Hampshire.

"I was not even subpoenaed," he said to himself. "I never knew. Marjorie did this by stealth—her father forced her." Then he began to vomit and for the first time in his strong young life he became ill and could not leave his bed for several days. He hoped he would die. In fact, he thought of suicide. He gave it long thought, for the dark impulse lurked in him as it lurked in his father.

A year later he was married to Miss Claudia Worthington in the ambassador's private chapel. Miss Worthington made a spectacular bride and the gushing newspapers spoke of the bridegroom's famous father, his own handsomeness "and serious demeanor during the ceremony, which was performed by his lordship, the Catholic Bishop of London, himself, and three Monsignori." There were nearly two thousand guests, "all distinguished," and three Royal Personages, not to mention "many of the nobility." The Pope had sent a Papal Blessing for the Nuptial Mass. The wedding was the event of the year, both in America and in England.

When Claudia lay beside him in the marriage bed Rory thought, O my God, Marjorie. My little darling, my Marjorie. O, my God, my God.

A year after that his first son, Daniel, was born, a year after that his son Joseph, and two years later twin daughters, Rosemary and Claudette.

Claudia Armagh was a most delightful hostess, and all spoke of her charm and gracious personality, her style, her taste, her savoir faire, her fascination, her wardrobes, jewels, furs, carriages, and even her large and stately limousine, one of the first to be manufactured in America, her house in London, her house in New York, her villas in France and Italy, "where the most distinguished members of international society gather for her fiestas and dinners and concerts, which are considered beyond any comparison. The most famous singers and violinists appear at musicales, at the summoning of Mrs. Armagh. She patronizes only Worth for her wardrobe, and only Cartier's for her jewels. Her taste is impeccable."

Claudia liked Washington immensely, for now her young husband was a congressman from Pennsylvania. It is true that there was some uproar about the election, the other party claiming that "dead men in cemeteries had voted for Rory Armagh, and live men had been bribed." Mr. Armagh had been elected, however, by a majority of

one thousand votes over his opponent, who seemed somewhat resigned and contented. After all, one does not quarrel with the generosity of an Armagh. Nor with their
power.

Once Claudia said to her husband pettishly, "I know that
gentlemen are not always faithful to the marriage vows.
My father was not. I do not quarrel with this fact. But I do
wish, Rory, that you were not always so—so blatant—but a
little more discreet."

Rory looked for Marjorie in every woman. He never
found her.

I am still Rory's wife, Marjorie would think in her lonely
little white bed at night, in her father's house. The marriage
was consummated. I don't care about courts and lawyers
and annulments. I am still Rory's wife and I will always be.
He's married to someone else, but he is still my husband,
before God if not before man. Rory, Rory. I know you
love me, and will always love me, as I love you. You will
never know that I watched you from an upper window
when you banged on Papa's door, and that I had to hold
myself not to run down to you and throw myself into your
arms, no matter what happened. Rory, Rory. How can I
live without you, my love, my dearest? Papa thinks I gave
you up for him, but I did it for you. Perhaps some day you
will know, though I will never tell you. Oh, my Rory, my
Rory. My husband, my darling. There will never be anyone
else.

There was never anyone else. Her father and her aunt
pleaded with her to "encourage" the young men who be-
sieged her, but she would say, "I'm not interested." How
could a wife be interested in any other man but her husband? It was infamous even to think of it. It was adultery,
even to think of it. She would hold Rory's old tie against
her breast at night, and kiss it and fondle it, and then sleep
with it under her cheek. In some way she knew that Rory
was thinking of her also, and that in spite of what divided
them their love reached out for each other and could never
be destroyed. This comforted her. Rory was her own and
she was his. Then she began a fantasy. One day, sooner or
later, Rory would return. It helped her through the years.

Chapter 11

Joseph Armagh built a magnificent mansion for his son, Rory, and Claudia and their children on a fine tract of land adjoining his own house in Green Hills. The property was known thereafter as the Armagh "Settlement." Claudia found it "dull." Though Bernadette was proud of her daughter-in-law, and boasted of her, the two women detested each other. Claudia considered herself far above the Armagh family, and resented Bernadette's "demands." Though she was not very intelligent Claudia was a good mimic, and she would imitate her mother-in-law for the amusement of her friends in Washington and in Philadelphia. She would lilt as Bernadette lilted, and exaggerate Bernadette's manners. Bernadette thought her daughter-in-law affected and pretentious, which she was, and was immune to the famous charm, which she never saw. When Claudia "put on airs" to her, Bernadette would utter a rude word, and laugh out loud, coarsely. She, and only she, was the grande dame of the Armagh family, and not this chit with the tiny bosom and the broad hips and big fat legs. Bernadette had discovered that Claudia had bowed legs, and this was always excellent for one of Bernadette's own mimicries. Who was Claudia Worthington, anyway? She boasted of her ancestry. But Bernadette was an acute woman, and intelligent, and she soon discovered that Claudia's grandfather on her mother's side had been a poor and impoverished carpenter, for all his boasting that he came of an aristocratic English family. The ambassador's father, in Bernadette's opinion, had not been much better. He had begun as a coal miner in Pennsylvania, at eight dollars a week, but had invented a certain machine which did away with the employment of women and children in the mines. (He had stolen the invention from a more intelligent but more gullible miner, a fact Bernadette's spies sedulously

688

discovered.) So, he had become rich and had put his sons through Harvard and Yale, and had emerged as an aristocrat. As for the ladies of Claudia's family, they had been ignorant nincompoops. Let Claudia wear her famous long white gloves everywhere. They were to conceal the fact that she had a slavey's or a barmaid's hands, angular, knotted, badly colored, and enormous. The noted ancestor related to the British Royal Family? Why, for God's sake, he had been but a guard at Windsor Castle!

"Never mind," Joseph had told his wife, with dark amusement. "Let the fiction prevail. Who does it harm? If Claudia wishes to be related to the British Royal Family—and they are vulgarians, themselves—let her be related. Coming down to it, as the Church teaches, aren't we all children of Adam and Eve?"

"Oh, shut up," Bernadette would say, with a laugh. "But that bow-legged snip is not going to wave her gloves in my face and breathlessly chatter to me and think she is impressing me. I told her once and for all that I knew all about her. I detest her, but for the sake of peace in the family I don't tell anyone else. Besides, her people are rich. I suppose Rory could have done worse. But all her fool remarks about 'low politicians!' And my father was a senator, and governor, when her people were picking coal cinders or splinters out of their bottoms. What a silly thing she is, with her soft gaspings and her infantile voice! I've heard her roaring at her children—like a hog-caller. And at the servants, too, if they forget the rose petals in her finger-bowl. Her grandmothers washed in zinc tubs and were glad to have them. My mother was a lady."

"Yes, I know," said Joseph.

"And your family was at least decent, intelligent, and literate, in Ireland," said Bernadette, with a passionate look of love at him. "Yes, I know. I used to gibe at you, but I think I was a little envious. My grandfather was only a blackbirder."

"But look at all the money we all have," said Joseph, and Bernadette could not understand his tone of voice, and why he turned away.

Bernadette was fond of her grandchildren, who were usually in the "Settlement," Claudia and Rory finding them impediments in Washington. This fondness surprised Joseph. He did not know that the fondness was composed partly of idle affection and partly malice. Daniel resembled

Bernadette's father, and she was particularly attached to him. Joseph, his namesake, was a vacant boy with his mother's petulance and pretensions of grandeur and his intolerance of servants. The twin girls were "lumps," in Joseph's estimation. He had little regard for them, and doubted their intelligence. "Blood will out," Bernadette would say. "Rosemary and Claudette are no brighter than their mother, and they have her legs. Peasants." But they were fond of her, for she was more indulgent to them than she had been with her own children, and had fewer theories regarding them. It was unfortunate that none of them resembled Rory, the colorful, the courtly, the man of style and presence, who could charm with a twinkle. True, the little girls had red-gold hair and big light blue eyes, but they did not have Rory's dash. Nor did any of them look like Kevin, or Ann Marie.

"You mustn't go upstairs and tease your poor auntie," Bernadette would say to her grandchildren. "She is just a child, herself. She had an accident. You mustn't make her cry, or take her dolls, or push her or make faces at her. You frighten her."

"She wets her drawers like a baby," Daniel, the eldest, would say. "It runs on the floor. Sometimes she stinks."

"Dirty girl, dirty girl," the little girls would sing.

"She can't help it," Bernadette would say, thinking of that day when Ann Marie had been changed from a lovely young woman into an idiot. Bernadette had confessed to her confessor, who had assured her that she had been quite correct in informing Ann Marie of the truth. What else could she have done? It was sad that the girl had not been informed as a child. Her conscience was pacified. It was all Elizabeth's fault, that shameless hussy, who was growing old too. And her disgusting son, Courtney, who was now a monk in Amalfi. Elizabeth's only son: a monk! It served her right.

Bernadette was queen of the "Settlement." She was the empress, the ruling mistress of the dynasty. She boasted that her grandchildren adored her. If Daniel, as some people said, had the teeth of a chipmunk, it did not matter. If Joseph whined perpetually and sulked, it was just his way. If the little girls were rude and not very bright, they were at least somewhat pretty. They trailed her contentedly as her own children had never trailed. For she was always indulgent, and always, especially before an audience, the doting grandmother. She would almost squat before them—before an audience—her enormous hams thrusting out behind her—and speak to them in a sugary rich fashion. Daniel, the most intelligent, was a born cynic, and he would smirk. But he would play this game also, for Grandma was always ready with an extra dollar, or a treat, if she were pleased. The children would cluster about Bernadette, before an audience, and everybody was deeply affected. Such a close family, such affection, such devotion and loyalty. In private Bernadette would admonish the boys: "We have a Name to live up to. We must do everything correctly. You have a future." To the girls she would say, "You must make good marriages. You owe that to your father and your grandparents." They hardly understood her, at their age, but they had some respect for her, which was more than they had for their parents. Bernadette still had a "hard hand on her," as Joseph once said.

There were many who wondered why the resplendent Rory Armagh, with his flair and style and color, his quick jesting ways, his twinkle and his general handsomeness, had married Claudia Worthington. (But these were those who were immune to her charm and who found her babyish voice annoying and her mannerisms a little ridiculous, and who thought her unattractive.) Had Rory been asked he would have answered: "I often wonder, myself." He would have smiled in his wryly jocular way, only half jesting.

Already numbed by the death of his young brother, the inexplicable desertion of Marjorie—which he still found incredible—made him feel, for many months, that he was not living at all, but dreaming in a dazed dark nightmare from which he could not wake. His apathy was frequently startled into savage rebellion, disbelief, hate, rage, like flashes of scarlet lightning in a night which would not end. He had spent himself in months of siege, which came to nothing, and which was haunted by the impulse to suicide. Then the apathy had set in, the dullness, the lightlessness, in which his color was quenched and his volubility reduced, to a great extent, for the rest of his life. He still kept the little flat—he kept it for six months—and visited it almost daily, hoping, blasphemously praying, that he would find Marjorie there, waiting for him with a full explanation. He would lie on the dusty bed in a state of physical and emotional exhaustion, staring blankly at the moldy ceiling.

When he would get up he would feel as old as death itself,
and broken. She had left nothing of hers behind but the
jewels, which he had sold at once. There was not even a
hairpin or a handkerchief, though he searched. It was as if
she had never sung or laughed in here, or lain in his arms,
or dusted or cooked. The little flat became a tomb to him,
and at last he knew that if he did not recover from this desolate horror, this terrible yearning, this dry weeping, this
lethargy, he would die. One way or another, he would die.

It was not until he began to hate Marjorie for what she
had done to him, in cold blood and indifference and rejection, as he thought, that his young body and young mind
could respond to outside stimuli again. Her conduct was
still inexplicable, but as his friends often said, women were
inexplicable in themselves. No doubt she had already forgotten him. To her it had been a light affair, of no lasting
consequence, otherwise her father could not have influenced her to abandon him and arrange for that execrable
annulment. Or, she was weaker and less intelligent and
more frivolous than he had guessed. She had made a fool
of Rory Daniel Armagh, and Rory's pride finally rescued
him and made him look about again. A damned wench—
making a fool of him, lying to him, laughing at him behind
his back, feeling herself superior to him, mocking him,
even when she lay with him! Self-preservation made him
hate her eventually, so that he could begin again. But never
again was his laugh so loud, his smiles so wide and skepti-
cally generous, his feet so always eager for dancing, his ear
always so ready for gay music, his warmth so spontaneous.
"Rory's growing up at last," said some of his many friends
at Harvard. They noted, with approval, that he had suddenly become more mature, more attentive to argument
and less happily belligerent, more thoughtful, and more
restrained. If his face were tighter and his light blue eyes
less gay than formerly, this too was noted with approval.
He was a man at last, and no longer a boy.

There was one who watched him, and that was his father, Joseph, who knew exactly what his son was suffering.
He will get over it, thought Joseph, but he himself was surprised at the tenacity of his son's love for that pretty young
creature who could not have advanced the Armagh fortunes. Young and full-blooded men like Rory, amorous
and with a wandering eye, did not stay attached very long
to any one female, and Joseph knew how amorous Rory

was, and knew of his little exploits even during his marriage to Marjorie. But Rory, apparently, had deeper emotions than Joseph knew, for all his perceptiveness, and Joseph, who dared not offer any sympathy but must remain apparently unaware of that unfortunate marriage, was concerned. Rory often had fits of gloomy silence when he came home on holidays, and had a way, very disturbing, of taking long and lonely walks through Green Hills, his red-gold head bent, his hands in his pockets, his feet listlessly kicking aside small stones. Joseph watched him.

Then, to Joseph's relief, after many long months, Rory seemed to "come out of it." He no longer shone like the sun nor did his voice and shouts and laughter echo all over the house—but perhaps it was better that he was more subdued. When Rory was graduated from law school Joseph gave him the gift of the Grand Tour abroad, and Rory went to Europe for several months. Joseph's associates and friends abroad kept him informed secretly of Rory's wanderings and actions. When it was reported to Joseph that Rory had become very much enamored of a beautiful young Italian matron, in Rome, and was conducting a wild affair with her, Joseph was profoundly relieved. Then there was a demimondaine in Paris, a lively interlude in Berlin, a vivid one in Budapest, and something resembling an orgy in Vienna with a number of other rich young men and a bevy of young ladies of a better stratum of the unvirtuous class.

Rory had then gone to London and had called on the ambassador and his family, and Claudia was still there. The ambassador gave a lavish round of parties for the young man. Claudia was in full and beguiling enchantment, for she was in love with Rory and feverishly wanted him. It was soothing to him to be pursued by so endearing a girl, of such enormous charm, who was in turn pursued by hordes of eligible young men including several of the high nobility of England. It was also flattering. He forced himself to be conscious of Claudia's allure, and not critical. She was devoted to him. Her eyes would become luminous and very beautiful when she stared at him silently. To Rory, whose pride had been so lacerated, this was like a warmth on a bitter black night. The engagement was announced. The marriage took place quite soon thereafter. Even Bernadette was abashed and impressed by the splendor of the occasion and the notable and famous guests, though she sneered to Joseph that her son could surely have done better than this dull and breathless piece with the ugly hands.

But only Rory knew that while he was waiting near the altar for his bride he felt a sudden desperate and insane desire to run, to return to America, to force Marjorie to see him, to take her away forcibly, if necessary, or even to beat her half to death. Anything but this strange girl in her white satin Worth gown and long lacy train and shrouds of white veiling, and that sickening stench of jasmine that hung about her like a cloud, on the arm of her stately father. The music and the singing of the choir seemed to him like the discordant noises of hell, and the whole chapel became one bizarre and jerking phantasmagoria to him, tilted and hot and icy and suffocating. He controlled himself, but he was covered with sweat and his color had left him, and his body trembled and he said in himself: Marjorie.

But, in self-preservation he had already taught himself not to think too deeply about himself or anyone else, or anything at all. Otherwise life would have continued unendurable. Claudia found him very attentive on their honeymoon, and grew to adore him more and more. He had a way fascinating to her, of appearing unaware of her presence on many occasions, and she who had always been pursued ardently since puberty by boys and young men, found this intriguing. Her husband was a man, and not a flirtatious and sweating youth. Rory was not married to her six weeks when he was unfaithful to her. This time he had sought out a low prostitute, and he felt both revenge on Marjorie and on Claudia. He was always, after that, to love women for their bodies while despising them as persons.

He did not resent nor deplore Claudia's manifest stupidity, her engrossment with clothes and jewels and appearances, her love of the trivial, her passion for little details, her crass materialism and her desire always to be noticed, seen, commented upon, and admired. She was photographed everywhere, and complained to Rory about their lack of privacy on their honeymoon, but Rory knew that she was pleased and would have been outraged had they indeed traveled obscurely. To Claudia, nothing really existed —not even Rory—as fully rounded and in three dimensions as herself. She was like an actress who knew that only lesser actors and actresses surrounded her, and that only the scenery and her own lines were valid and had meaning.

The scenery—especially the scenery—and her own embellishment of it, were of the most intense importance. The audience was just second in importance, and there must always be an audience for Claudia. Rory knew all these things about his wife, and was not irritated. Surely this self-absorption, this female stupidity, was safer than a woman's wit and tender mockery and intelligence. At least, they never intruded upon him, and he was rarely exasperated by Claudia, as he had been amusedly exasperated sometimes by Marjorie, whose sharp eyes had often darted too deeply into his nature and whose bluntness had been occasionally jolting, for all her gentle laughter. "You can't deceive me with all that artless prancing," Marjorie would say, hugging him and kissing him. "I know you, Rory, my love. Kiss me. I love you though I know all about you, my darling." Claudia would never say that to him, for she never knew him at all.

Rory lived in a half world for some time, smoothly flashing over its surface, enjoying himself. Hell, he would think, what else is there but pleasure in this world, to make it endurable?

He came to life, to painful life, on the occasion of President McKinley's murder in Buffalo, New York, in September 1901, when his son, Daniel, was a year old and Claudia was pregnant with Joseph. It was as if he had awakened from some dream and had been forced to live again. He did not want to live like this once more. He had been with his father's enterprises in several cities for some time, and was a member of his legal staff, and traveled a great deal and disported himself wherever any pretty woman was available. His father had not spoken in all this time of the financiers and the bankers and the industrialists he had met in London and New York, and Rory had begun to feel they were slightly unreal after all.

But President McKinley had been assassinated by an anarchist. An anarchist, thought Rory, flung into painful life again. Rory went to his father in Philadelphia and said, "Now, tell me, Pa. What did the President do that brought that down on him?" He smiled grimly at Joseph. "An anarchist. That means a Marxist, doesn't it, a Socialist?"

"Well, not exactly," said Joseph, leaning back in his stiff office chair and studying his son. "An anarchist really means a man who wishes to destroy all rulers."

"Yes," said Rory. "I know. All kings and emperors—and

Presidents. Down with duly constituted government. But what did the President do to deserve murder at the hands of an anarchist? Exactly?"

"I'm not sure I know what you mean," said Joseph, giving the impression that his eyes were hooded, though they were not. "There are many people who disliked him very much, though I hardly think they—incited—Leon Czolgosz to kill him. If they did, they never told me. After all, they are gentlemen, aren't they, and gentlemen don't get their hands bloodied. Haven't you been reading the newspapers? McKinley was accused of being 'imperialistic' by much of the radical press, and men like Czolgosz are fired by that word. I did hear that McKinley insisted over and over that the gold standard must be maintained in America, if our currency was to remain valid; he also said that money by fiat led to national bankruptcy, and he is quoted in the press as saying, in a conference, that America must never have a Federal income tax, if she were to remain free. I believe he called such a tax 'tyranny,' a 'gigantic spoils system for looting the people of their property, and so their liberty.' He was instrumental in the repeal of the temporary tax after the war—which, I believe, annoyed some people. He is or was against the establishment of a Federal Reserve System to coin money outside the province of the Congress. In short, I should say that Mr. McKinley was not very 'progressive,' was he?"

"So, he had to be killed, so that the 'progressive' Teddy Roosevelt could be President," said Rory.

Joseph smiled. "You are simplifying things, Rory. Nothing so crude was 'plotted.' I did hear that it would be best if Mr. Roosevelt were President, but I am not sure where and when I heard it."

"I bet," said Rory.

Joseph sat up in his chair and now his face was far grimmer than Rory's. "You will have to accustom yourself to things as they are. You are a lawyer. You know there are boundaries and statutes in law, and that they can be played with too often to be safe for the player. You have to be realistic. And you can't let your imagination run away with you."

"Such as imagining coups d'état."

"Exactly." Again Joseph studied him. "I always thought

you were a realist. I prided myself on that. I never thought you believed in a Child's Garden of Verses, where good and evil live, and honor and such. To live in this world safely you have to be a man, not a naïve child. Do you understand me?"

"Yes," said Rory. They looked at each other for a long moment and then Rory said, "I never thought myself an idealist. I've been a skeptic since early childhood. I am no white knight in shining armor. I'm an opportunist, too. But somehow, the death of McKinley disturbed me. I saw that the play I attended in Europe wasn't a play at all. It was real."

Joseph said nothing. Rory sat on the edge of his father's desk, tall and slender and elegant in his black broadcloth, his red-gold head shining in the late sun. He had lost his tendency to beefiness and even his mother now admitted that he looked "refined."

"Very real," said Rory. "And the players are like Lucifer: they have persuaded people they do not exist, or never existed."

"Perhaps," said Joseph, "you would like to inform the public and begin a crusade?"

Rory grinned, and his white teeth flashed and for a moment he was the younger Rory. "I might, I really might, if I thought there was a single chance that the public would believe me, and if I had more solid information."

Joseph smiled too. "But they wouldn't believe you, and isn't that fortunate? The people love to believe that the world is Pure and Good and Beautiful, and that God's in His Heaven and all's right with the world. They want to be free for their nasty little pleasures and little animal enjoyments, or their childish romping and eating and sleeping. A nation never forgives a man who tries to make it think. It will forgive murderers and liars and thieves and exploiters, oppressors and tyrants. But a man who says, 'Let me tell you about your enemies, and what you must do about them, in faith, in justice, in courage and fortitude, lest you die,' will indeed die himself. His people will kill him, themselves. There doesn't need to be any coup d'état, as you call it."

Rory nodded. "Yes, it is a very ancient story, isn't it? Almost banal, and always repeated. I think saints and just men should be strangled at birth. They do have a way of upsetting the plans of their betters, or trying to, at any rate. That, of course, is intolerable."

"I surmise you are not among those imbeciles," said Joseph.

"No. I prefer to live. I didn't make this world, but I have to come to terms with it." Joseph's face changed suddenly, and Rory saw it, and wondered. "This is the last time, Pa, that we'll have a conversation like this—I promise you."

"Good," said Joseph. "And now, coming down to your campaign for congressman. The people, on the one hand, will tolerate or even glorify a despot, but they are a little prudish about politicians being too overt concerning the beds of other men's wives. Let a leader kill half a million men in a war, and the people will set up statues to him. But let an aspiring politician be found with his trousers off in the bedroom of a woman not his wife and his career is finished, and not even death will wipe out his 'infamy.' Well, no matter. I should, though, suggest you become a model of conjugal devotion until you are at least elected. I am hearing some uncomfortable rumors."

"And all of them true, too," said Rory. "I have decided what to do, Pa. I have a very devoted wife. She's already spoken to me sweetly on the same subject. Tolerant."

Joseph frowned. "Well, be circumspect." Rory stood up and touched his forehead in a mock salute and left the office, and Joseph sat alone, still frowning.

A week later Harry Zeff suddenly died of a heart attack in his mansion in Philadelphia, leaving his beloved wife, Liza, and his twin sons, now both dedicated physicians and very upright if somewhat obtuse young men. Both were married to girls of sound family, and both had young children. Harry had been proud of them.

Chapter 12

He was three years younger than I, thought Joseph, who attended the funeral. I trusted him more than I ever trusted anyone in all my life. Harry was buried on a wet and windy autumn day, with the yellow rags of sodden leaves blowing about the headstones in the cemetery. The sky was the color of pewter, and poured pewter rain. "I am the Resurrection and the Life," intoned the priest. Liza stood beside Joseph, her sons behind her, and Joseph supported her with his arm and thought of the small girl in the house of Ed Healey and the young boy with the stormy curls who had saved his life, and who had laughed at him and had courage and gay fortitude. Joseph saw again the depot in Wheatfield, the night he had met little Harry, and suddenly he saw and smelled it all as if it had just happened.

It was not possible that Harry was dead. He was too much a part of Joseph's life. If they did not see each other with too much regularity they always wrote or telegraphed or used the telephone, and when they met it was as if it were a holiday, to Harry's jubilation. Harry never lost that curious mixture of childish trust and mature knowledge which had been his as a child, and his face had never hardened or become tainted, in spite of the things he had had to do in serving Joseph Armagh. He was like a workman who needs to use tar in his work, but who, on returning home, cleansed himself of it and did not see or smell it.

There were times when he seemed much older than Joseph, and times when he seemed only a youth. There were many who had said that he was the criminal agent of a powerful criminal, and Harry had heard this often, and it had not vexed him. "What is a criminal?" he had asked a reporter once, with unusual heat. "A man who never succeeded at criminality. He got caught." He angrily defended Joseph at other times. "Is it his fault that he has the intelligence to make a fortune?" he would ask. "You are just envious."

He wasn't even fifty-five, thought Joseph, seeing the wet black clods dropped on Harry's coffin and hearing the weeping of Liza. (She, herself, was only fifty-three, but she had become an old woman, white of hair, covered with soft heavy flesh, the result of fat living over the years, and contentment, and simple uncomplicated and motherly thoughts.) The sons resembled her, having the rather blank and characterless features of the common people, but their eyes were Harry's eyes, dark and lustrous, though not with Harry's intelligence. They were shrewd enough, and competent enough, to be successful in their own right, and the elder—by five minutes—Jason, sometimes had a sharply shrewd expression. They regarded Joseph as an uncle, and addressed him so. Jason would infrequently study him with a speculative gleam in his eye. The young men were not welcome at Green Hills, as they had discovered long ago from their mother, once awesomely intimidated by Bernadette who had referred to Harry as "that Turk," in Liza's hearing. The young men were short, powerful, square in body, with big strong heads, and moved with purpose if with some clumsiness.

He was a part of my life, thought Joseph, feeling the approach of the old pain again. He was the first I knew whom I could trust. Why, he was closer and certainly more loyal and faithful than any brother. He was my friend. I am just beginning to know that now.

Charles was there, at the funeral, in the wind and rain and under the canopy which protected the mourners, and Charles, as always, was urbane and composed and his hair was still ginger-yellow and his figure lithe and young. But Joseph thought, Charles is my age, and I am nearing sixty, and where have the years gone, the years of our youth? Is it possible that Harry is really dead? Joseph stared down into the grave and thought of the graves he had stared at before, and he wanted to turn away. But there were the photographers battling with plates and black cloths and cameras at a little distance, for Harry Zeff had been the powerful henchman of the powerful Joseph Armagh, and his closest friend.

Liza's sons took their mother to the carriage and waited for the family, and Joseph, usually adroit at avoiding reporters, found himself suddenly confronting three impudent young men with rain-wet faces and derbies and determination. "Mr. Armagh, sir," said one, "is it true that Mr. Zeff committed suicide, as it is rumored?"

Charles pushed his way to Joseph's side, and made a menacing gesture at the photographers. But Joseph put his hand on Charles's arm. He looked at the somewhat frightened young men and his face was bleak. "Tell me that again," he said. "Suicide? Mr. Zeff? You must be out of your minds. His sons are physicians. One of them signed the death certificate."

"Yes. We know," said the youngest and the brashest. This was the fearful Mr. Armagh, but a story was a story. "That's what seems funny about it. We heard—anonymously—that Mr. Zeff shot himself. And Mrs. Zeff called her sons. There was no other doctor."

"You're insane," said Charles. "Mr. Zeff died suddenly of a heart attack. See here, do I have to call those policemen yonder? Stop bothering Mr. Armagh."

"So Mr. Armagh denies the rumor," said the young man, and danced expertly out of Charles's way. "Thank you, sir. Mr. Devereaux, isn't it?" The rain and wind suddenly seemed like the sound of a cataract and a hurricane to Joseph, and he walked beside Charles to the second carriage, and he heard the cold squeak and sucking of mud at his heels. He sat in the carriage, with Charles beside him, and the black wet horses pulled them away, down the curving avenues of the dead under the dying trees, and through the bronze gates.

Joseph said, "It is a lie, of course. Harry died of a heart attack."

When Charles did not reply Joseph turned to him quickly and said in a harsh voice. "Well? He did, didn't he?"

Charles said, "We hoped to keep it from you, and then those damned reporters—they must have heard something, and not just rumor. No. Harry didn't die of a heart attack. He shot himself, as they said. We worked hard to keep it quiet, the news suppressed. But someone blabbed. Perhaps a servant, who overheard."

Joseph was appalled. The grayish light poured through the rivulets of water on the carriage windows, and it lay on Joseph's face making it stark and livid. "Why? Why should he do a thing like that? Was he ill, dying of some incurable disease?"

Charles hesitated, then sighed. He took off his wet hat

and smoothed his hair with his hand. "No. There was nothing wrong. His sons told me so. It was just that the other night—he went to his wife in their double bed, and kissed her good night, and told her—oh, some soft rambling story that he would always love her and be near her—and then he went down to his library and put a bullet through his heart. Not his head—where it could be plainly seen. He must have aimed carefully. Liza heard the shot and called the servants, and she wouldn't let them in the library, stood like a tigress, the sons told me, and they came." Charles shrugged. "There wasn't any note. There wasn't, isn't, any explanation. Harry was in excellent health. He was a multimillionaire. He hadn't been depressed, everybody said. It was just as usual, they said. I'm sorry, Joe. That's all I can tell you. As it was told to me."

"Burglars. Thieves," said Joseph, and his voice was thin and far away. "I saw Harry myself, less than two weeks ago." Then he stopped and his face changed subtly and became wizened, and Charles saw this.

Joseph continued. "I was feeling, well, depressed, and I happened to ask Harry what a man lives for. The average man. Even us. We work all our lives, struggle, plot, contrive, plan, aim, direct our activities. That is our major occupation. Sometimes we like what we do, and it absorbs us. But in the main the average man does not. So, I asked Harry, what in the hell do we live for. For our daily bread, and endless work, and fighting, and marrying and having children, and disappointment, or worse? What are our pleasures? A few hours of liberty a week, whether we live in a mansion or a hovel, a few opportunities for adultery and a few humdrum pleasures, which most of us are too tired to enjoy anyway. Then we die, and that is all there is. Even those born to great riches and luxury and idleness— for what do they live? Endless galas, parties, envies, traveling, dressing—and the same dreary recreations of a coal miner or a shopkeeper or a clerk or a factory hand. Is that all there is to a man's life? If so, I said to Harry, then it is not worth living."

Charles saw his dry and somber face and said nothing. "And Harry said," Joseph went on, "that there are little pleasures along the way, little satisfactions, and I asked him were they worth living for. He thought about it. Then he said, 'My grandmother was an old illiterate Lebanese woman, and she once told me that we lived for love.' We both laughed then. That was all of the conversation. My God, you don't think Harry was influenced by that conversation, do you, Charles?"

Charles shook his head. "No. Harry was too intelligent. He knew that we all lived because dying is infinitely harder to face—for most people. There may not be any satisfaction in living—I haven't found much—but an eternity of non-being is worse than that, even life at its meanest. Not to be. Not to exist. No wonder the very sick hold on to their last breath."

"But Harry didn't," said Joseph. "He preferred to die. Why?"

"Perhaps he was tired of living. Millions of us reach that stage."

"But Harry was a full-blooded, healthy man, not capricious, not complex."

"How do you know?" asked Charles. "Who knows any damned thing about any of us, including ourselves?" He looked through the window. The air was the color of sadness. The wind made the carriage rock.

"Do you think Harry might have been murdered, by thieves, perhaps, Charles?"

"Not in the least. The house was guarded like a fortress." Joseph pounced. "Why?"

"Why? Aren't your doors well-bolted at night, and your windows?"

"In town, yes. In Green Hills, no. You are putting me off, Charles, evading me. You know, as I know, that Harry killed himself deliberately, according to what you have told me. The unanswered question is why?"

Charles sighed again. "Look here, Joe, I asked Jason and Simeon myself, on the quiet, when they asked me not to tell you. They knew how attached you were to Harry. They didn't want you—disturbed, or being just as you are this very minute, probing, questioning, causing yourself misery. They told me they cannot think of a single reason why their father killed himself. There had been no hinting. Harry had been his jolly laughing self the night before, at dinner, to which they and their wives had been invited. He had even talked of buying a new yacht next year. He asked his sons' opinion. Just a family reunion."

He stared through the window again. "I remember what St. Paul talked about—the dark night of the soul. I suppose it comes to all of us, sometimes many times in our lives, sometimes only once. Perhaps it came to Harry just that once, and he hadn't any previous experience like it before to use as a frame of reference. Maybe he was—overwhelmed. After all, men of our age do get, I hear, storms of the spirit, to be a little fanciful, when we begin to weigh our lives and try to find out what they mean, who we are, and for what we have lived. I'll bet very few of us come up with a soothing and satisfying answer. Very few."

"Did you, Charles?"

"No," said Charles, almost cheerfully. "But, what the hell. I am here and I may as well enjoy the sights, as we say down South. It's like traveling. You look, you observe, you compare, you are interested and amused, it is enlightening or boring or exciting—briefly. And then, you come home."

"To that, back there," said Joseph. "A tombstone in a forgotten cemetery?"

Then Charles said, "Have you found out for what you have lived. Joe?"

Joseph thought, then answered in a heavy and gloomy voice. "I thought I knew. Once. But in some way I have forgotten. That is perhaps true of all of us. We forget our destination. Probably just as well. Just a grave."

"When you are young you believe the world is all yours, glorious and exhilarating and fascinating and full of promise and trumpets and drums and marches and new worlds," said Charles. "We don't ask ourselves what we are living for then. We know. But we forget, later, or it all seems a foolish dream. Well, here we are at the Zeffs'. Shall I let Jason and Simeon know that I told you, after all?"

"I have a feeling," said Joseph, as the coachman opened the door for them, "that this is a very banal conversation, and one that has taken place ten thousand million times before, between other men. In fact, I hear universal echoes, poor damned sods that we are."

Charles gave a subdued laugh. "That old Persian is very popular these days, Omar Khayyám. I like one of his verses in particular:

> "Ah, make the most of what we yet may spend,
> Before we too into the dust descend—
> Dust into dust, and under dust to lie,
> Sans song, sans wine, sans singer and sans end."

Just as he was about to step out he said, "Candidly, I

think vagabondage is the best life to live. If there is any-thing to reincarnation, I am going to be a tramp in my next existence. Now, that is living, Joe. Tramps end up in the same place we do, but they have a hell of a lot of fun and freedom on the way."

Joseph was asked by the family to be present when Har-ry's will was read. The day was cold and the color and the shine of steel. The house was opulent and even Oriental in its richness and furnishings, and it had always oppressed Joseph. The family sat in the library, with the weeping Liza and the crying sons, for they were emotional people. There was a large trust fund for Liza, larger ones for the sons, and the house for Liza and the money to maintain it. But the residuary estate was left, to Joseph's amazement, to charity, to be administered by the Archdiocese of Philadel-phia.

A package was placed in Joseph's hands, the paper brown and old and sifting. He opened it. He could not be-lieve what he saw. It was a worn Missal. Liza stopped her sobbing to look and wonder. "I never saw it before," she said in a broken voice. "Was it Harry's? Why, he never even went to Church!"

Joseph thought he had felt devastated before, but it was nothing to what he felt now. The Missal opened in his hands and he saw that it had been opened here many times before, and the passage was marked:

"Lamb of God, Who taketh away the sins of the world,
  Have mercy—"

Joseph had a terrible insight as he sat there with the opened passage before Him. He said to himself: He hated what he did for me, but because it was for me he did it. And that made him finally die.

Harry had never once spoken of religion to him, or to anyone else insofar as Joseph knew. His sons had been given as secular an education as Joseph had given his own sons. He had never revealed any religious interest, any speculative doubts or thoughts. Yet, this was his Missal, wrapped years ago for Joseph.

Was it a warning? If so, why?

He was suddenly desperately tired. The years do tell, he thought, as the lawyers consoled the bereaved. Charles was to remain for several days in Philadelphia and consult with

Harry's possible successor. Joseph was to go to New York. Then, suddenly, he thought of Elizabeth, and longed for her with a starved longing.

He returned to Green Hills alone, on the fastest train which roared majestically through the night. Then he felt the pain of his loss, the crouching, waiting pain. Even Kevin's death had not seared him like this, nor the loss of Sean and Regina, nor the destruction of his daughter. For Harry had been more than children, brother and sister. He had been the major part in Joseph's life, and possibly the most eager and full-bodied part, and the youngest. Joseph, through all those years, had doubted everyone else, all he had loved. But he had never doubted Harry. Now Harry had died for his loyalty, and a love Joseph had never suspected.

Exhausted by his pain he leaned his head against the window and he dreamed he was in that hot and dusty Washington room of so long ago, burning the papers which concerned Senator Bassett. He heard the senator speaking, but did not see him. "Too late," said the senator. "Too late."

A week later, when Charles was on the way home from Philadelphia his train was derailed and partially wrecked. Three men died in it. Charles was one of them.

"Christ, Christ," said Joseph, when he received the telegram from Philadelphia. He went upstairs to his study and stayed there three days and nights and did not come out. He never answered the door. He never touched the trays which were left at it. Whether he slept or not, no one knew. No one knew that for the second time in his life he got drunk.

Chapter 13

Joseph was having a long talk with the governor, who was afraid of him but who was not pleased by the conversation.

"Rory—and you know how fond of Rory I am, Joe, and know all about his excellent mind and endowments—hasn't exactly distinguished himself in his two congressional terms in Washington. Nothing too bad was ever said about him. He was never really controversial. But nothing positively good was said about him, either. He seemed to think being a congressman was a lark, a continuing social event, something with which a rich man and a rich man's son amuses himself. Galas, parties, garden affairs."

Then the governor frowned. "He did vote against a Federal income tax, but that didn't make him more popular. It was said in a lot of newspapers that he had done this for 'selfish' reasons, and that he didn't want his own fortune taxed."

"It is a strange thing," said Joseph, whose thick hair was almost white now, with only here and there a streak of russet. "Mankind is the most selfish species this world has ever spewed up from hell, and it demands, constantly, that neighbors and politicians be 'unselfish' and allow themselves to be plundered—for its benefit. Nobody howls more against 'public selfishness,' or even private selfishness, as much as a miser, just as whores are the strongest supporters of public morality, and robbers of the people extol philanthropy. I've lived a long time, but my fellowman baffles me more and more, which no doubt is naïve of me."

It didn't hinder you from plundering him, though, thought the governor, unkindly. But the governor owed his office to Joseph Armagh and his money. "And he voted against the Amendment to permit direct election of senators, instead of appointment by the State Legislature. In

707

fact, he delivered a speech, if I remember—notable for surprising eloquence and emotion—that that would be 'redundant,' and that two bodies of government were unnecessary, directly elected. If I remember, he said the Senate served the same purpose as the House of Lords, in England, to control the 'enthusiasm, sketchy consideration, superficial judgments and public exigency' of congressmen, who were directly elected by the people, and 'so subject to the greeds, vagaries, romances, and ignorant pressures of the mobs, under fear of defeat in the next elections. We must have a calm, unpressured, moderate, controlled and judicious body in the government,' he said, 'just as the Founding Fathers had decreed, to control the unseemly, hysterical and uneducated passions of the masses.' That did not endear him to many in Washington, or even in this state. He is now known as the 'Monarchist.' "

"Rory puts a lot of faith in the legislature of the state, though it, too, was elected," said Joseph, with not the slightest smile. But the governor laughed nastily and shook his head. "At any rate he was acclaimed as a 'Constitutionalist,' and many of the people are ardent Constitutionalists, so I don't think Rory is too unpopular."

Joseph thought of his angry conversations with Rory over these very matters, and his visits to Washington to influence his son. Rory, as always, was smiling and affable, though his lower eyelids relaxed innocently. "Pa," he had said, "I know what the decent electorate wants, in spite of the howling mobs of the Tuileries; pardon me, of New York and Philadelphia and Boston and Chicago, as such. If I am to have any political future at all I will have to rely on the honest men of America."

"Don't be a damned fool," Joseph had said. Then he had studied Rory. "Now, no joking, Rory, any longer. You and I know that honest men in any country are very rare. And they are totally impotent. You can't turn back the clock to McKinley's era, Rory. The vast mass of the American people want a Federal income tax, to take revenge on those they call 'the powers that be,' that is, the intelligent who have made money one way or another. If they don't believe, as you have told them, that that tax will eventually loot them and will be used to enslave them, rob them, and employed to promote wars for empire and tyranny, are they worth fighting for? No. Let them wallow in their own enslavement later, and die in wars. It is all they deserve."

"At least you're frank, Pa," said Rory. "Coming down to it, you always were. I inherited that from you."

"But I don't tell it to the imbecile public," said Joseph, and tried not to smile. "They want to believe in fantasies. Let them. Such fantasies are profitable—to us. That was a silly move you made when you quoted Lord Acton: 'The power to tax is the power to destroy.' Did that make the people think? On the contrary. They shouted that you wanted to be a 'privileged lord.' Like Lord Acton! That's how the public reasons. I once privately objected when Vanderbilt said, 'The public be damned.' But what else does it deserve?"

Rory did not answer, but he thought: Pa, it may surprise you. I happen to love my country, naïve though she is, ignorant though she is, gut-engrossed though she is, emotional and childish though she will forever be, and thoughtless and rampagious. She still is better than any other country, though some other countries may boast of a more intelligent electorate. But what did that famous intelligent electorate bring other countries, except oppression, the establishment of a vicious 'Elite,' and wars, constant wars? Intelligent electorates are no guarantee against Empire—in fact, they promote it—nor violence, nor tyranny, nor disorder and anarchy. They are usually against all that establishes law and order, tolerance, justice, liberty. It threatens the 'Elite's' mania for power. Pa, you shouldn't have let me see the deadly men of Zurich—and other places.

Rory had long known that his father was "fey," like all the Irish, and as he was himself, and so he was not too surprised when his father said very quietly, "Rory?"

Joseph had stood up then and had said, "Nothing in life brings much lasting pleasure, Rory. But power brings the most. It has an element of revenge in it."

Rory had never really pitied his powerful father before but all at once he pitied him so profoundly that he was shaken. He promised himself then that he would do as much as he could to please his father—but not overtly. Their quarrels would be private.

Joseph said to the govenor, "Let us not be diverted. I want my son appointed as senator by the State Legislature. You knew that in the beginning."

"But Joe, you were the most instrumental in the appointment of Lloyd Summers, for that post. You put a lot of pressure on our Party. This will be only his second term. You arranged it. Now you want him scuttled."

"Yes. I have nothing against Lloyd. A post in the state government? Yes, you can arrange that easily. But I want my son to be senator. It is that simple. He will be thirty in March. This is February. You have plenty of time, after March, when he will reach the Constitutional age."

"What the hell am I going to tell Lloyd?" asked the governor.

"Now, Jim. You know damned well that politicians don't have to worry over lies. They are born gifted with them."

It had not been very hard at all. Shortly after his thirtieth birthday Rory was delegated as the next appointee of his Party, by the State Legislature, to the august body of the Senate in Washington. His appointment was duly confirmed. Senator Rory Daniel Armagh moved to a finer and more luxurious, if more "refined," house in Georgetown. His wife, elated, said to him, "Rory, if you hadn't been married to me no one would have known about you at all!" Her father was no longer Ambassador to the Court of St. James's. He held a very lucrative and gaudy Cabinet post under President Theodore Roosevelt. The post did not demand much of him. But his parties were famous, and so were his women. He confessed that though he had enjoyed the pomp and circumstance of Empire in London, he was devoted to "democracy." He became a member of the Committee of Foreign Studies, in New York, and of the Scardo Society.

"All in all," said Mr. Jay Regan, the New York financier, "I think, therefore, that we are well satisfied with President Roosevelt. We had some doubt of him at first, but after I had had a few conversations with him. Joseph. I found him an eminently reasonable man. I think our support of him was justified."

"Dear old Teddy," said Joseph, and Mr. Regan laughed.

"Are you still bothered about his inroads into South America? Well, wasn't it planned that way? His very outrageous attacks on President Cipriano Castro of Venezuela —his language—inspired the native belligerence of Americans. 'Unspeakably villainous little monkey.' Ah, yes. 'I will show these Dagos that they will have to behave decently.' Indeed. That was truly inspiring—to the American masses.

They like strong noisy men, though some of them do call such men 'Caesars.' Lovingly. But doesn't everyone love Caesar? Yes."

"They also like thieves, big thieves," said Joseph. Mr. Regan continued to smile but his eyes fixed themselves on the other man. This Armagh frequently gave the impression, through his tongue, that he was "unreliable," and so he was not completely trusted. He also had a way of baiting his associates, and for this reason alone his son, Rory, was not as yet taken into what was ambiguously called "the Circle." The senator showed every symptom of being tractable and helpful, but there were some in the Committee of Foreign Studies who declared that he appeared to be making "mental notes" which might be "dangerous." Mr. Rockefeller, for instance, had openly declared that he was wary of the young man.

"I have a feeling," said Joseph to Mr. Regan, "that we are not inspiring love for the United States in South America. Roosevelt's seizure of Santo Domingo in 1904, for an alleged foreign debt of nineteen million dollars—which was not owed to America, not one penny—is not going to do us much good in the future. 'Roosevelt Corollary to the Monroe Doctrine,' indeed. It seems to me that I missed something in our last few meetings, or perhaps I wasn't told, Jay. I have often suspected, lately, that I am not invited to all the meetings."

"Now, now," said Mr. Regan. "Of course you are. But there are things of dull routine—"

"And didn't Teddy just jump for joy when Japan attacked Russia?" said Joseph. "What did he say? 'I was thoroughly well pleased with the Japanese victory, *for Japan is playing our game.*' I missed that, didn't I? Yes, I know. He finally, recently, intervened and demanded that the two nations make peace. I hear he is going to get the Nobel Peace Prize almost immediately. Who arranged that?"

"I am sure I don't know," said Mr. Regan, lighting a cigar. "We have no influence over that."

"Hah," said Joseph.

"Each of us in the Society owns a senator, who works for our interests," said Mr. Regan. "But who does Rory work for?"

"Me," said Joseph.

"Now, now, Joe," said Mr. Regan. "I doubt he even

works for you. This is the end of his first term, and no doubt he will be reappointed by the State Legislature. Yet, what has he done of value?"

"He has acquired a reputation for honesty, which even hostile newspapers can't deny."

"Very astute of him. But honesty doesn't serve our private interests, does it? I think there is nothing more valuable for a senator or any other politician to acquire as a reputation for honor and honesty—for public consumption. That can be done easily, with the help of a few newspapers and a little money and bought critics and lesser politicians, and large donations to the Party. But it is quite another thing when a senator takes himself so seriously that he ignores or refuses to serve—"

"His real masters," said Joseph.

Mr. Regan smiled. "Now, only a fool believes that the electorate is master over its politicians. 'Serving the people,' Joe—"

"I know," said Joseph. "An old nun I knew when I was a young boy used to say 'but that doesn't buy any potatoes,' though I don't think she meant it in this context. Still, it's valid."

"Moreover," said Mr. Regan, nodding, "the people are most ungrateful. A politician, as we know, who serves the people, really serves them out of conviction and idealism, is eventually despised by them as a naïve imbecile. But a scoundrel of color, who can invent a few deadly aphorisms of his own, and can laugh and twinkle and joke, gets their adoration, and even if he is later exposed for what he is—a thief, a time-server, a liar—the public becomes hysterical at the 'attacks' on him. In fact, the public will attack the outraged attackers of their darling. But, Joe, you know all this. You've been in this business almost as long as I have. See here, Joe, I'm Irish, like you, though Protestant. We have what my Granny used to call 'a sharp tongue on him, an Irish tongue.' More Irishmen have been hanged by their tongues than by ropes. We can't resist being sarcastic or ironic, at the very worst times."

"In short, are you warning me, Jay."

Mr. Regan, large and fat and rubicund—some said he resembled Mr. Taft—slowly lit one of his enormous cigars, and seemed to be ruminating. Then he said, "No, Joe. I'm just advising you. You want Rory to be the first Catholic President of what Bryan calls 'the Yew-nited States of Ammurrica.' We all know that. You must smooth down your spikes. We, 'the Circle,' know that you aren't devious nor overtly subtle, and that when you say something—shall we call it disturbing?—you mean it, and never regret its edge. So, you have a reputation for not being 'quite the gentleman.' In other words, you are not suave and urbane and serpentine, and you have a way of openly jeering at the delicate euphemisms of 'the Circle,' and laugh at its—you call it pretensions?—of 'ultimately serving humanity.' Yes. There is not a murderer who does not feel that he has served some purpose in murdering, nor a thief who does not think he is justified, nor a general who ever deplored a war. Men, even like our colleagues—and we know what they are—desire to be thought political philanthropists, of enormous intellect and understanding, with nothing but peace and harmony and enlightened government as their objectives. I don't care how intelligent a man is, or a country, they love to believe that his, and its, infamies, are committed in the name of a larger benefit to humanity. Aristophanes never wrote so broad a comedy, and I am constantly amused."

He looked at Joseph who had been listening with a dark expression. "What I am getting at, Joe, is that if you wish Rory to be President you will have to curb your tongue and serve us all, as we serve you, with your whole heart, and stop being sardonic. I confess that I often have your own thoughts but I am wise enough not to utter them. What good does it do, anyway? Does it advance your interests? No. It only heightens mistrust."

"I've served them damned well," said Joseph.

"Yes, and it sticks in your craw, and it's visible."

Joseph stood up and began to pace up and down the enormous paneled and carpeted office of Mr. Regan, in New York. He said, "Wasn't it Sophocles who said that when a vast force or power enters into the affairs of men, open or secret, it brings with it a curse?"

"We've been in business a long time, Joe, our fathers and grandfathers before us, and our sons will take our place. We have what the Romans called 'gravitas.' If you think that our growing and tremendous power is a 'curse,' then I cannot agree with you, for I, too, believe that humanity cannot bear what it calls 'democracy' but must have despotism. It is the Irishman in you which despises any sort of despotism, and you must hold your tongue."

He became annoyed. "Joe, you were to be subpoenaed to Washington to answer charges that you are a 'trust.' We helped you to evade that, as we helped others to evade it. You show no gratitude."

When Joseph did not reply Mr. Regan said, "You have objected occasionally to our promotion of revolutions throughout the world. Yet you know that revolutions increase the power of the State, and larger revolutions make the State absolute. That is our objective throughout the world. In many ways we are indeed philanthropists. We will remove the uneasy and unstable and hysterical power of the electorate—and it doesn't want the power anyway—and give it a firm, kind, benign government, which, to the relief of humanity, will remove the necessity for judgment, thought—particularly thought—and responsibility. Come on, Joe. You know all this. I am speaking to you as a friend now and not merely as a colleague."

But Joseph had been thinking of something else. He said, "Is it true that Roosevelt will not seek the nomination in 1908? He keeps on insisting on that."

"He has served his purpose," said Mr. Regan. "A little persuasion— The trouble with Mr. Roosevelt, Joe, is that he began to take himself seriously and to forget who really put him into power. His attack on 'trusts' came too close to the bone in the case of Morgan, Rockefeller, Depew, Mellon, Armour, and you, too. And I. You cannot trust a politician. Build him up, against all his inclinations, as a Benefactor of Humanity, a Warrior for Freedom, and he will eventually believe he is such, and act accordingly. He is working to make William Howard Taft President. Taft is not our man, but he is amiable and trustful and pedestrian."

"He will never know who pulls the strings," said Joseph. "We can spare him that, at least."

"Joe, it is that sort of remark that antagonizes people. I have warned you before, as a friend. If your plans for Rory are not to collapse, and perhaps you with them, and Rory also, learn a little discretion."

He looked at Joseph very hard now, and his light gray eyes were intent. "Rory is a good Catholic husband and father. We have worked on that, as you know. We are also mentioning that intolerance is evil, and Catholics are just as good Americans as Protestants, in spite of all the rampant anti-Romanism—"

"Which all of you initiated and stimulated for your pur-poses!" Joseph could not help exclaiming. Mr. Regan shrugged and sighed. "It served our purposes. But now we are interested in Rory. It will be some years before anyone will take him seriously as a candidate. I give him credit: He does not have your scalpel tongue, Joe. He is diplomatic, easy, devious, placating, which is very clever of him—and civilized. If he has thoughts he wisely keeps them to him-self. Perhaps even the things he does against us can be turned to our advantage. We are protean, as you know. Rory has impressed us. But, we can destroy Rory, if we wish. We know of his previous marriage—and the annul-ment."

I should have known, Joseph thought to himself. He controlled his fear. He said, "That is over and done with, and meant nothing. Do you know how many times Rory farts, too?"

Mr. Regan laughed heartily. "Indeed we do, Joe. Indeed we do."

Then he became stern. "If Rory wishes to be President then he must begin now to serve us—and not just you, if he indeed serves you, Joe, which I doubt. For instance, he must oppose that nefarious new bill, to be voted on by the House soon, the Child Labor bill. Hell, what do the people breed for, except to serve their masters? And don't parents have the right to decide the destiny of their children? Aren't their children their own, and not the State's? If they send their young children into the factories at five, six, seven years old, it is their affair, for who among them does not need money? I have simplified this a little, Joe. You know all the arguments. We have the clergy with us, too, in this. You might mention it to Rory. That bill must be stopped, if it reaches the Senate, though we will try to kill it in the House."

It was like an echo to Joseph, and he remembered Sena-tor Bassett in Washington, whose death had not prevented the passage of the Alien Contract Labor Act in 1882. He said, "Somehow, I feel the Child Labor bill will be enacted, though I will suggest to Rory that he oppose it."

Later he said to his son, "Rory, you and I want you to be President of this country. There are rumors that you will support the Child Labor bill, when it comes before the Sen-ate. Don't. I repeat, don't. The arguments are very good, as you know. 'Parents have the right to control their children, and the labor of their children. Their children are their own.' Yes. You will oppose the bill.''

When Rory did not answer, but only smiled his brilliant easy smile. Joseph said, "When you are President, you can, within limits, support what you will or oppose what you will.''

"No, Pa," said Rory, very gently. "You know that is not true. I will be the biggest puppet of all, and you know that. If I refuse—" and he drew his hand eloquently across his throat in a slicing gesture. "Well, I won't worry about that. No Catholic will ever be nominated for the Presidency, let alone be elected to it. Maybe we should thank God for that."

"This time we will succeed," said Joseph. Rory became grave. He looked at his father enigmatically. "Maybe I am interested in the Presidency, after all. Yes. Perhaps."

He voted against the Child Labor bill. "It is a violation of parents' Supreme and Divine Authority over their children," he said. He was much applauded in powerful newspapers. His father was congratulated by "the Circle."

Chapter 14

Ann Marie was thirty-six years old, and her brother, "The Senator," came from Washington to Green Hills—the "Settlement"—to celebrate their joint birthday. His wife came with him, querulous as always and expressing her opinion that this was a hardship considering that "the Season was in full bloom, and you need to be Seen, Rory." Her children, neglected and brought up by well-paid but indifferent servants and governesses, annoyed her. Mentally a child, herself, she thought of them as rivals. She reminded Rory that her parents had planned a birthday party for him in Washington, and now it must be postponed for several days. "After all," she would complain to Rory, "you owe everything to the fact that you married me and I am of a Distinguished Family, and your father is only a businessman."

She could not understand why Rory laughed himself almost into hysteria.

Ann Marie seemed more of a child than ever, rosy, fat, smiling innocently, babbling, playing with her dolls. Rory, her twin, sat in her rooms with her and tried to find, in that blank face and those luminous sherry-colored eyes, some trace of the sister he had loved, and who had grown in the womb with him. Once, when they were alone, he said to her very quietly, "Ann Marie? Do you remember Courtney?"

The rosy smile had widened. But all at once Rory saw, in those shining eyes, a shadow, a terror, an anguish which jolted him. Then it was gone. He was shaken. How much did Ann Marie remember? Was she lurking behind that plump and roseate facade, hiding? The soft lax hand in his had tightened, had grasped, and then it was limp again and she was talking about her new doll. When he stood up to go, sighing, she had looked up at him and the smile was gone. "Rory?" she said.

She had recognized him, then, though when he had appeared only an hour ago she had looked at him questioningly, with a child's shy and wary smile, shrinking at the sight of a stranger.

He bent over his sister, himself resplendent and shining even in the pale and bitter sunlight of March, and the icy reflection of the glittering snow outside. "Yes, dear," he said. She put her fat arms up to him and he held her, and he felt the trembling of her cheek against his. Then she moaned, "Rory, Rory. Oh, Rory—Courtney." She clutched him desperately, and he dared not move or speak.

Then she had dropped her arms and he had straightened up and she was giving him, once again, a very young child's wide-eyed stare. She giggled. She pushed a doll at him and said, "Kiss, kiss."

His mother said to him, with a weariness not entirely affected, "I wish to God your father would permit her to go to a fine private institution. You have no idea of the hopelessness, Rory, and the responsibility. Ann Marie is becoming so heavy that nurses complain, and leave, no matter what we pay them. She is walking less and less, and spends more and more time in bed, and she is so fat that I can't understand what the doctors mean by 'atrophy.' She certainly isn't wasting! She can't go for drives any longer. It is almost impossible to get her up and down the stairs, and now your father is installing an elevator for her. She looks like an infant. It is more than I can bear. Do talk to your father. When we have parties here, she sometimes screeches from upstairs and it unnerves people, and sometimes she fights with her nurses and is uncontrollable and shouts that she has to go to the woods. Really, Rory." She sighed. "Worse and worse. And Rory—sometimes the smell! It is disgusting, and I am ashamed to speak of it. The whole upstairs, sometimes— Complete degeneration, the doctors say, who agree with me that she'd be far better off in some institution."

"She never speaks about—anything?" Rory asked.

"No. If I don't see her for a few days, and God knows I am always here now, and I go into her rooms she stares at me and whimpers and doesn't recognize me, her own mother. It is very strange. She does recognize your father, no matter how long his absences are. I feel there is a curse upon this family, Rory, a curse."

"Now, Ma," he said, but he frowned. He did not speak to his father.

Joseph tried to be in Green Hills at least one week in every month to see his daughter. She always greeted him with such delight that he would dare to hope, for a minute or two, that she had returned to this world, for she knew him and would hold out her arms to him and cuddle against him, shyly. But within an hour or two she was withdrawn, smiling that childish smile, and babbling. He would smooth that soft brown hair, and notice the widening bands of gray, and the increasing wrinkles in the soft rosy face. Sometimes she seemed sixty years old, blubbery, almost massive in her fat, inert, blinking, not seeing, not knowing. But how can I send her away? he would think. This is all she has, her home, these rooms, her toys, her nurses. He would look into her eyes, childlike still, and try to find his daughter, to discover that "soul" that had once inhabited this bloated flesh. But it was like peering down into a deep well where only reflections rippled the surface.

He came back to Green Hills on a June morning so warm, so radiant, so full of brightness, that it was like a promise of coming joy. The roses rampaged from every bed on the estate, red and white and yellow, and were full of scent under the blowing trees. He remembered that spring day when he had first seen Green Hills and had heard the peepers in the trees and had seen the shine of blue water and the brisk arrowing of birds from limb to limb. What had he told himself then, what had he promised himself? He could not remember. I am an old man, he thought. I am tired, and old, and my hair is white and it is a burden to wake up in the morning and confront the day. Yet, I must. Why? I do not know. I have yet to find out what drives us. He suspected that the tiredness of his body came from his mind and not from his still vigorous lean body and his supple muscles, but that did not decrease the weariness, the mounting sense of futility that ran over him like a tidal wave when he was most vulnerable. He was no more interested in his grandchildren—about whom Bernadette was always prattling—than he had been when his own children were this young age. Their occasional presence in his house bored and annoyed him. The shrillness of their voices, the pounding of their feet on wood or marble, their empty faces, depressed him. There was a growing fad these days about "the Children," and he found it obnoxious and irritating, and when his friends spoke of their grandchildren he thought them fatuous, and knew that they knew they were.

Daniel and Joseph, nine and eight respectively, were already attending boarding school. ("Thank God," Joseph would remark.) The little girls, pretty but vacuous of face, were still at home. Now this was June, and the boys were in Green Hills and shouting "all over the damned place," thought Joseph. Why didn't that fool of a mother of theirs try to restrain them, or their governesses thrash them? When Joseph spoke of his grandchildren to their father, Rory, Rory would say with a curious smile, "I don't think they are too bad. Of course, they are not very intelligent, but neither is their mother. And you *did* want me to marry their mother, didn't you, Pa? Matter of inheritance. At least they are equal to Claudia now in their minds, if that is any consolation, which it isn't."

Marjorie's children, Rory would think, would be bright and witty and spirited, not "lumps," as Joseph called his grandchildren. Marjorie's children would be full of radiant mischief but gentle, kind, understanding, perceptive. Marjorie, Marjorie, my darling, Rory would think, looking at his children with their red hair and pallid blue eyes and big teeth. Rosemary was certainly no more aware of life than Ann Marie. Sometimes she drooled. "Blood will out!" Rory would say roundly to his father, with a strange grin. "Claudia's blood." But he could not understand why his father would then look so somber and turn away, for never had he suspected that Joseph had had any part in the annulment of his marriage. You can't make a silk purse out of a sow's ear, Rory would think, contemplating his children and their mother. But he did not speak of this to Joseph.

If only I could get rid of Claudia and not endanger my career, Rory would often say to himself. That foolish woman with her big backside and fat bowed legs and airs and graces! He no longer saw her charm, her formidable power of entrancement. He did not particularly like his mother but he resented Claudia's malicious imitations of her, the Irish imitations. Once he said to Claudia, "When your ancestors were grubbing for English squires and sawing wood my ancestors were noble in Ireland," to which she had replied, "Really! No one takes the Irish seriously. Hod-carriers, and such." She loved wine. She was always complaining of Rory's vulgar whiskey. "Whiskey is not civilized," she would say. "Only *brutes* drink it." Rory would look pointedly at her hands and she would darkly flush and hide them.

Now it was June and Rory and Claudia were in Devon —"to hear the nightingales!" Claudia would sing, throwing back her head and showing her huge white teeth. (Horse teeth, Bernadette would say.) Rory was in England for another matter, concerning the Committee on Foreign Studies, and was his father's emissary. "Gentlemen's affairs!" Claudia would carol in her infant's voice, when Rory went to London each week. They rented an estate in Devon each summer, for Rory, for a reason he would not explain to Claudia, refused to buy a house in England, though he remained in his father-in-law's house in London when he was in town. Unknown even to his father he would manage to visit Ireland for a few days also, and went to Carney where Joseph had been born. The poverty and misery of the Irish drove clefts about his mouth.

His children remained in the "Settlement" for the summer, ostensibly under the devoted care of Bernadette, their grandmother, who loved to parade them briefly before her friends, but only briefly. "I am not here very often," Joseph would say to her, "so is it necessary for them to be screeching in my house when I come? Send them home. I bought them a fine house, and let them stay there." The children feared him; they would look sideways with sly eyes at him, and hate him, but they obeyed him always and never muttered as they did with Bernadette. He could not endure the constant grins of the little girls, which showed the great white teeth they had inherited from their mother, and Daniel's whining and spoiled demands infuriated him. "I am afraid the girls are idiots," Joseph would say to his wife, "and Daniel is effeminate and Joe is a boor. Keep them far from me." But still, they were his grandchildren.

He came to Green Hills to be with his daughter, and with Elizabeth, when she was home. She did not visit him very often now in New York or Philadelphia or Boston. "I am almost sixty, my dear," she would say to Joseph, "and I tire easily now and travel is wearing. I don't know how you manage the travel so much, either." She had retained the figure of her girlhood, graceful and lissome, and Joseph thought she still looked like a young woman though the fine silky pale hair was more silver than blond now, and her complexion had faded. But her green eyes were pure and steadfast and calm. "You are much younger than I am," Joseph would say to her, holding her tightly in his arms. "You should not be so tired all the time." Neither of them spoke of Courtney, the monk in a cloister in Amalfi, who seldom wrote to his mother and then only to thank her for a gift she had made to his monastery. But Joseph knew Elizabeth's grief that the estrangement between mother and son had never been healed. She would say to Joseph, "I have no one but you, my dearest, no one in the world, no sister nor brother nor cousin nor nephew nor niece. I have only you." Her exhaustion seemed more pronounced each time Joseph saw her and he was becoming alarmed. Elizabeth smiled. "I am in perfect health, Joseph, but after all I am not young any longer."

It seemed to him this June that there was a transparency about Elizabeth which he had not noticed a month ago, a translucence in her face which made her appear ethereal. She had visited her doctor recently, she assured him, and her health was not impaired. Passion was not spent between them, but it had reached a stage of tranquillity, of profound acceptance, of absolute trust. They would sit, or lie, for hours, without speaking, their hands clasped together, and it was the only peace Joseph had ever known or would know. He thought of Elizabeth as his wife, and she thought of him as her husband. He was, as she often said, all she had in the world. Her one terror was that he would die and leave her. He had to reassure her over and over that he would not permit this, and he would smile. He came of a hardy, long-lived race, in spite of the early deaths of his parents. "You can't kill the Irish," he would say, "except with a bullet or far old age. We are made of steel and rope. We've had to learn how to survive." Elizabeth thought of Bernadette, fifty-five, coarsely vital if enormously fat and lumbering, with her heavy red complexion and loud voice and hair just slightly gray. Elizabeth had seen women like her in the markets of Europe, as strong as men and as vigorous. Elizabeth would sigh. Bernadette would live to be a very hearty old woman, into her nineties, eating and sleeping with zest and animal passion. Elizabeth had never known of Bernadette's great love for her husband which had never weakened at all through the years.

"You spend more time with That Woman than you do with your own family," Bernadette would complain to Joseph. "Managing her affairs," she would add hastily. "Doesn't she have lawyers, for God's sake? Yes, I know my father made you one of the executors, with his bank, but still— She lives like a nun in Green Hills. Her old friends hardly see her. She must be getting very, very old, and a recluse."

This June Bernadette said to her husband, making her voice regretful, "I have heard that Elizabeth is not very well. Some say she looks like a skeleton. She doesn't go—to town—much any more. Really. Well, at her age— Yes, I know she is younger than you, my dear, but then she isn't Irish. The English fade early. No stamina any longer. They're really decadent, you know. All the strength seems to have drained out of them. They're as bad, now, as the French."

Joseph thought of a recent meeting he had had with his colleagues in Paris. His face tightened. He said, "I think, in a war, that the English, whom I detest, would do very well. Very well, indeed. They are not so decadent as we'd like to believe they are. The Anglo-Saxon can be a tough old party. And the French, in spite of their everlasting wars, can be as bull-doggy as the English, if not more so."

"Well, there won't be any more wars," said Bernadette. It was nearly twelve years since Kevin had been killed, but she remembered. He had been the one child she had come close to loving, though she was proud of Rory and gloried in him. There were times when she was actually fond of him, for everyone spoke of his splendor and his glowing personality and his affable disposition and intelligence. "He is just like my father," she would say with pride. "He was the handsomest senator in Washington, and when he was governor no one could resist him. Rory is the very image of him. We expect wonderful things of Rory."

Bernadette could endure even Claudia when Rory was home, but now Rory was in London and Claudia was in Devon. That silly affected conceited creature! Bernadette thought. She gets worse every year. And that dark coarse complexion of hers, and her gloves! Common blood. Now she chatters all the time in French, to her children, and even her servants, and her accent is really abominable. Schoolgirlish. She may impress low and ignorant people, but not me, my girl, not me. And everyone knows how tight-fisted you are, except when it comes to your own clothes and jewels, and how you pare the cheese when you are here. Shameful. Self-indulgent creature, with no more brains in your head than a peacock. At least a peacock's pretty, which you aren't. Poor Rory. Bernadette knew that Claudia snubbed her. It made her at once hilarious and infuriated.

Ann Marie's doctors tried to soothe Joseph. It is true, they said, that she was degenerating physically, but she might still live for years. It is true, they said, that she had to be helped into chairs and bed now and could hardly walk. But her health was superb, considering everything. Her appetite was good, though her food was bland, like a young child's. But she thrived on it. Her mind, they would say, had not shown more degeneration, which was a hopeful sign. "Hopeful for what?" Joseph had asked them with bitterness, and they had not answered.

The elevator had been installed, and Ann Marie was helped into it by panting nurses assisted by the butler and the handyman, and she was taken into the gardens almost every day, to sit hugely in a chair, smiling in the sunlight and asking for flowers—which she promptly tore to shreds in fat rosy fingers, squealing all the time like an infant. She cried as easily and as loudly as an infant also, something which the doctors did not tell Joseph, and it was a mindless crying. It was only when she slept that she would suddenly awaken, wailing like a woman, and calling, calling in thick confused accents. Lately it had taken hours of cajoling—and sedatives—to soothe her back to sleep, and when she slept after the outbreak her face was the face of a heart-broken woman.

Joseph spent hours with her every day this June, reading books or newspapers in the shade of thick dark trees, sometimes listening to his daughter's babble, sometimes taking her hand, sometimes talking simply to her. She basked in his presence, and smiled, and if he had to leave her for a minute or two she cried, big tears running down her face. It would demand much of his strength to pacify her, while she clung to his hand on his return. Was he imagining it or was she showing a new fear this time, a new awareness of her desolation? He could not tell.

When he came to Green Hills he would invariably bring

his daughter a new doll, a new toy, which she would receive with delight and crows of pleasure. He had brought a Teddy Bear this time, which had been created in honor of Theodore Roosevelt. She hugged it to her flabby breast and murmured to it, and Joseph, with his book in his hand, watched her with a despair that never lessened. He knew, this June, that the long hope he had had was finally gone. His daughter had left long ago, on that ghastly day in the woods at the top of the hill. But, where had she gone? This piteous creature was not Ann Marie. It was only an animal which had long lost even a semblance of the slim shy girl of earlier years, except for the eyes. There, in those eyes, Joseph would often fancy, there was a distant tiny figure, the figure of Ann Marie, on a far plane, longing to leave, and as despairing as himself, lonely, isolated, existing in Limbo.

But still he could not bear the thought of this body dying, for the body held Ann Marie in thrall so she could not leave her father. She lingered, at an immeasurable distance it was true, but she lingered. At least, this was what Joseph believed and wanted to believe. When he looked into his daughter's eyes he would hail the infinitesimal figure of her in the clear pupil, and often he thought that she hailed him back, young, sweet, full of love and that delicate tenderness for him which he had known for years too brief and painful to remember.

There had never been a June day so perfect in temperature and shining quiet and fragrance, and the glistening green lawns spread all about the estate and the gardens shouted with roses and there was a singing fountain nearby, rainbowed in the sun. Leaf shadows fluttered over Ann Marie's face as she alternately murmured to her new Teddy Bear or crossly slapped it or hugged it. Her dry drab hair had been braided and then tied with pink ribbons, and the plaits lay on her gross bosom incongruously. She was fatter even than her mother, but her muscles were soft and weak and flaccid. Her legs, covered by a light blue rug, did not move. She wore diapers, like a baby. The big mansion gleamed like alabaster in the sunlight, and shadows tossed themselves radiantly over white wall and red roof and polished pillars. There was a breeze, and it made the far distant trees run greenly and nimbly up the hills.

Not even a gardener was in view, and the sunlight lay blindingly on the windows of the mansion and all was brilliant silence and peace. Joseph tried to read, sitting near his daughter on the lawn. Her babbling, softer now, was the only sound in that radiance.

Then Ann Marie was quiet. Joseph read. It was a confidential letter from Rory, in London, and though ambiguously worded it was important. His writing was small but black and concentrated, and if dispassionate to the casual eye Joseph could read between the lines. He almost forgot Ann Marie as he read.

Then he heard her say, softly and clearly, "Papa?"

"Yes, dear," he answered, not taking his eyes from the letter. Then suddenly it came to him, piercingly, that there had been a strange new note in Ann Marie's voice, aware, quickened, understanding. The pages of the letter fell from his hands to the grass as he looked up. Ann Marie was gazing at him, not with the rosy foolish fondness of all these years, the childish fondness, but with mature and sorrowful love.

She was transformed. The fat cheeks had flattened, the features sharpening instant by instant. The eyes grew large, widened, and Ann Marie was there, imminent, within touching distance. She had returned, was inhabiting her body again. A middle-aged woman looked at him, completely conscious, completely in the world, completely adult. The soul had come forward from vast spaces into the present. The loose mouth had dried, and all its contours were womanly and intelligent, and it was trembling.

But she was very pale. There was no color in her face now except for her eyes, those glistening and shimmering eyes which held Ann Marie.

O God, Joseph thought. O my God. His body began to shake; sweat broke out on his forehead. He leaned to his daughter to make sure, daring to hope, daring to accept this miracle. And she gazed back at him, faintly smiling, her eyes brightening moment by moment. "Papa?" she said again. The Teddy Bear slipped from her arms, her thighs, and tumbled to the grass, and she did not know it.

Joseph pushed himself to his feet, shaking like a palsied old man. He wanted to shout, to cry for help, to run for assistance. But he could only stand, clutching the side of his chair. It was a light garden chair and could not bear his weight, standing, and it fell away from him with a clatter, and he staggered.

He took a step to Ann Marie, his head roaring, his ears

clanging as if with bells, and he did not look away from her for fear that she would vanish again. He fell on his knees beside her. She held up her hands to him and he took them and stared into her face.

"Ann Marie," he said. "Ann Marie?"

"Yes, Papa," she answered, and smiled at him. The sorrow was deep in her eyes. "Poor Papa," she said. She took one hand from him and smoothed his white hair, and she sighed. Her pallor was increasing. There was a fine shine of moisture all over her face, and she had begun to pant a little, rapidly, with a shallow indrawing of breath. A deep pulse was thrumming in that massive throat.

"You've come back, my darling," said Joseph. His voice was dry and thick and choked.

"I never went away. I just hid," said Ann Marie. Her face was like white wet stone in the blowing shadows of the leaves. "I just slept," she said, and her hand gently smoothed her father's hair. "But I always heard you, Papa."

"You won't go away again?" said Joseph, and his heart was pounding so furiously that he felt faint. "You will stay this time, Ann Marie?"

She was shaking her head slowly and ponderously, but she still held his hand, and hers was cold and slippery in his. "Courtney is here; he is calling me. I am going away with him, Papa. He's come for me. You mustn't grieve. I am so glad to go. I stayed just now because I wanted to say goodbye to you, and tell you how much I love you and how sorry I am that I've caused you so much pain. Forgive me, Papa. I couldn't help it, but forgive me."

Then her face was brilliant with joy and love and ecstasy, and she looked beyond him and cried out, "Courtney! Courtney, I am coming!" Her eyes were like the sun, itself. She pulled her hand from her father's and held out her arms to something only she could see, and there was a murmurous sound of rapture in her throat.

"Ann Marie!" Joseph cried, feeling madness about him, and terror and coldness. "Oh, Christ!" he almost screamed, and took his transfigured daughter in his arms and pulled her against his chest. There was a quaking in him, heightened terror, a furious denial, and the bright day grew shadowy about him. Ann Marie resisted feebly, then she was still, and she collapsed against him and her head fell to his shoulder. He could no longer hear her breathe.

Then she sighed, and quivered all over her body, a long deep rippling of all her flesh. a final convulsion. She uttered one last sound, a fragile cry like a bird.

Joseph knelt and held his daughter to him, heavy against him, heavy in his arms. He said, over and over, "Ann Marie, Ann Marie." But only the wind answered in the trees. He began to stroke that fallen head on his shoulder.

Ann Marie Armagh was buried beside her brother under the pointed shadow of the tall marble obelisk, and the priest intoned, "I am the Resurrection and the Life—" The black grave yawned and the dully gleaming bronze casket was slowly lowered into it, sprinkled with holy water, and with earth. Bernadette sobbed beside her husband. Friends stood about them mutely. They watched Joseph, so gray and still and stiff, but so indomitable and grim and they thought —and later said to each other—that he had shown no grief at all and had not tried to comfort his wife. Unfeeling. they said. Yet it had been rumored that he had "adored" his daughter. Ah, well, it was merciful that she had died at last. Just a burden on her poor mother, who had been a slave to her all these years. The girl had never been very intelligent, and the accident had taken away her last glimmer of intellect. The roses, white and red and pink, covered the raw earth. Tombstones glowed palely all about them in the hot June sun. Leaf shadows ran over the grass.

That night Bernadette sobbed to her husband, "Yes, there is a curse on this family! I've known it for years! Now we have no child left but Rory. My last child!"

There was more fear in her than sorrow, superstitious fear. She said, "What will become of us if we lose Rory? I have such a feeling—"

"Damn you, and your feelings," said Joseph, and left her.

She forgave him, as usual, for only she knew how distraught he was, and how he prowled the house and the gardens at night, and how often he went to the cemetery.

A few days after Ann Marie had been buried Bernadette came to him in his rooms, carrying a newspaper in her hands, and her face, though swollen with weeping, was portentous and even a little excited.

"It is in the newspapers!" she exclaimed. "Courtney Hennessey, my brother, died of a stroke on the very day Ann Marie—passed away! Here, Joseph, read it for yourself! His mother was notified by cable. He's been buried in the monastery burial grounds. It's all here."

He took the paper in a hand that felt paralyzed and numb. He read, the lines blurring before his eyes. He said to himself, So, it was true. He came for her.

He threw the paper from him and turned away. "I feel sorry for her," said Bernadette. "He was all she had. My brother. I suppose I should feel sad, and I will have Masses said for his soul, but I really can't feel very much. Not very much. Maybe Courtney, and his mother, brought the curse on us." Joseph was leaving the room. "Where?" she asked him, but he did not answer. She began to cry, for she knew where he was going.

Chapter 15

It had been a hot July day and it was nearly sunset, but the sky was a darkish copper against which the trees were turned a fierce unnatural green, and the hills had become sharp and tawny. Everything stood out in that ominous light with a hurtful vividness and clarity and appeared too close, too insistent, too detailed. Every blade of grass was distinct, painful, like an emerald razor that could cut the foot, and the colors of the flowers in their beds had a nightmare intensity. There was a profound hush over all things; nothing moved, not a leaf, not a bud. Even the fountains in the gardens had become noiseless, and there were no birds in sight.

The countryman in Joseph knew that the absence of birds at this time of the day meant a storm. He went down the gravel path to the gate and then into the road, and down the road to Elizabeth's house. The copper of the sky had taken on a sheen, to the west, like brass. A hot breath, not a breeze or a gust, touched Joseph's set face, and it smelled of sulphur to him and burning dryness. He entered the gates of Elizabeth's house. He had not seen a carriage or a person on the road. All things had taken instinctive refuge. He heard, now, the explosion of gravel under his feet and it was like a shotgun being constantly discharged, the birdshot scattering.

There were white seats and tables under the heavy dark oak near the house, and there Elizabeth sat in a white dress too bright in that sinister illumination. She had a white shawl over her shoulders. Her pale soft hair, so severely dressed, her face and her still body, might have been the figure of a seated statue. She did not stir when she saw him. She only watched him leave the path and come towards her. Then, when he was almost before her she rose and threw herself soundlessly into his arms and they clung together without a word, held each other as if they were dying. Elizabeth's cold face was pressed against the side of his neck. His chest crushed her breast, his arms were like iron on her thin flesh. She held him as desperately. She did not cry or moan or utter a sound.

They did not even think of watchers, of curtains being held aside, of curious eyes looking. From her own window Bernadette could see those distant figures clenched together in an agony she was not permitted to share with her husband. She dropped the lace curtain and leaned her head against the side of the latticed window and cried silently, the slow and bitter drops falling one by one down her face without a sob. It was her child who had died, but Joseph had gone to a stranger for consolation, and was holding her as if they had become one motionless upright body, Elizabeth's white dress as still as stone. For the first time Bernadette knew that Joseph would never love her, and that he would most probably leave her. She let herself fall weightily on her knees at the window and bent her head on the marble sill and gave herself to sorrow as if she were a widow and her husband would not return. The tears made dark little stains on the marble and Bernadette pressed her open and tormented mouth against the sill, and she felt the slow agonized breaking of her heart. She had never known such abandonment, such suffering, such humble anguish, in all her life. There was no hatred in her yet, only a deep groaning.

A wild wind suddenly rose, and there was a flash of lightning, then another, and a stunning smashing of thunder. The brazen light was swept away by the turbulence of black clouds. Lightning flashed again and again, and the trees shook their green manes at it in fury. Then the rain came, sheets of glittering silver in the glare from the sky, pounding, rushing, roaring. It shut off all visibility. Bernadette lay supine and dumb on the floor of her room near the window, staring blindly at the terrible radiance that flashed over her.

Joseph and Elizabeth sat in the darkness and white fire that invaded the morning room. They sat side by side, their hands held together, staring at nothing, only half listening to the howling and raving of the storm, the wind, the thunder. They felt comfort in their nearness, and yet grief divided them so that they wanted to console each other and draw even closer. So Joseph told Elizabeth of Ann Marie's last words to him, and how she had cried out to Courtney and had appeared to "see" him, and that he had "come" for her. Elizabeth listened in silence, and now her eyes fixed themselves with a mournful absorption on Joseph's face, alternately hidden from her in darkness, and then revealed in lightning.

"I am glad," she said at last in her controlled voice which trembled only slightly. "I believe—I want to believe —that my son came for your daughter. Is there any other explanation for Ann Marie's knowing, and, as you have told me, her almost joyful dying?"

Joseph gently kissed her chilled cheek. He told her then of how his dying mother had apparently "seen" his dead father, who had come for her. Yet he knew surely that it had been only coincidence, the last desire of the dying. He did not tell Elizabeth this, but she sensed his resistance. "Don't you believe Courtney came for Ann Marie, Joseph?" she asked. "Don't you think your father came for your mother?"

He did not want to add to her pain. He hesitated. "I have heard of clairvoyance," he said. "It might have been only that."

"But what is clairvoyance?" she said. "It is a word, and we do have a habit of covering the inexplicable with a word and then thinking we have solved the matter by giving it a name. We have only added to the mystery. I believe—I believe— For the first time I truly believe. I have been only a nominal Catholic, skeptical and aloof, smiling at reports of miracles and simple mysteries, and now I think I was a fool. A sophisticated silly fool, who was too stupid to marvel and wonder—and hope. You have given me hope, Joseph, and please don't smile."

"I am not smiling," he said, and she saw his face in another burst of lightning and she thought he looked very ill. He thought of the three graves in the family plot, Sean, Kevin, Ann Marie, and the black earth which had swallowed those he had loved and he knew that he could not believe that they were more than their dead flesh and that they were aware, still, and conscious in some unfathomable place beyond the stars. It was against sense, against reason. A live dog, King David had said, was better than a dead lion, for he had being, and Sean and Kevin and Ann Marie and Harry and Charles had no being any longer, and had ceased to exist. He thought of Harry, and all the vitality and zest that had been Harry's and he thought of Charles, educated and intellectual and urbane. All that had gone out in the blink of an eye and there was nothing left, and no knowledge in them that they had ever lived. A rational man had to accept that, and not reach for mist and myths out of the torture of his heart.

But women were different. They had to be cosseted by comforting lies and made to believe the irrational. So Joseph said, "It may be true that they are together now, for Ann Marie had no way of knowing that Courtney was dead—" For the very first time Joseph thought of the mother of his children, and she had lost two of them, and she had loved Kevin and had been inconsolable for months, and he could hear her crying in the night, possibly not for her daughter but for the misery of the years of her daughter. Damn, he thought. I never even considered her. She knew, I am sure, where I was going tonight. Bernadette is no fool. Perhaps she had known about Elizabeth and me all the time. She would have had to be an idiot not to know.

He had felt compassion for Bernadette only on a very few occasions in their life together, a tight sour compassion. But now he felt a sick deep spasm of pity for his wife. He knew that she loved him, and really loved only him, and he revolted, as usual, against that love but now it was with pity also, even if that pity was tinged with his usual impatience. He had a horror of returning to that house and his wife, and confronting his sorrow again, his unbearable sorrow, in the silence of his rooms. He knew he would find himself listening for some sound from his daughter's suite, some childish babbling, some childish laughter, some cry or a call for him, as he had heard it for many years when he was home. But only the night would answer him. The rooms had been dismantled of their hospital equipment and utilitarian furniture, and had become, again, a pretty young woman's suite, to which Ann Marie would never return laughing from a ride on her horse, or singing at her little white piano, or running lightly over the polished wood. All at once the poor existing flesh which had been his daughter for years vanished from his memory, and it was the healthy shy Ann Marie he remembered now, with her soft little touches on his arm, her uplifted gentle face, her questioning dark amber eyes. At least that had returned to him like a ghost, but it did not relieve his grief. It made it worse, for it was as if Ann Marie, in full health and youth, had suddenly died and then had vanished, with her very voice in his ears and the very scent of her about him, and a last flash of her face.

The goddamn earth is one tomb, he thought, and we the walkers on countless graves. We would have been better if none of us had ever been born, to go through this, and for what? So we can have a few days of laughter, of hope, of ambition, of striving, and then nothing? Are they worth living for? I don't think so. What had Charles called this? "The dark night of the soul." But we have dark nights of the soul for the most of our lives, and only a brief dawn or two, or a little music, or the touch of a living hand occasionally, and I, for one, don't think it is worthwhile considering the whole of existence.

"Come to New York next week," he said to Elizabeth, but without urgency, for there was such a weight in his chest, such a despair.

"Yes," she said, and she knew what he was experiencing, for she felt it herself.

The storm was passing. Elizabeth did not ask him to stay when he stood up. But she looked at him and prayed as she had not prayed since she was a child, that he would be comforted, for there was no comfort any human being could give him, just as she could not be comforted even by the tenderest words. Only the dead could comfort the living, and they were silent. But hope was like a flowering star in her. She would think for hours of Ann Marie "seeing" Courtney and running out of her mountainous flesh like a bride to join him. She knew that Joseph had told her in order to comfort her, and she took his dropped hand and pressed it to her cheek and wished that he had this frail hope also. It was only a gossamer thread to hold on to in the dark whirlpool of grief, but it shone in one's hand and in one's heart and perhaps such fragility was the truth after all.

Joseph bent and kissed her with the gentleness of shared anguish, and then he went out into the warm diminishing rain and the almost violent freshness and fragrance of the new night after a storm. A full moon was now racing madly through tatters of black clouds, and Elizabeth stood at her door and watched Joseph as long as she could see him in that mingled white brilliance and utter darkness. She had willed him to come to her that night for she had been in frozen terror and despair, and she needed comforting and consolation and promises never to leave her. For she had heard, just before the news of Courtney's death, that she had inoperable cancer and that she had, at the most, only six months to live. Had not Ann Marie and Courtney died when they did she would have told him, lying in the strength and surety of his arms. But now he was as desolate as herself and he could not bear more grief at this time. She was thankful she had not told him. She would never tell him. Sharing suffering and fear did not decrease them; they only added to the burden, for then two suffered instead of one. I must have courage she said to herself, as she saw that Joseph was no longer in sight. What has to be will be and there is nothing one can do. At the end, we stand alone, just as we are born alone.

There was no sound except of servants in that great white mansion in the new night, and Joseph went upstairs. He passed Bernadette's room. The door was open and there was no light inside. He paused. Moonlight ran into the room and then was obliterated, but not before he saw Bernadette lying on the floor near the windows, not stirring, not speaking. He went to her at once and knelt beside her and then when the moonlight flared again he saw her wet and swollen face and the yearning and grief in her eyes.

He put his arms under her shoulders and drew her to him and held her, and she cried against him but said nothing, and he was ashamed and no longer impatient and he said, "There, there, my dear, it was for the best after all. Don't cry like that." But he knew that she was not at this moment crying for Ann Marie. He said, "Believe me, Bernadette, I will never leave you. I swear to God, I will never leave you."

The dinner bell rang softly, and at last they went downstairs together, hand in hand, and Bernadette's large red face was brighter and younger than it had been for years.

Joseph had sent a cablegram to Rory of the death of his twin sister and had urged him not to return at once, but to continue his mission. He had said in the cablegram that there was nothing Rory could do, and the death had not been unexpected, and that he was grateful that he had been in Green Hills when Ann Marie had died.

Timothy Dineen, solid, gray-haired, quiet and rocklike, had taken Harry Zeff's place in Joseph's affairs and now lived in Philadelphia. He had never married. He had loved Regina Armagh unswervingly all through these years, with the stubborn dedication of the Irish. He had not known until he was in Philadelphia that she had written to her brother twice a year, and that Charles had had to destroy the letters. He had not known, either, that Charles had taken to writing her briefly a few times a year, informing her of her family. As Joseph's confidential secretary as well as henchman and manager of The Armagh Enterprises now, he opened Joseph's letters in his absence. He opened Regina's, and after all this time he recognized the light delicacy of her writing. His heart jumped. He had thought of Regina as dead long ago, for Joseph had never spoken of her, and at first he could not think of her as Sister Mary Bernarde. As he began to read the letter, shamelessly, feeling the old pain and longing, he gathered that she had not known at all that Joseph did not read her letters. She believed only that he would not answer them, himself, but delegated others to do so. Apparently, however, Bernadette as well as Charles had written to her, and Rory, her nephew. She addressed Joseph with deep love and devotion as "my dearest brother," and begged, at the end, that he would eventually find it in his heart to forgive her for "any inadvertent pain I have ever caused you, my dear Joseph, in doing what I had to do. You are always in my prayers."

She wrote that Rory had written her of the deaths of Charles Devereaux and Harry Zeff and Ann Marie some time before, but that she, herself, had been ill for a number of months and could not send a letter of condolence. She did not mention the nature of her affliction, but here and there her writing wavered as if she were still weak and tremulous. Her whole letter was full of love and tenderness and consolation, and a simple faith which even Timothy found somewhat naïve and girlish. She did not mourn the dead, but only pitied the living for their loss. "The souls of those we love have ascended into the care and mercy of God," she wrote. "We must not trouble them with our tears and our grief. We must only pray for them and trust that they pray for us."

Timothy did not see the face of a woman of fifty-five, but the face of the young Regina, beautiful beyond believing, with that shining regard which was so moving and touching, and the mass of glossy black hair. He thought, She never lived in this world at all, at any time, and still does not live in it, but is kept from it not only by her cloister but by her innocence and faith. Perhaps only by her innocence. He saw that even if she had not lived in a convent when she was a child she would inevitably have been drawn to this life of seclusion—and flight. The world was no place for such as Regina Armagh. He thought of some of the nuns he had known during his own childhood, nuns like Regina. Perhaps the Church knew of these women and in mercy offered them a refuge from a battle and a struggle they could never have survived, for they were the eternal "little ones," in spite of intelligence and resolution. So the chronic yearning Timothy had known all this time lifted at last, and he answered Regina's letter as if he were a kindly older brother and said that Joseph was well. He took the simple holy card with its prayer, which Regina had sent to Joseph, and gently put it in his wallet.

He leaned back in his chair cautiously, for he was portly now, and he considered a rumor he had heard recently, that the Armagh family was "cursed." He could not remember who had mentioned this, and had laughed at it. All families, as they matured, suffered misfortunes and deaths, except for the very fortunate who were few. He smiled as he thought—I only hope the "curse" doesn't extend to me, as it seems to have done to Harry and Charles, who were outside the family! He chuckled as he blessed himself. As for Joseph, the extent of his fortune was staggering, even among his fellow "robber barons." That must be its own consolation, thought Timothy—to achieve what you have set out to achieve. It was probably the only consolation the world had to offer.

He considered again what Joseph had said to him a few days ago: "It is not too early to begin a boom for Rory for President in 1911. So, I want you to gather a competent staff in his behalf. No money will be spared. You have only to ask for it. You will manage his tours and go with him to the primaries. You will need several publicity men—hire them. And public relations men, too. Secretaries. Various subsidiary campaigners, who will arrange dinners, speeches, meetings with the public and politicians in all the big cities, and the smaller ones, too. Slogans. Posters. Interviews. Rory is personable. It is unfortunate that women can't vote, but men like him, too. He must be shown as the friend of the people— The brother of a war hero. Steve Worthington is boosting him from within—" Joseph paused and looked at Timothy narrowly, but Timothy's strong face was carefully bland. "You know what to do," said Joseph. "Every Irishman instinctively is a politician."

"It will cost a lot of money," said Timothy. "And you know, Joe, that the country is very 'anti-Papist.' Let just a whisper get out that Rory is going to strive for the nomination of our Party and there will be a national flood of vicious smears and hysterical accusations and denunciations. It will be worse than the anti-British propaganda in the country, and God knows that is violent and suspicious and hating enough. I've been doing a little quiet investigating myself, knowing that you've had the intention of Rory trying for the nomination of our Party. I've dropped hints here and there in Chicago, New York, Boston, Philadelphia, Buffalo, Newark, everywhere. And the response was very—shall we say—strenuous in opposition, even among the politicians in our Party, and even among Catholics. 'Does Armagh want to ruin our Party?' I've been asked. I've even been asked if you want to precipitate a religious war in this free land of ours. The prejudice is now even worse than it was thirty, twenty years ago, but you know that. We just aren't loved, Joe."

"I know," said Joseph with impatience. "But you've forgotten the priceless ingredient of any campaign: money. I'm willing to spend twenty, thirty, forty, fifty million dollars, and more if necessary, to make my son President of the United States of America. Even the Rockefellers wouldn't put up that much money for any of their sons. What do you think I've been living and working for?"

Timothy was startled at the angry question. He had often wondered what drove Joseph Armagh, and now he had an idea. It was a tight vengeful face that looked into his, the deep-set small blue eyes filled with fire and determination. Joseph's hair might be white, but it was still thick and vital, and the face was the face of a young man, and invincible. Timothy's father had been a jovial laughing Irishman, small and rotund and jolly, but he had often mentioned, with sad shakings of his head, the "black Irish," who had no humor but were relentless, full of mysticism, and imperious. "They never forget, Tim," his father would say. "Come what may, we never forget—a friend or an enemy. It's wise to keep out of our way. I am thinking, my bucko." But they have a terrible fascination, thought Timothy. They never surrender and so in a way they have grandeur as well as the Devil's own pride. The Irish kings must have been like this, until they were murdered by the English.

Timothy, who had never known want or adversity or starvation or cold or great sorrow or unbearable despair, suddenly understood and for the first time he was proud of his race who had survived all these things. He, himself, was somewhat of an Anglophile, and had felt himself congenial with the English, and England, when he had gone abroad. He had liked the aura of the enormous potency of the British Empire which he had detected in London. He liked the realism of the English, their drive for conquest and rule. He had admired the sensation of immutability in London, the incredible power, and the serenity which only power can bring. The English literally dominated the world. Gentlemen they might be, in their government and ruling classes, but they had an admirable sense of the realities and money and dominance, knowing they were unchallenged in the world. Unshakable materialists, they had created the industrial revolution. The throne of England was the center of man's universe, and the English did not care a damn for the opinion of "those lesser breeds outside the law." They preferred, if necessary, to be hated and feared than loved and merely accepted. Such pragmatism had appealed to Timothy.

Yet now, looking at Joseph Armagh, Timothy told himself that the Irish had all the qualities of the hated English, and something else that was intangible, but as formidable. It, perhaps, was the refusal to accept what others called the inevitable, and "limits." To the Irishmen—at least it was so in the case of many—there were no boundaries that could not be passed, no aspirations that could not be satisfied if one willed them strongly enough and never deviated or hesitated. Joseph Armagh was one such and Timothy began to believe that it was entirely possible that Rory Daniel Armagh could become President of the United States if his father wanted it. Joseph wanted it.

"I have half of Washington in my hand," Joseph said, and smiled sourly. "You know that, Tim. So, let us get busy. Money can buy anything. Do you think I've been idle all these years? I know what I know. So, get to work, Tim, and ask for anything you need."

"The Mugwumps and the Populists in Washington don't like Rory," said Timothy. "They call him a Monarchist, and worse. He has never yet supported a measure 'for the public weal,' as the Socialists call it. He has been accused of being an aristocratic 'member of the ruling classes.' He opposed the Child Labor bill and the unions, among other things."

"Now he is going to out-Bryan Bryan," said Joseph. "From this day on. Social legislation is going to be supported with zeal—and eloquence—by Senator Armagh. He isn't vulnerable like Bryan. He isn't a fool—and we have money. There is nothing about Rory which anyone can laugh at; he never makes an idiot of himself. He can't be lampooned; he lampoons back admirably. He has wit and appearance and intelligence—and money.

"Now, for our first move we will begin a campaign against prejudice—against any man by reason of race or religion. We will appeal to the famous sense of fair play in Americans. We will publish that Rory has been invited to meet the Pope—and Rory declined. Yes, I know that won't be true, but it will have an impact on Americans. Rory will mention that he is not in favor of 'parochial education,' though it should be tolerated in the name of freedom of choice. Rory will attack the men of great fortunes, 'who have no sense of obligation to their country and the Poor.' Rory will be the champion of the workingman, and social justice. He will be fervent. The people won't laugh. He has money. He has learned much. It is time for him to help himself, according to the advice I recently received.

"Rory," said Joseph, looking aside, his voice neutral, "will have the support of many of my friends. I can promise that. Rory will be more American than the average American. He will be as American as—"

"A five-cent glass of beer," said Timothy.

Joseph laughed, his low hard laugh. "Yes. Well, get to work as soon as possible, Tim. I've done a lot of the groundwork myself, over many years. Don't forget to mention Tom Hennessey, 'the friend of the people, the enemy of privilege,' Rory's grandfather."

He stood up. "I can tell you this again—my friends support Rory. They know what I want."

Timothy had known Rory from early childhood. He wondered if Joseph Armagh really knew his own son.

Chapter 16

Elizabeth Hennessey had not died in six months after all. She lived almost a full year.

She visited Joseph in New York and other cities only occasionally during the last few months of her life, for she was increasingly exhausted and neither lip rouge nor tinted powder could hide, any longer, the pallor that had come to her fine-boned face. Many lace ruffles at her throat and wrists, and the soft silk dresses she wore with their embroidered bodices, did not conceal too well her increasing thinness and fragility. The big hats, with their flowers and plumes, set high on her proud head, seemed too heavy for her strength. She endured the mounting and ruthless pain in silence, and when she met Joseph she was as reticent, calm, and smiling as always. She explained her few visits lightly. After all, she was growing old, and tired. After all, she had, as well as he, suffered a poignant loss in her only child, her only living relative except for a few distant cousins. She was a woman, not a man. She could not control her emotions, she said, as a man can control them. He had worldly affairs; she had nothing but her house and her gardens and a number of casual friends to take up her time. "I am bored, I think," she said once, and laughed. I am too tired to live any longer, she would say to herself, and in too much pain. The doctors had given her lozenges to suck when the pain was more intense than usual, and she took them sparingly, for they dulled her senses. She wanted to gather all the beauties of the world within the orbits of her eyes, and hold them, and the lozenges made her drowsy so that she slept and missed sunrises and sunsets and snow and rain and wind and the way a breeze turned a long lawn into the semblance of a sea, full of changeful colors. She was crushingly weary, and bereaved, but still the world was beautiful and it was all one could know and mysteries—or empty silence—lay beyond.

Joseph listened to all her explanations of her dwindling appearance, and her excuses, and insistently forced her to repeat what her doctors had said last about her "condition." She would lie easily then, saying that the "condition" was only aging, that she had never been of a strong constitution, but otherwise her health was reasonably good. He would listen, watching her closely, and then appeared satisfied. However, he would remark on her lack of appetite, apprehensively, and she would lightly change the subject.

She could never tell him, she thought. He had had enough suffering. She would die alone, and quietly. At the very least, that would be her last gift to him. She had never troubled him with her anxieties and her personal problems or her midnight fears, or any tempers or petulances or alarms, and she would not trouble him now.

Then it came to her one day in their suite in New York, as he sat beside her chaise longue and held her hand, that he knew, and that he had known for some time. She was startled deeply. She looked earnestly at his somber profile, suffused with the softened light that came through the lace curtains. He seemed sunk in himself. Yet she was aware that he was thinking of her with absolute concentration. The street noises were muffled; the shrieks and the howls of the elevated cars seemed far away. The hotel was quiet, for it was late afternoon and none was dressing for dinner yet or had returned from outings and shopping. It had been a warm early spring day and Joseph had bought her a bunch of yellow daffodils and narcissi from a street vendor, and they stood in a green vase on the velvet-covered round table where they often ate their meals together.

They had not spoken for some time. He sat like a devoted husband at her side, his opened book lying on his lean knee. He was staring at the opposite wall. Yes, he knew. She did not know how he had come to know, but he knew. The intuition of love had told him. It could never be deceived. Tears came into her eyes. But I am glad that I will be the one to go first, she thought. You are strong, but I am weak. You will bear this as you have borne other tragedies, but I could not have borne your dying. For that, if for nothing else, I thank God. All our lives are a giving up, one by one, of the things we love and enjoy, and finally there is the last abandonment and we are empty. But I have the memory of our love which I will take with me, if I may, for you are the only joy I have ever known, the only contentment and delight. And so, I am rich after all, richer than most. Others live lives of no color or vitality, and their existence is like nursery porridge, and as bland. But I have known all the heights that can be possible for a woman, all the raptures and the faith and the trust, all the excitements and the wonders, and even grief was bearable in your presence, my darling. I must not be greedy and try to cling to what I have had—for it is all fulfilled, full and overflowing. Nothing can be added. Nothing taken away.

For the first time since she had known of her mortal illness she was resigned, tranquil, no longer rebellious, no longer afraid.

He turned his head and looked down at her then, as if he knew this also, and their eyes met and held and everything they had been to each other, and all the long years, lay between them. They did not look away. Joseph's fingers tightened slightly on her hand, and that was all. She had accepted. He had been forced to accept. There was the difference.

Finally he said, "Elizabeth."

No, he must not ask. She put her hand to his mouth lovingly, and closed his lips. "It's all right, darling," she said. "Please don't say anything. It's all right."

She was so relieved that she almost cried. There was no need any longer for her to pretend, to paint her face, to try for soft animation, to force herself to laugh when the pain sprang upon her. So, she was granted this great mercy, knowing that he knew, and she no longer felt isolated in an iron cage of torture, afraid to cry out lest she hurt him. She had thought nothing could be added to what she had already had, but now she had this. She fell asleep, like a dying child who had been eased of suffering, blissful in the absence of agony, but prostrated, and he watched her until it was dark in the room and the street lamps outside began to bloom.

Her peace of mind made her seem stronger the next day, and they went to the opera for the last time together, and they knew it would be the last time, and so the music and the arias and the costumes were all the more intense to them and full of meaning. But they knew it was Elizabeth who sailed away in the swanboat and not Lohengrin, and they looked at each other and their hands tightened together. Yet never, not even in her youth, had Elizabeth looked so beautiful to Joseph, so translucent, so full of dignity and peace. He could not violate this courage by a single word, and he knew it.

He took her back to Green Hills himself the day following and she did not object, though this was the first time they had traveled home together on the same train. She was gathering last impressions as a gleaner gathers wheat against hunger and the night of hunger.

"In two weeks I will come back for a whole month," he said, when he left her at her door and her maid helped her across the threshold.

"Yes," she said, and her great green eyes were full of love and not sadness.

She had chosen her grave a month before, not near Tom Hennessey, who lay beside his first wife in a sunken grave near a heavy stone. She had bought a plot of land, and had even ordered her monument, to be graved simply with her name, the year of her birth and the year of her death. Oaks had always been her favorite trees. One stood there, ancient and mighty, and its branches would bend over her grave. She stood in the spring wind and was at peace, looking at the place where she would lie and sleep. When she had been young she had been horrified that people could casually choose their graves and what would be on their monuments, and could visit the spot. But now she felt comfort. It was beautiful here, and quiet.

A week later she died alone in her bed, at dawn, as she had hoped, and no one was with her. As the light increased a bolt of golden shadow shot through the window and lay on her sleeping face, and it was the face once more of a girl who had come home.

Bernadette telephoned Joseph in Philadelphia, to tell him that Elizabeth Hennessey had been found dead by her maid, that morning, and that the funeral would be held on Thursday. Bernadette's voice was subdued, though she was full of elation. Would Joseph return for the funeral? After all, he was Elizabeth's executor, and had managed her affairs.

"Yes," he said. "I will come." That was all. He began to work again. There was no feeling in him at all except a vast hollowness, a far desolation. He could not believe, in spite of all he had known for some time, that Elizabeth was dead, and that he would never see her again. His mind froze at the very approach to that reality, and then fell away. It was the way she had wanted it, he said to himself. He would go to Green Hills but there was no longer anyone there for him. Once he had been a stranger, staring at a stranger's house, and again he would be a stranger, and he would look again at a stranger's house, and as he thought he threw his pen from him and went to his apartments in Philadelphia and did not leave them until it was time to go to Green Hills.

Chapter 17

Before Rory Armagh had married Claudia Worthington he had attended informal classes in Fabian Socialism at Oxford. Had he not already been somewhat aware of the truth, as his father had told him and the "quiet, deadly men," the financiers, great industrialists, European and American aristocrats, bankers and the enormously rich, he would have been confused, incredulous, and then finally appalled, in spite of his natural cynicism and realistic approach to life.

For it was confirmed to him that the so-called "class struggle," of which he had heard in his secular schools, was an artificial struggle, created and manipulated by the "Elite," in their drive to power and control of all the world. There was really no quarrel between the American working-classes and their employers—the middle-class—for they had a common objective, which was work and survival and a small measure of happiness in a world that offered very little to anyone. They did not want power. They wanted peace, shelter, sufficient food, a sum left over for tiny pleasures, some area of privacy, families, and personal dignity. Above all, they wanted freedom to choose their lives, their God and their modest ambitions. They were not warlike or contentious. They were simple men. They did not particularly yearn for immense riches, and so were content. In their simplicity, in their great numbers, in their common beliefs and desires, in their native decency, they had weight and were formidable. Therefore, potential tyrants were impotent to use them, for they had the forthright man's skepticism of "ideals" and ideologies and "causes," and mass protests. If their lives were hard, it was the way of life itself, for competition and the struggle for survival were innate in all nature, beast, plant, man, and they knew this. Millions implicitly believed in their religion, that man was born to eat his bread in the sweat of his face, and labor itself, however onerous at times, had the dignity of natural causes. The admonition of Judeo-Christianity, as reuttered by St. Paul, was honored and understood by them: "He who does not work, neither shall he eat!"

If they thought of their "betters" at all—the men of inherited great wealth, and the bankers and the financiers and the "robber barons," it was not with envy or resentment, but with a sort of respectful amusement. William Jennings Bryan had not overly impressed them. But this normal health was only in America now. Socialism had eaten into the heart of France and Germany, into England even under King Edward, and into Italy in some quantity. France, therefore, had lost her status as a first-class power. Bismarck had almost destroyed Germany with his Socialism, but the Germans had hard-heads and had begun to recover by 1900 under a more intelligent Kaiser. Russia had been untouched by Socialism, due to the vigilance of the Czars and the Duma, always suspicious of West European fantasies and confusions. But the disease of Socialism was not easily eradicated, for it was the weapon of the "Elite" against all mankind, and was supported by "intellectuals," full of envy and greed, and opportunists.

The "Elite," through their prophets, Marx and Engels, had created the "class struggle," in order to divide, weaken, and finally conquer all nations. They were very clever. Tell the working people that they were unbearably oppressd, incite envy in them and lust, and you set them apart from their employers. On the other hand, secretly tell the employers that unions would destroy their profits, their very survival, and that the working class was bent on Socialism, anarchy, indolence, and loot, and you divided the employer from his workman. You created a climate of hatred, distrust, exigency, and enmity—the class struggle. You had prepared the field for dragons' teeth, for wars to deplete a nation's strength, for exploitation, and final despotism, and the "tranquillity" of slavery under a benign "Elite."

There were very few who knew that Socialism, and its daughter, Communism, were the oldest, most primitive, forms of government in the world, and had been invented in the Stone Age by cave-dwellers who lived in communes. Mankind, through eons, had advanced from Socialism-Communism into a dignified civilization where men were comparatively free. There were inequities, certainly, and injustices, for man was imperfect and would always be so, but left alone in an air of increasing freedom and choice and these would be more or less corrected, though not to an impossible Utopia. Human nature remained, and it was the one immutable in the world. America, though afflicted by child labor and untenably low wages, mostly imposed by the great barons of industry, was feeling her way surely if slowly out of the major injustices. She had laughed at the Socialists, the Mugwumps and the Populists, though admiring them for their frantic vehemence and color, and had realized their ideas were absurd and dangerous to the survival of the human race and the free spirit. Accordingly freedom was growing in America, and the desire for peace, and her prosperity stunned the world. Where men were free they could make a choice, and when they chose with common sense and awareness—as most did in America—they had natural power and liberty and mobility and strength.

So America was the huge impediment in the path to power of the "Elite." She must be infected with Socialism, and the "class struggle." How could this be accomplished, when Americans were the least revolutionary people in the world? Through wars, as well as through insidious and fiendishly intelligent propaganda from the capitals of Europe and from New York and Washington, all supported by limitless wealth and sleepless direction, chosen politicians and "intellectuals."

When he had been a youth at Harvard, and had learned of Socialism, Rory had asked himself: It seems incredible that the very rich would join forces with an ideology like Socialism which threatens their very wealth and their existence. He had been only eighteen then. But slowly, through his father and the men he had met over the following years, he had come to understand that there was no quarrel at all between the very rich and powerful, and Socialism. In fact, Socialism was their aim. So Rory understood, with good-humored cynicism, why his teachers did not directly attack the owners of great wealth. They were the tools of the "Elite." It was not against the wealthy that Socialism was directed, but against the masses of the people, and their liberty. All protests to the contrary, the truth remained. Socialism was a planned society for complete slavery for the majority of the people. It promised the safety and tranquillity of the grave, the dissolution of the human spirit. All who denied this were fools, or secret plotters. Never before in the world's history had there been so concentrated, so potent, a conspiracy against mankind, and it flowered in the twentieth century. Moses had shouted, when he had freed his people from slavery: "Proclaim liberty throughout the land, unto the inhabitants thereof!" But liberty was the foe of the "Elite." It must be destroyed, and barbarous Socialism re-established.

When Rory returned from Europe, after his sister's death, he had a long and quiet talk with his father. "I attended a session of Parliament in England, a full-dress session. It was said that Germany, with her superior industry and mechanical genius, was 'invading' the British 'traditional world market.' "

"Yes," said Joseph.

"So," said Rory, "there will be a war."

"Not immediately," said Joseph. "Perhaps by 1914 or 1916. I have seen the blueprints. But America can't be got into a war without money. So—there must be a Federal income tax. You have known this for years."

Rory nodded. The underlids of his eyes relaxed, artlessly. "The big move," he said. "Wars and taxes will create dissension in America, and weaken her. We've talked about this often, haven't we?"

"Yes," said Joseph. He stared at his son gloomily and did not pursue the subject. But Rory said, "And eventually we will be bankrupt. Very clever, isn't it?"

At the opening of the campaign to secure the nomination of his Party for the Presidency, Rory said, "I know all the objectives. I agree with them without reservation."

"Good," said Joseph, and his face was gloomier than ever.

"I don't think I will get the nomination."

"You will," said Joseph. "There are millions behind you."

And the Right People, thought Rory, and smiled at his father. "Faustian money," he said.

"Rory, remember this: No man ever failed by holding his tongue. You must accept things as they are."

"Oh, I do, I do. I assure you, Pa, I do."

He smiled at his father amiably. "It is really a struggle between money and blood, isn't it? And isn't it fortunate that the masses will never know—fortunate for us?"

"No man ever died of a surfeit of money," said Joseph.

"Remember that. In comparison blood is nothing—if it flows into money. Blood is cheap. Money is all-powerful. I once knew a very rich man, who also, though it seems unbelievable, had principles. He had a son full of idealism and faith in human nature, and a contempt for the money his father had earned and hoarded and increased. So the father said to his son, 'Tomorrow you will not receive your large allowance. I want you to go out into the city with empty pockets, for one week only. You love humanity; you've told me of natural compassion and generosity among men. You will go out as a beggar, to your famous fellow man.'

"So the son, smiling from ear to ear, and armed with his silly faith in his brother, left his father's house. I am sure it is sufficient to say that he was turned away from every door, rich or poor, and berated as a beggar. He could not afford to take a horsecar to apply for a job, and so walked until his soles were thin and broken. But as he had no skill, no trade, but only book-learning, he could not get a job. He suffered mockery and hate and hunger, for he had no money, not even for a meal in a saloon. He came face to face with the malice of humanity against the helpless, the cruelty which is part of the nature of man, and the scorn for the indigent. He finally was given a broom, at ten cents an hour, and told to sweep a factory. He discovered that his loving brother was an animal, and worse, and had no pity or charity.

"He returned to his father's house."

"A sadder if a wiser man," said Rory. "An old aphorism, and true."

"It's so old a story that it has become part of all our beliefs. Money is all, Rory. There is nothing else. The sooner you realize that the sooner you will become wise."

"I know," said Rory. "You've told me often, and quoted the Bible: 'Money answereth all things.' God bless money."

Claudia said to him, her greenish-brown eyes wide and stretched and glowing: "Isn't it delightful? You will be President of the United States! We will live in the White House! I will have such galas, such dances in silver slippers, such artistic performances, that they will dazzle everybody with their sophistication. After all, we are still a crude nation. It is time for Culture in political affairs, and discrimination, and the encouragement of the Arts."

"I'm not even nominated yet," said Rory. He rarely

talked with his wife. He was now as indifferent to her as his father was indifferent to his mother. At least Ma is not a fool, he would think. But my wife would take honors in a school for imbeciles. The Phi Beta Kappa of the feeble-minded. But Claudia was a marvelous hostess, gracious, charming, smiling, greeting, and she had fine taste and a certain shrewdness. She captivated almost everyone, including cynical politicians of the opposite party. She chattered in French to the French Ambassador, and delightfully tried to chatter in German to the German Ambassador, who was overcome by her charm, the scintillating aura that seemed to surround her. She wore gowns as if Worth had created only for her and no one else. At times she affected a beguiling shyness, and everyone spoke of her "jejune modesty." That all this concealed a powerful ego, a cold-blooded drive for eminence, was known to very few. Surely such a gentle lady, with such a flair for the fitness of things, incapable of being gauche though she was an American, refined, cultivated, sophisticated and fascinating, must have the soul of a "dew-drenched daisy." When Rory heard this he would laugh inwardly, and then go off to his lady of the day, the week or the month, where he could be assured of honesty, at any rate. Even honesty could be bought with money, if there was sufficient money, and temporary fidelity. But Claudia was a fraud even if she did not have the wit to realize that she was fraudulent and merely an echo. Papier-mâché, Rory would think of her. Nicely colored and jeweled with automatic gestures and graces, but papier-mâché for all that, except for native greed and expediency. No one can match her for that!

He was too good-tempered and cynically tolerant to hate her, but he came very close. So long as she did not try to inveigle him into what she called "significant conversation," he endured her. But when she pretended to intellect and seriousness he would stare at her with crescent-eyed and smiling incredulity, until even she was embarrassed and burst into tears. He had an idea that she loved him as much as she was capable of love, but that did not touch him. Claudia had few capabilities, and what there were were directed mostly towards herself.

Claudia was positive that he would be nominated as the candidate of his Party, though Rory was skeptical in spite of his father's power and money. But as the "boom" gathered weight and persistence throughout the country, as the money was spent on scores of managers and other politicians, and dozens of newspapers hailed him nationally, Rory had to admit that his father's dream might be possible. Money was all. It accomplished miracles, even in a nation obdurately obsessed by "Papism," and prejudice. The opposition newspapers began to mention his religion less and less, as if they were ashamed of their bias.

He began to be called "the Senator of the People," though few there were who could recall and point out anything he had particularly accomplished. Rory, under astute direction, decided to rectify this. Timothy Dineen, with a wry and understanding smile, consulted with him constantly. Timothy said, "I disagree with Abraham Lincoln. You can, if you are smart enough, fool all the people all of the time, and they will love it. Don't smile, Rory. You are not the worst politician in America. You are not even a first-class scoundrel. You never stole anything or accepted bribes. Tut, tut."

Rory had many consultations, too, with the Committee for Foreign Study, the American branch of which he had come to call, in himself, The Conspiracy. They found him serious and apparently dedicated to their international aims, respectful, pliable, intelligent, and agreeable. "We can make you President," Jay Regan said to him, "if we find you reliable. So far, Rory, I believe you are more reliable than Old Joe, your father, who has a nasty Irish tongue on him, and an irony which is unpredictable—and unsettling. You must never upset our foreign friends, you know. They have no sense of humor."

"Pa has a gallows humor," said Rory. "He likes to exercise it. But you've found him amenable, haven't you? Yes."

It was then that Mr. Regan began to study Rory. The young man was intent on being nominated, and elected. The question was, to Mr. Regan: Why? The usual answers were inadequate. There was something else. Mr. Regan distrusted intangibles. He also distrusted human nature and that worst of all manifestations of human nature: The capacity to employ independent judgment. He suspected that Rory was exercising that, though he had no proof.

Once Rory had said to him affably, "What if the newspapers learn something and the whole—thing—is exposed?"

"They won't expose it. We own them, Rory. They wouldn't dare to oppose us. Well, if there is even a hint, we can always say, 'Not we! The Jewish bankers are guilty!'

That will take care of everything. People will believe anything about the Jews. It exonerates them."

Rory thought. He remembered that the British government had blamed everything. including Acts of God, on the "detestable Irish rebels," and so had diverted wrath. He gave Mr. Regan an angelic smile. This disturbed Mr. Regan more than anything else.

There was a private railroad car for Rory. "The people affect to love rugged simplicity and democratic tendencies in their rulers and politicians," said Joseph. "But in fact if a man is simple and rugged and honest—and has money and position—they will despise him and consider him less than equal. After all, they reason, would they be simple and rugged and honest if they were in his position? No. They would be ostentatious and grand and overbearing. This man is not so. Ergo, he is no better than they are, and why should they honor him?"

So Rory had his private railroad car, and another car for his managers and secretaries and publicity and public relations men. Cars on other trains were filled with his "advance men," who went all over the country to prepare the way for whom they secretly called "the young Master," with snide chuckles but also with fawning. They engaged halls, were interviewed by reporters as skeptical as themselves, bought full pages of advertisements in newspapers, had brochures printed and posters. Rory's colorful face appeared everywhere, on lampposts and on walls and on fences, smiling, twinkling, handsome, engaging. Recalcitrant county chairmen, state chairmen, mayors and governors and delegates of the Party, were quietly bribed, threatened, promised, intimidated. The bribes were very large, the intimidations and threats not idle ones, as they soon learned. Rory had not one, but several campaign managers. They announced his intention of appearing in all the primaries. They talked of his personable appearance, his wit, his intellect, his devotion to the People, his determination to rectify "all injustices," his detestation of exploitation, his contempt for "men of great wealth who care nothing for their workmen but use them as cattle." He, though the son of a powerful and wealthy man, sought public office not for gain but for "equity" and a patriotic zeal to serve his country and his fellow American.

Rory came under tutorship by realistic politicians. He was not to be another Bryan, a gaudy and vociferous fool. He was not to stand on equal footing with the mobs who came to hear him in parks, on the streets and in halls. He was to be kind and gracious, attentive and sympathetic. But not overtly democratic. That would earn him contempt. At all times he was to be the gentleman, approachable to a certain extent but not all the way. Men liked leaders, not equals. They loved heroes, but not the rank and file even if heroes. They wanted men they could trust, not men who walked shoulder to shoulder with them. They loved jokes, but they also wanted dignity and the aura of potency. His dress must never be casual, rich but not overly rich, stylish but not extreme. Everything he wore was examined carefully before he put it on. As his thick red-gold hair was striking, he would take off his hat regularly in the open and let the sun, or lamps, shine on it. When he spoke—from meticulously written speeches prepared by astute men—he must let his natural eloquence add the emphasis, but he must never be coarse. An air of candor, yes, and at times even a little folksiness, accompanied by charming winks. But never familiarity. If questioned by men too familiar and too swaggering, he was to smile coolly and answer with formality and wit. At all times he must exude strength and purpose. If gibed at for his religion—which was never mentioned if possible—he was to say something to the effect that did not all men honor one God and worship Him, and was it not distinctly un-American and undemocratic to decide for all men in what way they should so honor and worship? He was to assume a regretful expression, as if the questioner had displayed boorishness and bigotry, which were not the traits of Americans at all. "We are all Americans. We honor God and our country, whether we are Presbyterians, Methodists, Catholics, Baptists, Jews or Episcopalians, and even to hint that any of these do not love their country devotedly and purely is a dishonor to all Americans."

Fundamentalist parsons in many backwoods communities did not believe in Rory's sincerity. If he were to be elected President—"God preserve us from that calamity!" —the Pope would take up residence in Washington, in the White House itself, and would soon dominate the Senate and Congress, and bring in the Spanish Inquisition and thumb-screws and the wheel, and within a year America,

Protestant America, would be a satellite of the Vatican. "Did not our ancestors flee such as these?" they cried from their pulpits. "Did they flee that their grandchildren should be the slaves of Popism and idolatry and priests?"

Rory's men used this very wicked bigotry for their purposes with an artfulness that was admirable and subtle. They even publicized the ravings of bigots, however obscure, and countermanded them by asking the American people to feel shame that they had such in their immaculate and tolerant midst. Multitudes did, indeed, feel shame and on seeing Rory for themselves, felt an emotional surge of affection and protection for him, to prove to themselves that they were just men and not ignorant fools full of hatred and vindictiveness. The other Party, therefore, was disarmed. If they mentioned Rory's religion it was only in passing, but the newspapers excoriated them, at least many of them did so to prove their tolerance. The opposition Party was left almost without an issue. It did mention that Rory had done nothing notable in Washington as a senator, but Rory's men cleverly used that very lack as propaganda. He had done nothing harmful to the People, though he had been in a position to do so!

A notable and famous minister in Philadelphia did timidly pose the question: Would Rory's first allegiance be to his country or to his religion? It had been put in private, but his colleagues publicized it. (They were amply rewarded.) The man had been notable for his intellect and integrity, his justice to all American faiths, his kindness and charity. It was unfortunate that he had slipped this one time, and he regretted it immediately as unworthy of him. But Rory's men blazoned it throughout the country via the press, and the minister was condemned vehemently. He was "intolerant" and "un-American." His own people ostracized him. When he was approached sympathetically by sweating bigots he repudiated them with anger at himself and disgust with them, and so earned more enemies. He never regained the authority and status he had once possessed, and he felt it a just punishment for his foolish and private lapse. He had many friends who were Catholic priests, and they were indignant, but he begged them not to intervene.

Claudia and her children were pressed into service. She appeared with Rory and her brood on the observation platform of his private car, a delectable and modish sight with her children clustered picturesquely about her. Audiences

were charmed. She had a natural flair for publicity, and so
was in her glory. She preened, she smiled, she cast down
her eyes modestly as befitting a woman; she breathlessly, in
her infantile voice, said she was not a feminist and did not
believe in votes for women, and was only a Wife and
Mother. She would look with passionate love at Rory, beside her, and touch his arm gently with her gloved hand.
But she never intruded, never asserted herself, never expressed anything but the most proper opinions. She asked
for votes for her husband, "because I know his deep love
for his country and for Social Justice, and peace and progress. He has talked with me often about these things, after I
have put the Children to bed and heard their innocent
prayers. We are simple people and speak to you simply." It
was excellent propaganda that this appeal for simplicity
was not accompanied by drab clothing and simplicity. Having been tutored well, she spoke shyly with farmers, workers, employers, and employees, about their "problems."
Rory would rectify them. He would be no "tool" of established and venal politicians. He would Serve his Country
and its Sons. He was beyond politics. He would be the
President of the People, without distinction of Party, race,
or creed. He had taken on this burden not for money or
position, for he possessed both in enormous quantity. He
asked only to give his life and his talents to America.

Even the suffragettes, who resented her as an anti-femi-
nist, were charmed by Claudia. She gave large teas for
women, though they could not vote. ("Why bother?" she
asked Rory's men. They told her seriously that women,
who could not vote, had great influence, however, on their
husbands. With unusual perspicacity she told them, "I
don't, gentlemen," and looked honestly sad. But these intervals were rare. Her eyes were fixed on the White House.)

Bernadette, too, was pressed into service. She was a far
better politician than Claudia. No one had to tell her what
to do. Fat, "unpretentious," an obvious matron and Mother, she was forthright and zestful, and appealed to Mothers,
who in turn appealed to their husbands and harassed them.
(She never made the mistake of talking with members of
Altar or Rosary Societies, and never talked with Catholic
women exclusively, if ever.) She talked only of the Children to women, and told them of her son's concern about
child labor and the exploitation of children. "Men, with all
their business affairs, are sometimes ignorant of these

things. It is necessary for us women to advise them." She hinted that Rory was really in sympathy with Votes for Women. Her teas were lavish and delectable and attended en masse, and her burly laughter and "honest folksiness" was applauded in many newspapers. Her father's record in the Senate was mentioned, though vaguely, for no one could exactly remember his record. However, it was hinted that it had been exemplary and guided by his deep concern for the American Character and Justice for All. Mr. Lincoln had often confided in him. (This little bon mot was not repeated in the South.)

If Rory ever talked—as he did privately—with members of the Holy Name Society and the Knights of Columbus, it was not mentioned in the press.

The duality of his nature was an asset to him. In speaking before exigent and brutal men he was honestly exigent and brutal. He could be rough, brutish and cynical when necessary, and even vindictive, and then with others he was suave, evasive, refined, casual, easy, intellectual. All his faces were equally sincere. His advisers admired this protean quality in him, but never let it be inadvertently displayed before the wrong audiences.

He was inexhaustible. He seemed never to tire. If his youth was sometimes mentioned doubtfully, he would counter that wisdom did not necessarily come with age and that perhaps this should be the Era of Youth. Freshness. A new approach. An Awareness that America was a young country, and why should not youth speak, too, in the conclaves of national affairs? After all, he would say with a jocular twinkle, youth was a malady that time would cure. In the meantime youth had something to say to America. He would quote the Bible—carefully, the King James Version, to the effect that "old men had dreams and young men had visions." Both were necessary. America had been born of dreams and visions. Without them, a nation was dead. "A people without a vision must perish." This was Rory's own touch, and it aroused the increasing admiration of his cohorts.

He never appeared to weary. He might talk at midnight, and then be fresh to speak at dawn at railroad stations, on the platform of his private car, to hordes of farmers and workers. He was eloquent and fiery, humorous and cajoling, amused and concerned. Sometimes his own men asked each other, "What is really driving him?" They never knew.

But there were those who suspected, knowing both Joseph Armagh and his son. These, however, were not among Rory's audiences. They met in New York and Washington. They read long obscure letters from Europe, and quietly discussed them.

There was seemingly no end to the millions of dollars Joseph poured out for Rory. They were not spent ostentatiously. But the power and weight of those pouring millions had their effect. "We will win," said Joseph to his son, and Rory began to believe it. "I have nothing left but you," Joseph would say. "Nothing."

Chapter 18

Joseph said to his daughter-in-law, "Are you going to Boston next week when Rory speaks there?"

"If you wish," said Claudia, who found it all exhilarating.

"I don't know," said Joseph. Claudia was far too stylish and sophisticated—at least in appearance and manner—for Boston. Boston was not susceptible to charm. It also did not like the Irish, though the Irish were growing in power and wealth in that city. But that very wealth and power was suspect. However, Claudia was not Irish, and she had Manners. Joseph considered it. Joseph had begun reluctantly to admire Claudia, who had the genius always to say the right thing at the right time. The voters were devoted to her. Perhaps Boston, who knew her assumed aristocratic pedigree, might be influenced. It was worth the chance. There would be teas for the ladies. Men were never invited to them, of course. It was all so charming, so feminine, so delicately urgent, so unobtrusive. So appealing, so shy, so modest, with the ladies all in silk and lace, carrying parasols and wearing dainty slippers. Joseph decided that Bernadette was not to go to Boston. She was too earthy for the ladies of Boston, though those ladies were earthy and ruthless and greedy enough. Even Irish ladies might be offended by Bernadette, and if invited would consider themselves her equal and therefore not be taken seriously.

Then Joseph received an abrupt if courteous invitation to attend "a very important meeting" of the Committee for Foreign Studies in New York.

He more than suspected that he had not been invited to the last four meetings, and to a certain extent he knew why, or thought he knew why. The Committee was apolitical. It supported any politician who would serve their purposes, and the purposes of their European colleagues. To them there were no Democrats or Republicans, no Populists, or "Wobblies," or Farmer-Labor Parties. There were only potential and obedient servants, whether Presidents or obscure delegates, mayors of big or small cities, governors, congressmen or senators. Every man was carefully scrutinized, his past records studied, his bent analyzed. On their judgment a man prospered politically or he fell ignominiously. They had supported Rory for congressman and senator, and had approved of him, or rather had approved of his father, their colleague. They had said nothing against Rory on his bid for the nomination of his Party. But insofar as Joseph knew they had not overtly approved of this either. Their whole attitude had been tentative. They had talked frequently with Rory and had been apparently impressed by him, and had complimented Joseph on his splendid son. "Nominal Catholic or not, he could be elected " they had told Joseph. "If he is—correct." Joseph had no reason to believe they had suddenly found Rory "incorrect."

Still, he was apprehensive. However, his relentless drive made him adamant, though he admitted he had no real reason to "set my back up." Everything had been smooth and perfect. A member of the Committee had even written a few of Rory's most telling speeches, which he had delivered with eloquence and elegance, and with spontaneity. Why the hell do I worry? Joseph asked himself on the way to New York. If they have changed their minds—which is not possible—it will mean nothing to me. My son is going to be President of the United States. He is all I have left. He is my justification.

"My son is going to be President of the United States," he said to his colleagues in New York, after the rich luncheon, with the best French wines, in the building. "I have nothing more to say."

He had stood up in the meeting room, tall, spare, ascetic, with his severe and hollow face under the thick mass of his white hair. His blue eyes were burning, and he had looked at them all, man after man, and they had felt his force and now his dominance.

"Who the hell is Woodrow Wilson?" he said, and he spoke with cold contempt.

They told him again, reasonably, quietly, and without reticence. They never spoke in ambiguities.

Woodrow Wilson was an Innocent. They had watched

and studied him for many years. He was naïve and an idealist, and an "intellectual." Therefore, he was their man.
He would never know who manipulated him. They had had
many talks with him recently, and had impressed him with
their solicitude for America and in turn he had impressed
them with his solicitude. He had quietly congratulated
them on their publications, "concerned with the advancement of America."

"I bet," said Joseph. "Did he ever guess who we are?
And what we want?"

They ignored that with pained expressions. It was their
intention to make him feel uncouth, which he did not.
They were gentlemen, they implied. They regretted that he
was not a gentleman. Joseph smiled. He looked at Jay
Regan, who soberly winked at him. But he knew in spite of
the apparent camaraderie that Mr. Regan would stand with
his colleagues, and not with Joseph Armagh. Together,
they had far more money than did Joseph, and far more influence. He was only a member, after all. He was not the
Committee.

Recent events were all recounted to him, in modulated
voices, as if he had violated decorum out of gross impudence and idiocy, and that all that had been said here before had escaped his feeble comprehension. He sat down
and listened with a parody of attention. They were not disturbed. They did not even look at him but stared down at
the papers before them on the great oval table, while the
Fifth Avenue traffic outside bellowed and the late summer
heat struck at the windows.

It was their intention that no Republican would be elected in 1912, and that no Democrat except of their choosing.
Mr. Taft was "impossible." He was not "amenable." He
had quarreled with Mr. Roosevelt, who had recently shouted that Mr. Taft was a "hypocrite." "My hat is in the ring!"
Teddy had cried. "The fight is on and I am stripped to the
buff."

"I know, I know," said Joseph with impatience. "We are
to divide the Republican Party with two candidates: Taft
and Roosevelt. And Rory, then, is supposed to win."

They ignored him with elaborate patience. "Mr. Roosevelt will run on the new Progressive Party ticket. We
coined a phrase for him, 'the New Nationalism.' The voters
are intrigued. They love the word 'new.' Mr. Roosevelt,
himself, has said he wishes 'a Square Deal.' It is a poker ex-

pression, and liked by the voters. People love him. He has a marvelous grin. Infectious. We have suggested a phrase for him: 'The Bull Moose Party.' He is, to use his own word, 'delighted.' "

"Yes, yes," said Joseph. "This was supposed to be in behalf of my son."

They pretended they had not heard him.

They recounted to him all they knew about Mr. Wilson. He had established the first potent Socialistic cell in Princeton in the early 1880s, when he had been a professor there. A fairly rich man, and a scholar, he had been most emotional concerning Karl Marx and had understood all that was necessary for the emergence of an "Elite" in America. He distrusted the common man, though he championed him, not having known, through all his six universities, in which he had studied and taught, any common men at all. He was an aristocrat by birth, and that made him respected by the common man. He feared and hated the "common men" who composed Congress, and he had quickly taken up what had been suggested to him concerning the power reserved to Congress for the coining of money. "Money trust!" he had proclaimed. He had declared himself in favor of an independent Federal Reserve System, a private organization, which would have the supreme power of coining the nation's money.

"I know, I know," said Joseph. "We have been working a long time to take away the power of Congress to coin money, and to give it to bankers, who will issue money by fiat. If you have anything new to tell me, please do so." His heart was beating fast with rage.

"We made him Governor of New Jersey."

"Really?" said Joseph, raising his white-russet eyebrows. "I didn't know that!"

They sighed. They hated sarcasm. They particularly hated irony and had always deplored Joseph's tendency to that.

"Mr. Wilson," one gentleman said, "understands that America must leave her traditional isolation from world affairs. We must now emerge as a world power."

"In short," said Joseph, "he will help get America into a war."

He was sorry immediately that he had said that, and many pairs of eyes looked at him in hurt rebuke as at a child who had been repeatedly told a self-evident fact.

"Mr. Wilson," said one gentleman, "understands that America must no longer be indifferent to World Injustices."

Joseph nodded. "Good for Mr. Wilson. He is now in our kindergarten, isn't he?" He was so infuriated that he lost caution. "I've missed a few meetings. Is Germany to be the 'enemy' or is France? Or England? I suspect Germany, of course."

"The Kaiser," said Mr. Regan, pursing his lips under his ambushing mustache, "is really an insufferable man."

"Teddy Roosevelt likes him," said Joseph. "Is that why he isn't going to get our support?"

They did not answer him. One said, "Mr. Wilson has shown us his program for what he calls 'the New Freedoms' for America."

"I thought the American people had all the freedoms they could handle," said Joseph, more and more aroused. "What else do they want?"

He was more than a little taken aback when they laughed decorously. "They don't want freedom, Joe," said Mr. Regan kindly. "They want Caesar. But you know that. We've talked about it often enough all through these years. So, we will help them. We will give them Caesar. Mr. Wilson, a gentle and unsophisticated man, who will follow our directives. He won't know he is Caesar, but we will. For—we are Caesar. Come on, Joe, you know that has been our aim for a long time. What's the matter with you, Joe?"

Joseph stood up again, and leaned his clenched fists on the table. "So Wilson is to be our candidate, our mannikin. Our Little Boy Blue who blows our horn. Mr. Wilson, the Defender of the common man, whom he despises. Mr. Wilson, who never did an honest day's labor in his life, with his hands, knows nothing of labor."

He looked at them all. "What do the Democratic bosses think about all this?"

A few gentlemen chuckled softly. "We haven't yet told them what to think, Joseph."

Then Joseph made a fatal mistake out of his anger. "Perhaps Rory can tell them the truth."

A deadly and absolute silence filled the great paneled room.

No one looked at him. The air became heavy, immovable, still. Joseph felt it. He began to sweat lightly. He felt a chill on his flesh. God damn me, for my Irish tongue, he thought. No one looked at him. He slowly sat down, but his clenched fists remained on the table.

He began to speak quietly. "Rory has followed all orders. He is speaking all over the country in favor of the Amendments for a Federal income tax, a Federal Reserve System, and the direct election of senators by the people, and not appointments by State Legislatures. You know that. You've read his speeches in the papers. He followed all your orders. All your directives. He has never deviated. You have written speeches for him. You have never, until now, indicated that he was not acceptable. Why now?"

Mr. Regan spoke, after a glance at the averted eyes around the table. "Joe, let us be reasonable. Rory is magnificent. But, he is young. And the young are naturally rebellious—and have their own ideas. Mr. Wilson will unquestionably take our orders, given discreetly through many politicians we know. For instance, Colonel House. He is our man, as you know. Mr. Wilson has had a long apprenticeship—in Socialism. He is ripe for us. Rory is not. Joe, again, let us be reasonable. In eight years, most probably, we will reconsider Rory. That will make him a little more mature, a little more understanding of our aims."

Joseph said, "You've talked often to Rory. Why have you turned against him?"

Again Mr. Regan consulted half-averted eyes. "Joe, I hate to say this, but we have a feeling that at this particular time Rory is not quite—reliable."

"And Wilson is, whether he knows it or not? To put it briefly, he is stupid enough, naïve enough, to swallow anything you tell him. Any noble phrase, any high-sounding aphorism: He will adopt them. You are afraid Rory won't. You think he will laugh, and then do what he wants.

"You've considered Taft. He is an old and able politician. He knows quite a lot about us, I have heard. He wouldn't be amenable. He would think, first, of America. He is suspicious. Teddy Roosevelt is too flamboyant. He might have individual thoughts, too. He is an internationalist, as he has proved. But still, he would think of America in sober moments, when he wasn't off hunting. So, Taft and Roosevelt won't be considered. They are, potentially, 'unreliable.' So is Rory."

He stood up again, and gathered all eyes to him. "I'm wasting time. I have only this to say: I am pouring out my whole fortune to get Rory nominated and elected. I don't give a damn for our European colleagues, who want Wilson, as you have told me. This time I will act independently. Rory is going to be President of the United States."

They listened and there was another silence. Then Mr. Regan said, "Joe, this is no time in history for personal vendettas. I know you have a vendetta. Wait, Joe. Suppose Wilson gets two terms as President. Then we will heartily reconsider Rory. What more can we promise you, in all reason, in all justice? We haven't abandoned Rory. We ask only that he, and you, wait for eight years. Come on, Joe. Be sensible."

He looked at them thoroughly. He said, "Compared to our European colleagues, we are little children. They have centuries of political manipulation, terror, revolutions, and chaos behind them. They have centuries of tyrants. They are old. They are very potent, more potent than we are. They know what they want. It is you who are following orders, not giving them."

They did not speak. Joseph drew a deep breath. "When are they going to move against Russia?"

It was as if he had uttered an obscenity in the presence of clergymen.

"A silly question, isn't it?" he asked, when they did not answer or move. "It is planned, isn't it? So I have been told. Yes, I am wasting my time and yours. But again I must tell you. Rory is going to be President of the United States, if it costs every penny I have, and even if I have to shout the truth from the rooftops and alert America—"

"To what?" asked a gentleman in the softest voice.

"To you," said Joseph. Without looking at them again or speaking, he left the room. He was sick with rage, but not frustrated. He felt no fear. He knew what he knew.

No one spoke after he left. One gentleman gently ruffled some papers. They avoided each others' eyes. A few sighed over and over. They looked at Mr. Regan. He sighed also. Then he put out his hand in an old familiar gesture, one known to the ancient Caesars.

Chapter 19

Timothy Dineen had kept Joseph well informed and up-to-date on Rory's publicity tours throughout the country, via newspaper clippings, editorials, Rory's speeches and the public reaction to them. Rory, himself, had coined a phrase: "The New Vision." It had taken the fancy of tens of thousands of people. The New Vision was all things to all men. If some caviled at this or that, they approved of other areas. The employer of many little children in mills and factories might purse his lips at Rory's demand that children not be exploited "for gain and small wages and deprived of their childhood and education." On the other hand that employer was appeased by Rory's fiery exhortations against "governmental interference," growing ominous lately, in the realm of private enterprise. "Private enterprise has made us a great and prosperous country, for individual judgment is superior to the conclusions of cloistered bureaucrats." He denounced the Trusts, and on the other hand he defended the right of companies to merge "so that they may operate efficiently, increase employment, set standards that are just to the employed and the employers, widen markets so that all Americans can participate in a growing era of mechanization and luxury, advance foreign trade and compete in world markets." He expressed sorrow at the "huge Tariffs which deny Americans foreign goods," and then he would suggest that Tariffs be lowered so that cheaper foreign goods would be accessible to the people at large. He laughed at the idea that lower-cost foreign products would put American workmen out of jobs. "Aren't our American workmen superior in skill and productiveness to foreigners?"

He teased, cajoled, laughed audiences out of ill-humor and suspicion, was serious and sober and light by terms, depending on the temper of those he addressed—and he always knew in advance. He was controversial only when those who listened to him were controversial and agreed with him. He was pacific or denunciatory, abusive or placating, as the occasion called for, and his natural intelligence informed him what to say.

He always concluded in this fashion: If nominated and elected by his Party he would not hide from his people in the White House. He would be open to all suggestions, "even from the most humble." In fact, he invited suggestions from workers and farmers. "All would be given the utmost and dedicated consideration. After all, aren't you the bedrock of America? Whose opinions are more valid?" He never failed to end with a passionate appeal to patriotism, national honor, and power. The band that accompanied him everywhere would follow his last words with a joyous—and loud—flourish of trumpets, and a military march, preferably one by Sousa.

Rory always said, "I appeal to the Conscience of the American People. I rely on their sound judgment, no matter their religion or position in society. I appeal to no Special Interests, or Groups. I am an American."

They were the words of a born politician. Only Rory knew that he meant them. It was not odd, considering human nature, that this sincerity had less weight than his adroit half-falsehoods, his appeal to local prejudices, his wooing of those despised, his evasiveness, and his deliberate use of his innate charm and handsome appearance. For when he spoke sincerely he was too simple. When he used his actor's rococo dissimulation he was far more believable.

Americans loved to be told that they had pre-eminence in the world of today, though Rory knew quite well that America was still a second-class country, unsophisticated, naïve, innocent, childlike, the butt of the jokes of the British and Austria-Hungarian and German empires, the derision of France. She was as immured from reality as was the lowering Russian Empire and its Oriental splendor and lingering despotism. Americans knew little of Europe, but Europe knew a disastrous lot about America.

He knew that when he had been a child in school the British had been hated vociferously, and always suspected and lampooned in the American press. To some politicians it might have been strange—as it was—that in very recent years the British were no longer so compulsively loathed. But Rory knew. The "hands across the sea" had been invented by the Committee for Foreign Studies, at the behest of their colleagues in all the European capitals. He also knew why, for his father had told him. I wonder, by God I do, what would happen if I told the American people the truth, Rory would think to himself, with deep wry humor. But he knew that no politician ever told the people the truth. He would be crucified. The people wanted fantasies and flatteries and dreams and excitements and color. There was one thing on which Rory was determined: If he were to be elected President, America would not be engaged in foreign wars. But of that he did not tell his father. Rory knew when to hold his tongue which unfortunately Joseph did not always know. Rory had no history behind him of starvation, exploitation, hatred, homelessness and oppression, and so he could easily refrain from lashing out at dangerous moments. Once Joseph had said to him, "It is said that the happiest nations are those who have no history. That is true of individual men, also." Rory had guessed the implications of that more than his father knew or understood. Joseph had manifold drives, many of them deeply and profoundly emotional. Rory had but one drive, not rooted in emotion but in reason and exigency. He could even be objective about the Committee for Foreign Studies. He courted it and deferred to it charmingly and obediently. He used its material. He thought he had deluded it.

He received a telegram from his father when he was in Chicago. Rory and Timothy Dineen were to meet with Joseph in Green Hills before the speeches and appearances in Boston. The telegram was urgent if terse. Rory raised his eyes at Timothy, and Timothy shrugged. "Old Joe must have some information we don't have," he said.

So they went to Green Hills.

Joseph had told Timothy something about the Committee for Foreign Studies, and here he had been discreet for even Timothy must not know too much. But Timothy guessed a great deal with his Irish intuition. He had "felt" a certain subterranean stir in the world, a certain heightening and obscure and hidden movement. The resentment against "the rich" in America had always been there, born of envy and inferiority and failure, just as it was naturally prevalent in other countries. That prejudice had given rise to the war "against the Trusts." (Timothy knew that the Trusts were not disturbed by this.) It was all talk, all propaganda, designed to soothe the envies of the proletariat and make them amenable. But now there was a quickening against "the powers that be." There were the Populists, the "Wobblies," the I.W.W., and now the Socialists, who had elected a number of men, especially from the Middle West, to Congress and the Senate. Timothy did not believe in "natural trends." He knew such trends were always carefully and deliberately invented and manipulated by anonymous and faceless men. If there was growing Socialism in American it had not happened by itself. It had been intruded delicately, and successfully, for a purpose which was still obscure, though Timothy had some thoughts on the subject. He had mentioned them idly to Joseph, but Joseph's face had remained carefully noncommittal. "Don't look for bogeymen," he told Timothy. "Don't search under your bed of a night." He smiled dourly.

Rory and Timothy met with Joseph in Joseph's study, all doors closed, all voices quietly modulated. Rory, who had not seen his father for some time, remarked to himself how the Old Boy had not been diminished in his almost visible aura of potency and power, focus and implacable strength. He had suffered not only the loss of two beloved children, and his best friends, and the earlier loss of his brother and sister: He had had to endure the loss of his mistress whom Rory suspected had had more of his father's love than even his children. Yet, if he suffered the bright and inextinguishable agony of loss, which could never really be dulled, he did not show it as he greeted his last son and Timothy. He was as quiet and as contained as usual, and as direct, as undramatic and as ruthless.

The first thing Rory noticed on entering his father's study was the "arsenal" on Joseph's desk. He knew his father kept guns but he had never known Joseph to wear one. Timothy looked at the array of very modern pistols on the desk but did not remark on them. He appeared to accept them as ordinary. There were a dozen of them.

There were brandy and whiskey and beer laid out. Joseph waved his hand at them, and at the glasses. Rory and Timothy, suddenly subdued—and always eying the arsenal —filled glasses. Then Joseph filled one for himself, and squirted soda into it. This was most unusual. Joseph, to their knowledge, rarely drank.

"I wouldn't have called you here if it weren't necessary," said Joseph. "By the way, Tim, you are a genius. The way you have handled Rory's appearances has been masterly."

Timothy, white-haired and stocky though he was now, blushed like a young boy. "Joe, we Irish are born politicians. We have an instinct for it. It doesn't call for too much effort, you know. We love it. It's our climate."

He toasted Joseph and his eyes were affectionate. "I think we will win in the primaries," he said, "and so the Party will have to take due notice. We've had a little trouble here and there with County Chairmen and State Chairmen—always jealous of their tiny powers—but we—ah—overcame them. The picture gets clearer all the time."

"Thanks to money," said Joseph. Timothy momentarily looked pained. One knew these things but was it always necessary to mention them? Joseph's irony was sometimes misplaced and unsettling. Then Timothy laughed, and Rory laughed with him. "Even Our Lord would not be heard nowadays unless He had a good Press," said Timothy.

Timothy did not always understand Joseph. Yet he did understand the sudden darkening on Joseph's face, the sudden instant withdrawal, which were the result of ingrained Irish prudery, and a hatred—even in Joseph, if unsuspected—of blasphemy. Rory considerately studied his glass. Timothy was abashed. He felt his own crudeness, though he had heard worse among other men. The three Irishmen were silent for a while. "Sad but true," said Timothy at last, and knew he was forgiven, and it amused his Irish irony. An Irishman might declare—and with full personal conviction—that he was "no docile son of the Church," and that he was an atheist and thought "tradition" amusing. He might declare himself emancipated from "priestly superstition." But let even a faintly blasphemous word be uttered, a single deprecation of that which was held holy by most men, and the atheistic Irishman bristled as if just that morning he had made his confession and had received, though probably he had not done this since his childhood. It was not a matter of mere teaching. It was a matter of the spirit, to revere the unknowable, to give it silent honor even if the mouth declared it deserved no honor. It made even the churchless Irishman fight to the death against English iconoclasts and military might.

Joseph began to talk. "What I must tell you now could be extremely dangerous if anyone outside this room knew of it. I repeat, it could be very dangerous, even fatal. So listen carefully."

He told them of his meeting with the Committee for

Foreign Studies. Rory listened alertly, with all his concentration. Timothy listened and thought: I suspected what they were, all the time, in spite of Joe's offhand remarks. The hot last sun of summer poured through the windows, as tawny as a lion's pelt, and it shifted imperceptibly as Joseph spoke. Rory and Timothy asked no questions. They said nothing, demanded no clarification. They knew. Lawnmowers clattered outside. There was a distant opening and closing of doors. The trees outside glittered as a breeze stirred them. The draperies at the windows inhaled and exhaled. There was a smell of cut grass, nostalgic and sweet, and the aromatic odor of dust and chrysanthemums. From far away a locomotive howled, melancholy and saddening. Bernadette had begun to play her favorite piano in the music room. She was one who liked the modern music, and her favorite was "Alexander's Ragtime Band." But now she was playing a sonata of Beethoven's, and the strong if mournful notes pervaded the atmosphere like a premonition, like an evocation of things past and things to come. For some reason that music disturbed Rory more than what his father was telling him. For all at once, incongruous, not relevant, he saw Marjorie Chisholm's face, and could not understand why it should come into his grave awareness now, for he had not thought of Marjorie acutely for more than a year.

Then Rory said, as his father stopped speaking, "So, I am now unacceptable to them. I would be unacceptable even eight years from now. They want Wilson—that innocent—who will tamely dance to their music, even if he doesn't know it is their music. They are afraid I wouldn't. How they guessed, I don't know."

Joseph said, fixing his small blue eyes on his son: "What do you mean? 'Guessed?' Is there something you haven't told me?"

Rory said quickly, "I am just conjecturing. I feel they would be doubtful of my—compliance. They ought not to worry. You've read my speeches. I know they've read them too." He hated himself for that slip of his tongue. He smiled at his father ingratiatingly. "I've never been there without you. Have I said anything 'wrong' to them?"

"No," said Joseph, but he continued to eye his son.

"It seems incredible to me," said Timothy, "that men in London, Paris, Rome, Geneva, and God knows where else, can decide who is acceptable as an American President!"

Joseph gave him a flashing and contemptuous glance, as if an infant had babbled without knowing what he had babbled. He said to Rory, "So, there it is. In 1885 Wilson attacked congressional 'power,' as he called it, with contempt and aristocratic disdain, when he taught at Bryn Mawr. In his subsequent collegiate career he 'democratized' learning and spoke of 'serious readjustments in national government.' What that had to do with academic learning and teaching—for which he was paid—no one has as yet questioned. He has intimated at all times that the American Constitution is 'outmoded,' or at least needs to be 'reformed.' He is an open enemy of conservatism, though he has not yet stated what conservatism is, except that he apparently fears it is rule by the people and therefore despicable. Champ Clark and Underwood, of our Party, laugh at him, but I hear he has William Jennings Bryan, that clown, behind him. Wilson knows no more of human nature than do the dogs we have around this house. He has eclectic notions, all rainbowed, and all unrealistic. Wilson talks of a 'national renaissance of ideals,' but when it comes down to it he also talks vaguely of 'trusts and money interest and privileged Big Business.' Phrases. Words. The Party distrusts him. They don't like prissy fuss-budgets, who don't know what the hell they are talking about, and they distrust large nebulous exhortations. All we know up to now is that he is and always was an immured man, and is totally unaware of practical issues. Therefore, he will be amenable to suggestion, if it is high-flown in words and empty of real content. Therefore, he is the ideal choice of our—friends— we don't want men they suspect might think, and irritate them."

"Do I understand that this is the first time they have moved in the direction of electing our Presidents?" asked Timothy.

Joseph hesitated. "Well, they had something to do with Teddy, who suddenly realized—something—and so after that was not acceptable. This is their first bold move to elect an American President. They are putting a lot of money behind Taft and Roosevelt, to divide and weaken the Republican Party and assure the election of Wilson. Taft is against removing the power of Congress to coin money, against—to some extent—a Federal income tax, and the direct election of senators. That was enough to assure enmity, and dismissal. So, they're backing Roosevelt, so Wilson will be elected. It is that simple. He is their man, because he will never know who pulls the strings. He will be surrounded by his fellow 'idealists,' all selected by the Committee."

"Will it do any good for you, Joe, and Rory, to expose this?"

Joseph looked at him incredulously. "Are you out of your mind? How many of the Democratic Party know anything of all this, anyway? They would laugh. So would the country. What! A quiet non-political Committee in New York determining who shall be elected or not elected? No one would believe it, true though it is. Americans love fantasics, but they are suspicious of any mention of 'plots.' They think it is 'foreign,' part of old monarchal institutions. Why, aren't Americans free men, free to choose their Presidents? Don't they vote in primaries, and choose? The fact that they are given few to choose from doesn't disturb them; they don't even think about it. They are persuaded that these men are 'the best the Party has to offer.' Democrat or Republican: They have no choice. For God's sake, Timothy, where have you been all these years, when you have been working for me?"

"Touché," said Timothy, wincing.

"If anyone told the American people that the Committee in New York—which is directed and ruled by the international bankers of Europe and America—chooses their rulers, they would say he was insane. Europe! Who cares for Europe, full of kings and czars? The new American arrogance is equal only to American naïveté and ignorance. And these things are encouraged."

Rory had listened in comparative silence, frowning, bent forward over his glass. "All right, Pa," he said at last. "Do you want me to withdraw, and the hell with the country?"

Joseph frowned deeply. "I don't know what you mean by 'the hell with the country.' What has the country got to do with it? I want you to be President of the United States. I will make you President of the United States. That's what I told them in New York. I will spend the last penny I have."

He touched the guns on his desk. "I want you and Tim to carry one of these all the time. I want your immediate bodyguard to carry them, too."

Rory sat back noisily in his chair and stared at his father

in smiling disbelief, his eyes inverted crescents of laughing incredulity. "For God's sake, Pa, who would take a pot shot at me?"

A heavy darkness spread over Joseph's face. He said, slowly and quietly, "I don't think you've really listened after all, nor listened in New York, London, Paris, Rome, Geneva. I think it was all wasted. You are as naïve as the average American, I am sorry to say. Have you forgotten Lincoln, Garfield, McKinley, all shot by those the newspapers called 'anarchists?' Did you think, as the newspapers said, that these murderers were insane zealots of something or other, and acted alone? Do you think these assassinations occurred in the tiny little minds of obscure little men, driven only by private individual passions? I thought you were taught better. The hand that fires the gun was directed from far away, perhaps in some European capital. When Czar Alexander was assassinated by an 'anarchist,' for God's sake, it was Communism which ordered it, and you've been told that a dozen times by me. It was planned months, years, before. He was a humane man intent on reforming and establishing the Duma and relieving the Russian people of tyranny and serfdom. So—he would remove the cause of catastrophic revolutions. So—he had to die. Christ! You knew that."

" 'Elemental, my dear Watson,' " Timothy murmured, and looked hard at the guns.

Rory studied his father. His ruddy color had diminished. He said, "Pa, if they want to get me, to kill me, they know they can surmount any guards or guns we have. They can kill me anywhere—if they want to. On the streets, in halls, even in church, or in my bed."

"Ah, so you've finally realized," said Joseph. "You've finally accepted what they are. But that doesn't mean they will 'get' you, as you say. I hate slang. Forewarned is forearmed. I don't think they will dare— They will only move very soon to discredit you, to make fun of you, to pour out more and more money for Wilson, to use propaganda against you. Your religion, for instance. Or, maybe not. There are millions of Catholics in America, of every race. They will find something, no doubt, besides guns. You aren't the President, yet. Still, we must be prepared. Rory, take one of those pistols. You've been taught how to fire."

He remembered what Mr. Montrose had taught him. He

said, "Never raise a gun unless you intend to shoot. Never shoot unless you intend to kill."

"Oh, Jesus," Rory muttered. But he took a compact heavy pistol and dropped it into his pocket. He felt foolish. But Timothy seriously studied the guns and finally selected one. Timothy looked straight at Joseph and said, "I will watch Rory every minute, Joe."

"Good," said Joseph. He did a rare impulsive thing. He reached over, shook hands with Timothy and Timothy reddened with pleasure.

"And the bodyguard must have guns, too," said Joseph. He refilled his glass, and sipped at it slowly. "Tim, you might mention to the bosses in Boston just exactly what that poor serious innocent of a Wilson is. Do they want a dreamer as President, who will disrupt the country? Do they want a man who will meddle in international affairs, to the detriment of America? I have prepared a whole dossier here, about him. Talk to the men in Boston. There are a lot of Irish there. They suspect high-flown idealists, men like Wilson. They don't like to be pushed. They suspect Europe. Without revealing your sources, you can have quiet talks with them. Hints. Raised eyebrows. Jokes. Ridicule. Have copies of this dossier made. Distribute them widely, before Rory speaks there."

He looked at his son and Timothy with care. "No man wants to believe in the reality of grave issues. He wants to believe only in frivolous ones. We will try something unique. We will give the voters a grave issue, even if their instinct is to follow soap bubbles. We will show them that the Pied Piper, the singer, Wilson, will lead their children to death. Be discreet. But not too discreet. Don't reveal your sources. But let your sincerity shine out. You know the truth. Imply it."

The atmosphere in the room was so heavy that Timothy tried for flippancy. "And may God have mercy on our souls."

Chapter 20

Joseph had carefully refrained from appearing with his
son anywhere. Some newspapers might mutter about "The
Armagh Enterprises, many of whose activities are reputedly nefarious," but they could never come out bluntly and
say, "Joseph Armagh travels with his son and finances his
public appearances everywhere." No one doubted the truth,
but as Joseph appeared uninterested in his resplendent son's
journeys all over the country, made no telling comments
which could be adversely misquoted, gave no interviews
and only smiled briefly at reporters who sometimes waylaid
him, and talked publicly with no one, he could not be
openly accused and pointed out and denounced. Only once
did he say to a Philadelphia group of reporters: "My son,
Rory? Oh, he's a born politician. I find politics dull myself,
now. If our Party wishes to nominate him—after all, I believe he made a good record as congressman and senator—
that is entirely in the hands of the delegates next year. No,
I don't at this time plan to attend the convention. No, gentlemen, thank you. I have nothing more to say." They did
not believe him, and he did not care. At least, they could
not quote him.

This did not prevent a number of influential newspapers
from implying that millions of dollars were being spent on
the senator in an effort to influence the primaries and the
delegates the next year. They had suddenly become bold
and contemptuous, and not with good-natured lampooning
such as calling Rory "The Golden Boy" as they once had
done. Lately editorials had lost their usual American
humor and had turned to rough derision and vicious cartoons. Joseph was not in the least surprised even when
papers who had written favorably of Rory were now expressing "serious doubts," as they called it, and some were

definitely hostile. "The Circle" had begun to work. The attacks on Rory, and his father, would increase in intensity until the nominations. On the other hand various newspapers became warmer in their admiration for Rory. Two can play at this game, thought Joseph. Still, it was not something to ignore, and Joseph prepared to take action, and began to plan. The bastards had not yet taken over America completely, though time was running out.

He decided that Claudia was not to accompany Rory to Boston. She was entirely too exotic for Boston ladies, after all. It was not that she was too stylish, too elaborate, or too obviously sophisticated. It was that she was too charming, though she was incapable of summoning up that charm at will. It flashed out like an enthrallment, when least expected, and dazed women as well as men. Boston ladies were a different breed.

"Thank God for small mercies, then," said Rory piously to Timothy and winked. Timothy smiled at him warningly. "No high jinks this time, boyo," he said. "We will be demure and serious as all hell in Boston, and high-minded, subdued, modulated, intellectual if you feel pushed, historical always, and above everything else, the Proper Little Gentleman."

"You don't have to tell me," said Rory. "Didn't I live for years among them, at Harvard, and—and in Pa's offices? I'll convince the Brahmins that I do, indeed, wash behind my ears and can sip sherry as elegantly as they can—God damn it—and my boots can be as discreetly polished. But don't forget the Irish there, Tim. A few little airs, 'The Wearing of the Green.' No, too brash, too much like Old Syrup, who dances an Irish jig on any table at the snap of a finger. How old is the old bugger now, anyway? He's got 'Kathleen Mavourneen' for his song, and I favored that for myself. How about 'Killarney?' No. Something light and haunting—"

"Like 'The Band Played On'?"

"Shut up, Tim. This is serious. How about 'The Harp That Once Thro' Tara's Halls'?"

"A Harp for a Harp," said Timothy.

Rory laughed, his deep ringing laugh, and Timothy would always remember it, for it was musical and manly and without affectation. "Now, that's it," said Rory. "Have posters made, strictly for the Irish section. 'A Harp for a

Harp.' It's good, Tim, really good." He sang a few bars, and for some reason Timothy's bright skeptical eyes became a little dim.

> "The harp that once thro' Tara's Halls
> The soul of music shed,
> Now hangs as mute on Tara's walls
> As if that soul were dead—"

Rory said, "Talk about the Israelites weeping in Babylonian captivity. Every Irishman always weeps for Ireland, and his 'exile,' but damned few ever go back, do they? But it does the heart good to mourn. All warm and sad and moist inside. The Jews and the Irish are the most sentimental people in the world, but you can't fool either of them. I've found that out about sentimental people. Yes, 'a Harp for a Harp.' "

"Well, just remember, even in Boston, that you are an American," said Timothy.

Rory gave him a sharp quick look and his face became heavy and firm, as if the muscles had tightened under it. "Do you think for a minute that I ever forget?" he asked. Timothy was surprised, not just by Rory's expression and his question, but by something that was intangible but real, almost grim, about Rory now.

The band went ahead to Boston. The proper, and satisfactory, audience was summoned to the train on which Rory rode—not his father's private coach. Men, women, and children had been given small American flags. It was a hot August morning, glittering and pleasant, for there was a slight cooling breeze. The band clashed and trumpeted and drummed: "The Stars and Stripes Forever!" The greeters cheered. There were hundreds of Irish faces there. Timothy gave a signal and the band became soft and haunting as it played "The Harp That Once Thro' Tara's Halls." Only half the Irish greeters had ever heard that mournful and moving song, but the music was familiar to their ancient spirits and some openly wept, and some who knew the song sang it in quivering voices.

And Rory stood on the steps of the train, waving his derby hat, his glorious red-gold head aureoled by the morning sun, his handsome face glowing and smiling. Timothy had seen him in that posture, with that very air and smile, on scores of occasions during the past months, yet for some reason Rory's appearance this morning was never to be dimmed in his memory. Had there been a special quality about Rory, then, a special brightening? Timothy would never be able to answer his own question.

They went to a fine almost new hotel near the Boston Common. Rory had spent many years at the university near Boston. He had spent weeks every year, until he was a congressman, in his father's office in that city. Yet, since Marjorie had deserted him the city had become strange and unfamiliar to him, a photograph of a reality he had once known and now half-forgotten and which he regarded with indifference. He stood at one of the windows in his suite and looked down at the trees of the Common. They were subtly turning yellow and russet, even so soon, in a glare of sunlight, and they moved and twisted on themselves, and it was, to Rory, a spot he had never known and in which he was not particularly interested.

"Like old times, eh?" said Timothy, watching him.

"Not particularly," Rory replied. He drummed with his fingers on the windowsill. He had been in good lively spirits, for he had inherited his mother's buoyancy. Yet all at once the sunlight beyond him appeared to lessen and the trees to turn cold and drab. He shook his head as if to shake a film from his eyes.

He and Timothy were alone in his bedroom, but in the rooms adjoining there were the loud and excited and burly voices of politicians, vehemently disputing, some shouting, some laughing. The smoke would be thick in there, and the whiskey and gin illimitable. They had been waiting for Rory for hours, and soon he would have to go into those rooms and meet them in a hullabaloo of greetings, back-slappings, finger-jabbings, shouts, yells, cheers, rude questions, ruder jokes. Most of them were Irish, and they were in a happy mood. The door of Rory's room had a separate entrance from the hall, and he knew that stationed without there were two of his armed bodyguards, quiet watchful men who knew their duty. They irritated Rory. He was too sanguine by nature to fear danger, or objectively to accept its possibility. If an assassin went gunning for a man, that assassin got his man, even a President, and he, Rory Armagh, had not yet even been nominated by his Party. Sure and the Committee for Foreign Studies had declared their preference for Woodrow Wilson, and Rory knew that they would not stop at discreet violence if necessary. But they would first wait for the convention, wouldn't they? By that time he hoped to have had many primary victories. Then there would be time for armed bodyguards, in the event he was nominated.

His changeful nature now turned melancholy. Without looking at Timothy he said, "I have the funniest feeling that I not only will never be President of this country but will not even be nominated."

"What's the matter with you?" demanded Timothy, startled. "Of course you will. Your Pa is putting out millions upon millions, and he's sure enough. Don't even start thinking of failure. That's fatal. Once you think you might be licked, you will surely be licked. And no Armagh ever gets licked, does he?"

"No. He gets killed," said Rory, thinking of his uncle, Sean, and his brother.

Timothy stood up abruptly, and his square pleasant face, tanned by the Western sun, had actually paled. "God damn it, Rory," he said in a low tone. "What's the matter with you?"

Rory himself was startled at the somberness in Timothy's voice, and he swung from the window and began to laugh. But Timothy did not laugh. He was staring at the young man whom he had tutored as a child, and whom he loved as a son, and his broad features were working. "What a hell of a thing to say!" he added.

"What? What did I say? Oh, about Sean and Kevin. And about the nomination. Well, I can have my doubts, can't I?"

But Timothy did not answer. He went, however, to the door and tested it. It was locked. He unlocked it and glanced out. The bodyguard came alertly to attention. Rory watched this with amusement, his hands in his pockets. He negligently leaned against the window. Timothy shut and locked the door. "Maybe you think I should have a nurse-maid, too," he said. He had never seemed so elegant, so alive, so vital and masculine.

But Timothy said, "You're not sleeping in this room alone. I'm going to share it with you." Rory burst out laughing. From far downstairs came the strains of "The Harp That Once Thro' Tara's Halls." The men in the ad-joining rooms began to sing, emotionally, passionately, and very loudly. Rory shook his head, his amusement growing. His mood had changed again from that nameless Irish melancholy to gaiety. "Get me a drink, will you, Tim, but don't let any of that mob in here yet. I want my lunch first. Never trust a politician on an empty stomach."

Timothy, in silence, opened an inside door and instantly everything was flooded in a tide of roaring, singing, laughter, shouts, and a flood of smoke. Rory had a quick glimpse of churning and sweating men beyond, milling about, waving glasses, smoking huge cigars, and it seemed to him that every man was obese and every man had a hot red face with starting eyes. It was these men, the ward heelers, the petty politicians, the chairmen of counties, the exigent rascals, who decided who would be nominated and who would not, and not State Chairmen or National Chairmen, for all their airs and urbane smiles and plottings.

Well, why not? thought Rory comfortably. Democracy is action. Long may she wave. She may stink at times, and stink mightily, but she's the best we have and probably will always be the best. Someone knocked on the outside door and Rory instinctively went towards it. He would have unlocked and opened it had not Timothy re-entered the big sunlit room, with its massive rich furniture. Timothy bellowed at him, and Rory stopped with his hand on the doorknob.

Timothy put down the soda and whiskey and the glasses, drew a deep breath and said, "God damn you, Rory. Haven't you any sense? Did you think your father was playing settlers and Indians?" His face was pallid and enraged.

He went to the door and roughly shouldered Rory aside, then shoved him against the wall. He was powerful, though Rory was a head taller than he. He shouted through the closed door: "Who is it?"

One of the guards answered. "It's me, Malone, Mr. Dineen. Somebody sent a card up for the senator. Want me to push it under the door?" Timothy gave Rory an irate glance, for Rory had begun to laugh again. "Yes!" said Timothy. A slim envelope was slipped under the door and Timothy, grunting, bent down and retrieved it. Inside was a fine card, faintly creamy, and finely engraved. Timothy read, "General Curtis Clayton, Army of the United States." On the back there was written in precise wooden letters: "I beg that Senator Armagh grant me a few minutes of his time. Urgent."

Rory plucked the card from Timothy's hand and read it aloud. "Well," he said. "The General, no less. What do you think he wants? Even the President's afraid of the old bastard."

"Would you know him if you saw him, Rory?"

"Of course I would. We've been at parties together, though never talked. I gather he thought me just a boy playing games at being senator. But he liked Claudia all right, all right. Well, let him come up."

Timothy put the chain on the door and cautiously opened it. He said to the bodyguards, "The senator will see General Clayton—for a few minutes." He nodded at the bellboy who was staring in awe at the obviously armed men near him.

"The senator will graciously grant an audience to General Clayton—for a few minutes," Rory mocked. "Tim, that is the most powerful old boy in Washington, outside of the President. When he farts bugles blow, drums rattle, armies come to attention, civilian authorities hide under tables, flags rush up poles. Even Teddy Bear runs for cover, as he wouldn't run from a charging elephant. The Cabinet quakes where he walks. He's got a Presence, Tim, a real Presence. An old warrior. And he hates civilians, especially senators who dispute his military budgets. Haven't you ever heard of him?"

"Yes," said Timothy. "Now that you mention it. If he's an old warrior, as you say, why did he oppose the war with Spain?"

Rory thoughtfully bit a fingernail and raised his red brows. "Well, so he did! I'd forgotten. Teddy practically called him a traitor. Since then, though, he's put the fear of God in Teddy Bear. I don't know how. Anyone who can do that to Teddy deserves the Congressional Medal of Honor for extraordinary heroism under fire."

There was another knock on the door. Timothy opened it but left the chain on. He motioned to Rory, who could hardly keep from laughing out loud, and Rory peered through the slit. "Well, well, General!" he exclaimed. "This is indeed an honor!"

General Clayton, not in uniform now, entered after Timothy had removed the chain. He watched Timothy replace the chain and then said in a grave voice, "An excellent idea, sir, an excellent idea." Then the general turned to Rory and ponderously took the younger man's hand and gave it a quick shake, military and precise. "Senator," he said briefly.

Though in civilian clothes, the general could not have been mistaken for anyone but a man of discipline and order and assurance and strength. He was almost as tall as Rory, but powerful of build, if compact, and though he was in his late fifties, self-control, self-restraint, made him appear much younger and very quietly vigorous. His face was absolutely rectangular, and so were his features, even the shape of his eye sockets. His hair was closely clipped, and brownish gray. He was a man of breeding, and his voice was deep and strong.

Rory said, "General, my manger, Tim Dineen. Tim, General Curtis Clayton."

Timothy and the soldier soberly shook hands. The general studied Timothy. He accepted Rory's offer of a drink, and he watched Rory pour it and his eyes narrowed thoughtfully as they ran over Rory's face and beautifully tailored suit and athletic body. He had not been mistaken, he thought. The Boy Senator was a man, suddenly a man. The general smiled again and gave Rory a small bow on accepting his glass. He sat down and Timothy sat near him. There appeared to be a warm confidence between them, a silent empathy. But Rory sat on the edge of a table and lightly swung an elegant leg and smiled sunnily. They all listened for a moment to the increasing uproar next door. Rory said, "My boys. Pols all. They aren't listening to each other, just to their own bawling. If they sound like bulls running after a cow in heat, it's just their way, General."

"I'm well acquainted, perhaps too much so, with politicians," said the general. " 'Civilian control of the military,' as the Constitution says, and it's an excellent thing—most of the time. But now I wonder—"

Rory waited for him to continue, but he had fallen silent, his eyes fixed on the glass in his hand. So Rory said, "What brings you to Boston, General?"

The general looked up. "You, Senator."

Rory lifted his brows and gave the general all his attention. "I?"

The general sipped at his drink. "While we military men are under the control of politicians we are alert to politicians. We dare be nothing else. So, I have been reading some of your speeches, Senator, from all over the country. I have studied them very closely, very closely indeed."

Rory's brows shot up, but Timothy became alert. "General," said Rory, "the speeches were just for the troops, as you would call it yourself. Happy generalizations. Handsome vague promises. Lampooning Taft and Roosevelt. Issues, excitable issues, not too well defined." He shrugged. "You know politicians."

"I know," said the general. "You are all genial frauds and expert liars. The public wouldn't have you anything else. But the reason I am here is because I think you will be elected President." ·

Rory grinned. "I wish I were that sure, General."

The general studied his glass again. "I am sure," he said at last. "The Republican Party is being divided by Roosevelt, and whether or not that is by design I don't know. So, if nominated by your Party you will be elected." He lifted his hand. "Let me finish, please. It is not just your father's wealth, though that is the main factor. You will be elected because the voters want something new, perhaps something more vital than the average politician, perhaps someone younger, someone more attractive and original. You are not a boring man, Senator."

Rory looked at Timothy with amusement, but Timothy was listening sharply to the soldier. "I wouldn't have taken this incognito trip to Boston if I did not think you would be nominated, and probably elected, Senator. Delegates? Local politicians? Your father has already bought them. So, let us confidently assume you will be nominated and elected."

Rory frowned a little. "I have heard a rumor," he said. "About the Governor of New Jersey, Woodrow Wilson, who may contest my nomination, if I am ever considered seriously by the pols. It is just a rumor."

The planes of the general's face suddenly became stonelike and expressionless. "Not a rumor," he said. He put down his glass. As if magnetized three pairs of eyes stared at the empty glass in silence. Then the general said, "But I feel you know that, Senator."

Rory's face became smooth, closed. He waited.

"I wish to refer to the clippings of your speeches," said the general. "The major newspapers left out a very salient ending to them. Only a very few and obscure newspapers printed it. No doubt the major newspapers felt it was irrelevant in these days. You end your speeches like this: 'Above all, I will work for peace not only for America but for the world.' "

The general's eyes became penetrating as they fixed

themselves on Rory. "Now," he said, "why should you speak of peace in a world at peace, except for a few minor skirmishes in remote parts of the globe, which are always skirmishing? Even the Balkans are quiet. The Hague never mentions wars any longer, but only a hope for a future league of nations. Russia is enjoying an unusual era of well-being, freedom and prosperity, under an intelligent Czar, and the elected Duma. The British Empire is well ordered, the balance wheel of the world. Germany is prosperous and enlightened. America is recovering from the Panic of '07. In short, Senator, peace is now an acceptable and taken-for-granted state in the world. So, why do you invariably speak of peace? There is no threat of war anywhere. So, Senator?"

Rory and Timothy looked quickly at each other and the general saw it, and he leaned back in his chair with a sigh, as if relieved. Rory's face was still closed and bland. He smiled broadly.

"Well, General, it does no harm to speak of peace, does it? A little flourish."

"Senator," said the general with deliberation, "I don't believe you. That is why I am here, with hope: I don't believe you. I think you know something only a few know, including myself. Tell me, sir, have you ever heard of the Committee for Foreign Studies?"

Rory, before he could control himself, felt his face involuntarily change, but after a moment he gave the general his candid relaxed blue look. "I may have heard of it, somewhere. Isn't it a private organization devoted to the study of foreign trends in business, banking, tariffs? Boring things like that?"

The general smiled again. "And no doubt, too, you have only casually heard of the Scardo Society of America, composed of self-declared intellectuals and 'liberals'?"

Rory shrugged. "I may have heard. Politicians hear everything."

But the general was still smiling. Rory felt a slight sweat between his shoulder blades. "Your father," said the general, "belongs both to the Committee for Foreign Studies and the Scardo Society."

"If he does, I don't know it, General." But Timothy was studying his hands.

The general closed his eyes briefly. "Senator, let us not play with each other. I am trying to be frank enough with you, but you are not frank with me. I can't be explicit. It isn't necessary. You know what I am talking about. So, let us assume that we have a mutual base of knowledge, if only as a hypothesis."

Rory nodded. "As only a hypothesis," he said. The general stood up and began to march around the room, his head bent as if he were alone and reflecting only to himself.

"There are those who believe that military men, like myself, can only be alive and functioning during wars, and that we are eager for wars. This is a fallacy. We do not make wars. The function of a military man is to defend his country, when called on by the President of the United States, and the Congress, who alone—up to now—has the power to declare war. It is being said now, and it is a lie, and I know the reason for it, that big military establishments 'provoke' wars. It is the civilians who goad a ruler into declaring war, who arrange for munitions, who buy munitions, who supply munitions.

"As of today, no nation is threatening another nation. Do you follow me, gentlemen? This is the twentieth century. No war will be fought in this century except by fiat alone of civilians—and not for mere conquest of territories or even solely for world markets." He paused, and said, almost humbly, "Soldiers are not eloquent. We have a hard time with words, and we are not politicians. Let me say this: Wars of this century will be fought to control men's minds and souls, to dehumanize mankind. It will be a war of powerful civilians against other civilians."

He looked at the others. "But you know that. You know all about Cecil Rhodes. He is dead now, but his ideas, and those of Ruskin, live on and are gathering force." He added, "Such ideas are hateful to military men like myself."

He stopped in front of Rory and his light brown eyes were almost fierce. "Wars won't be fought by one aggressive nation against another. They will be wars of governments against their own people, for tyranny over their own nations."

He threw out his hands. "If I did not believe that you gentlemen already know this I should not be here now." He waited for their comments, but they had averted their brooding faces. The general said, "I was a Rhodes scholar." He sat down, as if exhausted.

They knew all about the enormously wealthy Fabian English Socialist, Cecil Rhodes. They knew that his ideas, directed worldwide, were as jaded as worn stones, as ancient as dust, as hopeless for mankind as death. But modern political students and many politicians spoke of them as "new, exciting, progressive, dynamic, and above all, compassionate." And the ingenuous masses were listening, as if to humane good spokesmen.

The general said, "Though you can hardly believe it now, of course, I was a dedicated scholar in those days. But one year in England, as a Rhodes scholar, was enough! I returned and went to West Point. It was my way of learning to defend my country against the men who had taught me in England, during my scholarship."

Rory and Timothy were staring at him now, but they still said nothing.

The general continued: "You may, or may not, know it but the opening guns against mankind will be lifted in a few years, perhaps in 1917, or 1918, or 1920, or even earlier. We must try to teach our people that America is the ultimate target against which the money power of the world is directed, for she alone, now, stands in the way of ambitious men. This is the crucial issue: Military power versus Money. That is the modern, hidden struggle. There is no other."

He stood up before the silent men. He said, "Your friends in the other rooms have begun to shout impatiently for you, Senator. Now you know why I came to you today. I think you will keep your country out of war, or even prevent foreign wars. Diplomacy backed up by strength, and the willingness to use that strength in the suppression of wars; even the threat will be enough. When you are nominated, you can tell our people the truth."

"My God, no!" exclaimed Timothy. "That would never do, General. Even as it is—they—suspect Rory, though I don't know why. He's been amenable enough. They claim they are only 'doubtful' of his nomination because of his race and religion. You and I know about coups d'état. Rory must wait until he is President, and even then he would be in the most desperate danger—and you know that, too."

"A soldier is always in danger," said the general. "So is a man who insists on telling the truth." He held out his hand to Rory and his smile was suddenly warm. "Irishmen are rarely, if ever, traitors. They also know that only the strong can keep the peace."

"Yes," said Timothy, "but Rory still has to get the nomination of the Party, you know, against very—formidable —opposition."

"He will," said the general. "And that's why you must take the utmost care—" He hesitated. "Would you accept a contingent of my men, in civilian clothes, in addition to your own guards?"

"Yes," said Timothy at once, but Rory laughed. "No," he said. "It's ridiculous. Here I am—just letting the people see me throughout the country and get acquainted with me. I have broadly hinted that I'd like to be elected President next year, but I haven't even yet entered the primaries. But thank you, anyway, General."

The general looked at him long and hard and thought how splendid this young man was in both appearance and magnetism. He was to remember his last sight of Rory the balance of his life.

When the general had left Rory said, all his sunniness gone and his face as harsh as his father's: "There are New York reporters downstairs as well as other reporters. Bring them up here, Tim. I am going to tell them some truth."

Timothy was stupefied for several seconds. Then he said, "Are you out of your mind?"

But Rory said, "In spite of everything, I just don't feel I will get the nomination, let alone be President, and so I must tell some of the truth now—today—before it is too late. Go on, Tim. Bring them up here. I mean it."

Later Timothy was to wonder whether or not that interview with the Press had anything to do with what was to happen that night.

Chapter 21

It was five o'clock before Rory could return to his rooms with the heavily silent and desperate Timothy. Rory said, "Don't nag me, Tim. I'm too tired and I have a speech to make tonight in the ballroom—if I need to remind you."

The turbulent, half-sneering, partly derisive and skeptical and somewhat horrified Press had departed, after a session of wild questions, of smothered hoots, of eyes bulging with incredulity and excitement. "War?" one of them had shouted to Rory, waving both arms in the air. "With whom? Why? Are you serious, Senator?"

"I thought I explained all that, at least twice," said Rory. Some of his splendor had dimmed during the past two hours and he had not once been jocular as was his custom, nor joking. He looked much older. He had not sat down once during the interviews, but had walked up and down in controlled agitation. "I have said the 'enemy' has not yet been chosen, but I think it will be Germany. 'They' haven't told me too much, because they suspect me. Perhaps," he said, "you might consult the Committee for Foreign Studies, yourselves."

"But they are only businessmen and financiers and political students and political scientists, a private organization! Americans! They have no political influence—"

"You may eventually learn, to your death, that they have all the political influence," said Rory.

"Are you, sir," asked another reporter with a sly wink at his fellows, "just trying to throw dust into the voters' eyes because your Party indicates it prefers Mr. Woodrow Wilson, the Governor of New Jersey, to you? Or, at least, that is the rumor. Are you trying for a little personal revenge— or to influence the delegates, and the primaries to favor you and not Mr. Wilson?"

Rory felt that unique and desperate impotence men feel

who try to enlighten their people to the truth, and finally understand that the truth is one thing which will never be believed. It was a hopeless impotence. He had never experienced it before, and it shook him profoundly. He had expected some skepticism, some horror, some amazement. But the leering eyes below him, the knowing grins, the shakings of heads, the malicious glances, almost undid him. "You don't expect us to report this seriously, do you, Senator?" asked a young man who appeared to have taken the leadership.

"I had hoped you would take me seriously, for I have told you the truth," said Rory. "I know there is nothing so incredible as the truth—but, strange to say, I have a feeling that some of you—perhaps only two or three—know that I have told you the truth, and you are the ones who pretend to take what I've said with the loudest laughter and the most contempt. I don't know who you are—but you know. Well, gentlemen, that is all."

Timothy, very pale, stood up then and said, "The senator will speak fully on this tonight in the ballroom of this hotel. We have given you this interview so that you might make the morning newspapers. Essentially, what the senator has told you will be repeated tonight and perhaps enlarged upon. That is all. Please excuse us. The senator is very tired. He has been traveling strenuously all over the country, speaking and meeting tens of thousands of citizens, and needs to rest before the speech."

They straggled to their feet reluctantly when Rory turned to go, and there was not a single handclapping or show of respect. One reporter muttered to others, "What's he got against Socialism, anyway? 'Slavery!' 'Plotters!' 'International bankers!' 'Worldwide Conspiracy!' I heard the Armaghs were pretty levelheaded bastards. All that money," and he wet his lips with venomous envy. "The senator's gone dippy."

"Wars!" laughed another. "Can you imagine Americans agreeing to an international war, a war in Europe, for God's sake! 'To advance Socialistic-Communism,' he says. Who listens to Karl Marx, anyway? That boy senator has hot water on the brain! Wars! Didn't Governor Wilson say only last week that the world has entered on a permanent era of prosperity, peace, and progress? Now, there's a man I could vote for!"

"Me, too," said another. "Well, anyone going to report this drivel?"

"Not me," said still another. "My editor would fire me after asking if I'd been drunk. Well, let's listen to him tonight, if you can stand it. Wars! He's out of his mind."

Two or three only smiled, but they looked significantly at each other. Then one muttered, " 'The Golden Boy.' Well, he might just as well go and bury himself in the Armagh multimillions and forget the nomination. He's cut his throat as far as sensible men are concerned."

"Cecil Rhodes. Everybody knows what a philanthropist he was, humane and generous—"

"Ridiculous. War! He never did get very explicit, did he? Well, some politicians will try anything to get elected, but this is the worst I ever heard. His Dad should call an alienist for him, and let him be decently institutionalized."

They marched out together, laughingly chanting, "War, war, war! To arms!"

Rory undressed in his room in the heavy silence which Timothy had exuded. Timothy sat by the window, in despair. What had possessed the usually discreet and exigent Rory? Why couldn't he have waited until the primaries, at least?

He could not help himself. He turned his head and watched Rory pull his nightshirt on. "Why couldn't you have waited for the primaries?"

"Because," said Rory, behind the muffling silk, "I don't think I will even make the primaries."

The telephone rang and Timothy, cursing, answered it. There had been orders not to disturb the senator, yet the damned phone was ringing. "Who?" shouted Timothy. "Never heard of her! Tell her to go away, Jesus! What, she insists? 'Old friend of the senator's?' Well, damn it, what's her name, and I will report this intrusion to the manager."

Rory was sitting on the bed taking off his slippers. Timothy looked at him with sparkling eyes of rage out of proportion to the "intrusion." "Some damned female demands to speak with you, Rory. She won't go away. The assistant manager says she is of an 'old and notable family in Boston.' Knows the family well, and he doesn't want to tell her to get off. Well? She's on the telephone. Shall I tell her to go to hell?"

Maggie, thought Rory at once, and his haggard face was

excited and suddenly filled with color. He trembled, staring, sitting on the bed. Maggie.

"Some female you've bedded in Boston, no doubt," said Timothy with anger. He could not get over that infernal interview and took his rage out on Rory. "Maybe she's got a wood's colt to try to saddle you with; make good newspaper copy."

Maggie, thought Rory, and he pushed himself to his feet and took the telephone. He moved like one in a daze, and did not look at Timothy. He could hardly speak for a moment. Then he almost whispered, "Maggie?"

"Oh, Rory," she said, and her voice was filled with tears. "Oh, Rory, Rory."

"Maggie," he said. The receiver had become wet in his hand. Her voice rang over the years, all those long years. And the years vanished. "Where are you, Maggie?"

"At home, Rory. I don't know what made me call you, but I had to."

Timothy could not believe what he saw. Rory's exhausted face was illuminated and smiling and shaken. He was a youth again, excited, bursting with joy, transfigured. He held the receiver in both hands, as if holding the hand of a beloved woman. "Maggie, Maggie," he said. "Why did you leave me, Maggie, my darlin'?"

"I had to, Rory. Rory, I am still your wife. Your wife, Rory. I don't care that you married again. You are my husband. I've been faithful to you, Rory. I've loved you always." Her voice broke, and he could hear her sobbing.

"It was your father, who separated us, Maggie. He did it, the—"

She interrupted wildly. "No, Rory! It's time you knew the truth. I don't care what happens now. Papa and Aunt Emma are dead. I am all alone—your wife, Rory. It was your father who did it, who threatened Papa and me—and you, Rory. I did it for you, Rory. He would have ruined you, thrown you out, Rory. Your own father. We knew he meant it. So, I did it for you, more for you than for Papa and for myself."

He stood in numb silence for a long moment or two. Then Marjorie said, "Rory? Are you still there, Rory?"

"Yes," he said, in a most peculiar voice. He was staring at the wall now, and his pale blue eyes were wide and fixed, with the whites brightly glistening under the iris, and his face slack. Nothing showed in his expression, yet Timothy, watching with sudden intensity, felt that he was looking at a dangerous and deadly face, a mask that was terrifying.

"You believe me, Rory," Marjorie was weeping. "I never lied to you, except in that last letter. I had to do it for you, my dearest."

"Why didn't you tell me before, Maggie?"

"I couldn't, not so long as Papa and Aunt Emma were alive. Papa died a month ago. Rory, perhaps I shouldn't have told you after all. What good does it do? But, I read you were here. I saw your photograph in the newspaper. Oh, Rory, I must be out of my mind to talk to you now! But I couldn't control myself; I had to hear your voice, for the very last time, Rory. It will have to content me the rest of my life, I am afraid. Oh, Rory."

He shook himself all over, like someone shaking off dusty years and dead grass and rising from them, renewed, after a long and lightless dream.

"No, Maggie," he said. "Not for the last time. Maggie, I am giving a speech here tonight—"

"I know, dear. I am coming to hear you. I should have been contented with that and not have intruded on you now—at this late day. Rory."

"Maggie, afterwards, come up to my rooms." He paused. "Will you, Maggie?"

For God's sake, thought Timothy, who was astounded at the part of the conversation he was hearing. A trollop, apparently. But Rory had a taste for trollops. This was no time in his career for a flaunting of strumpets in the face of public opinion. She must have been a memorable doxy to stir the experienced Rory like this. He was actually trembling. "Rory," he said. "Not tonight, for Christ's sake, Rory! You're in Boston!"

Rory looked over his shoulder at him. "I am talking to my wife," he said. and his voice was full of a huge yet elated impatience. "Shut up."

Timothy had been half-rising. He fell back weightily in his chair, his head humming. His wife! Timothy's thoughts rang with wild surmises of bigamy, of madness, of polygamy, of threatened scandal, of a brood of unknown brats, of blackmail. The Press! He put his hands to his head and groaned.

Rory was giving the number of his suite. Now his voice was the voice of a boy. speaking with his first love, exuberant, joyous, excited. His face was the face of a lover. His weariness was forgotten. He was bending over the telephone as if he would kiss it, devour it. His eyes shone and glittered, became deeply blue. He glowed. He radiated delight. His voice was deep, shaken, stammering. Then he said, "Until tonight, my darling, my Maggie."

He hung up the receiver, slowly, lingeringly, reluctantly, listening to the last when only silence was there. He turned to Timothy. He tried to speak, then sat down on the bed, clasping his hands on his knees, staring at the floor. His throat worked. He said, "It was Maggie. My wife." Then his face changed, became savage and terrible. "That son of a bitch. My father."

Then he told the aghast Timothy. He spoke without emotion, but Timothy could sense the charge of rage and hatred that impelled his voice which was slow and without emphasis. "All these years," he said, and he seemed heavily indifferent. "All these wasted years. I haven't been alive. Only partly alive. He did that to me, and I thought he—I thought he had some feeling for me. He did that to me—He must have known what that would mean, but he didn't care. I could kill him. Perhaps I will." Now his look changed again, and his face was eloquent with sorrow and despair and incredulous acceptance. "He did that to me, his son."

"Now, wait a minute, Rory," said Timothy, who was sweating with his own emotions. "I've known your father a long time, since you were only a child. If he did that, then he did it for you. A nice Boston girl, who couldn't meet his ambitions for you. You had to have someone who was— important—and spectacular, though I hate that word. Someone who was known, who could do you proud, as your father would say. Someone perfect for your position. Claudia is that. Perfect for the wife of a politician. Come on, Rory. You are a man, not a boy in his first puberty. You must realize your father did it for you."

"For me, for what?"

Timothy tried to smile, and it was sickly. "You know what Kipling said about women. A woman's only a woman. But you are a man, with a future. Your father knew that. Give him his due, Rory. I know it must have hurt—when it happened. But you aren't a kid any longer. You have to be realistic. If the young lady is—willing— well, romp awhile with her tonight, though God knows how I'll manage it, to keep down scandal. She isn't a kid herself, any longer. How old? Thirty-three? Thirty-four? She should have had better sense than to call you, you a married man with four children. Women! A middle-aged woman, older than Claudia."

"My wife," said Rory. "I never had any other wife, all these years. I committed the worst kind of bigamy when I married Claudia."

"Who happens to be devoted to you," said Timothy, with pity.

"Claudia loves only her image in the looking glass," said Rory, and so dismissed his wife. "Maggie. Let her in tonight, Tim. She's the only thing I have, and I mean it."

He threw himself down on the bed and moved restlessly, as if his thoughts were too tumultuous to let him be still. "I'll take it all up with dear Papa, when I get home," he said. "I'll divorce Claudia. I'll marry Maggie again, and the hell with everything. 'Marry her again?' Why, I was always married to her, my Maggie, my darlin'."

"Jaysus," said Timothy, and threw up his hands. "All these years of planning, and it comes to this! Rory, think of your future for a minute, just a minute." Was it really possible for a man to give up his whole life for a woman—a woman! Incredible, nightmarish.

"I'm thinking," said Rory, and smiled, and turned on his side and slept like a contented child, satisfied at last after a long and weary day.

Timothy watched the sleeping man for some time and felt broken with hopelessness. Not only had Rory talked devastatingly to the Press this afternoon, and would probably talk so tonight, though the general, himself, had hinted at discretion. But he had just entangled himself in an impossible and scandalous situation. No doubt that woman would slyly talk to reporters, too, simperingly, calling Rory her "husband," for God's sake. She would want to be important in the eyes of the public, and the hell with Rory's prospects. Timothy could just see her, pretending to be meek and pliant, ogling her eyes, wetting her lips, affecting modesty, and burning with ambition. She would swing her little bottom seductively and look from under her lashes, and she would cling to Rory's arm publicly, and everything would fall into the trash barrel. The Press, already newly hostile to Rory, would go wild.

"Jaysus," groaned Timothy. It was all over now, as they said, except for the shouting. He could see big black headlines all over the country. He could hear the bellows of indignation and incredulity. The Committee for Foreign Studies would be coldly satisfied.

Timothy had a thought. It was very possible that that ambitious nobody had been induced to do this to Rory Daniel Armagh—for a great deal of money. Timothy tried to reach Joseph by telephone. He was not in Green Hills. He was not in Philadelphia. Where in the hell is he? thought the desperate and sweltering Timothy. Where is he? No one knew. Like father, like son, said Timothy bitterly to himself: Probably in some discreet hotel with a trollop, tonight of all nights. Timothy, to his shame, was taken with a childish desire to cry. He had served the Armaghs the greater part of his life, and he was full of grief for them, not for himself.

He could hear the distant band playing, "The Harp That Once Thro' Tara's Halls." All at once it sounded like a mournful dirge, of centuries of sadness. Why the hell did we pick that damned song? Timothy asked himself, and he wiped his eyes and cursed. All I need now, he thought, is to hear the banshees wailing the end of the Armagh ambitions —and a man's whole life. He was thinking of Joseph Armagh. Now he sniffled, and cried the bitter tears of a man, sparse and scalding.

Chapter 22

"Tim," said Rory, with a kind and admonishing look, as he dressed. "Don't take it so hard. Everything isn't lost, you know. What will be will be."

"Don't be so fatalistic," said Timothy.

"I come of a fatalistic race. Come on, Tim, Cheer up. Where's the Irish in you? Maybe what I say tonight to that big audience will—what is the phrase—ring round the world. Have a drink, Tim. This may even get me the nomination. I want a drink."

"You've had enough. All right, it is half-past seven. Let's go downstairs."

Never had he seen Rory so confident, so alert, so colorful, so potent. He also appeared larger and taller than usual, as if some power in him was expanding. His eyes glittered with excitement. He even hummed a little as he gave a last pat to his tie and shrugged his coat into position on his broad shoulders. He had brushed his hair until it shone like a red-gold helmet. Timothy, in the face of all that youth and romanticism, let himself hope a little. It was unfortunate that women could not vote. They would go mad for Rory Armagh, mindlessly mad. The younger suffragettes vowed that men thought through their bellies. But women thought with their organs of generation, and Rory was the erotic dream of women. "For the first time," said Rory, as they went to the elevators accompanied by six bodyguards, "I feel, I really feel, that I will capture the nomination. There's an old saying: 'Let the people know.' I have confidence in the American people and their common sense."

That's more than I have, thought Timothy. Still, he let himself hope. He blinked in the glare of the photographers' ignited powder as they took photographs of Rory near the

elevators. Rory smiled and waved, and even those cynical
members of the Press were surlily charmed.

The enormous lobby below was crowded from wall to
wall with heads, really nothing but heads, Timothy thought,
for the crush, shoulder to shoulder, above and below, obliterated body and feet. The heads moved constantly, wordlessly bellowing, back and forth, pouring into eddies, into
torrents, into swirls and backwaters and whirlpools, into
roaring brooks and rivers and tributaries, into seething
clots that dissolved to become bigger clots, larger whirlpools, broader rivers. There were hundreds of gray heads,
red heads, brown heads, black heads, and auburn and yellow heads, mingling, blasting apart, milling, disappearing,
reappearing. The noise was stupendous, a howling and
clamor to be found nowhere else but in a frantic zoo out of
control. Over them all floated one solid and writhing cloud
of smoke.

The lobby had gold damask walls and half-columns of
walnut or mahogany, and there were many scintillating
chandeliers, all lit, all swaying as if in a tropic wind. For it
was very hot in the lobby and smelled of heavy smoke and
sweat and pomade. There were few women here, except for
a small number huddled for protection against the walls
and absently guarded, from time to time, by their men who
kept plunging into the torrents that filled the major part of
the lobby. Doors at both ends of the lobby had been left
open, and through them poured more men intent on joining the contested and yelling throngs already there. Some
carried banners and flags. There were many white silk flags
with a green harp imposed on them with the legend: "A
Harp for a Harp!" "Erin go bragh!" was also seen on banners. A band was playing somewhere, patriotic songs and
marches, and Irish ballads, inspiring those nearest to sing
and enhance the general confusion and weltering roar.
There were stairs on each side of the lobby, one set leading
to dining rooms, the other to the ballroom. Men stood on
them, brandishing whiskey glasses and yelping jovially and
laughing, and milling up and down, and smoking, or happily pushing each other. All were sweating profusely and
mopping foreheads with handkerchiefs like banners themselves.

Uniformed men in blue and purple, employed by the
hotel, tried to coax those frenzied, drunken, and shouting
men up the stairs to the ballroom, and there was a large

blue contingent of the Boston police also trying for the same end. They were frequently swept off their feet, helplessly. Glasses were pushed into their hands, and cigars.

"Good God," said Timothy, half-pleased and half-dismayed. "This is far worse than Chicago." The elevators had opened on a shallow elevation above the lobby. The two men stood there, unseen for a moment or two, and surveyed the scene below. Hoarse voices surged up to them, clamoring, ebulliently babbling, and tumultuous pandemonium, senseless but joyous riot, feverish hubbub. And the heads seethed with increasing excitement, and the mobs increased and men fought to enter through the jammed doors and the band, losing its mind, devoted itself mainly to drums and trumpets, possibly in a last effort to be heard. Now a wave or breeze of air came to Rory and Timothy, and it was permeated with the smell of whiskey as well as sweat and pomade and smoke. It was both nauseating and choking and too hot and acrid.

"Good old pols," said Rory, in Timothy's ear. He had to bend and put his mouth almost against Timothy's ear to be heard. "How many do you suppose are here?"

"Thousands," said Timothy. The gold-colored carpet of the lobby could not be seen under that heaving carpet of heads moving in vapor. "Shouldn't wonder they'll start climbing the walls next or swinging from the chandeliers." Their bodyguard shifted uncomfortably close to them, in all that heat and stench, and new crowds were being disgorged by the elevators, all bawling, all waving to no one in particular, all bulging frenetically of eye, and all very, very drunk. To them the clot of men standing quietly close by was an impediment. They shoved against them, and cursed and glared, but did not as yet recognize Rory. "Nowhere into the ballroom but through this damned jungle," said Timothy.

"Come on," said Rory. "You'd be first to complain if the place were half empty."

Placards appeared, with Rory's overcolored portrait on them, and a thunderous shout went up: "Rory! Rory! Rory! Harp for a Harp! Long live the Irish!" They had been recognized at last. A tidal wave of wet men swarmed upon them, literally carrying them off their feet, bearing them with bellows and shouts and hoarse chanting into the center of the lobby. The bodyguard struggled and punched to keep up with the two men. Rory's red-gold head bobbed, sank, rose, turned about around and around, and his flushed and handsome face was laughing automatically. Timothy was close by, but having trouble even touching the floor.

Another group was struggling towards them, flailing arms and kicking, and the hysterical band began to play, "Kathleen Mavourneen!" and hundreds began to sing the song of Old Syrup, former Mayor of Boston, former congressman, former looter who had been discovered with both hands and both feet in the public trough. He had been consigned to "private life," and had never remained there, execrated and adored, incredibly fat and gross and huge of red wet face, and genial and honey-tempered as always, and perpetually engaged in politics, always regrettable and enjoyed by his public. Though he was in his seventies, married and with ten burly sons—now surrounding him and kicking and pushing too worshipful citizens—he had his "lady friend," as she was coyly called, with him, a tall slender woman with bright red hair and big protuberant green eyes and roped with pearls and pinned with diamonds and clad in her favorite virginal color—white silk— and showered with lace and wearing a huge plumed and flowered hat. Unkind rumor said she had been the esteemed madam of one of Joseph Armagh's most expensive houses of joy, but in fact she was really a burlesque queen from New York, though she had been born in Boston. At any rate, Old Syrup had been devoted to her for nearly two decades—she was now in her lush ripe forties—and her name was Kathleen, and he had adopted the old Irish song "as her own," in her honor. What Mrs. Old Syrup had to say about this was not recorded. Nor was the source of his wealth ever questioned. It was expected that politicians looted. It only became reprehensible when they were caught at it. Old Syrup was once reported to say, anent investigations: "Reform movements? I love them, now. They make money for me. Couldn't buy that advertising."

He and his sons, and his lady, fell upon Rory. Rory was wrapped in huge fat arms, encased in bursting broadcloth, and smacked on both cheeks. "Jaysus!" shouted Old Syrup. "And it's a gladsome sight for me, boyo, to see the son of that old rascal, Armagh, campaigning in me own town, then! Old Joe! God bless 'im! Never a better Irishman in this whole damned country, God bless 'im! How's old Joe?"

Rory had met Old Syrup many times before, and was always amused by him, and fond, for there was something charming about the old scoundrel. something both innocent and wicked, honestly goodhearted and kind, and ruthless, pious and blasphemous, ready to weep—and sincerely—at a story of want and suffering—and ready to exploit and rob the very same day, even those who were already exploited and robbed. "An Irishman," Rory once said to his father, "never makes a good Machiavelli. He can't master either his heart, his emotions, or his lusts. Nothing devious about us, sad to say. Whatever we are, we are with full soul and bad temper and our very, very uncontrollable tongues. Saint or sinner—we go all out on it. hammer and tongs, in spite of a lot of us trying to act like High Church bishops with gaiters, drinking tea and eating crumpets in genteel society. It galls us, finally."

Rory knew what Old Syrup was, and it amused him, and he let himself be heartily thumped and embraced and knew that for this moment, at least, Old Syrup was passionately honest in his greetings. (What he would think the next day, and before the primaries, and in close consultation with his cronies, was something else indeed.) Tonight he loved Rory like his favorite son. Tonight he was bursting with affection for "Old Joe." Tonight he desired nothing more than to establish Rory as the idol of the Boston Irish, and make him President. It was evident. His vast face, like the face of a happy child with naughty blue eyes, looked up at Rory with delight and affection.

"Mr. Flanagan," Timothy said, and had to repeat it several times before Old Syrup heard him. "Is there any way of getting Rory into the ballroom before he is stampeded to death?"

"Eh?" said Old Syrup, and looked up at his mighty belligerent sons. "Sure and we can. Bhoys, out with the feet and the fists."

But the crowd had become fully aware of the presence of Rory, and the boiling whirlpool surged towards him with the banners and the placards and the heat and the smoke. His clothing was seized, his shoulders. Arms tangled with his; he would have fallen if there had been anywhere to fall, an unoccupied spot. But every inch had legs and feet in it, struggling for advantage. Screams, howls, yells, expletives concerning trampled toes, rudely affectionate greetings shrieked in the highest and most penetrating tones, ruder questions, demands to shake his hand, demands to be heard, hoots and general bedlam, surrounded him almost visibly. The band went mad, pounding out "The Harp That Once Thro' Tara's Halls" in the most antic ragtime, which Timothy admitted was an improvement. He was fighting, together with the Flanagan brothers, to prevent Rory from being enthusiastically mashed to death, smothered or crushed. Above all that welter and happy fury Rory's shining head rose and bobbed, was lost, rose again. The crowd was trying to bear him somewhere, and rival contingents were trying to bear him somewhere else, and a few fistfights broke out merrily, to joyous cheers, and the smoke rose to the golden dome of the lobby and the heat became intolerable. Something fell thunderously somewhere, to heightened cheers, but no one seemed to know what it was, or where.

"Ah, it's a grand day, then!" cried Old Syrup, hugging one of Rory's arms determinedly and kicking out dexterously and without malice against pressing adherents. "God bless the Irish!"

"Somebody had better, or I'll be killed," Rory shouted back. One sleeve had been torn almost free from his coat at the shoulder, and his striped shirt showed in the gap. His tie hung at the side of his neck like a hangman's rope, and he was afraid he would be strangled. His feet had been stepped on so assiduously that they felt both burning and numb. His carefully brushed hair was disheveled, and fell and bounced over his wet forehead, which gave him a very boyish appearance. It was splendid to be hailed this way, but he wondered if he would survive. He was already drained, and had an important and momentous speech to make, and the ballroom was hardly nearer than in the beginning, and the noise made his head throb.

Then the Flanagans, man and boy, stood together like a football phalanx, and charged those nearest to Rory, and many of the crowd, cursing and waving fists, fell back and challenged the Flanagans to "come outside, then." Banners and placards tossed crazily, the band was shrieking its heart out and the drums were like thunder. But Rory found himself propelled towards the ballroom, three or four of his bodyguard with him, and Timothy, who ran with water and was bedraggled. The whirlpools swung together again en masse, and surged after Rory, and everyone poured and struggled and pushed and hit to get into the ballroom to the best seats. The band tried to enter, but was impeded by brass and drums. Trumpets and horn caught the dazzling light of the chandelier in hot gold, and splintered it. Flags blew as if in a hurricane. Throngs continued to struggle through the doors, shouting, hailing.

The river came to a brief halt as two men fell before it and tried to scramble to their feet and were either kicked impatiently or thrown off balance. Rory drew a deep breath; his lungs smarted from all that smoke and heat. He looked aside, still smiling widely. And near him, very near, almost within touching distance, Marjorie Chisholm stood, laughing and dimpling.

She was thirty-three or more years old and she looked like a fresh girl in her gray linen suit and gay sailor hat with pink ribbons. Her black eyes were merry—he had never forgotten them—and they shone and shimmered with love and joy at the sight of him, and her red mouth pursed in a kiss which she blew towards him, and her black hair began to tumble from under her hat in the way he remembered so dearly, all curls and tendrils and polished waves. In that instant he was not Senator Rory Armagh any longer, a husband and a father, a man aspiring to the nomination of his Party. He was Rory Armagh, the law student at Harvard, and he was meeting Marjorie here and in a moment he would have her in his arms, and there was nothing else in all the world and never was, and his whole body began to pound like one gigantic pulse.

"Maggie, Maggie!" he shouted over the hubbub. They were pulling the fallen men to their feet, and cursing them, and there was a little cleared space, miraculously, about Rory, and forgetting everything he plunged towards Marjorie, calling to her over and over, and his face was the face of a youth who sees his love, and it was lighted and passionate and urgent. She took a single step towards him, her gloved hands outheld, and she too saw no one else and every sound died from her awareness except the sound of Rory's voice, and she saw nothing but his face.

Someone seized Rory's arm. He never knew who it was. He tore that arm away, and turned his head furiously. It was the last conscious gesture he was ever to make.

For a shot rang out, stunningly, shockingly, and for a

moment or two the roaring stopped, and the seething diminished. Someone called plaintively, someone denounced
firecrackers in this place. Men looked about confusedly,
suddenly immobile, staring, glaring. There was another
shot, a great cry, and then a milling, of terror, of panic, of
an animal attempt at flight.

"My God, what was that?" asked Timothy. He turned to
Rory, for it was he who tried to restrain the other man. But
Rory was only standing there, blank and white and blinking, swaying from side to side, his eyes blind yet searching,
his mouth open. Then he fell like a post falling, but he
could not reach the floor. He fell into the arms of half a
dozen men, and they held him and whimpered and called
over and over, "Are you hurt? Anybody hurt?" A terrible
melee broke out. "Murder!" howled hundreds of men, who
still had seen nothing and had only heard. "Call the police!
Murder! Get that man! Who's this man, lying here? What
—what—what—"

The former noise was nothing like the noise which now
struck the lobby, wave upon wave of clamor, of curses, of
struggles, of yells and imprecations. Every man tried to run
in a different direction from his neighbor, and they collided, staggered back, fought, thrust, even bit, in their terror
and panic, their eyes starting from their pallid damp faces,
their mouths open and emitting grunts and squeals and
shouts. The floor of the lobby trembled; the walls trembled.
The flags blew straight out. Those who had sought walls for
shelter huddled together, panting, arms fending off those
who fell against them, feet kicking. Over it all came the
hoarse and gasping cry: "Who was shot? Who did it?"

Police were using their clubs, raising them and striking
down without discrimination. Men fell; others piled upon
them, wriggling like a heap of frenzied worms. The police
climbed on them, over them, smashing down, and with the
instinct of the law moving steadily to where Rory and his
bodyguard and Timothy and Old Syrup had been standing.
Their faces were fixed, not snarling or threatening. They
stared only in Rory's direction, and made for him, their
helmets invulnerable to blows, their arms rising and falling
like the arms of machines.

They had cleared a spot to lay Rory down. His chest was
pulsing scarlet. His eyes were open and vaguely searching,
though dimming rapidly. Only his hair remained in its re-

splendent condition, falling back from his forehead. His face was the color of wet clay. His mouth moved a little.

"Oh Christ, Christ, Christ," said Timothy and knelt beside Rory and took his hand. He looked down into that dying face and he burst into tears. Old Syrup, his hands on his knees, bent over Rory, muttering, gaping. Then a cry rose: "A doctor! A priest!"

"Armagh's down! Armagh's been shot! Armagh's dead!" roared hundreds, and they halted their flight as they realized, aghast, what they had said and what it meant.

"Oh, Christ, Christ, a doctor," groaned Timothy. "A priest. Rory? Rory?"

Several policemen had reached them and Timothy raised his distorted face and implored them, "A doctor, a priest. He's badly hurt, Rory." He repeated it over and over and clutched Rory's hand and a nightmare dazzle began to blind him and he said, "No, no, no." A ring of faces, appalled, pallid, loomed over him and he begged them to help, and finally someone said, "Its all right, Mr. Dineen. A doctor's getting through, and a priest." Hands touched him comfortingly, seeing his agony, but no one touched Rory. No one wanted to see what had been done to him, and many men about him began to cry like young children, turning aside, bending their heads, their features grimacing. Old Syrup staggered into the arms of two of his sons and he pressed his face against the chest of one and wept and whimpered, and they patted him, and were grim.

Timothy, who felt he was dying, himself, vaguely saw a woman kneeling beside Rory on the other side. She had lifted his head on her knee, her gray linen knee. Her hat was lost; her black polished hair fell to her shoulders. Rory's blood covered her gloved hands, her dress. She drew his head to her breast. She said, "Rory. It's Maggie, Rory. Maggie." Her pretty face was white and petrified. She pushed back his hair. She bent her head and kissed his cheek, his fallen gaping mouth. "Rory, my dearest, it's Maggie."

No one tried to remove her. They were all struck by the sight of the dying man in the arms of this strange young woman, dabbled with his blood, holding him as she would hold all the world.

Rory was in a dark and swirling place, filled with flashes of scarlet lightning. He was being tossed about on a black sea, helplessly. He could see nothing. But he could hear Marjorie's voice, and he thought he replied to it: "Oh, Maggie, Maggie, my darling. Oh, Maggie."

But he made no sound at all. He died an instant later in Marjorie's arms.

A priest was kneeling now, beside them, blessing himself, murmuring the prayers for the dying, for the dead. And Marjorie knelt there and knew that all her hopes were finally as dead as the man she held, but to the very last she would not let them take him away.

Chapter 23

Never had Old Syrup been so magnificent, so theatrical, so eloquent, and such a delight to the Press. Reporters came from all over the country to interview him, and then to write excited columns about him. The story was dramatic enough, but Old Syrup was not only a former congressman—they always called him "Congressman"—and very rich and politically powerful, but he was dramatically Irish and descriptive and never once did he repeat his story in the exact same words as before. There was always something remembered, something added, something imagined. This led to his later appointment as senator the next year by the State Legislature, and to an increase in his fortune. Queenie, "my lady friend," was his hostess in Washington, and a very discreet one. It was well known that Mrs. Old Syrup had no taste for politics, was very retiring, very charitable, and a joy to her parish, and disliked Washington. She was also a gentlewoman and never mentioned Queenie except as "my dear husband's assistant."

"There I was, with my bhoys, and my darlin' young friend, Rory Armagh, the senator—like a son to me himself, then—and we were all laughing and the band was playing, and hundreds, perhaps thousands, were struggling to get to Rory to shake his hand and shout their support of him, and there he was, shining like the damned sun, itself, now, and a sight for any sore eyes—his Dada was my best friend—and I tell you, gentlemen, that I'm a cynic and an old pol, but there was tears in my eyes, with joy. I couldn't have been prouder or happier if Rory had been of my own flesh and blood. Knew him since he was a little boyeen, and always ready with a smile, a joke, a sparkle. A scholar and a gentleman, as well as a senator. If Rory had lived to be nominated he would have been elected, yes sir, and he would have made the best damned President this country has ever seen. It's America's loss, gentlemen, even more than his parents' loss, and may God console them in His mercy.

"Well—you will excuse me a minute, now, won't you, while I wipe these old eyes. After all, it's a terrible thing, all that life and handsomeness and vigor, a young man, too, with a darlin' wife and four little children—my heart breaks for those little ones, and the young widow, so brave and beautiful and never breaking down, though you could see her heart was shattered, standing by the grave in her black veils like a statue, and never even shedding a tear. It's the easy grief that cries, not the deep one. Well, as I was saying, there we were in the lobby, and the crowds and the hails for Rory, and the band, and people pouring in through the doors just to look at the lad, and then all at once he moved—he must have seen someone he wanted to shake hands with—and he was exposed just for an instant, and me there with my sons and his bodyguard, and then there was a crack—a loud crack, like a firecracker. That's what we thought it was, for a minute, and we cursed the fool who'd do that in such a crowd.

"Then there was another crack. We all stood there, gowping, not knowing where to look, then men started to run and mill. Like hell, itself, yelling and shouting and pushing each other and somebody screamed 'Murder!' And, gentlemen, it was."

Genuine tears would stand in his crafty eyes for a moment, because of the picture he had drawn. Emotion broke his sonorous voice.

"Well, gentlemen, there was Rory on the floor—someone had cleared a space when he fell in the arms of his men—and a young lady, a most beautiful young lady, was kneeling beside him, holding him in her arms. Now, I knew that young lady's Dada well; an old and valued friend, a distinguished gentleman, Mr. Albert Chisholm, a lawyer of an old firm in Boston, honorable, upright firm. Miss Marjorie Chisholm. She'd known Rory in Boston when he was at Harvard. Rumors, there were, that they once was engaged, then. Young love. Miss Chisholm never married." Old Syrup would then look about him significantly, sigh, and shake his head. "I know, gentlemen, that she was first named 'the mystery woman,' but there weren't no mystery about Miss Chisholm. Belle of Boston when she made her day-boo. The pleece knew her at once. She wouldn't let

Rory out of her arms for a long time; had locked him in them, she had. It was pitiful. Then she went with him to the hospital, with the priest, old Father O'Brien, old friend of mine. But Rory was already dead. You'll excuse me a minute, gentlemen.— All Miss Chisholm could say, over and over, was 'Rory, Rory, Rory.' Like a Litany. Her father's associate had to be called to take her away, a Mr. Bernard Levine, a lawyer himself—trusted friend of the family.

"The murderer? Well, gentlemen, I never saw him, myself. But they found the 'black flag of anarchy,' as they called it, in his pocket, a little black flag, and a card saying he belonged to the I.W.W. Now, sir, I'm all for Labor, myself. Didn't I always fight for Labor when I was in Washington? Wobblies, they called them. Gentlemen, will you believe me when I say it is my conviction, my heart's conviction, that that murderer was no member of the I.W.W.? Rory always stood for the Working Man, when he was senator. Always spoke for the Working Man, all over the country. And another thing, gentlemen, there wasn't a single piece of identification on that foul murderer, not one. Even the name on the card was false. Never belonged to any union, and I.W.W. never heard of him. And there wasn't a handprint of his on the card, neither! What more proof do you want, then? Card as clean as a babe's mouth, and new as if it just come from the printing press. Young feller, they said, with a beard. Not more than twenty-one, twenty-two. Never did find out who he was. Never will, I'm thinking.

"Who shot him, right after he shot Rory? No one will ever find that out, either. Rory's bodyguards' guns had not been fired. No pleecemen had fired a gun. It came, now, out of the blue, as they say. Well, there were hundreds, thousands, there. Any man could have killed the assassin. And then melted off, like butter on a hot plate, oozing out of the crowd. I've heard him called a 'hero' by some newspapers, for killing the assassin, but if he's such a hero why don't he come forward to be praised? All I can say now is that that's the real mystery—outside the reason why Rory was murdered. If that assassin hadn't been shot, himself, we'd maybe have got the truth out of him. The pleece here in Boston, and I'm proud of the bhoys, have ways of making criminals talk. Now we'll never know the truth—who ordered Rory assassinated." Old Syrup looked about him weightily. "Maybe that's the idea, then, gentlemen, maybe that's the whole idea.

"What's that you say, sir? 'Disgruntled youth?' Now, begging your pardon, what the hell does *that* mean? Just words, now. Empty words. Is it hinting at a plot I am? Gentlemen, I don't know. Who would 'plot' against Rory? Finest young Christian gentleman I ever met, a lovely lad, never harmed a soul in his short life. Kind, charitable, full of fun, the best of sons and husbands. The whole Senate grieves for him, as well as his friends. You've read the eulogies. Weren't anything compared to what was said at the grave. In the family plot, in Green Hills, Commonwealth of Pennsylvania. Well, lots of you were there, too, so I don't have to repeat what was said. Assistant Secretary of State was there, and several senators and politicians, and two-three governors. And," said Old Syrup, impressively, "Old Joe's associates, many of them, Big Feenanciers and businessmen and bankers—never saw such a gathering. Mr. Jay Regan, himself, stood beside Joe Armagh and held his arm, and I'll never forget what he said to Joe, in that deep voice of his, at the funeral:

" 'Joseph,' he said, and many of us heard it, 'remember, you have four grandchildren.' Now, gentlemen, I think that was touching, then, don't you? 'Remember, you have four grandchildren.' Consoling, now. Reminding Joe he still had obligations, though all his three children lay in their graves before him, his son, the war hero, Kevin, his beautiful daughter, Ann Marie, and now Rory. And there was his brother's grave there, too, Sean Armagh, known to millions as Sean Paul. Greatest Irish tenor in the whole world, and don't deny it.

"What did Joe say? Well, he just turned a little and he looked at Mr. Regan—the Big Wall Street Feenancier— and it was as if there was a fire on his face for a minute— he being reminded of his dear little grandchildren, and that he had a Duty to them, even if his poor heart was broken. Joe's made of steel, gentlemen. As he always said, the same fire that melts butter hardens steel. And Joe looked right at Mr. Regan, one of his dear friends, and he smiled. Comforted, right there at the grave, thinking of the Little Ones, Rory's children. He smiled.

"Rory's poor mother? Ah, there's the tragedy. Lost her mind. She's in a sanitarium now, in Philadelphia, poor soul. Sent there last week, right after the funeral. God sent His angels to comfort her. They found her in the dark one night—wandered out of the house—and lying on her son, Kevin's, grave. Not crying, just mute. Like a dead creature, poor lady. Knew her father well, the old senator, when I was young, myself. Wonderful man. My Dada took me to see him in Washington; couldn't have been more than twenty or so.

"Ah, and a tragedy it all is, then. Mrs. Rory is with her parents, and the children. Under private doctor's care, in her father's house. Declared up and down, when she first knew, that Rory had 'died in the cause of Labor.' The Rights of Labor, she says. Well, who knows her husband's heart more than a wife does? So, who knows what Rory would have done if he had been President, for the Civil Rights of All Americans? Ambassador Worthington has hinted of them, himself.

"We mourn for the sorrow of the Armagh family. But, gentlemen, we should mourn for America, who suffered this tremendous—I say, tremendous—loss. God, in His wisdom, we say, Knows Best. We can only Hope. And don't, gentlemen, out of mercy, repeat any more about 'the curse on the Armaghs.' What curse? They never did anyone harm, now."

It was deep winter, but in Maryland it was dry and bleak and gray and black, the hills stark under a bitter sun. There was little snow, and this was in patches on the brown fields and in the ditches.

Timothy Dineen sat in an austerely clean room smelling of wax and fern and incense. Light came in faint and feeble shadows through the stained-glass windows. Before him was a screen and behind it he could see only the dim outline of a nun. Her voice was low and clear, the beloved voice he remembered, the young voice unroughened by the years, the melodious Irish voice he had adored in his youth. It was firm and gentle with courage and faith and consolation. But, he thought, I am old, old, old as death and as weary.

"You say, Tim, that dear Joseph died of a heart attack a month ago, in his bed, at night. I think he died of a broken heart. You see, Tim dear, Joseph never lived a single day for himself. He never once thought of himself, in all his life. Is that a sin? We esteem self-sacrifice— But we also must remember that one has one's own soul to save, too.

Ah, darling Joseph! He lived for Sean and me, and then for his children. I remember my young days in the orphanage. Sister Elizabeth would tell Sean and me of Joseph's sacrifices for us, his endless struggles for us, his endless devotion. Sean—" The gentle voice hesitated. "Ah, we are often blind, and our ears often deceive us, or we deceive ourselves. But I always knew, even as a very young child, what Joseph was doing for his family, and how he denied himself the simple joys and pleasures of youth so that we could have safety and security and a home. He was very young when he became the head of our family. Only thirteen, dear Tim. But, he was a Man. And that is something strange and rare and wonderful. A Man. He never asked for pity or for help. He never asked anyone to be generous or kind to him. He didn't even ask Sean and me to love him! But he loved us. He dearly loved us. Ah, God forgive me that I did not entirely understand! My youth was no excuse, no excuse at all, dear Tim. I do penance daily for my lack of understanding. I was drawn inexorably to this life, and always was drawn since my earliest recollections. But perhaps I was too stupid to make Joseph understand. He thought, always, that I had deserted him—as Sean had deserted him. I must do extra penance."

Timothy felt old and broken. He remembered:

> "The tumult and the shouting dies,
>   The Captains and the Kings depart.
>   Still stands Thine ancient Sacrifice—
>   A humble and a contrite heart."

If anyone's prayers would be heard by God—if there was indeed a God who heard and listened—then He would hear Sister Mary Bernarde's prayers above the prayers of anyone else, for surely, though she accused herself of "hard-heartedness and stupidity" she was as sinless and as good and pure as any human being he had ever known, even including his mother.

Then he thought: But the "Captains and the Kings" haven't "departed" at all! They were stronger than ever, since Rory Armagh's assassination. They would continue to grow in strength, until they had the whole silly world, the whole credulous world, the whole ingenuous world, in their hands. Anyone who would challenge them, attempt to expose them, show them unconcealed and naked, would be murdered, laughed at, called mad, or ignored, or denounced as a fantasy-weaver. The hell with the world, thought Timothy Dineen. Maybe these "quiet deadly men" were all it deserved. It would deserve the wars, the revolutions, the tyrannies, the chaos. For wicked men there was always the hope of remorse and penance. For the stupid there was no hope at all. The stupid invariably sacrificed its heroes, and raised statues to its murderers. The hell with the world. He, Timothy Dineen, was growing old. He would see the beginning of the last battle of man against his assassins—but, thank God, he would not see the final debacle. That was left to the coming effervescent and enthusiastic young, who would follow any banner and die in any carefully plotted war, and murder any potential rescuers.

He said, "Sister, pray for me." Then he was astonished, for the conviction had come to him that Sister Mary Bernarde's prayers might have some efficacy! She was only an immured nun, shut off from the world, living in an atmosphere of simple devotion and faith, unaware of the terrors outside her convent, unaware of all the ramifications of her brother's life of which he could not tell her, for she would not understand and be only confused. Yet he said, "Pray for me."

"I will pray for all the world," she said. "And especially for Joseph, dear Tim, and you."

He went out into the cold winter afternoon. The station hack was waiting for him. He heard the soft ringing of bells over the desolate landscape. The old bells, the ancient bells, the oldest voices in the world: Who knew? They might be eternal.

He leaned against the door which had gently closed behind him and he cried. But for what he cried he did not fully know.

Two months after Rory Daniel Armagh's assassination General Curtis Clayton attempted to address the Senate "to reveal what I know." He was denied. He wrote a book. It was never published, and the manuscript never found after his death. He implored the President to see him, and the President never answered.

He tried the Press and the reporters listened to him with grave faces and dancing eyes. They never reported what he said.

He died in the Army Hospital at Camp Meadows on the eve of the election of Woodrow Wilson. Some said he had committed suicide. His name was soon forgotten.

BIBLIOGRAPHY

(A few listings)

Allen, Fredcrick Lewis—"Morgan the Great," *LIFE* magazine, April 25, 1949

American Heritage, August, 1965

A Primer on Money—Subcommittee on Domestic Finance, Committee on Banking & Currency, House of Representatives, 88th Congress, U. S. Government Printing Office, Washington

Bryan, William "John"—*The United States Unresolved Monetary and Political Problems*

Budenz, Louis F.—*Bolshevik Invasion of the West*

Courtney, Phoebe—*The Council on Foreign Relations*

Dall, Curtis—*FDR, My Exploited Father-in-Law*

DeGoulevitch, Arsene—*Czarism and the Revolution*

Flynn, John—*Men of Wealth*

Forbes, B. C.—*Men Who Are Making America*

Gitlow, Benjamin—*The Whole of Their Lives*

Groscclose, Elgin—*Money and Man*

Hansl, Proctor—*Years of Plunder*

Huddleston, Sisley—*The Tragic Years*

Hull, Cordell—*Memoirs*

Lundberg, Ferdinand—*America's 60 Families*

Mises, Ludwig von—*Human Action*

McFadden, Louis T., Congressman—*On the Federal Reserve Corporation, Remarks in Congress,* (Congressional Record)

Myers, Gustavus—*History of the Great American Fortunes*

National Economy and the Banking System, Senate Documents, Volume 3, No. 23, U. S. Government Printing Office, Washington

Noyes, Alexander Dana—*The Market Place*

Papers Relating to the Foreign Relations of the United States—Russia, House of Representatives, Document No. 1868, volume 1, U. S. Government Printing Office, Washington

Patman, Wright—*Newsletter*, June 6, 1968—also Congressional Record, March 21, 1962, etc.

Quigley, Carroll—*Tragedy and Hope*

Rothbard, Murray—*Economic Depressions, Causes and Cures*
What Has Government Done to Our Money?

Senate Silver Hearings—*Testimony of Robert L. Owen*

Seymour, Charles—*The Intimate Papers of Colonel House*

Sparling, Earl—*Mystery Men of Wall Street*

Spengler, Oswald—*Decline of the West*

Sutton, Anthony—*Western Technology and Soviet Economic Development*

Viereck, George S.—*The Strangest Friendship in History*

Warburg, James—*The Long Road Home*

Warburg, Paul—*The Federal Reserve System*

White, Andrew D.—*Fiat Money Inflation in France*

Especially Recommended

Allen, Gary—*None Dare Call It Conspiracy*
The Bankers and the Federal Reserve

Skousen, W. Cleon—*The Naked Capitalist*, private edition

Report from Iron Mountain